APOCALYPSE LAW 4

John Grit

This story is 96,000 words in total and is of average length for novels. Design techniques have been utilized, such as font 11 text size to save in production costs and keep the price low, yet still be large enough for most people to read easily. In short, the paperback version of this novel is a lot longer than it appears to be (about 100 pages have been saved by design).

Chapter 1

Brian stood his ground and fired the first shot. That left ten of them, moving in for the kill. One large-framed but gaunt pit bull streaked across the street, deadly intent in his eyes, tawny hide rippling over straining muscles, teeth bared. When Brian dropped him with a shot to the chest, the other nine scattered, fleeing into an overgrown vacant lot. The poor creatures hadn't eaten in days, and it wasn't the first time hunger had gnawed at their guts. Their cushy lives as pets had ended more than a year before when their masters died in the plague, along with most of the human population. Hunger and natural instinct forced them to revert back to their primeval origins – creatures of the wild – and they had long since become as ferocious as wolves. Their world was ruled by the fang.

Brian and his friend Kendell had little enough food for themselves, much less extra food to feed stray dogs. They also didn't like the idea of being eaten alive, so they killed in self-defense, but with reluctance and some sorrow. Still, they were not about to let it bother them much, not after being forced to kill human beings who had suffered the same fate of the dogs, in that they too had reverted back to their primal origins and had become merciless predators armed with guns and cunning, rather than fangs and instinct.

Brian could hear them back in the thick brush, growling. "I think that last one was the leader."

His black friend moved closer, bolt-action rifle shouldered, the barrel held low. "Damn dogs are hungry. They've somethin' to eat now, though. Once we get back in the house, they'll eat the ones we shot."

At sixteen, Kendell was two years older than Brian and three inches taller. The growling seemed to be growing louder. "I hear 'em. They're comin' back!" he warned. He raised his rifle and fired at the same time Brian did. Two more dogs fell.

This time, the pack kept coming and was advancing on them fast, spreading out to make it more difficult to keep an eye on all of them at the same time. The safety of higher ground seemed the better part of valor. Without a word, the two ran for the truck in a panic. Kendell ran faster. Using the back bumper for a step, he catapulted himself up onto the overloaded flatbed, landing on his back. Two large boxes full of nails they had scrounged out of an abandoned hardware store flattened underneath him, leaving his back jabbed in a dozen places, but none of the punctures were deep.

Brian jumped onto the hood of the truck, landing on his stomach. One of the larger dogs, a German Shepherd, easily jumped right up on the hood with him and lunged for Brian's neck. He twisted around onto his back just in time and hammered his attacker with the butt of the rifle. Then he kicked the snarling animal off the truck. In two seconds, the enraged brute was back on the hood. He tried to kick the dog off him again, but the German Shepherd clamped his jaws down and ripped at his boot. Seeing his chance, Brian rammed the muzzle of his rifle against the dog's side and pulled the trigger. The big male went limp and slid off the hood onto the pavement, leaving a wide streak of blood on the side of the truck. Panting more than the barking dogs below, he sat up and started firing again, killing two more. Kendell joined in with his bolt-action and added one more kill before the few left alive turned and ran, evidently not liking the new odds.

"Run for the house!" Brian yelled.

Kendell was closer and made it into the front door first. He veered to the left, out of the way and left the door open.

Brian followed, checking for pursuit before closing the door behind him. "I think they've had enough. No sign of them now."

Kendell caught his breath. "I'm stayin' in this house anyway."

"Yeah." Brian glanced at the bedroom door, expecting his father's sleep to have been disturbed by all the gunfire. He peered inside the bedroom and found him lying still, eyes shut. Closing the door, he turned to Kendell and said, "Damn. He didn't wake up, even with all that shooting. I wonder if he's okay."

"Bullet to the head can be serious," Kendell said. "That doctor woman ain't got any of the usual stuff doctors have, like x-ray machines and drugs, so she's just guessin' how bad he's hurt." Noticing the look on Brian's face prompted him to add,

"But yesterday she said he seemed to be gettin' better. She also said there wasn't any infection. I think he'll be up and walkin' around soon."

"He better get well." Brian sat on a couch in the living room, one of the few things in the house that was not covered with a thick layer of dust from setting empty for many months until recently, when they brought Brian's wounded father there. Most of the homes in the little town, in fact most of the homes across the country and the world sat empty, or perhaps occupied only by the moldering skeletons of their long-dead owners. This modest home was not unlike millions of others. It just happened to be nearby when Brian's father was shot in a battle against a violent gang of youths. "He's the last family I have left." A shadow of sadness draped across his face, and he gave his friend a grave look. "Neither one of us will live long in this crazy world without him. I heard my friend Mel call what we have now WROL, meaning without rule of law. Both of us are pretty good shots and everything, but we won't make it without my dad. He knows things we don't, and not just about fighting."

"He'll be alright." Kendell sat in a worn-out easy chair. "It ain't likely he would die after makin' it so long. Besides, he's as tough as they come. I expect he won't leave you alone to fend for yourself. If death wants him, there'll be a fight." He pulled ammunition out of a jacket pocket and topped off his bolt-action rifle's five-round magazine. "You should reload yours, too."

They could hear the dogs outside snarling at each other as they ripped into their fallen comrades, devouring them with gulps of bloody flesh.

Brian nodded. "Yeah. You never know when trouble's coming. I just wish my dad would wake up and get better."

~~~

In a fitful and sometimes indecipherable dream, full of symbolism he didn't understand, perhaps brought on by the head wound, Nate Williams looked down from above on a day in his past life and watched his father cry. It was the first time in his life he had seen it. Before that day, he hadn't been sure his father had ever cried, even as a baby. But then, he had never been able to picture his father as a child, much less an infant. A younger man stood beside his father, a man he recognized as himself. Next to him stood Susan, holding their baby girl, and next to her stood Brian, nine years old and small for his age, or at least it seemed to Nate at the time. Later, he accepted the fact Brian wasn't going to be as big as his father and grandfather. The long line of big Williams men had come to an end. But Brian had a lot of Williams in him on the inside, and that was all that mattered. The rest of him came from Susan, and he loved Brian the more for it.

A preacher was saying something over a casket that would be lowered into the open grave below, to be embraced by the cold, dark earth. His mother was in it. It was at that moment he understood that his father loved his mother dearly. The tragedy was that understanding had come so late, too late. It had taken his mother's death to bring his father's feelings for her to the surface, where he could see it and know it for the truth that it was. He didn't know whether to be angry at his father for being so cold on the outside or at himself for being so blind and not able to see the truth that was before his eyes, a truth that had been there all along. He had had his doubts his entire life, and at that moment he realized he had been blind his entire life. The grief he saw on his father's age- and-weather-creased face, the sense of bewilderment and being totally lost, his soul adrift without its anchor, caused Nate to fear he was going to lose his father too, perhaps before he had a chance to see his mother buried. Without thinking, he put his arms around him. To his shock, his father didn't stiffen and pull away; instead he held Nate with his oak-limb arms and racked his shoulders that constant hard work had not allowed age to soften, his grief spilling out burning-hot, as lava from deep in the earth. The sight shocked Susan and Brian so much they stood there with their mouths open. A dozen friends and relatives also stood shocked.

Startled, the preacher stopped for a second to look at the faces of everyone around him, then went on reading from the Bible.

After only 30 seconds, his father's big shoulders stilled and the tears stopped flowing. He pulled away from Nate, no longer needing his support. Producing a handkerchief from a pocket and drying his face, he looked over at the preacher, who had finished. "Preacher," he said, the hardness in his voice already returned, "I think we've done all we can for her. It's time to put her in the ground. I'm sure she's already where she's going to be, whether we stop crying now or a month from now." The preacher and the farmer stood staring at each other from across the casket, neither one understanding the other. "But if you want, you can keep reading from the Bible while they lower her and put the dirt on."

The preacher nodded and went back to reading out loud.

The door had closed, and Nate never saw his father cry, nor did he ever hold him again. But he no longer had any doubts about what was hidden behind that broad, rust-colored iron gate of a face, padlocked to the outside world from the interior.

The experience made him realize he didn't want to be his father; it was too painful a life. And he wasn't going to wait until his wife was dead to let the world know he loved her. He held his wife and children every day after that and seldom raised his voice in the house. His father warned him he was spoiling his children, making them weak, but Nate let his words fall off his shoulders like rain.

In his dream, Nate relived the deaths of Susan and Beth, when the sickness took them. He remembered the boy he had been raising, spoiled to some degree, as his father had warned, but the world had changed, he had changed, and his son was no longer a boy. Had he gone too far in the other direction in his effort to give his son a chance to survive, becoming too much like his father? He prayed he had not.

~~~

The next day.

Nate's head still ached from the gunshot wound. Though he had been awake several times since he had been shot and even had spoken lucidly with Brian and friends, his memory wasn't clear. He vaguely remembered his son and friend explaining to him how they had taken him to the vacant home while he was still unconscious. That was when he had woken in the middle of the night for only a few moments. He wondered if seeing Brian and Kendell's relieved faces had not been a dream.

Dragging his bulk was an enormous task for the teens, but adrenaline helped. He wasn't that surprised the two had managed to carry or drag him so far. He had seen people accomplish many unbelievable feats in time of extreme emergency and in the defense of loved ones many times. Nothing really surprised him anymore. As a boy, he had heard many stories of World War II that were difficult to believe until he was able to later verify them. One veteran explained how American mechanics in England worked on heavy bombers for as long as 90 hours straight to keep them flying over Germany. He had never heard of a human being going so long without sleep or rest, especially while doing the hard work of repairing bombers that returned from missions heavily damaged. He thought it was the exaggeration of an old veteran whose memory had been warped from the passing of many decades and perhaps fueled by respect for those who kept the planes he relied on for his very life flying. Years later, Nate watched a documentary that supported the old vet's claims. He learned that the mechanics felt fortunate after witnessing the return of dead and wounded bomber crews and honestly believed they had it made as ground crew, where the enemy was much less likely to get a chance at them. Keeping those planes in top condition was the least they could do.

Tired of lying in bed and feeling the throbbing pain that kept time with his heartbeat, Nate sat up and touched the bandage. A roar emanated from between his ears and grew louder. After turning to sit on the edge of the bed with his feet on the floor, he looked around the room and listened. It took him ten seconds to realize the roar and pulsing was not coming from his head but outside the house. Fighting off dizziness, he stood and walked to look out the window. Helicopters flew low over the neighborhood of empty homes at high speed. He was not able to get a look at them, but in the distance, three more helicopters flew in formation – troop carriers. They appeared to be heading to the downtown area.

The bedroom door burst open and Brian rushed in, his face flushed with excitement over his father being awake and standing. His excitement over the helicopters was a close second, though; it meant friends might be arriving soon. "The Guard is back! I guess those choppers woke you up."

Nate turned from the window. "I couldn't tell. Might be regular Army."

"Do you think Deni and Caroline are with them?" Brian's face made it appear he was more pleading than asking.

"It looked like they were heading downtown." Nate held onto the back of a chair to steady himself. "There's only one way to find out."

Brian grew somber. "You okay? You remember who you are and everything?"

Nate smiled. "I remember I'm your father, and that's what defines who I am. Get your stuff and we'll see what's going on downtown."

Brian turned to run out of the room and yelled over his shoulder, "Your backpack's near the front door." Excited and not noticing his father's unsteadiness on his feet, he ran down the hall to grab his own pack and rifle.

Nate nearly fell over from dizziness when he bent down to grab his boots. He sat on a plain wooden chair and put them on, tying the laces military-style. He admitted to himself that he hoped Deni and Caroline were in one of those helicopters as much as Brian did. For a moment, a feeling of loneliness overtook him when he thought of Deni's face and voice. He shook his head and pushed away such thoughts. He was way too old for her, and she had a fiancé. He reminded himself that part of him died with his wife Susan.

Brian waited in the living room. When his father appeared from the hall, taking small, careful steps, realization washed over his face. "We don't have to go. If Deni and Caroline are with the soldiers, someone will tell them where we are. They'll come to us."

"No. We'll see what's going on." Nate braced himself by keeping a hand on the wall as he inched his way to his pack. He did not even try to swing it around and put it on. He grabbed his rifle with his other hand and said, "Let's go. I want to see them as much as you do – if they're with the soldiers."

Brian opened the front door and stepped aside to let his father pass.

Outside in the driveway, Nate dropped his pack on the bed of the diesel truck between two heavy boxes, where it would not bounce off.

Kendell sat on a wooden crate atop the flatbed with his rifle, keeping an eye out for feral dogs and dangerous men. All that was left of the dogs they had shot the day before were brown spots on the concrete and asphalt. More dogs had come in the night and dragged the bodies away to finish devouring them. "So, you're awake finally. I told Brian you'd be okay. Goin' somewhere?"

Nate slung his rifle on his shoulder. "Now, don't you boys fall over yourselves in happiness over me surviving a head wound." He smiled. "It looked like those choppers were heading downtown; we're going to check it out."

"Brian was sure excited about those choppers." Kendell smiled. "Does he have a girl in the Army?"

Brian walked up red-faced. "I never said that. She's just a friend of ours. She's like twenty-five or something – way too old for me." He threw his pack next to his father's.

Nate's eyes lit up, but he didn't rub it in. He had pretty much stopped ribbing his son many months back, when Brian started taking on the characteristics of a man. "Load up. We'll have to get there to find out what's going on. There's no point in sitting here and guessing all day."

The boys climbed into the cab and waited for Nate to pull himself up behind the wheel, which he did with some difficulty. He had trouble getting the engine started because the fuel was old, something they and everyone else had been dealing with for months. After three tries, he drove toward downtown, the truck's twin exhaust pipes spewing black smoke from poorly burned diesel fuel.

The neighborhood streets were empty of traffic as usual. Debris from the initial rioting and looting that took place more than a year before blocked the sidewalks and lined both sides of every street. Most of the homes they passed still contained skeletons from the mass die-off. There simply had not been enough healthy people to bury or burn all of the dead, and many refused to touch them even with gloves, for fear of the plague. Occasionally, Nate had to swerve around burned-out vehicles in the road. Many homes and businesses were windowless and doors swung open in the breeze. Someone had cleared some of the streets in the downtown area with a bulldozer, but no one had taken on the monumental task of removing all the trash from the sidewalks or clearing the streets of every neighborhood, where few people still lived anyway. Abandoned vehicles that had been pushed out of the most-used streets now sat in a jumbled mess on sidewalks and in front yards, along with other debris. There were more important tasks than cleaning up the town, like staying alive and finding enough to eat.

Besides the population reduction from the plague, one reason for the lack of traffic was the scarcity of fuel. Gas was either used up or too old and useless for vehicles, and diesel fuel was running out. Soon, there would be no fuel, and everyone would be on foot. Only those who managed to convert gas engines to liquid petroleum would have anything that ran, and that too would be used up someday. Anyone who had a horse or mule wasn't about to trade it for any price. The few who still held out hope the government would come and save them, bringing food, medicine, and fuel, were scoffed at. It was obvious there was no local or state government left, and many believed that not much of a federal government had survived.

Nate kept his speed under twenty miles per hour and thought about recent events. Over the last few months, Nate and his son had found new friends but had also lost nearly all their old friends to violence. The takers were making life hell for those who were already having the worst time of their lives. While dealing with cold-blooded killers, they had also met many good people, but too many of them had been killed by the takers. Something more effective had to be done. Some kind of law had to be put in place and enforced. Nate contemplated the coming of the military and what it may bring. Law and justice? Food and medical supplies? Was it the beginning of the old government coming back or a new government forming? He had only questions and worries. The last time the military showed up, they stayed only a short time and left.

It wasn't winter yet, but they had already experienced a couple cold spells recently, and Nate expected another winter of record lows and heavy snowfall like the last three, perhaps even worse. No one knew the reason for the weather change, but they certainly were not suffering from freakishly hot winters, and the summers had been basically normal, but for more frequent and unusually strong tornados. The oft-repeated phrase was, "Global warming my ass!" This day wasn't all that cold, but those in the truck considered the current temperature a bit too low for comfort. Not wanting the biting wind blowing in, they had the truck windows up. Nate saw Brian looking out of the dirty window on his side. "You checking the weather or looking for danger?"

"Both," Brian answered. "Might be a few of that gang left running around."

Nate barely recognized his son as the boy he knew before the plague spread around the world, reached into his family's home, and snatched away his wife and little girl. Before the plague, some thought he was too easy on his children, especially his own father, who died before the plague came. *Well, the world has more than made up for that. Brian's now a fourteen-year-old man, at least in the ways that count.*

Brian turned and looked past Kendell and at his father. "How are those boots Chesty scrounged up for you?"

"A little tight," Nate said. "They'll stretch."

Brian looked out his window. "Sorry they're too small. I told them but they couldn't find any bigger."

"They're a lot better than what I had. Those old boots were falling apart." Nate turned onto Main Street and sped up to twenty-five miles per hour.

A heavily loaded pickup passed them from the opposite direction. The driver blew his horn and waved. Nate waved back. He recognized him has one of the men who helped run a gang out of town that was terrorizing the few remaining residents, but could not place a name to his face. The boys waved, too.

"Looks like he's heading for the new place," Brian said. "Do you think they'll really be able to start a farm down by that big lake?"

"If they don't they'll starve." Nate blinked. His vision still blurred, he kept his attention on the street ahead.

As they passed two cars parked in front of a frame home that appeared to have been built in the thirties, Brian yelled, "Look out!"

Nate's first thought was an attack. He punched the gas. The right side of the truck rose several inches and fell, as the front wheel rolled over something in the road.

"You hit him!" Brian reached to open his door before Nate had the truck stopped. He jumped down when Nate slammed on the brakes. "It's a little boy," Brian yelled.

After pulling on the emergency brake lever, Nate looked around for trouble but saw no one. He opened his door and jumped to the street, his feet carrying him as fast as possible around the front of the truck to the other side, keeping his hand on the truck for balance. He found Brian on his knees, looking under the truck at a little boy about four years old. The boy appeared to be dead. Nate had stopped just before the rear tire rolled over him, but it was too late, the front tire had already done its damage. Blood trickled out of the little boy's mouth and nostrils.

Nate dropped to his knees beside Brian and reached for the boy's wrist. There was no pulse. He carefully pulled the boy out from under the truck and checked for breathing. There was no sign of life. The little boy's chest was caved in. "I never saw him." He cradled the child in his arms. His body racked in grief. "I never saw him." The little boy made him think of Brian when he was four.

"He ran out from between the two cars." Brian put his hand on his father's shoulder when he saw the grief on his face. "It wasn't your fault."

Nate sat there and held the little boy in his massive arms, shaking.

A woman's scream pierced the air. She exploded from the old house and ran to her son. Nate turned to hand him to her. Instead of taking the boy, she pounded Nate on his head and face. Brian and Kendell pulled her off him. By that time, the stitches closing Nate's wound were ripped loose and blood ran down his head onto his shoulder. No one noticed the HUMVEE that had pulled up and parked in the street behind them.

Three soldiers stormed out of the HUMVEE and pointed carbines at Kendell and Brian. One of the men yelled, "On your belly!"

A sergeant stepped up and appraised the situation. Her eyes widened. She ran to Nate and dropped to her knees. "Nate!"

Brian ran toward her. "Deni!"

A soldier stood in his way.

Deni yelled, "Bring a medical kit. I know these people."

Brian held her. "It was an accident. He never saw the little boy when he ran out into the road."

Nate sat by the truck staring into space, blood dripping onto his shoulder.

Kendell stood still and kept his hands up.

The woman took her son from Nate and cried, "He murdered my baby!"

Deni didn't look at her. She saw the pain on Nate's face, and something else that may have been related to the head wound. "Murdering a child is not in this man." She and Brian removed the bloody bandage and did their best to stop the bleeding by pressing gauze from the medical kit on it.

"They have a clinic a couple miles down the road," Brian said. "There's a doctor, but little supplies."

"We'll take him there," Deni said. She and Brian helped Nate up.

Kendell moved items out of the way and made room for Nate to lie in the back of the truck. A soldier struggled with Nate's weight and helped the others get him in a comfortable position. He placed a rolled-up sleeping pad under Nate's head.

Brian sat beside his father and smeared his face. "It wasn't your fault."

Nate looked up at him but said nothing.

Kendell headed for the cab. "I can drive. Someone should stay here with her." He motioned toward the grieving mother.

Deni had a carbine slung on her shoulder. She pulled it off and held it in her hands. "I'm going with them," she told the soldiers. "You three help her. Try to find some relatives or neighbors to leave her with. I'll radio you in half an hour." She had Kendell move over and got behind the wheel. Five minutes later, Kendell pointed at the church that was still being used for a clinic to take care of those wounded in the battle with the gang. Deni pulled into the parking lot.

Chapter 2

Doctor Sheila Brant looked up from a patient and saw Deni and Brian helping Nate through the church door. She pointed to a stool. They helped him across the room. While removing the bandage on Nate's head, she asked, "What happened? Last time I saw him he was in bed and doing fine."

Brian steadied his father on the stool. "I guess he should have stayed in bed longer. He seems to be dizzy or something."

Doctor Brant examined the wound. "What did he do, fall down? He's bleeding, and I was about to take the stitches out because the wound had pretty much closed."

Deni stayed out of Doctor Brant's way, but still managed to take a close look at the wound. "When was he shot, Brian?"

"It's been two weeks," Brian answered. "He seemed to be okay until now."

"Well," Deni said, "I'm sure the slapping he got from the distraught mother didn't cause him to be stunned and dazed like he is. It must be the wound."

"What mother?" Doctor Brant asked. "Never mind. Did she hit him with anything besides her hands?"

"No." Brian kept his worried eyes on his father. "She mostly just slapped him. I think he was already dizzy."

Doctor Brant cleaned the wound and put in more stitches. "All we can do is keep him in bed and give him more time to heal. It's very difficult to understand what's going on in his head without proper equipment."

By the time Doctor Brant finished with the new bandage, Nate became more alert. "Thanks. I'm okay now." His eyes focused on Deni. "It's good to see you again. How about Caroline?"

Deni flinched. "She's alive, but her leg couldn't be saved."

Brian showed no surprise Caroline had lost her leg. The gunshot wound she had suffered was severe. She had proven herself to be of great courage in their fight to save the farm from a large group of raiders. "Is she here?"

"No." Deni answered. "She's still with the National Guard. Your friend Mel has been making sure she's taken care of. Mel says he'll get her back to his place as soon as possible."

Brian's face tensed. "But no one's there. All the others were killed."

Deni caught her breath. "No! Even the children?"

Brian nodded, his face almost as anguished as when it happened. "All of them. They were killed while Dad and I were at Mrs. MacKay's farm."

Kendell walked away with his head down.

Nate struggled to get up from the stool. Doctor Brant steadied him. "Just sit there until we get a place ready for you lie down."

Nate ignored her and used all of his strength to stand. He looked at Deni and held his arms open. Deni stepped forward without hesitation and held him. Nate wrapped his massive arms around her and closed his eyes. "There were a couple times this world almost broke me," he said. "If not for Brian…"

Deni blinked tears. "You can't save them all. Believe me, I know. Death is everywhere. I've seen it, from Fort Benning to Miami. Soldiers from other parts of the country have told me it's the same all over."

Nate released her and sat down again before he fell. "So, what is your mission here?"

Brian brought a chair for Deni. She sat, keeping the M4 carbine in her hands, muzzle pointed at the ceiling. "Captain Mike Donovan should be here soon. I've served under him a while now. He's okay. Seems to be determined to keep the Army as professional as possible under the circumstances. Won't allow his soldiers to get too far out of line as far as excessive force against civilians goes."

Nate knew there must be a reason why Deni was informing him who he could trust among the officers she served under and knew there was another side to what she was telling him. "What about the noncoms?"

"Most of them are doing the best they can to help and have no interest in taking advantage of any civilians. I have one senior sergeant who's a pain, but I have yet to catch him doing anything he should be strung up for." She leaned forward and lowered her voice after checking the church entrance. "It's the Colonel I serve under I'm worried about. He's been issuing some strange orders lately, and more than a few of us noncoms are worried he may be losing it."

Nate leaned forward. "Strange orders?"

She started to speak but stopped when four soldiers walked into the church. She stood and snapped to attention, saluting a captain with red hair and a freckled face almost as red.

The captain was nearly as big as Nate. He returned her salute half-heartedly. "Where are your men, Sergeant?"

Deni stood in a brace. "There was a traffic accident, sir. A small child was killed. I left the men with the distraught mother and brought this civilian here to receive medical care. I was about to radio my men."

The captain gave Nate a once-over. "Looked to me like you were doing some fraternizing."

"I was getting a situation report from an ex-soldier. His name is Nate Williams, and he should be able to tell you a lot about what's going on in the area." She looked at Nate. "Nate, this is Captain Mike Donovan."

Nate stood and struggled to keep steady as he extended his hand. When they shook, Capt. Donovan used more force than he expected. *Oh, you're one of those.* Nate squeezed harder.

They stared at each other and cranked up the force until Donovan finally said, "Okay, enough." He massaged his right hand and smiled. "Sergeant Heath generally refuses to give men the time of day. You must have impressed her."

"We're just friends who have been through a few fights together," Nate said. His face grew serious. "The people here are hungry. Have you brought any relief supplies?"

"We're here to bring some stability – law and order – to the area."

Nate considered Donovan's words. "No food or medicine?"

"That will come later." Donovan looked at a small crowd of volunteers that had gathered and the wounded lying on sleeping bags on the floor in the church. "I need to speak to the one in charge here."

"I guess that would be me," Chesty Johnson had just walked in. "I was Town Marshal before the plague hit, and I've been kind of carrying on as if we still had a City Hall. The mayor's dead, and so is all but one member of the city council. Nevertheless, I'm still doing what I can."

Nate focused his attention on Deni. "Chesty's a good man. You can work with him."

Donovan glanced at the two of them and read something in their eyes. "Maybe I should put Sergeant Heath in charge of this town and move on to the next one. It seems she's already developed some trust with the locals."

Deni sighed and looked away.

Donovan noticed her reaction. "Don't get heated up, Sergeant. I was just joking."

"I'm sure she could handle the job," Nate said. "We had some trouble with a gang, but they left town recently. At the moment, things are quiet around here. What the people need is supplies. Some fuel would be great also."

"Hmmm." Donovan checked his watch. "You can expect some food and medicine within a week, but there'll not be any fuel for a while. Two tankers are on the way, but it's for the Army, not civilians."

Chesty broke in. "We can certainly get by for a week as far as food goes, but we're losing sick and injured every day. Our doctors need medicine."

"Doctors?" Donovan gave Chesty a dismissive glance. "You're lucky. Most people I've met the last twelve months haven't seen a medical professional of any kind since the first wave of death swept around the world."

"I'm sure that's true," Chesty said, "but we just had a battle with that local gang Nate mentioned and have many wounded. Don't you have any medical supplies you can spare? We have several children suffering."

Donovan raised his face to a tall depiction of Mother Mary on a stained glass window. "Anything I give you'll not be available for my soldiers, but I'll see to it you get something for your wounded."

"Thank you," Chesty and Doctor Brant said in unison.

"Sergeant Heath," Donovan said, "see to it."

"Yes sir." Deni said.

Donovan nodded to Chesty. "I need you to fill me in on that troublesome gang you were talking about."

Chesty said, "Sure. But they left town." He cocked his head. "So you're here more for law and order than relief."

"Let's step outside and we'll talk about it. I need you to show me around town." Donovan turned to Deni. "Carry on with the orders I gave you last night, Sergeant."

Deni responded, "Yes Sir." She used her radio to call the soldiers she left with the grieving mother and told them to come to the church.

Donovan and Chesty left.

Already tired from standing, Nate sat on the stool. "I wish you had showed up a few weeks ago. Things are quiet around here now."

"Better late than never," Deni said. She surveyed his face. "Of course I wish we had been here months ago."

Nate rubbed his eyes with the palm of his hands. "In a way you're too late. People here have decided to leave town and move to a lake south of us, so they can farm. They've been living on food from a warehouse, but that will not last much longer. The gang had taken possession of another warehouse until a couple weeks ago, but even with that extra food, they need to start farming."

Deni looked concerned. "How many have left?"

Nate shrugged. "I don't know. I've been out of it the last two weeks, but a considerable number. They've been hauling stuff to the lake and plan to take everything useful with them. It will take months to haul it all there, and they're low on fuel."

Doctor Brant spoke up. "I would guess maybe a third have already left town, but that's just a guess."

Nate noticed the concern on Deni's face. "Is that a problem?"

Deni raised an eyebrow. "It certainly means my mission will change. We were sent here to stabilize the area and provide protection for the people. Earlier flyovers gave pilots the impression there was a substantial number of survivors in this town, so we were sent here instead of a less populated area. Now you tell me the population is moving. I'm not sure my superiors will want us to relocate with you unless there are important resources at the new location."

"What about over two hundred people?" Doctor Brant asked. "Are they not important?"

Nate gently touched his head. "I too am wondering what important resources could be in this town – other than the people that is."

The look on Deni's face changed. "The food in the warehouses."

Nate sat up straight. "You mean your mission is to take that food from these people?"

"Well." Deni hesitated when she saw the face of everyone around her.

"Well what?" Nate asked.

"Taking control of the food supplies is part of our mission to stabilize the area. Higher-ups are concerned people may be hoarding it and keeping others from it."

Several people snorted. A few muttered something profane.

Brian stepped closer to explain, since his father was still not fully functioning. "The gang was keeping one warehouse to themselves, but the food in the one the townspeople had control of was being handed out and not hoarded. The gang is gone now, so we don't need the Army telling us how to take care of people. What we need is more food and medicine and fresh gas."

Deni nodded. "I know, Brian. People at the top often don't understand what's happening on the ground." She hesitated. "And of course they always know what's best for the little people who don't have brains enough to decide for themselves. As soon as I've had a chance to appraise the situation here, I'll file a report. But I'm just a sergeant."

"The military also tends to have a heavy hand," Nate said. "It's best to stay out of their way and not butt heads with them. I've seen indigenous people in other countries make that mistake and it's not pretty." He stood and tried to hide his unsteadiness. "I hate to leave you so soon, Deni, but I'm getting Brian and Kendell out of your area of operations before this turns bad."

Deni put her hands on Nate's shoulders to steady him. "You're in no condition to travel, and I promise it's not like that. I have yet to see any atrocities committed by any soldier I serve with."

"I hear you, but this country boy has had enough of big city life and is heading back to the farm." Nate took a step and grew dizzy. "Damn it." He sat down. "Brian, go get my pack and sleeping bag. I guess we'll have to stay here another day." A few minutes later, Nate was asleep on the floor.

Chapter 3

The next morning, Nate woke and saw Brian and Kendell sleeping on the floor next to him. He had slept all afternoon and night. He sat up. His head hurt. The room spun slowly. He considered that an improvement over the way he felt before his long sleep and decided it was time to suck it up and go on with life, so he grabbed his boots. After tying them, he woke Brian and Kendell up. The church was full of sleeping people with only one person awake to watch over the wounded. He whispered, "Keep it down and let's get out of here."

The two boys did as he said, putting on their boots and rolling up their sleeping equipment. In less than four minutes, they were in the parking lot and heading for the truck. All four stopped in their tracks.

"Someone's gone through our stuff." Brian shouldered his carbine and swept the area with his eyes, looking for danger.

Nate walked up to the truck and looked at the items scattered all around, items that had been on the truck. "Near as I can tell, they took our food, but everything else is still there."

Kendell's forehead wrinkled. "It's our fault. One of us should have kept watch. Now all the food we have is what little we have in our packs."

"Yeah," Nate said. "I've been of no use lately. We need to get this stuff loaded and head back to Mrs. MacKay's farm. Enough of this town already. Ramiro and his friends are probably worried, and I don't want them to come looking for us."

"I wanted to take you back with them, but the doctor said not to move you 'cause you might be hurt worse than she thought." Brian collected a few items and put them in the truck. "Can't we at least say goodbye to Deni first?"

"If we see her before we leave town." Nate wanted to talk to her again as much as Brian but did not admit it.

The three of them hastily threw everything on the flat bed of the truck, leaving a small space for someone to stand behind the cab. Nate stepped up onto the front pumper and onto the hood. Dizzy again and worried he might fall, he crawled across the hood, slid over the top, and stood just behind the cab, bracing himself against it. "Kendell, you drive. Both of you keep your guns ready but out of sight. Do not give any soldiers an excuse to kill you."

Kendell and Brian got in. This time the engine did not hesitate to crank, and they were on their way.

After driving three miles, they joined two overloaded trucks heading south to the lake. Nate felt safer with company, but did not relax his vigil.

A HUMVEE raced towards the convoy from the opposite direction, its horn blaring and lights flashing. The driver stopped in the road and got out. It was Deni. She held her carbine over her head.

The trucks stopped and the lead driver yelled out his window. "What's wrong?"

"You can't go this way," Deni yelled back. "There's a roadblock ahead, and my soldiers have orders to disarm all civilians." She ran to the pickup Nate and the others were in. "Did you hear me? You have to leave town another way. Take a back road."

"This *is* a back road," Nate said. "We might be able to use dirt roads and Jeep trails, but those big trucks of theirs won't make it." He looked at her, wanting to jump down to talk face-to-face, but he knew it would take him forever to get back up there with his head spinning. "Is it your crazy colonel?"

Deni nodded. "Col. Jamar Hewitt. He's ordered us to take all weapons from civilians." She watched the drivers and passengers from the trucks gather around. "He also has decided the townspeople are to stay in town and not move to the lake."

"You have to follow orders," Nate said. "If your colonel is crazy, he's likely to start ordering people executed. Thanks for warning us, but don't stick your neck out any farther. Go back to your post before you get into trouble."

She tilted her head and looked up at him. "Trying to get rid of me, are you?"

"I'm trying to keep you out of trouble," Nate said, "and you know it."

A man in his thirties, wearing torn coveralls and a bandage on his left arm broke in. "Good thing you warned us. There would have been trouble. I'm not giving up my guns. They've saved my family from harm too many times this last year of hell. They might as well kill me as disarm me."

Another man spoke. "We have a right to travel. No military officer has the power to tell us where we can go." He rubbed his whiskers. "Hell, where were they when we really needed them? Now they come and pull this? It doesn't appear they're here to help, just order us around. If you want to help, why didn't you soldiers bring food?"

Nate noticed the sudden change in the man's expression, as he glared at Deni. He was already seeing her as the enemy. He looked at the other men and saw the same thing on their faces.

"They're planning to ship supplies to the town," Deni said. "That's why they don't want the people moving away. The town is where the food will be."

"Bull. They can just as easily bring the food to us at the lake," the man in coveralls said. "We can't rely on the government for supplies. The last year taught us that. We have to start farming, and we need water, so we're moving to the lake."

"Yeah, she's lying," another man said, staring her down. "She's one of them."

Brian clicked the safety off his carbine and stepped back.

Nate noticed it but kept his eyes on the men. "I know Deni and trust her with my life. You're walking on thin ice here. And you don't want to go up against the Army. Keep your head working and maybe we'll work this out. The last thing you want to do is escalate things."

"Look, you don't have all day," Deni said. "It's true that I'm standing between the Army and your people." She looked at the men, trying to judge whether she was getting through to them. "But I'm not lying to you. I'm trying to help you. Now get off this road before a patrol comes along and escorts you back into town at gunpoint. If you want to get to the lake, you're going to have to go a back way and hurry up about it."

The man in coveralls rasped his whiskered face with his knuckles. "I know a back way, but these big trucks are bound to get stuck. We'll probably have to abandon them."

"You think this smaller truck can make it?" Nate asked.

Two of the men nodded.

"Then if you get stuck, we'll take you the rest of the way and you can come back with a four-wheel-drive to pull the trucks through the muddy or sandy spots later."

The man in coveralls nodded. "Let's get out of here." Before walking away, he said, "We'll give you a little time to say goodbye to her." The men climbed into their trucks.

The expression on Deni's face changed. She gave Brian a hug. "I miss you guys." She looked at Kendell. "You never introduced me to your friend."

"Oh, this is Kendell. We met him sometime back."

"He's a good kid," Nate added. "A lot of orphans are alive because of him."

"Any friend of these guys is a friend of mine," Deni said.

Kendell nodded. "Brian talks about you all the time."

"Oh?" Deni smiled. "That's why my ears are burning."

Brian gave Kendell a hard look. "I don't talk about her all the time."

Deni suddenly directed her attention down the road, in the direction of town. "Damn it! Col. Hewitt's motorcade. Go on. Get out of here."

Nate turned and watched the military vehicles coming fast. "It's too late. They'll see us leaving and you'll be left to explain why you let us go."

"Don't worry about that. Just get out of here."

Nate shook his head. "If they really want us, they'll catch us anyway. We can't outrun them." He handed Brian his rifle. "Here. You and Kendell put your guns in the truck. Hide them behind the seat. Then get over here with me and don't make the soldiers nervous."

"You still have your .45," Brian said.

Nate pulled his shirt over the pistol at his side while Brian and Kendell put the guns away.

Three HUMVEEs came to a sudden halt in the road and soldiers rushed out, their boots scraping on asphalt. Every man held their carbines at ready, looking over the sights. A sergeant screamed for everyone to lie on the ground.

"Do what he says," Nate told Kendell and Brian. He got down from the truck as fast as he could without falling on his face.

Kendell got down on all fours, but took time to look around before lying on his stomach. A soldier in his early twenties and so thin he looked emaciated, stepped forward, kicking him in the ribs. "On your belly!" he screamed, his eyes wild. Nate recognized the look of a young man who had seen too much and should be in a hospital, not carrying an automatic carbine.

Deni's protest was drowned out by Nate's. "What the hell's wrong with you?"

Deni got between the soldier and Kendell. "I had the situation under control before you showed up, Private. There's no danger here. I know these people."

The soldier pointed his M4 at Nate, who still lay prone on the asphalt. "Shut up!"

Deni rushed between them. "Get your finger off the trigger and point your weapon in a safe direction!"

The soldier did what she ordered only after some hesitation.

"Step back over there." Deni pointed to the shoulder of the road. "Don't kick anyone or point your weapon at anyone."

Kendell still had not caught his breath. He lay on his side and held his stomach, his face rigid in a futile attempt to mask his pain. Brian looked around at the surrounding soldiers, his eyes wide, his arms spread out on the asphalt as he lay on his stomach. Nate worried Kendell's ribs might have been broken. He glared at the private. "There was no need for that."

Deni knelt by Kendell and spoke without looking up at the man who kicked him. "What is your name soldier? I'm reporting this." She stood and snapped to attention when she saw an officer walk up.

Col. Jamar Hewitt gave her a strange smile. "Don't waste your time on a report, Sergeant. I would have kicked the boy's head off. Civilians around here must learn who's in charge now. They seem to think we're here just to serve them and pass out food."

"Colonel, there is no problem here," Deni said. "These people are not a threat to us or anyone else."

She was interrupted by a commotion at the two larger trucks. One soldier yelled, "Guns!" Soldiers yanked four townsmen out onto the road and began beating them.

A soldier walked up with a rifle and shotgun, displaying them to the Colonel. His demeanor foretold serious consequences, as if he had just found evidence of a murder. The four townsmen were on their bellies and bleeding from the result of rifle butts being applied to their heads. The Colonel motioned with a swagger stick. "Oh? No threat huh?"

One of the townsmen tried to protest. "My gun was just sitting on the seat. I never made any move to use it. Why would I?" He was kicked in the face, knocking him senseless. He collapsed onto the asphalt and lay motionless for a few seconds before coming to and spitting blood.

His friend protested, "Damn you! You're a coward and a bully! That uniform you're wearing has gone to your head."

Nate was worried. *I can't believe an officer would be carrying a swagger stick. Those things went out generations ago. Damn, this guy must have an ego.*

"Hell, sir, everyone's armed in this state, even during normal times." Deni looked at the Colonel for a second, thinking. "There has been no law for over a year. They need their guns for protection."

He raised his swagger stick, as if to say he'd heard enough. "We're here now, and the law came with us. A few executions will persuade the belligerent. We're moving in on that gang the indigenous personnel ran out of town. When we catch them, we'll hang two or three in front of the church. It'll be a sign to all these rednecks around here that the lawlessness has ended and they don't need their guns anymore."

Deni flinched but managed to keep her composure.

The Colonel gave the bleeding men on the asphalt a casual glance. "After the ten-day grace period, anyone caught with a firearm will be arrested."

A change came over Deni's face. Nate noticed it and thought his own reaction was probably the same as hers. *Disarming us is a death sentence in this world without rule of law. Even if the Army is here to stay, they can't protect us...unless...*

"So we're going to guarantee their safety?" Deni asked.

"Of course," Hewitt said, "after we get them all rounded up and concentrated in the downtown area."

Deni's shoulders slumped ever so slightly. "I see."

"It's the best way to see that they're fed and protected. These men caught with weapons will be taken into town." Hewitt barked orders to his men. "We're moving out!" He glanced down at Nate as he lay on the asphalt and then gave Deni a strange smile. "I'll let you decide what to do with your friends." He turned and headed for a HUMVEE, taking rapid, yard-eating steps. "Carry on, Sergeant."

The townsmen were marched at gun point toward a HUMVEE. The man who had watched helplessly as his friend was kicked in the face took a quick look around, turned his wide-eyed face to the woods, and bolted. Hewitt barked, "Stop him!"

A soldier snapped his M4 to his shoulder and fired two rounds into the man's back, dropping him in his tracks.

"Good work, soldier," the Colonel said, and got into a HUMVEE. He barked orders out of the window. "Drag his body into the woods and leave it. We've wasted enough time here."

One of the ashen-faced townsmen had been speechless, looking on in disbelief. He recovered from the shock enough to scream, "Oh God, no! You murdered him!"

Deni stood there watching them disappear around a curve in the road, her face turning more white by the second.

Nate rushed to Kendell. "Lie on your back." He felt Kendell's ribs, but couldn't tell if any were broken or not. He lifted Kendell by his shoulders. "See if you can sit up."

Kendell moaned, but managed. "Help me to the truck. Let's get out of here."

Brian helped Nate with Kendell. Once he was in the truck, Nate told Brian to get in beside him. "Both of you stay here. We'll be leaving in a minute." He found Deni standing near the HUMVEE, still not believing what she'd just seen.

Deni came out of her retrospection when he approached. "Things are turning bad fast. Kendell is right. You guys need to get out of here."

Nate put his hands on her shoulders and looked into her eyes. "You know that colonel of yours is playing with you. He expects you to let us go and then charge you for violating his earlier orders. He may even have you shot."

"I, I...can't desert my fellow soldiers." Deni looked inside herself. "I know he's acting strange, but –" She focused her eyes on Nate. "If he pulls something like that, there'll be an investigation, a trial."

"I wouldn't bet my life on it. Didn't you see the murder that just took place?" Nate pulled her to him, holding her. "I've seen that look in a crazy man's eyes before. And he has surrounded himself with soldiers who don't mind using unnecessary force. The mess the world's in, a crazy officer, soldiers who've seen too much – and lost too much. Probably their entire family. It all adds up to the shit hitting the fan around here in a way that may make our past troubles seem trivial."

"I didn't think you were the kind to run from your troubles." Deni looked away. Regret for her words on her face.

"There's no fighting the U.S. Army," Nate said. "They'll flatten us. You've got two boys and a farmer for a resistance force." He held her tighter. "If you go back, I can't help you, no matter what happens. And I'm telling you he's playing with you. He didn't really give you permission to let us go. You have two choices: Either take us into town to be put in his concentration camp, or –"

"I will not do that!"

"Then come with us."

"They'll find me."

"Your chances are a lot better hiding from them than taking them on in a fight. There must be a lot of deserters with the way things are. You'll just be one of many. I doubt he's going to expend much resources looking for you. I expect he wants soldiers with a conscience out of his way. He'll consider you good riddance."

She held onto him for support. "That might be a good reason to stay and help the other soldiers stop him. Donovan's a good man. I'm telling you most of the people I serve with will not follow illegal or immoral orders. Donovan can send a report up the chain of command, informing them Hewitt is off his rocker."

"And what if Hewitt is following orders straight out of Washington? Some have been trying to disarm the American people since the 1930s. Now, with more lawlessness than ever, they have a real excuse and a country under martial law to make it stick. You know the soldiers you serve with...how many will be on your side and how many on his? I mean when it comes down to life or death. Think about it. How are you going to know until the moment comes when each of them must decide on their own? That's not the time to learn who's who."

Deni shivered. "I know. And if Hewitt isn't acting on his own and Washington *has* ordered all guns confiscated, I fear the result."

"Yes. Blood will run in the streets. Anyone still living today is alive because of their guns and their ability to use them. They're not going to give them up and trust the same government that has been absent all this time to suddenly start protecting them. If he's following orders from Washington, things are going to get a lot worse, not just around here, but all over the country. And not many are going to allow anyone to corral them into a ghetto, where they'll be completely dependent on a government that's proven itself unreliable."

Deni put her forehead against Nate's chest. "I'll be branded with a dishonorable discharge the rest of my life."

Nate pulled away, so he could see her face and try to read her emotions. "Unless you were planning on making a career for yourself in the Army, I doubt it'll do much harm to your future under the circumstances. Don't look now, but there isn't much government or even society left." Nate looked over at Brian for a second, who sat in the pickup and talked to Kendell. "From what I've seen, we'll both be dead before things are anything like they were before the plague."

Deni stepped back. The look on her face told Nate she had made her decision. "There's a little food in the Hummer, and some ammo. We better throw it on your truck and get the hell out of here."

Chapter 4

Nate found a way around the roadblock by using several Jeep trails and backwoods dirt roads. The sandy trails were slow going, but they made it to Mrs. MacKay's farm by mid-afternoon, and only got stuck in the sand twice, making use of shovels they had in the truck to dig out.

Nate stopped in the dirt road in front of the gate and stood in the open, so those on guard duty could recognize him. Two men appeared from behind trees, one opened the gate while the other kept his rifle ready. Nate knew there were more armed men and women hiding in the woods, since he had helped to design their security measures. A tractor equipped with a front end loader had been used to push up dirt and logs, creating a barrier to vehicles and requiring any raiders to either crash through the reinforced gate or come in on foot – another suggestion of Nate's. The work had used up a lot of precious diesel fuel, but the extra security was worth it.

A man named Eugene seemed glad to see Nate. "Heard you got shot." He gave Nate's bandaged head a quick glance. "I see you're back on your feet. People around here will be happy to hear that. Uh, except Slim. He's on the warpath over you breaking his jaw." Eugene's eyes lingered on Deni and her uniform. She stood in the back, behind the cab, her carbine slung on her shoulder, so she wouldn't appear to be a threat. "We're watching him, but you might have trouble. I'd be careful. He's not the kind to forgive."

Nate said, "Thanks for the warning, but I don't understand why you keep someone like him around."

Eugene grunted and swatted at a fly. "Many of us agree with you. He may be kicked out of the group soon, now that he's almost healed up from that broken jaw you gave him. Sending him away while he was injured would've been a death sentence."

Nate shrugged. "It's none of my concern, as long as he stays away from me." He walked back to the truck. "I'm not planning on staying around much longer anyway. That town gave me enough of big city life."

Eugene canted his head and stared at Nate. "That town ain't exactly a big city. I hope you're kidding about leaving us. We need you around here."

"People mean danger. I risked my son's life for people I barely knew. That was a mistake. My main concern is Brian. And as long as Kendell is with me, I'm responsible for him, too." Nate slid behind the wheel and put the truck in gear.

Deni took notice of the security measures as they traveled the long drive. Any attacker who got past the first guards at the road would face another ring of armed men and women before they got to the buildings, and then there were more rifles waiting. Her eyes widened when she saw the large home and the outbuildings. A brick building that once housed many racing horses stood one hundred yards from the home. The few horses left were being used for farm work. Expensive racing horses worth hundreds of thousands, even millions, before the plague, were put to use pulling makeshift plows the maintenance man (who was a decent welder) had fabricated out of scrap steel. The horses had it relatively easy for the time being, though. When the diesel fuel ran out or the tractor broke down, they would have to do all the heavy work around the farm.

They were met by three more armed men standing in front of the house. A teen boy went inside. Twenty seconds later, he emerged with Mrs. MacKay. She gave Nate, Brian, and Kendell a warm welcome. "Ramiro tells me you had a lot of excitement in town. Are you well enough to help us complete the security measures you suggested?"

"I'll help while I'm here," Nate said. "But I won't be staying long. There's trouble coming from the Army. They've got a mad officer in town, and he's talking of disarming the people and gathering everyone up to put them in a downtown ghetto. He's not calling it that, of course, but that's what it'll amount to. People will lose their right to come and go as they please and will be completely dependent on the Army for all necessities. I sure don't want any part of it, and I'm certain few do. There's going to be trouble."

"As in violence?" MacKay asked.

"I don't see it any other way," Nate answered. "He spoke of hanging people in front of the church and arresting anyone caught with a gun after a ten-day grace period."

MacKay turned her attention to Deni. "And her? She looks like a soldier."

"She's a good friend." Nate motioned with his hand. "Deni, this is Mrs. MacKay."

The two shook hands. Deni wasted no time. "Nate probably should've warned you about the danger of Col. Hewett sending soldiers here. He plans to disarm everyone in the area, not just in town." She saw the reaction of her words on everyone around her. "A group this large isn't likely to escape his notice. Someday soon, they'll come for you."

"Well, we can't take on the U.S. Army, and we can't pack up and leave," Mrs. MacKay said. "Where would we go? How could we feed ourselves without this farm? And if we did run and hide, where could we hide that they couldn't find us? Where could we run that they couldn't follow? Someone's going to have to get in contact with this man's superiors and stop him. It's the only way out of this."

Mrs. MacKay's stoic reaction surprised Nate. "For all we know, his orders may have come straight from Washington. We have no idea what kind of government we have now, or who is in charge. There have been no elections that I know of, so we may have a dictator running the country. Who knows?" He turned to Deni. "Do you know anything about what's going on in Washington?"

She started to speak but Mrs. MacKay interrupted. "The four of you must be starving and exhausted. Why don't you come inside and rest? We'll talk about this later."

"Okay," Nate said. "I *am* tired." Actually, his head was still spinning, but not as much as in the morning, when he first woke. "But there isn't all that much time. They'll be here in a few weeks for certain."

"Until then," Mrs. MacKay said, "we need to appeal to higher authorities. We have had contact with the National Guard by HAM radio. Maybe we can explain to them what's going on and get something done that way."

"That's a good idea," Nate said. He was pleased to hear the group had been in contact with the ANG. "They certainly have communications with Washington and the regular Army. If we can convince them this Col. Hewitt is nuts, they'll order a junior officer to relieve him of his duties and send a replacement."

"See," Mrs. MacKay looked around at the growing crowd of nervous people. "Everything will be worked out." She turned to Nate. "Let's go inside and I'll ask someone to prepare you an early meal."

~~~

After the four had eaten, mostly beans and rice, Mrs. MacKay asked Deni and Nate to her office. "We need to talk," she said.

"You guys stay by the truck and keep out of trouble," Nate told Brian and Kendell.

Brian headed for the front door. "We don't have time to look for trouble; we're always too busy dealing with the trouble that comes looking for us."

Kendell added, "You got that right. At least there ain't any hungry wild dogs around here. And hopefully, no one is gonna take a shot at us."

"I hate shooting dogs," Brian lamented. "But I hate being chewed up and eaten even more."

Mrs. MacKay closed the door to her office. "I didn't want to talk about our troubles with the Army in front of the people. They were becoming frightened." She sat at her desk. "Do you have any suggestions on how to handle the problem?"

"I think you came up with the best idea yourself." Nate's gaze met Deni's. "What do you think?"

"Well, we should take the radio twenty miles from here before transmitting with it. Hewitt's bound to have soldiers listening to radio traffic, and we don't want them to DF the frequency."

"Yeah." Nate rubbed his chin and turned to Mrs. MacKay. "She's talking about them using radio direction-finding equipment to locate your signal. Also, whoever transmits the message had better be careful not to provide any clues as to who and where. One mention of your name or farm, and they'll be down on us quick. People in that town know of you. In fact, the town marshal knows you and Ramiro personally. The Army will question people to get info on whoever is transmitting to the Guard. If he learns we're calling him nuts and trying to have him relieved of duty, there's no telling how he might react."

"Well," Mrs. MacKay thought for a second, "do you think you could get an officer in the National Guard to come to you, so you could talk in person?"

"I doubt it," Nate answered. "They're busy, and they're low on fuel the last I heard."

Deni had an idea. "Maybe if we ask them to bring Caroline to us. Mel told me that Col. Greene had agreed to spare a chopper and crew to bring her back to the bunker after she had recovered."

"Col. Greene is my friend Mel's commanding Officer," Nate explained. "I think Deni is right. He seemed like the kind who keeps his promise, and he told me he would have Caroline back as soon as she was well."

Mrs. MacKay stood. "Good. We'll give that a try. I would feel better if you two went with one or two of my people and helped them set up the radio and went over what to say over the airwaves. You can rest today and leave early tomorrow."

Nate thought of suggesting they not wait, but decided he needed the time to further recover. He felt as if he would fall on his face at any moment.

~~~

Austin Stinson and his daughter Renee arrived at sunrise. They came from another surviving group of refugees twenty miles away, where people had squatted on another farm. The owners had died in the plague and they could not see starving while they let an empty farm go to waste. While eating breakfast, Austin offered to go with Nate and Deni and help set up the radio.

It was then Nate decided to leave Brian at the farm while he went with the others. Taking notice of how happy Brian and Renee were to see each other again, he asked, "Brian, why don't you stay here to help in the vegetable fields? Kendell, you might as well stay also. You guys can weed the fields or harvest vegetables."

Brian sat his glass of water down. "Are you sure? You might run into trouble."

Nate came back with, "I'll have a professional soldier with me. The three of us should be able to handle anything we run into."

"Yeah, she would be more useful in a fight than Kendell and me. I have to admit that."

Deni chuckled. "I promise I'll take care of your dad for you and make sure he gets back home before midnight."

Brian smiled impishly. "If you two are going on a date, you should leave Mr. Stinson here."

Deni chose her words diplomatically. "Col. Hewitt and many of his soldiers would recognize my voice and your father's too, so we won't be able to talk on the radio. Mr. Stinson told me he has never met Hewitt or any of the soldiers, so he'll be the one who does the talking over the airwaves."

"But it's going to mess up your date," Brian quipped.

"Enough of that now," Nate warned. "You're being disrespectful to Deni."

Renee couldn't quite stop herself from laughing.

Brian turned red for a second. "Oh, I forgot she has a fiancé." He lifted his eyes from his plate to Deni. "Did you ever find him?"

Deni clenched her jaw and swallowed. It was her turn to look down at her plate. "I've been told he died in the plague. So my efforts to try to get to him were in vain. He was already dead."

"Sorry," Brian said. Everyone at the table turned somber.

Ramiro and his wife Olga crossed their chests.

"If I had known, I wouldn't have been joking like that," Brian said. "I'm sorry." He got up from the table. "I might as well get to work out in the fields."

Deni reached out for him when he tried to pass on her side of the table. She stood and gave him a hug. "I've known for a long time now and had plenty of time to deal with it. You didn't cause me any pain." She let him go. "So don't feel bad about it. Just forget it."

"Take your rifle with you," Nate said. "And be careful while I'm gone. You and Kendell watch out for each other."

Kendell got up from the table. "I'm through eating. I might as well go with him and get to work also."

Austin cleared his throat. "We need to get moving, don't you think?"

Nate spoke to Mrs. MacKay. "If everything goes well, we'll see you late afternoon, or sooner."

Austin gave his daughter a pat on the shoulder as he went by. "Be good and listen to what Mrs. MacKay tells you."

She nodded. "Be careful."

They loaded the radio on the seat of one of the few pickups still running, along with a spool of wire for the antenna. One of Ramiro's men provided them with a fully charged 12 volt battery to power it with. Fortunately, the pickup was a four-wheel-drive. They were planning on traveling by back roads and Jeep trails to avoid contact with military patrols and would need four-wheel-drive for traction in the sand and mud. Another reason they were going to travel back roads was to make it more difficult to deduce where they came from if the point of their broadcast was located by military radio direction finding equipment. Col. Hewitt was bound to be pissed when he found out they were trying to get him relieved of duty for being mentally unsound, and they didn't want him ordering an airstrike or raid on the farm. The normal checks and balances of government and military went out the window when the plague killed most of the human population. They couldn't afford to take chances. The penalty could be death for dozens of people.

Chapter 5

Sitting in the truck, they inched along a narrow Jeep trail, overhanging limbs scraping paint off the truck in places and rust off where the paint had been long gone, all terrain tires spinning in the sand. Austin turned to go around a windfall that partially blocked the trail, the engine whining in first gear. A gunshot rang out from fifty yards to their left, and a bullet shattered the left mirror, sending shards of glass into Austin's face. Fortunately for him, he wore sunglasses and no damage was done to his eyes. He stomped the pedal, and the truck surged forward, throwing two fishtails of sand high into the air.

Nate yelled, "Stop! We have to bail and run into the woods."

Austin finally realized what Nate said and slammed on the brakes. Deni and Nate bailed out the right side, while Austin jumped out the left, landing on his stomach and fast-crawling to cover.

Nate lay on his belly in brush. He saw Deni lying twenty yards to his right, also on her belly, eyes wide, searching for danger. He scanned the woods for telltale movement. The towering gloom of the virgin forest seemed dark, even in midday. He was alerted by a frantic crashing through a patch of brush where the sun's tentacles managed to reach the ground and its warm rays brightened the leaves of undergrowth in a freckling pattern. Raising his rifle, aiming loosely at an opening, more of a tunnel through the brush, a natural firing lane just ahead of the rushing movement that he could only see as a blur, he squeezed off a well-timed shot.

A scream, obviously a feminine voice, echoed in the dark gloom. Somewhere behind the wall of green, lay a wounded girl or woman. Nate instantly regretted pulling the trigger. His body felt one hundred times heavier when he pulled himself up from the ground to work his way to her, dreading what he would find.

Deni flanked him, moving silently and staying in the darkest shadows of the forest, as Nate did the same.

Austin stayed where he laid, his face bleeding from shallow wounds on the left side. He licked his lips and strained to see through the forest underbrush, his finger on the trigger of his pump shotgun. The muzzle shook, as he looked over the front bead of silver and listened for the sound of steps on dry leaves. Someone was already hurt, and chances were someone was going to die in the next few moments. His heart pounded in his chest.

More rustling of leaves, this time much slower. Nate moved in, his rifle shouldered and ready. Reducing the yards between them allowed another sound to reach Nate's ears: crying. He swallowed and moved in closer, remembering the day he was forced to kill Carrie, a teen who wasn't right in the head – a result of being put through hell by sadistic captors. One day, she shot one of Ramiro's men, and Nate fired into the woods where she was hiding, not knowing it was her. It was one of the worst days of his life.

Nate looked down and saw what looked like blood on the leaf-carpeted forest floor. His eyes ran along a trail of crimson, ending in a stand of thick-growing palmettos, where the sound of crying emanated. He stepped behind a large pine. "I mean you no harm. If you give up now, we'll help you as best we can. If you keep shooting at us, you'll die."

The crying stopped.

Deni kept quiet, scanning the woods for danger in case the wounded one wasn't alone. She wasn't ready to reveal her position until she was certain no one was out there waiting for a shot at her or Nate.

Nate tried again. "Come on out. We have no interest in hurting you. Your shot only took out a mirror."

No answer came from the palmetto patch.

"We don't have all day," Nate warned. "We'll just drive away and leave you here."

A woman's nervous voice came from the palmettos, "I'm coming out. Don't shoot."

The palmetto fronds rustled for nearly a minute, then a woman appeared. She seemed to be in her late twenties, but it was difficult to tell, because she was so gaunt and her eyes so full of dread, giving Nate the impression she might be forty instead. Her right arm was crimson, and she was filthy. Her clothes were tattered and hung loose on her, especially around the waist. A rope tied around her kept her dirty jeans from falling down. She held a rifle backwards in her left hand, the muzzle pointing behind her. After dropping the rifle, she said, "I'm unarmed now. I guess you'll do with me as you please."

"We won't hurt you," Deni assured her. "The two men with me aren't the kind to abuse a woman."

Nate asked, "Are you alone? We just don't want to get shot at again."

"I'm alone," she answered.

Not taking her at her word, Nate kept his eyes searching the woods for danger. "Walk toward us and keep your hands in sight. Once we know there's no danger to us, Deni will take a look at your wound."

Something about the way her eyes flashed to her right for a second alarmed Nate, but he said nothing for the moment. She walked slowly toward them. When she was ten yards away, Nate said, "Stop there and turn around, so we can see if you have a gun hidden on you."

She did as he said. "See. I'm unarmed."

"Okay, set down where you are," Nate said.

After she sat on a rotten log, Nate asked her, "Are you telling us the truth about being alone? This is still a dangerous situation until we're sure there aren't any more people out there waiting to shoot us. The safest thing for you is to be honest and believe we mean you no harm. We would like to help you, but don't want to get shot doing it."

She seemed to be thinking over what to say next.

Deni lost patience. "Well? I think we've been very forgiving, since it was you who shot at us. I can tell Nate already feels bad about shooting you, but he can't undo that. We can help you, though, if you don't have more people out there waiting to shoot us."

"I'm the only one who had a gun," she answered.

Nate raised his rifle and pointed in the woods. "That may or may not be true, but I'm almost certain there are more people out there."

In a panic, the woman screamed, "Don't shoot! It's just my little children. They're not armed."

Suspicious, Nate wasn't about to expose himself until he was certain the danger was over. "Tell them to come to you."

"They're too far away to hear me," she replied.

If the children were that far away, there would be no danger of me hitting them by shooting into the brush. Nate whispered to Deni, "That doesn't make any sense. She's lying."

Deni looked at him and nodded.

Without a word, they backed off, staying behind cover.

The woman held her bloody arm and looked around, confused. "Where are you?"

There was no answer.

A barrage of gunshots rang out, coming from near the truck. Austin's shotgun boomed in response. Nate and Deni separated, moving in, ready to put a bullet in anything that moved. The woman was a ploy to draw them away from Austin and the pickup.

Fifty yards from the truck, Nate saw a man shooting at Austin from behind a pine tree. A buckshot load from Austin's shotgun sent bark flying. A cloud of powdered bark drifted off with the breeze, as Nate nailed the man in the back of the head.

Deni fired at someone on full-auto, her M4 chattering and echoing in the shaded forest.

As near as Nate could tell, there were four of them before the two were taken out – all men. One man saw Nate and took cover behind a pine tree that wasn't quite thick enough to stop a full metal jacket .308 round. He paid for his mistake with his life.

The last one ran, crashing through brush at top speed. His frantic dash was stopped by a load of buckshot that Austin sent his way. The bark of his shotgun echoed and faded into the distance.

The woods became deathly quiet. No one moved. Staying behind cover, they scanned the woods for more danger, their weapons ready. After five minutes, the woods came back to life. Insects buzzed, birds chirped. Nate could hear Deni's heavy breathing ten yards away, but there was no sign of anyone else in the forest besides Austin.

Deni moved in, making use of all available cover and concealment. Nate stood where he was, covering her with his rifle.

Approaching the truck, Deni called out in a low voice, "Austin, are you wounded?"

"No," he answered back.

"Well, hold tight and stay alert. There's another one out there we have to hunt down. I think we got all of them except her, but be ready if there's more."

"Will do," Austin said, as he stuffed shells into his pump shotgun.

Nate turned and headed for the woman, expecting her to be gone and hoping she would be. What if she surrendered? Where would they take her? There was no sheriff department to hand her over to. They might as well let her go. What if she fought? He didn't relish the idea of shooting a woman.

Deni and Nate moved through the woods with extreme caution, taking it slow, with more looking and listening than walking. When they got to where they had left the woman, she was gone. That was no surprise to either of them. One strange thing that bothered Nate was the fact he found no blood where the woman had been when they left her. How could that be, since her arm was covered in blood?

He did his best to follow her tracks, while Deni stayed off to the side and kept her eyes on the woods, so he could concentrate on tracking the woman. It didn't take him long to realize she wasn't bleeding much, if at all. Either she hadn't been hurt as seriously as it appeared, or she had managed to stop the bleeding someway. Since she had no pack with her, he wondered how she could have administered first-aid to herself. Worries of another ambush and doubts the woman wasn't alone forced him to consider stopping the hunt and turning back to Austin.

After another 100 yards of ever increasing anxiety, Nate froze in his tracks. He heard voices, many voices. Cocking his ear and listening intently allowed him to discern the voices of several children, perhaps as many as five or six. He moved quickly to Deni and whispered, "There are children with them. Sounds like there are quite a few people just ahead."

She cocked her head and appeared to be as puzzled as him.

He motioned to follow, and they turned back to Austin and the truck. On the way, they stopped near the place they had last seen the woman to talk quietly.

"I don't think the woman was ever wounded at all," Nate said. "She must have had some ketchup or something to put on her arm to fake a wound."

"Who the hell are they? What are they doing out here?" Deni wanted to know.

Nate thought for a moment. "I have a suspicion they were with that group on the road. Not the ones we fought at the bridge, but the other group, the one that was attacked by a helicopter. It seems some of them got away during the Guard's sweep of the area."

"You think they've been out here all this time?"

"I doubt it," Nate answered. "Not unless they managed to take a lot of supplies with them when they made their escape, and I know they didn't get much of my stuff, because Brian and I retrieved most of it. This is a long ways from where all of that took place, but still, I doubt they've been hiding here for so long. They live by stealing, and there isn't anything to steal out here."

"Until we came along," Deni added.

Nate nodded in agreement. "I'm sure their camp isn't far from the trail we came in on. They probably still have vehicles, and they wouldn't walk far from their transportation. I expect the trail we came in on turns to the left and they're camped right next to it – or right in the trail."

Deni furrowed her brow. "Good thing they took that shot at us. We would've driven right into their camp, and there's no telling how many there are."

"Maybe they wanted to keep us away from the kids," Nate suggested.

She nodded. "Maybe. It was certainly a tactical mistake for them to ambush us here, so you might be right. They were more concerned with protecting their camp than killing us."

"Let's get back to Austin and turn that truck around," Nate said. "We'll put some miles between us and them, then use the radio."

~~~

Other than their intense thirty minutes after someone shot at them, their trip proved uneventful. They were not able to contact anyone with the Army National Guard, but were able to contact several HAM operators who promised to relay the message to someone in charge. Arrangements were made to contact them again in two days. They loaded the radio up and headed home.

Chapter 6

A cool breeze came out of nowhere just before they reached Mrs. MacKay's farm, cooling the three occupants of the truck, as it rattled along the dirt road. Nate began to relax for the first time since the ambush. With Deni behind the wheel, the pickup pulled into the drive and passed through the open gate. Those on security duty all had stern faces for some reason.

Approaching the main buildings, Nate knew something was wrong. He noticed the long faces and furtive glances, eyes darting away when he looked back. He jumped out of the pickup before it stopped rolling and ran toward the house.

"Hey! What's wrong?" Deni yelled after him, jumping out of the pickup and running.

Austin went looking for Renee. He wanted to find her before someone told her about his injured face.

Mrs. MacKay met him on the porch, her face wet. "It's Brian. He's been beaten."

Nate grabbed her by her shoulders. "Where is he?"

"Come." She led him down a hall as fast as her old legs could carry her. "He's unconscious. We have done all we can for him. I don't know how badly he's hurt." Deni butted ahead of the others. Ramiro and two other men got out of her way to let her pass and followed.

Nate rushed by Mrs. Mackay when she entered the room. Kendell and a short, heavyset Hispanic woman got up from chairs and moved out of the way. Renee was sitting in a chair by the window, her face rigid with worry. Nate's breath caught at the sight of his son. He was unrecognizable. His eyes were swollen shut, nose broken and ripped at the bridge, his left arm in a sling. Nate held a wrist and checked his pulse. He tried to open one of Brian's eyes to check his pupil, but had no luck. It was too swollen. Nate ran his shaking hands over Brian's scalp and felt the back of his head, checking for any damage to his skull, knowing it could be fractured and he wouldn't be able to tell, but feeling his head anyway. He ran his hands down Brian's free arm and then gently removed the sling. His hand stopped midway down the forearm.

Mrs. MacKay spoke, her voice cracking. "You can see we set the break. We'll splint it later."

Nate carefully put the arm back in the sling and checked Brian's legs. Then he felt for broken ribs.

"We think he has two broken ribs on his right side," Mrs. MacKay said.

Nate had already felt the breaks. He checked Brian's jaw and opened his mouth. Two front teeth were missing, the inside of his mouth cut. His face was cut from being kicked with a boot. Someone had cleaned the cuts and sewn the deepest ones closed with fine thread. Nate straightened from where he leaned over Brian. Without warning, he collapsed to the floor.

Ramiro and Deni tried to help him up, but Nate pushed their hands away. "I'm all right, damn it." He got up and sat in a chair. His chest heaved as he stared at Brian. Without looking up, he asked, "Who did this?"

No one spoke. They looked away with their downcast eyes.

Deni looked around the room, her face wet. "Someone answer him, for God's sake!"

Kendell answered. "It was Slim, the guy you hit when he called me a nigger. I saw the last of it. Brian was workin' in the field. They were about two hundred yards away. I was runnin' to help and yellin' to make Slim stop kickin' him. Brian was on the ground. When he pulled a knife, I shot at him and he took off, disappeared into the woods. I don't think I hit him. Some men are after him."

Nate's breathing became erratic. He turned his head and looked up at Kendell. "Thank you for saving Brian's life."

Deni knelt beside the bed and held Brian's hand, her face streaming.

Kendell's face contorted with pain. "He's goin' to be alright. He's got to be." He smeared his tears. "That bastard took it out on Brian. He shoulda come after me or you. The coward. I bet he waited until Brian wasn't lookin' and caught him off guard. Otherwise he wouldn't have gotten close enough to take his gun from him. Brian woulda killed the bastard."

Nate waved them away. "Leave me alone with my son."

Mrs. MacKay was the last to leave the room. She closed the door to the sound of Nate crying.

Nate was in the chair when the sun rose in the morning, and he was still sitting there when Brian woke three hours after the sun had set again. He was alert for only a few seconds before falling back into unconsciousness. Nate could not be certain Brian could see him through his swollen eyes. He spoke to let him know his father was there, but he had no way of knowing if Brian understood. Despair weighed Nate down like a block of cold lead in his stomach. He reached up and rubbed his forehead with a shaking hand.

What would be the purpose of life if Brian died? Since he had lost his wife and little girl, everything had been about keeping him alive. There had been times when he hadn't liked himself so much, especially when he knowingly put Brian in a kill or be killed situation and did it over and over again. *My God. He was only thirteen years old when he was first forced to kill.* He regretted not protecting his son from that, from so many things, and regretted pushing him so hard, forcing him to grow up before his time. *I promised you it would get better someday.* He bent down and whispered in Brian's year. *I'm sorry. I should never have left you alone. It's my duty to protect you.*

Deni checked on them both several times during the day, but Nate didn't want to talk, and he didn't want anything to eat She concealed her shock when he turned his face to her; Nate didn't just look haggard and strained, he appeared to have aged ten years. She put her hand lightly on his shoulder and left the room in tears.

Late in the night, Ramiro checked on them but left when Nate said he wanted to be alone with Brian. Worry hid the boiling rage within him that grew by the minute. He kept his thoughts on his son and what he could do to help him recover. He tried not to think about hating the one who hurt him, but there were moments when the hate boiled over and came to the surface. In the back of his mind he knew there was nothing to be done for Brian. He would live or not, and it was out of his hands. He thought of praying but remembered how useless that had been when his wife and little girl were sick and dying. Fear he would just anger God kept him from praying. After all the things he had done over the last year, how dare he ask God to spare his son? His massive shoulders shook, and weakness overcame him. In desperation, he found himself on his knees begging God to punish him, but to give Brian a chance to live. He looked at his son, but Brian laid there, seemingly close to death, only his chest moving with each shallow breath. Suddenly embarrassed and grateful no one had walked in to see him act so stupidly, he got up and sat in the chair. He wasn't a believer, so why the hell was he grasping at straws? Because he couldn't lose Brian. More importantly, he couldn't allow Brian to lose his life. Brian was going to have a life, and if he had to pray to the sun and the moon, or to a God he didn't believe in, he would do it, do anything.

More long hours ticked by, and Nate had no choice but to get up from the chair and take care of himself. He was back in 55 minutes with a meager meal in his stomach, a bath and clean clothes. He sat there, watching Brian breathe. The lantern had been extinguished to save kerosene. The dim glow of a 12-volt automobile taillight attached to the wall above the headboard illuminated Brian's face. It was one Nate had wired and installed. Drained, he finally fell asleep in the chair.

~~~

When Nate opened his eyes again, the sun was up. He stood and stretched his aching back and stiff muscles, then looked out a window and judged it to be midday. He noticed people gathered around a pickup. Several men watched as a man was forcefully dragged from the pickup and into a nearby utility shed. The man's hands were bound behind him. Nate checked Brian one more time and then ran out of the room, down the hall, and out the front door, his rifle in his hands.

Two men saw him coming and yelled for Ramiro, who was in the shed. Ramiro appeared, his face showing concern. He threw his hands up. "No! We do not handle things that way."

Nate had nothing to say to anyone. He shouldered his rifle and clicked the safety off with the back of his trigger finger.

"This is a matter for a tribunal," Ramiro said. "We know how you feel, but cannot allow it." Several men lined up between Nate and the shed door. They were all armed but didn't point any weapons at him.

Nate raised his rifle higher but didn't point it at anyone. He wanted Slim but wasn't willing to kill innocent men to get at him.

Ramiro held his arms out. "Are you going to shoot us?" The compassion in his heart showed on his face. "We didn't hurt your son. We're your friends. I promise you he'll be punished. For now, we should be concerned most about Brian. My wife and I pray for him every night."

When they looked at Nate's face, they saw death staring back at them. The men gripped their weapons tighter, but didn't move. One man's chest heaved, and sweat ran down his face. He said nothing and stood his ground along with the others.

Nate saw good men standing before him, men he couldn't kill. His chest deflated, as he lowered his rifle and clicked on the safety. He turned and walked away without a word. The path he walked returned him straight to Brian.

One of the men pointed into the shed and told Ramiro in Spanish, "He brings nothing but trouble and pain to everyone he comes close to. If he is to die, I'll do the dirty job myself. God have mercy on me, but I'll do it."

A few minutes later, Mrs. MacKay entered the room Nate and Brian were in. "I was just told what happened. We cannot let you kill him. If you had caught him attacking Brian and killed him then, it would be different."

Nate's shoulders slumped. He kept his eyes on Brian. "I just want Brian to live and recover. I'll worry about Slim later."

Mrs. MacKay said, "Slim will be exiled."

Nate jerked his head and stared at her. Rage contorted his face. "If Brian dies?"

She looked back at him with understanding and compassion. "Then he will be shot. We decided on these things long ago. We needed laws, so we voted on what to do in cases like this."

Nate rubbed the stubble on his jaw. "I hope you're going to keep him locked up until it's certain Brian will live."

"Yes." She put her right hand on his shoulder. "I wish this hadn't happened, Nate. I really do. I'm sorry." She searched his face, perhaps for any sign Nate was blaming her as much as she blamed herself. "You left him in my care. I feel responsible."

"I'm responsible. I should've killed the bastard instead of just breaking his jaw. It was a mistake to create an enemy and then leave him alive. Mistakes like that are too costly now that there's no real civilization." Nate lowered his face to his open hands. "I'm afraid he may be bleeding inside. I knew soldiers who fell from helicopters or while repelling down cliffs that suffered the same kind of head injury." He looked up at her. "Did he bleed from his ears?"

"No. And he didn't fall from a helicopter," Mrs. MacKay said. "He was punched and kicked. The forces are less, and the damage should be less. Don't let worrying about what may happen eat you up. All we can do is take care of him. I think he'll be okay in a few days."

Nate straightened his back as he sat in the chair. "Well, there's nothing more to say about it. I will sit here and watch my son get better, or watch him die, as I watched my wife and daughter die."

"Until then," Mrs. MacKay said, "will you promise me there will be no more trouble from you about Slim? Will you let us handle him?"

Nate appeared twenty years older than he had only two days before. He looked at her and said, "I will not go after him here. But if you let him go, even if Brian lives, I'll hunt him down, but not here."

"What you do off my land and out of my sight is not my concern." She left Nate alone with Brian.

Ramiro waited for Mrs. MacKay in the living room. He saw something on her face, prompting him to suddenly stand.

"Come with me," she said.

He followed her in silence.

Taking much longer strides than normal for her, she crossed the distance from the house to the barn in a few short minutes. She stopped at a tool rack and picked out a broken wooden rake handle four feet long. Without a word, she fast-stepped to the shed where slim was being held, Ramiro following. The men guarding the door were alarmed by the look on her face. They had never seen her like that before and stepped aside, giving her a wide berth.

The sound of the rake handle coming down on Slim's back repeatedly and Slim moaning emanated from the shed's open door.

Inside the house, Nate stood, not sure what he was hearing. He walked to the window and opened it. Realization washed over his face. He closed the window and went back to the chair, trying to keep his mind on Brian.

~~~

It was time to contact the HAM operators again. The threat of a crazed military officer sending soldiers to arrest them or worse still hung over their heads, and Nate decided he had no choice but to go with Deni and Austin. Leaving Brian took all the will power he had. He did spend fifteen minutes with Kendell, training him on Brian's AR15.

"I'll stay with him," Kendell said. "When you get back, I'll be right here. Ain't nobody goin' to hurt him again."

"I doubt there's anyone here who wants to," Nate said. "Except Slim."

Kendell's eyes grew cold. "Slim ain't in no condition to move much, after what he got last night. I wish they would've asked me to do it."

Nate put his hand on Kendell's shoulder. "You leave him to me."

Renee was sitting on a chair next to the bed. "We'll take care of him while you're gone. Don't worry."

Deni waited outside the house by the pickup. When Nate appeared, she asked, "How's he doing?"

"The same," Nate said. "Other than that one time, he hasn't shown any sign of waking."

Austin sat behind the wheel. "He's just healing. He'll wake when it's time." They got in beside him and he cranked the pickup. "Which way?"

~~~

The radio crackled, and the man's voice sounded like he had been huffing helium. "We haven't been able to get in contact with Col. Greene. But we have been able to contact a

Capt. Boatswain of the National Guard. He's trying to get in touch with Col. Greene for us. The Colonel seems to be incommunicado for some reason."

Austin reiterated the severity of the situation and told the HAM operator he would radio him again in two days. "Well," Austin said, "we might as well pack up and head home."

~~~

Back at the farm, Nate and the others learned there had been no change in Brian's condition. Nate thanked Kendell and Renee, then relieved them from their vigil. Deni sat beside him for more than an hour. They talked quietly about Brian and their troubles with the Army.

"I'm thinking as soon as Brian can travel we should hit the road," Deni said. Their eyes met. "You know as well as I do there isn't anything we can do for these people if the army comes, except die along with them – or surrender our weapons and go to the concentration camp like sheep."

Nate rasped his whiskered face with his knuckles. "Brian isn't going to be able to walk for a few more days, even if he woke up at this moment. I don't disagree with you, but there's no reason to make that decision now. At least not until he's awake and able to travel."

"It's not that I'm heartless," Deni said. "But you know as well as I do I'm right."

The bedroom door was open, and Nate checked to make sure no one was standing there listening. "Yes you are. You also have the added worries of being a deserter. You're crazy colonel is likely to have you shot."

"Deserter?" Her voice rose both in volume and pitch. "So I've gone from being AWOL to being a deserter coward?"

"Whoa," Nate said. "You know me better than that. And I know you're no coward or deserter in time of war. There is no war. I'm the one who talked you into going AWOL in the first place. I meant you will be considered a deserter, even though there's no war going on. The people need help, and I know you would have preferred to stay and do your part. The fact is if Hewitt wasn't nuts you would actually be safer with the army than here with this small band of survivors, so you didn't leave because you feared to do your duty."

"I guess I'm touchy about the subject."

Nate nodded in understanding. "I know you feel bad about the whole damn thing. It was forced on you. Don't let it eat you up. You're not less of a person or less of a soldier, or less of an American. As to how it turns out in the end that depends on what kind of government we have now, and we don't know what kind of government we have. Not yet. It could be your going AWOL will be deemed justified, but to find out could be costly. I wouldn't advise turning myself in. Again, we have no idea what kind of government we have in Washington today. They might be hanging people on the Whitehouse lawn for all we know."

"Yeah," Deni agreed. "I know more about what's going on beyond this county than you do, and if you'd seen what I have, it would scare the hell out of you."

Nate tilted his head. "We have time. Why don't you fill me in?"

"Maybe later," she said. "When I'm not so worried about Brian. Mind you I only know what's going on in the Southeast. There are plenty of rumors, though, about the rest of the country and Washington."

Nate's thoughts drifted to worries about his son. Why wasn't he conscious yet?

Chapter 7

A helicopter flying low over the farm three hours before sunup woke everyone in the main house and outbuildings. Those on security duty were alarmed, searching the sky for more danger. Nate woke from the chair in the dark room, walked past the bed Brian was in, and pulled curtains aside to look out the window. A full moon glowed in the clear sky, and he could see the silhouette of the helicopter as it turned to buzz the farm again. *Damn it!*

Nate rushed out into the hall, where he was met by Ramiro and half a dozen other sleepy eyed men and women. Nate said to Ramiro, "I saw it, but can't tell if it's Army or Guard."

"What does it mean?" Rita, Ramiro's wife asked, as she stood in the hallway in her nightgown.

"I'm not sure," Nate answered truthfully. "Could mean trouble."

Mrs. MacKay waited in the living room, already dressed in her work clothes, as if she had not been awakened only moments before. "Nate," she said, "I think someone needs to get on the radio again and try to avert a potential tragedy. If that colonel is as crazy as you say, he may be about to order a raid on this farm." Her eyes betrayed her dread. "I'm not sure how to handle this. What do I advise the people here to do? Should they pack what supplies they can and flee now? But how will they survive without the farm? One thing that's completely out of the question is that we stay and fight. I know you told us we should defend the farm to the death because we'll starve without it, but this is different."

"Well, the last part is certainly true," Nate admitted. "One missile from a helicopter gunship would kill everyone in this house. No, we can't defend this farm against an airstrike."

"Perhaps the decision to flee or surrender should be left to each individual adult," Ramiro suggested.

"Who decides for the children who have no parents?" Mrs. MacKay asked. She was a woman who had always been confident of her ability to take on life's problems, but this was beyond her. She obviously felt she had no right to decide the next course of action for others, when the consequences of making the wrong move could be so terrible for so many innocent people. No matter how they reacted, if the Army was coming to disarm them and take them away to a concentration camp, the outcome was going to be bleak.

The sound of the helicopter coming back to buzz the farm a third time caught everyone's attention. Panic erupted in the house, as more people woke to gather in various rooms. People became loud and yelled at one another, demanding to know what they should do. Some were already gathering their children and preparing to flee into the surrounding woods.

Nate raised his voice above the clamor. "I think those with children should load packs with food and take their families to the backup camp you prepared for this kind of emergency. Volunteers will be needed to help the children who have no parents and the sick and elderly. A few of us will stay to guard the farm and stay on the radio, asking for help from the National Guard, Washington, or anyone else with the power to stop the mad colonel."

"Why should you stay?" Deni asked.

"Because Brian cannot be moved and I will not leave him."

"We'll make a stretcher," Deni said. "Since they've already found the farm, it won't matter if they recognize my voice on the radio. So I might as well stay and broadcast for help as long as I can."

Nate shook his head. "No. You may be shot on sight as a deserter. Go with the others."

The clamor subsided, as most of the men and women ran to other rooms to collect children.

"Then at least let Kendell and I take Brian with us. We can carry him with a makeshift stretcher."

"I would, but I'm afraid to move him. It's been so long since he woke up there must be something seriously wrong."

"I don't think you're making the right decision here," Deni said. "But Brian is your son, so it's your decision to make."

Austin and his daughter rushed into the room from outside. Austin had heard the last part of the conversation. "I'll stay at the radio," Austin said. "Just take care of Renee. See to it she gets away from here."

Nate hesitated.

"You're forgetting something," Austin said. "Slim. He's out there in that shed." Austin moved closer and whispered, "I'll take care of the bastard for you, while the others are at the camp."

"I couldn't ask you to do that." Nate was changing his mind about Brian as he spoke.

Austin smiled ever so slightly, softening the look of concern on his face somewhat. "You didn't ask."

"Thanks, but he's mine." Nate offered his hand and the two men shook. "We don't have all night. You get on the radio and try to get in touch with someone, anyone, who will help. I've got to make a stretcher and get Brian ready to travel." He turned to Kendell. "Stay with Renee. Make sure she makes it to the camp. Deni and I won't be far behind, carrying Brian. Go on now. The sooner you leave the safer it'll be for both of you."

"The kids," Kendell said. "I ain't leavin' them."

"Of course," Nate said. "You and Renee gather them up and take them with you, but be quick about it."

Kendell and Renee rushed upstairs.

Ramiro and his wife Rita had disappeared, but they came to the front door of the house carrying a military surplus stretcher. "For Brian," Ramiro said.

"Thanks." Deni took it. "That'll make things a lot easier."

"Set it on that couch over there, and I'll go get Brian. The hall's too narrow to use a stretcher." Nate squeezed by a line of half-awake children in the hall and turned into the room Brian was in.

Kendell stuck his head into the doorway. He had his pack on and his rifle in his hand. "We're leavin' now." Adults and children rushed by in the hall as he spoke.

"Go on. We'll be right behind you." Nate lifted Brian off the bed and headed down the hallway just behind Kendell. He could hear Austin on the radio pleading for anyone listening to contact someone in authority. Kendell and Renee disappeared out the front door, herding the frightened children before them.

Hurrying back into the bedroom, Nate grabbed his rifle and pack. Deni had followed. She scooped up Brian's rifle, backpack, and boots. The two of them headed back into the living room and prepared to travel. In less than a minute, they were out the door, carrying the still unconscious Brian.

Outside in front of the shed, Ramiro told the guards to grab their backpacks and follow the others into the woods. He walked in and held his rifle to Slim's head.

Slim begged. Tears ran down his face. "Please! This is murder. Don't do it! Don't!" He dropped to his knees, begging.

Ramiro couldn't pull the trigger. Instead, he found a coil of rope and tied Slim's hands more securely and then tied his feet, so he couldn't run away. "You're the curse of the devil. But I cannot murder you." He noticed that Slim had wet his pants but said nothing. Leaving, he turned at the door, and said, "The army may take you off our hands. Good riddance."

The house and outbuildings quickly emptied of all people. The horses were released into the pasture. Those on security searched the area and all the out buildings to be sure no one was being left behind but Slim. Mrs. MacKay was with Ramiro and his wife and entering the tree line. Having already been educated by Nate on the dangers of military aircraft equipped with forward looking infrared (FLIR), the group didn't cross the clearing between the house and the nearest trees in single file, but instead, purposely made so many tracks in the wet grass and in such a wide area that they left no discernible infrared trail to be detected, should aircraft fly over. Seen from the air, it would appear a lot of people had been walking around, perhaps going to and from the fields to harvest vegetables. In time, even that would fade away, as the heat left behind in their tracks cooled.

Many of the smaller children cried, picking up on the anxiety of the adults and sensing something was wrong. The swarming mosquitoes didn't help. The sun was rising by the time the large group of refugees made it to their fallback camp.

~~~

Austin worked the radio desperately. So far, he had not been able to raise anyone. It seemed everyone on the frequencies he tried was asleep, or at least every HAM operator. His ears perked up when military traffic came over a new frequency he had just switched to, and his heart jumped a beat. Fine tuning the frequency rewarded him with a clearer signal, but what he heard outside caused him to turn pale. From up the drive, probably at the locked gate, came a loud explosion. He grabbed up his rifle in one hand, but kept the radio mike in the other. "If there is anyone out there listening, Mrs. MacKay's farm is about to be raided by the Army. Please get in touch with Col. Greene of the National Guard."

Another explosion at the front gate momentarily startled Austin, but he was soon back on the air. Lights flashed outside in the foggy morning, and he could hear the rattle of vehicles coming down the drive. Still, he refused to give up and flee into the woods without first contacting someone who could help.

~~~

Thirty-five miles north of the farm, Capt. Mike Donovan walked into the abandoned office building that had been commandeered by the Army. The duty officer stood and saluted. He was behind a desk that was formally for a civilian receptionist. Donovan returned the salute casually and asked, "Has Col. Hewitt's entourage returned yet?"

Sergeant Silverstein answered, "Yes sir."

The look on his face prompted Capt. Donovan to ask, "What is it?"

"Sir, uh, Col. Hewitt has ordered the execution of a man caught with a weapon."

Surprised, he asked, "Is that his only crime?"

"Yes sir," the sergeant answered.

Donovan had been laboring hard for sixteen hours, tending to the myriad of details required to establish a base of operations in the downtown area, but now he had no intention of hitting the sack for a little shuteye. "Where is he?"

"Sir, the Col. is resting and is not to be disturbed."

That wasn't the question he meant to ask, but he let it go. "Where is the prisoner?"

"He's locked in a cell in the courthouse down on the corner." He pointed to his right.

"When are you scheduled to be relieved?" Donovan asked.

"At 6:00 hours, sir."

He checked his watch. "That's fifteen minutes from now. When you're relieved, stay here. I will need you. This morning's work has just begun."

"Yes sir," the soldier said.

Donovan rushed out of the building and headed down the sidewalk at a yard-eating gait, a sense of urgency on his face. Ten minutes later, when he had a chance to see the condition of the prisoner, his fears were confirmed. The man had been beaten nearly to death but was still conscious. He moaned as much in fear as pain, when Donovan's shadow fell on him in the cell.

"Hold on Mr. I'm not here to harm you." He pointed at the soldier guarding the cell door. "Is he the one that did this to you?"

The man shook his swollen head.

"Did an officer do this?"

The man nodded. "Hewitt," he said, through swollen lips.

Donovan's face grew rigid and pale. Visibly taken aback, he turned to the soldier outside the cell. "Did Col. Hewitt beat this man?"

The soldier stuttered, "I, I didn't see it."

"That was not my question. Do you know who beat this man?" Donovan raised his voice only slightly above normal, but everyone who knew him understood what that meant: he was madder than hell, because someone had screwed up and was about to pay for it.

"Sir," the soldier hesitated, "that's what I was told. It happened before my watch."

"Use your radio to call for a medical team. I want this man taken care of." Donovan headed for the door.

"Yes sir." The soldier saluted as Capt. Donovan walked by.

The soldier tried the radio several times. Finally, he woke someone up enough that he answered. "Get with it, will you? Capt. Donovan just left, and the shit has hit the fan. Too hardheads are about to go at it."

Back at the office building/headquarters, Donovan stormed in. The duty officer rose from his seat and snapped to attention. Donovan returned the salute. "It's past 6:00 hours. Where's your replacement?"

"He must have been detained, sir."

"See that goddamn radio on the desk?" Donovan pointed. "Does it work?"

Silverstein stood in a brace. "Yes sir. It worked the last time I tried it."

"Then use it, and find out what the hell's keeping your relief."

"Yes sir." Not comfortable with Capt. Donovan being so short and hard-edged in demeanor when no bullets were flying and no one was dying, he fumbled the radio, caught it in midair and regained his composure. Before he had time to speak into it, his relief arrived.

Donovan headed for the stairway. "Follow me; you've been relieved."

Sergeant Silverstein grabbed his M4 and tried to stay on Donovan's heels. Despite the age difference, he had trouble keeping up with him as they climbed several floors up. He was fifteen feet behind when they reached the radio room.

Capt. Donovan experienced another disappointment when he found the radio room empty and the radios unattended. "Son of a goddamn bitch," he exclaimed. "What kind of a chickenshit Army are we running, Sergeant?"

"Uh, I'll find the son of a bitch for you, Captain. He passed by my post when he went on duty at midnight, and no one has relieved him. The son of a bitch is supposed to still be here on duty. I knew he was a half-stepping goldbricker, but this is the first time I've caught him off post. I'll ream him a new ass when I get my hands on him."

Donovan had heard it all before and let the soldier's words hang in the air like a stale fart. After sitting in front of a radio, he said, "Just guard the door and don't let anyone in. Be prepared to use that weapon. Hewitt's not going to like what I have to tell Gen. Reardan. He's likely to order me arrested."

"Arrested?"

"Or executed."

Sergeant Silverstein began to sweat. "Sir, I guess you don't know about the raid on a farm Col. Hewitt ordered yesterday afternoon, do you? He learned of the general location of the place by beating the hell out of a prisoner. The man didn't know exactly where it was, but what he did know helped us locate it. After a few days of searching with choppers that is. Evidently it's a large group, and they're all armed. The Colonel wants to make an example of them. The raid should be happening right now."

Capt. Donovan turned a new shade of white. "Oh shit!"

Chapter 8

Voices out front told Austin soldiers were not far from the house. He pushed his luck and tried one last time to contact someone on the radio. Ominous sounds from outside, a noncom barking orders and soldiers' voices not far from the door, told him it was time to flee out the back. He grabbed his rifle and ran.

Twenty seconds later, soldiers burst through the front door, carbines ready. One tall, thin soldier sprayed the living room walls with his M4, even though it was obvious the room was empty. Photos of racing horses, past champions, fell from the wall and shattered on the tile floor. Trophies and awards on shelves were torn asunder and came crashing to the floor to join the photographs.

Sergeant Derek McCain tried to yell above the chatter of the M4, but was having no luck. "Cease fire!" When the soldier stopped to reload, McCain yelled again, "Stop the damn firing. What the hell are you shooting at?"

The soldier reloaded, glaring back at McCain.

One by one, soldiers yelled, "Clear!" as they checked every room in the house for occupants. A soldier rushed down the stairs and into the living room. "There's no one here."

Lieutenant Nelson Herzing walked in, dragging Slim by the collar, still bound tightly in a rope and looking much the worse for wear. He bled from his mouth and nose, and an ugly gash ran a ragged course down the side of his head. "They left us a present." Lt. Herzing unceremoniously flung Slim onto the floor. "He says a chopper buzzed the farm several times, long before we got here. Some asshole pilot warned them."

McCain scowled. "We get back, we'll find out who that damn pilot was. I'm tired of pussies in uniform going easy on the lawless civilians. Every time I turn around, someone's whining about how hard we're being on brigands."

Slim struggled and finally sat up, despite his hands being tied together. Lt. Herzing open-handed him upside his head, knocking him back to the floor. "Intel says they have children with them. They couldn't have gone far." He kicked Slim in the stomach. "I expect this one knows where they went to."

Slim spit blood and caught his breath. "Uh, yeah, they went to the fallback camp. It's only a couple miles into the woods. They figured they had to have a place to go if they were ever forced to abandon the farm." He looked up at the men around him, terror in his eyes. "I can show you where it is."

Lt. Herzing laughed. "No wonder they have your ass tied up."

Slim maneuvered his legs into position and sat on the floor again. "They were mad at me 'cause I told them I thought we should move into town, where we would be protected." He looked up from the floor, shivering. "They're meaner than you are."

Everyone who heard what he said laughed. Sgt. McCain pulled a telescoping baton out of a jacket pocket. "Oh, I doubt that." He brought the baton down on Slim's collarbone, producing a sickening cracking sound. Slim moaned and quivered in agony on the tile, rolling onto his side.

Lt. Herzing protested, "Enough of that. We need to take him with us. Unless you want to carry him I would hold off on that shit."

"My collarbone's broken." Slim moaned. "You broke my collarbone!"

Sgt. McCain yanked Slim off the floor, ignoring his screams of agony. "I don't give a damn if your legs are broken, you're going to walk, and you're going to lead us to that camp."

~~~

There wasn't much to the emergency camp, just a few pole barns with layers of overlapping brown palmetto fronds for rain-shedding shingles on the roofs and mosquito nets for walls. Wild-eyed children clung to Kendell, afraid they were about to suffer another ordeal, complete with weeks of hunger and sleeping on the muddy ground in a swamp. Renee helped to calm the children as best she could.

Ramiro ordered his people to set up a security perimeter. He insisted on security being so well-manned that it left mostly children in the camp, as nearly all of the adults were on picket duty.

Still, Mrs. MacKay was worried. "I'm thinking we should flee deeper into the woods until there is reason to believe the soldiers have left the area. This is too close to the farm."

After making certain Brian was as comfortable as possible, Nate and Deni sought out Ramiro and Mrs. MacKay. The two were discussing moving deeper into the woods, when Nate walked up and asked, "Where's slim?" He looked around. "Please don't tell me you left him behind. I thought someone was going to take him with us or kill him."

Mrs. MacKay looked at Ramiro, a question on her face.

"I, uh, left him tied up in the shed," Ramiro said.

Deni looked sick. "The soldiers know where we are. As sure as hell, Slim has told them by now."

"The chances of outrunning them are just about zero," Nate said. "With all the children and disabled we have to deal with, we can't move fast."

Deni added, "And we're leaving a trail in the woods a blind man could follow."

"We don't have much of a chance if we fight, do we?" Ramiro asked.

Nate noticed several people listening to the conversation, but decided to tell the truth anyway. "Our chances are a little better out here in the woods than at the farm. They went from zero to slim. The problem is our casualties would be grievous. Also, so far we haven't drawn any blood. Once we do, they're much less likely to go easy on us. Remember, they're willingly following orders they know are illegal and immoral. We kill and wound a few of them, they're likely to go animal on these people, including the children."

"Oh dear Lord," Mrs. MacKay said, her voice full of worry. "For the first time in my life, I have no idea what to do. Even if we give up without a fight, there's still no guarantee of humane treatment."

"You're right," Nate said. "There's danger at every turn. But none of it's your fault. Don't blame yourself." He thought for a moment. "There are things we could do, such as send the main group deeper into the woods, while the best fighters ambush the soldiers and lure them into more ambushes. That may give the main group time to get away."

Deni shook her head. "You're grasping at straws and you know it. This isn't the same as the situation we were in at the bridge that time. Those brigands didn't have airpower, and most of them had no training. I'll tell you what could be done: a few people, such as you and Kendell could sneak away, carrying Brian, while the rest of us give up and rely on the fact they're U.S. soldiers, and even after everything that's happened, everything they've experienced, everything they've lost, they won't slaughter innocent unarmed American civilians."

"Kendell will never leave those children behind," Nate said. "And I can't leave him, not and live with myself. Then there's the danger of you being executed for desertion." Nate's demeanor told everyone what he was about to say wasn't up for discussion. "You're the only one here actually wanted for a real crime, so you take off and don't look back. The rest of us will surrender. Maybe they'll even provide medical care for Brian."

Deni was about to protest, but Ramiro spoke up. "He's right. Unless the soldiers have lost all common decency, you're the only one that's in immediate danger. They'll probably take us to town and put us in some kind of so-called safe zone. There's a good chance higher authorities will intervene before too much time passes and things get too bad."

Nate pulled keys out of his pocket. "Go to the bunker and stay there."

She refused to take the keys. "No."

Nate held her. "Go on. There's no reason for you to be caught. You staying will only put you in danger. It'll change nothing as far as the rest of us are concerned. Use the radio there to get help for us."

Tears ran down her face. "It's not right. Why should I be the only one?"

Nate held her tighter. "Because you're the only one they're likely to shoot on sight and there's no reason for you to stay. You also know how to use the radio to get in contact with someone who can help." He released her. "Go on, now. There isn't much time before they're here."

She backed away, looking at Nate and the others through tears. "I'll be on the radio night and day."

"Do that," Nate said. "Just be careful you don't let them locate your signal."

She turned and ran into the woods.

Ramiro said, "Someone should to talk to the soldiers and tell them we're turning ourselves in. I'll do it."

"Why you?" Rita asked. "I need my husband. Let someone else do it."

Ramiro started to speak, but instead walked over and held her.

Mrs. MacKay thought for a moment. "Nate, will you come with me unarmed and try to reason with them?"

Nate nodded. "Yes." He handed Ramiro his rifle, and then his pistol. "We'll do it together." He removed his pack and set it on the ground. "We need to go now. They'll be here any minute."

Mrs. MacKay told Ramiro, "Call in the pickets and tell everyone to be ready to lay down their weapons when we return. Don't do anything to give them an excuse to fire on us."

Ramiro nodded. "We are facing a very dangerous moment."

Rita said, "We will face it together. If you are to die, let me die with you."

"Let's go." Nate nodded to Mrs. MacKay. They walked into the woods, both realizing they could be shot on sight.

After walking only four hundred yards, Nate could hear the soldiers coming. He whispered, "Get down behind that log." She did as he asked, getting lower to the ground when Nate motioned with his hand.

Nate yelled out, "Don't shoot. I'm unarmed." He was answered by a barrage of automatic gunfire. Taking cover behind a large pine tree, he waited for the gunfire to slack off. When it did, he yelled out once again, "I'm unarmed, damn it – don't shoot. I have a woman with me." This time there was no gunfire, but he could hear men moving in the brush, maneuvering, coming in for the kill. "We are no threat to you and are willing to come in unarmed. We have dozens of children with us. Please do not shoot."

A voice echoed among the trees. "Come toward me with your hands up."

Mrs. MacKay stood. "We are following your instructions."

Together, they moved forward slowly, staying in the open with their hands up. "We are just people trying to survive," Nate said. "We mean no one any harm."

A soldier stepped from behind a tree, holding his M4 on them. "Stay where you are and don't move."

Nate stood in a small opening in the brush, half expecting to be shot at any second. Mrs. MacKay stood beside him. Both held their hands over their head.

The soldier who had nearly broken Slim's collarbone stepped from behind a pine tree. "Where are the others?" Sgt. McCain demanded. "Before you answer make damn sure you don't lie to me."

"They're not far," Nate answered. "We came to contact you first, so there would be no unnecessary shooting."

Lt. Herzing had been watching from cover. He exposed just enough of his head to peer around a tree. "She stays here. You go get the others and make sure they leave their guns behind."

McCain pointed his carbine at Mrs. MacKay. "The old bat will be the first to die, if you try anything."

"We're not trying anything," Nate said, "except trying to keep dozens of children alive." He turned and walked away.

Approaching the camp, Nate faced the same danger of being shot before he had a chance to speak. He yelled out to identify himself.

Ramiro yelled back. "No one will shoot. Come on into camp."

Nate approached the nervous group slowly and emerged from thick brush. "So far, so good," he told Ramiro. "They promise not to shoot if we come in unarmed. Gather up the children and stretcher-ridden. Let's get this over with."

"Where is Mrs. MacKay?" Ramiro asked.

"She's with the soldiers," Nate said. He started for Brian, Kendell, and Renee before he finished speaking his last words.

Everyone deposited their weapons under the roof of one of the pole barns, leaving a large pile. Kendell helped Nate carry the stretcher Brian was on, while Renee kept an eye on the children, keeping them close. Almost no one but the smaller children spoke. The adults were so nervous, a dozen jumped when a branch fell out of a tall pine and crashed into the underbrush. In an orderly fashion, they wended their way through the woods, not knowing whether they would be treated humanely or slaughtered on sight.

<u>Chapter 9</u>

When Nate thought he was within hearing distance, he yelled out, "We're coming in unarmed. Don't shoot."

Lt. Herzing's warning came from out of a shadow, "Get your hands in the air!"

"I can't." Nate kept coming but slowed down. "I'm carrying a stretcher."

"Raise your hands or I'll fire." The Lieutenant could only see the upper half of Nate's body, because of brush in the way.

Nate stopped. "Put him down slowly," he told Kendell. "Stay here. I'll go in and explain to them."

Kendell spoke to the children, who practically considered him to be their father after all they had been through. "You kids sit down right where you are and don't make any noise."

Nate closed the last thirty yards with his hands in the air. "We have come unarmed as we promised."

"Yeah," Herzing said, "we'll see about that. Where are the others?"

"Back there," Nate answered. "I had to leave my injured son on a stretcher, because you demanded I come in with my hands raised." He moved toward Herzing, careful to keep his open hands in the air. "Where's Mrs. MacKay?"

She spoke up from back in the woods, "I'm here. They have not harmed me."

Moving in closer, Nate stopped ten feet away from Herzing. "Well, are you going to let me go back and get my son? If you do, the rest of the group will be coming with me. There are women and children with us. Let's not have any bloodshed here today, for God's sake. That's what all of this is about – avoiding bloodshed. We're staking our lives on your honor, Lieutenant."

He laughed. "Honor?"

"Remember the words 'duty; honor; country?' The people I'm with are part of that country."

Herzing laughed again. "I'm not so sure we have a country anymore."

"Yes we do," Nate said. "And these people are part of the few left alive."

Herzing gave Nate a strange smile. "Just don't start telling me what my duty is."

On the left edge of Nate's peripheral vision, someone took off running, crashing through the brush. Nate caught the sight of Slim's terrified face as he looked over his shoulder to see if he was being pursued. Sgt. McCain fired a short burst from his M4, cutting Slim down in mid-stride. The woods in front of Nate exploded in automatic gunfire. He hit the ground screaming, "Cease fire! Cease fire!" Bullets kicked dirt up all around him and whistled over his head. The forest was ripped to shreds, as the platoon had their mad moment of constant fire. When the firing diminished somewhat, Nate was still screaming, "Cease fire! Cease fire!" It was then he heard Herzing's voice.

The Lieutenant yelled, "Cease fire!"

The woods echoed with the sound of soldiers reloading. Nate took the opportunity to yell, "You're killing children! You bastards are killing children! Stop shooting."

Forty yards behind Nate, women and children screamed. He heard Ramiro and other men warning everyone to stay down. A mother staggered into the open, holding her headless four-year-old son in her arms, staring straight ahead blankly as she stumbled along.

An ashen-faced soldier stood up from behind a log. He walked over to Herzing and dropped his rifle at his feet. "God damn you. Look what you've turned us into. This whole operation was bullshit. Hewitt is a crazy mother, and you know it. Yet you follow his orders blindly like a stupid son of a bitch." He pointed at the dazed mother. "I'm going to help them." Before he walked away, he said, "Go ahead and shoot me in the back. You'd be doing me a favor."

McCain raised his carbine and aimed at the soldier.

Herzing yelled, "Do not shoot, Sergeant. Put your weapon away. Sling it and keep it slung." He yelled out to the other soldiers in the woods, "Do not fire unless fired upon. Move in cautiously, but I don't want any more unnecessary shooting." He looked around. "Where's the RTO?"

The radiotelephone operator rushed up. "Here sir."

"Request choppers to evacuate wounded civilians." Herzing saw Nate racing to check on Brian and the others. He ran to follow.

Nate was relieved to find Brian still on the stretcher unconscious and unharmed. Renee held two terrified children. Kendell was ten yards away, franticly trying to save a little girl's life. He looked up at Nate, simmering rage and hurt fighting to be the prominent emotion in his heart. "Why did they shoot? You said they wouldn't shoot."

"It was my fault," Herzing said. "He did everything he could to prevent this."

One look at the little girl told Nate there was no hope. He remembered her name. When he first met Melissa, she was nearly starved and had an infected foot from an ugly gash. They watched her take three more breaths and die.

Nate put his hand on Kendell's shoulder. "I'm sorry. She's gone."

Kendell's whole body wracked in grief. He looked up at Herzing with his wet face. "You're not soldiers; you're murderers. You kill little children." He rose to his feet and pulled a six-inch sheath knife.

A soldier aimed his carbine at Kendell's head.

Herzing yelled, "Don't shoot! No one shoots!"

Nate jumped to his feet. "Whoa! He didn't fire a single round. I saw that much. He's not one of them who shot. He also never gave any order to shoot." He stepped between Kendell and Herzing. "Put that away and check on the other children. They need you, and you won't be here for them if you keep this up."

Kendell smeared his face. "How can you take this and not fight back? The whole idea was to keep the kids from being hurt, but the bastards shot at us anyway."

Nate held his hands out and stepped closer. "It was a tragic accident. Slim tried to run away, and a soldier shot him. The other soldiers thought they were under attack and fired. It's exactly what I was afraid of, what I tried to avoid." He grabbed Kendell's wrist and took the knife. Kendell didn't resist. Instead, he broke down. Nate put an arm across his shoulders.

"I'm sorry this happened, but it did and we have to deal with it."

"I'm all right now." Kendell took two steps toward the crying children, then suddenly veered off and charged Herzing, plowing into him with both fists. Herzing didn't defend himself, taking three blows before pushing him away. Nate rushed in and grabbed him from behind.

By that time, several soldiers were about to get involved. Herzing raised his hands and barked, "Stay back. You men help these people."

Kendell yelled, "Let me go. I'm through. Let me help the other kids."

Nate released him. He picked up the knife he had dropped on the leaf-covered forest floor. "If I give this back, you must promise me you won't use it on anyone. They'll kill you. And I wouldn't like that."

"I promise." Kendell snatched the knife out of his hand and put it back in its sheath. He went to check on the other children. From then on, he acted as if Herzing wasn't even there.

A sound caught Nate by the ear. He rushed to Brian, where he still lay on the stretcher. Brian coughed again. He opened his eyes and saw Nate kneeling beside him. The first thing Brian said was, "I'm okay." He mumbled through swollen lips. Nate could only guess at what Brian said until he said it again.

Kendell rushed over, excited. "Finally, you wake up. Must've been all the gunfire."

Nate gave him a drink of water, but he coughed it back up. "Lie still," Nate told him. "You have broken bones."

Brian winced. "I guess that's why it hurts."

Nate tried to hide his worry. "Your left arm is broken, don't try to use it. Can you see okay?"

"Not good." Brian looked around. "I don't know where we are. It looks like we're in the woods."

Nate swallowed. "As long as you can see."

He saw Renee sitting on the ground looking at him, holding children in her arms, her face wet. "I can see. Don't worry. My head hurts, though."

Nate leaned over and put his heavy hand on Brian's head. "I have Aspirin in my pack, but you have to be able to swallow."

"Aspirin doesn't do much anyway."

"You need to drink water." Nate held the canteen to his mouth. This time Brian was able to swallow a small amount. He took the canteen from Nate and drank more. A spasm of coughs forced him to stop drinking. Nate took the canteen. "That's enough for now."

Brian forced his eyes open enough to see his father better. "Did you kill him?"

Nate flinched. "Slim is dead, but I didn't do it. I didn't get the chance."

Brian grimaced, his pain visible just under the surface. "A lot of stuff must've happened while I was out."

"That's an understatement," Kendell said.

"I'll worry about what's going on and where we are," Nate said. "You lie still and worry about getting well."

Brian became agitated when he noticed the soldiers for the first time. Then he saw Melissa lying dead. "What's going on? Who killed Melissa?"

Nate pushed him down. "I told you to let me worry about that. There's nothing we can do for her now."

Brian started to speak again but Ramiro interrupted. "Thank God." The smile on Ramiro's face could not be removed with a chisel and hammer. "A miracle amidst a tragedy. How are you feeling?" Rita appeared by his side. Tears of sadness turned to tears of joy, when she saw Brian.

Brian answered, "Like I got my ass whipped and was stomped on by someone wearing size fifteen boots." He looked at Nate. "But I'll be okay."

"I know you will," Ramiro said. "You're as tough as your father."

Brian gingerly touched his face. It was still swollen even after so many days had passed. "I wouldn't say that, but I think I'll live." He moved his head and took another look around. "I wish you would tell me what's going on. Looks like it's hit the fan around here." He noticed someone was missing. "Where's Deni?"

"She's okay," Nate answered. "Now lay back and don't talk anymore."

"But where is she?"

Kendell tried to signal for him to shut up about Deni, but it was too late.

"Sergeant Deni Heath?" Herzing stepped closer. "She's a deserter. If you know anything about where she is, you better speak up now."

Brian muttered, "Shit. I stepped in it, and I can't even walk. Don't ask me. I haven't seen anyone since I was beat up and knocked out."

Nate stood and faced Herzing. "Haven't you had enough? Look at that little girl over there."

"I can show you more dead and wounded," Ramiro broke in. "May God forgive you and your soldiers."

Herzing flinched. "That was an accident. The deserter's Army business."

Nate spread his arms. "There's no Deni Heath with us. That I guarantee you. Go ahead and look for her."

"But there was." Herzing glared at Nate. "You know where she went, don't you?"

"I assume you knew her well enough to be on a first-name basis," Nate said. "Yet you're already calling her 'the deserter.' I hear a hollow echo in your chest." He pointed at Melissa's body. "Do yourself a favor and take a good look at what happens when soldiers forget they're human beings. I remember a general telling me about a book he read at West Point. The last thoughts of the main character when he was dying in Vietnam were, 'if you have to choose between being a good soldier and a good human being, choose to be a good human being.' For a while there, after the shooting stopped, I thought I saw a spark of a human man in you. Now I'm wondering again and hearing that hollow echo in your chest."

Herzing glared at him. "Go to hell. You still have your son. I've lost everyone. You haven't seen what I've seen. The Army is all I have left."

Nate pointed at Melissa's body again. "Once you've seen children your own men killed, you've seen all you need to see."

Herzing stood there for a few seconds, and Nate wondered if he was thinking of putting his pistol to Nate's head and pulling the trigger. The Lieutenant called out, "Sergeant."

Sergeant McCain was back in the woods directing the soldiers. He came on the run, his carbine ready for trouble.

Before McCain came to a halt, Herzing barked, "Get these people back to the farm, and I don't want any of them abused. Take the bodies, too. We'll bury them on the farm."

"Uh, yes sir." McCain shook his head and went back to supervising the soldiers.

Chapter 10

A quarter mile from Mrs. MacKay's farm, Lt. Herzing asked his radio telephone operator, "How about those choppers? We need to get the wounded out of here."

"They're on the way," the soldier answered. "Sir, there's something going on."

Herzing rolled his eyes. "What? Spit it out."

"Capt. Donovan has barricaded himself in the com room and has contacted Fort Benning about how Col. Hewitt is insane and must be relieved of duty." He hesitated.

"What? Out with it."

"Capt. Donovan has been ordering you to abort this mission, but every time he does, Col. Hewitt comes on the air and orders you to not listen to the Captain."

"Shit." Herzing looked up at the sky and laughed. "How long has this been going on?"

"The Captain ordering you to abort the mission? Well, maybe fifteen minutes. The other stuff's been going on for over an hour."

Herzing shook his head in disgust. "The Army went to shit with the rest of the world. You should have told me about both events as soon as they happened. A direct order must be heard directly, not through an enlisted man. I'm going to need a new radio man when we get back. You're busted."

The young soldier wrung his sweaty hands. "You were busy, and I didn't know what to do. It's all so damn crazy."

"Crazy is the right word," Herzing admitted. "Since you're worthless on the radio, help with the stretchers. We've got to get these people to the farm."

"What about the orders?" the soldier asked.

Herzing gave him a strange look. "Last time I checked, a colonel outranks a captain. But, since I never received any of those orders from either officer, thanks to you, I'll use my own discretion. I'm certainly not going to play dueling officers with those two; I don't have the rank."

Nate heard the conversation and shook his head, as he carried one end of Brian's stretcher.

Brian looked up at his father. "So they have a crazy colonel?"

Nate answered, "We're down the rabbit hole, alright. Everything is snafu, not just the Colonel."

Brian changed the subject. "I can probably walk."

"The LT says he's going to take you to a doctor," Nate said. "I'd rather wait until a doc tells me it's safe for you to be on your feet. It's not far now, anyway."

Brian looked at Kendell, who was carrying the other end of the stretcher. "I just noticed you two don't have your guns." He checked the others walking close by. "Nobody has their guns, just the soldiers."

"When you surrender, you have to give up your weapons," Kendell said.

Brian was stunned. "I didn't believe anyone could make Dad give up his guns. God, I wish I was still unconscious. My head hurts. The whole damn world is snafu."

~~~

Bullets smashed through the communication room door and wounded the soldier who was inside with Capt. Donovan. The satellite phone in the com room was designed to use a microwave dish on the roof, but Col. Hewitt had ordered the dish antenna disabled just after Donovan contacted Gen. Reardan. All of the radio antenna wires on the roof of the building had been disconnected also, and he could no longer broadcast or receive transmissions, but not before Gen. Reardan had personally promised him the matter of Col. Hewitt's crimes would be dealt with and that he was sending an envoy from another forward operations base, complete with a one-star general, who happened to be there to inspect the FOB. He was told they should arrive by rotorcraft within two hours.

Donovan yelled through the bullet-hole-ridden door, "I've got a wounded man in here. I'm coming out unarmed, don't shoot." A chair had been propped up under the doorknob. He removed that and several heavy boxes. Then he slowly opened the door. A soldier waiting outside sprayed him in the face with pepper spray. Two more soldiers pounced on him and had his hands zip-tied behind his back in a matter of seconds. The pepper spray had everyone's eyes watering in the small room, and Donovan was gagging. They dragged him out into the hallway, and then dragged him down the stairway, his boots clunking on each step, until they reached the first floor.

Hewitt waited impatiently, fuming in the middle of the street. The soldiers dragged Donovan outside, dropping him on the sidewalk. Hewitt scowled and took three quick steps, ending with a viscous kick to Donovan's face. "I can't stand a traitorous bastard!"

Donovan spit out a tooth. "So now your superior officers are the enemy? I didn't radio China; I radioed Gen. Reardan at Fort Benning. By the way, Gen. Reardan has relieved you of duty, but then you know that." He looked around at the other soldiers. "Did you hear me? Col. Hewitt is no longer your CO. A BG is on his way to take the Colonel's place at this moment. Any order he gives you now is illegal. Follow his orders at risk of charges being filed against you." No one said anything. "You've been warned. Whatever happens now comes with a heavy price."

Hewitt wasn't concerned. "Yeah, they sent a brigadier general. I'm scared shitless." Spittle flew from his mouth, as he spoke. His face red with rage, he pointed at a nearby light pole. "Hang him!"

The soldiers hesitated. This was too much. Hang a captain? Hewitt *is* nuts! While everyone there had seen too much and was as rough around the edges as a soldier could be, unlike the Colonel, they were not crazy enough to hang a captain. With military discipline being the way it had been the last few months, thoughts of being tried and executed raced through their minds.

Staff Sergeant Steve Novak barked, "You heard the Colonel!" A dozen soldiers looked at each other nervously, not knowing what to do.

Sergeant First Class Quint Bartow rushed in from the edge of the crowd. "Col. Hewitt's orders are not legal. And I believe Capt. Donovan's claim that the Colonel has been relieved of duty." No one moved. Bartow let loose with a string of obscenities only a soldier could think of. "Use your goddamn heads! Since when does the U.S. Army summarily hang captains?" Still no one moved. "I'm the senior noncom here.

And Col. Hewitt is obviously bat shit crazy. Now detain the Colonel and let the Captain go. The Captain will be in charge until the BG arrives."

Novak raised his carbine to shoot Bartow. A private reached out and snatched the barrel, forcing the muzzle skyward just as a round went off. Two more soldiers moved in to help and forced Novak to the ground.

Novak screamed threats. "You pussies do not seem to understand that this is not the world we were in before the plague. Only the strong and hard will survive."

"Make sure they're both unarmed," Bartow ordered. "Then tie their hands and take them to the courthouse. Release the civilian locked in the cell there and put these two in his place." He looked around, his gaze as cold as ice. "If anyone here thinks I've committed a crime, report me to the BG when he arrives. In the meantime, write down what you've witnessed here, because you'll be expected to testify." He produced a knife from his pocket and bent down to cut the zip ties from Donovan's wrists. After helping him up, he asked, "What are your orders?"

Donovan rubbed his sore jaw and wiped blood off his chin. "Carry on, Sergeant." His eyes were still red from the pepper spray, but they lit up as he rubbed his cut and bleeding wrists. "You're doing a splendid job on your own. You don't need my supervision."

"Thank you sir." Bartow handed Donovan a canteen of water.

The first thing Donovan did after washing the pepper spray out of his eyes was check on the wounded soldier who had helped him in the radio room. Learning that the man had died pissed him off. He marched to the courthouse to confront Novak, ignoring the throbbing pain from having a tooth kicked out of his mouth. Standing in front of the cell door, Donovan glared at Novak. "Sergeant Silverstein died. Do you know who fired into the radio room?"

Novak sat on the edge of a bunk, looking at the floor. "Go to hell."

Donovan simmered long enough to hold his temper. Too much insane bullshit had already occurred, and he refused to add to it. "A man has been murdered, and you have nothing to say?"

Novak still didn't bother to look up. "I already said it. Go to hell."

Hewitt lay in a bunk on the other side of the cell, quivering and muttering to himself, showing more signs of a total breakdown. Evidently, there was still enough of a mind left in his head to allow him to understand he was in deep trouble.

~~~

Four helicopters were waiting when Mrs. MacKay's group arrived at the farm, escorted by the soldiers. A pilot called Lt. Herzing over. "Has your radio been on the blink?" he asked. "Capt. Donovan's been trying to raise you." He motioned with his head. "Come on and use the chopper radio."

Herzing got in the helicopter and waited until the pilot had Donovan on the radio and then took the mike and earphones. He listened intently as the radio crackled, his eyes growing wide at times and narrowing at other times. Afterward, he strode to Mrs. MacKay, a sense of purpose in his gait. "Call all of your lieutenants around," he told her. "I don't want to have to say this but once."

She looked confused. "Lieutenants?"

Seeming to be impatient, he answered, "Foremen, managers, closest confidants, people you rely on to help you run this place."

Mrs. MacKay pointed to Ramiro, who stood next to her. "My foreman's right here." There were more than a dozen others with her also, including Nate, Kendell, and Brian, still on the stretcher. Two dozen children were under a nearby large oak, most of them were asleep on the grass. Renee watched over them.

"Well." Herzing scratched his neck. "It's good news. I've been ordered to leave you people alone and allow you to keep your weapons. We're still going to take the wounded to town, though."

Kendell exploded. "It's a bit too goddamn late! You gonna bring back the dead?"

Herzing turned white under his suntanned skin. "I know it's all fu –" He glanced at Mrs. MacKay and Rita. "Uh, this has been a crazy morning for all of us. I'm sorry."

"Yes you are," Kendell said. He looked around and saw that most of the soldiers close enough to hear were looking down in shame. He swallowed and walked away twenty yards, then turned his back and cried.

~~~

The critically wounded were the first to be loaded onto the helicopters. Brian was not among them. He still lay on the stretcher, but it had been put on a couch in Mrs. MacKay's living room. He lay there and watched his father and Kendell help Mrs. MacKay clean up the mess left by the soldiers. Several times, he had started to get up, but Nate stopped him, insisting that he be checked out by a doctor before he tried to stand or walk.

Kendell carefully removed photos from their shattered frames and put them in a cardboard box.

"Careful you don't cut yourself on the broken glass," Mrs. MacKay warned.

"I don't understand why they shot up your house." Kendell placed a wedding photo of Mrs. MacKay and her late husband in the box.

Her hand shook as she repositioned a strand of hair to get it out of her eyes. "I would rather they had done all of the shooting in here. This house doesn't bleed."

"For a while there, it looked like it was going to get real bad." Kendell stopped short when he noticed everyone in the room was looking at him.

Nate had a broom in his hands. He stopped sweeping and said, "It was close. But there's no point in lingering on what might have happened."

"I ain't lingering," Kendell said. "But there ain't no forgetting the needless killing of kids."

"No, there isn't," Nate agreed. "But it was brought on by nervous soldiers who were afraid of being ambushed. It was an accident. As I told you before, no order to fire was given."

Kendell persisted. "People were killed for no reason."

Nate debated whether to respond or let Kendell's statement stand, when he noticed Brian had fallen asleep on the stretcher. He walked over and checked his breathing, finding it shallow and slow. He could tell something was wrong, so he shook him. "Brian. Wake up." He didn't respond.

"What's wrong?" Kendell asked, as he rushed over.

Nate's nervous response was, "He's out again, and barely breathing."

Renee was in the kitchen and helping to prepare a meal for the children when she heard. She ran into the living room. Standing near Brian and Nate, she reached down and touched Brian's forehead. "He's very pale and clammy. Something's wrong."

<u>Chapter 11</u>

Two soldiers helped Nate get Brian on board the helicopter, its rotor blade spinning overhead and jet engine roaring. Brian still hadn't woken. Nate reached in and put his hand on Brian's chest to check his breathing.

Ramiro and a dozen other men had gone back to get everyone's weapons and had just returned. He handed Nate his rifle and pistol. After handing Nate his backpack he said, "I'll put Brian's rifle and pack away where it'll be safe until he comes back. Good luck. We'll pray for him."

"Thank you," Nate said, sick with worry.

Renee stood by Kendell and watched the helicopter lift off, her face strained. She held Kendell for a second and then walked back toward the house.

Twenty-five minutes later, they were flying over the edge of town. Nate noticed right away that the number of soldiers had tripled since the last time he was there. The pilot changed the rotor's pitch and slowed the helicopter, then made a left turn and landed in the middle of a baseball field. A military ambulance waited nearby.

After Brian was loaded on board the ambulance along with several other patients, he was whisked away to the town clinic. Nate caught a ride in a HUMVEE. As they sped through town following the ambulance, Nate was in for more surprises, astonished at how much work had been completed since the last time he was in town. He estimated the Army's presence to be at battalion level, and that was going by only what he could see from the air earlier and then at street level. When the ambulance stopped in front of the clinic, Nate jumped out of the HUMVEE and followed those carrying Brian's stretcher to the front entrance. Soldiers guarding the entrance insisted he give up his weapons before entering. He handed them over without hesitation and then dropped his pack by the wall out of the way. A private promised he would take care of them, but Brian was the only thing on Nate's mind at that moment. He rushed in without a word.

Nate was ordered to wait in the lobby. In an air-conditioned room for the first time in over a year, he felt cold. The sunrise hour had been in the fifties, but as the day had worn on, it had risen into the eighties and grown humid. Folding his arms for warmth, he looked out the ground-level window, preparing for a long anxious wait. Two women in white walked by, chatting quietly. He turned and noticed for the first time that the ceiling lights were also lit up. It gave him reassurance to learn they had plenty of power and seemed to have a fully operating medical installation going.

After staring out of the window for more than an hour, Nate turned when Doctor Sheila Brant appeared, looking tired and harried, but somehow less strained than he had ever seen her before. There seemed to be a spring in her step and a purposeful confidence on her face. Following along behind her was a military doctor dressed in a blue surgeon gown. A face mask hung from his neck. He stopped at a trash can long enough to remove the mask and gown and throw them in.

Doctor Brant said, "I wish I had better news for you."

Nate turned white. "Tell me. Don't drag it out."

She said, "He's alive, but still unconscious. The problem is his skull was fractured and a piece of bone is protruding into his brain, producing hematoma. We performed a CT angiography and found no vascular injuries, but a blood clot is causing pressure on his brain. He's being prepped for surgery to relieve that pressure." She motioned with her right hand. "Doctor Millhouse will perform the surgery."

Brian was foremost on Nate's list of concerns, but in the back of his mind were thoughts of astonishment at the progress that had been made in so little time since he was last in town. Nate felt as if he had been brought back to the twenty-first century, and renewed hopes for Brian welled up within him, despite the dire prognosis. Sometimes the military can prove that government inefficiency and incompetence doesn't have to be the norm. He noticed the doctor's rank. "Major, what are his chances?"

Doctor Millhouse crossed his arms. "What has me worried is the length of time since the injury. It looks like it has been many days, maybe a week. It's a very small piece of bone and it's not very deep into the brain. His problem is the damage from waiting so long for treatment." He glanced at Dr. Brant and then back to Nate. "Has he been unconscious since the injury?"

Nate mopped his forehead with his arm. "No. He woke for a few seconds sometime back and again this morning for over an hour and seemed okay. He was talking and seemed normal. In less than two hours though, he was unconscious again."

"You must have kept him horizontal since he was injured."

Dr. Brant looked on waiting for Nate's answer.

"Yes," Nate said. "He wanted to get up several times, but I told him not to."

Dr. Brant commented, "That saved his life. If he had stood, his brain would've shifted in his skull, and that may have killed him. It certainly would have caused more hemorrhaging and a larger blood clot, resulting in even more pressure on his brain."

Nate had to sit down. He staggered to a nearby chair, remembering how he had almost allowed Brian to go ahead and stand. He just seemed to be so normal when he was conscious.

Dr. Brant sat down beside him. "Now that he has access to modern medicine, he has a good chance. The army has brought in a lot of equipment, including large diesel generators to power the clinic. Their medical personnel are the best there is. So Brian is in good hands. A lot has been going on around here besides Col. Hewitt's antics."

Doctor Millhouse tilted his head and gave Nate an intense stare. "What happened to the boy? Looks like somebody put a boot to him. He has broken ribs and a broken arm. I've seen plenty of spouse and child abuse in my time, so tell the truth."

Nate's eyes flared. "Someone did beat the hell out of him. A soldier shot the bastard this morning, before I had a chance."

Doctor Millhouse grunted. "I see. Time for me to scrub up." He rubbed his red eyes. "It's going to be a while, so try not to worry yourself to death. I think he'll be okay, but I won't know until I see what's inside. Problem is we're getting low on drugs, and he'll need anti-seizure medication while he's healing. A medical supply company's trying to jumpstart its production, but, of course, the plague killed off most of their qualified personnel and anti-seizure drugs aren't high on the priority list." He bent backward to stretch his tired back muscles and said, "We'll have to get by with what we have. It'll all be over for your son long before we get any new drugs." Seeing the look on Nate's face, he added, "I really do think, though, Brian will be back on his feet and out of here in a few days." He turned and disappeared down a hallway.

Dr. Brant changed the subject. "Capt. Donovan has already made a lot of difference in the short time he's been in charge. I've been told a brigadier general is taking over and Col. Hewitt is being held for trial."

Nate barely heard her words.

She touched his shoulder. "After all you've been through, I have no doubt you'll stand up to whatever happens. He's in good hands, so try to relax until it's over." She stood. "I have patients to see, but I'll check on him and report back to you later." She left Nate sitting there in the lobby with a dozen other worried people, who, like Nate, had the dread of impending loss on their faces.

~~~

Brigadier General Bernard Myers craned his neck to get a better look at the activities below as the helicopter approached the downtown area. He spoke into the mike. "Give me a one-mile circle at low altitude."

The pilot nodded. "Yes sir."

The bustle of little people far below reminded him of an anthill. Flying over the outskirts of town earlier, he had noticed a steady stream of vehicles heading for the lake. A tanker truck loaded with fresh gasoline straight from Texas and the one and only refinery that a company had managed to start up again stood in a parking lot that was once for school buses. Another tanker contained diesel fuel. The military still had the oil reserves that had lasted so long because most of the military was forced to shut down from lack of personnel. Refining the oil reserves into usable fuel had been a problem until the Texas company managed to restart operations. No one in government had planned for such a massive die-off outside of a full nuclear war with Russia, and every decision had to be made on the fly. Several eighteen-wheelers of food, mostly two-year-old MREs, were parked on the other side of the compound. The food wasn't for the civilians, though some of it had been handed out that morning to those who appeared to be near starvation. From what he had seen already, Donovan was already well on his way to getting things moving in the right direction. The fuel trucks were not his doing, but most of the rest was, and Myers was pleased with what he had seen so far. He anticipated a short stay before leaving Donovan in charge.

Myers spoke into the mike again, "Bring us on in."

The pilot flared, turned to the right, and touched down next to another helicopter. Donovan ran to greet him. He saluted. "It's been a while, General. I wish we were meeting under more pleasant circumstances."

The General instinctively bent over to keep low until he was out from under the spinning rotor. Yelling above the noise of the engine, he asked, "Where is Col. Hewitt?"

"Locked in a cell in the courthouse." The two climbed into a HUMVEE. "He is unharmed and comfortable enough. Do you want to see him now?"

"No," Myers said. "Take me to your headquarters. I want you to fill me in on what you've managed to accomplish and what you plan to get done over the next weeks and months."

The driver took them through the large parking lot and past the two fuel tanker trucks he had seen while in the air. Myers asked, "How much fuel have you distributed to the locals?"

"Not much. A few hundred gallons," Donovan answered. "Just enough to get their truck loads of stuff to the lake."

"What's the population of the locals here?"

"About two hundred, maybe a little more."

Myers seemed pleased. "Good. You're being stingy with the fuel. Those two tankers will probably be all you'll get for a long time. You'll need that fuel for your own vehicles." Myers looked out the window and watched a heavily loaded truck drive by, heading for the lake. He had questions, lots of questions. "Have you checked out the location they're moving to? Is it a viable place for agriculture? They'll be needing five pounds of food per day per person, and that'll require them to successfully work a very large and productive farm."

"I'm not a farmer," Donovan said, "but I've been told by people who should know that the rough plan they've worked out to irrigate the lowland there will probably work. Also, the land seems plenty fertile enough to grow beans and vegetables on. There's a lot of rich black peat there, so the lower part of that land is very fertile. They're planning an extensive network of irrigation ditches that'll be several feet below the lake's water level and will be controlled by dams. Basically, they're going back one hundred years and using old methods. If it works, they'll be able to irrigate over two thousand acres of land without use of pumps or the consumption of any energy whatsoever." He smiled and shrugged. "Every damn bit of it would've been illegal before the plague, as they're committing a hundred federal and state environmental crimes. The land is part of a state nature preserve. It seems all of the environmentalists must have died in the plague, since no one's protesting about it."

Meyers smiled back and nodded. "Even environmentalists like to eat." He immediately became serious again. "If they have a severe protracted drought, they'll have to dig the ditches deeper when the lake's water level drops, and that'll make it necessary to use pumps to get the water out of the ditches onto the fields. Chances are there still won't be much fuel for tractors or other equipment for many years, so they'll have to dig the ditches deeper and pump the water by hand. Even after they've had a few successful harvests, these people will not be out of the woods. The days of a guaranteed full belly in America are over. At least for a while."

"Yes sir," Donovan agreed. "These are a hearty people, though, and I expect we'll not have to stay here long before moving on to help another population center. They'll probably have a police or sheriff department up and running soon. They've already proven they can protect themselves."

Meyers watched another heavily loaded truck go by. "They're taking everything they might possibly need, aren't they?"

"Yes sir. There're a resourceful bunch, accomplished scavengers. It's one reason why they've survived for so long with no help from us. After what I saw in Miami and Orlando, it's refreshing to see people so self-reliant. They remind me of people I've read about in history books, those who pioneered this continent. It's also gratifying to see people not slaughtering and robbing each other. Instead, they've worked together to expel a violent gang."

Meyers nodded in silence. He looked out the window and saw people determined to survive and provide a future for their children. The clinic caught his attention as the convoy went by, because it had military vehicles parked in front of it. "Is that clinic your doing?"

"Yes sir," Donovan answered. "But Col. Hewitt had already gotten the ball rolling. He wanted the clinic for our personnel only, though. Also, there are two or three civilian doctors and a dozen nurses who've been helping since I gave them permission to treat civilians."

"Turn around. I want to see the clinic."

The driver heard. "Yes sir." He slowed and hooked a U turn on Main Street. The rest of the convoy followed his example.

Before Myers got out, he said, "From the looks of your face, you might want a doctor to take a look at you while we're here."

Donovan smiled, then grimaced from the pain. "What I need is a dentist. Col. Hewitt kicked a tooth out. I think the root broke off, and the remainder needs to be removed."

"You definitely need stitches," Myers said. "While you're being looked after, I'll take a look around; see what I can do to help as far as supplies go."

~~~

Nate heard a commotion near the entrance of the clinic. He momentarily forgot his troubles when he saw a general coming his way. His first instinct was to stand and salute, but he stayed seated. It had been a long time since he was in the Army. He did stand when Donovan and Meyers approached.

"General," Donovan said, "this is Nate Williams. Nate, this is General Myers." The two shook hands. Donovan said, "I heard about your son. How's he doing?"

"There's a blood clot on his brain from a splinter of his skull causing bleeding. They're operating now." Strain was evident on Nate's face. "They tell me he'll probably be okay."

"Who's the doctor?" Donovan asked.

Nate answered, "Major Millhouse is operating."

Donovan tried to reassure him. "Major Millhouse has been known to work miracles. If he says there's a good chance, there is."

Nate nodded and swallowed.

Myers gave Donovan a questioning look, as if he were asking why he had bothered to introduce this civilian to him.

"General," Donovan said. "We have a situation with a sergeant who went AWOL when Col. Hewett issued her illegal and immoral orders that she could not obey. She feared the Colonel would have her shot, and for good reason. Col. Hewitt, in fact, ordered that I be hanged. A noncom stepped in and saved me. It's all in my report." He touched his throbbing jaw. "The short of it is she had to flee for her life and is now on the run. I have reason to believe her action saved the lives of this man, his son, and a teenage boy." He motioned with his hand. "I believe Nate knows where she is. I was hoping you would reassure him that if she were to return on her own accord, she would suffer no repercussions. Personally, I feel she did the right thing under the circumstances."

Myers nodded as he listened. "Mr. Williams…" he turned to Donovan. "What is her name?"

"Sergeant Deni Heath," Donovan answered.

Myers continued, "You have my word no charges will be filed against Sergeant Heath, and there will be no punishment of any kind, if she returns to post as soon as possible."

"That's good to hear," Nate said. "There'll be no way to get in contact with her, at least until tomorrow. She has a long way to travel by foot to get to a radio. The plan was for her to try to get in touch with the National Guard and inform them of Col. Hewitt's mental illness and his crimes."

Donovan asked, "What's the earliest she could reach her destination?"

"She'll have to travel no more than a mile or two per hour to be safe, since she's traveling alone," Nate answered. "But I suspect she'll throw caution to the wind and get there as soon as possible, because she still believes innocent people are in danger. I would start listening for her transmissions on HAM radio tomorrow afternoon. I don't know exactly what frequency she's going to be on."

Donovan said, "I'll see that it's done."

The two officers left Nate standing in the lobby, relieved that it appeared Deni wasn't in any trouble, but still worried sick about Brian.

Chapter 12

Tired of staring at the clinic lobby walls, Nate got up to stare out of the window. A voice from behind caught his attention.

"Hey." Doctor Brant's smile was broader than Major Millhouse's. Nate knew the operation must have gone well.

"He's not out of the woods yet," Major Millhouse said, "but Brian's chances of a complete recovery are good."

Nate had to sit down. The sudden release of stress seemed to suddenly drain his energy. "I would like to see him."

"Okay," Major Millhouse said. "But only for a few seconds. He's going to be pale from the operation, but you know that. After you've seen him, though, you need to take care of yourself. Get a warm meal in you and find a place to sleep. There are plenty of empty homes in this town, so that shouldn't be difficult."

"Sleeping is what will be difficult," Nate said. He stood. "Thank you both for your help. I would like to see him now."

Doctor Brant glanced at Millhouse and saw how exhausted he was. "I'll take you to him. We've got a tired surgeon here who needs rest as much as you."

Chesty Johnson walked into the lobby. Seeing Nate and Doctor Brant, he walked over. "I just heard about Brian. How is he?"

"They tell me he has a good chance," Nate answered.

"Good." Chesty seemed relieved. "We can't afford to lose any more good people, and Brian is obviously going to be the man his father is."

"I'm on the way to see him now." Nate took a step and then stopped. "Why don't you come with me? There are a few things I want to talk with you about before I get some shuteye."

Chesty nodded. "Sure, I would like to see him myself. He's a good kid." Doctor Brant led the way. As they walked down a hallway, Chesty asked, "How's that teen, Kendell, doing?"

"He's safe at the MacKay farm." Nate kept his voice low, so as not to disturb resting patients. "He wouldn't leave those kids he's taken under his wing."

"That figures," Chesty said. "He's another one we can't afford to lose."

They entered the room and approached the bed. Brian was as white as the sheet he lay on, his head bandaged and an oxygen tube in his nose. Doctor Brant and Chesty left after staying only a few seconds, so Nate could be alone with him. He touched his son's chest to feel his heartbeat and his chest move when he breathed. "Everyone's okay at the MacKay farm and Deni will be back soon. The townspeople are hard at work moving to the lake. So don't worry about anything, just get better." He bent down and whispered in his ear. "I've got to get some rest, but I'll be here when you wake." He wiped his face and left the room.

Chesty waited in the hallway. Avoiding looking at Nate directly, he said, "Doctor Brant was called away to help with a patient." He finally looked at him, ignoring the anguish on his face. "You should get some rest now. I'll take you to a house nearby. It's within walking distance."

Nate acquiesced. He knew it was time for him to get some sleep. Brian wasn't going to wake until the drugs he was being given to keep him unconscious were reduced.

Outside the clinic, Nate picked up his weapons and backpack. He followed Chesty to a house down the street. To Nate's surprise, old Atticus and his adopted black son Deputy Tyrone were waiting for them with dinner ready to be warmed up in a camper's oven on a fire in the backyard. He had met them both when they were forced to deal with a violent gang in town.

The four men, all widowers who had lost family members in the plague and its after math, discussed the vast improvement in the townspeople's relations with the Army since Hewitt had been relieved of duty and arrested.

Tyrone washed down his rice and beans with water. "No one who isn't causing trouble has been disarmed, and no one has been prevented from leaving town and coming back for more scavenged supplies. The Army being here is actually turning out to be a good thing, so far."

"Yeah, but wait until they get a new officer or new orders from Washington," Atticus warned. "I don't trust the government, and after everything that's happened I trust them even less."

Nate didn't have much to say. Exhaustion and worry had drained him. "I think I'll hit the sack. Thanks for the meal." He got up from the table.

"Uh," Chesty said, "pick any room. We'll wake you if there's any news of Brian. I doubt he'll be waking anytime soon, though."

~~~

The next day found Nate back at the clinic. After checking on Brian, he decided to help Chesty and Tyrone coordinate efforts to protect the townspeople from the criminal element. Later in the day, Atticus joined them. Several more dependable men were needed to form the foundation of a sheriff department. Nate was asked to be a deputy but declined. "I'm not planning on staying long," he said. "As soon as Brian is well, we'll be heading for the sticks. There's just too much excitement around here to suit me."

Tyrone and Chesty tried to talk him into staying, but he would have none of it.

The Army worked closely with the fledgling sheriff department and learned a lot about the town's crime problems, mostly theft of needful items such as food, weapons, and tools. Since the gang had been run out of town, the crime rate had dropped drastically. There was one rape that had been committed six days before and remained unsolved. Chesty and Tyrone had exhausted all leads. The victim was only fourteen years old and of no help, not wanting to talk to anyone but her mother and unable to give any description of her attacker. Until she was able to provide more to go on, there was nothing the two men could do.

Donovan seemed genuinely interested in the welfare of the people and ordered his soldiers to treat everyone with respect but be ready to handle the troublemakers, stepping in only when necessary to keep the peace. There had been a few minor problems with parentless teens getting mouthy with the soldiers at checkpoints late at night, but things had gone smoothly enough.

The next day at the clinic, Doctor Brant asked Chesty when there was going to be an election. "After all, sheriffs are elected," she said. "They don't appoint themselves."

Chesty looked at her and the others sheepishly. "I guess it was a little presumptuous. My old position as Town Marshal was mostly symbolic. Tyrone should probably be Sheriff until we can arrange an election."

Tyron threw his hands up and shook his head. "Oh no. I don't want the job. Besides, the pay is terrible."

"It's exactly the same as a deputy's pay," Chesty quipped.

Tyrone came back with, "Yeah, exactly zero." They both laughed.

Nate wasn't in much of a mood for joking. "Once a harvest is realized at the lake, you can be paid in food."

Doctor Brant said, "That's more than I've been paid for my services. I wonder how many tomatoes setting a broken arm is worth in the current market." She massaged the back of her neck. "Speaking of broken arms, I've got to get back to work."

Chesty became serious again. "You need to get some rest and take better care of yourself. We can't afford to lose our best doctor. I doubt the military is going to stay more than a month or so. Best to let them take some of the load off you while they're here."

"Believe me, they have. I'm hoping they'll leave some of their equipment and supplies behind when they go. Maybe if I impress them, they'll get the idea I can put it to good use and decide to leave a little more for the town clinic." She walked away before anyone could reply.

"You know, her energy level makes me feel old." Atticus could see a smart-aleck response coming from Chesty before he spoke. "Oh, shut up."

Chesty threw his arms up. "I didn't say anything."

Tyrone laughed. "You probably *are* the oldest fart in town, now that you mention it."

Atticus feigned insult. "That's no way to speak to the man who raised you."

Nate stepped away, lost in his own thoughts.

"Hey Nate." Chesty said. "We found a couple springs near the lake, right where we want to grow vegetables. Besides irrigating the crops, what else can we use the springs for?"

"Potable water for one thing," Nate answered. "You can also build a springhouse over them for refrigeration."

Chesty knitted his brow. "How does that work? The water can't be that cold."

"I think most springs in Florida are a constant seventy-two degrees." Nate's mind was obviously still on Brian, but he continued. "That's a lot better than ninety or one hundred degrees in July."

Chesty nodded. "Oh, I see."

Atticus chimed in. "Before refrigeration, they used iceboxes. Up north, they would wait until the lakes froze and then saw big blocks of ice, put them on a sled drawn by a team of horses and drag them to the ice house. They usually had ice all summer before it melted. They could keep meat in the ice house without it spoiling. Down here, they used springhouses, but they weren't cold enough to keep meat for long."

Getting more interested in the conversation, Nate added, "Certainly, a springhouse will help vegetables stay fresh longer."

Chesty surveyed Nate's face. "We could use some help on the springhouses, also advice on laying out the irrigation ditches."

"I'm sure there are better qualified people in town to design your springhouses for you." Nate thought for a moment, remembering a film he saw about farming. It was produced during the Depression, and he remembered how the irrigation ditches were set up. "I might have an idea or two on the irrigation ditches, though."

"Anything we should be bringing with us from town?" Atticus asked. "I'll be loading a truck up and heading to the lake with another load this morning."

"Yeah," Nate answered. "Pipe. Three-inch diameter and about five-feet long. It needs to have a curve in it. Not a ninety-degree elbow, but like this." He scribed an arc in the air. "You'll need a lot of them, hundreds."

Atticus tugged on his grey whiskers. "Will two-inch diameter do? There's a lot of that grey stuff for electrical conduit out on the edge of town at a builder's supply place. No one wanted it I guess, but it's still there. The scavengers haven't touched it."

Momentarily forgetting his worries about Brian, Nate said, "Two-inch pipe's big enough. Electrical conduit can be heated and bent easily, so it'll work fine. Just take the stuff to the fields after you have the ditches finished. Cut and bend it to work. Right now, you don't know how high or wide the mounds of dirt on each side of the branch ditches will be, so it'll be better to wait and fit the pipe to work properly. That way you'll only waste one or two pieces of pipe if the first try turns out too short."

Tyrone narrowed his eyes in thought. "How do you pump the water from the ditch over the dirt mound and through the pipe?"

Nate's simple one-word answer was, "Siphon."

Chesty laughed. "Who's going to suck on the pipe to get the siphon started?"

Nate almost smiled, but Brian was still on his mind. "You don't. Just dip the entire pipe in the water to fill it and quickly bring one end over the mound and set it down, while keeping the other end in the ditch water. When the water in the pipe pours out, it'll cause suction and the ditch water will siphon out onto the nearest row of plants. No need to look for someone with a big mouth."

The others laughed.

"To tell you the truth," Nate admitted, "I've never done it. I just saw it in a film about farming during the Depression. My father said he had irrigated crops that way when he was young, but it was illegal to use lake or river water, since environmental laws were put in place over the decades. Hell, it's been illegal just to cut a cypress tree down on the edge of a lake or river in this state for decades. I always thought it was stupid to force farmers to by fuel or electricity to pump clean, drinkable water out of the ground to water crops, when there's a lake or river nearby with plenty of water that's too dirty to drink but plenty good for watering vegetables."

"But the government can dam up a river and ruin the fish population, or drain a marsh and fill it in to make room for another prison." Atticus shook his head.

"No one ever said that government has to be smart," Chesty quipped.

The conversation was interrupted when Doctor Brant appeared, her face showing alarm. "Brian woke ten minutes ago. Before Doctor Millhouse or I could go get you, he had a seizure." She raised her hands to Nate's reaction. "He's sedated. Brian's fine."

Nate rushed past her and down the hall.

Chesty paled. "Oh dear Lord."

She stayed just long enough to say, "If we only had the proper drugs, the seizures could be controlled." She ran after Nate.

Atticus followed. "I don't know about you two, but I want to be there in case Nate needs me. He's been there for us and the entire town."

Tyrone and Chesty followed in silence.

<u>Chapter 13</u>

She wasn't even sure what she had heard was human, but Deni decided to take precautions, so she stopped in heavy concealment and cover to listen. She knew she wasn't far from the dirt road that led to Nate's farm and was ready for trouble in case anyone was around, but the noise she had just heard made her skin crawl.

The sound came to her ears again. She suddenly realized it was a small child crying. Inching closer while staying in cover, she peered out into the clearing that was the road. Thirty yards away, she saw a ragged-out twenty-year-old pickup with a flat tire. Maneuvering closer enabled her to see from a different angle. She saw a filthy little raven-haired girl tied to the back bumper. The little girl was chewing at the rope in a desperate attempt to free herself. She kept looking down the road with frantic eyes, terror on her face. Deni searched the area for who or what she was terrified of. Seeing no sign of anyone, she moved closer, staying just within the edge of the woods and out of sight.

After another look around, Deni yelled to the little girl, "Who tied you up?"

The girl stopped chewing at the rope and jerked her head to face Deni's direction. "Please untie me before he comes back," she pleaded.

"Who is he?" Deni asked.

"A mean man," she answered. "He makes me call him Daddy but he's not my daddy. My daddy's dead."

"Where's your mother?" Deni asked.

"She's dead too."

"Is this man alone?"

"Yes," the little girl answered. "He went to get a tire off one of the cars back there in the road."

Deni knew she was speaking of a mangled mess of abandoned vehicles. "This man just took you?"

She began to cry again. "He killed my daddy and then took me away."

Deni's blood boiled. She wanted to stay there and wait for him to come back, so she could kill him. The little girl's frantic attempts to free herself and the fact there was no sign that the man was coming back anytime soon, prompted her to decide to free the girl and take her with her. The people back at Mrs. MacKay's farm were depending on her to get help from the National Guard, and she wasn't going to waste time waiting around to kill a man, no matter how much he needed it.

After one last look around before exposing herself to anyone who might be waiting out there with a rifle, Deni rushed to the pickup with a knife in her hand. The sharp blade cut the rope with one slash. "Come with me. Hurry," she told the little girl.

With residual fear in her eyes but glee on her face, the little girl stayed on her heels as they raced for the tree line and life-saving cover. They rushed through the woods one hundred yards before Deni stopped and turned to her. She kneeled down and set her carbine by her side, then looked the girl over for any injuries, finding only bruises and welts. "My name is Deni. What's yours?"

"Samantha." She sat down to tie her shoe lace. "My mommy and daddy called me Sammie, sometimes Sam."

"Okay, Samantha, are you thirsty?" She handed over a canteen. Samantha took it and drank eagerly. "Whoa!" Deni warned. "Take your time. You can have more later."

"I'm still thirsty," she pleaded.

"Okay. Just drink slower." Deni handed the canteen back. "How old are you, Samantha?"

She held up five fingers.

"Five years old. Well, that means you're a big girl now and can walk a long ways."

Samantha nodded. "We have to get away from him before he comes looking for me. I'm not thirsty now." She looked back toward the road. "Hurry. Let's go."

"Okay. We'll go, but no one's going to hurt you. Not that man or anyone else. You're with me now."

She looked up at Deni. "Why are you dressed like a soldier?"

Smiling, she said, "Because I am a soldier. And my job is to protect little kids like you. I promise no one is going to hurt you again." She picked up her carbine. "Can you follow along behind and try not to make any noise?"

She nodded.

"Good. If I'm going too fast or you get tired, just say my name."

"Okay, but we should go now. That man is mean."

Deni bent down and held her. "I told you not to be afraid. The last thing that guy wants is to catch up with us. It'll be the sorriest day of his life. I wish I had time to stay here and take care of him now, but there's something I have to do."

~~~

"We're almost there," Deni told Samantha. "I need you to stay in this brush and be quiet until I come back. I'm not expecting anyone to be around, but let me check and be sure." She kneeled to talk to Samantha at eye level. "Can you stay here, don't move, and be quiet?"

Samantha nodded. "Don't stay away too long."

"I won't. It'll only be a few minutes." She took her pack off. "Stay right here with my pack." Samantha nodded silently, her eyes revealing fear. "It'll be dark soon, but don't worry. I'll be back before then. In about an hour, we'll have something to eat." Deni patted her on the head and walked away.

Deni approached the bunker with caution. So far, she had seen no sign anyone had been in the area, but she wasn't going to risk her life on that slim evidence. She found the alarm system Nate and Brian had set up. It was a fishing line stretched around the bunker back in the woods and at chest level. One end led into the bunker. She could only guess at what Nate had devised to provide an alarm, if someone walked into the line. The line had been broken, by deer or falling limbs during a storm, probably. She wondered what the lines were attached to, probably empty food cans that would make noise when someone walked into the fishing line, she thought. Certainly, Nate wouldn't rig up explosives and risk an innocent person just happening by getting killed.

Finding only animal tracks, she moved on to the cave, where Nate's friend Mel had amassed supplies before the plague. It had taken him over a decade, and he endured many stinging remarks about him being a survivalist nut. In the end, the plague had proven Mel to be not so crazy after all, and the supplies of food and medicine had saved lives, including Brian's. She found no evidence anyone had been near it. A bush was growing in front of the entrance, and it was almost impossible to see the heavy steel door behind. The fact the door had been painted olive drab also made it more difficult for a casual passerby to notice. She turned back to the bunker.

The first thing she noticed was the radio antenna had been blown down. After gaining entrance by unlocking a series of locks with the keys Nate had given her and pulling several hidden bolts, she found the interior of the bunker to be as Nate and Brian had left it.

Five minutes later, she and Samantha were locked safely in the bunker. After using the hand pump to fill her canteens and watching Samantha enjoy a long drink of the cool, clean well water, she hooked up a hand-powered generator and set about recharging the battery that would power the radio. Nate had lost the solar panels when a tornado blew them away many months before. The small generator didn't put out much power, and she was tired long before the battery was half charged. Still, she thought it would give her a little air time, so she grabbed her carbine and went outside to set up the antenna. Samantha followed, not wanting to be left alone.

~~~

The first thing Brian saw when he opened his eyes was his father. Nate sat in a chair next to the bed, and his head was hanging down against his chest, rising slightly with each breath. His eyes were closed. Brian tried to clear his throat, so he could talk. The sound snapped Nate out of his fitful slumber. He raised his head and blinked his eyes open.

"Are you praying again?" Brian asked. "We tried that with Mom and Beth, remember? It didn't work."

Anger flashed across Nate's face for a second. "That's not exactly something to joke about."

"I'm okay. Don't be mad at the first thing I say after waking up."

Nate rose from his seat. Exhaustion forced him to steady himself by putting his hand against the nearby wall. "The operation certainly hasn't changed your personality. Do you notice anything wrong, such as blurred vision or a severe headache?"

Brian blinked and looked around the room. "Don't worry. I see the same as always. I do have a headache, but it's not bad. I've had worse, like when Big Jim tackled me in a football game in school."

"They're not supposed to allow tackle football in PE class." Nate wasn't interested in what happened in Brian's school before the plague, but it was a good way to test Brian's memory of his past life.

Brian shrugged. "We played a game of tackle while the coach wasn't looking."

"He must not have been looking for a long time."

Brian laughed. "You don't think teachers and coaches actually ever did anything to earn their pay, do you? At least 90% of school was a waste of time."

"That explains a lot," Nate's eyes lit up for the first time since Brian woke. His son seemed to be fully alert and lucid – a good sign.

"Well, don't worry about me being stupid. You're teaching me everything I need to know about how to survive."

"You know I didn't say that. It was a joke, and you certainly should know about jokes."

"You mean smart ass jokes."

"Yep." Nate moved to the end of Brian's bed and pulled the blanket up. "Move your toes."

Brian wiggled them. "So, you're worried I might be paralyzed? They must've operated on my brain."

Nate didn't want to worry him. "You had a blood clot that the surgeon had to remove. I think he just opened a small hole in your skull. Everyone agrees you're out of the woods now."

Brian reached up and felt the bandages around his head. He turned whiter than he was before. "So they did operate on my brain."

"I wouldn't call it that." Nate hoped his face was unreadable. "Like I said, the worst is over. We'll probably be home in a week or so."

Brian regarded his father closely. "Yeah, well, my vision is still good. Know how I can tell?"

Nate sighed. "I'm not in the mood for any bullshit, Brian. You're all I have, and this has been hard on me. A thousand times, I've wished I had either left Slim alone or killed the bastard. Making an enemy of someone like him and leaving him alive was a stupid mistake. It nearly cost you your life."

"Wasn't your fault." Brian's eyes were wet. He blinked. "I was going to say you were lying, but it doesn't matter now." He clenched his jaw and swallowed. "If there's any way I can recover, I'll do it. Even if I didn't want to, I'd get better so you'll stop blaming yourself for something that wasn't your fault. Slim was an asshole, and now he's dead. There's no point in even thinking about him anymore."

"Mostly I think about you. Calm down. I'm not the one who's hurt."

For the first time in his life, Brian seemed to be as concerned about his father as Nate was about him. "Yes you are," he said, "more than me."

~~~

Deni managed to contact two HAM radio operators before the battery ran down. Both knew about the problem with Col. Hewitt, as they were the same men Austin had talked to before. While she was talking with them, someone from the Guard broke into the conversation and informed Deni that Hewitt had been arrested and the crisis was over. It was then the battery voltage dropped below usable level and the conversation was cut short. Relieved, she put the radio away.

"Well," Deni told Samantha, "I'll recharge the battery later. Right now, we need to eat." She patted Samantha on the shoulder. "I'm sure you're as hungry as I am."

Samantha nodded. "Real hungry."

"I'll make extra then," Deni promised. "There's plenty of food here."

~~~

Deni woke before sunrise and set about making breakfast without disturbing her new little friend's rest, careful not to make any noise while starting a fire in the wood burning stove. She almost had the meal finished, when she dropped a stainless steel cup on the concrete floor.

Samantha woke instantly and ran to a back corner of the bunker, where she looked around the small room, wild-eyed.

"It's okay," Deni said. "I just dropped a cup." She bent down and picked it up. "I told you yesterday you're safe with me."

Samantha seemed to calm down. She stood there barefoot in the corner rubbing her sleepy eyes.

"Breakfast is ready." Deni sat a plate of the steaming freeze dried scrambled eggs on the small table. "I found some hot cocoa mix for you." She took a small packet out of her backpack and shook it. "And for me... I have Army issued coffee. It's three years old, but the Army promises it won't kill me. The water should be hot by now." She dug into the pack again. "Here are two MRE cookies for your dessert. You can eat them with a second cup of cocoa after you eat your eggs." She smiled warmly and motioned for Samantha to sit at the table. Producing a knife from a uniform pocket, she slit open a dull tan package. "Look at this. We even have flatbread for toast. It's MRE stuff and taste like mushy cardboard, but it's not really that bad."

Samantha sat at the table.

"Oh wait," Deni said. "I'll pump water so you can wash your hands, then you can do the same for me."

Deni's heart jumped into her throat, when she saw Samantha looking at the food with hungry eyes. "It'll only take a minute. Then we'll get right to eating."

~~~

After breakfast, Deni patrolled the perimeter to be sure no one else was around. Then she spent half an hour cutting more firewood and carrying it into the bunker, while Samantha watched. She spent the rest of the morning cranking the generator to recharge the battery.

When Deni stopped to rest, Samantha walked over without a word and cranked it for a while, using both hands on the handle. Five minutes was all she could take of it. "Are we going to stay here for a while?" Samantha walked to the table and sat down, rubbing her tired arms.

Deni pumped water into a cup and handed it to her. "We're going to recharge the battery some more, then I'm going to use the radio again. We'll probably be leaving tomorrow morning." She started to speak, but a sound outside caught her attention. Cocking her ear and listening more carefully, Deni said, "Helicopter."

Samantha's eyes grew large. "Are they coming after us?"

Deni turned from looking out a loophole. "No. They're probably coming to take me…home. There's a place where there are children your age. That's where I'm going to take you. You'll be safe there."

Samantha ran to her. "I want to stay with you."

Outside, the helicopter was landing.

Deni knelt and held her. "I'm not the only one in the world who will be good to you. There are a lot of good people where we're going. You may have an aunt or an uncle who wants to take care of you. These people can help find your relatives. And if you have no relatives, they'll take care of you themselves."

Samantha's fear manifested itself in tears.

Deni held her tighter. "This isn't good-bye. We'll be together a while longer. There's no reason for you to be afraid. Now stay here, while I go outside to see who's in that helicopter."

Samantha followed her to the door.

Deni slid the heavy bolt out of the way. The steel hinges squeaked when she swung the door open. Samantha wrapped her arms around her left leg. Deni held her hand. "All right. We'll go out there together." Samantha looked up at her. "Close your eyes," Deni said, "The helicopter's blowing a lot of stuff into the air." She led Samantha ten yards into the clearing in front of the bunker and stood in the open, so the soldiers could see she was unarmed.

A man in a soldier's uniform jumped out of the helicopter and ran toward them. She did not recognize him. He had a smile on his face and seemed to know who she was. Three other soldiers bailed out of the helicopter and formed a defense perimeter. "I didn't know you had a kid with you," the soldier said, yelling over the noise of the helicopter. "I was ordered to give you a ride. I guess she can come too."

When the soldier came close enough to hear without her being forced to yell, she said, "I thought you were Army at first. I see you're ANG."

"Yeah," the soldier said, "I'm with the Guard." But we have mutual friends. My name's Mel. The last time I saw you, you were unconscious." He looked around. "Nate and Brian wouldn't be here with you, would they?"

"No." Deni saw someone exiting the helicopter as she spoke. "I was out of it when we met before, but Nate and Brian have talked about you so much I feel I know you." She started to ask about Caroline but stopped short. The expression on her face changed, and she looked past Mel at a woman in civilian clothes, who seemed to have a stiff leg. "Excuse me," she said. "I see the bravest woman I've ever known standing over there, and I want to go talk to her." She picked Samantha up. "Close your eyes, my little friend. We're going for a helicopter ride."

Chapter 14

Chesty appeared at the clinic room door. Nate and Brian stopped talking about whether to go back to Mel's bunker or stay at Mrs. MacKay's farm after Brian recovered and waited for him to speak. The look on his face told him he had good news of some kind.

"A soldier just informed me that the Guard is bringing in your friend Sergeant Heath." Chesty enjoyed the two's reaction. "Also, they have another friend of yours with them."

Brian blurted, "Caroline!"

Chesty nodded. "And I'm told there's a third friend of yours."

"Mel!" Brian tried to sit up.

"Calm down. The doctors haven't said you can get out of bed yet," Nate warned.

Still enjoying Nate and Brian's reaction, Chesty added, "They'll be here anytime, so I'll leave now and try to be there to greet them when they land."

"Will you take them here so we can see them?" Brian asked.

"That's the plan," Chesty said, with a smile. "I better get moving, though." He rushed out of the room.

Only ten seconds later, Doctor Brant walked in. She stopped short, noticing the excitement on their faces. "Is something wrong? Chesty just bolted out of the place like there was a house fire somewhere, and you two look like you have something on your mind."

"We were just told several friends will be arriving soon," Nate said.

"So it's good news, then." She relaxed and checked Brian's chart. "We'll probably let you out of bed in a few days, but you'll have to stay in hospital a while longer. The probability of another episode or two like you had is high until you have healed."

"Will it always be like this?" Brian asked.

She shook her head. "Oh no. Once you've healed, the seizures should stop. As fast as you're recovering, in a few weeks you'll be back to your usual self. Your arm will take a little longer to heal."

"A few weeks?" Brian slumped back in his pillow. "Our friends will probably have to leave before then."

"Hey, be grateful you're going to be okay," Doctor Brant chided. "If you'd been hurt only a few days sooner, there would've been little I could have done for you. This clinic is operating only because of the Army."

"I guess you're right," Brian said, "but I still don't want to lie around here for weeks."

~~~

Chesty pulled up to the entrance of the Army's forward operations base just as the helicopter landed. The guards had been told to expect him and waved him on through after a quick ID check. He still had his badge and ID from his days as Town Marshal. Caroline approached close enough for him to see her scars, and he struggled to hide his shock. Nate had told him only that she had been put through hell by several sadists, and he wasn't prepared for what he saw.

Deni held Samantha's hand, as she walked up. She noticed Chesty's reaction. "Caroline, this is Chesty Johnson, the Town Marshal." She motioned to Mel. "This is Mel, another old friend of theirs – and mine."

Chesty smiled. "Nate and Brian say they cannot wait to see you three." He turned to the truck, but stopped short. "Uh, Brian's still in the clinic recovering from an operation, but he's doing fine. He's got a lot of his father in him."

"I'm afraid I can't go," Deni said. "I must report to my CO." A HUMVEE drove up as she spoke. When Donovan got out, Deni stood in a brace and saluted.

Donovan returned the salute. "At ease, Sergeant. I just dropped by to tell you no charges will be filed. General Myers has agreed that you did the right thing, considering that Hewitt ordered the men to hang me, as well as the execution of a civilian for the so-called crime of possessing a firearm."

Deni took several seconds to consider what she'd just been told. "I see you're okay, but what about the civilian?"

Donovan seemed to find her reaction amusing. "Hewitt beat the hell out of him, but he's alive and should recover."

"There was another man," Deni said. "He was with the man Col. Hewitt beat up." Her face hardened. "He was murdered and left beside the road."

Donovan didn't seem surprised. "File a report and we'll add that to the charges against him. I doubt he's going to be punished, though. He's most likely heading for a padded cell. The stress of losing his entire family and watching the world fall apart was too much for him." His eyes lit up. "Sometimes I wish *I* could go crazy, just for an hour or two. I tried getting drunk on moonshine about eight months ago, but when I woke up I realized it had just given me a hangover and the world was still snafu."

Deni almost laughed.

Mel broke into the conversation. "Sir, I have orders from Col. Greene to stay here awhile and report on how civilians in the area are doing." He pulled a folded sheet of paper out of a breast pocket. "Uh, you can read my orders if you want." He quickly added, "I'm not here to check on Army operations, or anything like that. My orders are to evaluate the most pressing needs of the people here, so when the Guard takes over after the Army leaves, we can hit the ground running and not waste time."

"I see," Donovan said. "Does the Guard often send a private on such missions?"

A bead of sweat ran down Mel's face. "Well, I know the area and some of the people. I lived south of here for years, not far from Nate Williams' farm."

"Even so," Donovan said, "Col. Greene must think a lot of your abilities. I expect there's a promotion in your future."

"I wouldn't know anything about that." Mel ignored the helicopter taking off, heading back to his National Guard unit. He spoke over the noise. "I asked for the assignment, and Col. Greene gave it to me because of my knowledge of the area."

"You're welcome to assess as much as you want, just stay out of trouble while you're here." Donovan turned his attention to Deni. "Sergeant Heath, I'll give you a few hours to visit your friends and get cleaned up, but I expect you to report this afternoon. I have a job for you."

Deni responded with a smile, "Yes, sir. Thank you. I have a little friend here I need to take care of, too."

Donovan patted Samantha on the head and smiled. "You're in good hands. Sergeant Heath is very protective of children." He turned and headed for the HUMVEE.

Chesty started for the truck. "Grab your packs, and let's get to the clinic. Nate and Brian are waiting."

~~~

It was Caroline who was overcome with emotion. The warm welcome she received from both Nate and Brian seemed to be more than she expected. "I thought you'd forgotten about me by now," she said. Everyone knew her as a stoic woman who never let anything get under her skin, a result of what she had been through, so everyone thought. But there she was overcome with emotion. She even managed a smile, revealing some of her new teeth, the gift of a kind dentist, who'd been told of her ordeal and how all of her teeth had been knocked out during multiple beatings.

"You helped us take on that bunch of killers," Brian reminded her. "And I would do anything to repay that debt. My dad says you're a good person, and I've never known him to be wrong about people."

"Jeez," Deni chided. "You guys are going to give her a big head. I'm jealous."

Mel gave her his infamous mischievous smile. "Don't be. I hear Brian's got a crush on you."

All playfulness left Brian. "Oh shut up. I've had enough of everyone claiming that. I know I'm too young for her. I just like her. I like Caroline, too. Hell, at one time I liked you and even considered you a friend, but not so much since you started ribbing me about Deni."

Mel put on a show of insult. "Well. If you're going to be that way…" He made a pretense of heading for the door.

Chesty walked into the room. "Tyrone just radioed me. A five-year-old girl has disappeared. I'm heading out there now to supervise a search. Anyone want to volunteer?"

Mel spoke up first. "Yeah, I'll go with you. I'm supposed to provide a situation report on the area, and this will be a good way to start learning what I need to know." He grabbed his pack that was leaning against the wall behind him. "Do you have a problem with kids being kidnapped around here?"

"No," Chesty answered. "And so far there's no reason to believe the girl didn't just go off with friends to play." He cringed. "I don't even want to think about some sicko grabbing children. We have more than enough to worry about."

"Just asking." Mel looked at Nate. "See you guys later."

Nate seemed to be making a decision.

Brian waved his father away. "Go ahead and see if you can help, Dad. It'd be better if you go with them. They might need someone who can track. She may have gotten lost in woods somewhere."

"I think I'll stay here," Nate said.

"Go on. I'm okay."

Caroline spoke up. "I'll stay with him. I would like to catch up on events. There are a lot of questions swirling around in my head."

Nate knew she planned to ask about the deaths of their friends. He wondered if he shouldn't stay and answer those painful questions himself, instead of putting Brian through bad memories while he was still recovering, but decided Brian was strong enough to handle it. "You coming, Deni?"

Samantha, who had been sitting quietly in a back corner of the room, looked up, her eyes catching Deni by the heart. "I would, but I have Samantha to take care of. I want a doctor to check her out. And then I have to find a place for her. After that, I must report to my CO."

"We have kind of an orphanage going," Chesty suggested. "They're good people and do a great job with little resources."

Deni started to speak, but the reaction on Samantha's face stopped her short. "We'll worry about that later. She can stay with me for now."

Mel scratched the back of his neck. "Hmm. Things must be different in the Army."

Deni flashed him a *shut up* look. "You guys better get going."

"Yes, we better," Chesty agreed "Follow me or be left behind." He rushed out of the room without another word.

Nate and Mel left right behind him.

Deni took Samantha by the hand. "Let's go see Dr. Brant." She walked by Caroline. "I'll leave you two alone to catch up on old times."

Out in the hall, Samantha looked up at Deni. "I don't want to see a doctor. I'm not sick."

Deni dropped to her knees and held her. "Don't worry. Doctor Brant is a nice lady."

Samantha appeared to be close to tears. "I don't care if she's nice."

"There's no need to be afraid. I'll be right there with you."

~~~

Dr. Brant handed Samantha a lollypop after her examination. "That's for being a good girl. Enjoy it. I'm almost out and there'll be no more. You stay here for a second while Deni and I have a chat."

Deni waited anxiously in the hall. "Well?"

Doctor Brant smiled. "No sign of sexual abuse. She had bruises all over her, though. The bastard beat her."

Deni released a load from her chest. "I must have happened onto her in time."

"Not necessarily."

Deni's eyes flared.

Dr. Brant put a hand up. "We don't know everything that *may* have happened, but we do know what *didn't* happen. She will not talk to me about the man other than to say he was mean."

Deni leaned against the wall for support. "Is there a child psychiatrist here?"

"Not as far as I know." She put a hand on her shoulder. "I know you have responsibilities as a soldier. Let me take care of her for a while. Come back tomorrow, if you can. Maybe by then I will have earned her trust and she'll have opened up to me enough to talk about what happened to her. If we're lucky, nothing but the physical abuse took place."

"Aren't you busy with patients?"

"I'll be off duty in less than thirty minutes. I can take her home." When Deni shook her head and blinked tears, she added, "You're not abandoning her. I promise I'll take care of

Samantha until you get back. Tomorrow, I can leave her with Brian, while I work my shift."

Deni dried her face. "I better explain to her that I'll be back tomorrow…and pray that I *can* come back. At least by tomorrow night. I don't want her to think I'm dumping her." She left Dr. Brant in the hall to say goodbye to Samantha. She had just enough time to get cleaned up before reporting for duty.

~~~

Chesty pulled up to the home of the missing girl's family and stopped at the curb. Tyrone had been busy organizing a search, and many people had volunteered to help. On the way, they had passed dozens of people out looking for her on foot, searching abandoned homes in the area, one by one. Others searched wooded lots and weed-choked ditches. Special attention was given to backyard pools. Long unmaintained and full of green slime, the only way to know if a child had drowned in them was to use a pole and feel for anything in the filthy water.

Chesty opened the truck door. Before getting out, he said, "I've got to touch base with Tyrone first. You guys might as well stay here until I learn something. Without information, we'll just be running around like a chicken with its head cut off." He ran to the front door of the house and disappeared inside.

Nate got out to stretch his legs.

Mel followed and stood on the littered sidewalk. "Looks like the people in this town are at least halfway organized. A lot of people came to help, anyway."

Nate looked down the street. "Yeah, and they're learning fast. With a little help from the government, they just might make it. There's a lot of work to do on that farm before they harvest their first crop, though."

"What are their chances of avoiding starvation?" Mel asked.

Nate turned to face him squarely. "They need enough supplies to carry them over until they get that farm going. And they need fuel for farm equipment and transportation. Shelters will have to be built down by the lake." He rubbed his forehead. "It's not going to be easy."

"You said 'they.' Does that mean you're not planning on staying to help?"

"No. I'm not staying. I've gotten off track lately. My main concern is Brian, and I've made serious mistakes, putting him in danger."

Mel tilted his head. "You're being too hard on yourself. And I don't believe you'll ever stop caring about other people. Yeah, you're Brian's father and he comes first, but you're not the kind to not care about others."

"I think Brian will be safer back at your place." Nate saw Chesty and Tyrone coming. "This conversation is over for now."

Mel cleared his throat and looked up at the sky. "Okay."

Tyrone didn't stop to talk. He just nodded at them, jumped into his patrol car, and took off.

"Does he have something to go on?" Nate asked. "I mean, there must be a reason for him to be taking off like that."

"Get in." Chesty slid behind the wheel of his pickup. "I think I have a job for you two."

Mel seated next to Nate and said, "You'll have to decipher that for me. I have no idea what the hell you're talking about."

The engine roared, as Chesty sped down the street. "Someone got another police radio working for us last night, and Tyrone gave it to a search team leader so he could radio us if his team found anything. While I was inside the house with Tyrone, we got a call from that team leader. They just found one of the little girl's shoes."

"Great," Mel said. "But why is that a job for us?"

Chesty had the tires smoking, as he made a sharp left turn. With fresh fuel in the tank, the engine was running better than it had in months. "I know Nate's a good tracker, and I was hoping you would be too, with your military training and all."

Nate spotted Tyrone's cruiser just ahead, parked next to tall trees. "A few dozen searchers stomping around in those woods will make it impossible for me to track her. Get them out of there."

Chesty slammed on the brakes and jerked the truck into park. "Will do." He jumped out and hit the asphalt running. He yelled at the first three people he came to, "Have everyone line

up along the road and wait for instructions. Get everyone out of the woods now."

"Why?" a man asked. "She's in those woods somewhere, and she can't be far."

"Maybe. Maybe not." Chesty brushed between him and two women standing next to him. "But if she's gone far, we've got a couple men here who can track her. They can't do that if you destroy the trail by stomping around in the woods."

"What we need is a police dog," one of the women said.

"That would be nice," Chesty muttered. "If you want to help, spread the word that everyone should line up along the road and wait for instructions."

After walking a quarter mile into the woods, Nate heard Tyrone giving orders somewhere up ahead. The men moved faster.

A patch of blue under a bush caught Nate's attention. He veered off to the left. On approaching the object, he could see that it was a little girl's shirt. "Hold up. I found something."

Other searchers in the area heard him and came running. In seconds, the woods echoed with the news that someone had found something.

Chesty picked the shirt up by its edge and examined it. "Mother says she was wearing a blue shirt. It's the right size. Got to be hers." He swallowed. "Don't see any blood on it."

"Not likely she would be taking her shirt off," Mel said. "It doesn't look good."

Nate suddenly became impatient. "Will somebody please show me where the shoe is?" He looked around and raised his voice before speaking again. "And for god's sake, everyone get out of the woods and go back to the road."

"Why?" a man standing nearby asked.

"To preserve the little girl's tracks," Mel answered. "Maybe we can track her."

The man spit and slapped at a mosquito on the back of his neck. "Hell, she can't be far away. Quickest way to find her is for everyone to spread out in a line and sweep these woods."

Mel waited for Chesty or Nate to say something, when they didn't speak up, he did. "If she's not far away, a small team of trackers can find her just as quick. If she's far into these woods, following her trail will be quicker. Depends on how many acres we have to search. But there won't be any trail to track if it's been stomped on by a large group wondering around lost."

"I guess you know more about it than I do," the man said. He raised his arms to get attention. "Hey, everyone back to the road. Let these guys do their job."

Mel quipped, "I didn't know this was my job." He caught up with Chesty and Nate, who were already heading deeper into the woods, following the sound of Tyrone's voice.

Nate kept walking and spoke without looking over his shoulder, his eyes constantly scanning the ground and brush. "You're here to learn about the people of this town. This stressful situation is certainly a good way to do that. As you can see, they work together fairly well, considering that there are always a few assholes and idiots in every crowd."

"Yeah, I guess," Mel said. "But my stomach's churning. I fear this is going to turn out to be a very bad day for all of us."

"We don't know that," Chesty reminded him. "She could've just wandered off."

Tyrone saw them coming and rushed to meet them. "I heard someone found a shirt."

"Nate did," Chesty said. "Looks like hers. Where's the shoe?"

"Come on." Tyrone turned and started walking.

When they got to the shoe, Nate didn't stop. "I'm going to have to walk in ever wider semicircles until I find tracks that weren't made by searchers."

Mel followed. "I'll ride shotgun for you, so you can keep your eyes on the ground. The bastard might be armed."

Chesty stiffened. "We don't know that someone took her." He handed Mel his radio. "Call Tyrone if you find anything."

"Yeah," Mel said, and kept walking.

Tyrone and Chesty's eyes locked for a second. They looked down at the small shoe. It was Tyrone who spoke first. "I couldn't find any tracks around the shoe, and I was one of the first to get to it."

"They won't be able to tell much until they get past where the searchers have walked," Chesty said, repeating what Nate had already stated.

Tyrone took a white handkerchief out of his pocket and tied it to a tree at eye level to mark the shoe's location. "We might as well sit down on that windfall over there. It could be a long wait."

It did seem like hours, but was in reality less than 90 minutes. Tyrone's radio squelched and Mel's voice came over the air, sounding flat and empty. "We found her. It's not good. Keep the sun at your back and come on in. Make a lot of noise and I'll lead you in by radio."

Tyrone spoke into the mike, "Is Nate still with you?"

The radio squelched. "Nate has gone on alone. I couldn't talk him out of it."

Chesty swore. "I was afraid of that."

<u>Chapter 15</u>

Mel had removed his uniform jacket. It covered the little girl's body ten feet away. He spoke into the radio mike. "Come on guys, move it! I need to catch up with Nate. Tracking isn't a one-man operation."

Tyrone pushed through a patch of thick brush, his black face full of dread and dripping sweat, though it wasn't that hot. Chesty followed not far behind.

As soon as the two men were close enough for them to see where he was pointing, Mel said, "She's over there." He took off on the run to find Nate.

When Chesty approached the body, he saw her little bare feet and ankles sticking out from under Mel's jacket. He knelt and waited long enough to take a few breaths and reinforce his constitution before lifting it.

Tyrone stood beside him. "It never gets any easier."

Chesty pulled his hand away, delaying the moment as long as possible. "Any easier? This is my first child murder. If anything serious happened in town, I always called in you guys at the Sheriff's Department and stepped aside."

Tyrone looked down at the jacket. "You're the sheriff now." He saw Chesty flinch. "But if you want, I'll do it. This is probably the tenth child murder case I've dealt with. Of course, we patrol officers just did the preliminaries and the detectives did the real work on a murder case."

"You should be sheriff. Come the election, you should run." Chesty reached for the jacket and pulled it aside far enough to see her face. His breath caught. "He beat her first."

"Strangled." Tyrone bent down to more closely examine her neck. "I would bet he used his bare hands, no rope or anything. With her little neck, it was easy."

Her half-open eyes were badly swollen. "There's a lot of damage to her face," Chesty said. "You think he did that with his bare hands?"

Tyrone had to look away for a moment. "A grown man using his fist on a little girl can do that much damage and more. This animal has an uncontrollable rage burning within him.

Could be women he hates, but little girls are easier victims, so he goes for the most helpless."

"Gutless." Chesty stood. "I hate to ask you, but I'm already about to throw up."

Tyrone put his big hand on Chesty's shoulder for a second. "Okay, friend. Take a break."

Chesty took ten steps and kept his back turned, while he blew his nose.

Three minutes later, Tyrone stood beside him. "Yeah, he raped her. If he beat her first, she was probably unconscious at the time. She may have been unconscious when he strangled her."

Chesty looked up at the sky and watched a thunder cloud approaching from the northwest. "Thought I heard thunder a while back. Now it looks like we're in for rain in a few minutes." He looked at Tyrone. "I doubt Nate and Mel are going to be doing any tracking in the rain."

Tyrone headed back to the body. "They have a small window of time left. Maybe they'll catch up with the bastard before the rain comes. Why don't you go on after them? I'll take her to the road and call off the search."

After thinking about what Tyrone said for a few seconds, Chesty shook his head. "It'll be more productive if I go back with you. We can gather some men in trucks and circle around. We might get in front of him, while Nate and Mel drive him to us."

Tyrone wrapped her in Mel's jacket and lifted her. "We'll do that. The trouble is she's been dead a while. I expect the killer's long gone." He took off at a fast pace. "Just in case he isn't, we need to hurry. There are dirt roads southeast of us. He could have a car waiting."

A bolt of lightning struck less than a mile away, and rolling thunder shook the ground. Unimpeded by the weight of a dead girl's body, Chesty ran on ahead. As he approached a few searchers who hadn't gotten the word to return to the road and wait for further instructions, he yelled, "We found her! Everyone get back to the road."

Word spread fast. She had been found, but was she alive. The woods echoed with excited voices. Then Tyrone broke out of the woods and into the street, where people could see the wrapped body. A wail rose up from the crowd. "No!"

Chesty tried to get their attention. "I need a dozen men in a couple pickups. Nate and Mel are tracking the killer. We'll try to get ahead of him and cut him off."

In five seconds, four pickups were loaded with armed, angry men.

Tyrone placed the body in the back seat of his cruiser. "If you catch him, you'll play hell keeping this bunch from lynching him on the spot."

Chesty nodded. "That's what I was thinking. But, like you said, I'm the acting sheriff, and it's my job to stop them."

"I'll back you."

"Someone has to take the body to the clinic and have a doctor examine it. If this guy's taken alive and put on trial, we'll need evidence." Chesty mopped his forehead. "The doctors at the clinic is all we have in the way of collecting medical evidence."

Tyrone gave him a strange smile. "This'll never go to trial, even if he's caught six months from now. If you think otherwise, you don't know people as well as I do."

"Even so, that poor little girl and her mother deserve as much of a formal process as we can possibly give them and as thorough an investigation as circumstances allow."

Tyrone regarded the faces of a dozen people in the crowd and then looked over at the men in the pickups. "I agree, but I still think I should go with you."

"No. You take the girl to the clinic," Chesty said.

If Tyrone had wanted to argue his point further, he would have been arguing with himself, as Chesty jogged away without a word.

~~~

The wind blew with ever increasing strength, and the sky grew darker. Nate stopped long enough to check his compass. "He's been heading generally southeast since he left the girl."

Mel kept his eyes busy, scanning the woods. "We'll lose his trail in the rain. When we do, we'll push on ahead at a fast clip. Unless this coward's smarter than I'm thinking he is, he'll stay on the same course and not veer off."

Nate didn't need Mel's words to know he understood what was on his mind. Besides his National Guard training, he knew Mel to be a competent woodsman and hunter. "That's the idea, but he obviously has a compass. And that means he might not be as dumb as we're thinking he is. The fact he's insane and a child-murdering bastard doesn't necessarily mean he's stupid."

Yeah." Mel kept his eyes working as he spoke. "I'm afraid you may be right."

Nate moved on, searching for the next partial track in the leaf-strewn soil.

Five minutes and only 30 yards later, the rain fell. It came in individual drops at first, and then it came down in windblown sheets. Nate rushed ahead to where trees would provide temporary protection from the rain and boot prints might survive a little longer. By going from tree to tree, he was able to find the trail here and there, in steppingstone fashion, until the rain had penetrated the heaviest tree cover and washed away all remaining sign of the killer's passing. From then on, it was Nate's compass that led them. They rushed through the stormy woods at a yard-eating gait, gaining on the killer, or so they hoped.

The storm cloud passed, and the rain stopped after only 35 minutes, but it had already washed away the killer's trail. Nate and Mel pushed on through most of the afternoon, following the same course. Their hope was they were not far behind and could cut across his trail again, finding tracks he had made since the rain stopped. Those hopes vanished when they came to a dirt road and one of the searchers took a shot at them.

After diving for cover, Mel got on the radio. "Chesty, will you tell that idiot to stop shooting at us?"

Chesty had heard the shot and was already wondering who was shooting at who. "Just stay where you are and I'll spread the word." He jumped in his truck and sped off, blowing his horn. Five minutes later, he got back on the radio. "You can come on out now. If anyone shoots at you after I've told them not to, you have my permission to shoot back."

Mel switched the radio off. "Shit." He looked at Nate, who was ten feet away and ensconced behind a large pine tree, lying in a mud puddle. "Did you hear that? He thinks we need permission from him to shoot back."

They both laughed, more to relieve the tension than because they thought it was funny.

Chesty's voice came back over the radio. "Give me a marker to go by and I'll come and get you."

Mel peered out of the brush, staying out of sight. "There's a tall lightning-killed pine tree across the road from us."

The radio squelched. "I see it. Be there in less than a minute."

Fifteen seconds later, Mel and Nate both heard Chesty's truck rattling down the road at high speed. "Well, here goes nothing," Mel said. They stepped out into the open with their hands raised.

Chesty raced up a hill and brought his pickup to a sudden halt next to them. He leaned over and yelled out of the passenger side window. "He didn't cross here. I've had men watching along this road for two miles."

Nate took his pack off and dumped it in the back of the pickup. "Well, that means he's gotten away this time. His trail had to have been colder than we thought. It was over when the rain washed away his tracks."

"Damn. I hate that," Chesty said. He got out and walked around to their side of the pickup. "Any suggestions on how to proceed from here?"

Nate reached into the back of the pickup and took a canteen out of his pack. After taking his first drink in hours, he said, "There's little chance of catching him today. The girl must have been dead longer than I thought, and the killer left long before we found her."

Mel relieved himself of his pack and placed it beside Nate's in the back of the pickup. "He's right. The bastard has gotten away this time."

Chesty kicked a rock, sending it flying down the road. "That means there'll be another little girl killed by this animal sometime soon." His face became rigid with impotent rage. It only lasted a few seconds before he was thinking again. "He must've had a vehicle parked on this road. Why else would he come this way?"

Nate had asked himself the same question before he even reached the road. "Still doesn't make sense. I mean him walking into the woods instead of just going back to the street not far from where he left the body. He had to have entered the woods from that street, so why didn't he leave his vehicle there, dump her, and go back to his vehicle?"

Mel snapped his fingers. "He left his ride in the woods, not on the street back there and not this road. He's on a motorcycle."

Chesty ran the fingers of his right hand through his hair, thinking. "How far back did you lose his trail?"

"Not long after it started raining, of course." Nate thought for a moment. "We hadn't walked far. Tracking is slow going." The look on his face suddenly changed. "Mel's idea is the only one that makes any sense. What we need to know is where he first took her. It may have been right there on that street. He probably waited until she came along, rushed out and grabbed her. He then carried her into the woods far enough no one would hear anything or happen on to them."

"I don't know," Chesty said. "That street's a long way from her home. Too far for a girl her age to walk."

"Well, you're the cop." Nate swung the pickup door open before getting in. "I've done all I can for you today."

Mel handed Chesty the radio. "The asshole's gone. You'll have to catch him another time."

"Yeah." Chesty looked totally beaten. He trudged to the driver side of the truck. "Just let me call off the search and send these people home. Then I'll give you two a ride back to the clinic." He got in and cranked the engine. "Another little girl's going to die because I failed today."

Nate thought about telling him he hadn't failed anyone, but realized it would sound hollow, no matter how true. After all, he still blamed himself for the death of the little boy he ran over. "Parents are just going to have to keep an eye on their kids. The more difficult it is for him to grab another victim, the more likely he is to make a mistake."

"And the more likely he is to move on to easier hunting grounds," Mel added.

Chesty looked sick. "I was hoping to catch him before he killed again." He started down the road. When two HUMVEEs appeared over the hill, he stopped and waited for them. "Maybe help has arrived. Better late than never."

The HUMVEEs stopped. Deni got out of the lead vehicle. "I just found out about the missing girl. Why didn't you coordinate with the Army? We're here to help."

Ignoring her question, Chesty said, "The killer may have gotten away on a motorcycle. I was just about to call off the manhunt."

Deni glared at all three men. "Damn it! You've left us in the dark on this, and we could've helped. Two dozen extra men and a chopper might've made the difference." She took a breath to hold her temper. "So you found the girl dead?"

"Beaten, raped, and strangled." Chesty looked down the road, rage surfacing on his face.

A soldier standing next to Deni spoke. "Just like the others."

Chesty stared at him. "Others?"

"Might not be the same one," Deni said. "But we had a similar problem in Georgia. Never did catch the freak."

Nate broke into the conversation. "Before the plague, there were sex offenders in every neighborhood. Unfortunately, the disease wasn't selective; it killed the good along with the bad and left some of the bad alive along with the good. Even if we caught this one, there are more out there and always will be."

"Yeah, but this bastard is killing children in my town," Chesty said. "And I'm going to get him."

~~~

Brian did not want to tell Caroline about how their friends were killed while she was away, but she insisted. Her reaction caused him to regret it. He knew that when a woman like Caroline cried it meant she was really hurting. "Things have been rough around here," he said. "But it's been getting better lately."

Caroline returned to her normal stoic self. "Yeah, that's why you're here recovering from being nearly beaten to death." She looked at Samantha. "And why this little girl is an orphan. And why your father and half the town are looking for a lost girl."

Brian examined Samantha's face for any sign Caroline's words had bothered her. "She has Deni now."

Caroline forced a smile. "She has all of us."

"Yeah," Brian said, "all of Deni's friends will help take care of you, Samantha. You're not alone. Not only do you have Deni, you have all the rest of us, too."

"That man will come back." Samantha's frightened face spoke louder than her words.

Caroline rose from her chair, her artificial leg slowing her only slightly, and walked across the room to Samantha. "If he does he'll be sorry."

Samantha looked up at her. "He wouldn't come after you. He'd be afraid of you."

There was an awkward five seconds of silence. "He might not be as stupid as I think he is, then," Caroline said.

Nate walked into the room.

"Did you find her?" Brian asked, glad for the interruption. He was certain Samantha was referring to Caroline's scars and just as certain Caroline took it that way, too.

Mel came in behind Nate. "You might want to talk about that later, after Deni picks up her friend."

Brian's chest deflated. He stared up at the ceiling. "I never even met her, but it feels like she was my little sister."

The fact Brian immediately assumed the girl was dead without it being told to him directly bothered Nate. He wanted to say something about how good things happen too, such as how the town came together to look for her. After struggling to come up with the right words, he decided it could wait until sometime when Samantha wasn't listening.

Caroline had not taken an interest in the conversation behind her; instead, she was looking at Samantha. "So, you're saying I'm bigger than that bad man who took you?"

Samantha nodded. "He's not big for a man." She pointed at Brian. "Not much bigger than him."

Caroline smiled and sat next to her on the bench she was on. "Was he the same height as Brian?"

"I think so. But I can't tell 'cause I never saw Brian standing."

Brian threw a sheet he had over him aside. "I can fix that."

Nate raised a hand. "No way. Not until the doctors say you can get out of bed."

He swung his legs around and prepared to sit on the edge. "This is important, Dad. We're finally learning something."

Nate rushed over and pressed on Brian's chest. "What did I tell you?" He raised his voice without realizing it. One look at Samantha told him he'd made a mistake.

"Never mind." Brian lifted his legs back in bed and lay on his pillow. "We just lost our chance. Did I ever tell you that sometimes you scare kids? She doesn't know you like I do. All she sees is this big man with a big voice." He gave his father an exasperated look. "It might be the same one who took the girl this morning. Did you ever think of that?"

"If you had just listened to me." Nate started for the door. "I'll see if I can find Dr. Brant. Maybe she'll okay you getting out of bed."

After he left, Mel chuckled under his breath, making sure he kept it down so Nate couldn't hear out in the hall.

Even Caroline thought it was funny. "Brian, sometimes you push your luck with your dad. You're probably the only one in the world who could get by with scolding him like that."

She and Mel broke out laughing. Samantha looked up at them and smiled, no longer afraid.

Chapter 16

Both Dr. Brant and Major Millhouse agreed it was time for Brian to get out of bed and test his balance, as well as start rebuilding his muscles. As soon as Brian was sure he could walk okay, he headed down the hall, through the lobby, and out the front door.

Dr. Brant was on his heels the whole way. "Hey! Hold up there, bud. I didn't say I was releasing you from my care."

Nate followed along behind, smiling at the fact his son seemed to be okay. "I guess he wants to feel the sun on his face, after being in bed for so long."

Dr. Brant glared over her shoulder as she tried to keep up with Brian. "Don't encourage him. He's already overdoing it."

Brian's atrophied legs and back muscles were already protesting, but he walked on to the bench under a stand of oaks out front. Sitting down next to a young, pretty Army nurse, he said, "Nice day, isn't it?"

She nodded and went back to reading a paperback.

The sun was just rising over the tree line to the east, and the dew had yet to melt away. Wet pine needles caught the sun's rays, creating diamonds of sparkling light. Brian drank in the sights and smells, noting that mornings were turning cool again. He turned to look down the walkway and saw someone with a stiff leg walking with a little girl and realized it was Caroline and Samantha. It was too far for him to make out their faces, but he knew it was them. The woman had an M4 in her right hand and the little girl's hand in her left. They seemed to be chatting away, which was unusual, both for the woman and girl.

Dr. Brant huffed up. "Now let's see if you can make it back. Maybe I'll have to call for a wheelchair."

The nurse got up and left.

Dr. Brant sat next to Brian. "Any dizziness?"

Brian looked at his father as he spoke. "No. Just give me a day or two to get my muscles working."

He enjoyed being outdoors for the first time since his operation. His gaze focused again on something only he saw, his eyes fixed on a point in space somewhere between the horizon to the east and the sun that was hiding behind the tree line, its glow escaping the earth's edge, rays radiating up and outward. The weather-faded boonie hat protecting his head rested in a way that announced he wasn't trying to look macho. No, it was strictly utilitarian. The rings of sweat salt and tattered brim declared he didn't care what it looked like to others; it was an essential part of his apparel, as important in bright sun as a poncho in a rain storm.

Nate regarded his son with amusement. Brian reminded him of himself at a slightly older age and knew he was relishing being alive. He had experienced the feeling many times after a battle, and he knew Brian had been in a multi-week-long battle for his life. "I tell you what; I think you've been in that room long enough. We'll hang around town a day or two, and then go back to Mrs. MacKay's farm."

Dr. Brant gave him a look of disapproval. "He still might have a seizure."

Nate started to speak, but Brian interrupted. "I haven't had one in weeks. Hell, it won't be long before it'll be time to take this cast off my arm."

"We'll stay close by for a couple days," Nate assured her.

She stood. "He's your son, and you're too big for me to argue with. I've got to get back to work."

Nate hooked his thumbs in his belt and looked at the ground. "We're both indebted to you. If you ever need anything…"

She smiled. "You're welcome."

Nate watched her walk away for a second, then sat next to Brian. "I want you to take it easy for a while."

Brian kept his eyes on the sunrise as he spoke. "Then it's back to Mrs. MacKay's farm?"

Nate nodded. "From there on to Mel's place."

Brian finally tore his gaze from the developing morning. He seemed concerned. "What about Kendell? He won't leave those kids, and we can't take care of all of them at Mel's."

Nate noticed that they had company. "I'm sure he'll stay at the farm with the others." He stood. "Would you two like to sit here and rest after your walk?"

Brian looked to his right and noticed Caroline and Samantha had already arrived. They had walked faster than he expected. He stood to make room for them on the bench. "You ladies walk fast. The last time I looked, you were way down the street."

Samantha smiled and looked up at Caroline, but said nothing, waiting for her to speak, instead.

Caroline was more interested in the fact Brian was out of bed. "What did you do, escape the clutches of Drs. Brant and Millhouse?"

"We left them tied up in a closet," Brian said, "and snuck out."

Samantha put her hand over her mouth and smiled.

Caroline motioned with a hand. "Sit down. There's enough room for three of us. I guess your dad will have to stand." Samantha sat down beside her.

Brian watched another heavily loaded truck go by, heading for the lake. He sat next to Caroline. "There were four people in the cab. Looked like a family."

"Did you notice the look on their faces?" Nate asked. "They had the same look all those heading for the lake have: a sense of purpose."

"They have a purpose all right," Brian quipped. "There's a lot of work to do out there."

Nate watched another loaded truck go by. The driver waved, and Nate waved back. "There's a future waiting for them by the lake. That's what I was talking about."

"Maybe," Brian said. "It won't be easy, though."

Caroline reinforced his thoughts. "More like almost impossible. They're going to need outside help. The Army's here in town now, but even they admit they're not staying, and there's no guarantee the Guard will move in behind them, as some have claimed. Mel says the Guard's resources are stretched thinner than the Army's."

Nate leaned against a nearby oak tree. "If they stay here, the warehouse food will run out, and they'll be *completely* dependent on outside help, help you and I agree isn't reliable. The quicker they get a farm going, the more secure their future will be."

"And farming requires lots of water," Brian added. "So the lake's their best bet."

A familiar flatbed truck came up the street. This one wasn't heading out of town for the lake. The driver blew his horn and waved out the window.

Brian jumped up and ran. His left arm was still in a sling, and he held it with his other hand. "It's Mr. Stinson and Renee! And he has Kendell with him."

Kendell jumped out of the passenger side door before the truck came to a complete stop and ran to meet Brian, obviously excited to see him on his feet. "Everybody was worried about you, especially Renee." He looked Brian up and down. "I guess I was right when I kept tellin' them not to worry so much."

Renee ran up and wrapped her arms around Brian's neck. By the time she let go, both of them were a little embarrassed.

Austin had parked the truck and joined them. He stood there smiling. All he said was, "Well."

No one had noticed Nate standing nearby and watching. He chuckled. "Well what?"

Austin shook Nate's hand. "I'm almost as happy as you are to see Brian back on his feet." He gave his daughter a wink. "And as you can see, Renee's happy, too."

Their reunion was cut short when Chesty's truck raced up the street and came to a screeching halt. Chesty stuck his head out the window. "Nate, I need your help."

All smiles vanished.

Nate stepped closer. "Don't tell me it's happened again."

Chesty swallowed. "Yeah, afraid so. Her name's Trisha Foreby. She may have been missing for hours, but the parents just got around to telling us. They thought she was in the backyard playing."

Brian was already standing next to his father. "Where's my rifle and pack? I'm coming with you."

"We brought 'em with us," Kendell said. "I'll get 'em out of the truck."

"Glad to see you on your feet." Chesty looked Brian over. "I can use all the help I can get – if you're up to it."

Brian's face was a picture of determination. "Don't worry about me." He pulled his arm out of the sling and flexed his hand. "The cast will protect it."

Nate took his broken arm and examined it. "It hasn't had time to heal completely yet, so be damn careful. Don't put any strain on it at all. Use it for nothing more than holding the other end of your M4. And don't forget your broken ribs."

"What's going on?" Austin asked.

Chesty motioned with his head. "If you want to help, hop in. I'll explain on the way."

"We'll follow you." Austin ran for his truck. Renee wasn't far behind. Kendell ran to Brian and handed over his pack and rifle.

Caroline looked on, obviously wanting to go with them and help, but she had Samantha to take care of.

Nate and Brian jumped in Chesty's truck. They were soon speeding across town. The Army had been alerted and soldiers were out in force, stopping every vehicle at strategic roadblocks, searching them for a little girl. After a short conversation, they waved Chesty and Austin through.

Chesty spoke into his hand-held radio. "Do you have anything new for me, Tyrone?"

Tyrone's voice came back, "Nothing yet. We've already covered most of the neighborhood and will finish the rest in about thirty minutes. Why don't you and your crew take 41st Street, east of 25th Ave., then work north from there?"

"Will do. I have five volunteers with me."

"Good. My team will work west of 25th Ave, after we're done here."

"Remember to tell them to concentrate on finding the girl," Chesty said, "but the guy we want may be a smaller white man. It's not much but all we have."

"I think it's best to tell them to look for the girl. If we find someone with her, that'll be another story. I expect if one of us doesn't get to him soon enough, he won't live long."

"Right on both counts." Chesty glanced over at Nate, who remained silent; though it was obvious his mind was racing.

He turned right onto 41st Street, left on 25 Ave., and stood on the brakes. "You and Brian work the east side of 25th Ave.

here." He pointed. "I'll work the west side of 26th, which means I'll be working the houses behind the ones you'll be working. If the home looks abandoned, go on in. If it's occupied knock and ask for permission to search. I'll leave it to your judgment as to how to handle any suspicious smaller man you might find inside. Be careful of your own safety, but also watch stepping on citizens' rights. Please don't shoot an innocent person."

"Great advice," Nate remarked. "But I doubt you think a few hurriedly spoken words have turned us into trained cops. Any way you look at it, Brian and I are vigilantes breaking into private homes. Excuse me while I put my son's life ahead of all other concerns."

Chesty gave him a strange look, and then chuckled. "Yeah, it's crazy. What else is new?" He exploded from the cab and ran to the rear, a pump shotgun in his hands. Yelling at at Austin, who had parked behind his truck, he said, "You, Renee, and Kendell come with me."

The house-to-house search was nerve racking. The fact Nate and Brian had found all of them empty so far did little to lower the stress of entering a home that may contain an armed madman lying in wait. Brian was forced to let his father lead the way, but he provided another set of eyes and ears, increasing his father's chances many fold. No one would blindside Nate while Brian watched his back.

Brian soon learned that his father never turned his back on an area he hadn't already searched. Not a single blind spot behind a couch or the inside of a dark closet was bypassed until it was checked out. He also had the opportunity to see his father work his way around many corners, a pie slice at a time, with rifle shouldered. Watching his father taught him a lot about clearing a house and how dangerous it was. He also realized that two men wasn't enough of a team to do it safely. He had been surprised to hear his father gripe to Chesty about the situation back in the truck. His father wasn't the kind to bitch and moan about anything. But he soon understood why he had spoken out. They had been put in a damned if you shoot/die if you don't position.

Dad was right: We're not cops.

After searching three homes that housed only the moldering skeletal remains of plague victims, they rushed to another home next door. This one was obviously occupied by a family. The uncut grass in the front yard was beaten down, and the sound of children playing could be heard through open windows. Nate knocked on the front door.

A woman in her thirties appeared, holding a revolver in her right hand. She scowled at Nate. "What do you want? My husband's asleep in the living room. If you wake him, there'll be trouble." She eyed their weapons. "Those guns don't scare us. We have guns, too."

"We don't want you to be afraid, Ma'am." Nate removed his boonie hat. "We're helping the acting sheriff search for a lost little girl. Her name is Trisha Foreby."

Her eyes opened wide, and she shook her head. "Well, she's not here. The only children in this house are mine."

Nate put his hat back on. "I'll take your word on that." He took two steps back. "Just keep in mind that a mother is worried sick at this moment, and we're trying to find her little girl for her."

She gave Nate and Brian a cold stare. "Searching here would be a waste of time. She's not here. Someone should've kept a closer watch on her little girl." She slammed the door in their face. They could hear her turning a bolt inside.

"Come on," Nate said. They rushed to the next home; this one they soon discovered was empty.

Brian's leg and back muscles had convened to register their complaints about how out of shape they were, after such a long recovery period spent in bed. His throbbing headache wasn't doing him any good, either. Fortunately for him, his broken ribs and arm seemed to be holding up well enough, but the arm barely had strength enough to hold up the rifle. Brian said nothing and just forced his way through the pain. He wasn't about to let his father down.

Nate didn't need to hear his son complain; he could tell he needed a rest. The tension was ratcheting up for them both every time they forced their way into another house and searched it room-by-room, looking over their rifle sights, ready to shoot in defense of their life. After clearing another home, they returned to the living room. "Hold on. We'll sit here a while and take a breather."

Brian protested. "Dad, that little girl…"

"I know." Nate slipped his pack off and sat on a dusty couch. "Nevertheless, we're taking five. Sit down and rest your nerves as much as your body."

Brian did as he was told, sitting down and massaging his left arm where it wasn't covered by the cast. "I know this is dangerous. The thing is I doubt this bastard has the spine to take on an adult. He likes to go after little kids."

"I'm not going to bet your life on that." Nate leaned back in the chair and looked up at the ceiling. "Drink some water, relax, calm your nerves. We'll be back at it soon enough."

Brian decided he was thirsty after all. He took a canteen out of his pack. "You're afraid I'm going to make a mistake."

Nate looked at him. "No. I'm afraid I already have. I can't save everyone in this town, not even lost little girls. But I just might be able to keep you alive a few more years and help you make it through the worst of what's to come. As much as I want to help these people, you come first."

Brian's eyes lit up. "You sure don't like this house-clearing stuff, do you?"

"We're kicking at rattlesnakes."

"Yeah, that's one of your favorite sayings." Brian looked at his father. "I know you're not going to quit now, so let's get back to work. We'll go slower, take our time."

Three gunshots from the house behind the one they were in cut their conversation short. In seconds, they had their packs on.

Brian crawled to a back bedroom window on his elbows to keep pressure off his arm and slowly stood, raising his head just enough to see. "Something's wrong with Renee!"

Nate yelled, "Stay down!"

Brian ignored his father. He ran down the hall and out the backdoor.

"Damn it, Brian!" Nate chased after him. Outside, he immediately saw that Renee was between two homes, bent over throwing up.

A four-foot-tall chain link fence stood between Brian and the next yard over. Forgetting his broken arm and ribs, he was over it so fast he would never even remember the fence at all. He hit the ground running, reaching her in seconds. Ready for trouble, he shouldered his carbine and scanned the area, looking over his sights.

Austin emerged from around the front of the house Renee was next to and rushed to console his daughter.

"Who shot?" Brian demanded. "Did someone shoot at you?"

Austin kept his eyes on Renee as he held her. "She fired to signal that we found the lost girl."

A crowd of searchers was already running toward them, cutting across yards, coming from other streets. Austin's ashen face and Renee's emotional state answered Brian's next question before he asked.

Nate ran up huffing. "Brian, the next time I tell you to stay down, do it!"

"I thought Renee had been shot."

Nate's heavy breathing was more from anger than the short sprint. "I've told you many times to never leave cover when bullets are flying."

Brian was astonished at his father's words. "Renee is our friend."

"Damn it, Brian, use your head. We could've covered her from where we were. If she was being shot at, you running up to her would've just resulted in you getting shot, too."

They went around to the front of the house just in time to meet Kendell as he emerged from the door. He pulled his T-shirt up and mopped his face on it. Then he lifted his face to the sky, his eyes focusing inward.

All anger fled from Nate's mind. "Damn it."

Chapter 17

Chesty emerged from the bedroom, his face taut, holding back emotion. "She's in there."

Nate blocked the dusty hallway, standing there, not wanting to go into the room.

For several seconds, they stood there in silence. Then Chesty said, "Looks like she was strangled like the last one – after he was through with her." He closed his eyes for a second. "Or before, who knows?"

Brian glanced at Kendell and turned to walk through the living room, past the disused, dusty furniture, out the front door, and onto the porch. Speaking to Kendell, he said, "Keep your eyes open. He might still be around."

Kendell followed. Standing beside Brian, he looked down the street. "Ain't no surprise. But it still makes me sick. This world ain't fit for little kids."

Brian looked away. "Damn it."

Nate and Chesty heard them. They stood in the hallway looking at each other. Without a word, Nate walked outside and joined the boys. "Brian, maybe you should stay with Renee."

Brian blinked and looked up at the sky. "Her dad's with her. We need to find this bastard."

It appeared to Nate that he was carrying the world on his shoulders. "Well, don't go running off. Stay right here. You wanted to be with her a few minutes ago; you might as well be with her now."

Word spread, and more people were gathering around the house. Nate heard people down the street yelling, "No!" A few openly cried and held onto a loved one. In less than a minute, the yard in front of the home Trisha's body was found in filled with people. Some combination of grief, shock, and anger could be seen on everyone's face.

Tyrone drove up in the dirty sheriff's cruiser that he always drove. He uncoiled his large frame from behind the wheel and ran to the front door. A few minutes later he emerged with Chesty.

Sick with a feeling of helplessness, Tyrone looked out over the crowd. "The diseased freak is probably not far away. But we don't even have a decent description. Hell, he could be right out there in front of us and we wouldn't know it."

Nate started to say something about how losing their cool wouldn't help anyone, but he looked to his right and saw Brian trying to console Renee. She spilled out her grief on his shoulder. He rushed over and held them both. "I'm sorry these things happen," he said, his own voice cracking a little.

"Why?" Renee asked, looking up at him.

Nate stepped back. "There is no why. Because there is no sane reason. All we can do is find him."

A man standing fifteen feet away heard. "Find him and kill him. That's all you can do. Kill the bastard before he does it again. He won't stop, you know. Not until someone puts a bullet in his head."

Austin walked up on them. "We have a sheriff and deputies. Let them do their job." He held Renee. "I'm sorry. They say she was a sweet little girl."

Renee's face turned hard. "The coward only goes after little children; they can't fight back."

Austin shook his head. "Don't count on it. You never know with crazies like this one." He lifted a warning finger. "Stay close from now on."

As word spread, the crowd grew larger. It wasn't long before anger began to overpower shock and grief, and the crowd grew ugly. Someone shouted, "How many more little girls have to die before someone stops this animal?"

Chesty faced the man who spoke. "If everyone keeps an eye on their children, this won't happen again." He sighed in frustration. "Stay calm and keep your eyes open. See anyone suspicious, keep an eye on him. But for god's sake, don't go shooting everybody that looks suspicious. We'll be killing each other the next thing you know. Just keep your children close and watch them. If you have any information, let me know about it."

The man who had spoken up before angrily asked, "And what're you going to be doing in the meantime?"

Chesty held his temper. "Tyrone's going to work the crime scene as best he can. Remember, we don't have the tools we would normally have, and there's no support from state police or federal agencies. Just as an example, we can collect fingerprints and DNA, but what can we do with it? Neither one of us is a fingerprint expert, and there's no crime lab to send the DNA to for testing."

"And what're you going to be doing while Tyrone's working the scene?" the same man in the crowd asked.

Chesty hitched up his pistol belt, his patience growing thin. "I have to tell the little girl's mother." He looked the man in the eye. "Unless you want to take that job off my hands."

The man looked down, suddenly taking great interest in the top of his boots. "Sorry. We're all keyed up and nervous as hell about this, Chesty."

After looking out over the crowd again, Chesty said, "The way to prevent you going through the hell other parents have is to keep an eye on your children. This person isn't likely to have the spine to take on armed parents and steal your children away from you by force. He doesn't operate like that. What he does is find a child alone that's not being watched by an adult. Keep your children inside for a while. Don't let them out of your sight. We'll catch this animal. But when we do, there'll always be more of them, so parents will always have to keep close watch on their smaller children." Before he left, he finished with, "It's always been that way. Unfortunately some parents learn too late."

Nate walked along with Chesty. "Do you want me to go with you?"

Chesty shook his head. "See if you can help Tyrone. It's going to be bad enough without someone watching me break down." He got in his truck and drove off.

Brian, Renee, and Austin joined Nate on the sidewalk. They all seemed to be looking to Nate for answers, and he had none. "Chesty's right," Nate said. "Everyone must watch their children." His words sounded hollow in his ears.

Austin spoke low, so others couldn't hear. "They tell me it's been days since anyone with small children did much work on the irrigation ditches. No one's getting any sleep, and progress on the farm has been slowed considerably. On top of that, people are wound up tight and ready to explode. I wouldn't be surprised if some poor innocent bastard gets lynched within a week."

Nate agreed, but said nothing.

"His luck's going to run out," Brian said. "If he keeps going after kids, some parent's going to catch him and blow his head off. There won't be a chance for any lynching."

Nate regarded his son, and for the thousandth time, found himself realizing that Brian had aged ten years in the last twelve months. "Either that or he'll leave town to look for easier victims. Once he learns people are watching their children so closely he has no chance to grab another one, he may leave the area."

"And go where?" Austin asked. "He'll have to travel a long way to find so many children in one place."

Brian furrowed his brow. "Mrs. MacKay's farm. It's the closest place where there are a lot of kids. It won't be so easy for him, though. They're not spread out like the people are here, and they guard that place well."

Renee looked sick. "How much hurting does it take to satisfy this freak?"

Austin put his arm over her shoulder. "None of us can answer that. I doubt if a psychiatrist could."

~~~

The days came and went, and no more children had been taken. Even non parents were keeping close guard over every child in town. It was thought the killer just hadn't been able to find a child alone that he could grab. Tyrone said he thought the killer was just staying low and might strike again anytime. Chesty agreed with most people's assessment of the killer's lack of courage and that he would never summon the nerve to take on a parent to get at a child.

Whatever the reason for the days of peace, everyone was grateful no more children had been murdered and agreed to keep up the vigilance, as it seemed to be working. They still had nothing to go on other than little Samantha's description of the man who killed her father and took her. Few thought it could possibly be the same man, though. After all, he had faced an adult, and an armed one at that. The child killer always avoided adults and preyed only on vulnerable little girls he caught alone, and he didn't wait long before killing them. Samantha had been held a lot longer than a few hours. Few really thought the two crimes were connected.

~~~

Austin, Renee, Nate, Brian, and Kendell were having breakfast on the front porch of a house near the clinic when Chesty and Tyron drove up.

Seeing the concerned looks on their faces, Chesty raised a hand. "No little girl's missing. At least none I know of. Relax. Finish your meal." He took his hat off and held it by the rim with both hands. "Word about town is you're leaving soon. Some people have asked if you might stop by the lake first and see if you can show them ways they can improve on the irrigation system they're putting in. They also are trying to rig some kind of a power generating capability with dammed water."

Nate put down his cup. "I thought they had an engineer helping them design their irrigation system."

"They do. But he's not a farmer. He's been a real help with the hydropower system they're working on, but says he needs some advice on the irrigation ditches."

Nate reluctantly acquiesced. "Well, Brian and I planned to catch a ride out of town with Austin. Caroline wants to come with us, but doesn't want to leave Samantha behind. She's been trying to get her to open up and talk about her surviving relatives, if any. If everyone's willing to stop at the lake, I'll take a look and see if I can help, but don't expect much. I'm no expert, just a dirt farmer."

"I'm sure they'll appreciate any help you can give." Chesty hesitated. "And Tyrone and I wish you'd stay in town… and… uh… maybe help us build a viable sheriff department."

Though not finished with his meal, Nate seemed to have lost his appetite. He stood and faced Chesty. "The answer is no. Besides the fact I don't know a thing about law enforcement, every time I postpone going home, Brian is the one who pays for my decisions. I've helped you as much as I can. There will always be more murders and other problems for you and

Tyrone to deal with. It'll never end. Well, my responsibility as a father never ends, and that responsibility comes first. The fact is Brian almost dying was my fault. I turned Slim into an enemy when I broke his jaw and then left Brian alone so Slim could get at him." He finished with, "I'm taking Brian home where I can keep him as safe as possible."

"Bravo Sierra!" Brian stood. "Bad things happen to people, and it's not your fault."

"It's not my fault little girls are being murdered, and it's not my fault the people of this town are facing hardships." Nate kept his eyes on his son. "But it *is* my fault Slim nearly killed you."

Brian thought for a moment. "Slim stopped breathing when you hit him. Maybe we should've let him die, but then you would've felt bad about killing a man just for insulting Kendell. See? There's no way you can win as long as you keep being so hard on yourself."

Nate and Brian stood looking at each other, neither one knowing what to say next.

Chesty ended the silence. "I guess I shouldn't butt in, but Brian has a point. It's impossible to protect your family from every danger."

"I'm taking Brian home before something worse happens." Nate stormed off the porch, stopping only long enough to snatch up his pack and rifle.

Austin tried to help Brian understand. "Being a parent has never been easy, but it's extra hard nowadays. In a short span of time, he's been shot and you were beaten nearly to death. None of those things would've happened if he hadn't taken you to this town. I can see why he thinks you'll both be safer in the woods. People are the source of most dangers."

"I know that," Brian said. "There's also the plague. It might come back. And with all these people living close together, it'll spread fast."

Everyone in the room exchanged worried glances.

Renee crossed her arms and leaned back in her chair. "I don't think we can survive as a society if we all live as hermits. We have to have communities, no matter how small."

Brian nodded. "Living alone also leaves you more vulnerable to attack. One of the reasons we left the farm was because we didn't have enough people to protect it from a large gang of raiders. When everyone was killed at Mel's place, it left just Dad and me to keep watch 24/7. That leaves no time to farm or anything else, so you either starve when you run out of food or take a chance on being murdered."

Kendell chimed in. "The fact is your father has kept you alive all this time, and that ain't no little thing. And the fact is it doesn't matter which path a man chooses, there ain't no safe way to go. Not with things like they are." He spoke directly to Brian. "Slim's doings were his own. He was a gutless bastard, almost as gutless as the child killer. He tried to kill you, but you were too tough, so you're here and he's in hell. It's best for your father to forget him."

"I wish he would," Brian said. "But he's never going to stop worrying. Losing Mom and Beth caused him to swear he wasn't going to lose me, too."

~~~

Out in the driveway, Nate had the tailgate down on Austin's truck, using it as a table while he rearranged the contents of his backpack. Austin planned to head for Mrs. MacKay's farm after eating, and he wanted to be ready to go with him. He still didn't know if Austin and the others were willing to stop off at the lake so he could check out the irrigation system the townspeople were building. Either way, he was ready to leave town. There were only two things he wanted to do first: Say good-bye to Deni and ask Caroline if she wanted to come with them. He knew that depended on what she had decided to do about Samantha. Saying bye to Deni was something he didn't relish.

__Chapter 18__

Nate stopped repacking his backpack long enough to look down the street and saw Deni driving up in a HUMVEE. He was glad to see Caroline and Samantha with her, since he had talk to Caroline.

Deni stepped out onto the asphalt. "I hear you're leaving town today."

Nate started to help Caroline out of the HUMVEE when he saw her having trouble with her artificial leg, but decided against it. She had her pride, and he wasn't about to run afoul of her temper. "Well Deni, it was no secret that I was only waiting for Brian to get better. I planned to look you up and say good-bye first."

Caroline ambled up with Samantha not far behind. "What about me? Were you going to ask if I wanted to go with you?"

"Sure was," Nate answered. "I'm glad you're both here so I can do all of that right now. We all really would like for you to come with us. And if you decide to take your little friend, she's welcome, too." He smiled at Deni. "You're welcome also, of course. But I doubt you want to go AWOL again. And you're a lot less likely to starve in the Army than with us."

"It seems Samantha has no relatives left," Caroline said. "At least that's what Samantha tells us. Deni and I have agreed it's best if she stays with me. Her being a soldier makes things too complicated for her to suddenly become a mother."

Deni checked Samantha's reaction. "It's not like Samantha and I won't be seeing each other. And the Army can't keep me forever." She patted Samantha on the shoulder. We'll always be friends."

Caroline started for the house. "Samantha and I'll go have a talk with the others while you two say good-bye."

Deni waited until they were on the porch and then opened her arms and stepped to him. "I wish I *could* go with you guys."

He held her. Seeing her wet face made him nervous for some reason, like he was a teen again and inexperienced with women. "Don't go and cry about it. We won't be that far away. It's likely we'll be coming into town again. I expect, too, the

Army will be stationing a few soldiers down by the lake, since that's where most of the townspeople are moving to."

"You won't be there."

"But the lake's closer to Mel's place and my farm."

Deni blinked, and a renewed flow started. "Don't lie. We won't be seeing much of each other after today." She looked up at him. "I think that would be a shame, because our age difference doesn't matter."

He felt like he had been hit over the head with an ax handle, not believing what he had just heard.

"Close your mouth," Deni said. "And stop pretending we don't have feelings for each other."

"Deni," he said, "there are a million men –"

"Shut up. There's just me and you." She held him tighter. "If you walk away, it'll be because you're afraid of losing another person you allowed yourself to care for. It'll just be about fear of getting hurt again and have nothing to do with age."

"Any way you look at it, it would be a dirty deal for you. I must be more than 14 years older. You can't possibly find a big ugly dirt farmer like me attractive."

"To hell with that. It's not like I'm a high school kid and you're 80."

He laughed. "Well, I guess I'm not quite old enough to be your father, but not by much. And you'd still be getting a raw deal."

"I think I'm old enough to decide what kind of *deal* I'm getting. So you need to come up with a better reason than that. Like maybe you don't have feelings for me."

He lifted her chin and looked into her eyes. "I never said that."

She looked up at him, smiling. "See, it wasn't so hard to admit what we both have known for a long time."

They decided to take a walk and talk things over. When they came back 30 minutes later, Nate had decided to stay at the lake a few days, doing what he could to help there and then come back to town. He wasn't sure what he'd do after that. His worries over Brian's safety and his belief he would be safer at

Mel's bunker wouldn't allow him to abandon his plan to leave the small community and head back to the woods.

Deni had to report for duty and left in a rush, fearing she would already be late.

Nate saw Brian watching from the porch. "You guys ready to head for the lake?"

"Yeah," Brian answered. "Caroline and Samantha want to go with us."

Nate reached into the back of the truck and tightened the top closure straps on his pack. "I told them they could come." It appeared to him that Brian knew things had changed. When Brian spoke next, he didn't have to wonder anymore.

Brian grinned from ear to ear. "When are you and Deni getting married?"

Nate stopped short. "You're being silly. I thought you had outgrown that."

"It was just a question. An obvious one."

"Well, you need to steer clear of the subject altogether and let us work it out. Have some respect for me and her both."

Brian grew serious. "I do. And I won't bother you about it anymore, unless you bring it up."

Nate walked up to Brian and slapped him on the shoulder. "Now you're acting more like a man again. I appreciate that." His eyes lit up. "And I promise not to rib you about Renee and how she's stuck on you."

"Hah! Yeah, I don't believe that."

"That she's stuck on you?"

"That too, but more the part about you not ribbing me."

~~~

Nate was amazed at how much work they had completed at the lake. Few buildings had been built, mostly tool and equipment sheds, but 400 acres of land had been cleared, and most of the main irrigation ditch had been dug. The question put to him was how to proceed with the branch ditches and then the smaller feed ditches.

He spent an hour looking the massive field over, starting at the concrete and steel dam that would hold back tons of lake water once the ground between the dam and the lakeshore was dug out. He walked the entire length of the main ditch that ran down the middle of the field. It was mostly dry, but some stinking dark ground water had leached out of the rich bottomland peat and 6 to 12 inches had accumulated. After all, most of the area they intended to farm was lowland and susceptible to flooding at times. A risk they had to live with if they wanted to use the rich peat for growing crops and the lake's water for irrigation. On the day Nate inspected the field, it was only two feet above the level of the lake's surface. This was all factored in from the start, as they needed the land to be as low as possible for the irrigation system to work on gravity alone, with no need for pumps and the diesel to fuel them. It was doubtful the hydro generators the engineer was designing for them and planning to fabricate from salvaged equipment would have the capacity to power all the homes and large water pumps, too. If they could build an irrigation system that worked on gravity alone, it would be better all around. Pumps would require fuel and maintenance. Pumps would break down and need unavailable spare parts.

A dozen soldiers were at the lake, with orders to help as best they could. Second Lieutenant (2LT) Colby Jacobson, who had just graduated from West Point when the plague hit, considered himself well versed on the science of engineering and he thought it doubtful this big hick farmer could offer any useful advice on the construction of the irrigation system. He was from the big city of New York and had no farming background. It showed. Unfortunately, he didn't realize that it showed.

2LT Jacobson's response to Nate's suggestion that the main ditch be dug deeper was, "I think that ditch is plenty deep enough. It's already below the lake's water level, and that's all it needs to be."

Nate wasn't about to argue with him; it wasn't his farm, but he had been asked to give his thoughts on how to design the irrigation system and intended tell it the way he saw it. "I've seen lakes and rivers drop ten feet during severe droughts. Best to dig the main ditch deeper than needed than to be forced to dig it deeper in the middle of a crisis, like a drought. Remember, this farm is supposed to prevent hundreds of people from starving." He raised his hands. "But, hey, I'm just here to offer my advice. There's no law that says you have to listen to me."

~~~

Renee and Brian had gone for a short walk together while the adults talked. Brian stopped regarding the large field long enough to look at her and comment, "This is going to be one big ass farm."

Renee laughed. "I'd say so."

Brian bent down and grabbed a handful of black soil. "Look at that. Pure peat. It'll grow veggies like crazy. This stuff holds moisture well, too. It'll require less irrigation."

Her gaze met his. "Your dad has taught you a lot about farming, hasn't he? Are you going to follow in his footsteps?"

He shrugged. "Don't have much choice. Looks like we're all going to be farmers. If we want to eat that is."

She turned melancholy. "There is need for other skills, too. Seems like there'll always be a need for people willing to protect the weak. Your dad would make a good cop."

Brian noticed the change in her. "Let's not talk about that. There's certainly nothing we can do about that crazy in town while standing here." He glanced toward his father and the other men, who were more than one hundred yards away, and smiled. "Besides, my dad would make a terrible cop."

She narrowed her eyes inquisitively. "Why do you say that? I think he'd make a good cop."

He turned cold. "If he caught that animal, the bastard would never make it to a jail cell. I probably would just shoot him on sight myself."

"Is that bad?" she asked.

"That's not what you'd really call law. Is it? That kind of thing is needed when there's no law and you have no choice. But we're talking about after we've pulled ourselves out of the jungle again and have restarted civilization. My dad would've made a good lawman back about 150 years ago when the West was being settled. And he knew how to keep us alive right after the plague when it was kill or be killed. But not now. Now, we're supposed to be returning to normal."

She regarded Brian with renewed admiration. "Your dad did what he had to."

"I know that. And he'll do it again if need be."

~~~

Despite Nate telling 2LT Jacobson he didn't want to argue, Jacobson took umbrage of Nate's advice on how deep to dig the main ditch, feeling that he was the expert on the subject, being an engineer and all.

Austin swatted at a mosquito and steered the conversation back on course. "So you think the main ditch should be dug deeper before any other work is done?"

Nate nodded. "I think the ditch should be dug several feet deeper, for two reasons. Besides the fact the water level of the lake will drop during the normal yearly dry season and infrequent extreme droughts, if the ditch is deep enough to be used as a canal, crops can be loaded on small barges or flat bottom boats and floated to the lakeshore and then transferred to larger boats. Since the lake is part of a chain of lakes connected by a river and canals, boats can be used to transport the crops to other areas and traded for needed items."

"All of that is just silly," Jacobson said. "Why are you planning that far into the future? In two or three years we'll have plenty of fuel, once the refineries are going again."

Austin's eyes lit up and he appeared to have something on his mind. "That would be nice. But I wouldn't want to bet my life on it, or the lives of the people who will be depending on crops from this farm. I think they've had enough of waiting on government to feed them. If they hadn't had those two warehouses – buildings built by corporations and filled with food produced by corporations and transported here by trucking companies with vehicles manufactured by companies on roads built by companies, the last, admittedly funded with tax dollars – they would have all been dead long ago."

"All tax revenue comes from the free market," Nate added. "So it was still the private sector that made it all work. Government governs best when it helps grease the skids of commerce with proper laws to prevent fraud and other problems, and then just steps aside. People say there should be a balance of government and free commerce. Well, my idea of proper balance is 99% free market and only 1% government."

"I seem to have gotten you two Southern front porch philosophers going," Jacobson said. "I didn't see any of you people turning down the Army's help when we showed up. The last time I checked the Army is government."

Austin almost laughed. "True, but you seem to forget that help came with a hell of a price. Some of our people were killed by soldiers, including children. And how long did it take you to get here? A lot of people have died over the last 13, 14 months, waiting for help. They paid dearly for that mistake, didn't they?"

"Come on," the butter bar lieutenant said. "Most of our personnel died in the plague along with everyone else. We've been struggling with little resources. And you can't blame us for a colonel going nuts."

Nate and Austin exchanged glances but said nothing.

"Austin, your little speech reminds me of something that's been worrying me about this farm," Nate said, carrying the conversation along. "I expect just about the time the government gets back on its feet it'll show up and start taking names. Anyone involved with this farm will probably be arrested for environmental crimes. They may even come after me just for giving advice on the irrigation system." He took note of Austin's reaction. "But I'll take my chances on that. These people must eat."

Austin nodded. "This is state land, so yes; they'll want it back someday. It's prime mosquito breeding grounds and valuable, don't you know." His eyes focused on Renee and Brian, who were more than 100 yards away and seemed to be enjoying each other's company. "But they'll play hell putting these people in prison for feeding themselves. How could they encourage people to commit armed robbery by proxy through the vote, telling the government to rob their neighbors to pay for so-called social programs, to the point there were sometimes more people on food programs than working a 40-hour job, and then turn around and arrest people for farming state land to feed their families during an emergency that made the Depression look like a minor problem? It seems to me if one wasn't a crime under normal conditions, this can't possibly be a crime when people are starving and there's no government at all."

Nate had a strange smile on his face. "You're going to hate me, 2nd Luey, but Austin has given me more food for thought, so get ready for more backwoods Southern philosophy."

"I can take it," Jacobson said. "Just don't blame everything on the Army."

"Before I get to my little history lesson, I might mention that the reason the military has been so short on resources is because it's the people in the private sector who normally provide those resources. The Army doesn't manufacture its own weapons, ammo, uniforms, and it doesn't grow its own food or drill for its own oil. When most of the civilian population died, it left the military with no support."

"I can't argue with that," Jacobson admitted. "Without the massive civilian manufacturing capacity companies built up, the U.S. would never have been the 'arsenal of democracy' and WWII would have lasted much longer and exacted a much higher price."

Nate thought for a moment about how to make his story as short as possible.

"Years ago, I read a journal written in the late 1700s. This guy from a Northeastern town described how some 'lazy' people went out into the wilderness and built a log cabin, cleared a field, and raised crops and a few chickens, hogs, and cows, plus hunted and fished to feed themselves. They did all of this with no modern equipment, just sweat, muscle, and backbone. But this guy called those pioneers lazy. Why? Because they didn't work in town for money.

"Mind you they didn't get a penny of welfare, food stamps, retirement, police protection, or any government services at all. Their children were not educated in a government school, and there were not even any roads. They cost the taxpayers nothing. Their lives entailed sunup to sundown backbreaking labor just to survive at a basic level. Yet, this guy called them lazy.

"Now. Fast forward to the last half of the 1900s and first part of the 2000s, when people who lived at others' expense took offense to being called leeches and many liberals almost worshipped them as some kind of noble victims of society." He shook his head and appeared to be sick to his stomach. "How in the hell did we go from calling pioneers, who worked long hard hours and didn't cost the taxpayer dime to calling bums on social programs, who just sat on their butts waiting for the government to rob a taxpayer noble victims of Capitalism?"

Austin laughed. "The first sign of federal government coming back will be the IRS showing up and demanding we pay back taxes. They'll need that money to restart the welfare state."

Jacobson steered the conversation back to the farm. "I hope everyone who wants some of the bounty will be willing to do their part. If not, they'll certainly be a burden to everyone else. Whoever's put in charge should come up with a system that requires every able-bodied adult to work before they get much of the crop."

"Yeah," Nate said. "But I don't want that job. Despite my rant, I fully understand it's not easy to let people go hungry, not even lazy bums."

Austin laughed again. "You're an old softy, Nate."

Nate almost rolled his eyes.

Chapter 19

Deni slept on a couch in the living room of an abandoned home. It was two o'clock in the morning, and she was dead to the world after a long hard day. Despite her deep sleep, the sound of distant screams managed to wake her. She jumped up with her rifle in hand. Running to the back door, she peered out the window, but couldn't see where the sound was coming from. Another scream sliced through the dark night. Her mind groggy, she unlocked the door and swung it open. Leading with her M4, she walked barefoot out onto the wet grass. A popping sound from somewhere in the neighborhood echoed in the gray fog, like a gunshot or a firecracker, followed by more screams. She couldn't tell where it came from.

After running back inside, she snatched up her radio from the coffee table. "Shots fired in the neighborhood. Is anyone on it?"

The radio squelched, and a voice came back, "This is Foster, Sergeant. We've got teams coming in from three directions. I'll report back once we know something. You might as well stay where you are and get some rest. Foster over."

"You do that," Deni said. "Report back to me in fifteen minutes. Heath out."

She sat down on the couch and rubbed her eyes, thinking she might try to get a little more sleep before the radio call came in. It took her all of 5 seconds to kill that thought. She slipped on her socks and boots. By the time Private Foster called back, she had rousted three soldiers and the four of them were in a HUMVEE heading in the direction she had heard the gunshots and screams.

Private Foster spoke over the radio. "It's a bad one. One dead woman. Shot in the chest."

"Just a woman?" Deni asked. "No children?"

"No one else in the house. Looks like a kid did live here, though. A little girl."

One of the soldiers swore under his breath.

Deni barked a series of orders over the air, starting with Foster. "Get your men outside and search the area around the house. Look for a blood trail – anything."

Capt. Donovan broke in after she requested that the entire neighborhood be cordoned off. "We're on it, Sergeant. Get to the scene and supervise, while I make sure no vehicle gets out of the area and no one sneaks out on foot."

"Yes sir," Deni said.

Racing down the last street, they were hindered by groups of alarmed and angry people in various stages of dress, almost all of them armed. A few carried kerosene lanterns. The driver laid on the horn and yelled out of the window, "Get out of the way. The killer's making tracks while you're wasting our time here. Get out of the damn way!"

"Stop!" Deni yelled. She jumped out and addressed the gathering crowd. "A mother has been murdered, and we believe a little girl has been kidnapped."

Several people moaned, "No! Not again."

Deni raised her voice. "Everyone. Quiet!" People continued to talk. "Shut up and listen!" The crowd quieted down. "First, no one leave any family members alone and unarmed. Make certain that all of your children are guarded. Once your family is secure, I need a dozen people to go that way." She pointed to her left, down the street. "And a dozen more to go this way." She pointed to her right. "See anyone with a little girl in tow, hold him for questioning."

"Hold him, hell," a man in the back of the crowd yelled.

"Just hold him until we get there," Deni warned. "Don't go killing everyone with a little girl! You're more likely to kill the wrong man than the one we want." She reiterated, "Just hold him until we get there. Once we're sure we have the right man, he'll get what's coming to him, I promise."

The crowd began to thin as people headed to their families, while single adults with no children headed down the street to do what Deni had asked. She jumped back in the HUMVEE. "Let's go."

The driver laid on the horn and took off.

When she got to the house, Deni found Chesty and Tyrone already there, searching for clues. Chesty had a lantern. The rest of the house was dark but for soldiers with flashlights.

Standing in a bedroom, Chesty's face looked distorted because of the angle of the light hitting him from below his face. When Deni walked in, he looked up from a photo he was examining. "Looks like a mother and daughter living alone. The mother's lying near the back door, dead. The little girl's missing."

Deni nodded. He wasn't telling her much she didn't already know. "There's a chance the girl's still alive, but we don't have much time."

Chesty handed her a photo. "Must be the girl we're looking for. It's probably more than a year old, though. She'll be about eight, older than the other victims."

She looked at it and handed it to Tyrone, who also committed the image to memory.

Chesty moved out of the bedroom into the hall. "The killer forced the backdoor, with his shoulder it looks like. There's no sign he used a pry bar or other tool. The only damage is where it splintered around the lock."

Deni followed. She looked down at the woman's body that was lying on the kitchen floor in a wide puddle of blood. "Wearing night clothes. She must have been woken up and came to investigate the sound of him beating the door open."

The victim appeared to be in her thirties. Family photos she had seen in the bedroom told Deni she had lost a lot of weight since the plague. She noticed something sticking out from under the body. "Help me turn her over."

Chesty bent down and turned the body on its side, revealing a butcher knife.

"She had a knife," Deni said. "The intruder got the door open and shot her when she tried to protect her daughter."

Tyrone was disgusted. "Why the hell didn't she have a gun?"

"Might not have believed in them, or some such nonsense," Chesty said. "Cost her her life and maybe her daughter's."

Deni stood. "I'm no cop, but I'm wondering if this is our child killer. This guy's got more spine than the little girl hunter."

"True," Tyrone said. "But we have a missing girl."

She raised an eyebrow. "And we have to find her, ASAP."

Chesty looked sick. "God, I hate to think we might have two crazies to deal with."

A soldier walked in and addressed Deni. "Sergeant. There's a civilian outside with a German shepherd. He says the dog is trained to track."

In seconds, everyone was outside on the front lawn.

A tall, thin man in denim coveralls stood in the street, a large German shepherd sat patiently next to him, panting and looking around at the crowd with calm interest. The man had him on a leash, but it appeared to not be needed, as the dog sat waiting his master's command. He spoke when Deni and the others approached him. "Before the plague, I trained dogs to search for children lost in wilderness areas." He swallowed. "I had to euthanize all but one of my dogs, couldn't feed them all. That was one of the worst days of my life. Anyway, you let me in the house so he can get the scent, Shep here will track the killer for you."

Chesty was doubtful. "Can it single out the killer's scent from all the other people who've been in and around the house?"

The man nodded. "Sure."

He had Deni's attention. "What's your name?"

"Jack Taylor," the man said.

"Come with me. I want you to track a little girl."

"Yeah," Tyrone said. "Give the dog a whiff of her clothes."

"Okay," Jack gave the leash a gentle tug, and the dog stood. "Come on, Shep. We have a lost girl to find." The dog yelped and became excited, looking up at his master, breathing heavy and coiled to take action. "Only thing," Jack warned, "Shep's going to have a problem tracking over asphalt, so I hope she stays on dirt. The oil on the street messes up a dog's ability to smell."

"Well, do what you can," Chesty said. "A killer has run off with a kid."

"Come on, Shep," Jack said, and they all rushed into the house.

Deni led Jack into the girl's bedroom. Jack yanked the pillowcase off the girl's pillow and said, "Find her, Shep! Find the little girl!" He held the pillowcase against the dog's snout. Shep grew excited and pulled at the leash, heading out into the hall, past the dead mother, and out the backdoor.

"I'll stay here," Tyrone said. "In case you need me to circle around in front with a vehicle."

A military helicopter arrived and circled overhead. Deni got on the radio and informed the pilot what they were up to.

The dog didn't hesitate, plunging ahead and across the yard behind the victims' home, straining at the leash. Jack took advantage of Shep's abilities and ran to keep up. The others followed along behind.

Shep never barked but whined excitedly, eager to drive on, and Jack struggled to let him close on the girl as fast as possible. When they reached the next street, Shep stopped and sniffed the asphalt.

"Has he lost the trail?" Deni asked, worried the hunt was already over.

Jack urged the dog on. "Find the girl, Shep." After ten seconds of Shep sniffing at asphalt and looking bewildered, Jack pulled on the leash. "Come on, Shep." He led his dog to the other side of the street and gave him slack on the leash. Shep worked back and forth excitedly in ever increasing arcs. His whining picked up and he took off across the yard of the next house over.

The hunt ended in the carport of what appeared to be an empty house. The dog kept walking in circles, sniffing at the concrete and whining. No amount of coaxing from Jack could change the fact his dog had lost the scent trail. The disappointment on the dog's face appeared to equal Jack's.

Without a word, Chesty kicked the front door down. His shotgun ready, he yelled into the dark house, "Sheriff Department. Anyone in there needs to come out with his hands up!"

Deni illuminated the interior with a powerful combat light attached to her carbine. It was powered by lithium batteries that can be stored ten years and the Army still had plenty of them in their supply line. "Come out with your hands up!" she yelled.

No answer.

Jack knelt beside his dog. "Is there anyone in there, Shep?"

The dog looked at its master and whined but didn't move. Instead, it sat down.

"Nobody in there," Jack said. "Shep would know if there was. He'd smell 'em."

Not taking Jack or his dog's word, Deni and Chesty endured many tense moments and carefully cleared the house. Deni's superior training showed, but Chesty had been to several state law enforcement classes and did his part.

Deni emerged from the house appearing dejected. "See if you can get your dog to pick up the trail again. We have to find that girl."

"I already have," Jack said. "The girl got into a car."

Deni nervously rubbed her forehead. "You sure? How can you tell?"

"This isn't the first time Shep and I've been at this," Jack answered. "She got into a car of some kind, and she's too young to drive, so she wasn't alone. In fact, the way Shep was acting while on the trail, I would say the killer was with her. There was certainly more than one person."

Chesty swore under his breath. "Last time he got away on a motorcycle. At least we think so." He thought of something. "Can you go back to the crime scene and get your dog to follow the killer's trail? More than likely it'll be the same as the girl's."

"Sure, but like you said, the killer took her. It'll be a waste of time because the trail will lead us right back here."

"Hold on." Deni thought for a second. "Nothing about this matches the other killer. Something else is going on here." She shook her head as if to clear it. "Whatever. Forget that for now. We have to find the girl."

"The perimeter is our last hope," Chesty said. "Just pray he didn't manage to get out of the area before your soldiers and the townspeople bottled him up. If not, he's long gone and that girl is lost."

"It's going to be a long night and day. Every house within the perimeter will have to be searched, one by one." Deni contacted her superiors by radio and gave a situation report.

After she had signed off, Jack spoke up. "Shep will make it faster. He can smell if she has been in a house. He can smell her scent where she got out of the car and walked in, of course, but he can even tell if she's been in a house recently, even if he doesn't catch where she got out of a car."

"Will you stay and help?" Chesty asked.

"Sure. Glad to."

"Thanks," Chesty said. "We appreciate it."

They were interrupted by a bright spotlight from down the street. The spotlight was instantly aimed in another direction to stop blinding them. A HUMVEE approached and slowed to a stop. Donovan got out. "Sorry about the light. My driver needed to ID you. Is this where the trail ends?"

"Yes sir," Deni answered. "We fear the killer may have gotten out of the area before the perimeter was cordoned off."

"Let's hope not," Donovan said. "I have more people on the perimeter now, so he'll not get past us. We have teams searching homes as we speak and every vehicle gets searched before passing our roadblocks. If he's still in the area, we'll find that girl and him both."

"Any trouble with the civilians complaining about *Posse Comitatus*?" Chesty asked. "Some people won't like the idea of the Army being involved in law enforcement."

"We just tell them a kid's been taken and they cooperate," Donovan answered. "Since the plague most people are so desperate for help they don't worry about that stuff. We've been acting as law enforcement since not long after everything went to hell."

Distant gunshots interrupted their conversation. Everyone instinctively flinched and ducked down behind cover. A burst of full auto fire told them it was likely soldiers had just shot someone.

Donovan ran for the HUMVEE, barking orders to the driver. "Get me there, now!" He jumped in and was on the radio as soon as he hit the seat.

Deni and Chesty moved out of the street onto the lawn. They had left their vehicles behind and couldn't follow.

Jack pulled his dog out of the way. "I hope that girl doesn't get caught in the fighting and take a bullet."

Deni saw a group of three men running toward them. "The shooting might not have anything to do with the killer and the girl." She looked down the street expectantly. "I wonder what this is."

Chesty followed her gaze and saw them for the first time. The men were yelling something, but he couldn't make it out. "Something's up," he said, and ran toward the men.

The others followed.

As they got closer, Deni could make out their words. They were saying something about a girl.

One of the men yelled, "We found her! She's okay."

Deni ran up to the men. Nearly out of breath, she asked, "What about the man who took her?"

One of the other men answered, "She was alone. The guy let her go."

Deni and Chesty's eyes met, relief and puzzlement on their face.

"Did she give you a description of the man?" Chesty asked.

"Yeah," one of the men answered. "He's her father."

~~~

Donovan looked through the HUMVEE's windshield. Three soldiers searched a pickup. A man's bloody body lay motionless in the street only five feet away from the open pickup door.

"Had to fire," one soldier said. "It looked to me like he wanted to die. He fired at me but wasn't really aiming. I wasn't going to take a chance, so I put him down."

Donovan nodded. "Where's the girl?"

"No girl. He was alone."

"What?" Donovan looked in the cab of the pickup without thinking. Worry washed over his face. "He must've killed her already." He looked for blood in the back of the truck.

Deni's voice came over the radio. "We have the girl. She's alive and unharmed."

Confusion replaced worry on Donovan's face. "What're we dealing with here?" His question was directed at no one and no one offered an answer.

A HUMVEE came racing up. Deni jumped out. "The girl says it was her father who killed her mother and took her."

"So this is a domestic thing?" Donovan asked.

"Well," Deni said, "the couple had been estranged for years. The girl says her father was always pestering her mother to take him back. He showed up tonight and broke in. Looks like he planned to kill his wife from the beginning. He may have been planning to kill his daughter, too, but changed his mind and dropped her off." Disgust washed over her face. "Who knows? Anyway, I had doubts from the start this was our girl killer; too much about this crime didn't match his MO."

Donovan looked at the dead man lying in the street. "Damn. The idiot should have been grateful he didn't lose his wife and daughter in the plague."

Deni remembered Donovan telling her he had lost his family early on, when the plague first hit the Eastern U.S.

Donovan directed his attention to Deni. "I'm glad the girl's okay, but after all of this, we still have a nut out there hunting little girls."

Chapter 20

Nate stood naked at a window and looked out into the dark night onto a street glistening from an earlier shower, reflecting the light of a dim moon. He felt a small hand on the back of his neck – massaging – as light as weightlessness, alternating into strong pressure and back to weightlessness, then two hands, flitting across his sun-darkened skin to his impossibly large shoulders, and pressing the worry-born kinks out. *This was a mistake,* he thought. *Like feeding a hungry stray dog, it'll come back to bite us both. It's too human. And human beings are too weak to live in a lawless post-plague world.*

"Stop worrying," Deni whispered in his ear. "It's already been done now. Worry won't undo it."

He turned and touched her face in the dark, cradling it in both his rough hands. He could tell she was smiling.

"I have to go," she said.

He heard her turn, felt her leaving the room. It felt as though something had already sucked the oxygen out of it. For a moment, it felt as though the dying air would suffocate him. But he couldn't allow it. He rushed to catch up, reached out and pulled her close, holding her in the dark. He heard her breath catch as their bodies pressed together.

A woman's love made a man softer, tempering the steel in him, leaving it less like a hard, brittle file with sharp teeth that rasped and cut into anything that came too close; but being soft, being human, could be a liability in a world ruled by the claw and tooth.

He remembered the bewilderment in Brian's eyes when he became much harder and colder, as the sickness took first his mother and then his little sister. He could tell that Brian was wondering if he had lost his father, too. He remembered wishing there was some way he could tell him the change was about keeping him alive, not loving him less. In fact, all the love for his wife and daughter had become directed at Brian, as well as the love he already had for his son. He didn't love him less; he loved him even more. To survive, Brian had to mature and become as hard as the new world around him. As his father, it fell on his shoulders to force a little boy who had led a relatively easy life to become a man strong enough to take anything. Even as he saw the change, he felt pangs of regret. Watching innocence – his boy – die was painful, though it was vital, if a man was to be born. Only a man could survive.

"I have to go," Deni said.

"I know." He didn't release his hold on her.

She laughed. "Am I supposed to wrestle my way out of your big arms?"

"Be careful out there," he warned. "Don't let this weaken you. It's still dangerous. Death is lurking, waiting for an opening."

She stiffened. "How could this weaken me?"

"Keep your mind on staying alive, not us."

"Uh, okay. I wish you'd stop worrying. As if you've done something wrong by being close to me. This doesn't put me in danger. I really don't understand why you think it does."

"It does," he said. "You'll see. When you're on patrol and you catch yourself thinking about us and you let your guard down at the wrong moment. The first time I was shot while serving in the Army, I was thinking of Susan when I should've been keeping my eyes and ears working, concentrating on staying alive."

She pushed away from him. "Oh hell, Nate."

"What?"

"Nothing. I must go."

He reached for her, but she pulled away. "First tell me what's wrong. I can't help worrying about you. I've seen too many people die not to worry."

"I *was* thinking of that," she said. "But…when you mentioned Susan…it made me feel like I'm competing with her memory."

"Damn it, I'm sorry. That's not it at all. It was all about trying to help you avoid a costly mistake. Just stay alert."

"I will. And I'm not mad anymore, so don't worry about that." She turned to the door. "I'll see you this afternoon."

Nate heard her in the bath down the hall. The water had been carried in buckets. It was cold, but wet. *Well, she misunderstood me. What else is new?*

~~~

Brian sat on the front steps of Chesty's house and enjoyed the sights and smells of the fresh new day. Dr. Brant had told him his arm and ribs were healing fast, but the arm cast would stay on another week, mostly to help prevent him from breaking it again, since he hadn't refrained from using it like she'd ordered him. Brian and Nate had been staying at Chesty's place after Austin left them in town before returning to Mrs. MacKay's farm, taking Renee and the others with him. That was two weeks before. He saw his father coming down the sidewalk, carrying his pack and rifle.

He was old enough to know Deni and his father had become lovers, that they had spent the night together, and that's why his father hadn't stayed the night at Chesty's. He was also old enough to know not to mention it. He expected his father might even feel guilt, as if he had cheated on his mother. The fact she'd been dead more than a year didn't mean his father wasn't still grieving inside. He would keep conversations on other matters and give the two distance and time to work out whatever there was to be between them.

Nate stepped up to the porch. He regarded his son, as if he might be wondering what he was thinking.

Brian looked up at him, revealing no clue what was on his mind. "What're we going to do today?"

He saw his father as permanent as anything he had ever known, as immutable and unchanging as the world itself, more so, since the world *had* changed. The plague changed everything in his life, and for a long time, he had thought his father had changed and grown hard and cruel with the world. But he later discovered that he was mistaken, that he had just been too immature to realize it, that his father had been the same man all along. His father, he had grown to realize, had not been hard on him those last 13 months; he had been hard on himself, denying himself almost all of the fun part of being a father and instead concentrating on survival. He had done much of the same with Deni and their relationship – until last night. And he knew his father would feel guilty about that too. If he let his guard down and someone was hurt, he would blame himself. If he was too cold and distant and someone was hurt, he would feel guilty of causing needless pain. Brian resolved to do his best to help him through that minefield.

"Chesty wants us to take a truck and patrol the streets," Nate said. "That killer is still out there, and he's determined to stop him before he kills another little girl."

Surprised, Brian raised a brow. "Okay. I'm ready."

The radio on Nate's load-bearing harness came to life. It was Chesty. "Nate, if you can hear me, answer."

Nate snatched the radio up. He had noticed Chesty and Tyrone's radio protocol was informal. That would most likely change over time as the number of deputies grew. For now, though, they were short on deputies and had no more radios, even if they had more personnel. "We're just about to go on patrol. What's up?"

"Just a radio check and to remind you to stay on your side of Division and that these radios have limited range, so don't go too far north or west. Remember, we don't have a repeater with a tall tower. These little radios are operating unsupported. Over."

Chesty was telling him nothing he didn't already know. He smiled at Brian and said, "We'll remember that. Over."

"Be careful out there and don't hesitate to call Tyrone and me for help. Out."

"Will do. Out."

Brian watched him put the radio away. "The Army'll be on the streets. Can you call them for help with that radio?"

"I'm sure they're monitoring all frequencies. We'll also stop to talk with any soldiers we come across. Best they can ID us and our vehicle from a distance. Also, we want them to know we're working with local law enforcement."

Brian nodded. "I guess that truck in the driveway's for us."

~~~

Nate edged out of his patrol area closer to where the last girl had been taken. There were several families on one street, and he wanted to check on them. He knew one couple had two young girls. They might be too much for the killer to resist.

"It's almost three," Brian said. "I have two MREs Deni gave me. We ever going to stop somewhere to eat?"

Nate pulled onto the street where the girls lived and stopped in the shade of a wide oak. It was out of habit, as the afternoon was cool and pleasant. "We can eat right here." He regarded Brian for a second, then opened the door and stepped out, taking his rifle with him. "I'm guessing you just offered me one of those MREs, otherwise, I'll have to go hungry until we get back to Chesty's place."

Brian smiled. "What made you think that I was going to give you one?" He got out and reached in the back behind the cab and pulled an MRE out, throwing it to his father. "Don't say I never gave you anything." He moved to the rear of the truck and swung the tailgate down to use as a table.

Nate reached into a pocket and produced a knife to open the MRE. "You're a gentleman, a scholar, and a horse's ass."

"You're welcome. Can I use your knife?"

Nate handed it to him.

Brian didn't use it. He stood there with the knife in his hand, looking like he had something on his mind besides a late lunch. "How long are we going to stay in town? You've always been in a hurry to get back to Mel's bunker."

"You know why we're still in town. I want to be near Deni."

"I know that. I was just wondering...Well, I guess you don't really know yourself, do you?"

"No. I don't know when we'll be leaving town. Soon. I haven't changed my mind on that." Nate waited for Brian to get at what was bothering him.

Brian cut his MRE open. "Just don't worry about me. Whatever you decide is okay."

"I always worry about you."

"What I mean is something could happen and you'll blame yourself. If it happens in town, you'll tell yourself it's your fault. If we go to Mel's bunker and something happens, you'll tell yourself it's your fault." He looked at Nate and said nothing for a few seconds, his eyes doing the talking.

Nate realized his son was looking back at him as an equal – a man, not a boy, but still his son.

Brian finished what he wanted to say. "So there's no point in leaving because something might happen to me here. It could happen anywhere. You might as well stay close to Deni."

"Well," was all Nate said. They started their meal. A few minutes passed before Nate could speak again. "Brian, there have been more times than I could count when I put you in harm's way, and every time I did my stomach was in knots. But not once was it for something trivial."

"Deni isn't trivial," Brian said, after washing down a bite with water from his canteen.

"No, Deni isn't, but the two of us being together is. Neither one of us would die without each other."

"That's not trivial either." Brian lost interest in eating. "So you're willing to help Chesty and Tyrone and kind of be their deputy and even take me with you, but you think it's too much of a risk to stay in town so you two can spend time together?"

"Some animal's killing little girls. Stopping him is worth some risk."

A thought brightened Brian's face. "So I'm not the only one in the world you care about. Why not care about yourself a little? And if you can't do that, care about Deni's feelings."

"I do. But hurt feelings won't kill her. It's all about what's most important – staying alive. You, Deni, me, our friends. That always comes first. Certainly it comes before feelings."

"Seems like you've made up your mind already. I guess we'll be leaving soon."

Nate threw his empty food pouches in the back of the truck. "I haven't made a decision on when. I'm thinking a few more days." He regarded Brian for a second. "Might stay a week if I can put you somewhere safe and get you to stay there. Maybe you can help out at the clinic. We certainly owe the doctors and nurses."

The radio on Nate's load bearing harness came to life. Tyrone was calling Chesty for help. There was a lot of static, but gun shots could be made out in the background.

Tyrone's area was on the south side of town, where the county road had brought so much trouble in the past, welcoming raiders. The road connected to an interstate highway and for a year, that highway had brought trouble from the north. Until recently, the townspeople had manned a roadblock there 24/7, but it had been judged no longer necessary. After all, the Army had arrived. They would protect them.

None of that mattered to Tyrone, who was left on the side of the road with a disabled patrol car, battered and bruised but otherwise unharmed. "Three big trucks – semis without trailers – came speeding into town. They had rigged cargo areas on the back and armed men were riding in them. The first truck forced me off the road and went on by. The second one rammed me. My vehicle's finished, but I'm okay."

"Who was shooting?" Chesty asked.

"Them," Tyrone answered. "I'm sure they're raiders. Notify the Army."

"Will do," Chesty said.

Nate and Brian had jumped in the truck and were racing south. After a lull in radio traffic, Nate spoke into the mike. "We'll pick up Tyrone."

"I'm closer," Chesty said.

Nate started to speak, but then he saw a truck turn onto their street and then another one, following only yards behind. Huge trucks, loud exhaust pipes spewing black smoke. One man shot a rifle in their direction, leaning out of the passenger side window as they barreled toward them. Bullets punched holes in their windshield. Nate yanked the wheel to the right and raced for cover between two houses. He didn't stop there; instead, he yanked the wheel to the left and plowed through a wood privacy fence to take refuge behind the house.

"Are you hit?" Nate reached over and pulled Brian to him, checking for wounds.

"No." Brian yanked away and exited the truck, his rifle in hand.

Nate bailed out on his side. He hit the ground running, keeping 15 feet back from the house. He yelled to Brian, "Stay back!" Stopping at the corner, he sliced the pie of angles, jerking his head back each time. The sound of the trucks continuing down the street wasn't enough for him to forego his training and just barrel around the corner, perhaps into a hail of bullets. Seeing no danger, he ran on to the front corner, where he repeated the same procedure, but this time he had the corner of the house to the left to deal with, also.

Brian kept his rifle trained on the corner to the left to back up his father. "They're gone, Dad."

Nate checked the front yards and the street as far as he could see. Finding it clear, he grabbed the radio out of its pouch on his chest. "A dozen men in two semis just shot out our windshield, heading north toward downtown."

Chesty's voice blared through the static, "Anyone hurt?"

"No."

"I just contacted the Army. They're on it. What the hell are these idiots up to? Don't they know the Army's in town?

Sweat beaded on Nate's forehead. "Looks like they plan to raid somebody. I have no idea who. Be careful. They're trigger happy."

"I have Mel with me. Follow your own advice. Out."

A shadow fell over Brian's face. "What part of town is Deni working today?"

"I don't know," Nate answered. "Let's check the truck out and see if it'll still run."

Chapter 21

Nate had the truck's engine roaring and the horn blaring nonstop. He blew through intersections in residential streets at 70 miles per hour. Fortunately, the neighborhoods were almost devoid of people and traffic. He slowed to turn a corner, heading for the clinic. All four tires smoked as he slid sideways through the intersection and stomped the gas, heading down the street.

Though strapped in tight, Brian held on with one hand and held his rifle with the other. He'd never seen his father drive on the razor edge of losing control of the vehicle before.

Someone was talking on the radio, but neither of them could hear above the engine and rush of wind. Nate slowed as he approached the clinic. A HUMVEE blocked the driveway and several soldiers aimed rifles at them.

"Stay where you are and don't let them see your weapon." Nate stopped in the road and got out unarmed, except for his pistol that was hid under his shirt. He approached the soldiers slowly, keeping his hands in sight.

When he was close enough, one soldier recognized him. "We're locked down, Mr. Williams."

"I figured that." Nate thrust a thumb over his right shoulder. "I would like to leave my son here where he'll be safe."

The soldier nodded. "Okay. Park your truck over on the sidewalk out of the way first."

Nate ran back to the truck.

Brian didn't wait for him to get in before saying, "I heard."

Nate slid behind the wheel. "Don't give me any trouble. I don't have time."

"I won't," Brian said. "Just because you might be safer if you're not worrying about me."

"Good." Nate parked on the sidewalk. "When you get out, put your pack on, then sling your rifle so some soldier doesn't get jumpy."

Brian got out and started to say something when his eyes flashed down the road. He yelled, "Get down!"

Automatic gunfire erupted.

It was at that moment Nate remembered Tyrone had said there were three trucks. Only two had raced by them when they shot up their windshield. He saw the truck turn off the street and ram the HUMVEE blocking the clinic entrance, despite the soldiers laying automatic fire into the windshield. Jumping out of the truck and throwing himself onto the sidewalk, Nate shouldered his rifle and began to fire into the attackers. He could just make out the report of Brian's rifle somewhere behind him.

It was over in less than three minutes. Nate yelled at Brian, "Are you hit?"

Brian lay on the ground, taking cover behind the truck's front wheel. "No."

"Don't move. Stay where you are. Remember, not every soldier knows us. Keep your rifle down."

Two soldiers were hurt, neither by gunfire. Their injuries were from the attackers ramming the HUMVEE and it slamming it into the soldiers behind it. Nate and Brian watched but never moved, not wanting to attract unwanted attention.

Capt. Donovan arrived with reinforcements, taking command. There had been several other attacks in town, the work of more truckloads of killers, and he'd been busy.

"Leave your rifle where it is and follow me," Nate told Brian. They moved onto a clear area of unkempt lawn, keeping their hands in sight and not making any sudden moves. They sat on the grass and waited while the soldiers secured the scene and made sure all threats had been neutralized.

Brian motioned with his head. "Chesty and Tyrone are here." The fact Mel was missing made them both nervous.

Chesty and Tyrone talked with the soldiers for a few minutes and then walked over to Nate and Brian.

"Is Mel okay?" Nate asked.

Chesty nodded. "He stayed behind to help with a wounded soldier."

Tyrone rubbed a bruised arm as he walked up. "One of the attackers is alive. He's wounded pretty bad but talking."

"Yeah, Chesty said. "Looks like they're some kind of anti-government group. He's not making much sense, but evidently they don't want the government to come back and don't like the Army being here."

Brian's brow furrowed. "Huh?"

"My reaction exactly," Chesty said. "A bunch of nuts. They basically committed suicide today. Unfortunately, they killed several people and wounded seven."

Nate's gaze was on the scene of the battle. "I hope that's all there was of their little militia. The bastards shot at everything that moved, not just soldiers."

"The wounded guy claims they have a big organization." Tyrone checked out the truck Nate was driving. "Look at that windshield. You guys are lucky."

Nate looked over at Brian and swallowed. "Yeah."

Brian broke the silence. "I wonder if Deni's okay."

~~~

A chunk of mortar flew off the front of the building next to where Deni stood, and she heard the zing of a ricochet. Instantly, she was in a flat-out run for the HUMVEE and cover. Another shot missed by only inches. The gunman was firing from a patch of woods in an overgrown lot.

The soldiers in her patrol team also dove for cover, two were already returning fire, but aiming blindly, as they had only a vague idea where the shooter was. The armorless HUMVEE wasn't equipped with a heavy machinegun, so all they had was their M4s.

Deni barked an order, "Bartram, get the SAW out."

A soldier jumped up and ran. Keeping low and behind the HUMVEE. Careful not to expose himself, he opened the nearside door, reached in, and pulled out a squad automatic weapon. He lay down on the concrete behind the HUMVEE and folded the bipod out. In seconds, he was spraying the woods in the general area where he thought the shooter was, limiting his bursts to four rounds.

Deni got on the radio and asked for a Black Hawk, but was told none were available. Attacks on other areas of town were keeping them busy. The shooting from the woods had stopped, anyway. She didn't know if that meant he had been taken out or if it was just because of suppression fire from the SAW keeping his head down.

Executing fire and maneuver techniques, Deni and two other soldiers worked their way closer to the wooded lot. She was grateful when they took no more fire. Still, she had no way of knowing whether the shooter was dead, had fled, or was just keeping his head down and biding his time, waiting for a clear shot.

The suppression fire had to stop when Deni and the other soldiers entered the woods, leaving her with a naked feeling. They spread out, staying just close enough to be in sight of each other. Immediately, they confronted thorny briars so thick they were forced to go around them. Bullying their way through would've made too much noise and let the shooter know exactly where they were. Keeping a close eye on the briar patch in case danger lurked there while moving on, Deni came to a small amount of blood, nowhere near enough to be debilitating, but evidence someone's bullet had connected. More importantly to her, the blood provided a trail to follow.

Though a cool day, it was uncomfortably hot under her helmet and heavy body armor. A slight breeze cooled her wet face, but when it picked up and tossed the brush around her she wished it would calm down. A brush-choked patch of woods busy with movement would make it difficult to see danger sneaking within range.

Three rapid shots rang out, and she caught the impact of the bullets as they slammed into a soldier on her right. She hit the ground and then belly-crawled to him. He lay on his back, gasping for air. A frantic examination of his vest told her the bullets had been stopped by his body armor. When he moaned and turned his face toward her, she saw that he had taken a grazing round across his left cheek. "Shit!" She pulled a battle wound dressing from a pouch on her vest and pressed it against his face. "Hold that, Horowitz."

"Is it bad?" he asked.

"No."

The look in his eyes told her he didn't believe her. "No shit. It's not bad." She searched the woods for more danger as she spoke into the radio. "We have a man down. Hostiles are still active."

The other soldier kept vigil while Deni calmed the wounded Horowitz. "You'll have a little scar to impress the girls. Nothing like a battle scar to give your looks character." She stretched to see above the brush while on her knees.

The soldier to her left crawled closer, his nervous eyes checking Horowitz's wounds. Blood poured from the soaked bandage and between his fingers to run down his forearm.

"Stay with Horowitz," she ordered, her eyes narrowing as she turned to look in the direction the shooter had fled. "I'm going after him."

The soldier gave her a *what the…* look.

Yeah, Deni thought. *I know it's nuts. But this bastard just shot one of my soldiers, and he's not going to get by with it.*

She didn't move until she had examined every inch of the woods ahead and was certain no one was waiting for her, at least not within 20 yards. Gripping her rifle tighter, she got to her feet and charged forward, bending low.

As soon as she'd moved 15 yards, she dropped behind cover and repeated the process, examining every inch of woods as far as her eyes could penetrate the wall of green before her. Repeating the process twice more brought her to the edge of the wooded lot. She'd lost the blood trail, and that told her the the shooter wasn't seriously wounded.

A quick scan of the open lot between her and the next house over gave her little comfort that death wasn't waiting for her to walk out of the woods into the open. She stayed where she was and contacted the soldiers at the HUMVEE by radio. "Reposition and give me cover on the east side of the lot."

The sight of Bartram with the SAW and another soldier taking position behind a house across the street overwatching the area between her and the next house gave her some reassurance, but she still involuntarily swallowed and asked herself if it was worth it as she stepped out into the opening. *Yeah, it's worth it. I can't let this bastard get away.* Besides, she wanted to know why he was shooting at soldiers. Was he part of the other attacks? What was it all about? Maybe he would be able to talk when she saw him up close, maybe not.

Rushing toward the house was a terrifying experience. She half expected to feel a bullet slamming into her at any moment.

Someone could be watching from any of three windows on her side of the house, taking aim.

Not slowing down, she slammed her shoulder against the house wall, grateful to have made it to cover in one piece. She knew she was doing almost everything wrong. Despite everyone being busy with other attacks, help would arrive soon, and she should wait. Her indecision over what to do next ended when a shot rang out from two houses over. The shooter wasn't aiming at her. She discovered that when Bartram rattled out a short burst and she looked that way to find another soldier down.

Damn it! As angry at herself for putting the soldier in danger as she was the shooter, she raced for the next house and cover. Two-thirds of the way there, a bullet shrieked by her head. She dropped to the ground and belly-crawled into two-foot-tall grass, which offered her concealment but not cover. Bartram's SAW spoke, unleashing two four-round bursts. Deni raised her head just enough to see and peered through the top edge of the tall grass. Out of the left corner of her eye, she caught a man with a rifle running across a yard. A snapshot rewarded her with the sight of a spray of blood from the man's upper torso just before he fell. A sense of extreme relief came over her. If the shooter was alone, the chances of another one of her soldiers getting hurt just dropped dramatically.

But was he alone?

One thing for sure, she was going to at least get close enough to the man she just shot to have a talk with him – if he was still alive. Why was this guy shooting at soldiers?

She turned her radio off to avoid it giving her position away and low-crawled to the next house, fully knowing there was nothing between her and a bullet if she were located in the tall grass. Making use of the shadow of a nearby fence, she made her way closer to the shooter, staying as low as possible. The wet gurgling of the wounded man laboring to breathe came to her ears, and she knew there was little time for her to reach him. It was most likely already too late. Even if he were alive when she reached him, he may not be able to talk. Still, she crawled closer.

Dirt exploded in her face.

A second shooter!

She rolled to her left until she landed in a depression and flattened herself against the ground. Another bullet kicked up dirt beside her. She saw a man with a rifle dash behind a house. The shooting stopped, telling her he may be the last one.

Taking a calculated risk that she would later shake her head over, she jumped up and ran to the man she'd shot, throwing herself on the ground next to him. He was still breathing and conscious. A quick look at his wound told her he probably wouldn't live long enough for the helicopter to arrive. She saw his rifle lying next to him (a Mini 14) and threw it ten feet away. A precursory search for more weapons produced only a sheath knife.

"Why did you and your friend shoot at us?"

"Kiss my ass." He coughed up blood.

"I don't think so. We just met. I want to know why you shot at me and forced me to shoot you."

He gave her a hate-laden glare. "Go to hell."

"Maybe later." Deni scanned the area for more danger. "You're dying. Are you sure you don't want to tell me why you shot at me?"

His voice became weak and difficult to understand. "I'm a POW and don't have to say shit."

She reared back a little, surprised. "What military are you with?"

No answer.

His chest no longer heaved and the wheezing had stopped. He stared up into the sky at nothingness.

"Damn it."

Bartram came running up. He dropped to his knees then lay on his stomach behind the SAW. "You're pushing it, aren't you, Sarge?"

"Has help arrived yet?" Deni asked.

Bartram mopped sweat off his brow. "Nah. No chopper, no soldiers. We're alone out here."

Deni's face turned hard with determination. "There's another one. Last I saw of him he ran behind that house." She pointed.

"Yeah," Bartram said. "I got a glimpse of him but couldn't get a shot. He may be in another county by now – or aiming at us through a window."

"Well, this one's not going anywhere. I'm going after the other one."

Bartram had been chewing gum, jacking his jaw nervously; he stopped and regarded her face in astonishment. "Now Sarge, that's just nuts. Why do you want him so bad?"

There were two reasons, but she wasn't about to explain herself to him. "You stay here. If help ever arrives, tell them I'm hunting the other one."

"Damn it, Sarge. At least let me go with you."

"Stay here like I said. Overwatch while I crawl to that house." Deni eased along the ground, staying as flat as possible. She made it to the house the last man disappeared behind without getting shot at, but as soon as she leaned out just far enough to see around the corner, a bullet slammed into the wall only inches from her face. She jerked her head back to safety.

The shot had come from down the street. Ducking behind the house, she ran through several backyards, closing the distance. She managed to catch the shooter off guard and get a hastily aimed round off while he watched the street, dropping him. Catching her breath, Deni stood behind the house and waited for the man to bleed and weaken before approaching. She did want him alive, though, and therefore didn't wait too long. Just as she started across the street, the man jumped up and ran behind a house before she could hit him again.

"Son of a –!" She noticed he left his rifle behind, leaving him with only a pistol, and he was bleeding from his right side. Without his rifle, he was a lot less lethal, so if she kept her distance, her odds weren't bad. That changed when she started across the street and confronted a man who popped up from behind an abandoned car thirty yards away wielding a rifle.

He cut loose with a long string of wild shots just as she dropped to the ground. Trying not to panic, she fired from prone and put three quick shots into him, centering his chest and killing him where he stood.

Where the hell did the wounded one go? Deni concentrated on slowing her breathing and heartbeat. *Damn it. I want at least one of these idiots alive.* Something was going on, and she was willing to continue the hunt to find out exactly what.

The bottom of her uniform jacket felt loose on one side, so she risked taking her eyes off the danger zone and looked down to see a hole and below that loose, tattered cloth on the right side of her waist. The bullets had missed her by no more than an inch.

A pistol round ricocheted off the concrete curb ten feet away. Evidently the wounded man wasn't so good with a pistol. His wound may have hindered his aim, also.

Where the hell is he?

A shot came from somewhere down the street. She had no idea where the bullet hit, but it didn't hit her. She didn't know exactly where the wounded man was either, but had an idea of the general area. Her main problem was every time she thought she was alone with only him to deal with, another man would pop up out of nowhere, and there was no way for her to know how many more were lying in wait.

By the time she had worked her way close enough to see him, she could hear a helicopter finally arriving, bringing reinforcements she hoped. He was in a driveway, peering over a concrete wall four feet high, trying to find her. His trouble was he didn't look in the right direction, and she had come up on his right flank.

Moving a few steps closer, she aimed to incapacitate him, and fired. The man jerked as his weapon clattered on the concrete, and then he lay still. Deni approached cautiously, rifle trained on his inert body. When she reached him, she kicked his gun away. Her mind registered that he carried a military model Beretta. The next thing she knew, her legs swept out from under her, and she was on her butt. The shooter had used his good arm, sweeping against her ankles and she hadn't seen it coming, realizing her error even as she went down. Her desire to bring him in alive for questioning may have gotten her into serious trouble. The pain from the impact shot up her back as she hit the hard driveway, but she ignored it and concentrated on maintaining her grip on her rifle even as she tried to roll far enough from the wounded man to train the muzzle on him and pull the trigger. *Enough of this. To hell with bringing him in alive.* As she rolled, her wrist struck the hard pavement and she lost her grip for a split second. He saw an opening and kicked at her while on his side, but she surprised him by doing some kicking of her own, planting the bottom of her left boot in his face.

She felt a satisfying connection with his nose and saw his head snap back, nasal area pouring blood. She followed it up with another brutal kick with the same boot and heard a crunch as his nose fragmented further and he fell on his back, lying inert.

On her hands and knees gasping, she thought it was over when the man sat up and punched. Her head snapped to the side and a blinding flash of light filled her vision as his fist smashed into her jaw, then she felt impossibly strong vise-grip hands wrap around her neck, preparing to choke the life out of her. She pulled away until she felt him resist, then instantly reversed direction and rammed the top of her head into his face, stunning him.

Deni followed with a thumb to the eye. Ignoring her aching body's protest, she drove her fist into his bloody face before he had time to recover.

His arms fell away from her as they lost their strength, and she completed her follow-through by snatching his head in both hands and hammering the pavement with it. The impact seemed to have knocked him senseless, but she wasn't playing with him any longer. Though still seeing stars and out of breath, she pulled cord out of a pocket and tied his hands securely behind his back.

Four soldiers ran up. "We got him, Sarge," one said.

Deni fell back onto the concrete and sucked air. "Just in time to save me," she quipped. "Watch it. There's at least one more of them." She took her helmet off and poured the contents of her canteen over her face while she gasped. "Please tell me that SOB's still alive."

A soldier reached down and felt the man's chest. "He's still breathing but unconscious."

She collapsed, too tired to feel any sense of victory.

Chapter 22

After seeing how overwhelmed the clinic personnel were, Nate and Brian decided to stay and help. Mostly they carried stretchers, so soldiers could go back out on patrol sooner. Before he left with Tyrone, Chesty told them the fighting seemed to be over, and most of the attackers had been eliminated, the rest had fled into the countryside.

A Black Hawk landed in a parking lot beside the clinic, carrying more wounded. One of them was being closely guarded. The soldiers wouldn't allow Brian and Nate to take him off their hands, insisting on carrying the stretcher themselves. They kept out of the way, realizing he must have been one of the attackers.

Nate nudged Brian. "Look."

They watched Deni jump out of the helicopter.

She tried to smile at the sight of their ashen faces. "Damn. I must look terrible. Don't cry guys. I'm okay, just banged up a little."

Nate looked her up and down for injuries. He said nothing, but the look on his face was saying plenty.

Brian rushed to her and put his arms around her. She held him for a second and let him go. "Calm down guys. I told you I'm okay."

Nate pulled him back. "She's on duty. Give her space."

"I'm telling you I'm okay," Deni said, smiling. "See you later. I've got a prisoner to keep watch over."

Nate's head jerked around and he watched the wounded man as he was carried into the front door of the clinic.

She saw death staring at the man. "Whoa! I worked hard to take him alive."

He turned to her. "They already have a live one. Supposedly it's some kind of self-proclaimed antigovernment militia."

Deni slumped. "You know how to make a girl feel better, Nate. I went through a lot to take him in."

Nate wished he had kept his mouth shut. "Sorry. Two talkers are better than one, anyway."

"Yeah," Deni forced a smile. "Nice try." She straightened her back. "I'll see you guys later."

The two kept busy for nearly two hours, knowing Deni was busy and she would be one of the last to be treated, since she wasn't seriously wounded. Though both were nervous and worried, the work helped to keep their mind off the horrible sight of her bruised and battered face.

~~~

Dr. Brant approached the father and son in a hallway. "I just treated her and she wants to see you both."

Their faces were displaying the same worried question mark.

Dr. Brant answered it. "She just has a lot of bruises, no broken bones, nothing that won't heal in a week or two. Obviously, she was in a hell of a fight."

"That was all about her taking one of those idiots in alive." Nate stared up at the ceiling for a second. "It wasn't worth it."

"I wouldn't tell her that," Brian warned.

Nate almost smiled. "Good advice. Let's go see her."

Dr. Brant had a smirk on her face but said nothing. She watched them walk away and then went to her next patient.

~~~

Nate touched Deni's face gently as she sat on the examination pad. "He almost broke your jaw."

"Na. Not even close." She smiled. "Stop feeling sorry for me. I'm a soldier, remember?"

Nate started, "You're my… friend."

She obviously thought his hesitation to say what he almost said was amusing. "Enough of this. Dr. Brant says I'm good to go." She stood. "So let's go." She regarded her two worried admirers. "But you can carry my pack for me."

Capt. Donovan walked in.

Deni stood in a brace.

"At ease, Sergeant." Donovan's eyes took in her swollen face. "I want you to rest until tomorrow afternoon, then report to me at 15:00 hours."

"Yes sir. Did you get anything out of my prisoner yet?"

"He's in surgery. What do you think about what little he said to you?"

Deni answered, "He didn't say anything. Another one told me he was a POW and didn't have to talk, but that's all I got out of him before he died."

Donovan contorted his face. "POW? Well, we have another wounded one that was captured in front of the clinic. He might live. So far, all we've gotten out of him was he's part of a militia that's against government, corporations, and Capitalism."

Nate grunted. "So what does that leave? Anarchy? I don't think you can have Socialism without a strong government. Who would collect the taxes to fund the programs?"

"Yeah, it's crazy," Donovan said. "We definitely have to learn more to understand what we're up against and how large of a threat this group represents." He started for the door, then turned around. "Take care of Deni for me, will you? Make sure she gets some rest."

"That's my plan," Nate said. "But she doesn't listen to me."

Donovan smiled. "Well, she has her orders from her acting CO. If she doesn't follow them, let me know tomorrow." He left Nate and Deni staring at each other.

~~~

The next day.

While Nate got dressed and prepared to spend the morning with Deni, who was in the next bedroom, he decided to carry his revolver instead of the heavy civilian version of the M14 that he usually carried. He didn't plan to go anywhere and would be spending the next several hours doing his best to make Deni comfortable. He thought she would spend most of the morning sleeping, anyway. The rifle would just be in his way. The 1911 would still be his backup weapon, a great combat handgun for ranges not much more than 20 yards. But even his skill level left it an iffy weapon to rely on at longer ranges. The power of the .45ACP, too, was lacking for longer shots. The .44 magnum Smith & Wesson revolver was another animal altogether; fully capable of killing a man at 150 yards with it, he felt it would be less cumbersome around the house while he took care of Deni as best he could. And if trouble showed up, he could grab his rifle from where it stood in a corner of the living room. Yes, there was some kind of a nut organization out there, but the chances of them coming to that particular house were a little above zero. As heavy as the .44 was, it was a lot lighter than the rifle and could be put in a holster at his side and forgotten unless needed. He wore it as a cross draw rig and kept the 1911 on his right side for speed at close range.

After slipping two speed loaders into a pocket, he went into the kitchen and prepared everything to cook fresh eggs for breakfast as soon as Deni woke. The eggs had come from a poultry farmer just outside of town.

Brian staggered in, sleepy-eyed. He noticed the big revolver and his eyes widened. "You haven't taken the .44 out of your pack in a while."

Nate responded with, "I missed it. After all, it's an old friend."

"How many .44 mag rounds have you burned in your life?' Brian wanted to know.

Nate didn't need to think about that question. "Over 100,000 rounds, not all through this revolver, though. Probably over 90% were through Smiths, with a few rounds sent down range through Ruger Super Blackhawks and Redhawks. Never owned a Super Redhawk or a Colt in .44 mag. I've traded off all of the other .44s I've tried but this Smith 629 Classic.

"Smiths are your favorite, aren't they?"

"Yep. A good trigger is paramount, and Smiths have a light, crisp single-action trigger, the best," Nate answered. "Warriors who didn't know much about shooting before their military training disdain the idea that a light, crisp trigger pull is needed for accurate handgun shooting, especially Glock lovers; but the fact is they're wrong. Handgun hunting and long range target shooting are part of an entirely different world from the use of handguns in combat, and they just have no idea what can be done with a good .44 mag revolver." He smiled at old memories. "I won lots of bets with fellow soldiers whenever I mentioned hitting coke cans at 100 yards shooting free-handed."

Brian perked up. "I remember you telling me about the man who got S&W to build the first .44 mag revolver and how good he was with them. What was his name? Elmer Keith wasn't it?"

Nate took a seat at the table and kept his voice down, not wanting to disturb Deni's sleep. "Yeah, that's true. During WWII, he was working at an arms factory and heard some of the managers talking about how the 1911 was useless in combat and no one could hit a thing with one past about 20 yards, baring a total accident. He told them they didn't know what they were talking about. The argument became heated and an Army officer got involved, giving Elmer Keith permission to bring his private pistol to the factory range and demonstrate long range shooting with the 1911.

"The next day during lunch break, nearly the entire factory emptied and gathered at the range where they test-fired new guns before they were sent to fighting men overseas. I don't remember the range but it was more than 200 yards – a lot farther than I can hit anything with a 1911, I'll freely admit to that. The target was about the size of a man's torso. Anyway, his first shot was either high or low and he overcompensated with his second. Then he proceeded to put the rest of the seven-round magazine on target. The officer addressed the crowd and asked if anyone wanted to go out there and stand next to the target to prove their theory that a pistol was useless in combat. There were no takers."

Brian snickered. "I used to get into arguments with kids at school whenever I told them you and I had spent Saturday afternoon shooting targets at long range with handguns. They just couldn't believe it was possible, and called me a liar. Then I took a video of you making a five-gallon plastic bucket dance at 200 yards. That shut them up."

"Believe me, there are plenty of people in the military with the same attitude," Nate said. "It's not worth arguing with them. Keep in mind you have to be a cool-headed shooter to be able to shoot as well in a firefight as at the range when shooting at targets that don't bleed and shoot back." He became serious. "That's the real limitation of handguns in combat, even at close range. Plenty of cops have emptied their handguns at extremely close range in a panic and didn't come close to hitting the suspect. The killer then just calmly walked up and killed them while they struggled to reload. That's the main reason cops switched from revolvers to pistols – more rounds in the gun and a much faster reload. Sometimes crazies have an advantage because they just don't give a damn and therefore don't panic, which allows them to hit what they aim at, while a cop who wants to go home to his wife panics and forgets to aim."

"Yeah," Brian said, "if you don't use that front sight, you're not going to hit a thing with a handgun." He looked down at the table. "When men are shooting at you, it's easier said than done, though."

Nate's voice came out almost as a whisper. "Yeah, but you've earned the right to talk about such things. You've seen the elephant, and at a very young age."

Deni walked into the kitchen, taking short, stiff steps. "You guys discussing who to invite to my wake?"

Brian jumped up and pulled out a chair for her. "We were about to make breakfast for you."

"Oh. That's nice." She sat at the table."

"The only painkiller I have is aspirin," Nate offered.

Deni sat back in the chair and slumped down. "I'll take a handful."

Nate got up to get the aspirin out of his pack. He came back with a bottle. "Might want to eat first and then wait an hour or two before taking these."

"At least you have until three before reporting for duty." Brian was already washing his hands, using water from a bucket near the sink. He could cook eggs as well as anyone and planned to do just that while Deni and his father talked.

Nate regarded her swollen face. "I'm sure your CO would give you the rest of the day off if you asked."

Deni rubbed her puffy eyes with the palms of her hands. "No. I'm anxious to learn what all of that shooting was about. It could be bigger than we're thinking. Even a small group of nuts can cause a lot of havoc."

After breakfast, Deni grew tired and decided to go back to bed for an hour or so.

Nate and Brian stepped out onto the porch to talk.

Brian glanced through the open front door. He seemed to have something on his mind. "She sure is beat up bad. How long will it be before she can leave the Army?"

Something down the street caught Nate's attention, but it didn't alarm him enough not to answer. "We've talked about that before. The Army can basically hold her forever under the extreme circumstances the country is dealing with."

"That's not right. When her time's up, they should let her go. It's too dangerous for a girl, anyway."

That made Nate smile. "It's not easy seeing a pretty woman hurt, is it?"

Brian's eyes lit up. "Have you ever thought about what actress she looks like?"

"I don't know." Nate appeared to be uncomfortable with the question. "She looks like Deni to me."

Brian started to say something when a potted plant that hung a foot from Nate's head exploded.

The crack of the rifle shot split the air just as Nate slid off his chair onto the concrete porch. Before he could say anything, another round buried itself in the wall.

Brian was close to the door and dove through it, landing on a throw rug that allowed him to skid several feet. He fast-crawled to the corner of the room and grabbed both his and Nate's rifle. Before he got to the door, Nate's revolver boomed once.

"I have your rifle," Brian yelled.

"Stay inside," Nate ordered.

Deni charged into the living room, her rifle in her hands.

Brian motioned for her to get down, and she dropped to the floor, her eyes frantically searching for Nate.

Nate's voice came in through the doorway. "He was a two-shot Charley. I saw him hotfooting it out of the area when he fell. Before he got back on his feet, I put a slug in him. He hasn't moved since. I think he's finished."

"Well, keep your head down while I go and get the radio," Deni warned.

"Near as I can tell, he was alone." Nate took her advice anyway and kept his head down as well as stayed in the shadow of the porch, constantly searching for trouble while looking over his sights.

Deni's cry for backup was almost instantaneous, as a patrol wasn't far away. The response came in waves. First a four-man rifle team and then a full squad. A few minutes later, the neighborhood was swarming with pissed off soldiers hunting for more of the assholes who'd killed and wounded their brothers the day before.

Chesty's old pickup screeched to a halt in front of the house, with Mel on the passenger side. Relief was evident on both their faces when they counted heads and no one was hurt.

"The idiot was a bad shot," Nate commented dryly.

"Unless he was actually aiming for the potted plant," Brian quipped. Coiled tension suddenly came to the surface. "I promised I wouldn't complain about the way things are, but I'm sick of people trying to kill us."

"I know," Nate said. "And with what happened yesterday and Deni being hurt… I know."

Chapter 23

Chesty looked down at the twenty-something-year-old dead man. "Ever see him before?"

Nate shook his head. "Looks like a college kid." He spoke to Capt. Donovan. "Did they find anything in his pockets to ID him or tell us where he came from?"

Donovan hooked his thumbs in his pistol belt. "All he had on him was his clothes, boots, and that SKS rifle with a bent back sight."

"Bent sight might be why he missed," Mel offered. "That's strange." He dropped to one knee and pointed. "He's got a half-inch entrance hole in the right side of his chest and the same size hole on the exit side." He raised his face to Nate. "What did you shoot him with?"

"My usual load," Nate answered. "A 250 grain hard-cast Keith-type bullet at 1200 feet per second. It's not exactly a hot load."

Mel smiled. "I should've known. You shot him with your .44 and not your rifle. That explains why the exit wound isn't the size of your fist."

Chesty grew impatient. "None of that explains why this fool took a shot at Nate."

Deni walked up. Glancing down at the dead man, she said, "I have a feeling he's part of what happened yesterday."

"Maybe," Donovan said. "But your intuition, as good as it is, just isn't enough without more to go on." He checked his watch. "Damn thing's quit. That five-year battery must've finally died."

Nate checked the position of the sun in the sky. "It's maybe thirty minutes or so past noon."

Donovan chuckled. "I never figured you for a smartass."

Nate took that as good-natured banter. "Well, I'm not going to stand here and look at a dead fool any longer." He took a step and then stopped. "Deni's still stiff and sore from being banged up. You think you could spare her until tomorrow morning."

Donovan rubbed the back of his neck. "I wish I could give her more time off, but I just got word the guy she brought in is conscious. Looks like the surgery they performed yesterday on him was successful. I would like for you and Sergeant Heath both to come with me to the clinic and help with the interrogation."

Brian had been standing fifty feet away, keeping quiet. "Uh, you don't want Dad or me anywhere near that bastard."

Donovan regarded Brian, obviously looking on him with respect. "That's the point. He'll be afraid of your father and Sergeant Heath both. After all, the good Sergeant whipped his ass yesterday."

A soldier's radio came to life. He listened intently for several seconds. Speaking to Donovan, he said, "A half dozen men shot up a checkpoint and ran into a house. It's about five miles northwest of here. The address is 307 Northwest 110th Ave."

Everyone raced to a vehicle. Mel, Nate, and Brian caught a ride with Chesty. Deni went with Donovan and the soldiers.

Chesty trailed behind the six-HUMVEE column as they raced through town. "Do captains usually get their hands dirty like this Donovan?" he asked Nate.

Nate checked on Mel, who was hanging on for life, sitting behind the cab in the back of the truck. He spoke past Brian, who was sitting in the middle, clutching his rifle, the muzzle pointing up. "No. But nothing's normal nowadays. Why should the military be different?"

Arriving near the scene, they soon found all roads blocked by HUMVEEs and edgy soldiers. Chesty pulled off onto the shoulder of the road. They were on the outskirts of town and it looked more country than town. "I think I know the house they're hold up in. The family died in the plague."

Nate got out. He pointed at Brian. "Stay in the truck. There's no need for you to be in this mess. I would have left you at the house, but hell, I just got shot at there. I don't know of any place that's safe."

Brian looked disappointed but said nothing, nodding.

Mel had already jumped down from the back of the truck. "I hope the house is constructed of cinderblocks. Bullets will go right through. They lose a lot of their velocity going through, though."

Chesty shook his head. He grabbed his rifle as he spoke. "It's a hurricane-proof house. Walls are solid poured concrete with plenty of rebars and covered by real stones, not fake flagstones. The windows are impact resistant, but I doubt they're bulletproof."

They ran to catch up with Donovan and his entourage.

The Captain looked the scene over with 7x10 binoculars. The house was on a hill in the middle of ten acres. There were a few trees on the land, but there was no way to approach closer than 100 yards without exposing yourself to gunfire. The grass, for some reason, hadn't grown very tall and would offer only concealment, anyway. "Get a SAW over here and extra ammo," he ordered. Directing his words to Chesty, he asked, "Do you know if anyone's living there?"

"The family died in the plague." Chesty rubbed his cheek nervously. "But that doesn't mean someone didn't squat in it the last few months. Can't promise there're no innocents in there with them."

"But most likely those bastards are alone in there."

Chesty guessed. "I would say so."

A soldier lying on the ground, taking cover behind a pine tree nearby spoke up. "Walls don't stop bullets. They're dead."

Mel coughed. "The walls of my bunker at my retreat stop bullets."

"You think so?" Nate asked the soldier. "Do trees stop bullets?"

"Depends on the size of the tree."

"So not all trees are the same, but all walls are the same? The walls of my farmhouse have stopped .308 and 30-06 full metal jacket bullets. Not all homes are made of wood or cinderblocks." He shrugged. "Of course if you have a Ma Deuce and plenty of ammo, you got it made. Cut loose and it'll reduce that place to smoking rubble. With enough ammo, even an old M60 would do it. Peck at it with thousands of rounds and chip away the walls little by little." He got out his binoculars and scanned the house. "It's dark inside of course, and I don't see anyone close enough to a window to catch any ambient sunlight. I notice there are no curtains. The place may have been stripped by looters. If so, that may make setting it on fire more difficult. There won't be as much flammable stuff left inside. Bullets are hot, but they pass through things so fast there's no time to transfer that heat to whatever it passes through. Might catch a sofa or mattress on fire, though, especially if it stops inside of it."

"Well, I'm not going to waste lives storming that house," Donovan said. "Those shitheads inside aren't worth one of my soldiers."

Nate let the binoculars hang from his neck. "Oh, I damn sure agree with that. And I'm going to the truck to check on Brian and let you do your job." He stepped back.

Chesty and Mel eyed Nate, but said nothing.

Donovan raised his hand. "Hold on. Stick around. I may need your advice before this is over."

Soldiers within listening distance looked like they couldn't believe what they'd just heard. A captain supervising this little operation was already overkill. They didn't understand that Donovan wasn't so much needing Nate's advice as worried about the look on his face. He knew something was wrong with him. Donovan asking for advice from Nate was in no way a sign of his incompetence; it was proof he was so at ease with carrying the load of his responsibilities he had no need for affectation. There was a reason he seldom raised his voice, and he damn sure didn't carry a swagger stick.

Nate kept walking. "I doubt that."

The Captain motioned for Deni to come closer. He leaned to her ear and spoke low. "What do you think is eating him?"

"I don't know," she answered truthfully. "This situation might be bringing back bad memories or something. He's a combat vet. Also, he's been through a lot since the plague hit. Hell, he was just shot at while sitting next to his son only an hour ago."

Donovan nodded. "Go with him. We have plenty of personnel to handle this mess."

Deni said, "Thank you sir."

She caught up with Nate, already halfway to the truck.

He heard her boots on gravel and looked back, then stopped.

She put a hand on his shoulder. "What's up, Nate?"

Nate looked toward the truck and Brian. "It's his job, not mine."

"True enough." She walked along beside him. "You know, my time was up months back. I might be a free girl soon."

"Maybe." Nate didn't sound too sure. "You're trying to cheer me up for some reason. Do I look like I need cheering up?"

She tilted her head and examined the features of his face as they walked along. "I don't know. It's hard to tell with you."

He gave her a look out of the corner of his eye and kept walking. After four steps, he stopped and pulled her to him, holding her tight. They held each other in silence for some time.

She rested her head on his chest. "What's going on, Nate?"

"I just think the Army can handle it."

"They can, but that doesn't answer my question."

He released her and started walking again. "I'm fine. That's all you need to know."

Several rifle shots boomed from the direction of the house.

Nate looked at Deni. "I would guess Donovan just gave them a chance to surrender and they gave him their answer."

A roar of full auto fire reverberated across the land. It lasted ten seconds and came to a sporadic stop. The SAW soon started up again, without the accompaniment of other weapons this time, keeping with short, three or four-round bursts.

By that time, Nate and Deni had reached the truck and Brian.

"Are you thinking there might be innocents in the house?" Deni asked.

Nate put his rifle in the truck. "That's certainly possible."

An explosion split the air.

"Sounds like Donovan's using grenade launchers." Nate saw smoke already rising above threes between them and the house. "He's having them lobbed in through the roof. I half expected him to call in a helicopter gunship."

Another explosion rocked the earth. "That one must've hit something inside," Deni commented. "Sounded like there was a secondary explosion a split second after the grenade went off.

Grenades will certainly circumvent the bullet-stopping solid walls."

Nate opened the truck door. "Might as well have a seat and rest your bruised body. It won't be much longer now that Donovan's figured it out."

The explosions stopped and there was no more firing. Nate guessed correctly that anyone left alive in the house was trying to surrender. Smoke billowed up above the trees in a large black cloud, then drifted downwind. A Black Hawk swooped in and landed beyond their line of sight. *Picking up wounded,* Nate thought.

Deni watched the smoke become blacker and rise into the blue sky until the tops of flickering flames rose above the tree line. Even at that distance, the snapping and crackling of a roaring house fire could be heard. After a few minutes, the black smoke turned gray. A sudden realization hit her when her stomach began to feel as if it held a cold block of lead, chilling her and weighing her down at the same time. *There's something dirty about using the power of a modern military against untrained civilians, even assholes who asked for it. Nate didn't want to witness it; he had seen it before.*

<u>Chapter 24</u>

Donovan stood in Chesty's living room and handed Nate, Tyrone, and Chesty each a copy of his report on the interrogation of the captured militia members, including two who had run from the burning house. Mel had gone on patrol with a team of soldiers to learn more about the town. Deni was on duty.

"It appears this strange political group's bigger than any of us believed." Donovan thought for a few seconds. "I'm still trying to come up with a label that fits their ideology, but there doesn't seem to be one, because the things they think society should be based on are totally contradictory. There's just no way any society or government could be all of the things they want."

"You mean Socialism without government, an economy where all necessities of life are free, and there is no monetary system?" Nate asked. "The closest example I could think of would be some Native American tribes."

Chesty raised a brow. "Did they feed the lazy?"

"I'm sure everyone had to work," Nate answered. "Survival was too tenuous to allow some to be a burden to the whole tribe. I know some tribes expected their men to die in battle before they got old and became a burden to others and women were expected to commit suicide if they lived to the point they were a burden. Eskimo women would walk out onto the ice in the dead of winter and walk into the wind until they dropped from exhaustion. Then they would die from exposure." He shook his head. "These nuts don't know what they want or what they're asking for."

Atticus stood next to Tyrone. He had stayed close to him ever since he learned of him getting banged up by the attackers in the large trucks, always with his shotgun in his hands and all of his pockets full of buckshot. "Sounds like a combination of One Percenters, Communists/Socialists, liberals, hippies, anti-Capitalists/corporation haters, anti-big-government, anti-military, anti-law-enforcement anarchists, who believe the government should provide everything free and with no taxes to pay for it." He smiled. "Simple really. I don't understand why you guys are having such a hard time wrapping your minds around this."

"Sounds like heaven," Nate quipped.

"And they're such a peaceful, fun-loving gang," Chesty added. "It's not like they're going around shooting at everyone they see."

"They're certainly not flower children of the 1960s," Donovan observed. "So far all of them have been white, but they deny being racial purists and bigots. We haven't come across any women in the group yet, either."

Atticus feigned surprise. "You think they're also anti-woman?"

Nate cleared his throat. "Might be they can't find a woman stupid enough to join their group." The expression on Nate's face changed. It was obvious he was having an epiphany. "On the other hand, they just might have women in their group."

"What are you thinking?" Donovan asked.

"Austin, Deni, and I ran into an ambush a while back. A woman faked a wound and led us away from the truck and Austin so others could attack him while he was alone. We had the impression there was a large camp nearby and the ambush was about keeping us away from that camp."

Chesty broke in. "I remember Austin telling me and Tyrone about that, warning us how dangerous it could be if we ever ran into that bunch."

Nate continued. "At the time, I was thinking the ambushers must be from the raiders the National Guard rounded up months back. I'm certain they didn't get them all. Well, maybe it's them. But they also might be part of this militia group."

Donovan listened with interest. "Either way, they need to be apprehended and incarcerated. They're a violent, lawless danger to the public. You should've told me about this sooner."

"A lot has been going on and it slipped my mind. I got the impression you were mainly interested in the town, not the countryside." Nate knew what was coming. "I'll go with you and point out their position on a map, but I think I should stay in town with my son." He glanced at Chesty and Tyrone. "Besides, I promised to help out the local sheriff a little longer while I'm still here."

Donovan nodded. "I understand. Let's get with it, though. It's still early. There's no reason why I can't put together a team and get this done today."

Nate walked to the corner of the room, where his rifle and pack were. "One other thing: There are children in that camp. While you're doing your planning, keep that in mind."

Donovan's chest deflated. "Wonderful. Already, it's going to take twice as many soldiers to get the job done clean with as few casualties on both sides as possible."

Nate moved for the door. "Chances are we scared them off. I doubt they're still camped in the same place, but they're somewhere, and you should be able to locate a large camp with no problem. Their noise and light discipline is lacking. You won't even need any infrared, just fly over the area at night and search for their big campfires."

"Okay." Donovan followed Nate out the door. "But that means the raid might not happen today or even tomorrow."

Nate started to say something about how life's full of trouble and toil, but instead spoke to Brian, who was taking a nap on the porch swing. "You want to stay here and sleep or come with the Captain and me?"

Brian sprung up and planted his boots on the floor. "Something going on?" He rubbed his eyes.

"Nothing to worry about," Nate answered. "Let's go."

Soldiers standing guard at the curb saw that the Captain was leaving and sprung to life, setting up a perimeter around him and preparing to head out. Those who had been guarding the back of the house ran to HUMVEEs and piled in.

The column cut through what was the seedy part of the downtown area before the plague and Donovan noticed a large crowd of young men; many appeared to be inebriated and too young to legally drink. "Looks like someone has reopened a bar. I wonder what they're selling as rotgut."

Nate looked on with interest as they rode by. "I guess Chesty and Tyrone can expect that to be a trouble spot." He glanced at Brian, who was looking at the rough men standing around drinking in front of a derelict building. "Dr. Brant can also expect more patients."

"From the drunks fighting?" Brian asked.

Nate looked out the window. "That and men going blind and dying from whatever moonshine they're pushing."

"Maybe it's just beer and they were careful about making the stuff the right way," Brian offered.

Nate directed all of his attention at his son. "I hope so, but I doubt it. Those men and boys looked hammered. The last thing we need are a bunch of drunk punks running around looking for trouble. I have no problem with drinking, but these people are facing starvation and can't be wasting time on nonsense. They should be helping at the farm." He snatched the radio up to his mouth and warned Chesty and Tyrone.

Brian's eyes narrowed. "What're they going to do? Do they have the power to tell people they can't drink?"

Nate put the radio down, "I doubt they're going to do that. Some of the ones I saw were underage, though. I expect they'll go easy on trying to enforce old laws that aren't as important as staying alive, but they can't let anyone sell poison and kill people. Anyway, they'll first have to go there and see exactly what's going on."

Brian narrowed his eyes. "If they're selling moonshine, what are they taking for payment? Money is worthless now."

"Food, gold, silver," Nate answered. "Also, ammo, guns, boots, anything useful."

Donovan joined in the conversation. "Chesty and Tyrone might need backup if that crowd gets rowdy."

"A few soldiers visibly out on the street can't hurt. It may keep them simmered down," Nate said. "They would appreciate it."

Donovan spoke to a soldier sitting in the front of the HUMVEE. The soldier immediately radioed orders to a patrol team, telling the team leader to head for the bar.

~~~

After locating the ambushers' camp on a map for Donovan, Deni, who happened to be at the FOB, was ordered to give Nate and Brian a ride back. On the way, Nate looked out of the HUMVEE and noticed Chesty's truck already parked in front of the bar. Four soldiers stood around a HUMVEE parked out front in the street, their rifles slung across their chests from combat slings. He assumed correctly that Tyrone, and probably Atticus too, was with Chesty.

He had Brian with him and planned to let the others handle it, but the radio on his vest squawked and Chesty's voice blared in the interior of the HUMVEE. "Nate, could you help us out? We have a few uncooperative drunken punks looking for trouble."

Nate made a face that made it clear he really didn't want to get into it with the locals in a bar, especially with Brian there.

Deni looked over at him and smiled. "No rest for the weary. Wouldn't you know that the first thing they start producing is alcohol."

"They should be making alcohol for fuel," Nate complained. "Don't they know they're still facing starvation? Do they think the Army's going to feed them the rest of their lives?"

Worry darkened Brian's face. "Don't let them hurt you, Dad. This isn't worth any risk. The same goes for Chesty and the others. If they want to go blind drinking poison, let them."

"You're right," Nate agreed. "This is Bravo Sierra, and these people should know by now that only those who work at staying alive 24/7 are going to pull through and last long enough to see society rebuild and come back to some kind of new normalcy that allows for a decent life."

Deni pulled in behind the HUMVEE parked in the street. "You guys have got me worried now. I think I'll call for more personnel out here. A show of overwhelming force might scare enough sense into them there won't be any trouble."

She reached for a radio.

"Shit! Brian, you stay here." Nate exploded out of the HUMVEE and raced to Chesty, who was motioning from the bar doorway for Nate to come and help.

Deni jumped out and ordered the soldiers in the street to follow her.

Brian looked down and noticed that his father had left his rifle. For a second, he thought about bringing it to him but decided against it. Him being in the bar would cause more danger for his father, because he would be worried about him. Besides, Nate had his pistol holstered under his shirt.

Not wanting to barge into something he knew nothing about, Nate slowed to a walk before ducking into the building. He found it dark inside, with only three dim kerosene lanterns for illumination. The smell of alcohol and sweat hit him in the face. Tyrone was having a heated argument with four young men. It seemed they took exception to Tyrone's "fake badge and uniform." Atticus appeared to be ready to start throwing buckshot at any moment. Everyone in the bar was armed, but most of the men didn't seem to want any trouble.

Chesty kept an eye on the rest of the crowd. So far most seemed content in just casually listening, taking it in as entertainment to go with their drink.

Tyrone's baritone voice reverberated throughout the building. "No one said you couldn't drink or that we were going to close this place down. We just want to make sure certain rules are followed, such as not selling or giving alcohol to minors."

The punk's drawl was thick as syrup, the taunt in every mispronounced word as obvious and old as bullying itself. "And whose rules are those, asshole? Yours?" the staggering drunk in his early twenties asked. "There ain't no law anymore. I don't care if you were a deputy before the plague. There ain't no law now." He looked blurry eyed around the room. "We can do as we damn well please, and there ain't no one to stop us."

Nate had seen his kind many times before, in many bars, in many countries. The young man was untested and unproven, and he knew it. That knowing was eating at him. Anxious to prove to himself he wasn't a coward, he was looking for unnecessary trouble, and the alcohol pickling his brain was giving him just enough false bravado to find that trouble. The accompaniment of the other three young drunks made matters worse.

Decades ago, as a strapping teenage boy full of energy and private dreams of making the world a better place for those that followed, Nate had been shipped to a South American jungle war. The war had taken much of the energy and dreams out of him and had both increased his respect for some people and completely killed it for others. When he'd returned, he'd come back a man hardened and sharpened to a fine edge, the product of enduring too long in the real hell of this world, and envisioning too little of the imagined heaven of the next. He'd seen too many young men suffer every inch of their personal paths to their 'reward.'

How in the hell, he'd asked himself a thousand times while in the jungle and years after he'd come home, can dying in agony with bullets or chunks of shrapnel burning red hot in your flesh and bone shards poking out of your body be called a reward? This was more of a sick joke than pinning a medal on a dead man or chiseling something poetic on his headstone. What wretched attempts to hide the ugliness of it all. He'd wondered who had come up with that bright and shiny lie. What reward? Having seen death in its most sickening, terrifying forms, he wondered... if this was their reward for bravery and devotion to duty, what would be their punishment for cowardliness?

Throw young men and women into a hell of unspeakable violence and rob them of their humanity. Then speak of them going to their reward? But only after they'd suffered. The lucky ones who died instantly, without pain or even knowing they would be dead in a few moments were few, and those who turned their lungs inside out with their last breath were many.

If he was going to fight these young men, it wouldn't be over something as trivial as giving them a chance to test their manhood. Screw that. The loud one reminded him too much of young guys he'd known in the Army, early on, before they tasted war, before most of the training even, before they had earned their 'rewards,' a bullet or a bomb or a rocket at a time. Everyone in the bar was armed, and if fighting broke out, someone was going to die, and Nate wasn't about to kill or die over nothing.

Nate stepped closer to Tyrone. "Let's back out of here and let this cool down."

Tyrone must've had the same thoughts. He stepped back. "Okay. We're leaving guys. Just keep it safe and peaceful."

Atticus and Chesty covered them with shotguns until they were all out the door.

The loudmouth laughed and taunted them, though it was obvious he was relieved they were leaving.

Chesty stood to the side of the door in case someone decided to send a bullet through it. He mopped his forehead. "I expect we'll be back to investigate a killing or at least a fight, but for now we should be patrolling the streets for that pervert and the militia nuts."

Still keyed up, Tyrone turned to Nate. "Thanks for defusing that."

Deni walked up, six soldiers with her. "Well, do you need any help?"

Chesty looked back at the closed bar door. "Nah. You guys might as well go on your way."

Deni ordered the soldiers to go back on patrol. They piled into HUMVEEs and drove away. She looked up and smiled at Nate. "I have the rest of the day off."

Nate started to say something when the four drunks emerged unnoticed from the bar. A bottle flew by his head and hit Deni in the face and temple area, knocking her to the ground. He rushed to her, kneeled down and held her face, turning it to appraise the damage. She was out cold, and a knot the size of an egg was already growing just above her eye. He put his ear to her mouth but couldn't hear if she was breathing or feel her breath. The one who'd thrown the bottle was laughing. The same one who'd laughed inside. Nate took her wrist and felt for a pulse. In his panic, he wasn't sure he felt any.

Nate's mind raced so fast it was tripping over a hundred thoughts and left him not able to react in a productive way. Movement caught his attention, and he looked up to see Brian charging, his rifle shouldered and murder in his eyes. He jumped up and raised his outstretched hands. "No!"

A shot split the air and Brian fell. Without any voluntary thought, he turned, and in one motion pulled his pistol. The front sight flashed in his vision, centered on the loudmouth's chest.

Tyrone's thick arm swept under his hands just before he squeezed the trigger. The shot that would have killed instead flew into the sky.

"It was Atticus shooting in the air!" Tyrone yelled. "Brian just fell." He held Nate's arm, keeping his hand and the pistol up. "Brian's okay. He just fell."

Brian's voice brought Nate out of his rage. "You're dead, you son of a bitch!"

Nate turned his head to the left and saw his son standing, pointing his rifle at the loudmouth. He blinked, yanked his arm from Tyrone's grip, and ran to Brian. "Don't shoot. Just keep your rifle on them." He motioned with his pistol. "Disarm yourselves or I'll kill you where you stand."

The eyes of the man who threw the bottle widened and he reached for his pistol.

"I'll kill you!" Nate warned.

The man froze, then slowly reached to his belt buckle and let the holstered pistol fall to his feet.

"That was close," Atticus said. "I came within a hundredth of a second of blowing your guts out."

Someone opened the bar door. Chesty threw down on him with his shotgun. "You don't want to join this party. Close that damn door and stay inside."

The man turned white and slammed the door shut.

Nate ran back to Deni. He found her still unconscious. Snatching her radio up to his mouth, he informed anyone listening that Deni had been injured and needed medical attention, his voice surprisingly professional under the circumstances. He checked her breathing again and was relieved to feel her breath on his hand. He could hear her heart beat slowly when he held his ear to her chest. Nate looked over and saw the worry in Brian's eyes. "She's breathing."

The tension somewhat released, Brian began to sob as he held the rifle on the one who threw the bottle.

Soldiers raced up in HUMVEEs. They bailed out ready for trouble, surrounding Deni. Sergeant First Class Quint Bartow checked her injuries. He looked up at Chesty. "What happened?"

Chesty pointed at the loudmouth. "That drunken idiot threw a bottle. He's under arrest."

"Oh, he's under arrest alright," Bartow said, his voice carrying a threatening edge. "If she dies he'll be executed."

The drunk swallowed. "Hell, she isn't dead. The little bitch just got in the way of my bottle. I was aiming for the big asshole." He started to say more, but what he saw in Nate's eyes took his breath away.

Chesty tried to stop him but got flung across the parking lot, not even slowing Nate down.

The only person there who had a chance of stopping Nate without shooting him stood in his way.

All it took was one word. "Dad."

Nate stopped.

"Remember Slim? You said it was a mistake to make an enemy of him and leave him alive. If you're going to kill him you might as well have let me shoot him."

"We'll take them off your hands, Mr. Williams." Bartow stared the four drunks down. "All of you put your hands in the air and march your asses to the HUMVEEs. Any of you give me any shit; I'll shoot your ass."

Chesty brushed himself off. "Holy shit."

Nate started to apologize to him, but Chesty held his hand up. "No time for that. You and Brian hop in my truck and I'll drive you to the clinic. I expect that's where they're going to take her."

The soldiers put Deni on a stretcher and loaded her in a HUMVEE. The column took off with Nate and the others following in trucks.

Chapter 25

Half way there, Nate saw Deni sitting up, holding her head. A soldier spoke to her and she turned to look back at the truck following. Struggling to smile, she waved at Nate and Brian.

Brian waved back. "She's going to be all right." He saw his father's reaction and looked away.

"Hey!" Chesty said. "She's already awake. She'll be okay."

Nate was relieved but still not so sure. She'd taken a severe blow, and he expected she had fractures and might suffer after affects from the concussion. *Damn that punk!*

~~~

Deni sat on the examination table in the clinic and glanced at Dr. Brant. "These two guys look like they're about to cry."

The Doctor didn't risk a response, changing the subject instead. "No fractures. You got a heck of a bump on the head and the side of your eye socket. When you first came in, I was concerned because the skull is thin there and you could have had damage to your right eye." She gave a reassuring smile. "But I'd say you dodged the proverbial bullet." She patted Deni on the shoulder. "You'll be fine in a few days. Sore as hell and carrying around a nasty bruise, but otherwise, no lasting damage."

Nate sat down on a folding chair against the wall. He still felt shaky and needed to rest his legs. "To think you came so close to dying or losing an eye over bullshit makes me sick."

Brian addressed Deni. "The idiot who threw the bottle must have nine lives. I almost killed him and Dad almost killed him twice."

Deni gingerly felt the knot on her head. "Twice?"

Brian glanced at his father and noticed the look on his face. "I'd better not get into that. Dad's still upset. Best to leave that alone, I think."

There were ten seconds of quiet in the room.

"Well," Dr. Brant said, "the Army has the four of them locked up in the courthouse. I have no idea what they're going to do with them. Maybe a public flogging."

Someone knocked on the open door. It was Chesty. Tyrone and Atticus were with him. They walked in, awkwardness and concern on their faces. A few seconds later, Mel walked in.

Dr. Brant answered them before they asked. "She'll be fine in a few days."

Relief visibly washed over the men.

Chesty stepped closer to Nate. "Donovan says he's going to let the other three go tomorrow morning. The one who threw the bottle, well... he's not sure what to do. He's a civilian and there are damn few civilian prisons in operation. Hell, people are going hungry. Who has time and resources for jails and prisons? If he was in the Army, it'd be different."

Deni stood, holding onto Brian for support. "Since the good doctor says I'm okay, I want to go home." She smiled at everyone in the room. "Shouldn't you deputies be out patrolling the town? There's still a child killer out there and the anarchists... or whatever they are."

Tyrone rubbed his chin. "And there's still that damn bar. I never believed in prohibition. All historians say it was a mistake and total failure." He shook his head. "But by God, that bottle-throwing fool almost got killed in the bar and then three more times outside. The trouble is I'm thinking the fool still hasn't been cured. Sometimes the only way to cure a dog of sucking eggs is to kill him."

Atticus scratched his head. "Tyrone, where did all this countrified wisdom come from all of a sudden?" He shot an inquisitive glance at him. "Egg-sucking dog? Huh?"

Tyrone laughed. No one else in the room felt like laughing, but the two thought it was funny.

Dr. Brant's tone changed. "Deni, I wish you'd stay the night for observation. You took quite a blow to the head and I'd feel better if we kept an eye on you until tomorrow at least. Certainly, you shouldn't go back on duty."

Deni started to protest.

Dr. Brant raised her hand. "If I have to, I'll ask Dr. Millhouse to have a talk with Col. Donovan."

Deni's shoulders slumped. "Oh hell. I'll be bored to death."

Nate stood. "I think you should do what Dr. Brant says." He caught a flash of something in her eyes. "I'm not telling you what to do. I mean like an order or something. But she's a good doctor and I think you should listen to her."

Deni reached back and slapped the examination table behind her. "I'm not sleeping on this thing tonight. The pad's only an inch thick. Might as well get out my sleeping bag and stretch out on the floor."

"I've got a comfortable couch in my office," Dr. Brant offered. "That way I can duck in and check on you every hour. This examination room will be needed for new patients coming in, anyway."

Nate stepped up to Deni. "Are you dizzy?"

"Are you offering to carry me?" Deni put her hands behind his neck and pulled him to her. They held each other. "Stop worrying. I'm okay." She let him go. "Now all of you get back to doing whatever it was you would be doing if I hadn't caught a bottle upside the head."

For some reason, Atticus thought that was funny. "You're alright, young lady. No wonder everyone likes you."

"Not everyone." Deni carefully touched the knot on her head.

~~~

Three days later, Deni seemed to be recovering well. There had been no complications, and the swelling had gone down to a degree, but a nasty black and blue mark an inch or more wide and three inches long remained. She had taken to wearing sunglasses to help hide it.

Nate had spent a lot of time with her, leaving Brian with their friends. She noticed he remained more alert than usual, and that meant he expected trouble. Since he never let his guard down even under normal circumstances, he must have had a good reason to be noticeably more alert than usual. Not an hour went by he didn't scan the area around the house for trouble. Any sound in the night prompted an immediate armed response from him. His edginess wore off on her to some degree and prompted her to wear a pistol in the house and keep her rifle in her hands at all times whenever they went outside for a walk or to check on Brian at Chesty's place. She was in the habit of taking precautions, but Nate seemed to think they were in a war zone. She chalked it up to the anarchists and her being hurt at the bar. She didn't know that Nate had Brian stay with the others because he considered Deni to be a target of the bottle-throwing punk.

Chesty, Tyrone, and Atticus also seemed to be on edge, keeping a close watch on Brian, and Mel stayed with him also. Deni correctly assumed they had promised to take care of him for Nate and were taking their promise seriously. Still, they too seemed to be on edge and expecting trouble.

Then the day came.

The Army released the man who threw the bottle. Donovan had asked SFC Bartow to give him a rough lecture on staying away from Deni and Nate, explaining how if he was found in a ditch with a bullet in his head, the Army wasn't going to waste time trying to learn who did it. In fact, it would be smart if he left town and never came back.

Unfortunately for the bottle-throwing punk, he let it all go in one ear and out the other.

Nate learned the man's name was Lance Vitrano, but he didn't care what his name was. The memory of his face was all he needed to ID him when he came after Deni, and Nate was certain he would.

When they'd stared at each other after the punk had thrown the bottle, a moment passed between them – a moment when the punk looked into the eyes of death and it looked back in rage. It was then Nate had taken the punk's measure and realized he'd been too generous inside the bar. And when Vitrano didn't apologize or show any hint of remorse – Nate did believe he wasn't aiming at Deni – he knew no amount of testing or maturing would change this punk. If Brian hadn't been there, he would've killed him at that moment. The next move was Vitrano's.

~~~

Nate hadn't been much company all afternoon, muttering something about the hairs on the back of his neck, and Deni had to go back on duty in an hour, so she went to her bedroom to get ready.

Nate made his rounds and scanned the neighborhood with his binoculars, slowing to look down the street. The weather had turned warm again, a respite from the winter that was coming. If it turned out like last year, it would prove unusually cold and not let up until far into spring. A scratch in his throat reminded him that he hadn't had a drink in hours. His eyes narrowed as he took another look, emotionless as he clutched his civilian version of the M14 rifle, then shifted his weight to another foot and glanced over his shoulder. A half-gallon plastic jug waited, sweating in the middle of the little dining table. He debated whether to go get it or keep watch.

Then he heard them coming, their airbrakes screeching and exhausts rumbling as only a big tractor trailer rig could. But he knew these trucks were sans the trailer. They slowed to make the turn and head toward the house, coming for Deni.

He watched through binoculars as the first one turned the corner and swung onto their street a quarter mile away, the big motor's throaty roar coughing during gear changes as the truck sped up, charging closer. A head-hurting, earsplitting racket pounded from inside the cab, generated by large speakers – angry music for angry punks.

Both trucks overshot the house. They must not have been sure of the address. One thing was certain, Nate had reason to believe they had spies in town and they had told the punk and his friends where Deni was staying.

The racket from inside the truck cab stopped, and chortles of laughter replaced it. They anticipated lots of fun coming their way.

Nate spoke without turning from the scene on the street. "Deni, prepare to defend yourself. Men have come to kill us."

The sound of Deni scrambling in her room came to Nate's ears as he watched the first truck come to a halt. The second truck slowed, its brake lights broken. Nate stepped out of the front door and flattened the nearest tires on both trucks with one shot each. It had taken him less than three seconds.

They bailed out; rifles in hand, and Nate got a glimpse of the punk as he frantically dove behind a chinaberry tree. There were six of them when they bailed. Four seconds later there were three behind cover and three who didn't make it before Nate put a bullet in them. They lay in the street dead or dying.

Deni fired from an open window. Her rifle chattered on full auto, keeping their heads down. The wall she was behind provided concealment but not bullet-stopping cover, so she moved to run out the back door and find a better place to fire from. She yelled, "Repositioning to the rear," as she ran.

Nate yelled, "Moving to the front," and ran to the large oak in a neighbor's front yard.

As the firefight went on, Deni managed to pick off one more of the attackers, putting a bullet through his head as he rose above cover to fire at Nate.

Nate bounded forward to new cover while Deni provided cover fire. Then she reloaded and moved forward while he kept their heads down.

Two bullets buried themselves in a tree to the left of Nate. He saw one of them dash for the trucks and took a shot as soon as his front sight was on target. The man fell screaming. More rounds passing his head forced Nate to duck back behind cover. He shifted position and checked on the wounded man. He was gone. Looking to his right Nate saw him under the nearest truck. He dropped to the ground and prepared to fire from prone while still out of the last attacker's sight. Deni was faster. Two rounds into his upper body finished him.

That left Vitrano. Nate just thought of him as 'the punk.' *Okay punk, how long before you realize you're alone and lose your nerve?*

A high-pitched voice screamed from behind the chinaberry tree, "I give up! I'm surrendering. Don't shoot!"

That was quick: five seconds.

"Throw your rifle out," Deni yelled.

Vitrano complied, throwing his rifle five yards. It clattered into the street. "I'm coming out!" He stood.

Nate rose up, his rifle shouldered and aimed at Vitrano. Two HUMVEEs turned onto their street, but Nate's attention was on the punk.

The punk caught the look in Nate's eye – dogged, merciless – and hesitated. The game had somehow changed. Something about Nate's eyes served as a warning more clear than the rattle on a snake's tail. He'd kicked at the diamondback once too often. In a sudden panic, he reached for the pistol hidden under his jacket.

Nate and Deni fired at the same time, she twice, Nate three times. He was dead before he hit the ground. Nate approached his prone body, rifle shouldered. When he was ten feet away, he put two more rounds into his chest.

Deni had approached Vitrano alongside Nate. She reached out and put a hand on his shoulder. "Nate, he's not worth it."

He turned to her and the shadow lifted from his face. It was over.

Chapter 26

Nate sat in Donovan's office. He and Deni listened to the Colonel inform them what his soldiers had learned about the anarchists.

Donovan pointed to several books on his desk. "We found this in one of the trucks."

Deni and Nate glanced down at the books. The one on top was titled "Anarchy for a better World."

Donovan continued. "Nate, your idea the six losers you and Sergeant Heath killed were part of the militia group seems to be accurate."

"I thought the trucks had to be too much of a coincidence," Nate said. "The first attackers were using trucks. The only difference was these two hadn't been modified to carry men on the back where the trailer normally hooks up."

"Would've made more sense to use dump trucks," Deni said. "At least the steel in the back would've provided some protection from bullets, and they would've had more room."

Nate nodded. "Yeah. They must have access to semis but not dump trucks or any other more suitable vehicles. That fact may help lead us to where they're hiding."

Donovan sat down behind his desk. "Well, Chesty and Tyrone say they know of no place in town where there would be a lot of semis. I've ordered pilots to keep an eye out for a gathering of trucks. They've covered a lot of this county and so far haven't seen anything suspicious."

Deni stood at ease in front of Donovan's desk. "There are certainly a lot of trucks that were caught in the traffic jams on the interstate highways. Early on in the plague when I was trying to get back home, I saw a lot of them parked at truck stops that couldn't go anywhere because the highways were jammed with pileups and dead people." She raised a shoulder. "I guess they may have been able to get a few through the jams and then gotten their hands on fuel."

"I don't know." Donovan clasped his hands behind his head and leaned back in his chair. "There must be a reason they're using semis. They could've used any kind of transport, so why semis?"

No one had an answer.

A soldier entered the office. "Sir, the soldiers stationed at the lake are under attack."

Donovan snapped out of his chair. "Are there any Black Hawks nearby?"

"Nothing," the soldier answered. "Everything in the air is either north of the town or west of us."

"Send an assault team."

"Yes sir." The soldier didn't move. "There's another problem. A civilian is asking for help on an amateur band. That group on the horse farm southwest of the lake is under attack."

"Follow my previous orders, soldier," Donovan said.

"Yes sir." He ran out of the room.

Deni started, "Sir, I request permission –"

Donovan shook his head. "I need you here."

"Are you going to send help to the farm?" Deni asked. As a noncom, she was pushing her luck by even asking but she asked anyway.

"I'm hoping the problem at the lake will be over quick and the team can then help the other group."

Worry darkened her face.

Donovan noticed it. "Keep your head on, Sergeant. Personal feelings have to be pushed to the back of your mind." He looked out the window of his office. "That was fast. They're loading onto the rotorcraft now. Must've already been loaded up with a full kit when they got the word."

The roar of three Black Hawks taking off rattled the building, even though the helicopters were some distance away.

Deni gave Nate a worried look.

Nate wanted to at least put his arm around her but knew better than to do that in front of her CO. "It's a big farm and they have good security measures. The chances Samantha and Caroline are even near the fighting are small. Then there's the fact I can attest to Caroline's courage and fighting abilities." He shook his head. "She doesn't quit. And she can shoot. They'll have to kill her to get to Samantha."

"I know," Deni said, her voice not sounding sure.

Donovan broke in. "Sounds like a vet."

"No," Nate said. "Well, she's a veteran of living through a hell that would make Ranger School seem like nothing."

"Are you going?" Deni asked Nate.

"It'll all be over by the time I get there. Depends on what the assault team reports. If there's anything we can do, I'll ask Chesty to gather up some people to go with me, but he and the people here will want to go to the lake first. That's where their neighbors are, not the horse farm."

She blinked and turned away. "I promised Samantha..."

Donovan cleared his throat. "I need to get to the radio." He rushed out of his office, leaving them alone. Once again, Donovan impressed Nate with his decency and leadership.

Nate held her. "That little girl's as safe with Caroline as anyone. We have others there to worry about also, at both places, but I really doubt those buffoons have mounted any kind of an effective operation. The soldiers there should take care of them in no time."

She nodded, girding her strength. "Austin and Kendell are reliable, too."

"Yes they are. Most of the people at the lake and farm have been through a few fights. They can take care of themselves. It's probably all over already."

"Yeah. You're probably right." She pulled away from him. "I have to go do my job." She left Nate standing there.

~~~

Nate left the Forward Operations Base and radioed Chesty while going to pick up Brian. In less than ten minutes, Chesty and Tyrone pulled in behind him in a truck. He pulled over and got out.

Chesty spoke before Nate had a chance. "Anything more about what's happening?"

"No." Nate leaned against the truck door. "They'll radio us if there are any important developments. You might want to gather up a posse in case the fight becomes prolonged and they learn they're up against a larger force than the usual punks that have attacked here." He stopped for a second. "You might also consider the possibility of another attack here in town and make preparations."

Chesty rasped the salt and pepper stubble on his face. "What did Donovan say about protecting them? I mean, is he committed to using everything he has if it turns out these idiots have more fight in them than we've seen so far? After all, we still don't know how large this anarchist group is."

Nate crossed his arms. "He was busy doing his job and didn't have time to discuss what his plans were. All I know is he immediately sent an assault team – three choppers full of soldiers. If all they have are a couple or three semis loaded with a few punks, the fight will be over PDQ."

Tyrone spoke up. "But they don't know how large a force the attackers have?"

"They didn't when I left." Nate looked down the street, his eyes looking inward. "If you want to be on the safe side, gather up some volunteers and head down there. Just remember the town could be in danger, too. I'm going to pick up Brian." He glanced at Tyrone. "And Atticus too, if he wants to come."

Chesty snorted. "Then what? Wait for word from the Army?"

Nate opened the truck door and put one leg in. "Perhaps you could stage them at the church. I'll be going back to the Captain for more info on what's going on at the lake as soon as I get Brian. I learn anything, I'll radio you."

Tyrone spoke to Chesty, "That's the best we can do right now."

"Let's go." Chesty ran for his truck, Tyrone at his heels.

~~~

Second Lieutenant Colby Jacobson was an engineer; he was not in the infantry branch. The plague and the resulting mass die-off had forced the Army to reorganize and replace empty positions with personnel from other Military Occupational Specialties and even other branches. He'd seen artillery captains doing the job of an infantry lieutenant and colonels doing the job of a platoon sergeant. So he shouldn't have been surprised to find himself in the middle of a firefight. He didn't consider himself to be a brave man or a warrior, but he was a soldier and an officer in the U.S. Army. On this day he was responsible for a dozen scared young privates and one very experienced Sergeant Dean Sullivan. Battle-tested and hard-bitten, he had taken command as soon as the bullets started flying. To his credit, 2LT Jacobson stuck to his side and listened when Sgt. Sullivan spoke.

It all began when two pickups loaded with armed young men, many just teens, sped up the dirt road, yellow clay dust billowing behind them, and refused to stop for the guard at the entrance to the fledgling farm, crashing through the gate and shooting the shocked townsman, killing him on the spot. There was supposed to be a soldier at the gate also, but he had gone to squat in the bushes. They immediately raced for the nearly finished dam and its hydro generator, firing at anyone they saw on the way.

Five-foot-seven, 120-pound "Big" Ben Tran was operating a backhoe, digging the main ditch deeper, when bullets started bouncing off the tractor. He jumped down with his old Marlin lever-action 30/30 rifle and ran for cover in a shallow branch ditch that was crosswise from the attackers. He landed on Sergeant Sullivan, who cut loose with a string of profane insults. "Sorry, soldier," Tran said. "In case you haven't noticed, those bastards are shooting at us." He pointed 100 yards away at the attackers, who seemed to be placing explosives on the dam. "Do you have a plan?"

Sullivan looked at him like he was a dog pile smeared on the bottom of his shoe. "Of course I have a goddamn plan, you dumbass!" A bullet screamed inches over his head, but he paid less attention than if it had been a fly.

Jacobson broke in. "Would you please let us in on it?"

The sergeant turned and glared at the lieutenant. "We live; they die." He turned to four soldiers in the same ditch with them and cranked up his voice to a level that would've impressed a megaphone. "At my command, concentrate fire on the men at the dam." He aimed. The soldiers and Tran also aimed and readied for the command to fire.

Sullivan yelled, "Fire!"

The three men working at the dam seemed to come apart where they stood.

Sullivan yelled, "Aim at the engine of the truck on the left and wait my command!" When he yelled "Fire!" everyone poured bullets into the truck's engine and flattened the near front tire. Two of the attackers had taken refuge behind the truck and paid for their mistake with their lives.

"Now the second truck!"

The same process resulted in leaving the attackers without transport and motorized escape.

The remainder of the attacking force had taken cover in the ditch behind the dam and in a line of tall cattails along the lakeshore. The cattails offered only concealment and wouldn't stop bullets no matter how much they may have wished them to. They lay shivering with fear in the mud with lake water covering all but their upper shoulders and head.

Sullivan noticed two soldiers taking refuge behind logs that had been bulldozed into a pile to be cut up later and carried off the field and used for firewood in the cold of winter. They were 75 yards away and too far for even his loud voice, with all the gunfire. He hand-signaled, telling them to provide cover fire on his command. This would force the attackers to split their efforts and fire in two directions, reducing their effectiveness.

The soldiers and townsman continued to receive haphazard, light, incoming fire. Judging by the Sergeant's lack of concern, he considered it nothing more than a mild annoyance. Bullets screamed by his head as he raised it up over the lip of the ditch and scanned the field, searching for cover he and his men could run to while closing on his enemies. Since they were in a field, cover was scarce. He needed several places where he and his men could take cover between their position and the enemy's position. They would be steppingstones to victory. He saw only two such places – both shallow ditches, barely deep enough to provide cover. He decided to divide his small force into two teams. Half would bound to the nearest ditch while the other half and the soldiers on their flank kept the enemies' heads down. Then his team would provide cover fire while the other half bounded past them to the last ditch. The rest of the soldiers on the farm should be there to assist by then and they would have the attackers' position fixed, meaning they couldn't maneuver or escape. Those left alive would have to choose: either surrender or die.

When the time came – to Sullivan's surprise – the civilian who'd landed on him in the ditch jumped up alongside of him, firing and working his lever-action rifle from the shoulder. He'd expected the man to stay in the ditch where it was safer. It had been too long since Sergeant Sullivan had been proud to risk his life for a civilian, and the feeling made him smile inside as he ran like hell. *The little bastard has balls.*

Jacobson fired as he ran, sweat dripping from his face. An increase in fire from the cattails along the lakeshore was answered with intense fire from the two soldiers behind the log pile, mowing cattails down, along with two of the killers hiding behind them. Those in the ditch added to the cover fire, managing to keep most of the men behind the dam hunkered down, where they couldn't see to fire over the top.

Running through a hail of bullets, throwing themselves recklessly into the shallow irrigation ditch, Jacobson and Sullivan looked around to learn that only they and the civilian had made it. Behind them in the open field, a twenty-year-old private lay dead.

Sullivan's attention turned to a mass of movement in the narrow Jeep trail that led to where several buildings were in the process of being hastily built. A train of trucks loaded down with armed civilians led by a HUMVEE full of soldiers sped toward them. In a second, he was trying to raise the soldiers in the HUMVEE to inform them where the enemy was and where to position for best effect.

The squad leader driving the HUMVEE followed Sullivan's directions explicitly. The civilians understood that the soldiers were the pros and they should trust them to know how to handle the situation. Working together in surprising efficiency, they managed to have the opposing force so well pinned in, with their backs against the lake and facing overwhelming force, everyone, including Sullivan, expected them to give up.

They were wrong.

It seemed there was more fight in this unorganized, untrained, and hopelessly outgunned gang of punks than anyone there could believe. Sullivan's request to surrender was met with sporadic, ineffective gunfire.

Sullivan looked at Jacobson. "A bunch of goddamn goosepimply assed brain-fart-headed losers. What, they're going to die for their cause? What chickenshit cause?"

Tran interrupted the conversation when he aimed his lever-action and fired at a young man who climbed up out of the ditch and tried to get at the explosives they'd placed on the dam.

Sullivan glared at the dead man. "What in the hell is their fixation on that dam about?"

Jacobson gripped his rifle tighter in preparation for another try at the explosives. "I too wonder why they think destroying that dam is worth dying for."

The standoff had lasted ten minutes, neither side firing, when a shot rang out from the tree line 300 yards away. Another shot followed.

A civilian fifty yards away was in a better position to see into the ditch behind the dam. He yelled over to Jacobson and Sullivan, "That guy shooting just killed two of them. Both headshots."

"Who is it?" Tran yelled back.

"I'd bet it's Trent Branningan and his wife. They went hunting this morning and haven't come back."

Ben Tran yelled back, "Yeah, it sounds like his 30-06 bolt-action."

Another shot boomed.

"He got another one," the man yelled.

Sullivan grunted and pointed. "White flag! Don't believe 'em. Not until they all walk out into the open unarmed."

Jacobson yelled as loud as he could, hoping most of the crowd heard him, including the other side. "No one shoot. But be ready in case this is a trick."

A soldier crawled along the ditch, trying to keep as low as possible. He stopped next to Jacobson. "Sir, I finally contacted the FOB. Captain Donovan has ordered an assault team to reinforce us. Three birds should be here soon."

Jacobson turned his ear to the sky. "Yeah, I hear them coming." He took the radio mike from the soldier and radioed the pilots, telling them to circle at altitude out of rifle range but within sight of the opposing force. "They're flying a white flag already, so just let them see you and I think this will be over quick."

It was. Or at least it seemed that way. The scared young men and teens, who had been wallowing in the mud for nearly 20 minutes watching their friends get shot, got up and walked into the opening with their empty hands up; but when they walked by the others in the ditch behind the dam, an explosion triggered by someone in the ditch killed all but two of the anarchists.

Sullivan stood and scanned the carnage. "Goddamn fanatics!"

Jacobson spoke into the radio mike. "It's over here. Go help the other group of civilians."

Chapter 27

Caroline was feeding the horses when she heard the first shots. They came from the road, at the gate. Her rifle was slung across her back, so she didn't have to hunt for it when she ran for the house, where Samantha was last seen playing with the other children. Her 'store-bought leg', as she called it, couldn't slow her down by much; the strength of her heart wouldn't allow it. Whatever was going on at the gate, she intended to keep it away from the children. Besides, her backpack was in the house, and in it she had more ammo.

The sporadic popping of distant gunfire continued as Caroline dashed past a nervous armed man and into the front door, scanning the living room, she didn't see Samantha, so she rushed into the dining room, finding no one there. Rushing down the hall, she came to the third room and heard children's voices. The tension on her face relaxed as she swung the door open and saw three armed women ready to shoot if she had been a threat. That relief washed away when she couldn't find her little friend among the other children.

"Where's Samantha?" she demanded.

"I think she is with the other children," a Hispanic woman answered.

Caroline's face grew rigid with worry. "Where?"

"Under the big oaks in the front yard," another woman answered, in thick Mexican accent.

Caroline's suntanned face blanched and a sudden chill flowed through the marrow of her bones. The big oaks were halfway between the house and the gate by the road, not far from the shooting. Turning on her stiff, artificial leg, she stepped into the hallway and aimed for the living room, intending to rush back out the front door. Suddenly stopping in her tracks and reversing course down the hall, she remembered she had only the 30-round magazine in the M4 she carried. It had been taken off a dead member of the murderous gang on the road so many months back. The unfortunate brigand had probably stolen it from a National Guard Armory early in the plague or killed a soldier for it. Either way, she had put it to good use since the day Nate gave it to her, sending many evil men to hell.

The thud of her hard replica foot in a worn-out boot hitting the scratched and scarred wood floor of the hallway gave evidence to her quick progress, ending with her in a room where she had left her pack and magazine pouch vest. Slipping into both, she headed down the hall and out the front door in a rush that would have left many younger women with two good legs in the dust. The firing at the gate had intensified. What concerned her more was the fact it seemed to have moved closer. Fear spurred her on.

Running among massive oaks hundreds of years old, she darted from tree to tree, using them for cover as much as possible and scanning the grounds for danger. Other men and women were doing the same; forming an inner ring that those at the gate would fall back to if they couldn't repel the assault.

The firing grew louder and closer still. And Caroline had yet to reach Samantha and the other children. Throwing herself behind a three-foot-tall limestone rock, she paused to look around and realized the others had stopped advancing, taking up their assigned positions instead.

She was alone.

Damn it. She should've yelled to the nearest ones and explained that the children were between them and the attackers. Certainly, they didn't know, otherwise, wouldn't they have kept coming on? Wouldn't they have risked all to protect the children? The slow deliberate firing of Kendell's bolt-action 30-06 gave relief, but at the same time signaled an alarm – he was already under attack.

She pressed on.

Movement to her right, where a ring of large limestone rocks had been arranged around a massive oak for decoration many decades past, caught her eye. She readied to fire. The report of Kendell's bolt-action alerted her not to shoot. She turned her attention to the direction she thought he was shooting at. A young man rose up and fired at Kendell with what looked like an M1 carbine, or a cheap copy, from behind a pile of oak logs someone had gathered the day before while trimming limbs from the oak trees.

A snap shot from her M4 took the young man down permanently.

She saw Kendell straining to see who had shot and waved at him. He waved back, not smiling, but appearing somewhat relieved. The strain evident on his face. She wondered if the children were there with him and realized they must be. He chose that position for a reason. Most likely, the children were all lying flat on the ground within the protection of that ring of rocks. The urge to run to Samantha was strong, but she resisted. Providing cover for each other by her staying at a distance made more sense than her repositioning within that ring of rocks alongside of Kendell. Why make it easier for the attackers to concentrate their fire? Her being off to the side would force them to divide their attention, as well as fire, reducing the effectiveness of both.

A bullet sent stone fragments flying, stinging her face. She ducked and dropped onto her left side, allowing her to see around the stone and keep her low at the same time. It was awkward for her to aim from that position, but her third shot took down the woman who'd fired at her from only 50 yards away. *Damn! How did she get that close without me seeing her? She almost got me.*

Caroline told herself to stop worrying about Samantha and keep her mind on the fight. There would be plenty of time to worry later – if they both were still alive. Kendell's rifle cracked the air, and she thanked God for sending such young men to protect children. They would have to kill him to get to Samantha and the others.

Two men in their twenties rushed her. She sat up and cut them down with two well aimed shots. A desperate three-shot string from Kendell's bolt-action warned her he needed help. She looked that way and her eyes widened. Four men and two women, all in their early twenties, were bounding from tree to tree, working closer to Kendell. Their coordination was poor and they were not covering one another while they bounded forward. Kendell had already killed two of their group, the evidence their still bodies lying on the ground.

She worked on those closest to Kendell and wounded two of them. That was good enough for the time being, as they were not going to rush Kendell's position while writhing on the ground in agony.

As they worked their way closer, Caroline could make out their voices. *What the hell?*

A young woman yelled out, "Nature gave us Eden, Heaven on earth. But then came Capitalism and they raped the land."

A man added, "The one percenters took food from the poor and charged too much for gas."

The first woman finished with, "Corporations sent a plague to kill us all, but we survived and will exact revenge."

Caroline aimed and fired. *They're all nuts. This is about hatred of the corporations that all went under when the plague hit? So, they hate Capitalism. What does that have to do with us? I haven't seen a dollar or anyone lift a finger for a buck in a year. This farm is about feeding ourselves and surviving, you morons!*

She fired and dropped another one. Bullets hitting the rock forced her to duck before she was blinded by fragments. A thought sent shivers down her spine. *If those freaks get to the children there's no telling what they'll do. Hell, they may be doomsdayers wanting the human race wiped out. Children are the future of the human race, so they may kill them all.*

Caroline took advantage of a lull in the fighting and reloaded. Thinking it would also be a good time to reposition in case they were planning a flanking maneuver, she scanned the scene for good cover she could rush to.

The attackers had other ideas and never gave her the chance to reposition. It took all she had to shoot them off her. A human wave of screaming maniacs almost overran her position, despite Kendell's frantic, but accurate shooting and her resorting to full auto fire when they got within twenty yards.

Sickened by the slaughter, Caroline wished it would end. She didn't harbor the hatred for these misguided young people that she did for men in general. Logic told her that most men were not sadistic rapists and she shouldn't hold every man responsible for what her captors did to her and her family and what she witnessed done to a teen girl named Carrie, but her emotions were not so easy to control with logic. Even so, on this day, she found herself killing not out of hatred of men but in defense of herself and other innocents, and she wished it would all be over soon.

The roar of an engine and the rattle of a vehicle racing down the drive caught her attention. She couldn't see it from her position, and all she could do was hope the others stopped it before the killers inside reached the house. A teen boy trying to sneak up on Kendell took her attention from the driveway and the approaching danger long enough for her to take careful aim and fire. The result was the boy's head erupting into pink mist. She grimaced and ducked back down behind the rock, just before a bullet screamed by where her head had been.

Realizing how close she'd come to suffering the same fate as the teen, she slumped down behind the rock and began to shake. Running her hand over her sweaty face, shame and anger at herself took over, and she resolved to be strong. She refused to be afraid of any man, especially a punk teen. Never again would any man have control over her or make her afraid. They could kill her, but they would never take her dignity or her freedom.

She peered around the left end of the rock and saw a young woman with a shotgun rushing between trees. Just before she squeezed the trigger, Kendell's rifle spoke and the woman fell on her face. She never moved.

Caroline felt her stomach grow sick again. *Damn it. Why don't they give up and leave?*

Shouting from the direction of the ring of rocks Kendell and the children had taken refuge in alerted her that something had changed. The bolt-action cracked the air several times in quick succession. She strained to see what he was shooting at but to no avail.

Motion out of the left periphery of her eye caught her attention. She turned to fire and squeezed the trigger in the face of a man only ten yards away. A mass of attackers were coming on even as she fired into them. Forced to retreat from behind the rock, she fired until it appeared she had stopped the human wave attack and then struggled to get up fast, despite of her stiff leg hindering the effort. Finally on her feet, she ran toward Kendell in a panic.

Kendell looked her way and his eyes rounded in shock. He pointed, shouting, "Behind you!" Warning her was all he could do, as she was in his way and he couldn't shoot without hitting her.

She turned to look over her shoulder and stumbled on her fiberglass and steel leg, landing on her backpack. The impact caused her finger to involuntarily fire off a round. By utter luck, she had the muzzle pointed at a man's chest when it went off. Before she had time to fire again, they were on her. Three men and a woman.

It seemed they were trying to take her alive, and that frightened her more than being killed. She'd been a prisoner before and under the mercy of sadists who knew no mercy. Never again! She fought with everything she had, screaming like a wild woman, but they had her trapped under the weight of four adults. Constantly squirming and resisting, her eyes wild with horror, she felt her body tiring, but fear surged through her nerves and adrenalin mixed with oxygen-rich blood, giving her the strength to tear her right hand lose long enough to reach for her hunting knife. She slashed out and cut a man's throat so fast the others were shocked when blood spurted across their faces. The woman holding her left hand down was disemboweled instantly, intestines rolling out onto Caroline's hand before she had time to lift it way. Screaming, her eyes wild, she slashed at the others, leaving them cut and bleeding. Before any of them had time to recover their wits, Caroline drove the six-inch blade into a man's heart and rolled for her rifle.

A bullet hammered one man in the chest and Kendell's rifle boomed from the rocks. Another shot from his bolt-action took out the last one within arm's length of Caroline, just as she got her hands on her rifle and raised it up while still on her back, ready to take on any threats. Looking over the sights, she swung the muzzle in a great arc, screaming. Finding no nearby threats, she grabbed her artificial leg and repositioned it. Her chest heaved as she struggled to stand. Using the rifle for leverage, she pushed herself off the ground and stood. With one more look around, keeping the rifle ready, she turned her determined face to Kendell and the children and ran, her uneven lope eating up yards.

Kendell covered her with his rifle. When she dove behind a rock next to him, he glanced her way and nodded, then pulled his knife and reached it out to her, handle first. "You lost yours back there and I think you can use mine better than me, so you might as well take it."

She did. "Is Samantha with you?"

Before he could answer, Samantha yelled, "I'm over here!"

Relief washed over Caroline's face. "Are you hurt?"

"No." Samantha answered, her voice sodden with tears and fear.

"You stay where you are, girl. I'll come and get you when it's time. Just lay flat on the ground and keep as low as possible." She reloaded as she spoke.

"That was a hell of a fight," Kendell commented. "I ain't seen anything like it." He scanned the area for danger. "I couldn't do nothin' for a while; they were too close to you. Sorry I couldn't help until the end."

"Don't worry about that." Caroline looked around for someone to shoot. "I would much rather you wait for a clear shot than to shoot me accidently." The truth she would never admit to was, there had been flashing thoughts of her begging Kendell to shoot her rather than let them take her alive. The thought lived and died only while it appeared she wasn't going to get away, but once she had her hand free and wrapped around the knife handle, all thoughts were on killing them and freeing herself with no help from anyone.

She looked out from between two limestone rocks and almost smiled. She did it! Even with those odds. And her leg hadn't stopped her. Looking over at the dead men and women who'd just tried to capture her alive – and she could only guess what they had in mind to do with her – she mentally told them, *No one will ever have the power of life and death over me again, and no one will ever make me beg.*

Shooting and shouts from the direction of the house prompted both Caroline and Kendell to look that way.

The vehicle on the drive! Caroline remembered hearing a car or truck heading for the house. The gunfight seemed to increase in intensity over the next five minutes. She held her rifle tighter in her sweat-soaked hands. Feeling a sickly stickiness, she looked down and realized it was blood, not sweat. She ignored it long enough to snap her rifle to her shoulder and fire at a fleeting target, when a man darted between trees. She had doubts she had hit him, but screaming from behind trees near the man she shot at changed her mind. For some reason the man's screaming irritated her. "Oh, shut up," she yelled, "it's not like you didn't ask for it, you whiney son of a bitch!"

A glance at Kendell told her he was a bit put off. He remained silent, though, and didn't give her any dirty looks. *Probably feels sorry for me. Thinks I've lost it.*

A spike of pain shot through her leg from the bullet she didn't expect, a bullet from nowhere. It smacked into her flesh with a loud thud, followed by the report of the rifle that had sent the deadly chunk of copper-coated lead on its way. She jerked in response to the pain and turned onto her back. Her mind barely registered the vague silhouette of Kendell, leaning over her, tightening a cord around her leg. Her assailant, who had been hiding behind one of the trees to the rear of their position, made the mistake of moving closer before taking another shot. He could have killed Kendell, who was in the open while trying to stop Caroline's wound from bleeding her to death. Caroline saw him and sat up, pushing Kendell out of her way and firing. She saw the impact of the bullet on his chest. His knees buckled and he fell forward as he lost consciousness, his rifle clattering on small rocks at his feet.

She glared at Kendell. "Don't do that again! He almost killed you."

Kendell stared back in surprise.

Samantha came running out from where she'd been hiding with the other children. "Caroline! You're hurt!"

Caroline's face revealed terror as strong as during her desperate struggle with those who tried to take her alive. "No! Get down!"

When she ran by Kendell, he reached out and grabbed her, pulling her to him and keeping her protected with his body. Shots kicked up dirt just over his shoulder.

Caroline fired into the trees from sitting position but without the support of either leg. "Get her back with the others," she yelled, and fired twice more. She didn't hear the helicopters landing in the pasture behind the house, some 300 yards away, as she fired until her rifle was empty. Reloading while lying on her left side, she kept watch as Kendell carried Samantha to cover, ignoring her screaming for Caroline.

A burst of gunfire near the house told Caroline and Kendell both the fight was heating up, but Caroline had stopped shooting out of a lack of targets. The shaded ground under the trees suddenly appeared empty. She continued to scan the area, seeing no movement. It dawned on her that shooting at the front gate had also stopped. All of the fighting was between them and the house.

Kendell yelled at Caroline as he reloaded his bolt-action rifle, one round at a time. "Tighten that tourniquet," he warned, "or you'll bleed too much."

She paid him no mind and kept scanning the perimeter. Then she heard Samantha crying along with the other children. Reaching down, she twisted the extra cord, tightening the loop around her leg, and the blood flow slowed. *Why didn't the asshole shoot me in the other leg? It doesn't bleed and can be replaced easier.*

Caroline felt herself growing lightheaded and wondered how long she could hang on. Movement among the trees between them and the house snapped her out of her growing stupor and she readied to raise the rifle, not quite yet wanting to let go of the cord and allow what blood she had left to leak out. A man in camouflage clothing and armed with an M4 emerged from the trees and moved into a more open area. He was followed by several more. She strained to raise her rifle but found it had gained 100 pounds since she last shot it.

The men kept coming closer, spread out and alert with weapons ready but not bounding in teams. One came close enough to see Caroline sitting there staring at him with her rifle at her side. He raised his rifle and she thought she was dead. There was nothing she could do, as her own rifle had become too heavy to lift.

But he didn't shoot. He yelled to cross the distance between them. "Lady, take your hand away from that weapon. I don't want to shoot you, but I don't know if you're friend or foe."

Kendell yelled out, "Who are you?"

"US Army. Sent to protect the people who live on this farm. Come out with empty hands and you won't be harmed."

Kendell raised his head enough he could see Caroline sitting there. As their eyes locked, she fell over on her side and was out. On seeing that, Kendell yelled at the soldiers, "We have children with us. Don't shoot." He left his rifle on the ground and stood with his hands in the air.

A soldier approached, barely paying any attention to the children, keeping his eyes on Caroline and Kendell.

Kendell motioned with his head. "We have a wounded woman."

The soldier yelled over his shoulder, "Marcel, get over here."

A wet-faced seven-year-old boy cried out while sitting on the ground next to the other children, "Please don't hurt us."

A soldier looked over the group of children, his face softening. "Don't be afraid, kids. It's over."

Chapter 28

Brian and Kendell listened with great interest to the adults talking about Caroline. She had just come out of surgery and Brian's father was discussing her prognosis with Drs. Brant and Millhouse.

"The main threat to her life was the loss of blood," Dr. Millhouse said, "but the medic on the scene gave her an IV, which kept her alive until she was flown here."

Nate's eyes were on Brian when he asked, "What about her leg?"

Dr. Millhouse smiled. "It should heal up fine. It'll be sore and she may have another limp to deal with when she walks, but I see no threat of her losing it. We have antibiotics in her IV now, and the wound seems to be clean and free of damaged flesh that could later go septic. I had to trim a little off but not much."

Kendell leaned against the hallway wall and turned away, wiping his face.

Brian noticed. "She's been through a lot, but she's tough."

Kendell turned to face him. "You have no idea."

"Oh, I think I do," he countered. "I was with her when she was shot in the leg she lost, and she wouldn't stop fighting. It's probably why she lost it. She wanted Dad to operate without any painkiller."

Raising an eye, Kendell started to speak but didn't.

"You don't believe me?" Brian motioned with his head. "Ask my father."

Mel and Chesty walked up.

"How is she?" Mel asked.

Drs. Millhouse and Brant excused themselves, explaining they had patients waiting.

Nate answered Mel's question. "The docs say she'll be okay."

Relief crossed Mel's face. "I've got a HAM operator waiting. He promised to give the folks at the horse farm the word on Caroline's condition as soon as I got the message to him." He turned and rushed down the hall, disappearing when he turned left for the stairs.

~~~

Mrs. MacKay limped wearily down the hall and heard Samantha in a bedroom asking a woman about Caroline for the hundredth time, her voice full of worry. The woman tried to calm her but to no avail. Few of the children were asleep, though it was nearly midnight. They lay in bed or on mattresses on the floor crying and were still too upset and nervous for sleep. The little child Mrs. MacKay worried about most was Samantha. She had wanted to go with Caroline, but her pleas didn't produce the results she so desperately wanted. Everyone knew there were two people the little girl trusted; one was Caroline, the other Deni. On this night, she didn't hide the fact she felt alone, despite all those around her.

Ramiro approached his former employer in the hallway, the grief of losing his wife Rita in the fight still on his face, but also the look of a man with a purpose, a man fulfilling a duty to others. His sense of responsibility drove him on through the pain.

He leaned forward so she could hear when he spoke softly so as not to disturb anyone who had managed to fall asleep. "The soldier Mel, he radioed that Caroline will live and keep her other leg." There was no smile on his face, but his eyes little up a little at the elderly woman's reaction.

She reached out for Ramiro's hand and he gave it to her. She held it in both of hers and said, "Thank you for your kindness, my friend. I grieve so painfully for Rita, one of the finest women I've ever known." After looking him in the eyes, she said, "I must tell little Samantha that her friend will be back soon."

Ramiro nodded. "Yes, please do. It pains me to hear her cry for Caroline."

She turned and walked to the bedroom door, stopping to rub her bruised right shoulder for a second. It was sore from firing a pump shotgun her late husband left her. She had only 3-inch magnum 00 buckshot and the recoil had been a bit too much for her slight frame. Even at this late hour, there had been no time away from her worries for others, no time for herself. Later, she would come to terms with the fact she had taken human life in her desperate struggle to protect the people on her farm. Giving Samantha the message that at that moment glowed warmly in her heart would be one of the few chores of the day she expected to enjoy.

~~~

As the nights grew longer and colder, progress on the large farm allowed for a small cold weather crop, and the fresh produce – as limited as it was – supplemented dry and canned goods from the warehouses and military handouts, mostly MREs. A three-family cooperative had successfully started a catfish farm, but they had yet to solve the problem of finding a source for enough feed, so their production was temporarily limited. A hog farm that also raised chickens, turkeys, and goats had struggled to get established and was producing a little food to add to the community's supply. They too, were having trouble coming up with a source for enough feed for their livestock. Some men had taken to not only running long trotlines in the nearby lakes and rivers for catfish and anything else worth eating, such as soft-shelled turtles, but had also started night hunting for alligators. The meat from the younger ones was prized, and their skins made tough leather.

There had been little recent trouble with the anarchists, as people had started calling them, though no one was sure exactly what kind of ideology they espoused with such fervor. It was clearly not just simple Anarchy, but held elements of Socialism and anti-Capitalism, also. Interrogations of the captured fanatics produced rambling rants and tirades that were almost indecipherable. There were obvious common threads in each individual's rants, though. Besides hatred of government, Capitalism, and technology, they hated corporations in particular, blaming all of them for the plague. Many of them also harbored a deep hatred for the U.S. military. The farm by the lake, Mrs. MacKay's little group on her horse farm, the town, and even the Army represented a new start of all the things they blamed for the plague and every social ill that existed before. As such, they considered them all a threat to the human race. This explained their motivation for the bloody attacks. Unfortunately for them, most of the blood spilt was theirs.

Donovan had expended considerable resources hunting for the main Anarchist group, never finding a clue as to where they were hiding out. He never even found the group that attacked Nate, Deni, and Austin. The few campsites they found had been abandoned months or at least weeks before. Many of his officers and noncoms suggested they had moved on to where they didn't have the Army to deal with. He had to agree that was possible, but his gut told him he hadn't seen the last of what he considered to be fanatical terrorists. They may have been incompetent as warriors, but they were still deadly enough and a threat to civilians.

~~~

Deni had Nate and Brian over for dinner. Kendell and Caroline had long since returned to Mrs. MacKay's horse farm, and their other friends were patrolling the streets of the town.

The menu included fried gator tail, lima beans, and cornbread, the conversation light, covering the local news, such as a mother of three giving birth to her first daughter.

Nate sipped a glass of water. "Well, good for her and her husband, they're doing their part."

Brian dropped his spoon back in his lima beans. "Doing their part?"

"Rebuilding the human population," Nate answered.

"The birth rate in town *has* started to rise." Deni eyed the small nugget of gator tail on her plate but passed it over. "As food and healthcare have become more plentiful, people have started to act more like normal people in normal times." She sliced more cornbread for herself. "Marriages are up too," she added.

Brian suppressed a smile and continued to chew.

"On a related subject," Nate said. "Have you heard anything new about you being discharged from the Army?"

They had decided not to get married until the Army let her reenter civilian life. As long as she was a soldier, she could be transferred to another part of the country or even another part of the world, and Nate didn't want to face being separated from his new wife.

Deni's expression changed. "No. As shorthanded as they are, they're reluctant to let anyone go."

Nate's chest rose and held, as if he were about to lose his temper. "I think they've gotten enough of your blood sweat, and tears. Your time was up months ago. As for your service to the country, you can do just as much good for the American people as a civilian."

She raised her hands. "Hey, you have my vote. I've driven Donovan nuts lately, badgering him about it. If he were not such a patient man, he'd have busted me back to buck private by now."

The crevasses on Nate's face that were not there before the plague deepened. "Of course he says it's out of his hands."

Coming to her CO's defense, Deni said, "Well, it is."

Nate reached over and lightly touched the discolored skin left by the impact of the bottle the punk had thrown, and then went back to eating without a word.

She regarded him in silence for some time. "Hard to hide that one with my hair," she said, indirectly referring to the ragged scar that ended just below her hairline in the front, a scar left by a bullet that came within a fraction of an inch of killing her. Nate had sutured her scalp himself and his handiwork was none too professional.

Nate tried to read her emotions. "I was just thinking of how loyal you are to those you know. Donovan's your CO, and that compelled you to defend him."

She smiled. "Well, it *is* out of his hands."

"It's not right," Nate said. "You've done your part. I'm sure there are plenty of hungry young people who would sign on just for the three squares. It's time they let you go."

They went back to eating, and the conversation became light again.

"Hey." Brian reached for another slice of cornbread. "People have been gathering at radios at 8PM to listen to a new program that started a couple days ago. Someone has gotten a shortwave radio station restarted. I guess they found enough fuel for a generator big enough to power the equipment." His eyes were question marks when he looked at his father. "There's time to finish with dinner and listen at the church."

Nate didn't seem very interested. "What kind of program is it?"

"I think it's a news program," Brian answered.

Nate raised an eyebrow. "Well, that might be informative. It's always a good idea to know what's going on beyond the horizon."

~~~

After dinner, the three of them piled in a truck and drove to the church – the one place they knew a shortwave radio was available for the public to listen to. All three brought their weapons. They weren't so complacent that they no longer thought it necessary to keep weapons close by, and Deni had orders to keep her rifle and pistol with her at all times.

The entrance to the parking lot was guarded by soldiers and so were the front and back doors of the church. Such a large gathering would be a tempting target for the strange nihilist militia. There had been no trouble of late, but someone in the Army wasn't taking chances. Most likely it was Capt. Donovan.

They found the church half full. The crowd enjoyed ice cream someone had made. A man at the door handed the three each a bowl and a spoon. It was strawberry. Where enough sugar and other ingredients had been found, Nate had no idea. The milk and strawberries were easy enough, but the sugar in particular was something no one had seen in many months.

It turned out the ice cream was made from real cream and had a much stronger taste than what Brian was used to. Even the fresh strawberry taste was stronger. "This is good," he commented. Other than MRE cookies and powdered drink mix, it was the only sugary food he'd tasted in months. They had cows on the farm before the plague and he had drunk whole milk much of his life, but no one in the family had ever found the time to make ice cream with it.

Deni smiled. "You have a mustache."

"It's real ice cream," Nate said, "not the mass-produced fake stuff people are used to. That's why it tastes different. They finally got an ice company's machinery going and somebody must've found some rock salt."

It seemed everyone had on their best clothes. About a third of the men were wearing tattered jeans and shirts, but they were clean. Most wore handguns under their coats and jackets, and at least half of the people there had a rifle or shotgun slung across their back.

The radio produced only noise until the program started, even then, the noise to signal ratio wasn't the best, but with a little effort, most could make out the words. The church's PA system helped. It was powered by 12-volt batteries and a power inverter that jumped the 12 volts of direct current to 120 volts of alternating current. A man turned up the volume and the chattering crowd grew silent and began to sit in the pews, ignoring the blood stains on the floor that wouldn't wash off – a reminder to all of the days when the church had housed wounded from the battle with the gang they finally ran out of town.

Everyone was eager for news from another part of the country, and it had been said this program broadcasted from out west somewhere, maybe Denver. A few people in the church had relatives in Colorado, or prayed they still did, and took intense interest.

Heavy metal music blared out of the speakers for 30 seconds of acoustic torture, while a young man who must have thought he could sing screamed at the establishment and how the last generation had ruined the world, startling everyone and irritating the older people there.

Then there were several seconds of silence. People glanced at each other, wondering if something had gone wrong, when an excited loud voice that sounded like it came from a man in his early twenties proudly announced, "This is Chip Horace."

Another man with a weak monotone voice chimed in. "And this is Doug Shifler."

They spoke at the same time, finishing with, "Together, we're the Chip and Doug Show!"

"Now, let's get the less important stuff done and out of the way," Chip said. "Since our first broadcast, we've received many requests from local listeners here in Denver – many of them accosting us on the street or beating the studio door down – to reach out to lost relatives for them, asking if anyone knows if Uncle Billy Bob is alive, or whatever. Well, this ain't that kind of show folks. We're here to talk about the so-called rebuilding and the crimes Washington is committing nowadays. You'll just have to wait until a few other morons waste their time getting a radio station up and running and start their own program, if you want to know how Uncle Billy Bob and Aunt Bee are doing."

"Yes," Doug added, "we're just two morons blabbering on the airwaves and have only seven listeners. So please stop pestering us. Chances are you could scream down your street and find out more about what happened to your lost family members than by pestering us to ask about them on our show." He waited a second then added, "So please stop it."

"Morons? Seven listeners? I guess that's supposed to be funny," a woman whispered to her husband. Both sat in the pew in front of Nate.

"I guess," her husband answered, a pained expression on his face. "Sounds like they've been sipping the moonshine."

Nate coughed and looked up at the ceiling, examining the religious paintings. He liked the way they were washed in the yellowish flickering light of several kerosene lanterns, making the images dance like spirits coming down from Heaven.

Deni squeezed his hand.

He lowered his eyes from the ceiling and looked at her.

She smiled and whispered in his ear, "You get bored quick, don't you?"

"I've already lost nearly all hope this is going to be worth listening too," he whispered back.

Her shoulders racked in silent laughter.

"I'm sorry I mentioned the program," Brian muttered. "Maybe it'll get better."

Chip continued. "We know our seven listeners don't want to hear us ramble on. After all, we're morons. So we have a recording of an interview we did a few days ago with General Creedmoor of the National Guard. Listen up folks. We think you'll find it sickening, uh, interesting."

The General explained how they had been working with the remains of local and state law enforcement and had made great strides in restoring law and order to Colorado and several surrounding states. Reading between the lines told those in the church he was painting a rosy picture, but his words were somewhat reassuring just the same. Federal law enforcement, evidently, was out of the picture, since he didn't mention a single federal agency other than to discuss the Border Patrol briefly.

Nate caught several signs the recording of the General's comments were many months old. One of those hints was his mention of the plague still killing people in great numbers. That made him wonder how he could trust anything the two radio 'morons' told them. Unfortunately, many in the crowd believed he was saying the plague had returned and were upset by the 'news.'

The General went on to inform them the Border Patrol had collapsed early in the pandemic, with most agents refusing to report for duty. The resulting invasion of illegal immigrants into California was unstoppable, and the state had been written off as a lost cause. Much of LA was burned to the ground within a week of the plague hitting the U.S., and there was no one to care how many illegals snuck in and no one in authority to stop it. Illegals from Mexico had pretty much taken California back and destroyed it in the process. They tried the same tactics in Texas and New Mexico but met with such violent resistance, they soon retreated back across the border. The trouble with Mexico was complete news to everyone in the church, and a low murmur began to rise. Nate and Deni eyed each other, and Brian's eyes kept darting to them both, checking their reaction.

Nate whispered in Deni's ear, "Certainly the higher ranking officers knew about this. Did you have any idea what was going on in the Southwest?"

She shook her head. "They've kept us completely in the dark. I doubt even Donovan knew."

Nate gave her a look that said he didn't believe a captain wouldn't be privy to such intel.

She shrugged. "Why would they keep this secret? What's the point?"

Nate had no answer. "It could all be BS. This guy might not even be a general. For certain, if it's true, the U.S. would've taken California back by now, even with a weakened military."

Deni furrowed her brow. "I'll ask Donovan about it tomorrow, but I expect he'll tell me it's bull."

The recording of the interview with the General ended. The next words out of the mouths of the radio duo shocked everyone listening.

"Can you believe that shit?" Chip asked. "This asshole general was talking as if the immigrants had done something wrong. After all, they just took what was theirs back. The U.S. took the Southwest from their people in the first place."

"Right on," Doug said. "For the first time since governments began to cast their dark shadows over mankind, we have a chance for real freedom under Anarchy. But the right-wing Nazis never give up. They're busting their ass to bring back their tyranny. The next thing you know, they'll have us all slaving for the almighty dollar again."

"Not me," Chip countered. "And not if the Warriors of Anarchy keep fighting."

Mouths dropped, and the crowd buzzed. A few listeners laughed.

The laughing ended abruptly when Chip added, "If we have to, we'll kill every Capitalist in the former U.S. to stop them from enslaving us all over again! It's the government's job to provide for us, not help the corporations force us to work to earn money so we can buy things that should be free in the first place. How could anyone with a conscience charge for food, healthcare, energy, and anything else that people need to survive?"

I guess farmers, doctors, nurses, and oil producers should work for free, Nate thought. *And these nuts complain about Capitalism enslaving them.*

Doug continued the rant. "Capitalism and technology caused the plague. I think everyone knows this, but a few will not admit it. They're the ones who are trying to 'better their lives' by bringing back all of the things that enslaved mankind. Some towns have even managed to tap into solar and wind power plants and now have electricity and running water." His voice became shrill. "The crazy bastards must be stopped!"

"Well, the ice cream was good," Brian quipped.

"Morons isn't the word," Deni said, "they're nuts. Maybe it's the stress of the plague and its aftermath."

Nate sat there with a worried look on his face. He tried to speak to Deni over the buzz of the shocked crowd. "If this is coming out of Denver, it means this movement is more widespread and larger than I ever thought."

"Great. That's all we need." Deni tugged on Nate's arm. "I must report this to my CO. Let's go."

Nate stood and rearranged his slung rifle. "Okay, but if he's doing his job he already knows about this."

Chapter 29

A month later.

Caroline edged away as the weasel-faced man walked by.

His cold eyes flashed to Caroline for a second and then to Mrs. MacKay. He nodded and exposed perfect teeth. The smile was as cold as his eyes. If there was any humanity behind either, it didn't show. "I hope you're doing well on this fine morning," he said, overly pleasantly.

Caroline waited until the man was out of hearing range. "That man makes me uncomfortable, Mrs. MacKay. I'm not sure why, but the way he looks at little girls makes me shiver."

Mrs. MacKay stopped walking along with her and pondered her words. "Thom Noley? He seems to be harmless. He showed up a month or so back and has worked hard and caused no trouble. I don't think I've ever seen him pay any attention to the children at all. He stays away from them."

They went on to the horse stalls to examine an injury on a horse's leg. It was swollen, and Caroline was worried it may have been bit by a rattlesnake.

Samantha was there with one of the women who watched after the small children.

Inside the stall, Mrs. MacKay checked the leg while Caroline held the horse by the bridle and calmed it with soft words.

"That's no snakebite." Mrs. Mackay sounded sure. "It's just a bruise." She straightened her back and rose to her full height. "I'm getting too old to lean over like that for more than a few minutes," she complained, rubbing her back. "Just give her a few days' rest. Make sure everyone knows she's not to be worked until the leg has had a chance to heal."

Caroline followed her out of the stall and closed the gate. "I'll do that. In fact I think I'll hang a sign on the gate in case someone doesn't get the word."

Samantha looked up at the two adults, her eyes revealing worry. "Is she going to lose her leg like Caroline?"

"No," Caroline answered. "She wasn't shot. It's just a bruise. She'll be fine. People don't always lose an injured leg. My leg has healed just fine."

Samantha hugged her. "I'm sorry I said that. I made you feel bad. I could tell."

Caroline patted her shoulder. "Oh, no you didn't. I was just surprised you'd think the horse was going to lose its leg is all. Don't worry about it. It was nothing."

"Samantha looked up at her. "I wouldn't want to hurt your feelings."

"I know that. But the fact is my feelings aren't so easy to hurt. Don't worry about it, my little friend."

~~~

Three hours before sunrise, on the coldest night of the dying year, dipping down into the low twenties, voices in the hall woke Caroline. Her first thought was to check on Samantha, still fast asleep on her pallet next to other children and bundled in blankets for warmth. Her next action was to put her leg on and then her boot. She grabbed her rifle and opened the door to be met by Ramiro in the hall, holding his fist up to knock. The two locked eyes.

"Have you checked to make sure all of the children who should be in your room are there?" Ramiro asked.

Caroline nodded. "No one is missing." Her eyes flashed down the hall and she saw frantic parents holding their sleepy eyed loved ones.

Kendell stood in the hall in front of a bedroom, not knowing what was going on.

"A little girl is missing," Ramiro told him. "Please check if any children who should be in your room are missing."

Kendell said, "They're all here," and rushed back inside the room to put on his boots and prepare to help search.

Ramiro waited until Kendell took his rifle in hand and rushed out the door, closing it behind him. "You and Caroline please search the horse stalls, while others search the tool shed and other outbuildings."

Kendell and Caroline took off for the stairs, then rushed through the house and out the backdoor.

"Don't wait for me," she said. "I won't be far behind." But he didn't have to wait; she was right on his heels.

Both immediately noticed a dark trail of tracks in the frosty grass. They followed at top speed, their breaths misting in the cold. Approaching the horse stalls with caution, they slowed the last twenty yards, keeping their rifles ready. When they heard a little girl crying, Caroline pushed Kendell out of the way and pulled on the heavy double doors, finding that someone had chained them from the inside. The clank of the chain gave warning, and they heard him flee out the backdoor. Kendell ran round the left side of the building to catch him.

The sturdy building was constructed of brick and heavy timber, the windows all protected with one-inch-thick steel bars in jailhouse fashion – a relic from the days when horse breeders were worried their multimillion-dollar race horses could be stolen or even poisoned to eliminate competition. There was no way Caroline was going to gain entry on the front side of the building, so she rushed to the right and around the corner. The moon was out and the building cast a shadow that she couldn't see into. From out of that shadow, a knife slashed at her throat. Only her quick reflexes saved her life. Thrusting the rifle up and in the way protected her neck. The blade drew blood only from the back of her left hand. She threw herself on the frosty ground, landing on her back, and fired just as he came at her again.

Kendell raced around the building and pointed his rifle at the prone figure writhing on the grass. "Caroline! Are you hurt?"

The man was moaning loudly, but Caroline's voice carried over his. "Yeah. My hand." She struggled to her feet and pointed the rifle at her attacker. "You have a flashlight?"

"Yeah. Batteries are almost dead." Kendell dug around in his pocket and pulled out a small light. In a second, he had the man's face lit up.

The weasel-faced man Caroline never trusted grimaced in pain and blinked in the light, holding a hand over a bullet wound in his left side.

"Check him for weapons." The tone of Caroline's voice was flat and hard.

Kendell searched him and found him unarmed. The knife was lying on the ground out of his reach.

They heard the little girl screaming. Hate burned in Caroline's eyes. She took careful aim, compensating for the height of the sight above the barrel, and shot much of the man's right hand off at the wrist as he held it up in response to Kendell's light blinding him.

He screamed in agony and horror.

"What's wrong?" Caroline asked. "I thought you liked to hurt? It's not so fun when it's you that's hurting, is it?" She put a bullet through his right knee. He howled in agony. "That should hold him. Watch him while I go check on the girl."

The man moaned and held his bleeding wrist with his good hand while Kendell kept his rifle aimed at him. People came running in groups of two to six, gathering around, asking what was going on. Caroline reappeared with a hysterical three-year-old girl in her arms, covering her eyes so she couldn't see the man's condition. Caroline had put her warm wool shirt on her, leaving her with only a thin T-shirt in the cold. The mother rushed up crying and took her away, heading for the house.

Caroline yelled, "Get back everybody!" The rage in her voice compelled them to move fast. She aimed and fired again; taking off most of the man's other hand at the wrist, the bullet crashing on through and ripping the right wrist lower down than before, as he was holding it to stem the bleeding.

The man's renewed screaming seemed to be more from terror, than pain.

A woman held her stomach and screamed, "Have you lost your mind?"

"Yes," Caroline answered, "I have."

She took off the man's other knee with two quick shots, nearly amputating his leg. Without another word, she walked back to the house, not about to ask for approval or forgiveness. If they didn't understand, that was their problem.

Kendell held his rifle on the screaming man as he bled to death. Not knowing what to do, he stood there and watched as the man grew weak and became silent. Finally, he passed out.

Kendell said, "He ain't goin' nowhere. And he ain't hurtin' no more little girls." He left the others and went to check on Caroline. He had seen she was bleeding heavily from her hand.

Ramiro and Mrs. MacKay met Kendell halfway to the house. He stopped just long enough to say, "The child murderer attacked her and she defended herself."

No one even remembered the weasel-faced man's name when they buried him the next day, and no one bothered to pray over him or mark his grave.

~~~

Mrs. MacKay and Caroline sat at the dinner table talking over the events of four hours past.

"How's your hand?" Mrs. MacKay asked.

"I'll live." Caroline wondered what was coming. Banishment?

The elder woman persisted. "Don't you think you should allow someone to take you to town and have a doctor look at it?"

"If it starts to look like it's infected, I'll go. Kendell promised he would drive. I'd rather not get him involved, though, the trip could be dangerous."

"Ramiro and I haven't decided yet if there should be a tribunal to investigate what happened last night."

"What's to investigate?" She held her bandaged hand up. "He came at me with a knife while running from the scene of the crime. I shot in self-defense."

"The first shot, yes. There were witnesses who saw the last shots. Kendell will only say it was self-defense, but the others…they say you lost it."

That Kendell is alright. Caroline had no patience for weakness. He needed killing and she killed him. What was the problem? "It took more than one shot to do the job. I figured if he didn't have any hands he couldn't hurt me anymore."

Mrs. MacKay blinked and regarded Caroline for a few seconds. "I don't think anyone believes you were afraid of him at all. You mean he couldn't harm children anymore. Did you hate him that much?"

"He left his mark on me." She held her hand up again. "I also saw his handiwork on the girl." She looked away. "He was the kind of asshole you had to get to know to depreciate."

The corner of Mrs. MacKay's mouth moved ever so slightly. "Under the extreme emotional stress you were under, no one judges you. The problem is some people are afraid to have you around after what they witnessed last night. They think you have an uncontrollable temper."

"Tell them as long as they don't rape and murder little children or come at me with a knife, they're safe." She sighed. "Or don't. I don't care. If you want me to leave; I'm gone."

Warmth radiated from the widow's wrinkled face. "You're too valuable an asset to lose. It's not like you killed someone who didn't deserve it… and we would miss you." She rose from her chair. "Rest today and don't worry. Most here are grateful you removed a threat to their children and couldn't care less how it was done. This is a problem Ramiro and I will have to work out with those who witnessed the bloodshed last night."

~~~

Chesty and Tyrone had taken over the lower floor of the courthouse and turned it into a sheriff department office of a sort. The Army still used the holding cells occasionally, but had no use for the rest of the first floor and was more than happy to let Chesty and Tyrone use it. The former sheriff office was too far out of town as far as Chesty was concerned, and it had been burned to the ground during the early days of rioting, anyway. All of the sheriff department branch offices had suffered the same fate. Millions had blamed the government for the plague and expressed their anger on any symbol of authority, especially law enforcement officers, vehicles, and buildings.

Nate and Brian sat at a table in the courthouse cleaning their rifles and discussing how the serial killer had been caught and killed.

Nate reached for a small bottle of bore cleaning chemical. "In a way, Caroline is the kind of person this country needs right now."

"Yeah." Brian pushed a cleaning rod down the barrel of his rifle. "But it sounds like some of the people who saw it are now afraid of her. You and I both know she's not quite normal."

"Normal?" Nate set his rifle on the table. "What would be normal after what she's been through? So far she hasn't harmed a single innocent person."

Surprised and a little stung by his father's reaction, Brian spoke in an apologetic tone. "I know she was put through hell and most people would have gone completely nuts. I wasn't criticizing her."

"It's obvious she's been through a lot," Chesty said. "And I bet the scars that show are nothing compared to the ones on the inside. Scarred or not, there are children who will not be murdered thanks to her, and not just the one her and Kendell saved that night."

Tyrone listened but kept most of his attention on his task at hand and didn't say anything. He busied himself with compiling reports of people running across small groups of suspicious-looking young people who might be members of the radical gang. It appeared they were probing the town, learning where the spots most vulnerable to attack were. The Army was still trying to understand exactly what the group was about. The term terrorist organization was already being used among officers and noncoms.

Nate's eyes peered unfocused into his past. "Growing up, I knew Vietnam and elderly WWII vets. Those who served during WWII seldom if ever talked about their experiences in the war, unless it was to tell some story completely unrelated to combat. Don't think I'm diminishing their service, what they went through, or what they achieved. My grandfather died in Europe, so I know many of them lived with nightmares their entire lives. Well, the fact is the great majority of them never suffered that experience. Most of the 16 million who served in uniform never left the U.S. Maybe that's why most of them looked on the war in calm retrospection, though there were certainly some who were deeply scarred by their experiences. Those captured by the Japanese in particular. Seeing others tortured to death and experiencing some of that torture yourself, knowing that it would resume the next day and the next without end until death, can break the strongest mind."

He looked at his son, hoping he would understand. "Caroline was never a soldier, yet she went through the same hell, watching her own family murdered in horrible ways and witnessing Carrie put through unimaginable hell. She deserves respect and understanding. She might not be the life of a party, but so what."

Chesty hesitated, then decided to speak. "And the Vietnam vets? Why were there so many news stories in the 70s and 80s of them committing suicide or going nuts and killing people? How could that war have been worse than WWII?"

Nate leaned back in his chair. "Growing up, I heard of those old stories. Later, I also read that claims of veterans of that war being half nuts were grotesquely exaggerated. The great majority of Vietnam vets went on to live happy, productive lives, many becoming very successful." His eyes locked on his son while he answered Chesty's question. "As to your question of why a smaller war could be harder on those who fought it... Ponder this: I read that during WWII, a U.S. infantryman averaged 10 days of combat in one year. In Vietnam, an infantryman averaged 240 days of combat in one year. If there's any truth at all to that, it explains a lot."

Chesty whistled. "Damn."

Brian swallowed. "And what about that little jungle war *you* were in?"

Nate regarded his son with unblinking eyes. "By your 14th birthday, you had more true stories of life and death struggles than most military retirees, and you had been wounded." He shook his head. "I don't want to bore you."

Brian looked down at the table for a second and then at his father. "I wasn't expecting to be entertained."

Chapter 30

Capt. Donovan walked into the courthouse with a roll of maps under his arm. Sergeant First Class (SFC) Quint Bartow was with him.

Donovan looked around the office at everyone. "Bad news."

Chesty was about to go out on patrol. He put his shotgun back in the rack. "Oh hell. Is it the crazies?"

"Yes," Donovan answered. "The ones in Washington. They're already raising hell about your people using state land go grow food on."

Nate immediately saw trouble. "What's it to them? That land belongs to the State of Florida, not the Feds. I expect there are national forests being farmed right now. Let them bitch about that."

Donovan unrolled his maps on a table. "There are still a few environmental wackos in Washington that lived through the plague, and they're raising hell." He looked as guilty as a priest caught handing money to a whore. "Don't ask me how they found out about your farm."

"Uh, how *did* they find out?" Chesty asked.

"I told you not to ask."

"I just did."

"Well shit." Donovan froze for a second. "A certain Army Captain included in a report a short paragraph about how the locals were feeding themselves by farming a wildlife preserve." He looked as if he expected rotten tomatoes to be tossed at him any second. "A general decided to brag to a Senator on how well things are going in parts of Florida. The Senator told reporters. It wasn't long before the enviro wackos were buzzing like hornets after a cow kicked their nest open."

Brian broke in. "Reporters? They must be farther along in the rebuilding than down here in the South."

"Don't get the wrong idea." Donovan shook his head. "Things are no better in Washington for the common citizen. The people are starving and crime is worse."

"What do you expect?" Chesty said. "It's full of politicians."

Nate steered the conversation back to Washington's plans for the farm. "Have they ordered you to kick everyone off that land? You know that would be a death sentence. Many of these people will starve without that farm. They just now have been able to enjoy a few meals from those fields after all of their work."

"It's not quite like that but almost as bad." Donovan looked around the room. "They are thinking about taxing you."

Chesty's mouth dropped. "How? I haven't been paid in over a year, and neither has anyone else I know. What are they going to tax?"

Donovan's answer was, "They want one third of your crops."

Nate's voice echoed in the room. "There is no way they can spare that!"

"They'll starve," Brian added. "They'll be lucky if they don't starve this summer when the warehouse food runs out. *If* they work themselves to death, and *if* they have good weather, and *if* the bugs and animals don't eat most of it, they just might scrape by another year."

"Add another if to that," Nate warned. "They must also preserve and store enough food to last till the next harvest."

Chesty raised a hand. "Hold on. I'm confused. How in the hell did this thing go from environmental concerns to confiscating a third of the crop? Only in Washington could they go from one to the other without skipping a beat."

A smile played around the edges of SFC Bartow's mouth, but he managed to keep quiet.

Donovan found a chair and sat in it. "I have more news for you, but I guess it can wait a few minutes until everyone has digested the tax nonsense."

"Nonsense?" Nate glanced at the top map in the stack Donovan left on the table. "It might be nonsense but the hunger it causes will be just as real."

Donovan rested his hands behind his head and leaned back in the chair. "Relax everyone. They have put me in charge of collecting that tax." He looked around the room. "Thirty percent? They'll be lucky if they get ten. We'll send them the worst of your produce. There are hungry people all over who need anything you can spare, but the fact is your people worked for it and produced it. It's yours. Forced wealth redistribution is bad enough, but when you take food out of the mouths of those who produced that food and expect them to go hungry the same as if they had never put any effort at all into coaxing it out of the ground and harvesting it…well, that's a recipe for civil war."

Nate still wasn't ready to let it go. "And when they replace you with someone less reasonable?"

"We'll have to deal with that when it happens." Donovan pointed. "I saw you looking at one of the maps. It marks the location of dozens of small garden patches in the county. Most of them belong to regular folks trying to survive. A few are being worked by the radicals."

Brian feigned surprise. "You mean they actually work? Isn't that against their belief that everything should be free? Working a garden is the same as paying for food."

"Even anarchists will work if they get hungry enough." Nate became interested in Donovan's map. He lifted it aside and scanned the next one in the stack. After twenty seconds, he stopped and cast his eyes on Donovan. "It appears Washington has inventoried every garden patch in the county. Looks like they put satellites and drones to use, flying over every inch of land and taking photos. Is that for the tax?"

"Yep," Donovan answered. "The military is running out of food and will be in the same starvation boat as the rest of the population by sometime next year. Washington says the Army and Marines will be the new IRS, but we'll be collecting crops and livestock, not money."

Chesty looked sick. "You *do* realize that you're talking about the government turning the American people into serfs. Sounds like we're going to be like feudal Europe."

Brian's eyes rounded. "I remember reading about serfdom in Europe and how those who couldn't pay their taxes to the land-owning warlords would 'pay through the nose,' meaning a soldier would punish them by putting a knife in their nostril and yank, slitting their nose."

"I think that nose slitting was in Ireland," Nate added.

"None of my soldiers are going to be slitting anyone's nose," Donovan promised. "As for Europe, they've already returned to the Dark Ages in many ways. Citizens have been drafted, not to serve in the military, but to work in coal mines, slaughterhouses, and meat-packing plants, as well as on farms. In countries like China, it's even worse, because they've had massive hunger riots that dwarf those in Europe and have been on the verge of civil war for many months."

Nate's mind raced. "So the people will soon be expected to feed your soldiers, even though they're going hungry themselves? How much are you going to lean on them to extract your portion of the fruits of their labor?"

Donovan flinched. "That's a moral dilemma everyone in the military is losing sleep over."

"You mean those with a conscience," Nate added.

"Yeah," Donovan said. "Those with a conscience. Keep in mind, though, even they have to follow orders. I'm thinking cooperation will be more productive than intimidation. Soldiers can work in the fields as well as anyone and carry a rifle while they're doing it. Still, I think our protection and other assistance is worth something and we should get some consideration from the local people for that. I'm just hoping we can hold things together until the country is back on its feet." He bit his lip. "If not, we'll soon be looking like Europe and Asia." He didn't seem to have much faith his hopes would be realized.

Nate tapped the stack of maps with his index finger. "The tax aside, what are you planning to do with this information? And if you order airstrikes, how can you determine which of these garden patches are being worked by the violent anarchists and which are being worked by peaceful citizens?"

Donovan crossed his oversized arms. "That's *the* question."

"I would expect most of them are just folks trying to survive." Brian looked to his father for support. "I mean, the crazies can't be more than a small percentage of the people in this county."

Chesty walked over and looked at a few of the maps. "Wow. There's a lot of gardening going on out there."

"If there wasn't," Nate said, "there would be a lot of starving going on out there. People are hungry as it is. I think being slaughtered by the Army for the crime of trying to feed yourself would be just a little unjust. Brian is right; most of these people are not violent radicals. They're just people struggling to survive. Using aerial photos of garden patches to hunt for terrorists is about the stupidest thing I've ever heard of government doing."

"Oh?" Donovan turned to Bartow. "What do you think, Sergeant?"

"I think the Army isn't in the justice business. On the other hand, we're not in the business of slaughtering Americans either. As for how stupid government is, that goes without saying."

Donovan rubbed his chin. "According to Washington, we're now in the 'social justice' business, meaning we're to take from those who have food, no matter how hard they worked to produce that food, and give it to those who are hungry, no matter how lazy those hungry are."

Nate winked at Brian as he spoke to Donovan. "Like you said, you've taken over for the IRS."

Chesty laughed. He stopped short. "What's wrong with me? There's nothing funny about this."

"Might as well laugh as cry," Donovan said. "The government painted itself into a corner by starting up and then expanding all of those entitlements. They couldn't end them without facing economic disaster and a voter uprising, and they couldn't sustain them through taxes and printing more money, not forever. Buying votes with social programs for generations would've been the downfall of America, if the plague hadn't come along. America was broke, fiscally and morally.

"Now they face a problem not unlike the one that was solved by the massive die-off. They must feed the hungry to avoid a civil war, but to do that they must take food from the industrious, since government has no food of its own left, or won't in about six months. But how do they do that without pissing off the industrious and causing the civil war that they're trying to prevent? What's worse, if they piss off the industrious, they'll be facing a much more dangerous foe than if they just allowed the lazy to go hungry. On top of that, they know it's the industrious they need if we're ever going to rebuild, not the lazy."

Nate smiled. "You putting it that way makes it seem like the plague never happened. Government has been taking from those who work and giving to those who don't for generations, only now that there's no economy and money is worthless, they're going to take food. Someday they'll be taking our labor by 'drafting' us to work on government farms like in Europe. Remember, the UK did the same thing during WWII. Not everyone who was drafted served in their military and fought in the war, many worked in coal mines, factories, and on farms. Anyway you look at it it's slavery."

Chesty snorted. "Damn Nate, you're scaring the shit out of me. If I didn't know the good Captain and Sergeant to be reasonable men, I'd be reaching for my shotgun already."

"Enough civics and history." Donovan leaned over the stack of maps. "We'll deal with Washington later. How to handle the radicals; that is the question."

Chapter 31

Deni told Mel to stay where he was. Mel wasn't part of her team, wasn't even in the Army, and she wanted him out of the way. His superiors must have really liked his reports, because he had managed to talk someone in the Guard into letting him stay months longer than the original days he had been allowed. Whatever. She liked him and considered him a friend and a competent soldier. Any friend of Nate's and Brian's had to be okay. Nevertheless, she wanted him out of the way and instructed him to stay with the vehicles on the Jeep trail. The next thirty minutes would prove to be either boring or culminate in a bloody firefight and violent death for many. She planned to make sure none of them were her soldiers.

Mel caught movement down the trail. It was another convoy, this one made up of civilian vehicles, three pickups loaded with armed men. He recognized the driver and front passenger of the first vehicle, and saw Chesty and Atticus in the cab of the second. "No offense, but if you're going to make me stay by the vehicles, I think I'll join Nate's team. He has men with him who were military contractors, and they claim to be high speed operators. Just out of curiosity, I would like to see them work."

Deni looked down the trail and saw Nate driving the lead pickup. "Good. Nate might need a real soldier when it hits the fan. I'm not so sure about those contractors. Where have they been all this time? The townspeople could've used them. Now all of a sudden they decide to volunteer for this operation? I notice Nate wouldn't let Brian come to this little party. I suspect he has the same worries."

Mel reached into the HUMVEE and grabbed two grenades. "May I borrow these?"

She shrugged. "Yeah, if you bring them back in one piece."

He gave her a half-smile. "I'm not going to carry them just to weigh down my ass against the wind." He grew serious. "I'll watch his back. You keep your mind on your problems. Nate asked me to watch out for you, so he'll be pissed if you let some asshole kill you after I went with his team instead."

She smiled. "And I'm going to be pissed if you let some asshole kill him." She waved at Nate, still 50 yards away, and led her team into the woods. Already behind schedule, she couldn't wait to talk to him.

Mel stepped out into the Jeep trail and waved for Nate to stop. He walked up to the open window. "Deni doesn't like my company, says for me to watch your back."

Nate obviously didn't like it. "Damn it, Mel! I asked you to watch out for her."

Mel appeared to be genuinely embarrassed. "Sorry, friend. She ran me off."

Nate stabbed his left thumb over his shoulder. "Hop in. We don't have all day. Our target's miles from here."

Mel yelled, "Make room or I'll use you for a landing mat!"

Two irritated men scrambled to get out of his way and pushed others in the process, resulting in a storm of profanities from all.

Mel grabbed onto the truck a foot behind the cab with his left hand and swung his lower body up over the side and into the back with one motion, using nothing more than his leg muscles and pivoting on his hand. He landed on his feet as if he did that kind of thing every day. With the full kit he had strapped onto his body, weighing close to 100 pounds, it impressed more than one of the contractors. He stood in the truck and cast his smirk on the others. "Damn boys, I only needed two square feet. I think a couple of you are going to have to get married now that you've become so familiar with each other."

A mixture of laughter and more profanities ensued.

Nate smiled and shook his head. He spoke to Tyrone, who was sitting on the passenger side, "Mel always was full of shit. You either like him or hate him."

~~~

Though the weather was bright, clear, and crisp, sweat dripped from Deni's chin as she peered through brush and scanned the area around a small shack. Chickens in a coop clucked peacefully and scratched at the bare ground in a futile search for something edible. A boy, who appeared to be about nine, was hoeing weeds in the winter garden. They had a greenhouse made of scavenged materials. The walls were a mosaic of windows that had been removed from abandoned cars, and the roof was made of tempered glass that appeared to have been pilfered from store fronts. A decades-old diesel pickup sat near the shack, more rust than paint covered its dented body.

Deni thought her first raid was going to be a bust. This looked to her to be nothing more than a family surviving the hard times, not terrorists. A little girl of around seven years of age walked out of the shack and skipped to the garden to join the boy. Worries over losing one of her soldiers diminished and transformed into a resolve to be sure no innocent people were hurt.

Her radio squawked. She hurriedly turned the volume down and put it to her ear. The soldier's message changed everything. "We found a pole barn back here. Two white males, early twenties. One white female, a little older. All armed with rifles. It looks like they're making bombs."

She spoke into the mike, "Don't move in until I give the word." She was waiting on a team of soldiers kept in reserve to report.

She didn't have to wait long. Her radio came to life and a soldier reported three more armed men around another shack 70 yards back in the woods. The shack was so small and well hidden under three large oaks growing close together, air surveillance hadn't spotted it.

Deni issued new orders over the radio. "That shack and its occupants are now your responsibility. The other teams will have to do without your backup. Be careful. There are at least two children with the civilians at our position."

Only a few feet from Deni, Private Brenner scanned the area with binoculars, kneeling behind a pine tree and leaning only enough of his upper body out to allow him to see. He had stuck a few green leafy branches into the webbing of his helmet cover and the upper half of his pack to provide extra camouflage. The lower part of his face was covered with an olive-drab mosquito net veil. "Wish we knew how many people are in that shack and how many are armed."

"And how many children there are inside," Deni added. "If only we could take these people down quietly without alerting the other hostiles."

Deni looked on as the boy dropped his hoe and ran into the woods behind the vegetable patch, unzipping as he ran. "That might be an opportunity." She spoke into the radio. "Reserve team. Four men move to the west side of my position and be quick about it. Grab that boy who just ran into the woods behind the garden. Stealth and silence are of the essence."

A few minutes later, a soldier reported to her on the radio. "We got him."

Deni watched as the little girl stopped working and yelled for the boy to stop playing in the woods and get back to work. When he didn't appear, the girl yelled something at someone in the shack. A woman came out. The little girl pointed at where the boy ran into the woods and conversed with the woman, who promptly tramped off to go after the boy, the girl right behind her.

A radio report confirmed that the woman and girl were in custody.

"Well," Deni said. "So far so good." She tried to see into a near window of the shack, but saw nothing because it was too dark inside. "We'll wait a minute or two and maybe get lucky again. Waiting a couple minutes is worth a life or two. It's early, we have all day."

Several soldiers within hearing distance glanced at each other and nodded. Their expressions revealing that they liked what they'd heard.

Deni was about to order the soldiers to move in when a man in his late twenties appeared at the door of the shack, yelling someone's name. He wore an undershirt that was so dirty it was difficult to tell it was once white, and tattered blue jeans so faded there was little blue left.

"Reserve team, move in behind the shack," Deni ordered.

The man reached under his shirt and scratched his belly. He yelled something again and then walked around to the side of the shack, where he was met by a soldier's rifle muzzle only feet from his nose. In seconds, two other soldiers had him on the ground and tied up.

Deni spoke into the radio. "Reserve team, clear the shack now."

Two soldiers rushed into the open door. After what seemed like an eternity to Deni, the reserve team leader reported that no one else was in the shack.

"Great," Deni said. "Leave one man to guard the prisoners and get back to the rest of your team. My team will join Bravo Team at the pole barn."

Keeping low, she retreated from the edge of the clearing. The other soldiers backed into the woods and followed her.

Though it had all gone well so far, the weight on her shoulders swelled. As a junior sergeant, she had been given responsibilities beyond the norm on this mission, a necessity grown out of the fact they were short on junior officers and senior noncoms, and there were many other raids taking place on the same day.

She found herself in an Army that once employed many female soldiers, but quickly had so few she hadn't seen a woman soldier under the rank of Colonel in almost a year. Almost all female soldiers who survived the first part of the plague went home to their families, especially those with children. Being surrounded by young men with hungry eyes and sometimes profane speech could be unnerving, but she demanded the respect due her and got it. Capt. Donovan wasn't the kind to tolerate any sexual harassment, and they knew anyone who went too far would face swift punishment. In recent months, there had been another reason to keep their attitude toward her professional: Nate. But before the Captain, before Nate, they would first have to deal with her, and she had proven herself deadly in a fight. The end result was hungry eyes were usually all she had to deal with, and that she could ignore.

Gunfire echoed in the trees. Deni and her team hadn't yet made their way to the pole barn, and she immediately became worried. Rushing in could just get some of her soldiers killed, so she continued on at a safe pace.

The intensity of the firing increased. Deni picked up the pace a little but didn't let her guard down and was certain to keep all of her team under control, using normal patrol tactics.

An explosion from the direction of the pole barn left everyone's ears ringing.

Deni's team wasn't far away when Bravo Team's leader came over the radio and informed her that all of the hostiles were dead, killed by the explosion that may have been set off by the soldiers' fire.

"Any of your team hurt?" she asked.

"The answer came back, "No.""

Relieved, but still worried things could change at any second and some of her soldiers pay with their lives for something she overlooked, thoughts raced through her mind. Decision made, she gave her orders. "I am taking my team to reinforce the others at the second shack. You secure your location and await further instructions."

She hand-signaled her team and changed directions. To avoid crossing the open field, she was forced to reverse course, go back to the front of the farm, and then skirt the clearing, staying just inside the woods. After crossing the narrow drive, her team swung around toward the other shack to join her third team. On the way, she met the soldier who was guarding the two children and the man and woman.

Deni asked, "Did anyone pass by here?"

The soldier answered, "No."

Approaching the area where she thought the shack should be she saw a soldier watching a well used trail. His attention was on the opposite direction, and he didn't see her or any of the rest of her team. When they were nearly close enough for her to speak to get his attention, he turned his head and was momentarily startled by them being able to approach so close without him noticing, but soon recovered.

Deni kneeled beside him. "Fill me in on the situation."

The young soldier gave her a dirty faced smile. "We got all of the men at the shack disarmed and rounded up. We're just laying low in case a straggler or two comes along."

Deni didn't quite understand. "How did you do that without firing a shot?"

"When the shooting started at the pole barn, the three men came running to join the fight and ran right into our team. We stuck rifle muzzles in their faces and they dropped their weapons. A quick check on the shack proved it empty. So far, those three are the only ones in our area."

Using the radio, Deni spoke to the team leader. "Tighten up your perimeter by falling back and decreasing its size around the shack. My team will search the premises to gather any intel on the terrorists' plans. Shouldn't take more than five or ten minutes. Then we'll move out."

Private Brenner was close by and listening. "We need to be careful over there. They're likely to have more improvised explosive devices laying around, maybe even some set as booby traps."

She nodded. "Yeah. These people seem to be kind of wacko. They just might have booby traps out."

At the shack, Brenner went in first before Deni had time to stop him. She kept everyone else out until he reappeared with an a few pamphlets and books about anarchy and how all forms of government were slavery. He handed them to Deni. "There are also stacks of hand-written flyers they must be handing out to people." He held a sheet of paper up and read a passage. "Any man who must work for a living is not truly free. Never again will we allow the greedy corporations to force us to work for money to buy things that should be provided at no cost." He chuckled. "I wonder how that would work, since they're against government. Who is going to provide everything free? They seem to blame the plague and all of society's ills on technology and government and are trying to prevent both from reemerging."

"Yeah, but that's nothing new." She took the leaflet from him and read it. "Same old stuff about how their mission is to prevent America from rebuilding and turning the country into what it was before it hit the fan."

She handed the flyer to Brenner. "Take that stuff with you when we leave. The rest of you search the area for caches of weapons and explosives. Be careful and go slow. I don't want to lose anyone." She disappeared into the shack to search it herself in case Brenner missed something important.

Chapter 32

Nate scanned the ten acres surrounding the small house with binoculars. "We have three teen boys – all armed – near the shed. Looks like they might be siblings. They seem to be working on something on a table. Can't tell what it is."

Mel listened to Deni's team on his radio and took notice of Nate's remarks at the same time. "Might be bombs they're working on. Deni's people have caught a gang of turds building bombs."

Nate looked through his binoculars again. "I can't make it out. They have tools in their hands. I can see that much."

"What kind of tools," Mel asked.

"Too far. Can't tell." Nate handed his binoculars to Mel.

While his friend used his binoculars, Nate looked over the four men who told him and everyone else who would listen they were ex-Special Forces and had been contractors in a recent Mideast war. They kneeled in thick brush to his left, their rifles shouldered and pointed at the three boys, their fingers on the trigger. He took note that they were behind concealment but not bullet-stopping cover, such as the thick pine trees he and Mel were kneeling behind. He had already asked them twice to each find a thick tree for cover.

The men Nate suspected were posers seemed to be too excited for the circumstances. Even if they were really ex-contractors he still thought of them as 'demisoldiers.' They were all outfitted with what would appear to the casual observer to be the kind of equipment many people had seen soldiers wearing on news reports covering the last Mideast war just before the plague hit and America suddenly became too preoccupied with survival of the country to be killing people over politics. They wore Kevlar helmets and civilian-available body armor. Their trauma plate carriers had MOLLE pouches attached and they were ready for war, with eight thirty-round magazines for their civilian-legal semi auto M4-style carbines, all topped with $1,000+ ACOG sights. On their right legs, they wore dropdown holsters, a 9mm Glock strapped inside. All of them wore clear goggles for eye protection. Nate thought the fingerless gloves and snazzy patches on their dessert-tan uniforms that said, "Risk Control Services, Inc." were a bit much.

All four claiming to be ex-Special Forces was something that pegged-out Nate's BS meter. He hadn't had time to ask them a few casual questions that would tell him if they really were what they claimed to be, and until he had, he wasn't going to call them liars. Then there was the fact they had worked with Chesty once, when the town had a little trouble with home invaders many months back, and he had told Nate they seemed to be the real thing and handled themselves well. Chesty told him they had stayed in town a few days and then went back to their survivalist retreat in the backwoods. At least that's what they told Chesty before they left town. They were closed-mouthed on its location, he said. That was understandable, of course. No survivalist would want to reveal the location of his retreat.

We'll see, Nate thought. *A lot of those contractors never served in any real military. Some were in law enforcement; some had no experience at all. The government often contracts with shady companies and those companies will hire anyone when they need lots of warm bodies.*

Chesty and Tyrone had taken their half of the team and skirted around to the right side of the small home. The plan was to get them in a simple crossfire and either take them prisoner or kill them, depending on how reluctant they were to surrender.

But before the first shot was fired, they first needed to determine if these people were violent terrorists or just folks trying to get by.

Mel handed Nate his binoculars. "I can't tell what they're working on either; it's too far to see that much detail. They're just teens, though, I can see that. The youngest one is at most, about thirteen."

The contractor known as Race glared at Nate. "What are we waiting for? We can kill them from here."

Nate jerked his head around and stared the younger man down. "I do not want any of you to shoot unless fired on! If any of you can't live with that, get your ass back to the trucks and stay there."

"This is bullshit," the man kneeling beside the first one said. "You pussies are going to get one of our team killed."

Nate and Mel had been told his name was Lawson.

Mel took a quick look at Nate and saw a short fuse burning. He tried to calm the situation down. "Chesty is acting sheriff of this county and Nate is one of his deputies. You four are here as volunteers and are under Nate's authority. I wouldn't argue with him anymore." He clicked his M4 to full auto. "This isn't the time to get stuck on dumbass."

Race stood and sneered at Mel. "Come on, weekend warrior. I'll take that M4 from you and stick it up your ass."

Nate rolled his eyes. "Get down, idiot."

Shouts from the boys near the shed prompted everyone to look that way.

Too late.

The boys ran for the house, yelling an alarm to someone inside.

Race shouldered his rifle to fire. "They saw us!" His hasty shots went high, plowing into the house above the door, just as the last boy rushed in and slammed it shut.

Surprisingly, no shots came from inside the house.

Nate yelled, "Do not fire! Do not fire!" He and Mel stayed behind the thick pine trees.

Mel didn't even look in the direction of the house. He kept his eyes on the contractors, careful to stay behind the tree in case someone from the house shot in their direction.

Race continued to stand while aiming, exposing himself to the sight of those in the house. He diverted his attention long enough to glare at them, looking like he wanted to kill Mel and Nate both.

Mel calmly advised, "You think it might be time for you geniuses to get behind something that can stop bullets? Hint: That brush isn't going to do it for you."

Mel's advice seemed to have registered, and Race started to lower himself behind brush, but then his face washed over with anger, and he froze for a second to say something. His words never had a chance to become anything more than thoughts. A bullet punctured his Kevlar helmet – in one side and out the other. A gush of blood and matter spilled down the side of his face. The man's eyes went blank and he fell in his own shadow.

His friends turned white with shock and froze for several seconds. The first one to recover yelled obscenities and fired at the house, emptying his magazine in one long string of poorly aimed shots. The other two soon joined in.

"Stop firing, you stupid sons of a bitch!" Nate yelled. "I told you not to fire." He repeated his words when they stopped to reload and they finally heard him.

Kneeling next to his dead friend Lawson asked, "Why the hell not? They're shooting at us."

Losing his temper, Nate's voice rose. "That piece of shit shot at them first, you idiot! What do you expect? If someone shot at my boy from the woods, I would kill him too."

Chesty's voice emanated from Nate's radio. "Who fired? Goddamn it, who shot?"

"Mel," Nate said, "If anyone one of them shoots again, empty your mag into all of them."

The men's eyes rounded.

Mel shouldered his rifle. "I can't miss at this range."

Nate spoke into the radio, "One of the contractors shot at the boys. Someone inside the house killed him, then his friends cut loose. Mel has orders to kill them all if they shoot again."

"Shit!" Chesty waited a few seconds before asking, "What do you think? Are they terrorists?"

"Who knows?" Nate glared at the kneeling men. "I have no reason to believe they're anything but people who want to be left alone and don't like their children being shot at. This thing is over as far as I'm concerned. The best thing to do is back away."

"Let me try a white flag," Chesty suggested.

Nate didn't hesitate. "It's too late for that and it's not worth it. Let's back off now before more people get killed."

Chesty responded with, "I'd hate to waste the whole day. Stand by while I try to talk with them under a white flag."

Worried, Nate tried again. "There's no way to salvage this now. It's time to leave."

"He's raised a flag," Mel warned.

Nate looked across the field in disbelief. "Damn it. Has everyone gone nuts?"

A shadow fell over Mel's face. "What can we do?"

Nate spoke into the radio in urgent tones and tried to talk Chesty into listening to him. "Chesty, if I were the father of those boys, I'd shoot you on sight. Do not expose yourself. Stay behind cover. They will kill you!"

The contractor named Ernie complained, "Hell, that house is made of wood. We can shoot right through the walls and kill them from safety."

Nate had enough of worrying about loose cannons. He pointed his rifle at the three men. "Drop your rifles!"

All three scowled at him, making it known how they felt about being relieved of their weapons. After a few seconds, they dropped their rifles on the ground.

"Now your handguns." Nate aimed at the nearest man's head.

"In case you're wondering," Mel warned, "I'm backing Nate all the way. What happens next just depends on if you want to die."

They fumed in silence for several seconds and then slowly pulled their pistols out of their holsters and dropped them at their feet.

"Now lie down in the depression over there behind you." Nate motioned with his rifle. "Move it. Mel is going to keep his rifle on you until this is over. You'll get your guns back then."

Nate spoke to Chesty on the radio. "It's time to back away from this."

Chesty's subdued voice came back, "Hold on. I see movement in a window."

A rifle shot cracked, and Lawson, who hadn't kept low while moving to cover, was shot through the back of the head.

His two friends turned white and hugged the earth as if they were afraid they would fall off into space.

"Oh shit!" one of them screamed. "It's your fault they're both dead. Assholes!"

"He should've belly crawled," Mel said, sounding irritated. "He committed suicide by stupidity. Now shut up before I shoot you myself."

Bark flew from the pine tree Mel hid behind. He pulled his left hand in to prevent it from being shot off. This meant he couldn't keep his rifle trained on the two men, but it would take only a tenth of a second to bring it up if need be. He looked back at Nate, who was checking to see if Mel had been hit. The expression on Nate's face made him laugh.

"Somebody in that house can shoot," Mel said.

Nate nodded and grabbed the radio when it blared out Chesty's voice, asking if anyone had been hit.

"The first shot killed another one of the deadly high speed operators Mel and I have been blessed with," Nate answered. "No one else was hit." He added, "Now can we get the hell out of here before more people are killed?"

"Yeah," Chesty answered. "Everyone back off and keep behind cover. We'll meet at the vehicles."

Nate dropped to the ground and crawled to a tree 20 yards away. He took position behind the tree and signaled for Mel to retreat while he kept watch on both the men nearby and the house.

The man named Reggie asked, "What about our guns?"

Nate had no time for him. "To hell with your guns."

After crawling farther back in the woods, Mel sat against a thick tree, making sure those in the house couldn't get a shot at him. "Maybe those people will send them to you by UPS in a week or two."

"Kiss my ass," the nearest man spat.

"You have me mistaken for a different type of man." Mel smiled. "I don't swing that way."

Nate said, "Moving," and dropped to his belly. He crawled to a tree 30 yards farther back in the woods. "Send those two," he told Mel.

"Crawl to Nate." Mel motioned with his rifle. "Remember what happened to your buddies. Drag your peckers in the dirt the whole way and keep your head down."

As soon as the contractors and Mel had joined Nate, they took off on a run, knowing they were far enough into the woods they couldn't be seen from the house.

When everyone was standing by the pickups, Chesty and Tyrone took a headcount. Everyone was accounted for – minus the dead contractors.

Atticus sauntered up to Nate and Mel while others climbed into the pickups. "Who started shooting?" He kept his shotgun pointed skyward and his finger straight but near the trigger.

Mel stabbed a thumb over his shoulder. "He's back there dead, along with his friend."

Atticus raised an eyebrow. "I was going to kick his ass, but now I feel sorry for him."

"Don't," Nate said. "He shot at those boys without cause."

"And he put us all at risk," Mel added. "It was just luck that none of my friends were shot." He gave the two ex-contractors sitting in the back of a pickup a cold stare. "If they had, *I* might be pissed right now and ready to kick ass."

Reggie jumped out of the pickup and rushed at Mel. "Bring it on, you little prick!"

Chesty shouted across the distance. "We don't have time for that bullshit. Anyone not in a truck in 20 seconds will be left behind. We're out of here."

Everyone scrambled to pile into pickups. Mel purposely jumped in the one the two supposed 'ex-Green Berets' were in. Sitting across from them, he winked. "Later."

Reggie said, "Two of my friends are dead and you think it's funny."

The truck took off on the rough Jeep trail and jostled the men riding in the back.

"No, I don't," Mel contradicted. "I do think they both caused their own deaths and put a lot of other people in jeopardy." He gave them a hard stare. "And that pisses me off."

Nate drove the rear pickup. He glanced at Tyrone. "It could've been worse."

Tyrone looked through the windshield at the pickup in front. Mel and his two new enemies seemed to be under an uneasy truce. "Yeah, but it's still embarrassing to even be a part of such a snafu." He tried to shake unpleasant thoughts from his head. "Damn!"

Nate slowed for a shallow creek that crossed the trail. "What we witnessed today shows how dangerous, tricky, and downright dirty the job ahead is. Ferreting out terrorists that hide among the population has always been a dangerous, dirty job."

Chapter 33

All involved in leading the raids had gathered in what was a courtroom. The room was full of soldiers and civilians alike. Donovan stood in front of the assembly next to the empty witness stand, scanning written reports as the leaders took their turn and gave a brief account of their mission.

When it was her turn, Deni gave a quick synopsis of how her raid went perfectly, showing some amount of pride and heaping praise on the soldiers under her. She later regretted her glowing words on how well the mission had gone and the great results, when Chesty explained how he had lost two civilians and was forced to abort the mission to avoid further bloodshed before it could even be determined if the people at the homestead were terrorists or not.

Sergeant Derek McCain, who had led a raid of his own that had gone fairly well, got a verbal punch in. "If you want professional level results, you need to send professionals."

Donovan gave him a look that would wilt a sturdy oak tree. "Sounds like you had bad luck, Chesty."

Tyrone's baritone voice reverberated in the office. "We had a few trigger-happy fools with us. It happens when you use a team that's made up of the general population. It's not easy to vet a posse that you gather up only hours before going on the mission." He glanced at Chesty. "It was embarrassing to be a part of that total snafu."

Chesty examined the top of his boots for a second. His eyes met Donovan's. "Those four men who claimed to be military contractors before the plague helped us out before and proved themselves to at least be sane. I don't know what happened this time."

Tyrone said, "This time there was a real chance of a gunfight and they couldn't take the pressure, so they started shooting, that's what happened."

"Maybe," Chesty said in a voice that made it clear he was through discussing it.

The meeting went on for another hour until the last team leader gave his oral report.

"Okay," Donovan said. "I think we have done some good as far as disrupting the plans of the terrorists in this area, such as they were. In addition, we have gathered more intel and were able to peer deeper into their twisted minds, shedding a little more light on their motivations. All in all, it was a good day's work."

He rubbed the back of his neck before continuing. "I've had a conversation with Dr. Brant, and she tried to explain to me why these people have glommed onto this weird ideology. From what I understand of her explanation, people who have been severely traumatized need to have someone or something to blame for their pain. Even before the plague, corporations and the wealthy had become almost the new Jew to blame everything on. The government was a convenient target, but many looked to the government to take care of them, so they were less likely to blame government for everything. Those that saw the government as their keeper and provider tended to blame the wealthy and corporations for every societal problem, while criticizing politicians for being bought out by those corporations, tending to steer clear of demanding a reduction in governmental power, size, and expense. In fact they usually wanted more government in the form of more social spending. Well, the plague ended any chance of the government expanding to take care of everyone and the corporations have collapsed. I guess she was saying the reason their half-baked dogma has attracted so many devotees is because there are now millions of traumatized people with a deep need to blame someone for the tragedy they have witnessed and lived through."

Chesty raised his hand. "Uh, since I'm not in the Army, I guess it's okay to ask a question."

Donovan nodded. "Go ahead."

"I don't get why they don't want the farm in operation, so the town can feed itself. For some reason they don't even want people to improve their lives at all. Do they want what's left of the human population to die out like a doomsday cult?"

"No. I'm certain that's not it. They fear recovery, rebuilding." Donovan took a leaflet off a table and quickly scanned it to refresh his memory. "They are afraid society will rebuild in its old image with the same government and economic system and then the cycle will repeat, culminating in another mass die-off they blame on Capitalism and the wealth it creates." He looked around the room. "And they are willing to kill to stop it."

"Obviously," Chesty said. "They remind me of people who wanted to drag down the wealthy to remove inequality, instead of lifting up the poor through opportunity in the free market. They seem to want to keep everyone at starvation level."

Donovan appeared to be pressed to move on to a topic he could do something about. People had the right to think whatever they wanted, no matter how wrong they might be. He needed to understand the anarchists' motivations only because he had to stop their terrorism, and he had no interest in getting into a philosophical debate over how wrong their ideology was. It was his job to protect the American people. Politics and philosophy wasn't part of his job. Sure, a lot had changed since the collapse caused by the plague, but his core job of protecting the American people was still there. Just because *Posse Comitatus* had been repealed and he wasn't protecting the people so much from a foreign threat but more from each other didn't mean he had any business telling people what to think or believe in. If they were not violent, he couldn't care less. Besides, there was a more dangerous threat looming, and he wasn't sure how to respond to it. Decisions had to be made soon, and those decisions would determine the future of the soldiers who served under him and hundreds of civilians he had grown to respect.

Time for Donovan to call a halt to the meeting. "Dr. Brant said this kind of thing was bound to happen. There are probably many different political groups and cults doing their own thing out there in this post-plague world. We just happen to be dealing with the most violent group at the moment." He looked around the room. "I think we've covered everything as best we can for now. Sergeant Heath, I need you to stay. The rest of you are dismissed."

Deni's face revealed concern Nate had not been at the meeting. She stood silently until the two were alone. "Sir, do you have any idea where Nate is? I expected him to be here with everyone else who had been involved with the raids."

"Come on," Donovan said. "He and Mel are waiting for us."

Curious, she kept her questions to herself and followed him out the door into the parking lot where they got in a waiting HUMVEE.

Donovan's driver headed for the street, needing no orders from the Captain. Another HUMVEE full of soldiers followed to provide security.

Donovan's demeanor became less professional and more like someone talking to a friend. "I have good news for you. Your discharge from the Army has come through."

Deni's face broke into a wide smile. "Wow!" She rubbed her forehead with her hand, appearing to be totally surprised. "Great! Nate will be ecstatic! We didn't want to get married until –"

Donovan's eyes lit up. "I know. You wanted out of the Army first."

Still showing complete surprise, she asked, "Why now? Did you do something to hasten their decision?"

"Well, please don't take offense, but Washington has a policy of letting women out of the military if they plan to have children. It's their effort to rebuild the population." He waited until they got through a checkpoint at an intersection. The driver slowed just enough to allow the soldiers to see their CO was in the HUMVEE and wave them through. "I told them you wanted to get married and start a family."

She started to laugh, but caught herself. "From soldier to brood mare."

Donovan was quick to say, "It's no one's business whether you plan to have children or not, but I told them that to speed things up and get them to give you your honorable discharge."

She shook her head and smiled. "I understand. And thank you. It's those in Washington and the Pentagon I'm aghast at."

"I hate to lose a good soldier, but you served the time you signed up for long ago and you've earned this."

"Thank you Captain," she said.

He looked out the window at a modest house that hadn't been maintained since the plague. All outward appearances suggested it had been abandoned long ago. The driver pulled in behind a familiar pickup parked on the street next to the curb.

Donovan's eyes met Deni's. "Nate and Brian have been told the news. I need to go inside to talk to you and Nate about something in private, then I have to get back to work. You have another two weeks before you'll be officially free. Until then, you'll be on leave. As you know, the usual procedures have pretty much been abandoned, but you will have to turn over all of your equipment, including your issued weapons."

She opened the door. For some reason, she stopped and turned to him. "I feel like I'm deserting you and the others with a big mess that still needs cleaning up."

Donovan shook his head. "Don't. You did more than your share. And I'm certain you will continue to help people in other ways as you live your life with Nate and Brian." He got out, ending the conversation.

Soldiers in the following vehicle had already scrambled out and formed a defense perimeter. They kept watch for any threats as the two walked.

The front door of the house opened and Nate appeared. Brian squeezed past him and ran to Deni. They held each other for a few seconds.

"Dad is happier about you getting out of the Army than he'll probably let on," Brian said, keeping his voice low.

She laughed. "Oh, you think?"

They headed for the house. Brian looked up at her as he walked. "I hope you're not too tired from dealing with the nuts. Dad and Mel made dinner for you."

Nate met them at the porch, giving her a hug. "I'm glad you're free now."

All of them went inside, where Mel noticed something on Donovan's uniform Deni and Nate hadn't. He put a glass of wine down on the table and stood in a brace. Saluting, he said, "Good evening, Colonel."

Taken by surprise, Deni finally noticed the insignia on his uniform.

Donovan casually saluted. "Stop that nonsense." His eyes lit up. "You're in the Guard, not the Army."

"Wow," Deni said. "You didn't even mention you had been promoted. I hope I didn't call you Captain on the way over here."

Donovan pretended to be trying to remember. "I think you did, but I'll let it go."

Nate shook his hand. "Congratulations. Well earned. So they skipped Major and promoted you to Lieutenant Colonel. I guess nothing is the same as it was before the plague."

"It's certainly not the Army you knew, Nate. And thank you, but the promotion doesn't mean a thing," Donovan said. "Except I might have a little more pull with the Pentagon and that could prove helpful with what's to come."

Nate's smile vanished. "Is there something we need to know?"

"Well," Donovan rubbed the back of his neck, "that's why I intruded on your celebration. But it will only be for a few minutes, then I'll leave you to your dinner." He moved to a chair. "It's been a long day, so I'll talk while sitting."

Everyone sat and waited for what would probably be bad news.

"I received new orders along with the promotion," Donovan said. "I expected to be transferred, but that didn't happen. I'm still responsible for this area, but it seems our fears of Washington wanting a pound of flesh from the people here have come to reality."

"How much of these hungry people's food do they want?" Nate asked, his voice flat and hard.

"It will be my job to determine that." Donovan looked at Mel. "You might want to leave the room, unless you can promise to never speak of what you hear over the next few minutes."

Mel raised his face and looked Donovan in the eye. "Everyone here is my friend. It will be a cold day in hell before I do harm to people I respect."

Donovan nodded. "Okay then. Washington has grown impatient and feels the people of this town owe them for the MREs, fuel, and protection they have received from the Army. I have been ordered to assess how much food you can spare without starving you. This is solely my decision. I will be sending them very little at first, just enough to pacify them."

"At the moment, they can't spare any food," Nate said. "Its winter and it will be getting colder soon. If the last few winters are the new norm, we can expect record cold and snow in January, February, and even March." He looked around the room. "Global warming seems to have turned into global freezing."

"Yeah, I think they got that one wrong," Mel quipped.

Deni asked, "How long to do think you can hold them off before they get wise to you? You're between us and your superiors. If you follow orders, the people here will grow to hate you for taking food out of their children's mouths; if you don't, Washington is going to lose patience."

Donovan stood. "My oath is to the people of the United States. If Washington thinks I'm going to take food from people who would go hungry without it, they'll learn soon enough where my allegiance is."

Nate got up from his chair. "You're telling us you're willing to risk everything for these people?"

"Unto death," Donovan answered. "I have no surviving family to miss me and little to live for but to do my best to help this country get back on its feet. I understand Washington's plight. There are millions going hungry. The minute this town has an excess of food, I will ask for donations, but I refuse to take it by force."

"Wow," Brian said.

"I hate to load bad news on top of good, but it's better that you know now rather than later." Donovan looked at everyone in the room as if it might be the last time he saw them. "Good evening and enjoy your dinner."

He left them standing there wondering what was to come.

Chapter 34

It had been a long tiring day, and Chesty wanted to fall into his bed and pass out. The raid being a bust seemed to make his weariness heavier on his shoulders. He unbuckled his pistol belt and removed his boots. That's as far as he got before he blew the kerosene lantern out and fell asleep.

Two hours before daylight, his eyes snapped open. Something had awakened him. He reached for his pistol just as the bedroom door exploded, sending splinters across the room. He fired at the same time the nineteen-year-old sent a load of buckshot into his chest. They both died instantly.

~~~

A pounding on the front door woke Nate. He grabbed his rifle and entered the hallway to meet Deni, holding her rifle at the low ready. Brian and Mel had been sleeping on couches in the living room. They had lain down on the floor, their rifles pointed at the windows.

Nate could see them in what little moonlight made it into the room. He motioned for them to stay down, and then yelled, "Who is it?"

"It's Atticus. Chesty has been killed!"

Nate rushed to the door and opened it. "Where's Tyrone? This may be a reprisal for the raids – a hit on all local law enforcement."

"Tyrone's at the scene." Even in the dim moonlight, it was obvious Atticus was upset. "A punk shot him before he even had a chance to get out of bed. Chesty must've shot at the same time, because the bastard's lying in the bedroom doorway."

Deni noticed Brian standing barefoot in the living room, ashen-faced. She rushed to him. "I'm sorry. I know he was a good friend."

"This stinks," Mel said. "We can't afford to lose people like him."

Nate turned to Brian. "Get dressed. We're getting out of this house." He spoke over his shoulder, "Atticus, don't stand in the doorway like that. They may be coming after us."

Deni rushed to her room to put on her full kit in preparation for battle. In ten minutes, all of them were racing down the street in two pickups.

When they arrived at Chesty's home, Donovan was half in a HUMVEE speaking on a radio. A squad of soldiers surrounded the area. Tyrone leaned against a pickup.

Atticus approached his adopted son cautiously. "I know, Tyrone, I know."

Tyrone lifted his wet face and handed Atticus Chesty's badge. "I'm not taking his place. I can't."

Atticus laid a hand on Tyrone's big shoulder for a second and backed away several steps. He looked at Nate with wet eyes and reached out his open hand. "Tyrone needs you. At least for a while."

Deni snatched the badge out of his hand. "No! All he's wanted for months is to leave other people's problems behind and get back to his farm with Brian. In two weeks, I'll be out of the Army and we'll be free..." She stopped, tears running down her face. "It's useless." She handed the badge to Nate. "If you're going to appoint yourself Sheriff, then I appoint myself deputy. Maybe Tyrone and I can watch your back."

Atticus said, "You've got an old man and his shotgun to help you."

Nate lightly touched her face with his rough hand. "Two weeks."

She blinked tears and looked away. "Yeah. Two weeks."

Also by John Grit

Feathers on the Wings of Love and Hate:

Let the Gun Speak

(Volume 1 in the series)

Feathers on the Wings of Love and Hate 2:

Call Me Timucua

(Volume 2 in the series)

Apocalypse Law

(Volume 1 in the series)

Apocalypse Law 2

(Volume 2 in the series)

Apocalypse Law 3

(Volume 3 in the series)

Patriots Betrayed

Short Stories
To Kill a Cop Killer
Fierce Blood
Old Hate

Made in the USA
San Bernardino, CA
21 February 2015

Dieter Wunderlich
EigenSinnige Frauen

Zu diesem Buch

Was verbindet Madame Pompadour, Marie Curie, Coco Chanel und Simone de Beauvoir? Sie alle weigerten sich, ein konventionelles Leben zu führen, wie es den Erwartungen ihrer Zeit entsprochen hätte. Statt dessen verfolgten sie ihre Ziele und setzten sie durch – oft gegen massiven, meist männlichen Widerstand. In diesem Band hat Dieter Wunderlich zehn besonders eigensinnige Frauen porträtiert. Der Bogen reicht vom Bauernmädchen Johanna von Orléans, das an seine Bestimmung glaubte und König Karl VII. in den Sieg führte, bis zu Frida Kahlo und Ulrike Meinhof. Bei aller Genauigkeit und Sachkompetenz sind Wunderlichs Darstellungen »so unterhaltsam und spannend wie ein Roman zu lesen« (Frankfurter Rundschau).

Dieter Wunderlich, geboren 1946 in München, Diplompsychologe, war von 1973 bis 2001 im Management eines großen internationalen Unternehmens tätig. Seit 1999 hat er sich mit Büchern wie »Vernetzte Karrieren. Friedrich der Große, Maria Theresia, Katharina die Große«, »EigenSinnige Frauen« und »WageMutige Frauen« als Autor farbiger und sorgfältig recherchierter Biographien einen Namen gemacht. Er lebt in Kelkheim am Taunus. Weiteres zum Autor: www.dieterwunderlich.de

Dieter Wunderlich
EigenSinnige Frauen

Zehn Porträts

Mit zehn Abbildungen

Piper München Zürich

FSC

Dieses Taschenbuch wurde auf FSC-zertifiziertem Papier gedruckt.
FSC (Forest Stewardship Council) ist eine nichtstaatliche, gemeinnützige
Organisation, die sich für eine ökologische und sozialverantwortliche
Nutzung der Wälder unserer Erde einsetzt (vgl. Logo auf der Umschlag-
rückseite).

Ungekürzte Taschenbuchausgabe
Piper Verlag GmbH, München
1. Auflage September 2004
7. Auflage Mai 2007
© 1999 Verlag Friedrich Pustet, Regensburg
Umschlag / Bildredaktion: Büro Hamburg
Isabel Bünermann, Friederike Franz,
Charlotte Wippermann, Katharina Oesten
Umschlagabbildungen: François Boucher (»Kopf der Marquise de
Pompadour«, 1756, Detail; München, Alte Pinakothek; Foto:
Bayer & Mitko / Artothek) und Bildarchiv Preußischer Kulturbesitz
(»Coco Chanel«, um 1930)
Satz: Friedrich Pustet, Regensburg
Papier: Munken Print von Arctic Paper Munkedals AB, Schweden
Druck und Bindung: Clausen & Bosse, Leck
Printed in Germany   ISBN 978-3-492-24058-1

www.piper.de

Inhalt

Johanna von Orléans (1412–1431)
Ein Bauernmädchen glaubt unbeirrbar an seine
Bestimmung – und führt den König zum Sieg   9

Maria Ward (1585–1645)
Ein Leben lang ringt die Nonne mit den Männern der
Kirche um die Verwirklichung ihrer Vision   38

Maria Sibylla Merian (1647–1717)
Eine Forscherin reist nach Südamerika –
100 Jahre vor Alexander von Humboldt   59

Madame de Pompadour (1721–1764)
Eine Mätresse greift in die große Politik ein   75

Rahel Varnhagen (1771–1833)
Eine Jüdin im Gespräch mit großen Deutschen   99

Marie Curie (1867–1934)
Ein Leben für die Radiumforschung   121

Coco Chanel (1883–1971)
Der märchenhafte Aufstieg einer Näherin aus der
Provinz zur Pariser Modeschöpferin   144

Frida Kahlo (1907–1954)
Auseinandersetzung mit dem Schmerz:
Die Tragödie einer großen mexikanischen Malerin   161

Simone de Beauvoir (1908–1986)
Mit den Männern von gleich zu gleich   178

Ulrike Meinhof (1934–1976)
Moral und Terror   206

Anmerkungen   234

Bildnachweis   256

Mein wichtigstes Werk ist mein Leben

Simone de Beauvoir

Johanna von Orléans

*Ein Bauernmädchen glaubt unbeirrbar
an seine Bestimmung –
und führt den König zum Sieg*

Ein Bauernmädchen reitet zum König

Mit einem Gefolge von sechs Männern reitet ein siebzehn-
jähriges Bauernmädchen durch Lothringen. Sie wagen sich nur
im Dunkeln auf den Weg, bei Tagesanbruch schlüpfen sie in
abgelegene Scheunen, denn sie durchqueren ein von Engländern und Burgundern besetztes Land; und es herrscht Krieg.

Wenn sie in ein Dorf reiten, um etwas Brot und Wein zu
besorgen, begegnen sie alten Männern und Frauen, die dort
ausharren, obwohl sie sich kaum noch sattessen können, weil
die Äcker brachliegen und auf den Wiesen nur noch vereinzelt
Kühe weiden. Wer nämlich kräftig und mutig genug war,
setzte sich in die vom Krieg verschonten Gebiete ab; und
die Daheimgebliebenen müssen damit rechnen, daß durch-
ziehende Soldaten ihre letzten Hühner schlachten und die
Getreidefelder zertrampeln.

Johanna und die Männer frieren nicht selten in ihren feuch-
ten Kleidern, denn im Februar 1429 regnet es häufig. Die
Flüsse führen Hochwasser; Furten werden sich erst wieder im
Sommer bilden, und weil sich die Flößer nicht in die reißende
Strömung wagen, müssen die Reiter Brücken suchen – obwohl
sie dabei riskieren, entdeckt und aufgegriffen zu werden.

Trotz der Strapazen läßt das Mädchen die Männer nie aus-
schlafen: Johanna springt nach einer Rast stets als erste hoch
und brüllt die Männer an, wenn sie nicht rasch genug aufbre-
chen. Woher nimmt sie die Kraft? Was treibt sie vorwärts?

Der Bauerntochter stehen ein königlicher Bote, ein Bogen-schütze und zwei Edelmänner mit ihren Dienern zur Verfügung. Bevor sie sich in Vaucouleurs an der Maas auf den Weg machten, hatte der Anführer dem Stadtkommandanten schwören müssen, Johanna sicher nach Chinon zum König zu bringen. Auf ihre Begleiter ist sie angewiesen, weil sie weder die sechshundert Kilometer lange Strecke kennt noch Näheres über die Kriegslage weiß und es selbst in Friedenszeiten nicht wagen dürfte, ihr Heimatdorf ohne männlichen Schutz zu verlassen.

Ein Schäfer, an dem der Trupp vorbeireitet, nimmt nur Männer wahr, denn Johanna ist groß, schlank und schmal in den Hüften, sie schneidet ihr schwarzes Haar kurz und kleidet sich wie ein Junker: Schon von weitem fällt der wehende Umhang ins Auge. Lange Strümpfe mit Ledersohlen umhüllen die Beine. Hin und wieder faßt sie unter ihr Hemd und zupft an der kurzen Hose, einem Wäschestück, das sie erst seit wenigen Tagen trägt, denn Mädchen und Frauen haben unter den Röcken nichts an.

Selbst wenn sie sich zwischen den nach Schweiß riechenden Männern zum Schlafen ins Heu legt, wagt es keiner, sie zu berühren. Die Jungfrau bleibt zugeknöpft und begeistert sich nur, wenn sie von ihrer Sendung spricht: dem Auftrag, Frankreich zu retten.

Endlich überqueren die Reiter die Loire. Von da an brauchen sie sich nicht mehr zu verstecken, denn in diesem Gebiet halten die Territorialherren dem französischen König die Treue.

Rasch verbreiten sich Gerüchte und Nachrichten über Johanna. Mit Karl VII. will sie sprechen! Wird der König das Dorfmädchen empfangen? Was macht sie so selbstbewußt, daß sie es wagt, vor ihn hinzutreten? Eine Jungfrau will Karl VII. zur Krönung in Reims verhelfen und die Engländer aus Frankreich vertreiben! Von Gott sei sie dazu ausersehen. Gewiß, auf so ein Wunder hoffen die Franzosen. Aber weiß sie denn nicht, wieviele Frauen bereits auf dem Scheiterhaufen verbrannt wurden, weil sie behaupteten, über besondere Kräfte zu verfügen, während Vertreter der Kirche sie für Hexen hielten?

Nach einem zehntägigen Ritt, ein paar Stunden von Chinon

Johanna von Orléans (1412–1431)

Französische Miniatur, um 1505. Nantes, Musée Dobrée

entfernt, diktiert die Analphabetin abends im Quartier einen Brief an den König, in dem sie ihr Kommen ankündigt und ihre Mission beschreibt. Damit schickt sie ihren Herold voraus.

Am nächsten Tag steigt sie in einem Gasthaus von Chinon ab und wartet ungeduldig auf eine Nachricht aus dem Schloß.

Der Hundertjährige Krieg

Warum hoffen die Franzosen so verzweifelt auf ein Wunder? Weil sie sich seit hundert Jahren gegen die Engländer wehren müssen: Seit das französische Königshaus der Kapetinger 1328 ausgestorben ist, machen die englischen Könige der Dynastie Valois das Erbe streitig und versuchen, ihren eigenen Anspruch auf die französische Krone mit militärischen Mitteln durchzusetzen.

Karl der Weise, der Frankreich von 1364 bis 1380 regierte, eroberte die meisten der bis dahin an die Engländer verlorenen Gebiete zurück. Aber als sich nach seinem Tod herausstellte, daß sein Sohn Karl VI. geisteskrank war, entzündete sich an der Frage, wer die Regentschaft führen sollte, ein neuer Machtkampf – dieses Mal zwischen dem Herzog von Orléans, der dem Haus Valois treu blieb, und dem Herzog von Burgund, der sich mit den Engländern verbündete.

Im Oktober 1415 schlugen dreizehntausend Engländer das mehr als dreimal so große französische Ritterheer in die Flucht. Der vierundzwanzig Jahre alte Herzog Karl von Orléans, den man zunächst für tot gehalten und auf dem Schlachtfeld liegengelassen hatte, wurde gefangengenommen.[1]

Die Könige von England und Frankreich starben 1422 innerhalb weniger Wochen. Während die Anhänger der Valois den Dauphin Karl VII. als französischen König ausriefen, übernahm für den erst neun Monate alten englischen Thronfolger dessen Onkel Herzog Johann von Bedford die Regentschaft.

Als der geisteskranke König starb und von seinem Sohn abgelöst wurde, schöpften die Franzosen neue Hoffnung. Aber bald merkten sie, wie schwach Karl VII. war: „In seiner überängstlichen Frömmigkeit hörte er dreimal täglich die Messe und hielt jede liturgisch vorgeschriebene Andacht peinlich genau ein ... Zur Finanzierung des Krieges gegen England verpfändete er seine Juwelen und beinahe die Kleider am Leib; aber er fand keinen Gefallen am Krieg und überließ ihn Ministern und Feldherren, deren Begeisterung und Fähigkeiten im Widerspruch zu ihren Eifersüchteleien standen."[2]

Mit vereinten Kräften schoben England und Burgund den Herrschaftsbereich Karls VII. auf das Territorium südwestlich der Loire zusammen; und in den besetzten Regionen widerstanden nicht mehr als zehn isolierte Orte dem Feind. Der französische König krallte sich im Tal der Loire fest, um nicht völlig den Halt zu verlieren, aber der englische Regent und der Herzog von Burgund beabsichtigten, ihm auf die Finger zu treten.

Die Stimmen

Das Reich des noch ungekrönten Königs endete im Osten an der Maas. Am westlichen Ufer des Flusses liegt Domrémy, der Ort, in dem Johanna 1412 zur Welt kam.

Sie war das dritte von vier Kindern einer Bauernfamilie. Die Mutter stammte aus einem Nachbardorf; der Vater war aus der Champagne gekommen und hatte sich in Domrémy Respekt verschafft.

Wie die anderen Mädchen des Dorfes half Johanna von klein auf beim Säen und Ernten, Füttern und Melken, Putzen und Flicken – aber im Alter von dreizehn Jahren sonderte sie sich ab und entwickelte eine auffallende Frömmigkeit. Das geschah, nachdem eine Horde englischer und burgundischer Soldaten das Vieh aus Domrémy fortgetrieben, den Ort geplündert und die Kirche in Brand gesteckt hatte.

Johanna begann Stimmen zu hören.

„Als ich dreizehn Jahre alt war, hatte ich eine Stimme von Gott, die kam, um mich zu leiten."[3] Im Garten erschien ihr der Erzengel Michael mit einer Engelschar. Sie sah auch zwei Frauen: die heilige Katharina, die Schutzpatronin eines Nachbardorfes, und die heilige Margareta, deren Statue trotz des

Feuers in der Kirche von Domrémy unbeschädigt geblieben war. Anfangs fürchtete sich Johanna vor den verwirrenden Erscheinungen, aber bald freute sie sich, wenn die Heiligen zu ihr sprachen, und es gelang ihr allmählich, sie absichtlich herbeizurufen. Solange sie in Domrémy blieb, behielt sie freilich das Geheimnis für sich.

Weil Domrémy im Sommer 1428 erneut von Soldaten heimgesucht wurde, flüchtete Johannas Familie mit anderen Dorfbewohnern nach Süden in die zehn Kilometer entfernte Stadt Neufchâteau. Von dort aus sah Johanna die heimischen Felder brennen. Jeden Tag erfuhr sie Neuigkeiten über den Krieg und sie hörte, wie besorgte Leute einander fragten: „Wird Karl VII. in der Lage sein, die Engländer und die Burgunder aus Frankreich zu vertreiben?" „Aber wißt ihr schon, was man sich erzählt?" flüsterten sie sich zu: „Frankreich wurde durch eine Frau[4] verraten; aber eine Jungfrau wird kommen, um das Land zu befreien."

Als die Sechzehnjährige nach zwei Wochen mit ihrer Familie heimkehrte, forderte eine Stimme sie auf, sich nach Vaucouleurs zu begeben, eine gut befestigte Stadt zwanzig Kilometer nördlich von Domrémy, die zu Karl VII. hielt, obwohl sie auf burgundischem Gebiet lag. „Die Stimme sagte mir, daß ich nicht länger bleiben könne, wo ich war, und daß ich die Belagerung der Stadt Orléans aufheben müsse. Sie befahl mir außerdem, zu Robert de Baudricourt in die Festung Vaucouleurs zu gehen, deren Stadtkommandant er war. Er würde mir Leute geben, die mit mir gingen. Ich antwortete, daß ich ein armes Mädchen sei, das nicht zu reiten und Krieg zu führen verstünde."[5]

Heute halten wir Visionen für Halluzinationen: Wir gehen davon aus, daß Johanna damit unbewußt auf ihre Angst reagierte und die Stimmen ihre Hoffnungen wie ein Echo reflektierten. „Die ‚Stimmen' bieten uns eine direkte psychologische Materie, denn ihre Ermahnungen, Anweisungen, Ratschläge, Ermutigungen, Absichten, Hoffnungen und Versprechungen sind nur die Triebe, Sehnsüchte, Absichten, Hoffnungen und Wünsche Johannas, die unbewußt durch ein allegorisches System ausgedrückt werden, das seine Gestalten von einer kollektiven ‚mit religiösen Vorstellungen gesättigten Mentalität' ableitet: Johannas ‚Stimmen' sind Johanna selbst."[6]

Damals glaubten die Menschen an Feen, Elfen, Kobolde, Hexen, Gespenster; Erde und Himmel waren nicht klar voneinander abgegrenzt: Niemand bezweifelte, daß sowohl Gott und die Heiligen als auch der Satan das irdische Geschehen über Mittelsmenschen beeinflußten. Das Problem bestand allenfalls darin, zwischen göttlichen und teuflischen Eingebungen zu unterscheiden – aber dafür gab es die Inquisition.

Heimlich bereitete Johanna ihren Aufbruch vor: Sie überredete einen Onkel, sie in sein Haus zu holen. Ihren Eltern log er vor, sie wolle seiner Frau helfen, die gerade ein Kind geboren hatte; aber nach wenigen Wochen quartierte sich Johanna in Vaucouleurs ein, statt nach Hause zurückzukehren.

Um dem Stadtkommandanten ihr Anliegen vorzutragen, ging sie zur Festung, doch die Posten wiesen sie mit hämischen Bemerkungen zurück. Johanna gab nicht auf, sondern kam wieder und wieder.

Robert de Baudricourt wollte sie zunächst zu ihren Eltern zurückschicken und dem Vater empfehlen, sie mit Ohrfeigen zu empfangen. Dann holte er Erkundigungen über sie ein und beobachtete, was geschah, wenn ein Priester ihr – aus sicherer Entfernung – das Kreuz hinhielt: Da sie sich nicht in Schreikrämpfen wand, sondern demütig niederkniete, verwarf er den Verdacht, sie sei vom Teufel besessen, und nach einigen Wochen empfahl er sie dem König in Chinon.

Der Empfang beim König

Im Kronrat wird darüber gestritten, ob Karl VII. Johanna empfangen soll oder nicht: Einige Mitglieder treten dafür ein, sie kurzerhand wieder nach Hause zu schicken, aber eine andere Fraktion, die zunächst mehr über sie herausfinden will, setzt sich durch.

Also suchen einige der königlichen Ratgeber Johanna in ihrem Quartier in Chinon auf, um sie – so neugierig wie es ihre steife Würde erlaubt – zu befragen. Die unerfahrene Bauerntochter mißtraut den feinen Herren; erklärt ihnen zögernd, daß der Himmel sie beauftragt habe, dem König zu helfen und sie mit ihm selbst sprechen wolle.

Tatsächlich wird sie am zweiten Abend ihres Aufenthalts in das die Stadt überragende Schloß gerufen. Ungestüm springt sie vom Pferd. Ohne auf ihren niedrigen Stand zu achten, führt ein Graf sie gemessenen Schrittes durch die Flure an den Wachen vorbei in die Empfangshalle. „Der Saal war von fünfzig Fackeln erleuchtet und gedrängt voll mit über dreihundert Menschen einer glanzvollen Versammlung von Soldaten, Höflingen und Prälaten, von denen einige feindselig eingestellt, andere leichtfertig belustigt, alle aber neugierig waren, dieses neue Schauobjekt zu sehen ..."[7] Die Grüppchen brechen ihre Gespräche ab; es wird so still, daß das Knistern der Fackeln zu hören ist. Johanna läßt sich von der ungewohnten Szenerie nicht überwältigen und zeigt „kein Anzeichen von Unschlüssigkeit, Ratlosigkeit, Schüchternheit oder Verlegenheit".[8] Ein Spalier öffnet sich, ihr Begleiter führt sie vor einen der Herren und sagt: „Du stehst vor dem König." Aber Johanna durchschaut die Täuschung: „Der ist es nicht. Ich würde den König erkennen, obwohl ich ihn nie gesehen habe."[9] Karl VII. betritt den Saal, unauffälliger gekleidet als die meisten der Höflinge, die ihn aufgrund einer Weisung kaum beachten. Es ist charakteristisch für ihn, daß er sich nicht gleich zu erkennen gibt, sondern erst versucht, sich einen Eindruck von Johanna zu verschaffen. Aber dafür bleibt ihm keine Zeit, denn sie überlegt nicht lang, geht geradewegs auf ihn zu, blickt in sein überraschtes Gesicht, senkt erst einige Meter vor ihm den Kopf, beugt ein Knie und begrüßt ihn: „Edelster Dauphin [so nennt sie ihn, bis er gekrönt ist], ich bin gekommen, von Gott gesandt, um Hilfe zu bringen – Euch und dem Königreich Frankreich."[10] Der Angesprochene deutet auf einen prunkvoller gekleideten Herrn und behauptet: „Ich bin nicht der König. Der König steht dort." Aber Johanna erwidert: „In Gottes Namen, edler Fürst, Ihr seid es und kein anderer."[11]

Die Anwesenden sind verblüfft: Wie konnte sie den König erkennen? – Gewiß ließ sich Johanna vor dem Empfang beschreiben, wie der König aussieht: den melancholischen Blick, das schüchterne Auftreten und die schlurfende Art zu gehen. „Ein Trauerkloß ... und dabei erst 26."[12]

Karl VII. spricht mit dem Mädchen, das aufrecht vor ihm steht und wie ein Edelmann aussieht. Er hört sich an, was Johanna ihm über ihre Sendung berichtet. Anfangs schweift sein Blick noch zwischen den Umstehenden herum, dann beugt er sich vor, die Querfalten auf seiner Stirn weichen Runzeln über der Nasenwurzel, und er schaut ihr fragend in die Augen: „So werde ich meinen Feinden widerstehen?"

Den König hat Johanna für sich eingenommen, aber kann sie auch die Kirche – deren Segen für das Vorhaben unerläßlich ist – von ihrer Sendung überzeugen?

Die Prüfung

Zwei, drei Wochen später begleitet ein königliches Gefolge das Bauernmädchen in die hundert Kilometer südlich von Chinon gelegene Stadt Poitiers.

Gleich nach ihrer Ankunft diktiert Johanna einen Brief an die Engländer: „König von England und Ihr, Herzog von Bedford, der Ihr Euch Regent von Frankreich nennt, ... gebt dem König des Himmels Sein Recht! Übergebt der Jungfrau, die von Gott, dem König des Himmels, gesandt ist, die Schlüssel von allen guten Städten in Frankreich, die Ihr eingenommen und geschädigt habt! Sie ist hierhergekommen durch Gott, den König des Himmels, um das königliche Blut zurückzufordern. Sie ist gern willens, Frieden zu schließen, wenn ihr von Euch Gerechtigkeit widerfährt und Ihr von Frankreich ablaßt und zurückerstattet, was Ihr Euch angeeignet habt. ... König von England; wenn Ihr es nicht tut, so wißt: Ich bin Kriegsherr, und wo immer ich auf Eure Soldaten in Frankreich stoße, werde ich sie vertreiben, ob sie wollen oder nicht. Und wenn sie nicht gehorchen, so werde ich sie töten lassen. Ich bin hierher von Gott, dem König des Himmels, gesandt, um Euch Mann für Mann aus ganz Frankreich zu schlagen ..."[13]

Eine Chance, ihre Mission durchzuführen, hat Johanna nur,

wenn sie Jungfrau ist. „Denn Jungfrauen sind dagegen gefeit, vom Teufel besessen zu sein, eine Jungfrau kann also nicht zugleich Hexe sein. In einer Welt, in der jeder, der Außergewöhnliches leistet, mit einer der beiden außerirdischen Mächte, Gott oder Teufel, im Bunde sein muß, käme bei einer Jungfrau nur Gott in Frage. Und dann: Jungfrauen genießen einen Sonderstatus. Sie sind Grenzgängerinnen – nicht nur zwischen den Geschlechtern, sondern auch zwischen den Sphären des Irdischen und Überirdischen. Jungfrauen werden daher übernatürliche Fähigkeiten zugetraut...“[14] „Sie konnten Erlöser gebären – oder selbst Erlöser werden.“[15] Wenn Johanna glaubhaft machen kann, daß sie eine von Gott auserwählte Jungfrau ist, kommt es nicht mehr auf ihre niedrige Herkunft an; im Gegenteil, sie steht dann mit dem König auf einer Stufe, denn auch er beruft sich auf die göttliche Legitimation.[16]

Sie muß deshalb in Poitiers eine Prüfung ihrer Jungfräulichkeit über sich ergehen lassen und vor einem Untersuchungsausschuß der Kirche wochenlang Fragen beantworten. „Was sagten die Stimmen?“ „Welchen Auftrag haben sie dir gegeben?“ „Warum kleidest du dich wie ein Mann?“ Als ein Dominikaner von ihr wissen möchte, in welcher Sprache sich die Stimmen an Johanna wenden, antwortet sie schnippisch: „In einer schöneren als der Euren.“[17] Da lachen selbst die ehrwürdigen Kirchenmänner, denn der Fragesteller benutzt den ungehobelten Dialekt einer mittelfranzösischen Landschaft.

Nachdem sich das Tribunal von ihrer Lauterkeit überzeugt hat, kehrt sie nach Chinon zurück, wo der Kronrat sich dafür ausspricht, sie mit den Soldaten nach Orléans ziehen zu lassen.

Die Lage Frankreichs ist so verzweifelt, daß die königlichen Berater auf keine Chance verzichten wollen, zumal mit der Entscheidung kein Risiko verbunden ist: Sollte es nicht gelingen, Orléans von den englischen Belagerern zu befreien, würde die Anwesenheit Johannas dies auch nicht verschlimmern. Aber im Fall des Erfolgs kann die Jungfrau als Hoffnungsträgerin der Franzosen aufgebaut und zur Abschreckung der gegnerischen Streitkräfte eingesetzt werden.

18

Die Befreiung von Orléans

Orléans kommt im Hundertjährigen Krieg eine strategische Bedeutung zu, weil es sich um das Zentrum eines politisch besonders engagierten Herzogtums, eine Stadt mit dreißigtausend Einwohnern, einen wichtigen Binnenhafen und entscheidenden Loire-Übergang handelt: Gelänge es den Engländern, den Ort zu erobern, könnte sich Karl VII. auch in seinem Rückzuggebiet südlich der Loire nicht mehr halten.

Ein fünftausend Mann starkes englisches Heer marschierte im Oktober 1428 vor Orléans auf. Die Truppenstärke reicht jedoch nicht aus, um Orléans vollständig abzuriegeln, etwa zu verhindern, daß mitunter eine Schweineherde in die belagerte Stadt getrieben wird.

Johanna schließt sich einem Nachschubtransport an: Dreitausend Mann sichern vierhundert Schlachttiere und sechzig Wagen auf dem Weg von Blois nach Orléans.

Ein Waffenschmied paßte ihr eine wertvolle Rüstung an, „genau richtig für ihren Leib": Helm, Harnisch, Arm- und Beinschienen. Die Panzerung schützt vor Schwerthieben und Lanzenstichen, Pfeilschüssen und Steinschleudern; andererseits müssen selbst kräftige Ritter darauf achten, daß sie wegen des Gewichts nicht aus dem Sattel kippen.

Jean d'Aulon führt ihre persönliche Begleitmannschaft, zu der zwei weitere Edelleute, der Beichtvater, Johannas Brüder Jean und Pierre sowie zwei Herolde und zwei Pagen gehören: eine Eskorte wie sie normalerweise nur hochrangigen Offizieren zusteht.

Weil die Engländer den Herzog von Orléans gefangen halten, kümmert sich dessen fünfundzwanzig Jahre alter Halbbruder Johann der Bastard[18] um die Verteidigung der Stadt.

Er kommt dem französischen Konvoi am 28. April 1429 ein Stück entgegen und wendet sich an Johanna: „Ich bin froh über Eure Ankunft." Aber sie hält sich nicht mit Höflichkeitsfloskeln auf, denn sie bemerkte gerade, daß Orléans auf der anderen Seite des Flusses liegt; wütend ist sie, weil die königlichen Befehlshaber eine Marschroute am südlichen Loire-Ufer gewählt hatten, um den Engländern aus dem Weg zu gehen. Da sie darauf brennt, nach all den zeitraubenden Vorbereitungen endlich in die Schlacht zu ziehen, fühlt sie sich vor den Kopf gestoßen und läßt sich nur schwer davon überzeugen, daß es in diesem Fall nicht aufs Kämpfen ankommt, sondern auf die zuverlässige Versorgung der zu befreienden Stadt.

Im Augenblick zweifelt Johann der Bastard selbst an dieser Entscheidung, denn seine Leute müssen den Nachschub nun auf Booten und Flößen gegen die Strömung über den Fluß bringen, doch der Wind bläst ihnen genau entgegen. Unschlüssig steht er am Ufer. In diesem Augenblick dreht der Wind und er kann Befehl geben, die Segel zu setzen. „Von diesem Augenblick an setzte ich große Hoffnung auf die Jungfrau, mehr noch als vorher",[19] erinnert er sich später.

Am Nachmittag des folgenden Tages reitet Johanna an der Seite des Kommandanten und mit einem Gefolge von Edelleuten in Orléans ein. Schon von weitem sind die Trommler und Trompeter zu hören. Dann taucht das in Blois für Johanna genähte weiße Banner auf: damit schreitet ein Fahnenträger dem Zug voran. Jubelnd drängen sich die Bewohner um Johannas Pferd, küssen ihr die Hände und den Saum ihres Umhangs, während die Kinder wie bei einer Prozession brennende Kerzen in der Hand halten. Das also ist die von Gelehrten geprüfte, von Gott gesandte Jungfrau, die gekommen ist, um Orléans zu befreien!

Vertraut man ihr das Kommando über einen Truppenteil an? Häufig wird Johanna zur Heerführerin verklärt, aber das Bild ist falsch: Die aristokratischen Offiziere glauben an ihre Sendung, aber sie würden keine Befehle eines Mannes aus dem Volk befolgen, und schon gar nicht die eines unerfahrenen Bauernmädchens. Johanna mag eine Visionärin sein, aber worauf es bei der Kriegsführung ankommt, kann sie nicht sehen, und wie sollte sie ohne militärische Kenntnisse eine Einheit führen? Nein, ihre Rolle wird eine andere sein.

Einer der beiden Herolde, die Johanna ins englische Hauptquartier schickt, um die Gegner zum Abzug aufzufordern, wird gefangengenommen. Sie tobt, denn sie versteht: Durch diesen Verstoß gegen das Kriegsrecht drücken die Engländer aus, daß sie die Jungfrau und deren Sendung mißachten.

Mit einem Pfeil läßt sie einen Fehdebrief ins feindliche Lager schießen.

Am 7. Mai frühmorgens erschallen in Orléans die Fanfaren. Die königlichen Truppen greifen die in einer Festung vor der Stadt verschanzten Feinde an. In den vorderen Reihen sehen die Soldaten Johanna: Hoch aufgerichtet sitzt sie im Sattel und reckt ihr Banner zum Himmel.

Ihre Landsleute rennen gegen das Bollwerk an, werden zurückgeworfen, sammeln sich, stürmen erneut nach vorn – aber die Engländer wehren die Attacken ab.

Um die Mittagszeit hilft Johanna mit, eine der zahlreichen Sturmleitern an die Festungsmauer zu lehnen; da trifft sie der Bolzen einer Armbrust an einer ungepanzerten Stelle unterhalb des Halses. Sie stürzt zu Boden. Kameraden tragen sie weg und legen sie im Schutz einiger Sträucher ins Gras. Laut schreit sie auf, als ihr ein Soldat das Geschoß herausreißt. Ein anderer reicht ihr ein Amulett, aber Johanna weist es zurück: „Ich würde lieber sterben, als das tun, was ich für Sünde halte und gegen Gottes Willen."[20] Sie wimmert vor Schmerz, während ihr zwei Männer den Harnisch öffnen, die Wunde mit Olivenöl beträufeln, Speck auflegen und sie verbinden.

Nach kurzer Zeit sehen die Angreifer das Mädchen mit dem weißen Banner erneut an ihrer Spitze.

Gegen Abend ermatten die Franzosen und glauben nicht mehr, die Engländer überwältigen zu können.

Wenn sie Orléans aufgeben, ist der Krieg entschieden!

Lange redet die Jungfrau auf den Kommandanten ein, bis sie ihn davon abbringt, den Rückzug zu befehlen. Johanna stürmt nach vorne. Ihr Fahnenträger steigt bereits in den Burggraben hinunter, da greift sie aus irgendeinem Grund nach ihrem Banner, packt es an einem Zipfel und rüttelt daran. Die Franzosen, die das für ein Zeichen halten, greifen noch einmal an – und nun gelingt es ihnen, die englische Abwehr zu überwinden und die Feinde aus der Festung zu vertreiben.

Ist das nicht paradox? Gerade weil sie die Realität nicht wahrhaben will, glaubt Johanna noch an den Sieg, wenn die erfahrenen Soldaten aufgrund ihrer wirklichkeitsnäheren Einschätzung der Lage bereits aufgeben – und am Ende behält die Bauerntochter recht.

„Sie tritt auf mit einem simplen Programm, das auf wenigen simplen Ideen beruht ... Und nur, weil sie die wirklichen Zusammenhänge nicht kennt oder schlicht ignoriert, gelingt es ihr, zu denken und zu wollen, was andere für unmöglich halten."[21] „Ihr Mut und ihre Überzeugung waren übermenschlich. Sie waren von der Art, die keinen Zweifel und kein Hindernis kennt. Ihr ungebrochener Glaube war das Geheimnis ihrer Stärke. ... Ihre Grundehrlichkeit war es, was sie befähigte, verzagte Männer mitzureißen und widerstrebende Fürsten ihrem Willen zu beugen."[22]

Am nächsten Morgen verlassen die Engländer auch die anderen Stellungen: Für einige Zeit stehen die feindlichen Heere einander drohend gegenüber. Ein Chronist schildert diesen Sonntag morgen: „... räumten die Engländer ihre Schanzen, hoben ihre Belagerung auf und zogen in die Schlacht. ... Darum kamen die Jungfrau und mehrere andere tapfere Kriegsleute und Bürger mit großem Aufgebot aus Orléans heraus und stellten sich vor ihnen in Schlachtordnung auf, eine ganze Stunde lang und einander sehr nahe, doch ohne sich zu berühren."[23] Johanna schärft ihren Leuten ein, sich an das sonntägliche Kampfverbot zu halten, im Fall eines englischen Angriffs jedoch unverzüglich zurückzuschlagen.

Nach einiger Zeit zieht die englische Streitmacht ab.

Orléans ist frei!

Den Erfolg verdanken die Franzosen ihren gut geführten Truppen – und Johanna, weil sie durch ihre unerschütterliche Siegeszuversicht die Soldaten mitriß. Die wundergläubigen Zeitzeugen sehen in der gelungenen Befreiung von Orléans das erhoffte Zeichen: Offensichtlich wurde die Jungfrau von Gott gesandt, um den Franzosen zu helfen; gewiß wird sie auch den zweiten Teil ihrer Mission erfüllen und Karl VII. zur Krönung nach Reims führen. In dieser Zuversicht scharen sich die Franzosen um ihren König, und es entsteht ein französisches Nationalgefühl: „Der alte Glaube und der neue Patriotismus"[24] verbinden sich zu einer unwiderstehlichen Kraft. Die Jungfrau von Orléans, die ein zu Boden getretenes Frankreich seelisch wieder aufrichtet,[25] wird zum „Symbol der Freiheit und zur Integrationsfigur des nationalen Befreiungskampfes."[26]

Niemand beeinflußt 1429 den Verlauf der Geschichte mehr als sie; ihr Auftreten stellt eines der bedeutendsten Ereignisse des Hundertjährigen Krieges dar, vielleicht sogar „eines der merkwürdigsten bzw. wunderbarsten Ereignisse in der Geschichte der Menschheit".[27]

Aber nicht aus Dankbarkeit, sondern wegen der Propagandawirkung beeilt sich die königliche Kanzlei, die Jungfrau von Orléans zur Heldin einer von Gott gewünschten Rettung zu stilisieren und eine Legende zu begründen.[28]

Die Krönung in Reims

Die Jungfrau drängt nun darauf, mit dem Dauphin geradewegs nach Reims zu ziehen: „Erlauchter Dauphin, haltet nicht so langen und ausgedehnten Rat! Kommt so bald wie möglich nach Reims, um Eure würdige Krone zu empfangen!"[29]

Aber der König will zuerst die englischen Garnisonen aus der Umgebung des Loire-Übergangs bei Orléans vertreiben, um zu verhindern, daß die Feinde das Loch in der Front schließen. Denn was nützte ihm die Krönung, wenn er anschließend nicht zurückkehren könnte und obendrein vom Nachschub abgeschnitten wäre?

Der siegreiche Loire-Feldzug festigt das Ansehen der Jungfrau: Wenn sie den Männern Mut macht, können ihnen die Gegner offenbar nicht widerstehen. „Die Feinde fliehen, sobald sie Johanna von Orléans erblicken!" Das gehört zwar in den Bereich der Legende, aber die Vorstellung von ihren übernatürlichen Kräften wirkt wie ein Stabmagnet: Während sich zahlreiche englische Soldaten vor einem Einsatz auf dem Kontinent drücken, weil sie das Mädchen wie eine Hexe fürchten, verbreitet es auf der anderen Seite Hoffnung und zieht immer neue Freiwillige an, die sich in die königliche Armee drängen und sie rasch auf zwölftausend Mann anwachsen lassen.

Die militärischen Aussichten der Franzosen sind selten günstiger: die eigenen Truppen hoch motiviert, das Volk begeistert, die gegnerischen Streitkräfte geschlagen und hoffnungslos. Das königliche Heer könnte in vier Tagen nach Paris marschieren, um die Feinde aus der Hauptstadt zu vertreiben, aber Karl VII. nutzt weder den eigenen Schwung noch die Verwirrung der Feinde, sondern verhandelt mit Herzog Philipp dem Guten von Burgund, weil er glaubt, zuerst die feindliche Allianz spalten und die Burgunder auf seine Seite ziehen zu müssen.

Allerdings zieht er mit seinem Heer tief in das besetzte Gebiet, zur traditionsreichen Krönungsstadt Reims[30]. Am 16. Juli – einen Monat nach dem Loire-Feldzug – überbringt ihm eine Abordnung die Schlüssel der Stadt, und die englisch-burgundische Garnison macht sich davon. Begleitet von Würdenträgern und Truppenführern reiten Karl VII. und Johanna noch am gleichen Tag durch die von neugierigen Bürgern gesäumten Straßen. Die Nacht verbringt Karl in der gotischen Kathedrale. Am anderen Morgen werden die Tore geöffnet; die Orgel ertönt. Prälaten und Herzöge, der Magistrat und die Patrizier der Stadt nehmen ihre Plätze in der nach Weihrauch duftenden Kirche ein, während sich das Volk auf dem Platz davor drängt, um nichts von der fünf Stunden dauernden Zeremonie zu versäumen.

Die Bischöfe tragen ihre goldverzierten Prunkornate, Karl VII. ist zunächst nur mit einem langen weißen Hemd bekleidet. Mit dem Gesicht nach unten liegt er auf dem Boden vor dem Altar, bis ihn der Erzbischof auffordert zu knien und ihn an Stirn, Brust, Schultern und Armgelenken salbt. Nachdem er den Krönungseid gesprochen hat, helfen ihm die Bischöfe in einen karminroten Mantel. Der leuchtend blaue Umhang, den sie ihm um die Schultern legen, ist mit silbernen Bourbonen-Lilien bestickt. Als der Erzbischof dem König die Krone aufsetzt, kann sich die Jungfrau, die mit ihrem Banner neben dem Altar steht, nicht mehr zurückhalten: Sie kniet schluchzend vor Karl VII. nieder und umfaßt seine Beine.

Auf Umwegen nach Paris

Die burgundischen Unterhändler verständigen sich mit ihren französischen Verhandlungspartnern auf einen vorerst zweiwöchigen Waffenstillstand. Karl VII. übersieht, daß er sich damit verpflichtet, zwei Wochen lang abzuwarten, während die Engländer ebenso wie die Burgunder die gewonnene Zeit eifrig nutzen, um ihre Stellungen zu verstärken. Obwohl Johanna das burgundische Doppelspiel zunächst ebensowenig wie der König durchschaut, hält sie nichts von dem Waffenstillstand und drängt statt dessen zum Aufbruch, um Paris gewaltsam zu befreien. Sie neigt mehr zum Kämpfen als zum Verhandeln. Anders als die bedenkenlose Draufgängerin zaudert der König: Aufgrund seiner Bildung und der ihm zugetragenen Nachrichten verfügt er über eine komplexere Vorstellung von der Lage und muß mehr Argumente gegeneinander abwägen, bevor er eine Entscheidung treffen kann. Es fehlt ihm aber auch an Zuversicht und Selbstvertrauen.

Während sich das königliche Heer in Compiègne endlich auf den Angriff vorbereitet, erhält Johanna folgenden Brief des Grafen von Armagnac: „Hochverehrte Herrin, ich wende mich in aller Bescheidenheit an Euch und bitte Euch um Gottes willen angesichts der gegenwärtigen Spaltung der heiligen allgemeinen Kirche in Sachen der Päpste[31] um Rat: Denn es gibt drei, die einander das Papsttum streitig machen: Der eine, der sich Martin V. nennt, lebt in Rom, und ihm gehorchen alle christlichen Könige; der zweite, der sich Papst Clemens VII. nennt, lebt in Peñiscola im Königreich Valencia. Von dem dritten, der sich Papst Benedikt XIV. nennt, weiß niemand, wo er sich aufhält ... Ich bitte Euch nun inständig, Unseren Herrn Jesum Christum anzuflehen, daß Er uns durch Euch zu wissen tue, welcher der drei genannten Päpste der wahre sei und welchem man von nun an gehorchen solle: Martin, oder Clemens, oder Benedikt, und welchem wir glauben sollen, im geheimen oder offen, denn wir sind unbedingt bereit, nach dem Willen und Gefallen Unseres Herrn Christus zu handeln."

Johanna antwortet: „... Darüber kann ich Euch im Augenblick nicht die Wahrheit sagen, ehe ich nicht in Paris oder anderswo in Ruhe bin, denn im Augenblick beschäftigt mich die Kriegführung zu sehr. Aber sobald Ihr wißt, daß ich in Paris bin, sendet mir einen Boten, und ich lasse Euch ehrlich und nach bestem Vermögen wissen, wem Ihr glauben sollt, so wie ich es durch den Rat meines allerhöchsten Herrn, des Königs der ganzen Welt, erfahre, und was Ihr zu tun habt."[32]

Wegen des bevorstehenden Kampfes kümmert sich die Jungfrau wieder verstärkt um das Seelenheil der Soldaten, aber als sie eine Lagerdirne verjagt und dabei mit dem flach gehaltenen Schwert zuschlägt, bricht die Klinge. Ein böses Omen?

Am 8. September halten Johanna und die Truppenführer das Warten nicht mehr aus. Die Jungfrau spricht mit ihrem Beichtvater:[33]

„Ich will die Gräben von Paris überschreiten."

„Heute?"

„Ich weiß: am Tag von Mariae Geburt. – Gott wird mir verzeihen."

„Prüfe dich wohl, Johanna, an einem Feiertag zu kämpfen, ist eine schwere Sünde. Eine noch schwerere ist es, gegen sein Gewissen zu handeln."

„Ich habe mich entschieden."

„Du bist ganz bleich."

„Ich habe heute morgen gebetet, mit aller Kraft. Meine Stimmen waren da. Sie haben mir nicht verboten, zu kämpfen."

„Haben sie dir geraten, zu kämpfen?"

Johanna schüttelt den Kopf: „Sie haben mir viele Dinge gesagt, viele gute und viele freundliche."

„Warum weinst du?"

„Nun, weil ich Komplimente eigentlich nicht wollte. Was ich wollte, war ein Befehl, eine Anweisung. Doch nichts, nichts; weder dafür noch dagegen. Vorher war es klar, es war einfach: Orléans, danach Reims. Und was ist jetzt? Was soll ich machen?"

„Du solltest bist morgen warten. Ein Wort von dir, und sie lassen die Vorbereitungen ruhen."

„Nein, ich will Paris. Es ist das Herz des Königreichs ..."

„Was willst du von mir?"

„Eure Absolution; ich will Euren Segen."

„Gott sei mir dir." Er macht das Kreuzzeichen. „Ego te absolvo. Amen."

„Amen." Und nach einer Pause murmelt sie: „So wird es gehen."

Wieder ist Johanna mit ihrem Banner in den vorderen Reihen zu sehen. Vor einem tiefen Festungsgraben, hinter dem die mächtige Stadtmauer aufragt, kommen sie zum Stehen. Johanna verlangt von den Männern, daß sie Karren und Reisig ins Wasser werfen und Bretter darüber legen, damit sie auf die andere Seite gelangen können. Inmitten des Lärms prüft sie mit einer Lanze die Wassertiefe. In diesem Augenblick durchschlägt ein Armbrustbolzen ihre Beinschiene. Sie wird fortgetragen, verbunden und kann nicht mehr aufstehen. „Und als sie getroffen war, verlangte sie nur noch eindringlicher, alle sollten sich über die Mauern hermachen und die Stellung nehmen."[34] Von ihrem Platz aus kann sie zwar den Franzosen nicht länger Mut machen, aber sie verfolgt deren vergebliches Anrennen gegen die Pariser Stadtmauern laut schimpfend – und gegen Abend protestiert sie gegen den vom König befohlenen Rückzug.

Die Gefangennahme

Einige Wochen nach der Niederlage begleitet Johanna eine kleine Armee, die gegen einen Abenteurer auszieht, der sich vom burgundischen Herzog dafür bezahlen läßt, daß er mit seiner Bande gegen die Franzosen kämpft.

Was für ein Abstieg!

Jean d'Aulon, der bei Johanna geblieben ist, wird am 28. Mai 1456 in Lyon schildern, was vor einer Festung des Gegners geschieht, als die königstreuen Soldaten nach einem gescheiterten Ansturm abziehen und Johanna zurückbleibt: „Ich fürchtete Schlimmes, bestieg ein Pferd, hielt sogleich auf sie zu und fragte sie, was sie da so allein täte und warum sie sich nicht wie die anderen zurückziehe. Und sie? Sie nahm ihren Helm vom Kopf und sagte mir: ‚Ich bin nicht allein. Ich habe in meiner Gefolgschaft noch fünfzigtausend Mann. Und ich werde von hier nicht weichen, bis die Stadt unser ist!' Und ich versichere, daß sie in diesem Augenblick nicht mehr als vier oder fünf Männer bei sich hatte."[35] Wie bei der Befreiung von Orléans lassen sich die Soldaten durch die unbeirrbare Zuversicht der Jungfrau auf einen neuen Angriff ein, der ihnen zum Sieg verhilft.

Trotzdem scheitert der Feldzug gegen die burgundischen Söldner.

Als sich Herzog Philipp der Gute sicher genug fühlt, versucht er nicht länger, seine wahren Absichten zu verbergen: Er zieht im Frühjahr 1430 Truppen zusammen und bereitet sich auf neue Schlachten vor. Karl VII. sieht ein, daß er sich von dem Burgunder täuschen ließ. Und während dieser einen klaren Plan verfolgt und mit englischer Unterstützung rechnen kann, ist der französische König auf die kommende Konfrontation nicht vorbereitet.

Im Mai 1430 – ein Jahr nach der Befreiung von Orléans – reitet Johanna an der Spitze von Freischärlern nach Compiègne, denn Philipp der Gute zieht eine starke Streitmacht um die nordfranzösische Stadt zusammen. Aber Johanna wagt einen Ausfall: Sie führt fünfhundert Männer zu einem der feindlichen Truppenlager, und weil man sich dort in Sicherheit wähnt, gelingt die Überrumpelung.

Doch zufällig reitet zur gleichen Zeit der burgundische Befehlshaber Johann von Luxemburg mit einigen Offizieren zu dem überfallenen Stützpunkt und beobachtet von einem nahegelegenen Hügel aus, was sich dort abspielt. Sofort galoppieren Reiter zurück, holen Verstärkung. Auf diese Weise gelingt es den Burgundern, die Angreifer nach Compiègne zurückzudrängen.

Der Stadtkommandant ließ während des Ausfalls die über die Oise führende Brücke besetzen, um den Freischärlern den Rückzug zu sichern, aber als die Burgunder seine Männer in die Flucht schlagen, befiehlt er, das Stadttor zu verriegeln.[36]

Ein Chronist berichtet über das Geschehen vor dem verschlossenen Tor: „Und die Jungfrau, die ihre weibliche Natur

28

verleugnete, bekam die ganze Last zu spüren und bemühte sich sehr, ihre Truppe zu retten, indem sie als Kommandant und als die Tapferste der Herde hinter ihnen und die letzte blieb ... Einen [burgundischen] Bogenschützen, einen unbeugsamen und recht mürrischen Mann, verdroß es sehr, daß eine Frau, von der man immerfort gehört hatte, so viele tapfere Männer zurückschlagen sollte, er packte sie bei ihrem Umhang aus Goldstoff und zog sie vom Pferd, so daß sie flach auf den Boden fiel."[37]

Im Kerker

Nach einigen Tagen läßt Johann von Luxemburg seine an Händen und Füßen gefesselte Gefangene auf dem Rücken eines Pferdes in eine Festung bringen. Um aus ihrem Kerker zu entweichen, reißt die Achtzehnjährige Bretter aus dem Fußboden; den ahnungslosen Turmwächter sperrt sie ein, aber von der Torwache wird sie entdeckt und aufgegriffen. In einer anderen Burg springt sie von einem Turm, zwanzig Meter tief. Wollte sie fliehen oder sich das Leben nehmen? Jedenfalls erwacht sie nach kurzer Zeit aus ihrer Bewußtlosigkeit und stellt fest, daß sie sich nur leicht verletzte.

Während der französische König weder ein Lösegeld noch einen Gefangenenaustausch anbietet, um die im Jahr zuvor gefeierte und für politisch-militärische Zwecke ausgenutzte Jungfrau von Orléans zu retten, hängen sich die Engländer wie Kletten an sie und setzen alles in Bewegung, um sie zu vernichten. Übersieht Karl VII., daß er damit selbst in Mißkredit gebracht werden soll? Die Engländer wollen nicht nur Johannas lähmende Wirkung auf ihre Truppen beseitigen, sondern zugleich beweisen, daß Karl VII. seine Krönung einer Ketzerin verdankt.

Monatelang verhandelt der französische Bischof Pierre Cauchon im Auftrag des Herzogs von Bedford mit den Burgundern über die Herausgabe der Gefangenen. Die Universität von Paris drängt: „Wir sehen mit äußerstem Erstaunen, daß sich die Übergabe dieser gemeinhin die Jungfrau genannten

Frau zum Schaden des Glaubens und der kirchlichen Recht-sprechung so lange verzögert."[38]

Die Engländer treiben in der Normandie eine Sondersteuer ein, um Ende 1430 ein Vermögen für die Auslieferung Johannas bezahlen zu können.

Pierre Cauchon soll auch das kirchliche Gerichtsverfahren leiten. Der Herzog von Bedford wählt dafür einen Ort, an dem er weder einen Aufstand der Bevölkerung noch einen Angriff des französischen Königs fürchtet: Rouen, die bedeutende Hafenstadt an der Seine, die sich 1419 nach monatelanger Belagerung ergab.

Die Vertreter der Kirche wollen mit dem Prozeß zwar beweisen, daß Johanna von Orléans keine übernatürlichen Kräfte zur Verfügung stehen, aber um ganz sicherzugehen, daß sie nicht durch einen Zauber entflieht, sperren sie die Jungfrau nicht in ein Kloster, sondern in einen der Türme des Stadt-schlosses und lassen einen engen Eisenkäfig für sie schmieden. Der wird zwar nicht benutzt; aber man legt ihr Fußeisen an und verbindet diese mit einer kurzen Kette, um ihr das Gehen zu erschweren. Nachts wird sie damit an einen mächtigen Holzklotz gefesselt.

Acht englische Kriegsknechte bewachen sie.

Während die französischen Soldaten ihr Idol niemals sexuell belästigten, machen sich die englischen Bewacher einen Spaß daraus, die wehrlose Gefangene durch obszöne Gesten zu er-schrecken und ihr eine Vergewaltigung zumindest anzudrohen.

Der Prozeß

Am 9. Januar 1431 eröffnet Pierre Cauchon das Verfahren.

Ein Notar ermittelt in Johannas Heimat gegen sie, befragt mehr als ein Dutzend Zeugen, erfährt jedoch nichts Belasten-des. (Cauchon wird deshalb so wütend, daß er sich weigert, ihm die Reisekosten zu erstatten.)

Seit dem Tag, an dem sie ihr Heimatdorf verließ, hört Johanna auf ihre Stimmen, auf niemand sonst, und es gibt keinen Menschen, dem sie sich anvertraut. Einen Verteidiger lehnt sie ab. Allein tritt sie den bis zu sechzig Gelehrten und Würdenträgern gegenüber, spitzfindigen Doktoren der Theologie, die im Gegensatz zu dem Bauernmädchen Erfahrung mit solchen Gerichtsverfahren haben. „Nie trat ihre Glaubensgewißheit, ihre Lauterkeit, ihre Standhaftigkeit, ihre geistige Kraft und Wachheit heller zutage, und nie war sie menschlicher, rührender und größer in ihrer Menschlichkeit."[39]

Gelegentlich ermahnt Johanna die durcheinander auf sie einredenden Herren, ihre Fragen der Reihe nach zu stellen. Unerschrocken sagt sie aus, und kaum jemals verliert sie ihre Standfestigkeit. Selten läßt sie sich von einer der Autoritätspersonen einschüchtern; nie gibt sie auf. Mitunter geht sie sogar zum Angriff über, etwa wenn sie Pierre Cauchon droht: „Du sagst, du bist mein Richter. Sei mit dem, was du tust, vorsichtig, denn ich bin in Wahrheit von Gott gesandt, und du begibst dich in große Gefahr."[40]

Erstaunlich ist es, wie sie sich in der für sie ungewohnten verbalen Auseinandersetzung zurechtfindet; wach und instinktiv umgeht sie viele der ausgelegten Fallen, zum Beispiel als sie gefragt wird: „Johanna, seid Ihr gewiß, im Stande der Gnade zu sein?" (Das könne niemand wissen, lehrt die Kirche. Also: Behauptet Johanna, im Zustand der Gnade zu sein, wird ihr das als ketzerische Anmaßung ausgelegt; sagt sie das Gegenteil, gibt sie ihre Schuld zu.) Sie erwidert auf die Fangfrage: „Wenn ich es nicht bin, möge mich Gott dahinbringen, wenn ich es bin, möge mich Gott darin erhalten!"[41]

Bisweilen reagiert sie mit Spott und Ironie, obwohl sie weiß, daß es um Leben und Tod geht: Ob die heilige Margareta englisch geredet habe? „Warum sollte sie englisch sprechen, da sie nicht auf der Seite der Engländer ist?"[42]

In der Präambel der Anklageschrift wird das Gericht aufgefordert, Johanna zu verurteilen, und zwar „als Hexe und Zauberin, Wahrsagerin und falsche Prophetin, die böse Geister beschwört und mit ihnen im Bunde ist, als abergläubisch, die Schwarze Kunst betreibend, in Sachen unseres katholischen Glaubens falsch denkend, schismatisch, am Artikel ‚Unam Sanctam'[43] und vielen anderen Glaubensartikeln zweifelnd, als Lästerin Gottes und Seiner Heiligen, ärgerniserregend, aufsässig, den Frieden störend und ihn verhindernd, als Kriegshetzerin, die grausam nach Menschenblut dürstet und zu seinem Vergießen anspornt, die Ehrbarkeit und Schicklichkeit ihres Geschlechts verletzend und unehrerbietig und unpassend Kleid und Beruf der Krieger annehmend, weswegen sie vor Gott und den Menschen verabscheuungswürdig ist, als Verächterin göttlicher und natürlicher Ordnung, wie der kirchlichen Disziplin, als Verführerin von Volk und Fürsten zur Schmähung Gottes, die es zuläßt, daß man sie verehrt und anbetet und ihre Hände und Gewänder zum Kusse darbietet, die sich göttliche Verehrung und göttlichen Kult anmaßt ..."[44]

Die in siebzig Abschnitte unterteilte Anklageschrift wird ihr Ende März im Gerichtssaal vorgelesen, und zu jedem einzelnen Punkt muß sie Stellung nehmen.

Dann fassen die Gelehrten das Ergebnis des Verfahrens zusammen. Die überzogenen Formulierungen können nicht darüber hinwegtäuschen, daß das Gericht sie keiner schweren Schuld überführt hat. Sieht Pierre Cauchon überhaupt noch eine Möglichkeit, sie als Ketzerin zu verurteilen, wie es die Engländer von ihm erwarten?

Johanna erkrankt Mitte April, fiebert und übergibt sich. Der Kommandant der Burg beschwört die Ärzte, sie zu retten: „Der König hat sie teuer bezahlt; er will sie keinesfalls eines natürlichen Todes sterben lassen."[45] Die Kranke vermutet, ein Karpfen, den ihr Pierre Cauchon schickte, sei verdorben gewesen. Da brüllt sie einer der Ankläger an: „Du Lästermaul! Du Hure! Du hast Heringe und andere salzige Dinge gegessen, die dir nicht bekamen."[46]

Wollte Cauchon sie vergiften? Eine Tote kann man nicht publikumswirksam wegen Ketzerei verurteilen und hinrichten; sie wird statt dessen zur Märtyrerin. Wenn der Richter jedoch befürchtet, einen Freispruch nur auf diese Weise verhindern zu können, würde Johannas Ermordung ihm und den Engländern nützen.

Drei Wochen später führen die Theologen die Gefangene vor den Henker und zeigen ihr die bereitliegenden Folterwerkzeuge: „Johanna, seht, alle Anwesenden sind bereit, auf Antrag des Vorsitzenden Euch der Folter zu übergeben, um Euch auf den Weg und zur Erkenntnis der Wahrheit zurückzuführen, und daß Ihr dadurch das Heil der Seele und des Leibes erlangt, das durch Eure lügnerischen Erfindungen ernstlich gefährdet ist."[47] Aber auch durch diese Inszenierung läßt sie sich nicht entmutigen.

Noch glaubt sie fest daran, daß die Stimmen sie retten werden.

Das Urteil

Am 24. Mai drängt sich das Volk frühmorgens vor dem Friedhof neben der spätgotischen Abteikirche Saint-Quen, einem der wenigen Plätze in Rouen, die für die geplante Veranstaltung groß genug sind. Man hat zwei Podien gezimmert, damit möglichst viele Menschen das Spektakel sehen können: Während die Angeklagte zu einem der Podeste geführt wird, nehmen die kirchlichen Würdenträger auf dem anderen Platz.

Wieder beweist Johanna von Orléans Mut und Standfestigkeit: Obwohl Karl VII. sie im Stich läßt, versäumt sie es nicht, dem Prediger, der ihn als Ketzer beschimpft, ins Wort zu fallen und ihm zu widersprechen: „Ich schwöre bei meinem Leben, er ist der edelste Christ unter allen Christen, der den Glauben und die Kirche am meisten liebt und durchaus nicht so ist, wie Ihr sagt."[48]

Schließlich beginnt Pierre Cauchon, das Todesurteil zu verlesen.

Die Menge kreischt; aufgebrachte Zuschauer werfen mit Steinen nach Johanna, und sie erblickt den Karren, auf dem sie zur Richtstätte gefahren werden soll.

Da fällt sie auf die Knie, stammelt, daß sie ihrem Irrglauben abschwören will, klagt, sie sei von den Stimmen getäuscht worden. „Ich will alles befolgen, was die Richter der Kirche sagen und verfügen. Ich will ihrem Befehl und Willen gehorchen. Da die Geistlichen sagen, daß meine Erscheinungen und Offenbarungen weder aufrechtzuerhalten noch zu glauben sind, so will ich sie nicht mehr aufrechterhalten. Ich überlasse mich gänzlich dem Urteil der Richter und unserer Heiligen Mutter, der Kirche."[49]

Pierre Cauchon blickt auf und läßt die Hand mit dem Schriftstück sinken. Weil das Publikum schreiend protestiert, verstehen nur die Umstehenden, was er sagt: „Wir haben Sorge zu tragen für das Heil der Seele und des Leibes auch dieser Frau und dürfen sie nach ihrem Widerruf nicht mehr zum Tod verurteilen." Er entfaltet ein für diesen Fall vorbereitetes zweites Papier und verurteilt sie „zu immerwährendem Gefängnis beim Brot der Schmerzen und dem Wasser der Trübsal".[50]

„Der König hat sein Geld schön an Euch vergeudet!" schreit einer der Kirchenmänner. „Verräter!"

Im Tumult endet die Veranstaltung.

Rückfall?

Johanna hofft inständig, nun endlich in ein Kloster gebracht zu werden. Aber die Soldaten erhalten den Befehl: „Führt sie dahin zurück, wo ihr sie hergebracht habt."

Gefängnis statt Todesstrafe: dafür zahlten die Engländer nicht das viele Geld! Aber an dem Urteil läßt sich nicht rütteln, die Hinrichtung ist nun ausgeschlossen – es sei denn, der Verurteilten kann ein Rückfall nachgewiesen werden. Verfolgt Pierre Cauchon einen Plan?

Johanna legt die Männersachen ab und zieht erstmals seit ihrem Aufbruch in Vaucouleurs vor mehr als zwei Jahren wieder ein Kleid an, eines, das die Herzogin von Bedford bereits vor Beginn des Prozesses für sie schneidern ließ. (Übrigens ohrfeigte Johanna den Schneider, weil dieser bei der Anprobe versuchte, ihre Brust zu betasten.)

Drei Tage später wird Pierre Cauchon berichtet, daß sie sich erneut wie ein Mann kleidet.

Warum tut sie das? Ein Gerichtsdiener sagt später aus, man habe Johanna die Frauenkleider weggenommen, aber auch wenn wir bezweifeln, daß sie auf diese Weise gezwungen wurde, rückfällig zu werden, drängt sich eine mögliche Erklärung auf: Wir brauchen uns nur vorzustellen, wie das mittlerweile neunzehnjährige Mädchen in Röcken und ohne Unterwäsche wehrlos angekettet vor den Männern liegt, die Tag und Nacht bei ihr wachen.[51] Kann es nicht sein, daß Pierre Cauchon mit dieser Entwicklung rechnete, als er Johannas Widerruf annahm?

Als er sie verhört, beteuert Johanna, sie trage die Männerkleidung nur, um ihre Keuschheit schützen zu können: „Ich habe sie freiwillig angezogen. Ich habe sie angezogen, weil es dienlicher und ziemlicher ist, wie ein Mann gekleidet zu sein denn wie eine Frau, da ich ja mit Männern zusammen bin. ... Doch wenn man mich zur Messe gehen läßt, mir die Fesseln abnimmt und mich in ein anständiges Gefängnis bringt und eine Frau bei mir läßt, dann will ich mich fügen und tun, was die Kirche mich heißt."[52] Sie wolle lieber sterben als in dem von Männern bewachten Kerker bleiben. Erklärt sie deshalb, daß sie nicht aus Überzeugung widerrufen habe, sondern aus Angst vor dem Feuer? Der Protokollführer vermerkt am Rand: „Responsio mortifera. Tödliche Antwort".[53]

Eine von Pierre Cauchon einberufene Versammlung von Theologen und Prälaten befindet, daß die Angeklagte wegen des Rückfalls ihr Leben verwirkt hat.

Der Feuertod

Frühmorgens am 30. Mai 1431 erfährt Johanna von zwei Dominikanern, daß man sie auf dem Scheiterhaufen verbrennen wird.

Entsetzen packt die Neunzehnjährige: „O Gott, verfährt man so schrecklich und grausam mit mir! Muß denn mein reiner Leib, der nie geschändet, nie entstellt war, heute verbrannt werden, in Asche verwandelt? O, ich wäre lieber siebenmal enthauptet worden als so verbrannt! Wehe! Wäre ich in einem kirchlichen Gefängnis gewesen und von Männern der Kirche bewacht und nicht von meinen Feinden, es wäre mir nicht so furchtbar ergangen!"[54]

Barfüßig, die Hände vor dem Gesicht und mit einem ungefärbten, grob gesäumten Nesselhemd bekleidet, wird Johanna um neun Uhr auf einem Karren zum Alten Markt gefahren. Eine Papiermütze hat man ihr auf den Kopf gesetzt. Darauf steht in großen Buchstaben: „Ketzerin, Abtrünnige, Götzendienerin". Eine Eskorte von achtzig Soldaten bahnt ihr den Weg durch die johlenden Gaffer.

Auf dem Marktplatz drängen sich Tausende von Schaulustigen um die Holzpodeste, die für die Geistlichkeit, den Vogt und Johanna errichtet wurden.

Ein Magister der Sorbonne predigt und läßt sich dabei von einem Einfall zum anderen forttragen. Endlich hört Johanna, wie Pierre Cauchon das neue Urteil verkündet: „Dieses vom Satan mit Ketzerei angesteckte Glied muß aus dem Leib der Kirche weggeschnitten werden, bevor andere Glieder von dem Übel angesteckt werden." Er überantwortet Johanna dem Vogt. Während die Todgeweihte kniend die gefalteten Hände zum Himmel streckt und stammelnd betet, verlassen die kirchlichen Würdenträger den Platz – um ihre Hände in Unschuld zu waschen.

Weil es bereits auf Mittag zugeht, murrt die erregte Menge, bis zwei Soldaten Johanna vor den Vogt schleppen, der mit einer unwirschen Handbewegung und den Worten „Fort mit ihr!" die sofortige Hinrichtung anordnet – ohne einen eigenen Urteilsspruch zu fällen, wie es das formale Recht erfordern würde.

Es ist üblich, die Opfer im letzten Augenblick zu erdrosseln oder auf dem Scheiterhaufen mit Pech getränktes Stroh aufzuschichten, damit sie in den lodernden Flammen rasch ersticken, bevor das Holz richtig zu brennen beginnt. Aber in diesem Fall kennt der Henker keine Gnade.

„Die Schreie des im prasselnden Feuer stehenden Mädchens, die über den alten Marktplatz gellten und das Stimmengewirr der Menge übertönten, gingen allen Anwesenden und auch einigen Engländern sehr zu Herzen."[55]

Als Johanna verstummt und ihr der Kopf vornübersinkt, scharrt der Henker das Feuer mit einem Schürhaken von ihrem Körper weg, damit die Umstehenden sich davon überzeugen können, daß wirklich die Jungfrau von Orléans und nicht eine andere Frau verbrannt wird.

Dann facht er den Brand noch einmal an.

„Tatsächlich sind Anklänge ihrer Lebensgeschichte an die

Jesu Christi – einfache Geburt, Berufung, Sendungsbewußtsein, Erlösungsauftrag, Verrat und früher, schmählicher Tod nach einem politischen Prozeß – nicht zu übersehen."[56]

Rehabilitation

In den folgenden Jahren gelingt es den Franzosen, an die militärischen Siege anzuknüpfen, die sie mit Hilfe Johannas errangen: 1436 gewinnen sie Paris zurück; dreizehn Jahre später ist auch Rouen wieder in französischer Hand.

Als König Karl VII. feierlich in Rouen einreitet, weiß er, daß er sein wichtigstes Ziel – die Vertreibung der Engländer – in absehbarer Zeit erreichen wird.[57]

In dieser Situation erinnert er sich daran, daß mit der Verurteilung Johannas auch seine Krönung in Mißkredit gebracht wurde. Jetzt ist der Zeitpunkt gekommen, den Vorwurf zu entkräften, er habe sich von einer Ketzerin helfen lassen.

Als Repräsentant der weltlichen Macht kann er zwar das Urteil eines kirchlichen Gerichts nicht widerrufen, aber er beauftragt ein Mitglied des Kronrats, den Prozeß von Rouen zu überprüfen und Zeugen zu befragen. Aufgrund des zusammengetragenen Materials führt die Kirche 1452 – einundzwanzig Jahre nach Johannas Hinrichtung – eine offizielle Untersuchung durch, aber es dauert noch einmal drei Jahre, bis der Papst drei französische Bischöfe beauftragt, über das Gerichtsverfahren zu urteilen.

Am 7. Juli 1456 heben die Richter das Urteil von 1431 auf und zerreißen in einem symbolischen Akt eine Abschrift des fünfundzwanzig Jahre alten Protokolls.

Am 18. April 1909 spricht Papst Pius X. Johanna von Orléans selig und am 16. Mai 1920 verkündet Papst Benedikt XV. ihre Heiligsprechung.

Maria Ward

Ein Leben lang ringt die Nonne
mit den Männern der Kirche
um die Verwirklichung ihrer Vision

Gespräch mit einem Jesuitenpater

„In ein Kloster möchtest du aufgenommen werden."

„Ja, das wünsche ich mit der Glut meines Herzens. Ich habe mich noch gar nicht umgezogen. Nach dem Ritt kam ich gleich hierher, um Euch das Empfehlungsschreiben meines Beichtvaters zu übergeben."

„Wie ich höre, bist du einundzwanzig Jahre alt. Und ich sehe, daß Gott dir einen gesunden Leib geschenkt hat. Es ist also nicht zu spät: Gewiß würdest du noch einen Mann finden, der dich heiratet und eine Familie ..."

„Ehrwürdiger Vater! Hier in Flandern schützen die spanischen Statthalter die Katholiken, aber in meiner Heimat müssen sich diese verbergen und jederzeit damit rechnen, eingesperrt, gefoltert, vielleicht sogar gehenkt zu werden. Glaubt Ihr, das sei ein Land für Kinder? Wer kümmert sich um die unschuldigen Knaben und Mädchen, deren Väter, Mütter, Brüder, Schwestern man verhaftet, und was soll aus den Unglücklichen werden, wenn sie erwachsen sind? Nein, um nichts in der Welt möchte ich heiraten! Ich will mein Leben Jesus weihen; ich sehne mich danach, Seine Braut zu werden."

„Und dein Vater?"

„Als man den vielen Sprengstoff unter dem Parlament in London entdeckte, wurde auch mein Vater verhört – meine Mutter, meine Geschwister und ich haben wochenlang um ihn gebangt –, aber er denkt nicht daran, England zu verlassen, und er hätte es lieber gesehen, wenn ich nicht fortgegangen wäre."

Maria iſt ſo 1621 von Trier nacher Rom in pilgramß kleider Zu fueß gereiſt

Maria Ward (1585–1645) auf ihrer Pilgerreise nach Rom

Augsburg, Institut der Englischen Fräulein

„Höre auf deines Vaters Warnung ..."

„Pater peccavi.[1] Aber ich konnte nicht anders, und Vater hat mich schließlich in Frieden ziehen lassen. Eine Freundin half mir am Donnerstag nach Pfingsten, auf eine Fähre zu kommen; in Calais kaufte ich ein Pferd, und damit bin ich hierher geritten, um in einer der Burgen Christi Zuflucht zu finden."

„Die Armen Klarissinnen warten bereits auf dich."

„Aber ich habe mich noch gar nicht für einen Orden entschieden."

„Gott hat für dich gewählt."

„Wie das?"

„Wie sonst könnten wir erklären, daß die Klarissinnen mit Ungeduld auf dich warten? Sie kennen dich überhaupt nicht. Es kann nur der Wille Gottes sein!"

„Gern füge ich mich."

„Der Geist bei den Armen Klarissinnen ist vortrefflich. Sie leben von Almosen. Weißt du, daß es Chor- und Laienschwestern gibt? Du mußt also eine wohlbedachte Wahl treffen." Der Jesuitenpater hustet. „Und ich will dir dabei helfen." Er räuspert sich. „Väterlich und vernünftig will ich dir raten."

„Als Chorfrau werde ich in strenger Klausur leben, schweigen und fasten, mich nicht ablenken lassen von irgendwelchem Tand: In dieser Ruhe – so hoffe ich zuversichtlich – vernehme ich die Stimme Gottes klarer."

„Es gefällt Gott, daß du bereit bist, in einen strengen Bettelorden einzutreten. Jesus wies irdische Habe zurück ..."

„Und hat Jesus nicht auch seine Mutter und seinen Pflegevater verlassen, um ...?"

„Natter! Hüte deine Zunge! Willst du dich mit Gottes Sohn vergleichen?"

„Nein, Vater, nein, das war eine Falschheit des Mundes. Jesus, verzeih' mir. Gott, bewahre mich vor bösen Worten. Heilige Jungfrau, Mutter Gottes, steh' mir bei!"

„‚Latet anguis in herba.'[2] Nimm dich in acht! Satan kennt viele Möglichkeiten, von dir Besitz zu ergreifen. Anathema sit![3] Das Blendwerk der Hölle: Die ein oder andere Aspirantin kann es kaum erwarten, die Aufgaben einer Chorschwester zu übernehmen. Sie ahnt nicht, daß der Teufel sie durch ihren Hochmut verleitet. Ein solchermaßen verirrtes Geschöpf wird die Dämonen hienieden nicht mehr los."

„Das muß schrecklich sein."

„Gott sei davor; es ist qualvoll! Aber jeder Schritt von der Lüge weg ist ein Schritt zur Wahrheit hin."

„Was wollt Ihr, daß ich tue?"

„Prüfe dich. Wähle dann das Sichere vor dem Unsicheren."

„Wohlvorbereitet bin ich auf das gottgeweihte Leben einer Chorfrau."

„Höre auf mich. Wie könntest du besser zwischen Lüge und Wahrheit unterscheiden, als durch demütiges Dienen? Wie deine Ernsthaftigkeit überzeugender beweisen, als durch die gewissenhafte Erfüllung der Pflichten einer Laienschwester?"

„Laienschwester! Da müßte ich für den Orden betteln."

„Fürwahr, es ist eine besonderes Vorrecht, für den Lebensunterhalt des Ordens zu sorgen."

„Aber ich kann das mitnichten."

„Du wirst es lernen, Dei gratia[4]."

„Die irdische Welt ist voll von bösen Gedanken und schändlichen Taten: Das ängstigt mich im Innersten."

„De hoc satis![5] Blicke auf das Kreuz. Gottes Sohn bewies wahre Demut: Er ließ sich geißeln und bespucken. – Kannst du da noch zögern?"

„Ehrwürdiger Vater, mit ganzer Seele höre ich, aus tiefem Herzen danke ich für Euren weisen Rat; mit allen meinen armseligen Kräften will ich nach dem rechten Weg suchen, aber ich fürchte, ich bin zu verwirrt."

„Bete. Suche Kraft in Gott. Die ehrwürdige Mutter Oberin wird dir Zeit lassen, den Orden kennenzulernen und dich zu entscheiden."

„Ich vertraue auf die Vorsehung Gottes."

„Geh mit Gott."[6]

„Pater, wie seid Ihr mit Maria Ward verblieben?"

„Ehrwürdige Mutter, ich habe so mit ihr gesprochen, wie Ihr es empfohlen habt: Ich glaube, sie ist ehrgeizig, ehrgeizig genug, um sich selbst prüfen zu wollen."

„Es ist gut, wenn es geschieht, wie Ihr sagt, denn ich denke nicht daran, eine neue Chorfrau aufzunehmen, solange wir keinen Ersatz für die beiden gefallenen Laienschwestern gefunden haben und gewiß sein können, daß unser schwer geprüftes Kloster ausreichend Nahrung und Kleidung bekommt."

Katholiken im Elisabethanischen England

Am 23. Januar 1585 brachte Ursula Ward in Yorkshire ihr erstes Kind zur Welt. Das Mädchen wurde auf den Namen Johanna getauft; Maria nannte es sich seit der Firmung.

Eltern, Großeltern, Onkel und Tanten hielten am katholischen Glauben fest, obwohl Katholiken unter Elisabeth I. gefährlich lebten: Die jungfräuliche Königin verstand sich nicht nur als Oberhaupt der anglikanischen Kirche, sondern zugleich als Vorkämpferin der europäischen Protestanten – und nachsichtig durfte sie dabei nicht sein, denn die konfessionellen Streitigkeiten vermischten sich mit den machtpolitischen Auseinandersetzungen zwischen England, Schottland, Frankreich und Spanien. In ihrer Regierungszeit wurden 127 katholische Priester und 62 Laien hingerichtet. Das prominenteste Opfer war Maria Stuart: Ihr wurde 1587 der Kopf abgeschlagen.

Jakob I., der Sohn der Hingerichteten, der nach Elisabeths Tod die Kronen von England und Schottland vereinigte, „war zumeist ein toleranter Dogmatiker. ... Er träumte in seiner zerstreuten philosophischen Art davon, die katholische und protestantische Christenheit zu versöhnen. Als sich aber die Katholiken unter seinem Wohlwollen vervielfachten und die Puritaner seine Nachsicht öffentlich anprangerten, ließ er wieder zu, daß elisabethanische Gesetze erneuert, erweitert und verstärkt wurden ...“[7]

Dagegen verschworen sich einige fanatische Katholiken, darunter drei Onkel Maria Wards: Thomas Percy, John und Christopher Wright. Durch einen in monatelanger Arbeit gegrabenen Tunnel schleppten die Männer dreißig Fässer Schießpulver unter den Palast von Westminster. Am 5. November 1605, während einer Sitzung des englischen Oberhauses mit König Jakob I., wollten sie die Sprengung auslösen.

Doch in der Nacht vor dem geplanten Anschlag entdeckten Agenten der Regierung den Stollen.

Die Attentäter, die bei der Verfolgung nicht ums Leben kamen, wurden hingerichtet.

Laienschwester im Klarissenkloster

Am 10. Mai 1606 trifft Maria Ward in der flämischen Bischofsstadt Saint-Omer ein. Am folgenden Tag wird sie von den Armen Klarissinnen aufgenommen.

Die Oberin hat es eilig: Sie drängt Maria Ward, bereits nach einem Monat die Ordenstracht anzulegen. „Von den Ordensoberen des Klarissenklosters, die dringend eine Ausgehschwester brauchten, kann der schwerwiegende Verdacht nicht genommen werden, in eigennütziger Absicht geraten zu haben, und zwar einem unerfahrenen jungen Menschen, der eine sehr harte Entscheidung für sein Leben treffen wollte. Das war in moralischer Hinsicht ein mehr als fragwürdiges Vorgehen.“[8]

Die Laienschwestern putzen, kochen und bedienen die Chorfrauen. Mit einer anderen Novizin verläßt Maria Ward jeden Tag nach der Frühmesse das Kloster. Bettelnd ziehen sie in Saint-Omer von Haus zu Haus oder sie wandern zu den Bauernhöfen in der Umgebung. Hier legt ihnen eine Magd eine Handvoll Bohnen und einen Laib Brot in den weiten Korb, dort erhalten sie von einer Bäuerin ein paar Eier; ab und zu dürfen sie auch Blumen als Schmuck für die Klosterkirche mitnehmen. Manchmal werden sie freundlich behandelt, meistens mürrisch abgefertigt; und es kommt vor, daß ein fluchender Bauer sie vom Hof jagt.

Der Jesuit, der Maria Ward überredete, als Laienschwester bei den Armen Klarissinnen einzutreten, bereut sein Verhalten, als er beobachtet, wie die zierliche Frau unter der harten Arbeit leidet. In dem Maße, wie sich ihr Körper an das stundenlange Schleppen des Korbes gewöhnt, wird ihr Denken unruhiger: Ist das die Erfüllung, die sie suchte? Sie weiß aber auch, daß der Orden auf Almosen angewiesen ist und fürchtet sich vor dem Hochmut. Die Äbtissin beobachtet, daß sie ihre Lippen zusammenpreßt und die anderen Nonnen kaum noch ansieht.

Als der Schnee das letzte Gemüse in den Gärten zudeckt, dauert es noch länger, bis die Laienschwestern ihre Körbe gefüllt bekommen; und das Winterwetter trägt nicht dazu bei, Maria Ward auf freudvolle Gedanken zu bringen.

Ein spanischer Franziskaner, der im März zur Visitation kommt, fragt auch nach der neuen Laienschwester, erfährt von den Zweifeln an ihrer Eignung und bestärkt Maria Ward in ihrem Bestreben, das Kloster zu verlassen.

Die Vision

Maria Ward stiftet ein eigenes Klarissenkloster. Das dafür vorgesehene Anwesen erwirbt sie mit ihrer eigenen Mitgift und der großzügigen Spende einer angesehenen Adelsfamilie. Mit einem Empfehlungsschreiben des Bischofs von Saint-Omer reist sie nach Brüssel – und muß sich dort als Gast in einem Kloster ein halbes Jahr lang gedulden, bis die spanischen Statthalter im Oktober 1608 ihr Vorhaben billigen.

Fünf Nonnen aus dem Orden der Armen Klarissinnen schließen sich ihr an, und der Bischof ernennt eine von ihnen zur Äbtissin des Klosters. Maria Ward kommt für dieses Amt nicht in Betracht, denn sie absolvierte noch kein Noviziat, und ohne diese Vorbereitung darf sie die Gelübde nicht ablegen. Selbst für die Gründerin des Klosters gibt es keine Ausnahme: Sie schuldet der Oberin uneingeschränkten Gehorsam.

Am 2. Mai 1609, als Maria Ward Franziskusgürtel knüpft, weiße Stricke, die den Habit der Klarissinnen zusammenhalten, hat sie eine Vision:

„Das Erlebnis schien von Gott auszugehen und ergriff mich mit solcher Gewalt, daß es mich ganz vernichtete. Meine Kraft war erloschen, und ich fühlte in mir keine andere Tätigkeit als die, welche Gott wirkte. Was mir zu tun verblieb, war nur dies, geistig zu schauen, was geschehen war und was in mir vollbracht werden sollte, ob ich wollte oder nicht. Ich litt sehr, denn die Macht ging weit über meine Kräfte; mein größter Trost war es, daß ich sehen konnte, Gott wolle sich meiner nach seinem göttlichen Wohlgefallen bedienen. Es wurde mir dabei gezeigt, daß ich nicht im Orden der hl. Klara verbleiben sollte; ich sollte etwas anderes tun, doch was und welcher Natur dies wäre, das sah ich nicht und konnte ich nicht erraten. Ich verstand nur, daß es etwas Gutes und der Wille Gottes sein werde."[9]

Maria Ward erschrickt: Zum zweiten Mal scheitert sie als Nonne. Nur ihrem Beichtvater erzählt sie von der Vision. Aber im Herbst verläßt sie ihr Kloster und reist nach England, um mit sich ins reine zu kommen.

In ihrer Heimat begeistert Maria Ward einige junge Frauen aus guten Familien für die Idee, in Saint-Omer eine Ordensgemeinschaft für die Unterweisung von Mädchen ins Leben zu rufen.

Die „Englischen Fräulein" kaufen ein Anwesen und eröffnen eine Schule, in der sie vormittags und nachmittags jeweils zweieinhalb Stunden lang unterrichten. Im Mittelpunkt steht der Religionsunterricht; aber sie lehren auch Lesen, Schreiben und Rechnen, zeigen den Schülerinnen, wie sie Kranke pflegen sollen und vermitteln ihnen Kenntnisse über Heilkräuter, leiten sie zu gutem Benehmen an und üben mit ihnen Singen und Malen, Nähen, Weben und Sticken. Dabei fördern sie individuelle Begabungen, erziehen die Mädchen zu selbständigem Denken und bleuen ihnen den Lehrstoff nicht – wie üblich – mit Stockschlägen ein.

Das ist revolutionär, denn es herrscht die Auffassung, ein wenig Schulunterricht könne allenfalls Knaben nützlich sein. „Religion war wichtig, um ein sittliches Leben zu führen; Rechnen konnte beim Einkaufen auf dem Markt nicht schaden, Lesen war noch geduldet, wie sollte man sonst die Bibel lesen, aber alles andere war unnötig, um Hausfrau zu sein oder die Kinder zu erziehen."[10] Angesehene Familien schicken zwar ihre Töchter vor der Pubertät in strenge Klosterinternate, aber dabei kommt es ihnen nur darauf an, deren Jungfräulichkeit zu bewahren, bis sie einen Bräutigam gefunden haben.[11] Eine öffentliche Tagesschule für Mädchen – noch dazu eine, die ihnen ungeachtet ihres gesellschaftlichen Standes offensteht – ist etwas völlig Neues.

Während sich Maria Ward von einer lebensgefährlichen Masern-Erkrankung erholt, wird ihr klar, daß der Sinn ihres Lebens nicht in Klausur und Kontemplation liegt, wie sie anfangs glaubte, sondern in der apostolischen Arbeit nach dem Vorbild der Jesuiten. Zur „Verteidigung und Ausbreitung des katholischen Glaubensgutes unter den drei feierlichen Gelübden der Armut, der Ehelosigkeit und des Gehorsams"[12] will sie ein zentralgeleitetes Institut aufbauen, das keinem anderen Orden und keinem Bischof, sondern nur dem Papst gehorchen soll. Sie besorgt sich eine Abschrift der Regel des 1534 von Ignatius von Loyola gegründeten Ordens und entwirft nach diesem Muster die Konstitution der „Schola Beatae Mariae"[13].

Eine überarbeitete Version sendet Maria Ward Ende 1615 an Papst Paul V. und bittet ihn, die Ordensgründung zu bestätigen. Die Kurienkongregation, die das Anliegen prüft, schickt ihre Antwort im folgenden Frühjahr an den Bischof von Saint-Omer und den Nuntius in Brüssel: Die Kardinäle loben den Glaubenseifer der Englischen Fräulein und fordern den Bischof auf, deren Wirken zu beobachten. Maria Ward hofft nun, daß ihr Institut in absehbarer Zeit von der Kirche anerkannt wird; aber ihre Gegner jubeln, denn sie interpretieren die Floskeln als Ablehnung.

Bald unterrichten die Englischen Fräulein sechzig Schülerinnen in Saint-Omer: Ein zweites Haus wird erforderlich; und wenig später richten sie weitere Niederlassungen in Lüttich, Köln und Trier ein.

Nächtelang grübelt Maria Ward, wie sie das Leben und die Arbeit der Gemeinschaft finanzieren kann. Ohne die päpstliche Approbation fehlt es an Geld, denn die Eltern einiger Novizinnen weigern sich, deren Mitgiften herauszugeben, solange sie ein Scheitern der Ordensgründung befürchten.

Zu Fuß nach Rom

Nach jahrelangem Warten auf das kirchliche Plazet beschließt Maria Ward, selbst nach Rom zu gehen.

Im Oktober 1621 bricht sie auf; fünf Gefährtinnen, ein Priester und ein Diener begleiten die Sechsunddreißigjährige auf der 1500 km langen Wanderung. Um wenigstens von gottesfürchtigen Marodeuren nicht überfallen zu werden, kleiden sie sich wie Pilger: Die schwarzen Umhänge und hohen, breitkrempigen Hüte schützen sie außerdem vor Schnee und Regen. Die Gruppe führt nur zwei Pferde mit: Auf dem einen reitet die jeweils schwächste Person, das andere trägt die Körbe mit dem Gepäck. Zu Fuß gehen die Englischen Fräulein und ihre Begleiter durch Elsaß-Lothringen, über den verschneiten St.-Gotthard-Paß ins Tessin, durch die Lombardei und die Toskana. Bis zu fünfunddreißig Kilometer am Tag legen sie zurück. Am 24. Dezember treffen sie in Rom ein – mittellos, weil sie unterwegs bestohlen wurden.

Der neunundsiebzigjährige Botschafter der Spanischen Niederlande in Rom, der die kostbaren Gewänder der kirchlichen Würdenträger und die laute, ausgelassene Lebensart in den Mittelmeerländern gewöhnt ist, traut seinen Augen nicht, als er der ernsten und ärmlich gekleideten Maria Ward zum ersten Mal begegnet.

Insgeheim lehnt er Maria Wards Vorstellungen ab und ist überzeugt, daß sie damit scheitern wird, doch auf Anordnung der spanischen Statthalterin in Brüssel begleitet er sie zur Audienz bei Gregor XV.: Wortreich schildert er dem Papst die Arbeit der Englischen Fräulein, weist auf ihren guten Ruf hin und bittet ihn, der Gründung zuzustimmen.

In das Gespräch, das die Würdenträger in lateinischer Sprache führen, wird Maria Ward kaum einbezogen, aber sie übergibt dem Papst eine Bittschrift, in der sie ihr Vorhaben beschreibt. Mit Zuversicht erfüllt es sie, daß der Heilige Vater freundlich auftritt, sie seines Wohlwollens versichert und zu ihr sagt: „Wer ausharrt bis ans Ende, wird gekrönt werden."[14]

Am Neujahrstag schreibt sie der spanischen Statthalterin: „… der Botschafter Eurer Hoheit, Monsignore Vives, … hat die

Gründe unseres Kommens hervorragend und wirkungsvoll erklärt, die Frucht unserer armseligen Bemühungen, unseren guten Ruf an allen Orten, wo wir uns aufgehalten haben, erwähnt, und auch die Gnade und Zuneigung, die Eure Hoheit uns erwiesen haben und den dringlichen Wunsch Eurer Hoheit, daß Seine Heiligkeit uns die Gnade erweisen möge, uns mit der Bestätigungs-Bulle zu beglücken etc., worauf Seine Heiligkeit mit geneigtem Wohlwollen reagierte."[15]

Die Bittschrift überantwortet der Papst einer Kurienkongregation, deren Mitglieder Maria Ward einzeln aufsucht, um ihnen das Anliegen zu erklären.

Einer der Kardinäle weist sie darauf hin, daß das Konzil von Trient[16] für Frauenorden die Klausur ausdrücklich vorgeschrieben habe; sie müsse deshalb auf die skandalöse apostolische Arbeit verzichten. Darauf läßt sich Maria Ward nicht ein, denn es würde ihren Vorstellungen in einem zentralen Punkt widersprechen.

Verleumdungen

„Im Lügen und Betrügen hat das Weib den Vorzug über alles, was da kann verlogen, betrogen und arglistig sein."[17] „Schwach, dumm und auf sündige Lust bedacht – das ist das Klischee der Frau, wie es die frühen Kirchenväter entworfen haben."[18] „Die Zeiten sind hart für die Frauen, besonders die frommen, denn es gibt keine Tugend einer Frau, die den Richtern – lauter Männern – nicht verdächtig ist."[19]

Argwöhnisch belauern die Männer der Kirche Maria Ward. Sie assoziieren Weiblichkeit mit Sünde, betrachten sie als „Symbol von Natur, Sinnlichkeit und Sexualität"[20], verlangen von den Frauen, daß sie sich entweder hinter Klostermauern zurückziehen oder heiraten, ihren Ehemännern blind gehorchen, Kinder gebären und das Haus nur verlassen, um die Messe zu besuchen oder auf dem Markt einzukaufen. Irritiert reagieren sie auf eine selbstbewußte Frau, der es zwar nie in den Sinn käme, gegen den Heiligen Vater aufzubegehren, die aber in geistlichen Angelegenheiten mitredet, eigene Wege geht, ihre unkonventionellen Absichten innerhalb der Kirche durchzusetzen versucht und zu ihren Anhängerinnen sagt: „Was soll der Ausdruck ‚nur Frauen' anderes bedeuten, als daß wir in allen Dingen einem anderen Geschöpf, dem Mann, wie ich annehme, nachstehen. Das ist, wie ich zu sagen wage, eine Lüge … Es gibt keinen solchen Unterschied zwischen Männern und Frauen … Die Wahrheit können Frauen ebensogut besitzen wie Männer. Mißlingt es uns, so geschieht es aus Mangel an der Wahrheit, aber nicht, weil wir Frauen sind … Es gibt keinen solchen Unterschied zwischen Männern und Frauen, der Frauen hindern könnte, Großes zu vollbringen, wie wir am Beispiel der Heiligen sehen … Ich hoffe zu Gott, daß man in Zukunft sehen kann, daß Frauen Großes vollbringen."[21]

Die Englischen Fräulein geraten zwischen die Fronten: Die Gegner der Jesuiten beschimpfen sie als „Jesuitinnen"; andererseits hält sich die Gesellschaft Jesu zurück, um sich den Rücken freizuhalten. „Die Einbeziehung des Jesuitenordens in den Kampf gegen Maria Wards Institut macht dann auch die konsequente Zurückhaltung des Jesuitengenerals verständlich, der Ruf und Wirksamkeit der Gesellschaft Jesu zu schützen hatte."[22]

Der Erzbischof von Canterbury klagt, Maria Ward schade der anglikanischen Kirche mehr als sechs Jesuiten. Im März trifft ein Beschwerdebrief des englischen Klerus in Rom ein. Katholische Geistliche entrüsten sich darüber, daß die Englischen Fräulein mit ihren Schülerinnen nicht in klösterlicher Abgeschiedenheit leben. Sogar mit den Vätern ihrer Zöglinge sprechen sie; wie soll man da nicht an ihrer Keuschheit zweifeln? Andere Briefschreiber weisen auf die finanziellen Schwierigkeiten der Gemeinschaft hin und behaupten, daß Maria Ward naive Mädchen aus wohlhabenden Familien anlocke, um sich deren Mitgift zu verschaffen. Die meisten Feinde agitieren in geheimen Sitzungen gegen sie und verbergen sich hinter Kongregationsbeschlüssen, ziehen hinter den Kulissen die Fäden oder setzen – wie der Kardinalvikar[23] – fünfundzwanzig Spione auf sie an.

Um die Verleumdungen zu entkräften, ihren Feinden den Mund zu stopfen („turara la bocca") und die Kurie vom Nutzen ihrer pädagogischen Arbeit zu überzeugen, eröffnet Maria Ward im Herbst 1622 in einer römischen Mietwohnung eine Tagesschule. Am 25. Februar 1623 schreibt sie nach Brüssel: „Täglich kommen ungefähr 120 junge und ältere Mädchen, verschieden nach Stand und Alter. Wegen des Winters und weil die Mädchen wenig auf die Straße kommen, besonders die größeren, wundert man sich gerade in Rom, wie sie in unsere Schule eilen. Die Mütter begleiten ihre älteren Töchter, die nicht allein auf der Straße sein dürfen. Sie holen dieselben am Ende des Unterrichts wieder ab. Auch angesehenere Leute hier wollen ihre Kinder zum Unterricht und zur Erziehung in unser Haus bringen."[24]

Von dieser Erfolgsmeldung läßt sich die Statthalterin in den Spanischen Niederlanden nicht mehr überzeugen: Sie beginnt am Gelingen der Ordensgründung Maria Wards zu zweifeln und stellt einige Wochen später ihre regelmäßigen Geldüberweisungen ein. Da weiterhin einige Eltern Englischer Fräulein deren Mitgiften zurückhalten, sind diese nun noch mehr auf Zuwendungen anderer Gönner angewiesen.

Die Kirche läßt sie vorerst gewähren.

Hoffnung auf den neuen Papst

Als Gregor XV. am 8. Juli 1623 stirbt und ihm nach einem achtzehntägigen Konklave Urban VIII. auf den Heiligen Stuhl folgt, hofft Maria Ward auf eine Wende zu ihren Gunsten. Sie ahnt nicht, wie konservativ Urban VIII. denkt. (Zehn Jahre später zwingt er Galileo Galilei zum Widerruf der Behauptung, die Erde bewege sich um die Sonne.)

Maria Ward versucht eine Audienz zu bekommen, aber die Kurienkardinäle schirmen den Papst so ab, daß es selbst für kirchliche Würdenträger schwierig ist, ihn zu sprechen.

Erst im Oktober 1624, als er sich wegen einer Erkältung nach Frascati zurückzieht, gelingt es ihr, zu ihm vorzudringen. Sie überreicht eine Bittschrift und erläutert, wie dringend sie auf die päpstliche Approbation warte. „Ich sagte Seiner Heiligkeit, wir seien gekommen, ihn um Bestätigung dessen auf

Erden zu bitten, was von Ewigkeit her im Himmel bestätigt gewesen sei, nämlich um die Bestätigung unserer Lebensweise; daß besagte Lebensweise seit sechzehn Jahren bestehe, in so vielen verschiedenen Ländern und Städten geübt werde und von Paul V., der sie zu bestätigen versprochen hätte, gutgeheißen worden sei; daß vor Bestätigung derselben die Eltern der Mitglieder das Vermögen ihrer Töchter nicht herausgeben wollten, worunter wir (ich meine unsere ganze Gesellschaft) gar sehr litten, daß während dieser sechzehn Jahre die meisten Ordensgenossenschaften der Kirche Gottes ihr Möglichstes getan hätten, um uns Hindernisse zu bereiten."[25]

Urban VIII. hört sie an, versichert ihr freundlich: „Wir werden so handeln, wie Gott es uns eingibt." Aber vor Zusagen hütet er sich.

Ein halbes Jahr nach der Audienz ordnet die Kurie an, die Einrichtungen der Englischen Fräulein in Rom, Neapel und Perugia – wo sie inzwischen ebenfalls Schulen gründeten – zu schließen.

Fünf Jahre nach ihrem Eintreffen in Italien sieht Maria Ward ein, daß ihre Bemühungen dort gescheitert sind: Am 10. November 1626 – acht Tage vor der Weihe des Neubaus der Peterskirche in Rom – bricht sie mit einer kleinen Gruppe nach Norden auf.

Anfang Januar trifft sie in München ein. Kurfürst Maximilian I. von Bayern[26] lädt die Englischen Fräulein ein, in einem Gasthaus zu logieren, bis das – nach dem ehemaligen Besitzer benannte – Paradeiser-Haus instandgesetzt ist und sie dort einziehen können. Der Kurfürst entlohnt die Handwerker, stiftet eine Glocke, zahlt die Rechnungen für die Einrichtung und kommt für den Unterhalt von zehn Englischen Fräulein auf, die eine Tagesschule, ein Pensionat und ein Noviziat eröffnen.

Auseinandersetzungen in Wien

Im Sommer 1627 fährt Maria Ward nach Wien, wo ihr Kaiser Ferdinand II. ein Haus in der Gasse „Stoß am Himmel" neben der Kirche Maria am Gestade überläßt.

Mit der Feindschaft örtlicher Kirchenfürsten rechnet sie nicht. Aber im November erscheinen drei Geistliche aus dem Stephansdom zur Visitation bei den Englischen Fräulein und werfen der Gründerin vor, ihr Institut ohne bischöfliche Erlaubnis zu betreiben. Zwei Monate später kehrt der Wiener Kardinal Melchior Klesl aus fast zehnjähriger Verbannung zurück.[27] Er beschwert sich bei der Kurie in mehreren Briefen über die Englischen Fräulein und er vergißt nicht, darauf hinzuweisen, daß sie mit ihren Schülerinnen Theaterstücke aufführen. (Das tun die Jesuiten auch – sie haben damit neben der Predigt ein weiteres Medium zur Belehrung in Glaubensfragen geschaffen –, aber Frauen und Mädchen auf der Bühne auftreten zu lassen, gilt als sündhaft, weil es zu den Aufgaben der Schauspielerinnen gehöre, „unsittliche, verführerische Weibspersonen so überzeugend darzustellen, daß ihnen die Rückkehr zur Tugend außerhalb der Bühne nicht mehr möglich sei."[28])

Die Wiener Nuntien[29] schreiben lange Briefe nach Rom, in denen sie Gerüchte über die Englischen Fräulein wiedergeben und Vorwürfe gegen sie aufzählen, auf ihre Ablehnung der Klausur hinweisen und meinen, „die Mädchen ihrer Schule würden nur die Aufmerksamkeit der jungen Männer auf sich ziehen."[30]

Im September und im November wird Maria Ward vom außerordentlichen Nuntius in Wien empfangen. „Er kann sich dem Staunen nicht entziehen und wohl auch nicht der Kraft und dem Charisma der Persönlichkeit dieser über vierzigjährigen Frau, die einen weiten Weg im Geistigen wie im Geographischen zurückgelegt und Strapazen auf sich genommen hat, um einen geistlichen Auftrag zu erfüllen. Verwundert, staunend berichtet er nach Rom, daß dieses geplante Ordenswerk ein großartiges Unterfangen sei – aber zu groß für eine Frau ..."[31] „... er fürchte mehr als früher für diese Frau, wenn sie nicht richtig gelenkt werde."[32]

Der Nuntius drängt seine Besucherin, noch einmal selbst nach Rom zu reisen, verschweigt ihr aber, daß die Kurie – nicht zuletzt aufgrund der Briefe aus Wien – angeordnet hat, alle Einrichtungen der Englischen Fräulein zu schließen.

Verhör und Verhaftung

In München bereitet sich Maria Ward auf die zweite Romreise vor, die sie Anfang 1629 antritt, obwohl sie kaum etwas essen kann und bis Trient in einer Sänfte getragen werden muß. Ob sie bis ans Ziel ihrer Reise durchhalten wird, ist unsicher. Sie schafft es, aber in Rom kann sie wochenlang nicht aufstehen; erst am 25. März ist sie in der Lage, eine weitere Bittschrift an den Papst zu diktieren.

Sieben Wochen später wird sie von Urban VIII. in Castelgandolfo empfangen. Maria Ward weiß noch immer nicht, daß eine Kurienkongregation unter seinem Vorsitz vor zehn Monaten beschloß, das Institut der Englischen Fräulein zu verbieten, und der Heilige Vater deutet es allenfalls mit diplomatischen Floskeln an, deren Bedeutung sie nicht durchschaut. Sie bittet darum, ihr Anliegen noch einmal von einer Kurienkongregation prüfen zu lassen, und Urban VIII. geht darauf ein, verrät ihr allerdings nicht, daß er seit Monaten beabsichtigt, den Fall der Inquisition zu übergeben.

Fast eine Stunde lang trägt Maria Ward ihr Konzept vier Kardinälen vor. Sie freut sich über diese Möglichkeit; daß es sich um ein Verhör handelt, sagt man ihr nicht. „Sie konnte über ihr Werk sprechen und es verteidigen. Sie erklärte den Eminenzen, sie wolle in Gemeinschaft tun, was einzelne Frauen mit dem Segen der Kirche immer schon getan hätten. ... Sie sei bereit, von ihrem Werk abzustehen, wenn Papst und Kardinäle dies für richtig fänden; abändern könne sie es nicht. Die Angelegenheit gehöre mehr den Kardinälen als ihrer Person und sei Gottes Sache."[33]

Als Maria Ward im Mai 1630 wieder in München eintrifft, wird sie von ihren Anhängerinnen bestürmt: Ob sie bereits wisse, daß die Häuser in Köln, Lüttich und Saint-Omer geschlossen sind? Den Englischen Fräulein dort wurde untersagt, Stiftungen anzunehmen und sich einheitlich zu kleiden, sie dürfen nicht mehr gemeinsam beten und die Glocken nicht länger läuten.

Maria Ward hat schon in Rom davon erfahren und die Betroffenen in einem Brief aufgefordert, „den Versuchen zur

Aufhebung in Höflichkeit und Bescheidenheit Widerstand [zu] leisten."[34] Sie klammert sich an die Hoffnung, der Heilige Vater wisse nichts von dem Verbot und schickt von München aus ihre engste Mitarbeiterin, Winefrid Wigmore, nach Lüttich, um die Englischen Fräulein zu ermutigen, trotz des Dekrets weiterzumachen. Winefrid Wigmore muß sich deshalb im September vor dem Kölner Nuntius verantworten, und aufgrund der Vernehmungsprotokolle läßt die Kongregation der Universalen Inquisition sie einkerkern.

Wieder wendet sich Maria Ward mit einer Bittschrift an den Heiligen Vater, aber mit ihrem Aufruf zum Widerstand hat sie ihren Gegnern entscheidende Argumente geliefert: Der Papst unterzeichnet am 13. Januar 1631 eine Bulle, in der ihre Gründung rigoros abgelehnt wird: Es gelte, den Weinberg von wucherndem Unkraut freizuhalten. „Denn diese Frauen oder Jungfrauen haben unter dem Scheine, das größere Heil der Seelen zu fördern, Werke unternommen, die sich dem weiblichen Geschlechte bei der Schwäche seines Verstandes, für die weibliche Bescheidenheit und für die jungfräuliche Sittsamkeit nicht geziemen, Werke, welche kaum ein wohlunterrichteter, geübter und reiflich erprobter Mann ohne Sorge und nur mit großer Umsicht auf sich nähme."[35]

Am 7. Februar 1631 fährt Jakob Golla, der Dekan der Münchner Liebfrauenkirche, mit zwei Kanonikern beim Paradeiser-Haus vor. Eine Schwester führt die Besucher ins Haus. Der Dekan entfaltet ein Schreiben und eröffnet Maria Ward, daß er den Auftrag habe, sie als „Häretikerin, Schismatikerin, Rebellin gegen den Heiligen Stuhl"[36] gefangenzunehmen.

Von der Bulle hat sie nichts erfahren; sie kann es nicht glauben, daß der Papst ihre Verurteilung billigt, aber Jakob Golla setzt ihr auseinander, daß er sich an die Anordnungen aus Rom halten müsse – er habe ohnehin schon zwei Wochen lang gezögert, die Verhaftung durchzuführen. Maria Ward beruhigt ihn: „Ich werde keinen Widerstand leisten."

Der Dekan hebt hervor, er habe einen ehrenvollen Ort für Maria Wards „Besserung" gefunden; sie entgegnet ihm: „Euer Gnaden sprechen von ‚ehrenvoll', nennen mich aber eine Häretikerin und behandeln mich als solche."[37]

Sie darf sich nicht von den anderen Schwestern verabschieden; diese müssen in ihren Räumen bleiben, während sie niederkniet, kurz betet und dann den Männern zur Pforte folgt, wo eine Kutsche bereitsteht, mit der sie ins Klarissenkloster gefahren wird.

Weil ihre Gesundheit angegriffen ist, darf ein Englisches Fräulein sie in der Zelle pflegen.

Vier Klarissinnen, denen es verboten ist, mit den beiden Gefangenen zu sprechen, wechseln sich Tag und Nacht bei der Bewachung der Zelle ab. Als Ketzerin darf Maria Ward weder die Messe besuchen noch Sakramente empfangen. Obwohl die regelmäßigen Wäsche- und Lebensmittellieferungen aus dem Paradeiser-Haus überprüft werden, gelingt es den Englischen Fräulein, mit Zitronensaft auf Einwickelpapier geschriebene Nachrichten und tröstende Worte heimlich auszutauschen. (Die Schrift wird erst sichtbar, wenn das Papier gegen eine Kerzenflamme gehalten wird.) Auf einem der Kassiber beschreibt Maria Ward ihre Zelle: „Unsere Wohnung war zuvor das Krankenzimmer für jene, die von den Ärzten aufgegeben waren. Wie es scheint, haben wir eine solche verjagt, die jeden Augenblick sterben kann; sie ist schon drei Jahre krank und hat bereits ihre ganze Lunge in das Zimmer gehustet, wo wir bald braten und bald erfrieren... Die zwei kleinen Fenster sind ziemlich vermauert und unsere Türe, mit einer Kette und einem Doppelschloß versehen, öffnet sich nur beim Ein- und Austritt unserer zwei Wärterinnen und der Äbtissin, unserer Oberaufseherin ..."[38]

Nach einigen Wochen verschlimmert sich Maria Wards Leiden so, daß sie nach den Sterbesakramenten verlangt.

Jakob Golla zögert, will sich gegen Vorwürfe seiner Obrigkeit absichern und setzt deshalb ein Schriftstück auf: Maria Ward bereue es von ganzem Herzen, wenn sie jemals etwas gegen die Kirche oder den Glauben getan habe. Die Schwerkranke fragt, ob das Papier vom Papst oder von der Inquisition stamme; und als man ihr sagt, der Münchner Dekan habe es verfaßt, läßt sie es zu Boden gleiten, ohne es zu unterzeichnen: „Nein, nein, eher will ich mich in die Arme der göttlichen Barmherzigkeit werfen und ohne die heiligen Sakramente sterben!"[39]

Schließlich signiert sie ein Dokument mit folgendem Wortlaut: „Niemals habe ich etwas, weder Großes noch Unbedeutendes, gegen seine Heiligkeit ... oder die Autorität der heiligen Kirche gesagt oder getan ... und ich möchte auch jetzt nicht für tausend Welten noch um ein gegenwärtiges oder zukünftiges Gut zu gewinnen, das Geringste tun, was sich mit den wahren Pflichten einer treuen Katholikin und einer gehorsamen Tochter der heiligen Kirche nicht vereinbaren ließe. Wenn dennoch das Werk, das vom Oberhaupt der Kirche und der heiligen Kongregation der Kardinäle zunächst gestattet und gutgeheißen wurde und bei dem ich nach Maßgabe meiner Armseligkeit der heiligen Kirche zu dienen bestrebt und beflissen war, von denjenigen, denen eine solche Entscheidung zusteht (nachdem sie den wahren Sachverhalt erfahren haben), als in irgendeinem Punkt den Pflichten eines wahren Christen und dem Seiner Heiligkeit und der heiligen Kirche schuldigen Gehorsam widersprechend beurteilt wird, so bin ich bereit und werde mit der Gnade Gottes stets bereit sein, meinen Fehler anzuerkennen, wegen der Ärgernisse um Verzeihung zu bitten und außer der öffentlichen Schande, die mir schon angetan wurde, auch mein armseliges und kurzes Leben zur Sühne für die besagte Sünde aufzuopfern."[40]

Nachdem sie die Letzte Ölung empfing, bessert sich ihr Gesundheitszustand: Sie ist schwach und ruhebedürftig, aber sie schwebt nicht mehr in Lebensgefahr, als Papst Urban VIII. die Klosterhaft aufhebt und sie Mitte April 1631 ins Paradeiser-Haus zurückkehren darf.

Freispruch

Ein halbes Jahr später bricht Maria Ward zum dritten Mal nach Rom auf, dieses Mal, um sich vor dem Inquisitionsgericht zu verantworten. Sie ist jetzt sechsundvierzig Jahre alt.

Im folgenden Frühjahr gewährt ihr Papst Urban VIII. eine weitere Privataudienz. Maria Ward beteuert: „Heiliger Vater, ich bin keine Häretikerin und bin nie eine solche gewesen." Und er versichert ihr: „Wir glauben es, wir glauben es, wir brauchen keinen weiteren Beweis. Wir und alle Kardinäle sind nicht nur zufrieden, sondern auch erbaut über Ihr Vorgehen. Nehmen Sie es nicht so ernst, daß Sie so geprüft wurden, wie es geschehen ist; denn so sind auch andere Päpste mit anderen Dienern Gottes verfahren."[41]

Einige Monate später spricht die Inquisition Maria Ward vom Vorwurf der Häresie frei und unterrichtet die zuständigen Nuntien über diese Entscheidung: „Gegenwärtig leben in dieser Stadt Donna Maria della Guardia[42] und mehrere ihrer englischen Gefährtinnen, die in Demut und geziemender Ehrerbietung gegen den Heiligen Stuhl allen Befehlen des Papstes bei der Aufhebung ihres Instituts bereitwillig Gehorsam leisteten zu höchster Zufriedenheit der Eminenzen … Auf Nachfrage können Sie bestätigen, daß das Heilige Tribunal die Englischen Fräulein, die dem Institut der Donna Maria della Guardia angehörten, keines Verstoßes gegen den heiligen und orthodoxen katholischen Glauben schuldig findet noch je schuldig gefunden hat…"[43]

Daraufhin wird auch Winefrid Wigmore aus der Haft entlassen, und die Kurie weist den Englischen Fräulein in Rom ein Haus zu, in dem sie eine neue Schule eröffnen: Sie dürfen wieder Mädchen unterrichten, müssen allerdings das Verbot ihrer Ordensgründung respektieren.

Epilog

Im Sommer 1637 erkrankt Maria Ward abermals und erhält wieder die Sterbesakramente. Doch sie erholt sich noch einmal, und sobald sie dazu in der Lage ist, reist sie mit Winefrid Wigmore nach Spa zur Kur. Von dort kehrt sie im Frühjahr 1639 nach England zurück.

Sechs Lebensjahre sind ihr noch vergönnt: Am 30. Januar 1645, sieben Tage nach ihrem sechzigsten Geburtstag, stirbt sie in Yorkshire.

Mehr als drei Jahrzehnte lang bemühte sich Maria Ward, die Vorurteile der Kardinäle zu überwinden und ihre Vorstellungen durchzusetzen. Doch erst 334 Jahre nach ihrem Tod wird das Institutum Beatae Mariae Virginis als Ordensgemeinschaft anerkannt. „Auch für sie gilt das Wort von Papst Johannes Paul II., mit dem er das Geschick Galileo Galileis zusammenfaßte: ‚Una tragica incomprensione reciproca – Ein tragisches Mißverständnis auf beiden Seiten.'"[44]

Heute kümmern sich weltweit etwa zweitausendfünfhundert Englische Fräulein in zweihundertfünfzig Häusern um die Bildung und Erziehung von Mädchen in Kindergärten, Schulen und Internaten.[45]

Maria Sibylla Merian

Eine Forscherin reist nach Südamerika –
100 Jahre vor Alexander von Humboldt

Teufelsbrut

Sooft er in Frankfurt am Main zu tun hat, steigt der Amster-
damer Kaufmann Mynheer Scheven im Gasthaus „Zum Roten
Mönch" ab. 1664 bringt dieser weitgereiste Mann der siebzehn
Jahre alten Maria Sibylla Merian einen präparierten exotischen
Schmetterling mit, den sie für ihn malen soll. Voll Freude
rennt sie nach Hause, doch auf dem Weg lauern ihr Burschen
auf, packen sie, reißen ihr das Kästchen aus der Hand und zertrampeln den kostbaren Falter: „Was für eine eklige Teufelsbrut!"

Der berühmte Vater

Mit in Kupfer gestochenen Stadtplänen und -ansichten wurde
Matthäus Merian berühmt.[1] Der dreiundzwanzigjährige Sohn
eines Baseler Sägewerksbesitzers war schon kein Unbekannter
mehr, als er 1617 in Oppenheim die Tochter eines erfolgreichen Verlegers heiratete.

Nach dem Tod des Schwiegervaters übernahm er dessen
Verlag und zog damit nach Frankfurt am Main. Der Rat der
Messestadt stimmte zu, weil Matthäus Merian in seinem
Antrag persönliche Gründe wie den „baufälligen Leibzustand"
seiner Schwiegermutter erwähnte, aber auch nicht vergaß, darauf hinzuweisen, daß „sich etliche Buchhändler schon hiervor
beklagt, wie es an einem Kunst- oder Kupferstecher mangelt
und sie ... daher mich anhero gen Frankfurt wünschen möchten."[2]

Zweiundfünfzig Jahre war er alt, als seine Frau starb. Acht Kinder hatte sie geboren. Matthäus Merian wartete das übliche Trauerjahr nicht ab, sondern heiratete bereits nach acht Monaten ein zweites Mal, damit sich wieder eine Frau um ihn, die Kinder und den Haushalt kümmerte, denn zu diesem Zeitpunkt kränkelte er bereits.

Im Juni 1650 starb er während eines Kuraufenthaltes in Bad Schwalbach.

Seine Witwe Johanna Sibylla heiratete im Sommer 1651 den ebenfalls verwitweten Jacob Marrel, einen Maler feiner Stilleben, der auch mit Bildern handelte, die er in Holland erwarb.

„Die Kunst der Künste in den Niederlanden war die Malerei. In der ganzen bekannten Geschichte – das Italien der Renaissance nicht ausgenommen – errang nirgendwo eine Kunstgattung solch allumfassende Popularität. ... Die Kunst wurde durch den beinahe völligen Ausfall kirchlicher und aristokratischer Gönnerschaft in neue Kanäle der Häuslichkeit und des Realismus gelenkt. ... Einfache Bürger ... schmückten ihre Häuser mit Gemälden, die sie oft zu bemerkenswerten Preisen kauften; so bewies ein Bäcker seinen guten Geschmack dadurch, daß er sechshundert Florin für ein Bild von Vermeer bezahlte."[3] Reich wurden allerdings seltener die holländischen Maler als einige der Kunsthändler.

Jacob Marrel war zwar nicht besonders geschäftstüchtig, aber er verdiente genug, um eine Familie ernähren zu können, und von seinen zahlreichen Reisen wußte er viel zu erzählen. Mit ihm kam wieder Leben ins Haus.

Er wird eine der außergewöhnlichen Begabungen seiner am 2. April 1647 geborenen Stieftochter Maria Sibylla Merian erkennen und fördern.

Tulpendiebin

Hin und wieder besucht Maria Sibylla Merian ihren zwanzig Jahre älteren Halbbruder Caspar: Er arbeitet als Radierer im Merian-Verlag und führt ihr vor, wie Schraffuren dunkler wirken, wenn die feinen Linien, die beim Druck die Farbe auf-

Maria Sibylla Merian (1647–1717)
Kupferstich-Porträt von Houbraken, 1717

nehmen, dichter nebeneinander liegen, zeigt ihr, was geschieht, wenn er Gravuren verbreitert und wie er die Metallspäne entfernt, ohne die polierte Kupferplatte zu verkratzen.

Jacob Marrel hantiert mit Pinsel und Farbtöpfen, Papier und Pergament, und wenn er verreist ist, schaut Maria Sibylla Merian zu, wie sein Schüler Abraham Mignon die Farben mischt, den Pinsel führt und die Bilder komponiert.

Man erzählt sich, sie habe heimlich Malutensilien aus der väterlichen Werkstatt genommen, um auf dem Dachboden Blumen zu malen.

Eines Tages soll sie sich dafür eine echte Vorlage geholt haben. Wir stellen uns vor, wie sie einen Gartenzaun überklettert und eine Tulpe ausgräbt, nach Hause eilt, die Pflanze aquarelliert und sie zurückbringt. Aber der schlaffe Blütenstiel richtet sich nicht wieder auf. Der Besitzer, dessen Vater noch zwölf Schafe für eine einzige Tulpenzwiebel tauschte,[4] ertappt die kindliche Diebin bei einem weiteren Versuch. Wütend schickt er einen Dienstboten zu ihrer Mutter. Die hastet herbei, und Maria Sibylla hört schon von weitem ihr Gezeter. Aber der Graf, dem die Tulpen gehören, wird neugierig, als das Kind schluchzend beteuert, nur eine Malvorlage gesucht zu haben: Er fordert es auf, ihm die Aquarelle zu zeigen, und weil sie ihm gefallen, akzeptiert er sie als Schadenersatz für die echten Tulpen.

Die Mutter beruhigt sich nicht so rasch: Sie jammert wegen der Schande, schimpft, und als Jacob Marrel einige Tage später aus Holland zurückkehrt, erzählt sie ihm gleich von dem Vorfall: „Das kommt davon, wenn ein Mädchen zu wenig im Haushalt hilft und seine Zeit mit solchem Unfug vertrödelt!" Doch Jacob Marrel erkennt, daß Maria Sibylla Merian die künstlerische Begabung ihres berühmten Vaters geerbt hat; er richtet ihr in seiner Werkstatt einen eigenen Arbeitsplatz ein und läßt sie Meisterwerke kopieren, um ihren Blick für Proportionen und die Bildaufteilung zu schulen.

Woher kommen die Sommervögelchen?

Als Maria Sibylla Merian begreift, daß sich die „Sommer- und Mottenvögelchen" – so nennt sie die Tag- und Nachtfalter – aus Raupen entwickeln, beginnt sie, diese in Schachteln zu sammeln und zu füttern. Dabei findet sie heraus, daß die Raupen nicht wahllos fressen, sondern auf bestimmte Wirtspflanzen angewiesen sind und selbst auf knackfrischen Blättern verhungern, wenn es die falschen sind. Sie beobachtet, wie sich die Raupen aus Eiern entwickeln, häuten und verpuppen; und schließlich sieht sie auch den ersten Schmetterling schlüpfen, versteht, daß das Tier in verschiedenen Stadien seines Lebens Ei, Raupe, Puppe, Falter ist. „Wochen- und manchmal monatelang ist sie hinter einer bestimmten Raupe her. Sie gibt nie auf, bevor sie nicht das fehlende Glied in einer Verwandlungskette gefunden hat."[5]

Tausend Fragen stellt sie, aber in ihrer Umgebung antwortet niemand darauf; niemand hört ihr zu, niemand teilt ihre Begeisterung: Man hat andere Sorgen.

Der Dreißigjährige Krieg[6] ging zwar eineinhalb Jahre nach ihrer Geburt zu Ende, aber von den Folgen erholt sich Deutschland nur langsam. „Die Ernten wurden zur Ernährung der Armeen gebraucht, und was übrigblieb, wurde verbrannt, um die Ernährung der Feinde zu verhindern. In manchen Ortschaften waren die Bauern dazu gezwungen, versteckte Vorräte oder Hunde, Katzen, Ratten, Eicheln und Gras zu essen. Tote wurden mit Gras im Mund aufgefunden. Männer und Frauen stritten sich mit Raben und Hunden um das Fleisch toter Pferde. Im Elsaß wurden erhängte Verbrecher von den Galgen geschnitten und gierig verzehrt; im Rheinland wurden ausgegrabene Leichen als Speise verkauft; in Zweibrücken beichtete eine Frau, sie habe ihr Kind aufgegessen."[7] In einzelnen Gebieten fielen bis zu vier Fünftel der entkräfteten Einwohner den Seuchen zum Opfer. Scharen von Bettlern und Marodeuren lähmten den Neuanfang.

Kann ein gütiger Gott das gewollt haben? Waren die Greuel Teil der göttlichen Vorsehung? Der ein oder andere beginnt an der Schöpfungsordnung zu zweifeln. Die Mehrheit hält zwar am christlichen Glauben fest – aber seit die abendländische Glaubenseinheit durch die Reformation zerbrochen ist und Katholiken, Lutheraner und Calvinisten sich streiten, fragen auch Christen: „Was sollen wir glauben?"

Bodenständige Menschen, die am Hergebrachten festhalten, sind verunsichert. Von ihnen kann Maria Sibylla Merian kein Verständnis erwarten.

Das gilt auch für ihre Mutter: Sie hält das Geld zusammen; Waschen und Putzen, Spinnen und Weben, Kochen und Einwecken – davon versteht sie viel, aber wenn sie etwas aufschreiben soll, wird es schwierig, und zum Lesen hat sie ohnehin keine Zeit, denn sie arbeitet von früh bis spät. Wenn ihre wissensdurstige Tochter sie fragt: „Woher kommt der Regen?", „Benötigen Blumen keine Nahrung?", „Warum zwitschern die Vögel nur im Frühling?", fehlt es ihr sowohl an Neugier als auch an Energie, um darüber nachzudenken, und je erschöpfter sie ist, desto heftiger schreit sie Maria Sibylla an: „Zerbrich dir nicht den Kopf über unnützen Kram; hilf mir lieber, den Fußboden schrubben!"

Bestärkt wird sie in ihrer Haltung von ihrem Bruder Wilhelm, einem sittenstrengen Prediger in Hanau, bei dem sie vor ihrer ersten Ehe wohnte. Der nimmt an, daß Raupen als Teufelsbrut aus Schlamm entstehen, Maikäferplagen durch Exorzisten bekämpft werden müssen und Hexen in Gestalt von Schmetterlingen frische Milch in ranzige Butter verwandeln.

Das glauben die meisten. Wie sollen diese Menschen verstehen, was Maria Sibylla bewegt? Daß sie sich künstlerisch betätigt wie ein Mann, ist verdächtig genug. Aber ein Mädchen, das Raupen züchtet, wird argwöhnisch belauert, riskiert, als Hexe verfolgt und auf dem Scheiterhaufen verbrannt zu werden.

Eine unglückliche Ehe

Inmitten dieser engstirnigen Umgebung teilt Maria Sibylla Merian mit dem sieben Jahre älteren Abraham Mignon die Vorliebe für das Malen. Sie lernt viel von ihm, und beide leben unter einem Dach. Bahnt sich eine Romanze an? Der eine oder andere Biograph vermutet es, aber sicher wissen wir nur, daß der Künstler fortzieht, als Maria Sibylla siebzehn ist.

Zur gleichen Zeit tritt ein anderer Maler in ihr Leben.

Sie sieht Johann Andreas Graff nicht zum ersten Mal, denn er lernte fünf Jahre lang bei Jacob Marrel, als sie noch ein Kind war. Danach bereiste er Italien, Griechenland, Spanien und die Niederlande, um seine Ausbildung als Architekturmaler abzuschließen.

Nun will der Siebenundzwanzigjährige in Frankfurt am Main sein Meisterstück einreichen. Er beabsichtigt, von einem anderen Werk „abzukupfern", aber Maria Sibylla Merian durchschaut das und hilft ihm, einen eigenen Kupferstich zu gestalten.

Nach der bestandenen Prüfung hält er um ihre Hand an. Den Sohn eines Nürnberger Schulrektors hält Maria Sibyllas Mutter im Vergleich zu Abraham Mignon für die bessere Partie. Deshalb setzt sie sich bei Jacob Marrel für ihn ein, und am 16. Mai 1665 wird Hochzeit gefeiert.

Am 5. Januar 1668 wird Maria Sibylla Merian von einer Tochter entbunden, die sie auf den Namen Johanna Helena taufen läßt.

Als das Kind gut zwei Jahre alt ist, übersiedelt die Familie nach Nürnberg – vier Tage dauert die holprige Kutschfahrt – und bezieht das geerbte Familienhaus der Graffs unterhalb der Burg.

Maria Sibylla Merian ist keine Schönheit, jedoch bescheiden, tüchtig und strebsam, in sich gekehrt, kraftvoll und charakterstark. Ihr Ehemann begeistert sich zwar rasch für etwas, aber es fehlt ihm an Ausdauer; er bleibt oberflächlich, läßt sich treiben, kann hübschen Frauen nicht widerstehen und fühlt sich im Wirtshaus wohl. Heute schwelgt er im Glück und morgen fühlt er sich niedergeschlagen. Seine Frau klagt: „Er ist immer noch ein Verliebter; ach, und ich wünschte, er könnte ein Liebender werden!"[8]

Johann Andreas Graff bildet Lehrlinge aus, malt Blumen, Stilleben und Landschaften, aber seine Hoffnung, der berühmte Geburtsname seiner Frau werde ihm neue Türen öffnen, erfüllt sich nicht: Er bleibt erfolglos und verdient kaum genügend für den Lebensunterhalt. Im gleichen Maß, wie seine finanziellen Schwierigkeiten zunehmen, steigen die Mengen, die er trinkt; immer häufiger bleibt er nachts fort, von Monat zu Monat kümmert er sich weniger um seine Arbeit und die Familie: ein Teufelskreis.

Kunst und Wissenschaft

Um das Einkommen aufzubessern, eröffnet Maria Sibylla Merian eine Stick- und Malschule für die Töchter der Nürnberger Patrizierfamilien; sie bietet eigene Aquarelle als Stickvorlagen zum Kauf an und handelt mit selbst hergestellten Farben.

Blumenbilder, die sie für den Unterricht gemalt hat, veröffentlicht sie 1675 und 1677; 1680 fügt sie einen dritten Teil hinzu und gibt alle sechsunddreißig Kupferstiche zusammen in einem Band heraus.

Obwohl ihre Zeitgenossen annehmen, Ehrgeiz sei eine den Männern vorbehaltene Tugend, hört sie nicht auf, ihr handwerkliches Können im Malen, Radieren und Kupferstechen zu verfeinern. Was sie an Raupen und Schmetterlingen in den verschiedenen Entwicklungsstadien beobachtet, hält sie mit Schreibfeder, Pinsel und Stichel fest. Mit ihrer künstlerischen Fähigkeit zur detailgetreuen Wiedergabe hängt ihre genaue Beobachtungsgabe eng zusammen; daraus ergibt sich „eine geglückte Verbindung wissenschaftlicher Beobachtungen und künstlerischer Darstellung"[9], die selbst Goethe bewundert.[10]

1679 bzw. 1683 erscheinen die beiden Bände ihres Buches „Der Raupen wunderbare Verwandlung und sonderbare Blumennahrung". Zu Beginn wendet sie sich an den „hochwerthen, kunstliebenden Leser": „... suche demnach hierinnen nicht meine, sondern allein Gottes Ehre, Ihn, als einen Schöpfer auch dieser kleinsten und geringsten Würmlein zu preisen; alldieweil solche nicht von ihnen selbst ihren Ursprung haben, sondern von Gott, welcher sie mit solcher Weisheit begabt, daß sie in gewissen Stunden die Menschen (wie es scheint) fast zu Schanden machen: Indem sie nemlich ihre Zeit und Ordnung fleissig halten, und nicht eher hervorkommen, bis daß sie ihre Speise zu finden wissen."[11]

Anders als den meisten Naturforschern ihrer Zeit geht es ihr nicht darum, Lebewesen zu klassifizieren, sondern sie spürt den Vorgängen nach, durch die aus einer Raupe ein Schmetterling wird und stellt auf jeweils einer Doppelseite die Entwicklungsstadien einer Tierart dar: links auf einer Bildtafel veranschaulicht, rechts im Text erläutert. (Diese Kombination von Bild und Beschreibung behält sie auch in ihren folgenden Büchern bei.) Statt der bis dahin üblichen Abbildungen einzelner Tiere und Pflanzen zeigt sie deren Zusammenspiel in ausgewogenen Bildkompositionen[12]: „Im Zentrum des Kupferstichs steht gewöhnlich eine Pflanze ..., die Futterpflanze, auf die ein Tier angewiesen ist: Auf sie legt es seine Eier; von ihr ernährt sich die gefräßige Raupe ...; auf den Blättern oder von den Stielen der Wirtspflanze hängen die Puppen, aus denen schließlich die Schmetterlinge kriechen, die sich paaren und ihre Eier wieder genau auf der richtigen Futterpflanze ablegen. Jede Tafel stellt eine kleine Welt für sich dar, einen Kreislauf."[13]

Trennung

„Deß Menschen Leben ist gleich einer Blum", schreibt Maria Sibylla Merian 1675 in ein Album.[14] Nicht nur als Künstlerin und Forscherin entfaltet sie sich, sondern mit ihrer gesamten Persönlichkeit und sie findet ihre unabhängige Identität; heute würde man sagen: sie verwirklicht sich selbst. Johann Andreas Graff gelingt es nicht, aus dem Schatten seiner Frau herauszutreten, „steht ihrem kompromißlosen Schaffen hilflos gegenüber",[15] und aufgrund ihres Fortschritts erscheint ihm sein Mißerfolg noch größer. Zwar kann er diese Einsicht selbst in seinen Räuschen nicht mehr verdrängen, aber abfinden mag er sich damit auch nicht: Das Zusammenleben wird für die Familie unerträglich.

Als ihr Stiefvater am 11. November 1681 stirbt, packt Maria Sibylla Merian ihre Sachen, und einige Wochen später zieht die Vierunddreißigjährige mit Johanna Helena und der drei Jahre alten zweiten Tochter Dorothea Maria wieder in ihre Geburtsstadt, um ihrer Mutter beizustehen. (Johann Andreas Graff folgt seiner Frau, aber nach zwei weiteren Ehejahren resigniert er und kehrt allein zurück.)

Jacob Marrel hat Schulden hinterlassen. Matthäus Merian d. J. behauptet gehässig, seine Stiefmutter habe mit ihrem Mann „das gute Geld verzehrt, also daß sie nach seinem Tod das Gnadenbrot bei ihrer Tochter essen mußt".[16]

Obwohl Maria Sibylla Merian aufgrund ihrer Veröffentlichungen finanziell unabhängig ist und sich auch innerlich von Johann Andreas Graff gelöst hat, fällt ihr die Trennung schwer, denn über eine Frau, deren Ehe gescheitert ist, tuscheln die Nachbarn, und es gilt als anstößig, wenn eine Mutter nicht bei ihrem Gatten wohnt, sondern ihre Kinder allein aufzieht. Aber Maria Sibylla Merian handelt nicht aus einer Laune heraus, sondern nach reiflicher Überlegung, und sie steht zu ihrem Entschluß.

Bei den Labadisten

Der französische Jesuit Jean de Labadie verließ mit neunundzwanzig Jahren seinen Orden, konvertierte elf Jahre später, ordnete sich aber auch in der reformierten Kirche nicht ein, und 1669, als Neunundfünfzigjähriger, gründete er eine urchristliche Sekte.

Als er fünf Jahre später in Hamburg starb, trat der Eiferer Pierre Yvon die Nachfolge an. Dessen Frau und deren Schwestern überredeten ihren Bruder Cornelis van Sommelsdijk, den Labadisten Schloß Waltha in Wieuward südwestlich von Leeuwarden zu überlassen. Dreihundertfünfzig Deutsche, Holländer und Franzosen leben dort in einer klösterlichen Gütergemeinschaft; sie versorgen sich selbst, indem sie ackern und Kühe züchten, töpfern, schmieden, weben und Leder gerben. Dabei haben Frauen und Männer gleich viel zu sagen.

Als Maria Sibylla Merian erfährt, daß ihr Halbbruder Caspar – der sich 1677 den Labadisten auf Schloß Waltha anschloß – krank ist, reist sie im Sommer 1685 mit ihrer Mutter und den beiden Töchtern nach Holland, um ihn zu pflegen, bis er im April des folgenden Jahres stirbt.

Daraufhin kommt Johann Andreas Graff, um seine Frau und die Kinder zurückzuholen, aber die Mädchen weigern sich, ihren Vater auch nur zu begrüßen, und Maria Sibylla Merian zieht es vor, bei den Labadisten zu bleiben.

Bei ihrer Entscheidung läßt sie sich nicht nur von religiösen Überzeugungen, sondern auch von praktischen Erwägungen leiten: Die Labadisten akzeptieren sie, obwohl sie ihren Mann verließ, und in der Gemeinschaft fällt es ihr leichter, neben dem Malen und Forschen für ihre Mutter und die Kinder zu sorgen.

„Die Trennung von ihrem Mann, die Übersiedelung nach Schloß Waltha, das Leben dort bedeuteten einen gewaltigen Einschnitt in ihr Leben. Sie scheint Bilanz gezogen zu haben, Bilanz über ihr Leben, Bilanz aber auch über ihre Forschung."[17] Vor dem Hintergrund ihrer weiteren Entwicklung erscheint der Rückzug in die Sektengemeinschaft wie eine Verpuppung. Voller Tatendrang wird sie daraus hervorgehen und ihre Persönlichkeit für den Höhepunkt ihres Lebens entfalten.

Cornelis van Sommelsdijk regiert die niederländische Kolonie Surinam[18] im Nordosten Lateinamerikas als Gouverneur. Als er 1688 bei einem Soldatenaufstand ermordet wird, greifen die Erben auch nach seinem Schloß in Holland, und allmählich zerfällt die Labadistengemeinde.

Maria Sibylla Merian will ihrer Mutter keinen Ortswechsel mehr zumuten. Aber nachdem die alte Frau gestorben ist, kündigt sie ihr Frankfurter Bürgerrecht auf, läßt sich von den Labadisten ihren Besitz zurückgeben und übersiedelt mit ihren Töchtern 1691 nach Amsterdam – wo die Dreimaster anlegen, die für den Überseehandel benutzt werden.

Amsterdam

Im Jahr darauf vermählt sich die inzwischen vierundzwanzig-jährige Johanna Helena mit dem Kaufmann Jacob Hendrik Herolt, der sein Geld mit Kolonialwaren aus Surinam verdient. Fast zur gleichen Zeit läßt sich Johann Andreas Graff von seiner Frau scheiden.

Maria Sibylla Merian verkauft weiterhin ihre Bücher, wobei sie – wenn ein Käufer dies wünscht – die Stiche gegen einen beträchtlichen Aufpreis koloriert. Sie erteilt auch wieder Malunterricht und handelt erneut mit Farben. Außerdem verkauft sie einen Teil ihrer Insektensammlung.

Mit dem Geld will sie eine Forschungsreise finanzieren: Sie träumt von Surinam, seit sie die präparierten Schlangen und Schmetterlinge sah, die Cornelis van Sommelsdijk nach Waltha geschickt hatte. Da nicht einmal ihre Gönner glauben, daß eine Frau die Strapazen einer solchen Expedition durchhält, findet sie niemand, der bereit ist, das Unternehmen zu finanzieren: Sie ist auf sich selbst angewiesen.

Über die vor zweihundert Jahren von Kolumbus entdeckte Neue Welt weiß man noch wenig. Seeleute erzählen schaurige Geschichten von Riesenkraken, die „Dreimastsegelschiffe überfallen und mit ihren Armen in die Tiefe reißen. Meeresungeheuer, schiffsgroße Fische mit Eberköpfen, je drei Hauer auf jeder Seite, zerknacken damit Menschen, und Riesenkrebse umklammern winzige Menschen mit ihren Scheren. Feuerspeiende Seedrachen mit zwei kleinen Kaminen auf dem Kopf, Dampf ablassend. Menschen ohne Kopf soll es in den Urwäldern geben, die Augen, Nase, Mund auf der Brust, die Ohren in den Achseln."[19] Was Johanna Helena und ihr Mann berichten, nachdem sie von einer Handelsreise aus Surinam zurückgekehrt sind, steigert die Neugier der Mutter. Sie schildern zwar auch die Gefahren der Überfahrt, die Qualen der Seekrankheit, das mörderische Klima, das Risiko einer Malaria-Erkrankung, die Bedrohung durch Vogelspinnen, Nattern und Skorpione, aber das schreckt Maria Sibylla Merian nicht ab. Statt dessen erkundigt sie sich, welche Medikamente, Kleidung und Ausrüstung sie mitnehmen soll.

Trotz ihrer Furchtlosigkeit schätzt sie das Wagnis realistisch ein und hinterlegt bei einem Notar in Amsterdam ein Testament zugunsten ihrer Töchter.

Surinam

Im Juni 1699 schifft sich die Zweiundfünfzigjährige mit ihrer um dreißig Jahre jüngeren unverheirateten Tochter[20] auf dem Dreimaster „Willem de Ruyter" nach Südamerika ein – genau einhundert Jahre vor Alexander von Humboldt.[21] Und das in einer Zeit, in der eine Frau ohne männliche Begleitung noch nicht einmal mit der Postkutsche in die nächste Stadt fahren darf! In die Kolonien reist eine ehrbare Frau nur mit Männern aus ihrer Familie. Allein überqueren in der Regel nur „Zuchthaushuren, betrunkene Straßenferkel und Diebinnen"[22] den Atlantik.

Als das Schiff in den Wellen schlingert, kann Maria Sibylla Merian nicht mehr aufs Wasser schauen; ihr wird schwindelig, übel; kalter Schweiß bricht ihr aus, und sie übergibt sich, bis sie glaubt, Teile des sich krampfenden Magens hochzuwürgen. Erst nach Tagen kann sie wieder etwas essen.

Während der drei Monate dauernden Schiffspassage gibt es Zwieback, Hirsebrei, Erbsenbrei, Gerstensuppe und Stockfisch, abgestandenes Wasser, mal ein Glas Rotwein, selten ein Stück Käse oder eine Scheibe Pökelfleisch.

Nur wenige wagen eine solche Reise. Wieviel mutiger muß eine Frau sein, die sich dazu entschließt! Aber nicht genug damit: Maria Sibylla Merian und ihre Tochter beabsichtigen, auch noch in den tropischen Regenwald vorzudringen. Réaumur zeigt sich tief beeindruckt von der Kühnheit der Naturforscherin: „Sie bietet dem Sturm die Stirn, sie trotzt den Wellen; Sibylla sucht in Surinam die Natur, mit dem Geist einer Weisen und dem Herzen einer Heldin."[23]

Am Rand der zwanzig Kilometer von der Suriname-Mündung entfernten Hauptstadt Paramaribo richten sich Mutter und Tochter in einem Holzhaus ein, das ihnen ein gutmütiger Pflanzer zur Verfügung stellt. Kopfschüttelnd beobachten die

Siedler, was die Neuankömmlinge auspacken: Präparierinstrumente, Gläser und Schachteln, Pergament, Pinsel und Farben. Keiner der Kolonisten begreift, wieso zwei Frauen solche Risiken und Anstrengungen in Kauf nehmen, um Tiere und Pflanzen zu studieren.

Ein halbes Jahr nach der Ankunft in Surinam fahren sie 65 km weiter stromaufwärts zur Plantage Providentia. Den einzigen Weg durch die Sümpfe, Mangrove- und Regenwälder bildet der braune Fluß: Während Myriaden von Mücken die Insassen des Einbaums verfolgen, paddeln drei Indianer zwei Tage lang gegen die Strömung; dann erblicken die beiden Forscherinnen die ersten Anpflanzungen der Siedlung.

„Der südamerikanische Regenwald überrascht und überwältigt jeden, der ihn zum erstenmal erlebt. Ein lautes Urwaldkonzert empfängt den Besucher: Affen brüllen, Insekten zirpen, fremdartige Vogelschreie mischen sich mit tropfenden und klopfenden Geräuschen; überall im Unterholz raschelt es. Die Wipfel der Urwaldriesen bilden ein fast undurchdringliches Laubdach, durch das kaum ein Stück Himmel scheint. Dieses tropische Universum birgt eine so reiche Tier- und Pflanzenwelt, daß diese auch heute – bald 300 Jahre nach Maria Sibylla Merians Aufenthalt in Surinam – noch nicht vollständig erforscht ist."[24]

Um nicht in der Mittagshitze arbeiten zu müssen, klettern Maria Sybilla und Dorothea Maria Merian frühmorgens aus ihren Hängematten. Indianer führen sie durch einen Urwald, „so dicht mit Disteln und Dornen verwachsen, daß ich meine Sklaven mit Beilen in der Hand vorwegschicken mußte, damit sie für mich eine Öffnung hackten."[25] Körbeweise sammeln die beiden Europäerinnen Schmetterlinge, Käfer und Spinnen, Schlangen und Eidechsen, Guajavefrüchte, Wunderbaumblätter und blühende Jasminzweige, die sie abends präparieren und als Vorlagen für spätere Ausarbeitungen malen. Außerdem hält Maria Sibylla Merian ihre Beobachtungen in einem Journal fest.

„Ihr Ruf verbreitete sich, und da Frauen bei den Indianerstämmen und in den sozialen Verbänden der Afrikaner oft als magische Heilerinnen und Kräuterfrauen tätig waren, mögen die Indianer und Afrikaner sie für weniger verrückt gehalten haben als die Kolonisten."[26]

In dem ebenso feuchten wie heißen Klima erkrankt Maria Sibylla Merian Anfang 1701: Kopfschmerzen wecken sie aus dem Schlaf; sie erbricht Blut und wird tagelang von Fieberanfällen geschüttelt: wahrscheinlich Gelbfieber.

Die Siedler staunen, daß sie die Krankheit überlebt. Allerdings kann sie nicht daran denken, ihre Forschungen in Surinam fortzusetzen.

„Metamorphosis Insectorum Surinamensium"

Ihr Schiff läuft Ende September 1701 im Hafen von Amsterdam ein.

Nach der zwei Jahre dauernden Trennung freut sich Dorothea Maria auf das Wiedersehen mit Philipp Hendriks, dem Arzt, der sich auf der Hinfahrt um die Passagiere und die Besatzung kümmerte. Zehn Wochen später heiratet das Paar.

Am 8. Oktober 1702 schreibt Maria Sibylla Merian dem Nürnberger Arzt und Naturforscher Johann Georg Volckamer, sie bringe jetzt alles, was sie in Surinam entdeckt habe, „in Perfektion aufs Pergament". „Darum habe ich vorher in dem Land die Würmer und Raupen, wie auch die Arten ihrer Speise und deren Eigenschaften gemalt und beschrieben. Aber alles, das ich nicht vonnöten hatte zu malen, habe ich mitgebracht, wie die Sommervögel und Käfer und alles, was ich in Branntwein einlegen konnte und alles, was ich trocknen konnte, alles das male ich nun ... Aber alles auf Pergament in Großfolie, dabei die Tiere lebensgroß, sehr kurios, da viele verwunderliche und seltene Sachen dabei sind, die da noch nie ans Licht gekommen sind, und auch so leicht niemand eine solche schwere kostbare Reise tun wird um solcher Sachen willen."[27]

Vier Jahre lang arbeitet Maria Sibylla Merian an einem Buch über ihre Beobachtungen: Nach den in Surinam gemalten Vorlagen und mitgebrachten Anschauungsobjekten gestaltet sie sechzig Aquarelle und beauftragt drei Kupferstecher, Druckvorlagen davon herzustellen, während sie unter ihren Bekannten Subskribenten anwirbt, um die Veröffentlichung finanzieren zu können. In den Texten, die sie zu den Bildkompositionen verfaßt, beschreibt sie nicht nur die Tiere und Pflanzen, sondern sie kritisiert auch die Engstirnigkeit der Kolonisten und berichtet, daß die Indianer- und Negersklavinnen die Pfauenblume als Abtreibungsmittel verwenden, um ihren Ausbeutern keine Söhne und Töchter auszuliefern.[28]

„Mit dem gleichen Wagemut und der gleichen Entschlossenheit, mit der sie vor zwei Jahren ihre Reise angetreten hat, wird die fünfundfünfzigjährige Frau jetzt ihre eigene Verlegerin."[29] 1705 erscheint das Buch „Metamorphosis Insectorum Surinamensium" (Metamorphose der Insekten Surinams) in holländischer und in lateinischer Sprache.[30]

„Ihre schon beim Raupenbuch erwiesene Meisterschaft, den Pflanzen und Tieren bei der Darstellung ihre Eigentümlichkeit zu erhalten und sie trotzdem in eine wirksame Bildkomposition hineinzubauen, hat mit dem Surinam-Werk einen unvergleichlichen Höhepunkt erreicht. Es gehört nicht nur zu den besten alten naturwissenschaftlichen Werken, sondern ist eines der prachtvollsten illustrierten Bücher, die je geschaffen wurden."[31]

Johanna Helena geht 1711 mit Jacob Hendrik Herolt nach Surinam. Zur gleichen Zeit verliert Dorothea Maria ihren Mann und ihr einziges Kind infolge einer Typhuserkrankung. Drei Jahre später vermählt sie sich mit dem geschiedenen Schweizer Kunstmaler Georg Gsell und zieht mit ihm zu ihrer Mutter, die seit einem Schlaganfall teilweise gelähmt ist. Die beinahe Siebzigjährige wird von ihrer jüngeren Tochter gepflegt, bis sie am 13. Januar 1717 stirbt.

Madame de Pompadour

*Eine Mätresse
greift in die große Politik ein*

Die neue Geliebte des Königs

1745. In der Gerüchteküche von Versailles brodelt es: Die Höflinge sind zwar Seitensprünge des Königs gewohnt, aber in diesem Fall handelt es sich bei der Geliebten um eine Bürgerliche. Und die Beziehung hält an!

Mißgünstig tuscheln die Gräfinnen darüber, wie es Jeanne-Antoinette Lenormant d'Étioles bereits im vergangenen Herbst gelang, Ludwig XV. aufzufallen: Als er im Wald von Sénart jagte, richtete die Dreiundzwanzigjährige es so ein, daß sie seinen Weg zweimal kreuzte – wobei sie zunächst ein himmelblaues Kleid trug und in einer rosafarbenen Kutsche saß und für die nächste Gelegenheit ein rosafarbenes Kleid und eine himmelblaue Kutsche wählte.

Sofort griff die Herzogin von Châteauroux ein, um ihre Stellung als offizielle Mätresse Ludwigs XV. zu verteidigen: Wütend ließ sie der Rivalin ausrichten, daß sie keinen weiteren Annäherungsversuch dulden werde. Das genügte, um die junge Dame vorläufig zurückzuhalten, denn einen Wunsch der Maîtresse en titre ignoriert niemand ungestraft.

Die Herzogin von Châteauroux starb jedoch am 8. Dezember 1744 im Alter von siebenundzwanzig Jahren an einer Lungenentzündung.

Als König Ludwig XV. im darauffolgenden Frühjahr einen Maskenball veranstaltete, nützte Jeanne-Antoinette Lenormant d'Étioles die Gelegenheit: Ein entfernt verwandter Kammerdiener half ihr, sich als Jagdgöttin verkleidet unter die Gäste zu mischen. „Es herrschte an diesem Abend bald ein solches Gedränge, daß die Türdiener es aufgaben, Neuankömmlinge beim Eintritt öffentlich anzukündigen."[1] Gespannt warteten alle auf das Erscheinen des Königs. „Schließlich öffnete sich die Tür ... und heraus traten acht Gestalten, die alle auf die gleiche, höchst eigenwillige Art – nämlich als geometrisch gestutzte Eibenbuschgebilde – verkleidet waren!"[2] Einer der Verkleideten war Ludwig XV., aber welcher? Eine der jungen Damen glaubte, die Maskerade durchschaut zu haben und schlüpfte mit einem der „Eibenbüsche" in den Garten. Doch als sie später – etwas derangiert – wieder in den Saal kam, erblickte sie den König, der die Kopfmaske abgenommen hatte – und sich mit der schönen Jagdgöttin unterhielt.

Nach dem Ball kam Jeanne-Antoinette Lenormant d'Étioles häufiger ins Schloß, angeblich, um Ludwig XV. Bittgesuche ihres Mannes vorzulegen. Am 3. April saß sie unter den Zuschauern im Schloßtheater – im Blickfeld des Königs. Dann wurde sie eingeladen, mit Ludwig XV. und anderen Gästen zu speisen.

Jeanne-Antoinette Lenormant d'Étioles – „ein Paradigma weiblichen Abenteurertums"[3] – hieß zwar nicht Étoiles[4], aber sie sah ihren Stern aufgehen.

Jeanne-Antoinette Poisson

Wer ist die Frau?

Ihr Vater, François Poisson – „ein dicker, robuster Mann, von grober Gestalt und grobem Benehmen, allen Genüssen des Lebens zugetan"[5] – stammte von Tagelöhnern ab, war Kutscher, arbeitete sich bei einem Bankier und einem Heereslieferanten hoch und verdiente am Ende als Händler so viel, daß er sich ein Haus neben dem Palais Royal in Paris leisten konnte. Vermutlich war er nicht korrupter als seine Geschäftspartner, aber als man ihn wegen einer Unterschlagung anklagte, floh er für einige Zeit aus der Stadt, um nicht aufgehängt zu werden.

Verheiratet war er mit einer um fünf Jahre jüngeren, hübschen und lebensfrohen Fleischertochter, die seit dem Besuch bei einer Wahrsagerin glaubte, sie werde eine zukünftige

Madame de Pompadour (1721–1764)
Gemälde von François Boucher, o. J. Paris. Musée du Louvre

Königin gebären. Als erstes Kind kam am 29. Dezember 1721 Jeanne-Antoinette zur Welt. Als das Mädchen sechs Jahre später einen Bruder bekam, lag die 1724 geborene Schwester bereits im Grab.

Wahrscheinlich wußte nur die Mutter, wer die Kinder gezeugt hatte, denn mit der ehelichen Treue nahm sie es nicht so genau. Jedenfalls glaubte Charles-François-Paul Lenormant de Tournehem, er sei der leibliche Vater der Kinder, und Louise-Madeleine Poisson wird so oder so nicht versucht haben, ihm das auszureden, da der ebenso reiche wie gebildete Steuerpächter für seine tatsächlichen oder vermeintlichen Sprößlinge aufmerksam sorgte.

Er beauftragte Hauslehrer, das Geschwisterpaar im Deklamieren, Tanzen, Musizieren zu unterrichten und ihm aristokratische Umgangsformen beizubringen. Schließlich überredete er seinen Neffen Charles-Guillaume Lenormant d'Étioles, um die Hand des Mädchens anzuhalten. Obwohl Jeanne-Antoinette Poisson den „äußerst kleinen, ziemlich häßlichen und schlecht gebauten"[6] Bewerber verabscheute, sträubte sie sich nicht gegen die Heirat, denn auf diese Weise kletterte sie auf der Gesellschaftsleiter einige Sprossen nach oben; ihren ordinären Familiennamen (Poisson – das heißt nichts anderes als Fisch) legte sie ab[7], zog in ein Schloß und erhielt wertvolle Kleider, kostbaren Schmuck und ein eigenes Haus in Paris.

Am 10. August 1744 brachte sie eine Tochter zur Welt – und im Wochenbett reifte ihr Plan, den König auf sich aufmerksam zu machen.

Madame Lenormant d'Étioles legt Wert auf geschmackvolle und nach der neuesten Mode geschneiderte Kleider: Die Röcke, die sich über einem ovalen Reifrock bauschen, zwingen sie, seitwärts durch Zimmertüren zu gehen, und dabei wippen sie so raffiniert, daß die Umstehenden einen Blick auf ihre Fesseln und die zierlichen Schuhe erhaschen können. Der pastellfarbene Seidenrock fällt vorn auseinander, um den prächtigen Aufputz des Unterrocks zur Wirkung zu bringen. Das Mieder betont die eng geschnürte Taille; sie trägt es wie eine Jacke, vorn offen, zeigt das reich mit Rüschen und Schleifen verzierte

Bruststück des Korsetts und – im weiten Dekolleté – den kostbaren Spitzenbesatz des Hemds. Das Haar kämmt sie schlicht zurück und schmückt es mit erlesenen Perlen.

Ein Zeitgenosse schwärmt: „Jeder Mann hätte sie gern zur Mätresse gehabt. Groß, aber nicht zu groß für eine Frau, herrlich gewachsen, hatte sie ein rundes Gesicht, regelmäßig in jedem Zug. Teint, Hände und Arme waren wunderschön, die Augen eher klein, aber von so viel Glanz und Geist und Feuer, wie ich bei Frauen nie gesehen habe. Nichts an ihr war eckig, alle Formen, jede Bewegung abgerundet. Sämtliche Damen bei Hof, unter denen manche sehr schön waren, stellte sie in den Schatten."[8]

Auch der Forstmeister von Versailles ist des Lobes voll: Sie „war schlank, ... geschmeidig, elegant ... Sie besaß schöne Haare, die mehr hellkastanienbraun als blond waren ..."[9] „Ihre Augen hatten einen eigenen Reiz, vielleicht war es ihre unbestimmte Farbe – kein schwarzes Gleißen, keine zärtlich sehnsuchtsvolle Bläue, nicht der feine Schimmer grauer Augen, nein, eine unnennbare Tönung, geschickt, auf alle Weise zu verführen und jede Regung einer sehr beweglichen Seele auszudrücken. Ihre Miene wechselte in einem fort ..."[10]

Die etwas traurigen Züge in ihrem fein geschnittenen Gesicht überspielt sie mit einem gewinnenden Lächeln. Obwohl sie dazu neigt, beim Sprechen lebhaft zu gestikulieren und das Gesagte mimisch zu verstärken, wirkt sie eher nachdenklich und zurückhaltend. In den Pariser Salons[11] wird sie gern gesehen, weil sie bei der geistvollen Konversation Funken schlägt. Aufgrund ihrer überragenden Intelligenz versteht sie es, witzige Bemerkungen einzuflechten, doch über Humor verfügt sie nicht: den lassen ihr Mangel an Gelassenheit und ihr außergewöhnlicher Ehrgeiz nicht aufkommen.

Der Hof von Versailles

In der absolutistischen französischen Monarchie verkörperte der König den Staat und verfügte über die uneingeschränkte Macht. „L'état c'est moi!"[12] behauptete König Ludwig XIV. Ein strenges Zeremoniell hob ihn von den gewöhnlichen Menschen ab und unterstrich sein Gottesgnadentum. Selbst aus seinem Aufstehen und Schlafengehen machte der „Sonnenkönig" einen formellen Akt: „Morgens um acht begann die erste Zeremonie des Tages, das *lever*, das öffentliche Aufstehen des Königs. Dazu wurden die Höflinge in Etappen zugelassen, wobei es als höchste Ehre galt, wenn man der ersten und zweiten Phase des *lever* beiwohnen durfte. Während der ersten Phase lag der König noch im Bett, und seine Kleider wurden für ihn bereitgelegt. Nun durfte die zweite Gruppe zusehen, wie er das Nachthemd ablegte und Hemd und Wams anzog. Dann folgten das Anziehen des Rockes, das Schließen der Schuhschnallen und das Umhängen des Degens. Ludwig XIV. hatte wie viele seiner Zeitgenossen nicht die Gewohnheit, sich zu waschen."[13]

Zuerst Hunderte, dann Tausende bildeten den königlichen Hofstaat in Versailles. Dessen Strukturen und Abläufe entsprachen bis ins kleinste einem allgegenwärtigen Reglement, das die hierarchische Stellung jedes einzelnen Höflings ebenso festlegte wie seine Pflichten und Vorrechte. Ohne die ausdrückliche Erlaubnis des Königs „durfte man nichts, weder tagsüber nach Paris, noch sich gegen die Pocken impfen lassen, geschweige denn seine Kinder verheiraten."[14]

Infolge seiner pompösen Hofhaltung und verschwenderischen Bautätigkeit hinterließ Ludwig XIV. 1715 einen riesigen Schuldenberg, aber den Kosmos der Versailler Schloßanlage betrachteten die europäischen Fürsten jahrzehntelang als Vorbild.

Das Hofleben bestand aus einem raffiniert-maliziösen Netzwerk von Intrigen[15]; Ehebrüche und Schurkereien tolerierte man, solange sie mit eleganten Manieren und „pflichtschuldiger Heiterkeit"[16] überspielt wurden.

Bei der Liaison zwischen Ludwig XV. und Jeanne-Antoinette Lenormant d'Étioles handelt es sich um einen doppelten Ehebruch: Nicht nur der König ist verheiratet, sondern auch seine Geliebte. Was aber die Gemüter bei Hof wirklich erregt, ist die Abstammung der Auserwählten: Eine Bürgerliche droht in die sorgsam abgeschottete Welt des Adels einzudringen! Das stellt die gesellschaftliche Ordnung auf den Kopf. Gibt es nicht genügend schöne Töchter adeliger Familien? Einer von ihnen stünde die Ehre zu, vom König begehrt zu werden – zumal die Höflinge überzeugt sind, daß die neue Favoritin Ludwigs XV. wegen ihrer Herkunft keine Maîtresse en titre werden kann.

Ludwig XV.

Ludwig XV. kam am 15. Februar 1710 in Versailles zur Welt. An seine Eltern konnte er sich später nicht erinnern, denn sie starben innerhalb einer Woche an Pocken, als er zwei Jahre alt war, und da auch sein Großvater seit 1711 tot war, folgte er 1715 seinem Urgroßvater auf den Thron, während ein entfernter Verwandter die Regentschaft übernahm.

„Jede Vorsichtsmaßregel wurde getroffen, um ihn für die Herrschaft unfähig zu machen."[17] In ständiger Sorge um seine Gesundheit schützte ihn die Gouvernante vor jedem Luftzug, und niemand wagte, den vergötterten Knaben zu tadeln.

„Sinnbildlich repräsentierte dieser Herrscher die Hinfälligkeit und Schwächen der Epoche ... immer begleitet und verzehrt vom Gefühl des Ekels, der Mattigkeit und von äußerster Entnervung. Die Langeweile war der böse Geist des Herrschers: sie lähmte alle glücklichen Gaben seiner Natur, sie drückte seinen Geist hinab, reduzierte ihn aufs bloß Geistreiche, auf Skepsis und Spott – sie ließ ihn unproduktiv werden. Sie schwächte und entwaffnete seinen Willen, sie erstickte sein Gewissen ebenso wie seine Begierden. Sie ließ ihn gleichgültig werden seiner geschichtlichen Verantwortung wie seinem Land gegenüber."[18]

1721 wurde Ludwig XV. mit der zweijährigen Tochter des spanischen Königs verlobt, aber als einer der Ratgeber zu bedenken gab, daß man noch lange auf einen Thronfolger warten müsse, obwohl der König bald zeugungsfähig sei, schickte der Regent das Mädchen wie eine abgelegte Puppe nach Madrid zurück und arrangierte 1725 die Hochzeit des inzwischen fünfzehnjährigen Knaben mit der Tochter des verjagten polnischen Königs Stanislaus Leszczynski.[19]

Da es sich um eine Vernunftehe handelte, überraschte es niemanden, daß der schüchterne König mit seiner um sieben Jahre älteren Gemahlin Maria wenig anzufangen wußte und diese an seiner Seite vereinsamte, obwohl sie zehn Kinder gebar.

Zwar rühmten die Höflinge ihre Güte, aber im nächsten Halbsatz lästerten sie über ihren fehlenden Esprit.

Immerhin wartete Ludwig XV. jahrelang, bis er sich eine Mätresse nahm. Louise Julie de Nesle Comtesse de Mailly diente der Königin als Zofe, und ihr Gemahl gehörte zur königlichen Leibgarde. Nach und nach holte er sich auch ihre drei Schwestern ins Bett. Zwei von ihnen ließen sich ohne weiteres überreden; die dritte gab sich dem König erst hin, als er sie zu seiner offiziellen Mätresse und zur Herzogin von Châteauroux erhob.

Obwohl es zum guten Ton gehörte, sich als Würdenträger eine Mätresse zu leisten, plagten Ludwig XV. wegen seines ehebrecherischen Lebens von Zeit zu Zeit Gewissensbisse – und einige Männer der Kirche träufelten scharfe Ermahnungen in die Wunden.[20]

Offizielle Einführung in Versailles

Im Frühjahr 1745 richtet sich Jeanne-Antoinette Lenormant d'Étioles im Schloß von Versailles ein.

„Ludwig XV. besuchte sie häufig. Während der Sitzungen mit seinen Ministern im Arbeitskabinett begab er sich manchmal über eine Geheimtreppe zu ihr. Die Minister mußten auf ihn warten, um dann gemeinsam mit ihm den Raum zu verlassen. So wurde bei den Höflingen der Eindruck erweckt, als habe er erst in diesem Moment aufgehört zu arbeiten ... Die früheren Mätressen Ludwigs XV. hatten mit vielen rauschenden Festen in ihren Appartements Entrüstung gesät. [Die neue Geliebte] dagegen ... verwandelte die Gemächer in einen dezenten Speisesaal, in dem sie exklusive Essen gab. Es galt als besondere Gunst, zu diesen intimen Soupers in Gegenwart des Königs geladen zu werden. Der Herzog von Croy, der 1746 zu den Glücklichen gehörte, beschreibt den Verlauf eines solchen Abends ...: ‚Es wurde nur von zwei oder drei Dienern serviert, die sich zurückzogen, nachdem jeder genug auf seinem Teller hatte. ... Der König war fröhlich, ungezwungen ... Er schien überhaupt nicht mehr schüchtern zu sein, sondern ganz natürlich; er sprach sehr gut und viel ...'"[21]

Charles-Guillaume Lenormant d'Étioles fällt ihn Ohnmacht, als er erfährt, daß seine Frau die Mätresse des Königs ist; er schreibt ihr flehentliche Briefe, droht, sich das Leben zu nehmen, aber schließlich findet er sich mit der Trennung ab – zumal ihm der Monarch dafür das einträgliche Amt eines Steuerpächters verschafft.

In dem Schloß, das ihr der gehörnte Ehemann überläßt, verbringt Jeanne-Antoinette Lenormant d'Étioles den Sommer: Der König hält sich vier Monate lang bei seinen Truppen im Feld auf, und sie nutzt seine Abwesenheit, um sich in den Feinheiten höfischer Umgangsformen unterweisen zu lassen. Da ist es mit Tischmanieren und Höflichkeitsfloskeln nicht getan, denn wer in dieser Gesellschaft bestehen möchte, muß Tausende von Regeln beherrschen: die Körperhaltung, das Gehen, die Mimik, das Sprechen und das Briefeschreiben – jede Äußerung wird nach minuziösen Regeln beurteilt. Die Umgangsformen sind ebenso graziös-verschnörkelt wie die Verzierungen der Rokoko-Architektur. Hier besteht nur, wer diese Klaviatur beherrscht, und um zu brillieren, hilft es, in dieses virtuose Spiel scharfsinnige Intrigen einzufügen.

Der König schreibt seiner dreiundzwanzig Jahre alten Geliebten in dieser Zeit mehr als achtzig Briefe – die letzten adressiert er bereits an die „Marquise de Pompadour" – und gleich nach seiner Rückkehr sorgt er dafür, daß sie als Maîtresse en titre bei Hof eingeführt wird: Zwei Damen der Gesellschaft stellen sie entsprechend der Etikette dem König vor – und alle tun so, als würde sich das Liebespaar zum ersten Mal sehen. Die Höflinge drängen sich, damit es ihnen nicht entgeht, wenn die erste aus dem Bürgertum stammende Mätresse etwas Unpassendes sagt, stolpert oder eine falsche Verbeugung macht. Doch nichts dergleichen geschieht. Nachdem Ludwig XV. verlegen einige Phrasen mit ihr ausgetauscht hat, sucht Madame de Pompadour die Königin auf. Maria empfängt die achtzehn Jahre Jüngere in ihren Privatgemächern und fragt sie nach einer gemeinsamen Bekannten. Die Umstehenden zählen mit: Zwölf Sätze wechseln die Damen! Das hätte niemand erwartet.

Werden sich die Königin und die Mätresse arrangieren?

Mißgunst und Feindschaft

Ein höhnisches Schreiben der Pompadour beweist, daß andere Damen versuchen, sie von der Seite Ludwigs XV. zu verdrängen: „Ich weiß, daß Sie sich seit einiger Zeit ganz hervorragend im Sinne jener schönen Damen betätigen, die Absichten auf das Herz des Königs haben. Sie folgen ihm auf Schritt und Tritt. Sie sind immer irgendwo im Hinterhalt anzutreffen, um ihn zu überraschen – was uns viel Spaß macht. (Ich bitte Sie um Verzeihung, Madame: man müßte eigentlich Ihre Torheit beklagen, statt darüber zu lachen.) Ich persönlich, Madame, habe das Unglück, die Größe Ihrer Qualitäten nicht zu kennen. Aber auch der König weiß nichts davon, obgleich Sie alles tun, was in Ihren Kräften steht, ihn damit bekannt zu machen."[22]

In einem anderen Brief berichtet Madame de Pompadour einer Freundin, ein Geistlicher habe sich dem König zu Füßen geworfen und ihm eine Bittschrift überreicht: „Im Auftrag Gottes verkünde ich Eurer Majestät die unbedingte Notwendigkeit, Madame de Pompadour so schnell wie möglich fortzuschicken. Sonst wird Gott seine Rächerhand über Ihr Königreich ausstrecken und Ihre Untertanen für die Schwachheit des Herrschers bestrafen."[23]

Die Höflinge entrüsten sich über die enormen Rechnungen, die für ihre verschwenderische Einrichtung, ihre Kleider und Juwelen bezahlt werden. „Sie ist teurer als der Krieg!", sagt jemand und verdreht die Augen. Neider und Klatschbasen lauern auf einen Fauxpas, und sogar Voltaire – der ihr eine königliche Pension und die Aufnahme in die Académie française verdankt – weist sie wegen eines unpassenden Worts

84

in einer Abendgesellschaft zurecht und steigert so ihre Blamage. Über die Königsmätresse, die „aus nicht allzu feinen Verhältnissen, doch mit dem geballten Einsatz ihrer weiblichen Mittel und Möglichkeiten emporgestiegen war, um aus dem Bett des pflichtvergessenen königlichen Erotomanen das Zepter über Frankreich zu schwingen",[24] werden Kalauer zum besten gegeben und Spottgedichte kichernd herumgereicht.

Dem Kronrat mißfällt, daß sich der König sogar in geheimen Regierungsangelegenheiten mit Madame de Pompadour bespricht, und die Drahtzieher registrieren mit Unbehagen, daß eine Frau politische Entscheidungen unkontrollierbar beeinflußt.

Klug und zielstrebig setzt sich die Angegriffene zur Wehr. Es fällt ihr nicht immer leicht: „Ich fange an einzusehen, daß der Ehrgeiz eines Frauenherzens die größte aller Martern ist."[25] Sie weiß, daß Erotik und Prostitution zwar das Startkapital für ihren Aufstieg bildeten, aber nicht genügen, um das Erreichte dauerhaft zu sichern. Deshalb verläßt sie sich nicht nur auf den Schutz des Königs, sondern sucht Verbündete, und es gelingt ihr, sogar die Königin für sich einzunehmen, indem sie ihr respektvoll begegnet und Ludwig XV. dazu überredet, seine Gemahlin nicht länger wie Luft zu behandeln.

Ohne ihr politisches Gespür würde sie dennoch über kurz oder lang einer Intrige zum Opfer fallen.

Noblesse oblige

Innerhalb von vier Jahren erhält Madame de Pompadour vier Schlösser – und bei keinem gibt sie sich mit dem Vorgefundenen zufrieden, sondern sie läßt hier einige Räume restaurieren, da einen Park neu gestalten und dort einen Trakt anbauen. Ganz nach ihren Vorstellungen entsteht auf den Seine-Ufer-terrassen von Meudon ihr Lustschlößchen Bellevue, um das sie die Fürsten in ganz Europa beneiden. Sie meint dazu: „Man spottet immer über die Bauwut: Ich für meine Person kann diese angebliche Torheit nur billigen, die so vielen Armen Brot gibt. Mir macht es keinen Spaß, das Geld in meinem Kasten anzuschauen, ich bringe es lieber in Umlauf."[26]

Im Schloß von Versailles richtet sie ein Theater ein. Selbst die Königin besucht eine der Aufführungen. Die begehrten Rollen vergibt Madame de Pompadour vorzugsweise an Grafen und Gräfinnen, Herzöge und Herzoginnen, die ihr dafür einen Gefallen erweisen, etwa einem ihrer Anhänger zu einem einflußreichen Amt verhelfen.

. Im Zeitalter der Aufklärung wird Gott an den Rand seiner Schöpfung geschoben und der Kosmos als Maschine aufgefaßt, deren Räderwerk sich aufgrund erforschbarer Gesetze dreht. Die Philosophen untergraben die Fundamente der etablierten Ordnung. Denis Diderot propagiert den aufgeklärten Menschen, „der die Vorurteile, die Tradition, das Überalterte, die universelle Übereinstimmung, die Autorität, mit einem Wort alles, was das gesamte Denken unterjocht, zu Boden reißt und wagt, selbst zu denken."[27]

Ein absolutistischer Herrscher wie Ludwig XV., der sich auf das Gottesgnadentum beruft, fürchtet diese geistige Entwicklung – und verbietet die umfangreiche Enzyklopädie, in der Denis Diderot und andere Intellektuelle ohne Rücksicht auf Dogmen und Traditionen niederschreiben, was sie wissen.[28]

Von Diderot um Hilfe gebeten, wartet die Marquise de Pompadour auf eine günstige Gelegenheit, und als bei einem Souper niemand die Frage beantworten kann, woraus Schießpulver gemacht wird, klagt sie: „Ich weiß nicht einmal, woraus das Rouge besteht, das ich mir auf die Wangen lege."[29] Und einer der Gäste meint: „Es ist schade, daß seine Majestät unsere enzyklopädischen Wörterbücher konfisziert hat, die jeden von uns hundert Pistolen gekostet haben. Wir würden dort bald die Erklärungen für alle unsere Fragen finden."[30] Daraufhin läßt der König die Folianten aus seiner Bibliothek holen. Eifrig schlagen die Herren nach und lesen sich gegenseitig vor, wie Rouge, Schießpulver und viele andere Sachen erzeugt werden. Auf diese Weise erreicht die Pompadour, daß Ludwig XV. das Verbot aufhebt.

Die Schlüsselposition der Marquise de Pompadour läßt sich am ehesten mit der eines Kultusministers vergleichen.[31] Aber nicht nur um Kunst und Kultur kümmert sich die königliche Mätresse, sondern auch um praktische gesellschaftspolitische Angelegenheiten: Der Besuch einer Mädchenschule, die Ludwig XIV. für Töchter verarmter Adelsfamilien einrichtete, bringt sie auf eine Idee: 1751 unterschreibt Ludwig XV. die Gründungsurkunde der königlichen Militärschule in Paris, in der jährlich fünfhundert mittellose Edelmänner als Offiziere ausgebildet werden sollen, um verarmte Adelsfamilien zu unterstützen und das Ausbildungsniveau des französischen Offizierskorps zu heben. Wegen finanzieller Schwierigkeiten wäre das Projekt beinahe gescheitert, aber die Pompadour gibt nicht auf, bis die École Militaire fünf Jahre nach dem Gründungsakt eröffnet wird.[32]

„Sie erging sich täglich in tausend Zerstreuungen, war immer in Bewegung, immer geschäftig. Sie zeigte sich überall, kümmerte sich um alles und verausgabte sich an hundert Orten und in tausend Dingen mit einem Fieber, einer nervösen Willenskraft, die wahrhaft erstaunlich waren in einem so zarten und so kränklichen Körper."[33] Neben ihren Eingriffen in die staatlichen Angelegenheiten und ihren Bemühungen, den König zu unterhalten, findet sie noch Zeit, zu lesen. Mehr als dreitausendfünfhundert Bände stehen in ihrer Bibliothek. Ist diese gescheite Frau nicht die Tochter eines groben Lebensmittelhändlers? Jedenfalls wird deutlich, wieviel sie ihrem Gönner (leiblichen Vater?) Charles-François-Paul Lenormant de Tournehem verdankt: Die Bildung, zu der er ihr verhalf, bildet ein Substrat, auf dem ihre Neigungen blühen. Und Ludwig XV.? Würde er sich mit einer weniger kultivierten Frau nicht bald wieder langweilen?

Liebe

In den ersten Jahren ihres Zusammenlebens mit Ludwig XV. erleidet die Marquise de Pompadour mehrere Fehlgeburten. Sie gibt sich dem König hin, aber sie scheint im Bett nicht besonders leidenschaftlich zu sein, denn ihre Kammerfrau erinnert sich später: „Ich hatte bemerkt, daß Madame sich

schon einige Tage lang Schokolade mit einer dreifachen Portion Vanille und einer Dosis Amber zum Frühstück bringen
ließ, daß sie Trüffel aß und Selleriesuppe."[34] Diese vermeintlichen Aphrodisiaka sollen ihr helfen, mehr Gefallen an
der „etwas ruppigen, waidmännischen Liebeskunst"[35] Ludwigs XV. zu finden – aber sie wird krank davon.

Einige Zeit tut sie sich Gewalt an, um ihre „trauerenten-
hafte" Kälte, wie sie es selbst nennt, zu überwinden, aber sie
ist weise genug, sich nach einiger Zeit damit abzufinden, daß
ihr Körper den König nicht mehr erregt: Sie ermutigt ihn, sich
mit anderen Frauen zu befriedigen, sorgt dafür, daß in einem
versteckten Anwesen im Versailler Hirschpark stets ein, zwei
Mädchen auf den Unersättlichen warten, achtet jedoch darauf,
daß aus den Liebesabenteuern keine Rivalinnen hervorgehen,
weil sie weiß, daß ihre Position trotz der inzwischen erworbe-
nen Macht ohne weiteres durch ein Wort des Königs zerstört
werden kann.

Wenn die Beziehung lediglich auf Sexualität beruhte, zer-
bräche sie jetzt.

Ludwig XV. schläft zwar kaum noch mit seiner Mätresse,
aber er verbringt jeden Tag einige Stunden mit ihr. Er liebt
diese Frau, weil sie schön und klug ist, energisch und nie um
einen Einfall verlegen. Während er sich schwer entscheiden
kann, weiß sie stets, was sie will. Sie reißt ihn aus seiner
Melancholie, indem sie ihm unermüdlich neue Zerstreuungen
vorschlägt und ihn dazu bringt, daß er sich schulterzuckend
darauf einläßt. Sie überredet den König, mit ihr in eines der
anderen Schlösser zu fahren, lädt Gäste ein, arrangiert Feste,
bringt ihn mit komischen Geschichten zum Lachen, zeichnet,
deklamiert und singt – hört jedoch auf, bevor er dessen über-
drüssig wird: „Der allerchristlichste König ist, wie ich, bald
traurig, bald fröhlich. Wenn ihn Schwermut überkommt,
nehme ich meine Zuflucht zu kleinen Liedern, die er sehr
liebt. Dann singen wir und sind scheinbar vergnügt."[36]

Er schätzt ihren Rat in persönlichen wie in politischen
Angelegenheiten und vertraut ihr, denn sie läßt sich von keiner der rivalisierenden Hofcliquen vorschieben.

Macht und Einfluß

Bald gehört es zum guten Ton, daß Besucher des Königs in Versailles nicht nur der Königin, sondern auch der Mätresse ihre Aufwartung machen. Obwohl Madame de Pompadour kein staatliches Amt bekleidet, empfängt sie ausländische Diplomaten – wobei sie sitzt und selbst Herzöge vor ihr stehen. Was sie für richtig hält, trägt sie dem König vor, und häufig stimmt er ihren Vorschlägen zu. Aber nicht nur auf diesem Weg greift sie in die Politik ein: Sie pflegt auch mit anderen Meinungsmachern und Entscheidungsträgern gute Beziehungen.

Wer Madame de Pompadour überzeugt, hat bereits halb gewonnen; wer ihr jedoch im Weg steht, muß mit schwerwiegenden Nachteilen rechnen.

„Eine absolute Härte gegen sich selbst, eine überlegene Beherrschtheit aller Regungen, Sinne und Instinkte, das Talent zu Lüge und Komödie, ein vollkommener Egoismus, der den des Königs ergänzte, das Kalkül eines Politikers, dem alles Mittel zum Zweck war, kennzeichneten die Marquise. Ein unbedingter Wille auf ein angestrebtes Ziel, ein philosophischer Geist, ironisch und skeptisch, kaltblütig und ohne zärtliche Regungen oder religiöse Gefühle, ein Herz ohne Gnade, ohne Verzeihung, unerbittlich im Groll und in der Rache, taub gegenüber den Bitten und Klagen jener, die in Ungnade gefallen waren ... – so war die Favoritin im Innern beschaffen. ... Der Ehrgeiz regelte ihre Leidenschaften, die Vernunft ihr Gewissen."[37]

Einer der ersten Gegner, an denen sie ein Exempel statuiert, ist Jean Frédéric Phélippeaux de Maurepas, ein eifriger Verfasser von Spottgedichten über die Pompadour. Der Marineminister platzt vor Wut, denn wann immer er den König aufsucht, ist sie da, und obwohl dieser ihm seit vielen Jahren vertraut, muß er seine Papiere zusammenraffen und sich zurückziehen, wenn Madame de Pompadour meint: „Monsieur de Maurepas, der König wird gelb, das bekommt ihm nicht. Adieu, Monsieur de Maurepas."[38]

Der Marineminister hält sich für unersetzbar und wird sowohl von der Königin als auch vom Dauphin unterstützt, aber Madame de Pompadour arbeitet geduldig und ausdauernd daran, sein Ansehen beim König zu untergraben. Als Ludwig XV. dennoch mit einer Entscheidung zögert, redet sie ihm ein, de Maurepas habe ihre Vorgängerin, die Herzogin von Châteauroux, vergiftet und wolle nun auch sie ermorden. Mit vorgespielter Angst fällt sie dem König wohldosiert auf die Nerven – bis er ihren Widersacher verbannt.

Das gibt anderen zu denken. Trotzdem läßt sich Kriegsminister Marc Pierre Comte d'Argenson nicht davon abschrekken, gegen Madame de Pompadour zu intrigieren; gerade wegen ihrer außerordentlichen Macht will er sie aus ihrer Position verdrängen.

Zu diesem Zweck plant er 1753, dem König eine harmlosere Mätresse zuzuführen, und seine eigene Geliebte, die Comtesse d'Estrades, hilft ihm dabei: Für die Rolle der Verführerin gewinnt diese Vertraute der Pompadour die nicht besonders schlaue, dafür aber junge und gut aussehende Gräfin von Choiseul-Romanet, die als Kammerzofe in Versailles dient.

Ohne Verdacht zu schöpfen, lädt Madame de Pompadour den Lockvogel wiederholt zu gemeinsamen Ausfahrten mit dem König ein.

Als Ludwig XV. die Schöne in sein Bett holt, können es die Verschwörer kaum erwarten, bis sie ihnen noch in der gleichen Nacht Bericht erstattet. Sie nimmt sich nicht einmal Zeit, ihre Kleider zu ordnen: „Ja, ja, ich werde geliebt, er ist glücklich und sie geht, er hat mir sein Wort gegeben."[39]

Im Überschwang der Gefühle hat der König versprochen, seine Maîtresse en titre zu verstoßen.

Da nimmt das Geschehen eine unerwartete Wendung: Der König schreibt Charlotte-Rosalie de Choiseul-Romanet nach der ersten Liebesnacht einen leidenschaftlichen Brief; das naive Mädchen zeigt ihn einem Vertrauten und bittet diesen, eine stilgerechte Antwort für sie zu formulieren. Graf von Stainville verspricht, sich etwas auszudenken, nimmt das Billet doux an sich – und bringt es Madame de Pompadour.

Die stellt den König zur Rede. „Madame de Pompadour war eine der wenigen Frauen, die genau wissen, wann und wie man eine Szene macht. Als der König wie gewöhnlich gegen Abend zu ihr kam, um ein Stündchen zu verplaudern, ehe er mit den Ministern an die Arbeit ging, brach das Ungewitter über ihn herein. Es traf ihn gänzlich unvorbereitet, er hatte gar nichts für sich anzuführen. Als er aber in den Händen der Marquise den Brief erblickte und hörte, wie sie dazu gekommen war, da entlud sich ein Zorn auf Madame de Choiseul ...“[40] Die Achtzehnjährige muß sofort das Schloß verlassen.

Es dauert nicht lang, bis Madame de Pompadour durchschaut, wer bei der Intrige die Drähte zog, aber sie muß zwei Jahre warten, bis sie sich rächen kann. Eine Gelegenheit ergibt sich, als sie krank im Bett liegt und ein Brief des Königs von ihrem Nachttisch verschwindet. Sie dramatisiert den Vorfall, betont, das Schreiben habe sich auf eine brisante politische Angelegenheit bezogen und lenkt den Verdacht auf die Comtesse d'Estrades – die deshalb aus Versailles verstoßen wird. (Der Graf von Argenson muß sich 1757 auf sein Landgut zurückziehen.)

Die Gegner der königlichen Mätresse schüren Mißgunst gegen sie. „Es blieb nicht bei Beleidigungen und Spott; Madame de Pompadour bekam auch zahlreiche anonyme Drohbriefe, die sie um ihr Leben fürchten ließen.“[41] Sie muß „jeden Tag aufs neue um ihre Machtstellung kämpfen: Es war eine nie endende Schlacht, eine Anspannung, die sie nicht zur Ruhe kommen ließ, eine Aufgabe, um die ihr ganzes Denken kreiste. Jeder Tag brachte die gleiche Mischung aus Intrigen, Heimlichkeiten und listigem Taktieren, ohne die es der Mätresse unmöglich gewesen wäre, sich dauerhaft in dieser labilen Stellung allerhöchster Gunst zu halten, um die sie ständig beneidet und derentwegen sie ständig angegriffen wurde, in der sie unentwegt Gefahr lief, in eine Falle zu gehen ...“[42]

Sie muß auf der Hut sein – zumal ihre Feinde neidisch beobachten, wie ihre Anhänger in begehrte Positionen aufsteigen.

Madame de Pompadour sorgt dafür, daß der König ihren Bruder François-Abel kennenlernt. Dessen schüchternes Benehmen gefällt Ludwig XV., und obwohl der junge Mann im Gegensatz zu seiner Schwester von keinerlei Ehrgeiz getrieben wird, erhebt man ihn zum Marquis. Damit nicht genug: Die Pompadour arrangiert 1747 für ihn eine mehrjährige Bildungsreise durch Italien, damit er sich auf die Rolle des Generalinspekteurs des königlichen Bauwesens vorbereitet.[43] Dieses Amt verwaltet der alternde Charles-François-Paul Lenormant de Tournehem, der es ihrem Bruder überlassen will. Das geschieht schneller als erwartet, denn der väterliche Freund der Geschwister stirbt 1751, und François-Abel muß vorzeitig aus Italien zurückkehren, um – vierundzwanzigjährig – die Nachfolge anzutreten.

Madame de Pompadour ermahnt ihre Tochter Alexandrine: „Nur nicht hochmütig sein! Es steht niemandem an, und Dir noch weniger als anderen. Wenn ich Dich wie eine Prinzessin erziehen lasse, so bedenke, daß Du weit davon entfernt bist, eine zu sein. Das Schicksal, das mich emporhob, kann mir auch untreu werden und mich zur unglücklichsten aller Frauen machen. Dann würdest Du, genau wie ich selbst, gar nichts mehr gelten."[44]

Auch für Alexandrine entwickelt die Pompadour hochfliegende Pläne: Sie träumt davon, das Mädchen mit einem illegitimen Sohn Ludwigs XV. zu verheiraten. Aber in diesem Fall versagen ihre Überredungskünste: Sie kann den König nicht für ihren Plan gewinnen, und während sie weiter nach einer „guten Partie" sucht, stirbt Alexandrine vor ihrem zehnten Geburtstag.

Der Tod ihrer Tochter erschüttert die sonst so beherrschte Marquise: Sie ißt tagelang kaum etwas, schläft so gut wie nicht und sucht vergeblich Zuflucht im Glauben.

Herzogin und Palastdame

Der König erhebt seine Mätresse zur Herzogin, aber damit gibt sich die Pompadour nicht zufrieden: Palastdame der Königin will sie werden.

Königin Maria lehnt ihre Ernennung jedoch ab, denn für das angesehene Amt kommt nur eine tugendhafte Frau in Frage, keine exkommunizierte Ehebrecherin.

Trotzdem hält Madame de Pompadour an ihrer Absicht fest und findet auch in diesem Fall eine Lösung: Sie schreibt ihrem Ehemann, sie bereue ihr Verhalten, er möge ihr vergeben und sie wieder bei sich aufnehmen. Bevor der Brief bei ihm eintrifft, läßt sie ihm jedoch ausrichten, daß der König über eine Zustimmung nicht erfreut wäre, und erwartungsgemäß antwortet Charles-Guillaume Lenormant d'Étioles, er verzeihe ihr, aber sein Junggesellenleben wolle er beibehalten. Der Briefwechsel dient Madame de Pompadour als Beleg für die Behauptung, sie habe versucht, zu ihrem Gatten zurückzukehren; man könne ihr also nicht länger die Schuld an der gescheiterten Ehe zuweisen.

Tatsächlich hebt die Kirche die Exkommunikation auf, und sie erhält den begehrten Posten – eine weitere Stütze ihrer Macht.

Zur gleichen Zeit beeinflußt sie die Politik der europäischen Großmächte. Davon handelt der folgende Abschnitt.

Von der österreichischen Regierung umworben

Nach dem Tod ihrer Väter im Jahr 1740 stehen sich der preußische König Friedrich II. und die Kaiserin Maria Theresia gegenüber: Vierzig Jahre lang wird die warmherzige fromme Wienerin, die sechzehn Kinder gebiert, von dem zynischen Anhänger der Aufklärung bekämpft.

Obwohl sich Bourbonen und Habsburger seit jeher feindlich gegenüberstehen, tritt Wenzel Anton Graf Kaunitz, der 1750 als österreichischer Gesandter nach Paris geht, für eine Annäherung an Frankreich ein. Er trägt Madame de Pompadour seine Ideen vor, und um die Meinungsmacherin für das Vorhaben zu gewinnen, stachelt er ihren Ehrgeiz an: „Madame, Sie sind in der Lage, die große Politik zwischen Wien und Paris mitzugestalten!" Maria Theresia sähe es lieber, wenn ihr Gesandter nicht eine Frau als Vermittlerin einschalten müßte, „die von ihrer Auffassung von Sittlichkeit wie ihrer Anschauung des Herrschertums meilenweit entfernt"[45] ist, aber Graf Kaunitz überzeugt die Kaiserin, daß nur auf diesem Weg ein Fortschritt erzielt werden könne.

Seinen Plan verliert er auch im neugeschaffenen Amt des Staatskanzlers in Wien nicht aus den Augen: Im August 1755 schickt Maria Theresia einen Kurier nach Versailles, um Ludwig XV. erneut auf ihre gemeinsamen Interessen hinzuweisen, und Georg Adam Graf von Starhemberg, Kaunitz' Nachfolger in Paris, unterrichtet unverzüglich Madame de Pompadour über den Vorgang.

Der König geht einem Treffen mit dem österreichischen Gesandten vorsichtig aus dem Weg und beauftragt statt dessen seine Mätresse und einen ihrer langjährigen Vertrauten, mit Graf von Starhemberg Geheimgespräche aufzunehmen. Auf Madame de Pompadours Landsitz Babiole findet die erste Begegnung statt. Zu den weiteren Verhandlungen wird sie zwar nicht mehr hinzugezogen, aber die österreichischen Politiker bleiben mit ihr in Verbindung und sie wirkt unermüdlich auf den König ein. „Sie lockte, erschreckte und ermutigte. Sie appellierte an die Instinkte Ludwigs, die ihn zu einer Allianz mit der Kaiserin drängten, und schoß gleichzeitig auf geschickte Weise Giftpfeile ab, die seiner alten Abneigung gegen den häretischen Preußenkönig neue Nahrung gaben. Sie appellierte sogar an seinen Glauben und ließ vor seinen Augen die Idee einer großen katholischen Allianz erstrahlen, die in Europa das Gegengewicht gegen die wachsende Macht der protestantischen Partei bilden würde. Endlich gaukelte sie dem Herrscher, der sich nach Ruhe sehnte, das Bild eines langwährenden Friedens vor, an dem er sich in seinem Alter erfreuen könnte ..."[46]

Ihre Beharrlichkeit trägt Früchte, als sich Preußen und England 1756 – einige Monate vor dem Beginn des Siebenjährigen

Krieges[47] – verpflichten, jeden Angriff einer fremden Macht in Deutschland gemeinsam abzuwehren: Ludwig XV. und Maria Theresia schließen daraufhin einen Neutralitäts- und Verteidigungspakt, der im Jahr darauf zur Offensivallianz erweitert wird.

Starhemberg schreibt Kaunitz über Madame de Pompadour: „Es ist gegenwärtig der Augenblick, da wir sie mehr denn je nötig haben. ... Es ist sicher, daß sie es ist, der wir alles verdanken, und daß sie es ist, von der wir alles in Zukunft erwarten müssen."[48] Staatskanzler Kaunitz versichert ihr: „Es ist Ihrem Eifer und Ihrer Weisheit, Madame, zuzuschreiben, was bisher zwischen den beiden Höfen vereinbart wurde."[49] Und Maria Theresia bedankt sich bei der Mätresse mit einem wertvollen Schreibzeug.

Die Franzosen aber sind entrüstet: „Auf einmal sollten sie Schulter an Schulter mit den Mördern ihrer Väter, Onkel und Brüder kämpfen? ... Dem Volk und den Generälen war das Bündnis von Anbeginn verhaßt, wie viel mehr noch, als nach den ersten Siegen das Blatt sich wandte und die Armee empfindliche Schlappen erlitt. Schuld an allem war nur eine, die Pompadour."[50]

Das Attentat

Versailles, 5. Januar 1757: Der Monarch kommt die Stufen herunter, um seine Kutsche zu besteigen. Ein Mann drängt sich durch das Spalier der Höflinge. In seiner Hand blitzt ein Dolch auf. Damit sticht er auf den König ein. Leibgardisten stürzen sich auf den Unbekannten. Ludwig XV. meint zunächst, der Mann habe ihn nur gegen die Schulter gestoßen; erst als er an die schmerzende Stelle greift und das Blut an seiner Hand bemerkt, weiß er, daß er verwundet ist. Erblaßt dreht er sich um und kehrt ins Schloß zurück. „Als er nach oben in sein Schlafzimmer kam, schien er stärker zu bluten. Ihm wurde schwarz vor den Augen, er glaubte sein Ende nahe und verlangte nach einem Beichtiger. Jetzt begann die Verwirrung. Der Hof residierte schon einige Tage in Trianon, das Bett war nicht bezogen, kein Nachthemd zu finden, schlimmer noch, kein Arzt. Der König wurde bewußtlos, kam wieder zu sich und bestand darauf zu beichten."[51]

Der Schock ist groß, aber der Souverän wurde nur leicht an der Schulter verletzt.

Den Attentäter verurteilt man zum Tod: Eine große Menge sieht zu, wie ihm der Henker die Hände abhackt, ihn mit flüssigem Blei übergießt, ihm die Zunge aus dem Mund reißt, bevor er ihn mit Armen und Beinen an vier Pferde bindet und dann die Tiere auseinander peitscht.

Die Hintergründe des Anschlags werden nicht aufgeklärt, aber wie Fieber eine Infektion anzeigt, so ist die Tatsache, daß der König ermordet werden sollte, ein Symptom für den Aufruhr: Im Volk brodelt es. Das Elend treibt die Menschen auf die Straße, während die Hofgesellschaft in Versailles feiert. Als Personifizierung der höfischen Verschwendung zieht Madame de Pompadour den Haß auf sich, und der Erzbischof von Paris macht sie und ihre gottlosen Freunde Diderot und Voltaire in seinen Predigten für das Attentat verantwortlich. „Jeder trägt dazu bei, mir das Leben zu verbittern. Man legt mir das allgemeine Elend zur Last, die verkehrten Pläne des Kabinetts, den Mißerfolg des Krieges und die Triumphe unserer Feinde. Man klagt mich an, daß ich alles verkaufte, in allem meine Hand hätte, alles beherrschte."[52]

Ludwig XV. schließt sich tagelang in seinen Privatgemächern ein und überläßt die Regierungsangelegenheiten dem Dauphin. Wieder einmal von Angst und Reue heimgesucht, bittet er seine Gemahlin, ihm die zahlreichen Ehebrüche zu verzeihen.

Währenddessen wartet seine Mätresse sorgenvoll auf eine Botschaft von ihm. Die Hofetikette läßt es nicht zu, daß sie den König aufsucht – und der läßt nichts von sich hören. „Während der König sich in den Händen der Kirche und der Mediziner befand und der Dauphin elf Tage das Regiment ausübte, blieb Madame de Pompadour in ihren Gemächern ohne Nachricht. Von draußen drangen Drohungen und Schreie des Volkes, das sich unter ihren Fenstern zusammengerottet hatte, zu ihr herauf ..."[53]

Ihre Befürchtungen trügen nicht: Der Großsiegelbewahrer fordert sie im Namen des Königs auf, den Hof zu verlassen. Zunächst neigt sie dazu, sich zu fügen – vielleicht stammt ihr Ausspruch „Nach mir die Sintflut!" aus dieser Zeit –, aber wenige Tage später überwindet sie die Resignation und beschließt, weiter um ihre Stellung zu kämpfen.

Endlich kann sie wieder mit dem König sprechen. Sie jagt nun ihrerseits den Großsiegelbewahrer davon.

Der Tod

Im Februar 1764 erkrankt Madame de Pompadour an einer fiebrigen Erkältung. Das ist seit ihrer Kindheit häufig geschehen, aber dieses Mal erwarten die Ärzte selbst nach mehreren Wochen keine Genesung; im Gegenteil: der Zustand der Dreiundvierzigjährigen verschlechtert sich so, daß sie die Letzte Ölung erhält.

„Vor Atemnot konnte sie nicht liegen, sie saß auf, in einem Morgenrock über weißem Taft. Noch immer ein wenig geschminkt, lächelte sie jedem zu, der hereinkam, kein Wort der Klage kam über ihre Lippen."[54]

Am Palmsonntag sagt sie zu dem Geistlichen, der gerade gehen will: „Einen Augenblick, ich komme mit."

„Sie starb, inmitten luxuriösesten Wohlstands, an der Armeleutekrankheit Tuberkulose, die noch in ihren letzten Lebenstagen ein Pariser Arzt dadurch heilen wollte, daß er ihr schwere Steine zu heben und im Zimmer hin und her zu laufen empfahl."[55]

Ihr Leichnam wird auf einer Bahre aus dem Schloß getragen und mit einer Kutsche nach Paris gebracht. Obwohl es stürmt und regnet, schaut der König von einem Balkon aus zu, wischt sich die Tränen aus dem Gesicht und klagt: „Das ist die einzige Ehrerbietung, die ich ihr erweisen kann."[56]

Ihrem letzten Willen entsprechend wird die Tote in der Gruft der Kapuzinerinnen in Paris bestattet.

Voltaire trauert um sie: „Die echten Freunde der Literatur, die wahren Philosophen müssen den Tod der Frau von Pompadour beklagen. Ihr Denken und Streben war richtig; niemand weiß das besser als ich. Mit ihr verloren wir wirklich sehr viel ..."[57]

Rahel Varnhagen

Eine Jüdin im Gespräch mit großen Deutschen

Der Traum

„Ich befand mich immer in einem vornehmen bewohnten Palast, vor dessen Fenstern gleich ein großartiger Garten begann. ... Die Zimmer des Gebäudes waren immer erhellt, offen, und die Bewegung einer großen Aufwartung darin; so sah ich immer eine ganze Reihe geöffnet vor mir da, in deren letztem eigentlich die Gesellschaft der vornehmsten Personen war, wovon ich jedoch keinen einzelnen mir denken konnte, obgleich ich sie alle kannte, zu ihnen gehörte und zu ihnen hin sollte. Dies aber ... konnte nie geschehen. Mich hinderte ein Unvermögen, eine Lähmung, die in der Luft der Zimmer und in der Erhellung zu liegen schien; ich dachte mir diese Hemmung nie im ganzen und glaubte nur jedesmal von anderen Zufälligkeiten gehindert zu sein; und gedachte auch jedesmal zu meiner Gesellschaft zu kommen.

Jedesmal aber, wenn ich noch sechs bis acht Zimmer von ihr entfernt war, stellte sich ein Tier in dem Zimmer ein, wo ich war, welchem ich keinen Namen geben konnte, weil seinesgleichen nicht in der Welt war; von der Größe eines dünneren Schafes als Schafe gewöhnlich sind; rein und weiß wie unbetasteter Schnee; halb Schaf, halb Ziege, mit einer Art von Angorahaaren; bei der Schnauze rötlich wie der reinlichste, reizendste Marmor, Aurorafarbe, die Pfoten ebenso. Dieses Tier war mein Bekannter. Ich wußte nicht woher: es liebte mich unendlich; und wußte es mir zu sagen und zu zeigen: ich mußte es behandeln wie einen Menschen. Es drückte mir mit seinen Pfoten die Hände, und das ging mir jedesmal bis ins

Herz; und es sah mich so voll Liebe an, wie ich mich nicht erinnere eine größere in eines Menschen Auge gesehen zu haben; am gewöhnlichsten nahm es mich bei der Hand, und da ich immer zur Gesellschaft wollte, so durchschritten wir die Zimmer, ohne jemals hinzukommen; das Tier suchte mich zärtlich und als hätte es wichtige Ursachen, davon abzuhalten; weil ich aber hinwollte, so ging es in Liebe gezwungen immer mit ..."[1]

Juden im friderizianischen Berlin

Der Philosoph Moses Mendelssohn, der 1743 nach Berlin gekommen war und sich dort mit Lessing befreundete, „glaubte, die Juden müßten sich aus dem geistigen Getto, in dem sie seit Jahrhunderten lebten, dadurch befreien, daß sie ... ihre Religion überholter ritueller Formen entkleideten, um sie somit als ein Bekenntnis unter anderen akzeptabel zu machen. Er suchte die gesellschaftlichen Schranken zwischen Juden und Nichtjuden niederzureißen, indem er sein Haus zu einem Treffpunkt für Intellektuelle, bedeutende auswärtige Besucher und die Berliner Hautevolee machte in der Hoffnung, das gegenseitige Verständnis zu fördern und zu beweisen, daß die Juden kein exotisches Volk waren, sondern Deutsche mit den gleichen Interessen wie andere aufgeklärte Mitglieder der deutschen Gesellschaft."[2] Christen und Juden sollten sich zuerst einmal als Menschen achten.[3]

Jüdische Bankiersfamilien folgten dem Beispiel: Sie bemühten sich, „dem moralisch Dubiosen, dem Widrigen, Kleinlichen und Ungeistigen, das allem Handel, allem bloß Geschäftlichen anhaftet, zu entrinnen und sich in die reinere, die geldlose Sphäre des Geistigen zu erheben ..."[4] Sie brachen mit Traditionen, die sie von der übrigen Gesellschaft ausgrenzten und fanden in der protestantischen Elite den einen oder anderen, der es wagte, sie zu besuchen und sich durch die persönliche Begegnung von antisemitischen Vorurteilen wenigstens teilweise zu befreien.

Schleiermacher schrieb 1798: „Daß junge Gelehrte und Elegants die hiesigen großen jüdischen Häuser fleißig besuchen

Rahel Varnhagen (1771–1833)

Bronzerelief von Christian Friedrich Tieck, 1796.
Berlin, Nationalgalerie

ist sehr natürlich, denn es sind bei weitem die reichsten bürgerlichen Familien hier, fast die einzigen, die ein offenes Haus halten, und bei denen man wegen ihrer ausgebreiteten Verbindungen in allen Ländern Fremde von allen Ständen antrifft. Wer also auf eine recht ungenierte Art gute Gesellschaft sehen will, läßt sich in solchen Häusern einführen ..."[5]

Die Familie Levin

Auch die Familie Levin entwickelte sich zu einem Zentrum des Kulturaustausches.

Markus Levin stellte während des Siebenjährigen Krieges[6] im Auftrag Friedrichs des Großen Silbermünzen mit Kupferkernen her. „Außen schön und innen schlimm – außen Friedrich, innen Ephraim", hieß es im Volksmund. Durch den Betrug füllte er nicht nur die Kriegskasse des Königs auf, sondern erwarb auch selbst ein Vermögen und eines der wenigen Generalprivilegien für Juden in Preußen.

Seine beiden ersten Ehen blieben kinderlos, aber seine dritte Frau gebar am 26. Mai 1771 Rahel und in den folgenden vierzehn Jahren eine weitere Tochter und drei Söhne.

Sie alle fürchten den geistreichen, launenhaften und despotischen Vater, einen autoritären „‚pater familias', der seine Frau schweigen heißt und den Kindern seinen Willen aufzwingt."[7] „Sein Hohn und Spott pfeift über die Kinderköpfe, als spiele einer mit der Peitsche über ihren vor Angst gesträubten Haaren."[8] Vergeblich suchen sie Wärme und Geborgenheit bei der stumm ergebenen Mutter.

Anders als die Mutter steht der Vater der Religion eher fern. „Seine Leidenschaft für Ballett, Theater und Oper ... und die Gewohnheit einer luxuriösen, ästhetisch verfeinerten Lebensführung hat Rahels Vater seinen Kindern offenbar leichter einzuprägen gewußt als die Religion seiner Vorfahren."[9]

Sooft einer der vornehmen Besucher über kluge Bemerkungen Rahels staunt, blickt Markus Levin stolz auf die Tochter – und prägt sie dadurch: Nach Anerkennungen für geistreiche Einwürfe und Ausführungen wird sie zeitlebens streben.

Rahel wirkt zart und sensibel. Sie ist blaß, schmächtig; häufig kränkelt sie, und seit früher Jugend leidet sie unter rheumatischen Beschwerden. „Rahel ... ist von der Natur wenig verwöhnt, einer ihrer Freunde wird ohne Bosheit über sie sagen: ‚ein hervorragender Kopf auf einem minderwertigen Körper'. Wäre da nicht die Lebhaftigkeit des Blicks, so bliebe sie unscheinbar."[10] Und sie meint selbst: „Gott hat mir in die Seele gelegt, was Natur und Umstände mir für das Gesicht versagt haben."[11]

Als der Vater im Februar 1790 stirbt, übernimmt der älteste Sohn die Rolle des Familienoberhaupts, die Führung des Geschäfts und die Verwaltung des Familienvermögens. Die bald neunzehn Jahre alte Rahel möchte in dem Unternehmen mitarbeiten, aber das lehnt die Familie ab: Frauen gelten als ungeeignet für Geschäfte. Sie darf lediglich die überforderte Mutter im Haushalt und bei der Erziehung der jüngeren Geschwister unterstützen.

Das von Markus Levin angesammelte Vermögen und die laufenden Einnahmen erlauben es der Witwe Chaie Levin zunächst, mit ihren Kindern auch weiterhin in einem Wohlstand zu leben, den nur ein paar hundert Berliner Familien mit ihnen teilen.

Höhere Schulen bleiben Mädchen verschlossen. Das gilt selbstverständlich auch für die Töchter arrivierter jüdischer Familien. „Was aber die jungen Männer schon als Recht betrachteten, kam für ihre Schwestern noch nicht in Frage. Ihnen wurde neben Hand- und Hausarbeiten das Lesen und Schreiben beigebracht, gewöhnlich in hebräischer Schrift; ferner erwarben sie mehr oder minder gründliche Kenntnisse in Französisch und Deutsch. Im übrigen waren sie jedoch auf sich selbst gestellt – abhängig von der Bereitwilligkeit der Eltern, Hauslehrer zu engagieren, und auf die intellektuellen Anregungen und Mitteilungen von Freunden, Brüdern und Ehemännern angewiesen."[12]

Rahel erhält Musikunterricht und liest nicht nur hebräische Bücher, sondern auch Werke von Dante, Shakespeare, Diderot und Goethe in den Originalsprachen.

Ihr erster Vertrauter und mehrjähriger Brieffreund ist David

Veit. Obwohl er Jude ist, durfte er ein christliches Gymnasium besuchen und studiert jetzt Medizin. Aufgrund seiner systematischen Schulbildung verfügt er über ein umfassendes, „schubladisiertes" Wissen. Doch Rahel ist ihm intellektuell weit überlegen, und sie denkt leichter als er in neuen Bahnen, denn ihr steht kein Karteischrank der Bildung im Weg. David Veit sieht deshalb in ihr ein entrücktes Idol, dem er sich kaum zu nähern wagt.

Der Salon

Im Alter von vierundzwanzig Jahren schart Rahel Levin eine Gruppe regelmäßiger – vorwiegend männlicher – Besucher um sich. Jede Woche treffen sie sich in der Wohnung, die Chaie Levin nach dem Tod ihres Mannes mit den Kindern bezog.

Besitz und Standesunterschiede bedeuten hier ebensowenig wie religiöse Gegensätze. In Rahels Salon begegnen sich Künstler, Philosophen und Staatsmänner: der schwedische Diplomat Karl Gustav von Brinckmann[13], Antoni Henryk Fürst Radziwill; ein Neffe des Königs: Prinz Louis Ferdinand und dessen Mätresse Pauline Wiesel; Wilhelm und Caroline von Humboldt, Friedrich Schleiermacher, Moses Mendelssohns Tochter Dorothea Veit[14], Friedrich Schlegel, Jean Paul, Ludwig und Friedrich Tieck, Clemens Brentano und viele andere.

„Rahels angebliche ,Wahllosigkeit' in der Auswahl ihrer Gesellschaft, die ihr wegen der Vielschichtigkeit der Gäste von einigen von ihnen ... bisweilen auch vorgehalten wurde, geriet zum Markenzeichen ihres Salons. Nicht nur, daß bei ihr Menschen mit jeglicher Konfession und Weltanschauung zu Worte kommen konnten; Rahel war darüber hinaus auch bekannt dafür, einen jeden ihrer Gäste nach seinem ganz eigenen Maßstab und keineswegs der gesellschaftlichen Konvention und Etikette folgend zu klassifizieren und zu behandeln."[15]

„Man spricht über Literatur, Kunst, Philosophie, das Leben, über neue Bücher, Theateraufführungen, Universitätsvorlesungen, hört Autoren und Autorinnen zu. Über Politik spricht man nicht",[16] denn für eine Dame schickt es sich nicht, eine Meinung über politische Themen wie zum Beispiel die Französische Revolution zu äußern.

Auf Witz und Verstand kommt es bei der geistreichen Unterhaltung an. Hier wird „eine Geselligkeit gepflegt, die nicht gleichzusetzen ist damit, was man heute, oft mit gequältem Lächeln, ‚zwangloses Beisammensein' nennt."[17] Wer in dieser narzißtischen Gesellschaft glänzen möchte, muß auf Stichwörter achten, die es ihm ermöglichen, einen Geistesblitz aufleuchten zu lassen – wobei der Gedankenschnörkel oft wichtiger ist als der inhaltliche Zusammenhang. Immer wieder springt einer der Teilnehmer auf die virtuelle Bühne, um sich vor den anderen zu präsentieren, und meistens spielt Rahel selbst die Hauptrolle: Erregt durch das eigene Sprechen und berauscht von ihren Einfällen kultiviert sie ihren Esprit.

Wilhelm von Humboldt erinnert sich später: „Man suchte sie gern auf, nicht bloß weil sie wirklich von sehr liebenswürdigem Charakter war, sondern weil man fast mit Gewißheit darauf rechnen konnte, nie von ihr zu gehen, ohne nicht etwas von ihr gehört zu haben und mit hinwegzunehmen, das Stoff zu weiterem ernstem, oft tiefem Nachdenken gab, oder das Gefühl lebendig anregte."[18]

Der Salon stellt ihre Akademie dar: Im Salon saugt sie Wissen auf und übt ihren Verstand. Der Schriftsteller Theodor Mundt bezeichnet Rahel als „das alles am feinsten durchfühlende Nervensystem ihrer Zeit".[19] Sie nutzt immer zugleich ihren Scharfsinn und ihr Einfühlungsvermögen – zwei Eigenschaften, die sich bei den meisten Menschen gegenseitig ausschließen –, beweist Phantasie, beobachtet nuancenreich, versteht rasch und lernt ständig dazu, hört nie auf, sich und andere zu ergründen. Karl Gustav von Brinckmann meint: „Vielleicht gehörte aber auch eine solche Allseitigkeit des Geistes dazu, wie die ihrige, um auch aus noch so gemischten Gesellschaftsverbindungen nicht bloß Vergnügen, sondern Nutzen zu schöpfen. So reich ihre Menschenkenntnis war, so bewunderungswürdig gewandt und leicht abgewogen war ihre Behandlung der verschiedensten, sich einander oft völlig widersprechenden Charaktere ... In meiner Seele las sie, wie in einem offenen Buche mit breiten Rändern, wo sie überall etwas hinzuschrieb und verbesserte; und wo irgend die Handschrift meines unruhigen Geistes mir selbst unleserlich schien, entzifferte sie solche oft schneller und fertiger als ich selbst."[20]

Johann Wolfgang von Goethe

Ins Schwärmen gerät Rahel Levin, wenn sie in ihrem Salon über „Die Leiden des jungen Werthers", „Wilhelm Meisters Lehrjahre" und Johann Wolfgang von Goethe spricht.

Im Juli 1795 begleitet sie die berühmte Schauspielerin Friederike Unzelmann nach Teplitz. Von dem mondänen Kurort am Rand des Erzgebirges aus unternehmen die beiden Damen einen Abstecher nach Karlsbad, wo der Dichterfürst gerade kurt, und tatsächlich gelingt es ihnen, von der dänischen Dichterin Friederike Brun eingeladen und dem Abgott vorgestellt zu werden.

Goethe zeigt sich von Rahel Levins Eigenständigkeit des Denkens beeindruckt: „Ja, es ist ein liebevolles Mädchen; sie ist stark in ihren Empfindungen und doch leicht in ihrer Äußerung. Jenes gibt ihr eine hohe Bedeutung, dies macht sie angenehm. Jenes macht, daß wir an ihr die große Originalität bewundern, und dies, daß diese Originalität liebenswürdig wird, daß sie uns gefällt ... Sie ist, soweit ich sie kenne, in jedem Augenblick sich gleich, immer in einer eignen Art bewegt und doch ruhig – kurz, sie ist, was ich eine schöne Seele nennen möchte."[21]

Männer

Rahels erste Liebesaffäre bahnt sich während eines Opernbesuchs im Winter 1795/96 an: Bei dieser Gelegenheit fällt ihr der gleichaltrige Karl Graf von Finckenstein auf. Es geht ihr vermutlich mehr um das Erlebnis des Verliebtseins als um eine tiefere Verbindung mit einem anderen Menschen. Sie lehnt zwar die konventionelle Ehe ab („Ist intimes Zusammenleben ohne Zauber und Entzücken nicht unanständiger als Ekstase irgendeiner Art?"[22]), aber als der Diplomat um ihre Hand anhält, zögert sie nicht mit ihrem „Ja", denn durch die Vermählung mit einem Grafen könnte sie den Makel der Geburt vergessen und in die Gesellschaft aufgenommen werden: „Gleich hat sie ja gesagt, hat zugegriffen, als hätte sie nur auf ein solches Ereignis und nie auf einen Menschen gewartet. Als hätte sie nur Fortgenommenwerden ersehnt, Heirat."[23]

Karl Graf von Finckenstein stammt aus einem der ältesten märkischen Geschlechter: Als Mitglied seiner Familie ist er hoch angesehen. Rahel aber zerrt ihn in den Kreis ihrer geistreichen Freunde, wo seine persönliche Farblosigkeit auffällt.

Da flieht der Graf in den Schoß seiner Familie – die entsetzt ist über seine Verlobung mit einer Bürgerlichen, einer Jüdin ohne Mitgift noch dazu.

Er drückt sich vor einer Entscheidung, bis er im Herbst 1799 an die Preußische Gesandtschaft in Wien versetzt wird und Rahel ihm einige Monate später einen endgültigen Abschiedsbrief schreibt: „Ich imponiere Dir und darum kann ich auch kein Glück bei Dir finden."[24]

Einmal stand sie im Traum mit ihm auf einer Festungsmauer. Die Menschenansammlung hinter ihnen wollte Rahel in den Abgrund stoßen und verlangte von ihm die Entscheidung: „Er stand grausam verbissen da, und sah nach der Tiefe: man schrie stärker und heftiger und forderte sein Ja; immer dichter an mir; sie faßten, mit den Augen auf F., an meine Kleider; ich suchte ihm in die Augen zu sehen und schrie immer: ‚Du wirst doch nicht Ja sagen?' Er stand unbeweglich verlegen da, verlegen gegen das Volk, noch nicht Ja gesagt zu haben. ‚Du wirst doch nicht Ja sagen?' schrie ich wieder. Das Volk schrie auch: und er, ‚Ja!' sagte er."[25]

Rahels Versuch, sich in die preußische Gesellschaft einzuordnen, ist gescheitert: Sie wurde abgewiesen. Die Scham quält sie ein Leben lang.

Mit einer Freundin, die ein uneheliches Kind erwartet, wohnt sie vom Sommer 1800 bis zum folgenden Frühjahr in Paris. Dort läßt sie sich auf ein flüchtiges Abenteuer mit dem

acht Jahre jüngeren Hamburger Kaufmann Wilhelm Bokelmann ein, der so schön ist, daß man ihn „le beau Kelmann"
nennt.[26] „In der Freundschaft mit dem viel Jüngeren taucht sie
unter wie in der fremden Stadt, verzichtet auf eigene Kräfte
wie auf die quälende Sorge um sich selbst."[27]

Dann reist sie nach Amsterdam, um ihre Schwester Rose zu
besuchen, die seit wenigen Wochen mit einem holländischen
Juristen verheiratet ist.

1802 verliebt sich Rahel in den spanischen Diplomaten Don
Raphael d'Urquijo. Sie liebt ihn „bis zur Tollheit", ist außer
sich, fühlt sich verzaubert, schwelgt in Gefühlen und möchte
ihre Gedanken mit ihm teilen. Aber „er will ihre Seele gar
nicht kennen. Wenn er schon selbst eine Seele hat, wozu soll
er sich mit noch einer Seele beladen. Er mag auch gar nicht
ihre maßlose und schrankenlose Liebe. Abgesehen von allem
anderen schickt es sich nicht für eine Frau, einen Mann um so
viel mehr zu lieben, als der Mann sie liebt … Außerdem fühlt
er sich bei ihr nie sicher. Je weniger er ihre Briefe versteht, die
ihn um eine Liebe anflehen, die er nicht kennt und sicher
nicht gewillt ist zu geben, desto eifersüchtiger wird er."[28]
Rahel klagt, er sei „borstig" und sie finde kein Herz bei ihm.
Weil der cholerische Spanier ihre Liebe nicht versteht, sie mit
seiner Eifersucht verfolgt, sich durch ihren Intellekt eher
bedroht als beflügelt fühlt, und weil Rahel nicht bereit ist, das
Klischee vom vernunftbegabten Mann und der gefühlsbeton-
ten Frau zu übernehmen, scheitert nach eineinhalb Jahren
auch diese Beziehung, die Rahel später ihr „spanisches Purgatorium"[29] nennen wird.

Napoleon in Berlin

Gut einen Monat vor seinem 34. Geburtstag fällt Prinz Louis
Ferdinand in einem Gefecht; Rahel Levin verliert einen ihrer
Freunde. Vier Tage später wird die preußische Armee von den
Franzosen vernichtend geschlagen.[30] Der preußische Hof flieht
nach Königsberg, und in Berlin heißt es: „Jetzt ist Ruhe die
erste Bürgerpflicht."[31] Am 27. Oktober 1806 reitet Napoleon

durchs Brandenburger Tor. Zwei Jahre lang bleibt die französische Besatzung in Berlin.

Die Katastrophe verändert das Leben in der preußischen Hauptstadt; und Rahel bleibt von dem Umbruch nicht verschont.

Das Unternehmen der Levins gerät in Schwierigkeiten. Rahel – die von regelmäßigen Zahlungen aus dem Familieneinkommen lebt – muß ihre Ausgaben einschränken und sich trotzdem wegen ihres vergleichsweise noch immer kostspieligen Lebensstils Vorwürfe der Brüder und der Mutter anhören.

Aber es kommt viel schlimmer: Die Fremdherrschaft reißt die Intellektuellen in Deutschland aus ihrer politischen Gleichgültigkeit. Heinrich von Kleist fordert seine Landsleute auf, die Franzosen totzuschlagen. Rahel sitzt unter den Zuhörern, als Johann Gottlieb Fichte an den Sonntagen im Winter 1807/08 in seinen berühmten „Reden an die deutsche Nation" zur geistigen Erneuerung aufruft. Um den Deutschen wieder Mut und Selbstachtung zu vermitteln, erinnert er sie an die Höhepunkte in ihrer Geschichte und die kulturellen Glanzlichter; er verherrlicht das deutsche Volk, „das in einer verdorbenen Welt das einzig noch echte, ursprüngliche Volk sei. Das war Unsinn, das war nicht wahr, Fichte kannte die Welt nicht; was er den Deutschen über ihre Weltaufgabe sagte, hatte er sich rein ausgedacht. Aber der gewaltige Rhetor machte tiefen Eindruck auf seine Hörer."[32] Das aufkeimende Nationalbewußtsein verdrängt den Kosmopolitismus der Berliner Salons, und der aufflammende Hurrapatriotismus richtet sich nicht nur gegen die Franzosen, sondern auch gegen die Juden.[33] In einer durch den Nationalismus verpesteten Atmosphäre breitet sich das Gift des Antisemitismus wieder aus. Ludwig Börne klagt darüber, daß die Frage, ob jemand Jude sei oder nicht, bei jeder Gelegenheit gestellt werde, von Antisemiten sowieso, aber auch von allen anderen Leuten: „Es ist wie ein Wunder! Tausendmale habe ich es erfahren, und doch bleibt es mir ewig neu. Die Einen werfen mir vor, daß ich ein Jude sey, die Anderen verzeihen mir es; der Dritte lobt mich gar dafür; aber alle denken daran."[34]

Rahels Gäste bleiben nach und nach aus. Sie treffen sich

nun bei Ministern, Grafen und Fürsten; Achim von Arnim gründet eine „christlich-deutsche" Tischgesellschaft, zu der Franzosen, Juden, Philister und Frauen keinen Zutritt haben. „Rahel Varnhagen mußte entdecken, daß selbst diejenigen, die sich voller Stolz auf ihren glänzenden Abendveranstaltungen hatten sehen lassen, nicht bereit waren, sie als ihresgleichen zu akzeptieren – das heißt, als Deutsche wie sie – und daß es nichts gab, wodurch sie sich befreien konnte von dem, wie sie es sah, Unglück, als Jude geboren zu sein. Sie vergaß ihre Scham darüber nicht eine Stunde."[35]

Einsam sitzt sie an ihrem Teetisch und klagt: „Rang, Stand, Zerstreuung, Freunde, Gesellschaft, alles fehlt mir."[36] „So ist alles anders! Nie war ich so allein. Absolut. Nie so durchaus und bestimmt ennuyirt. Denken Sie sich, ennuyirt! Denn nur Geistreiches, Gütiges, Hoffnunggebendes, kann eine so Gekränkte, eine so Getödtete noch hinhalten. ... Sie sind Alle weg. Meine deutschen Freunde, wie lange schon; wie gestorben, wie zerstreut! ... Ich bin wie ich war, Brinckmann; die Schläge haben das Alte in mir gestählt, und bewährt, und mich wahrlich neu, und weiter urbar gemacht. Ich bin noch des Scherzes, der Freude und des höchsten Leides fähig, nur ganz umwerfen kann mich nichts, denn ich liege."[37]

Ihrer Jugendfreundin Pauline Wiesel, die sich keiner Konvention fügt, schreibt sie: „... auf verschiedenem Wege sind wir zu einem Punkt gelangt. Wir sind neben der menschlichen Gesellschaft. Für uns ist kein Platz, kein Amt, kein eitler Titel da. ... Und somit sind wir ausgeschlossen aus der Gesellschaft, Sie, weil Sie beleidigten. (Ich gratuliere Ihnen dazu! So hatten Sie doch etwas; viele Tage der Lust!) Ich, weil ich nicht mit ihr sündigen und lügen kann."[38]

Der Tod der Mutter

Zur gleichen Zeit, als Rahel ihre Einsamkeit beklagt, überwirft sie sich so mit ihrer Mutter, daß diese 1808 die gemeinsame Wohnung verläßt. Da Rahels Geschwister längst ausgezogen sind, hätte sie die Miete nun allein bezahlen müssen.

Aber dafür reicht das Geld nicht: Die Siebenunddreißigjährige richtet sich deshalb in einer kleineren Wohnung ein, läßt sich jedoch weiterhin von einem Diener und einem Zimmermädchen aufwarten: „„ein Mann im Haus' und eine Begleitung in der Stadt, ohne die Rahel als alleinstehende Frau nicht auszukommen meint."[39]

Als die Mutter im folgenden Sommer schwer erkrankt, versöhnt sich Rahel mit ihr und widmet ihr viel Zeit. Trotzdem: Vor ihrem Tod im Oktober 1809 legt Chaie Levin fest, daß der älteste Sohn seinen Geschwistern keinerlei Rechenschaft über die Vermögensverwaltung schuldet. Rahel bleibt auf seine Gutwilligkeit angewiesen: Die Höhe ihrer Rente hängt vom Erfolg der Geschäfte ab, in die ihr kein Einblick gewährt wird – und sie kann sich nicht wehren, als der Bruder zwei Jahre später die Zahlungen an sie noch einmal zusammenstreicht. Jetzt muß sie auch auf den Diener verzichten und in eine bescheidenere Wohnung umziehen.

Karl August Varnhagen

Karl August Varnhagen wurde 1785 in Düsseldorf geboren. Sein Vater begeisterte sich anfangs für die Französische Revolution und gab seine erfolgreiche Arztpraxis auf, um – zunächst nur mit dem Sohn – nach Straßburg zu ziehen. Als die Revolutionäre König Ludwig XVI. am 21. Januar 1793 köpften, kehrte er entsetzt nach Deutschland zurück und fand in Hamburg eine Wohnung. Dorthin ließ er die Familie nachkommen. Aber er fand keinen Boden mehr unter den Füßen und starb einige Jahre später.

Obwohl er sich vor allem für Literatur interessierte, folgte Karl August Varnhagen dem Rat eines väterlichen Freundes und studierte Medizin, schloß das Studium jedoch nicht ab, sondern schlug sich einige Jahre lang als Hauslehrer durch.

1803 wurde Karl August Varnhagen Rahel Levin vorgestellt, aber die beiden verloren sich rasch wieder aus den Augen, bis sie sich im Frühjahr 1808 zufällig bei einem Spaziergang Unter den Linden über den Weg liefen.

Rahel erschrickt über die Leidenschaftlichkeit des vierzehn Jahre jüngeren Bekannten, aber im Sommer mietet sie eine Wohnung in der vornehmen Gartenstadt Charlottenburg, wo sie ungestört zusammen sein können, und sie beginnt schließlich, „auch ihn mit ihrem unerschütterlichen Glauben an die Bildungsfähigkeit begabter Menschen zu leiten."[40]

Sie spornt ihn an, sein Studium ab September in Tübingen fortzusetzen. Doch im folgenden Sommer meldet er sich zur österreichischen Armee.

Im Sommer 1811 zeigen sich Rahel Levin und Karl August Varnhagen in Teplitz erstmals in der Öffentlichkeit als Paar.

Im Gegensatz zu Karl Graf von Finckenstein und Don Raphael d'Urquijo versucht Karl August Varnhagen seine Geliebte zu verstehen. Er sammelt alles, was ihm Rahel über Goethe geschrieben hat, stellt eine Auswahl davon mit eigenen Erwiderungen zusammen und veröffentlicht das Manuskript 1812 im „Morgenblatt für gebildete Stände" unter dem Titel „Über Goethe. Bruchstücke aus Briefen".

Karl August Varnhagen meint über sich selbst: „Mein Gemüt ist ganz arm auf die Welt gekommen und muß sich, wenn andere in der Erdengesellschaft jeder gleich anfangs einen Einsatz gegeben hat, oder doch jederzeit, es liegt nur an ihm, geben kann, scheu zurückziehen vor dem Spiel. Leer ist es in mir, wirklich meistens leer, ich erzeuge nicht Gedanken, nicht Gestalten, weder den Zusammenhang kann ich darstellen als System, noch das einzelste heraussondern in ein individuelles Leben als Witz, es sprudeln keine Quellen in mir! ... Aber in dieser völligen Leerheit bin ich immer offen, ein Sonnenstrahl, eine Bewegung, eine Gestalt des Schönen oder auch nur der Kraft werden mir nicht entgehen, ich erwarte nur, daß etwas vorgehe, ein Bettler am Wege."[41]

Diesem „Bettler am Wege", dessen Neugier aus seiner eigenen Hohlheit entsteht, vertraut sich Rahel an. Er bewundert ihren Esprit, rühmt ihre Klugheit und macht sich zum Priester dieses Idols – wobei er „letztlich ihr Leben zur Anekdote degradiert ... [und] in ihr im Grunde nur ein gewaltiges Kuriosum sieht".[42]

Alexander von der Marwitz

Im Winter 1812/13 kehren Napoleon und die kläglichen Reste der geschlagenen „Grande Armée" vom Rußlandfeldzug zurück.[43]

Einige Monate später stellt sich Karl August Varnhagen wie viele andere Deutsche den russischen Streitkräften zur Verfügung. Und am 27. März 1813 erklärt der preußische König dem französischen Kaiser den Krieg.

Mit Truppen von Knaben und Veteranen besiegt Napoleon die verbündeten Preußen und Russen, aber während des folgenden Waffenstillstandes – den er später als die größte Dummheit seines Lebens bezeichnet – schöpfen seine angeschlagenen Gegner Atem, und nun stellen sich auch Schweden, Großbritannien und Österreich gegen ihn: Als der Waffenstillstand ausläuft, stoßen die Alliierten mit drei gewaltigen Armeen gegen den Kaiser vor. Nach der „Völkerschlacht", die vom 16. bis 19. Oktober 1813 bei Leipzig tobt und hunderttausend Menschen das Leben kostet, muß sich Napoleon endgültig hinter den Rhein zurückziehen.

Rahel hat sechs Wochen nach der preußischen Kriegserklärung Berlin verlassen und wohnt ein Jahr lang als Zimmernachbarin des Komponisten Carl Maria von Weber im Haus der Schauspielerin Auguste Brede in Prag. In der überfüllten Stadt organisiert sie die Unterbringung von Flüchtlingen und die Versorgung von Kriegsopfern. Sie „arbeitet achtzehn Stunden am Tag, um Verwundete zu verbinden, Leiden zu lindern, Hoffnungen zu pflanzen."[44]

Einen der verwundeten Soldaten, die sie in Prag pflegt, hatte sie kennengelernt, kurz bevor er im Mai 1809 in den Krieg zog: Der preußische Junker Alexander von der Marwitz verachtet die Welt, sehnt sich nach Erhabenem, möchte ein Held werden und weiß zugleich: Das bleibt ein Traum. Seine Familie ist reich und angesehen; aber das widert ihn an – während Rahel in ihrem Traum verzweifelt, weil sie nicht zu der im Haus versammelten Gesellschaft vordringen kann.[45]

Alexander von der Marwitz betet die sechzehn Jahre ältere Rahel Levin an, liebt sie „wie man das Meer, ein Wolkenspiel,

113

eine Felsschlucht liebt"[46]: platonisch. Sie nähern „sich einander im wohlverstandenen Sinne der intellektuellen Begegnung jener Zeit, nicht in Liebe, aber auch nicht nur in Freundschaft, sondern in einem tiefen menschlichen Verstehen."[47]

Rahel spielt mit dem Gedanken, Varnhagen für ihn aufzugeben, aber Alexander von der Marwitz zieht im Winter wieder in den Krieg und fällt am 11. Februar 1814 in Frankreich.

Diplomatengattin in Wien und Karlsruhe

Als sich die Dreiundvierzigjährige im Sommer 1814 erneut mit Karl August Varnhagen in Teplitz trifft, nimmt sie seinen Antrag an.

Weil eine Eheschließung zwischen einer Jüdin und einem Christen unmöglich ist, muß Rahel konvertieren, also – mit den Worten Heinrich Heines – das „Entréebillet zur europäischen Kultur" erwerben: Am 23. September 1814 wird sie evangelisch getauft, und zwar auf den Namen Friederike Antonie. Die Hochzeit findet vier Tage später statt. Da ihr Mann inzwischen einen alten Adelstitel seiner Familie entdeckte, heißt sie nun Friederike Antonie Varnhagen von Ense.[48]

Karl August Varnhagen von Ense wird Diplomat. Anfang Oktober 1814 reist er im Gefolge des preußischen Staatskanzlers Karl August Fürst von Hardenberg zum Wiener Kongreß[49]. Rahel folgt zwei Wochen später.

In Wien trifft sie alte Freunde wieder: Friedrich Gentz, Wilhelm und Caroline von Humboldt, Friedrich und Dorothea Schlegel, Josephine Gräfin Pachta und Charles Joseph Fürst de Ligne, dessen Ausspruch „Le congrès danse beaucoup, mais il ne marche pas"[50] in die Geschichte eingeht. Allerdings beklagt sich Rahel, daß man sie häufig allein läßt.

Karl August Varnhagen muß im Juni 1815 zurück nach Berlin und folgt einige Wochen später Fürst von Hardenberg nach Paris. Dort bilden König Friedrich Wilhelm III. von Preußen, der österreichische Kaiser Franz I. und Zar Alexander I. am 26. September 1815 eine „Heilige Allianz" gegen den Liberalismus, und am 20. November schließen Großbritannien, Preußen, Österreich und Rußland einen neuen Friedensvertrag mit Frankreich.

Rahel Varnhagen bleibt zunächst in der Nähe von Wien, wo ihr eine Freundin ein Landhaus zur Verfügung stellt. Erst zwei Monate nach ihrem Mann reist auch sie ab, aber nicht nach Berlin und auch nicht nach Paris, sondern nach Frankfurt am Main, wo sie Entscheidungen über den nächsten Einsatzort ihres Mannes abwartet.

In der Wohnung, die sie dort bezogen hat, stattet ihr Johann Wolfgang von Goethe am 8. September einen kurzen Besuch ab.

Karl August Varnhagen kommt im November.

Im März 1816 wird er zum preußischen Geschäftsträger am badischen Hof ernannt. Das ist ein vielversprechender Karriereschritt, und er freut sich auf die verantwortungsvolle Position. Im Sommer zieht er mit seiner Frau nach Karlsruhe, um sein neues Amt anzutreten.

Wilhelm von Humboldt, der zwar Rahels Intellekt bewundert, aber aus seiner Abneigung gegen Juden immer weniger ein Hehl macht, kommentiert Varnhagens Berufung folgendermaßen: „Ich sagte ja lange, daß die kleine Levy Exzellenz werden würde. Wieviel fehlt nun daran? Die Lohnbedienten nennen sie gewiß schon in Karlsruhe so. ... Ich hätte noch nichts gegen den sogenannten Jakobinismus von Varnhagen, wenn wahrer Ernst dabei wäre ... Dabei die Dame, der Stamm Levy, die Bundeslade! Wie soll das auf den Großherzog wirken ...?"[51]

Rahel Varnhagen sträubt sich gegen die Repräsentationspflichten, sie leidet darunter, daß sie keine Meinungen äußern darf („Keine Meinung haben ... wird Klugheit, Betragen genannt."[52]) und vereinsamt in der Gesellschaft, die nicht ihrem geistigen Niveau entspricht. Dennoch spricht man in Karlsruhe „mit Liebe und wirklichem Enthusiasmus"[53] von ihr, und sie ist nicht erleichtert, sondern entrüstet, als ihr Mann nach drei Jahren ohne Angabe von Gründen abberufen wird.

Gerüchten zufolge verlangte der österreichische Staatskanzler Fürst von Metternich die Entlassung des Gesandten, der

seine liberale Gesinnung nie verleugnet hat. Obwohl er ge-
warnt wurde, fuhr er fort, „entgegen den Aufgaben seines
Amts und über seine Befugnisse hinaus die liberalen Kräfte zu
unterstützen. Anscheinend war er überzeugt, daß die Revolution bald eine radikale Änderung der politischen Verhältnisse
schaffen würde, und daher nicht allzu sehr um seine Stellung
besorgt. In Wirklichkeit aber waren die konservativen Kräfte
im Aufstieg."[54]

Als der Theologiestudent Karl Ludwig Sand am 23. März
1819 August von Kotzebue erstach, „weil er die nationale und
liberale Begeisterung der studentischen Jugend sarkastisch
abqualifiziert hatte",[55] machte Metternich daraus „ein Ereignis, beinahe so bedrohlich wie der Bastillensturm, und das nun
nach den allerenergischsten Maßnahmen rief, wenn Deutschland vor dem Chaos errettet werden sollte."[56]

Karl August Varnhagens Karriere endet so jäh wie sie
begann; dagegen kann er nichts unternehmen, aber als er in die
USA abgeschoben werden soll, reist er mit seiner Frau Anfang
Oktober 1819 nach Berlin, um in Gesprächen mit der preußischen Regierung wenigstens das zu verhindern.

Wieder in Berlin

Jahrelang hält der preußische König Karl August Varnhagen
hin. 1824 wird er in den Ruhestand versetzt; er darf sich
Geheimer Legationsrat nennen, und der Staat zahlt dem Neun-
unddreißigjährigen eine Pension. Um so mehr Zeit bleibt ihm,
für zahlreiche Zeitungen im deutschsprachigen Raum zu
schreiben und zu Hause gemeinsam mit seiner Frau Gäste zu
empfangen.

Die Varnhagens begrüßen in ihrer Wohnung zum Beispiel
Carl Maria von Weber: Rahels ehemaliger Zimmernachbar
besucht sie einige Tage nach der Uraufführung seiner Oper
„Der Freischütz", deren sensationeller Erfolg auch auf die
patriotische Begeisterung zurückzuführen ist – unter der Rahel
zu leiden hat.

Alexander von Humboldt, Georg Wilhelm Friedrich Hegel,

Hermann Fürst von Pückler-Muskau, Achim und Bettina von Arnim, Leopold von Ranke, Heinrich Heine und viele andere besuchen das Ehepaar Varnhagen.

Da für die Zusammenkünfte kein Jour fixe festgelegt wird, wechselt der Teilnehmerkreis von Mal zu Mal. Die Gesellschaft sitzt nicht – wie in Rahels erstem Salon – ungezwungen bei Tee und Gebäck, sondern an einer festlich mit Kerzen und Blumen gedeckten Tafel: „Gespeist wird nach genau festgelegter Sitzordnung und Menüfolge. Als Vorgerichte abwechselnd kalter Fisch, Salate, Suppen, Makkaroni, manchmal auch Kaviar mit Champagner. Als Hauptgericht serviert ein Lohndiener Wild, Kapaun, Geflügel; Dore legt in der Küche Rinderbraten mit Rosinen auf die angewärmten Platten; der für das Abendessen extra engagierte Koch ist für seinen Fasan mit Ananas bekannt. ,Alles in Perfektion', darauf legt die Hausfrau Wert."[57]

Gebannt hören die Gäste Rahel Varnhagen zu. „Wenn in ihrer Umgebung Lachen oder Zustimmung ertönt, kommt [ihr Mann] näher und fragt: ,Was hat sie gesagt?'"[58] Gewöhnlich steht er hinter ihrem Sessel, um eifrig mitzuschreiben – „wie Rahels Adjutant, immer ein wenig zu beflissen, geradezu versessen, sich an Rahel hochzuranken, Bedeutung durch die ihre zu gewinnen."[59]

Widerwillig läßt sich Franz Grillparzer im September 1826 während eines Berlin-Besuchs von Karl August Varnhagen mit in die Wohnung nehmen: „Varnhagen ging mit mir nach Hause. Als wir an seiner Wohnung vorüberkamen, meinte er, er wolle seiner Frau – jener später bekannten Rahel, von der ich aber damals nichts wußte – meine Bekanntschaft verschaffen. Ich hatte mich den ganzen Tag herumgetrieben und fühlte mich müde bis zum Sterben, war daher herzlich froh, als man uns an der Haustüre sagte, die Frau Legationsrätin sei nicht daheim. Als wir aber die Treppe hinuntergingen, kam uns die Frau entgegen, und ich fügte mich in mein Schicksal. Nun fing aber die alternde, vielleicht nie hübsche, von Krankheit zusammengekrümmte[60], etwas einer Fee, um nicht zu sagen Hexe, ähnliche Frau zu sprechen an, und ich war bezaubert. Meine Müdigkeit verflog oder machte vielmehr einer Art

Trunkenheit Platz. Sie sprach und sprach bis gegen Mitternacht, und ich weiß nicht mehr, haben sie mich fortgetrieben, oder ging ich von selbst fort. Ich habe nie in meinem Leben interessanter und besser reden gehört. Leider war es gegen das Ende meines Aufenthaltes, und ich konnte daher den Besuch nicht wiederholen."[61]

„Eine schöne Seele"

Rahel Varnhagen schreibt mehr als zehntausend Briefe an dreihundert Menschen,[62] „poetische Passagen, philosophische und gesellschaftliche Einsichten, Aphorismen, Literaturkritiken, Abhandlungen über Schauspielkunst, Tanz, Malerei und Musik, sogar Tagebucheintragungen."[63] Obwohl dieser Gedankenaustausch immer privat und häufig intim ist, findet sie nichts dabei, wenn die Briefe anderen Menschen zum Lesen weitergereicht werden; sie denkt sogar darüber nach, die Korrespondenz für eine spätere Veröffentlichung zu sammeln.

„Nichts charakterisiert Rahels Stil prägnanter als seine Angemessenheit zu ihrer Lebensart: sie schreibt, wie sie geht und steht. Ihre schriftliche Rede wirkt so mündlich, daß man mitunter verblüfft ist, sie tatsächlich schwarz auf weiß vor Augen zu haben. Ihr ungemein spontaner, sprunghafter, drauflosfahrender Ton will keine elaborierten Argumentationen transportieren. Er konfrontiert den Leser mit Paradoxen und Hyperbeln, kühnen Metaphern und gewaltsamen Umstellungen, vor allem aber mit Auslassungen und Brüchen."[64]

Ihrer Schwester Rose schreibt Rahel: „Weiber ... haben der beklatschten Regel nach gar keinen Raum für ihre eigenen Füße, müssen sie nur immer dahin setzen, wo der Mann eben stand und stehen will; und sehen mit ihren Augen die ganze bewegte Welt wie etwa einer, der wie ein Baum mit Wurzeln in der Erde verzaubert wäre ... Mache dir auch Zerstreuung ... geh an Orte, wo neue Gegenstände, Worte und Menschen Dich berühren ... Wir Frauen haben dies doppelt nötig; indessen der Männer Beschäftigung wenigstens in ihren eignen Augen auch Geschäfte sind, die sie für wichtig halten müssen, in deren

Ausübung ihre Ambition sich schmeichelt; worin sie ein Weiterkommen sehen, in welcher sie durch Menschenverkehr schon bewegt werden: wenn wir nur immer herabziehende, die kleinen Ausgaben und Einrichtungen, die sich ganz nach der Männer Stand beziehen müssen, Stückeleien vor uns haben. Es ist Menschenunkunde, wenn sich die Leute einbilden, unser Geist sei anders und zu andern Bedürfnissen konstituiert, und wir könnten z. E. ganz von des Mannes oder Sohnes Existenz mitzehren."[65]

Rahel Varnhagen leidet zeitlebens darunter, daß sie eine Frau und noch dazu eine Jüdin ist. Aber sie betrachtet sich nicht als Opfer eines Schicksals, sondern nimmt ihr Leben selbst in die Hand und statt sich aufzugeben, gewinnt sie ihre geistige Unabhängigkeit, indem sie anregende Gespräche und Briefwechsel führt. In ihrem kleinen Kreis versucht sie eine humanistische Gesellschaft zu verwirklichen. „Das nenn' ich eine emanzipierte Frau. Mit Stricken festgebunden zu sein an die Vergangenheit, die Herkunft, das Geschlecht, die allgemeine Meinung – und sich doch befreien können. Nicht durch Flucht, denn wir können nicht flüchten, sondern durch Damit-fertig-werden. ... Das nenn' ich emanzipiert sein: Sich frei machen von allem, ‚was die Leute denken', nicht nachbeten, nicht nachtun. Sich selbst finden, und den Mut haben, selbst zu sein."[66]

Nachlaß

1829 verschlechtert sich Rahels Gesundheitszustand; sie fühlt sich schwach, leidet unter Beklemmungen, Gicht und Rheuma. Zwar erholt sie sich bei einer Kur in Baden-Baden ein wenig, aber völlig gesund wird sie nicht mehr.

Rahel Varnhagen stirbt am 7. März 1833 im Alter von zweiundsechzig Jahren.

Sieben Tage später läßt Karl August Varnhagen ihren Leichnam in einem metallummantelten Eichensarg auf dem Berliner Dreifaltigkeitsfriedhof vor dem Halleschen Tor bestatten.

Rahel bleibt der Mittelpunkt seines Lebens: Im Juli 1833

verteilt er den Privatdruck „Rahel. Ein Buch des Andenkens für ihre Freunde", im Jahr darauf läßt er eine erweiterte dreibändige Ausgabe folgen, und die restlichen vierundzwanzig Jahre seines Lebens verwendet er darauf, ihre Briefe zu sammeln und zu veröffentlichen.

Marie Curie

Ein Leben für die Radiumforschung

Studienbeginn in Paris

Professor Paul Appell beendet seine Einführungsvorlesung in die Zahlentheorie. Als die Studenten höflich applaudieren, blickt er noch einmal kurz in die Runde; dann klopft er sich den Kreidestaub vom Frack, rückt den Zwicker zurecht, streicht mit der Hand über den Kinnbart und verläßt das Auditorium.

In der ersten Reihe steht eine Studentin auf und packt ihre Notizen in eine abgewetzte Mappe. Mit gesenktem Blick eilt sie aus der Sorbonne auf die Straße, wo sie mit hochgezogenen Schultern im Nieselregen auf den zweispännigen Pferdeomnibus wartet, der zum Pariser Nordbahnhof fährt.

Ängstlich achtet sie beim Abzählen des Fahrgelds darauf, daß keine Münze aus dem Portemonnaie fällt. Ohne die anderen Fahrgäste zu beachten, nimmt sie Platz und beugt sich über ihr Mathematikbuch. Einer jungen Mutter, die ihr schlafendes Kind auf dem Schoß wiegt, kommt sie in dieser vom Eiffelturm überragten Weltstadt vor „wie ein Gänseblümchen im Treibhaus".[1]

Es handelt sich um eine Polin, die in den nächsten Tagen ihren 24. Geburtstag feiern wird. Unter dem Namen Marie Sklodowska (eigentlich heißt sie Marya) schrieb sie sich für Vorlesungen in Mathematik, Physik und Chemie an der Sorbonne ein, wo heute – am 3. November 1891 – das neue Semester angefangen hat.

An der Gare du Nord wechselt Marie Sklodowska den Bus, und nach einer weiteren dreiviertel Stunde Fahrt steigt sie in La Villette aus, einem Arbeiterviertel, in dem sich die Pariser

Schlachthöfe befinden. Sie wohnt bei ihrer um drei Jahre älteren Schwester Bronislawa, die seit einigen Monaten mit dem siebenunddreißigjährigen Arzt Kazimierz Dluski verheiratet ist und ihm seit dem Abschluß ihres Medizinstudiums in der Praxis hilft.

„Kazio besucht noch einen Kranken, aber es wird nicht lang dauern. Inzwischen mache ich das Abendessen und backe einen Kuchen."

„Ich hoffe, du machst das nicht meinetwegen, Bronia."

„Sag: Wie war dein erster Tag an der Universität?"

„Mein Französisch ist noch zu schlecht: Ich muß meine Sprachkenntnisse verbessern."

„Das wirst du hier schnell lernen."

„Es fehlen mir aber auch mathematische Grundlagen, an die in Warschau niemand dachte. Ich muß also nicht nur an der Sprache arbeiten, sondern auch fachlich aufholen, damit ich den Anschluß nicht verpasse. – Bronia, ich habe Angst, daß ich das nicht bewältige!"

„Unsinn. Natürlich stürmt jetzt viel auf dich ein. Aber ich habe es geschafft, und dir wird es auch gelingen."

„Ich versuche jedenfalls alles – und fange gleich damit an."

„Willst du mir nicht in der Küche von Vater erzählen?"

Marie kommt zum Abendessen aus ihrem Zimmer, läßt aber die Bücher aufgeschlagen liegen und zieht sich gleich nach der Mahlzeit wieder zurück. Wie an jedem Abend kommen Bekannte der Dluskis unangemeldet zu Besuch: andere Polen, die ebenfalls in Paris wohnen. Marie versucht, nicht auf das Stimmengewirr und das Gelächter im Nebenzimmer zu achten, aber als ihr Schwager Ohrwürmer aus der Operette „Pariser Leben" auf dem Klavier spielt, fällt es ihr schwer, sich auf mathematische Ableitungen zu konzentrieren.

Einmal steckt Bronislawa den Kopf zur Tür herein, um ihr Tee und Kuchen zu bringen.

Eine Stunde später klopft Kazimierz: Widerstrebend folgt Marie ihrem Schwager in das andere Zimmer, wo sie fröhlich begrüßt wird.

Endlich brechen die letzten Gäste auf. Marie sitzt noch ein paar Stunden über ihren Büchern und schlüpft dann ins Bett.

Marie Curie (1867–1934)
Foto: undatiert

Aber während der vier Stunden, die ihr zum Schlafen bleiben, schreckt sie zweimal hoch, weil Kazimierz Dluski zu Patienten gerufen wird.

Das hält Marie nur wenige Wochen lang aus. Zögernd spricht sie ihre Schwester darauf an. Werden Bronia und Kazio das auch nicht mißverstehen und als Undankbarkeit auslegen? Marie ist erleichtert, als das nicht der Fall ist und die beiden ihr helfen, in ein billiges Hotel im Quartier Latin zu ziehen.

Kurze Zeit später findet Marie ein Mansardenzimmer in einem sechsstöckigen Mietshaus, zwanzig Minuten von der Sorbonne entfernt. Das Tageslicht fällt lediglich durch eine Dachluke in die Kammer; und es gibt weder elektrischen Strom noch fließendes Wasser. Gewöhnlich geht Marie erst heim, wenn der Lesesaal der Universitätsbibliothek geschlossen wird. Bis tief in die Nacht sitzt sie dann im Schein einer Petroleumlampe auf ihrem einzigen Stuhl am weiß lackierten Holztisch. In besonders kalten Nächten, wenn das Wasser in der Waschschüssel gefriert, heizt sie ihren kleinen Eisenofen mit einem Brikett.

Wochenlang nimmt sie kaum etwas anderes als Tee und belegte Brote zu sich. „Bei dieser Lebensweise wird aus dem kräftigen, frischen Mädchen, das Warschau vor einigen Monaten verlassen hat, bald ein blutleeres, erschöpftes Wesen."[2] Marie magert ab; häufig tanzen ihr die Zahlen und Buchstaben vor den Augen. Als sie in der Universität taumelt und beinahe zusammenbricht, benachrichtigt eine Kommilitonin die Dluskis. Kazimierz kommt unverzüglich und diagnostiziert einen Erschöpfungszustand, besteht darauf, daß Marie ihn nach La Villette begleitet, und obwohl Bronislawa für ihr Neugeborenes zu sorgen hat, kümmert sie sich darum, daß ihre Schwester wieder ausreichend ißt. Einigermaßen erholt kehrt Marie nach einer Woche in ihr Mansardenzimmer zurück – mit guten Vorsätzen, die Schwester und Schwager ihr abgerungen haben.

Nach drei Semestern schließt sie das Grundstudium in Physik als Jahrgangsbeste ab, und im Jahr darauf beendet sie auch das Grundstudium in Mathematik.

Ihrem Bruder schreibt sie: „Man muß daran glauben, für eine bestimmte Sache begabt zu sein, und diese Sache muß man erreichen, koste es, was es wolle."[3]

Kindheit in Warschau

Wladislaw Sklodowski unterrichtete an einem Warschauer Gymnasium Physik und Mathematik, während seine Frau ein Mädchenpensionat betrieb. Nach drei Töchtern und einem Sohn brachte Bronislawa Sklodowska am 7. November 1867 Marya zur Welt.

Während der letzten Schwangerschaft waren die ersten Anzeichen einer Tuberkulose-Erkrankung bei der Mutter aufgetreten. Sie gab ihre Berufstätigkeit auf. Um ihre eigenen Kinder nicht anzustecken, wehrte sie deren Liebkosungen ab. Gefühle spielten ohnehin nur eine untergeordnete Rolle im Zusammenleben der konservativen Lehrerfamilie; statt dessen erzogen die aus dem verarmten polnischen Landadel stammenden Eltern die Kinder zu strenger Disziplin und Pflichterfüllung. „Der Vater setzte seine viktorianischen Vorstellungen von Anstand durch."[4] Die Mutter „verlangte von ihren Kindern vor allem dieselbe klaglose Pflichterfüllung, die sie ihnen vorlebte."[5]

Obendrein kontrollierte die russische Polizei das Leben in Warschau. Polen existierte nur noch in der Erinnerung.

Rußland, Preußen und Österreich hatten 1772 ein Drittel des polnischen Territoriums unter sich aufgeteilt. Inspiriert von der Amerikanischen und der Französischen Revolution verabschiedete das Parlament des verbliebenen Rumpfstaates am 3. Mai 1791 die erste schriftlich fixierte Verfassung Europas, aber noch im gleichen Monat ließ Katharina die Große ihre Truppen in Polen einmarschieren, um ein Übergreifen der „französischen Pest" auf Osteuropa zu verhindern. Die polnische Armee kapitulierte; Preußen verständigte sich mit Rußland über die zweite polnische Teilung. Dagegen erhoben sich zwar die polnischen Patrioten, aber den Aufstand schlugen russische Truppen blutig nieder, und 1795 tilgten Rußland,

Preußen und Österreich den polnischen Staat von der Landkarte.

Aus der Stadt Warschau und ihrem Umland kreierte der Wiener Kongreß[6] ein vom russischen Zaren in Personalunion regiertes Pseudokönigreich.

Damit begann eine rücksichtslose Russifizierung des Landes: Wenn ein russischer Schulinspektor auftauchte, mußten die Schüler die Reihe der Zaren fehlerfrei aufsagen können. „Polizisten, Lehrer und Verwaltungsbeamte waren Russen, und zwar meistens besonders polenfeindliche. Es war verboten, polnisch zu reden; Zeitungen, Bücher, Schulen, Kirchen – alles wurde kontrolliert und überwacht, und jeder Pole machte sich einfach schon dadurch verdächtig, daß er Pole war."[7]

Als ein russischer Aufsichtsbeamter 1873 Wladislaw Sklodowskis Gehalt zusammenstrich, holte dieser bis zu zehn Schüler als Pensionsgäste in die Wohnung und erteilte ihnen Nachhilfeunterricht, um die Miete bezahlen und seine Familie versorgen zu können. Marya mußte auf einem Sofa schlafen und aufgeräumt haben, wenn die jungen Herren morgens um sechs Uhr in dem Zimmer frühstückten.

Einer von ihnen steckte 1876 zwei Töchter der Familie mit Typhus an, und Maryas älteste Schwester starb daran.

Zwei Jahre später beweinte Marya auch ihre Mutter: Bronislawa Sklodowska erlag ihrer Lungenkrankheit.

Der Traum vom Studium

Marya verließ das Gymnasium 1883 mit einer Goldmedaille für das beste Abschlußzeugnis des Jahrgangs.

Ihre ältere Schwester reiste zwei Jahre später nach Paris, um Medizin zu studieren. „In dieser Entscheidung lag für die ganze Familie etwas Atemberaubendes."[8] Beim Abschied versicherte Marya ihrer Schwester: „Glaub' mir, das ist der richtige Schritt. Du mußt unbedingt studieren, und für uns Polinnen gibt es dafür eben nur im Ausland eine Möglichkeit." Marya hätte Bronislawa gern begleitet, aber für zwei reichte das Geld nicht. Deshalb studierte zuerst die Ältere, und danach – so hatten sie es sich versprochen – sollte diese ihrer jüngeren Schwester weiterhelfen.

Um Bronislawa genügend Geld für den Lebensunterhalt in Paris schicken zu können, nahm Marya eine Stellung bei der Familie eines Warschauer Rechtsanwalts an: „Es ist eines jener reichen Häuser, wo man vor Gästen französisch spricht – ein erbärmliches Französisch –, Rechnungen ein halbes Jahr lang nicht bezahlt, aber das Geld aus dem Fenster hinauswirft und dabei an dem Petroleum für die Lampen spart. Es gibt fünf Dienstboten, man posiert auf Liberalismus, in Wirklichkeit aber herrscht finstere Dummheit. In süßestem Ton wird bösartiger Klatsch getrieben – ein Klatsch, der an keinem ein gutes Haar läßt."[9]

Nach drei Monaten kündigte Marya und begann als Gouvernante bei einer wohlhabenden Familie auf einem Gut hundert Kilometer nördlich von Warschau zu arbeiten: Sie unterrichtete die beiden zehn bzw. achtzehn Jahre alten Töchter, und nach ein paar Monaten durfte sie in ihrem Zimmer auch für einige Dorfkinder Schulstunden halten. Im Dezember 1886 berichtete sie in einem Brief: „Die Anzahl meiner Schüler ist nun auf achtzehn gestiegen. Selbstverständlich kommen sie nicht alle auf einmal, denn das könnte ich nicht bewältigen, aber auch auf diese Weise habe ich zwei Stunden täglich damit zu tun. Mittwoch und Samstag nehme ich mir mehr Zeit, bis zu fünf Stunden hintereinander... Mit allen meinen Verpflichtungen bin ich meistens von acht bis halb zwölf und von zwei bis halb acht ununterbrochen beschäftigt. Von halb zwölf bis zwei ist Spaziergang und Mittagessen ... Um neun Uhr abends stürze ich mich in meine Bücher ... Ich habe mich daran gewöhnt, um sechs Uhr aufzustehen, damit ich mehr arbeiten kann – aber ich bin nicht immer fähig dazu."[10]

Die drei Söhne der Familie studierten in Warschau. Als einer von ihnen in den Semesterferien nach Hause kam, verliebte er sich in Marya und dachte sogar ans Heiraten. Aber seine Eltern unterbanden die Romanze: Obwohl, oder gerade weil die Mutter selbst Gouvernante gewesen war, galt die mittellose

Lehrerstochter nicht als standesgemäß. Marya wird die Enttäuschung nie vergessen.

Mißtrauisch belauerte die Frau des Gutsbesitzers die Gouvernante nach dieser Auseinandersetzung, und die Zurückgewiesene schrieb an ihren Bruder: „Mein lieber Josef, ich klebe auf diesen Brief die letzte Marke, die ich besitze ... Wenn Du wüßtest, mein Lieber, wie schwer es mir ums Herz ist, wie ich mir wünschte, für ein paar Tage nach Warschau zu kommen! ...meine Seele tut nicht mehr mit. Ach, könnte ich für Tage nur dieser eisigen, erkältenden Atmosphäre entfliehen, der fortwährenden kritischen Beobachtung meiner eigenen Worte, meines Gesichtsausdrucks, meiner Bewegungen! Ich brauche das wie ein frisches Bad an einem schwülen Tage."[11]

Doch Marya hielt durch, blieb auf dem Gut, weil sie und ihre Schwester auf den Verdienst angewiesen waren. Erst als ihr Vertrag im Sommer 1889 auslief, wechselte sie zur Familie eines Warschauer Großindustriellen.

Im Frühjahr 1890 war es soweit: Bronislawa konnte ihrer Schwester Kost und Logie anbieten. Marya antwortete: „Liebe Bronia, ich war dumm, ich bin dumm, ich werde dumm sein, solange ich lebe, oder, um es mit anderen Worten zu sagen: Glück hatte ich nie, habe ich nicht und werde ich nie haben. Ich habe von Paris wie von der Erlösung geträumt, aber seit langem schon habe ich die Hoffnung aufgegeben, je hinzukommen."[12] Sie zögerte, den alt gewordenen Vater allein in Warschau zurückzulassen. Eineinhalb Jahre lang schwankte sie, dann warf sie ihre Bedenken über Bord und fuhr mit der Dampfeisenbahn von Warschau nach Paris – auf einem Klappstuhl in der 4. Klasse.

Pierre Curie

Als Marie Sklodowska im April 1894 einen ebenfalls aus Polen stammenden Professor wegen eines Forschungsauftrags um Rat bittet, lädt dieser sie zu einem Gespräch ein und zieht den fünfunddreißig Jahre alten Physiker Pierre Curie hinzu. Marie Curie schreibt darüber in ihrer Selbstbiographie: „Beim Betreten des Zimmers erblickte ich einen jungen, großen Mann mit kastanienfarbenem Haar und großen hellen Augen, der in der offenen Balkontür stand. Ich bemerkte den ernsten und netten Gesichtsausdruck und eine gewisse, scheinbar lässige Haltung, die einen in seine Gedanken vertieften Schwärmer auszeichnet."[13]

Weder Pierre noch sein älterer Bruder Jacques gingen jemals zur Schule: Ihr Vater, der Pariser Arzt Eugène Curie, ließ sie von Privatlehrern ebenso sorgfältig wie freigeistig unterrichten. Sie studierten Physik und veröffentlichten einige bahnbrechende Arbeiten zur Piezoelektrik[14], bevor Jacques einem Ruf nach Montpellier folgte, während Pierre eine schlecht bezahlte Stelle als Laborleiter an der Städtischen Schule für industrielle Physik und Chemie in Paris übernahm.

Pierre Curie ist ebenso wie Marie Sklodowska von der Forschung besessen. Beide wollen nichts anderes – und diese Gemeinsamkeit bildet die Brücke, auf der sie sich allmählich näherkommen.

Seinen ersten Heiratsantrag lehnt sie ab, weil sie nicht vorhat, in Paris zu bleiben. Im Sommer 1894 verbringt sie einige Wochen mit ihrem Vater in der Schweiz und begleitet ihn dann nach Warschau. Dort fragt sie vergeblich nach einer Arbeitsmöglichkeit und beschließt deshalb, nach Paris zurückzukehren – wenigstens für ein weiteres Jahr. Pierre schickt sie ein Foto. Sein Bruder Jacques kommentiert es mit den Worten: „Sie macht einen entschlossenen Eindruck, geradezu eigensinnig."[15]

Im Juli 1895 schreibt die siebenundzwanzig Jahre alte Marie einer Freundin: „Wenn Du diesen Brief erhältst, wird Deine Mania[16] einen anderen Namen tragen. Ich werde den Mann heiraten, von dem ich Dir im vorigen Jahr in Warschau erzählt habe. Es ist mir sehr schmerzlich, für immer in Paris zu bleiben, aber was soll ich tun? Das Schicksal hat es so gewollt, daß wir uns tief verbunden fühlen und den Gedanken, uns zu trennen, nicht ertragen können... Ein ganzes Jahr lang habe ich gezögert und wußte nicht, wozu ich mich entschließen soll. Endlich habe ich mich mit dem Gedanken abgefunden, mich hier niederzulassen."[17]

Marie und Pierre heiraten auf dem Standesamt in Sceaux, einem Vorort im Süden von Paris, wo die Familie des Bräutigams seit dreizehn Jahren wohnt. Das Paar lehnt eine kirchliche Trauung ab, verzichtet auf Ringe und ein großes Fest. Von dem Geld, das sie zur Hochzeit geschenkt bekommen, kaufen sich Marie und Pierre Fahrräder und fahren damit in die Flitterwochen.

In der Pariser Dreizimmerwohnung, die sie zu Beginn des folgenden Semesters beziehen, beschränken sie sich auf die notwendigsten Möbel – nicht nur, weil sie sparen müssen, sondern auch aus Überzeugung: Ihr eigentliches Leben ist ohnehin die Forschungsarbeit, das Labor ihr Zuhause.

„Ich richte nach und nach meine Wohnung ein, aber ich gedenke, einen Stil beizubehalten, der mich jeder Sorge enthebt und keinerlei besondere Pflege erfordert, denn ich habe sehr wenig Bedienung: Eine Frau kommt täglich für eine Stunde, um Geschirr zu waschen und die groben Arbeiten zu verrichten. Ich koche und räume selbst auf. Alle paar Tage fahren wir nach Sceaux, um die Eltern meines Mannes zu besuchen. Unsere Arbeit ist davon nicht gestört: wir haben im ersten Stock zwei Zimmer, die alles, was wir brauchen, enthalten, wir sind also wie zu Hause und können dort ohne weiteres den Teil unserer Arbeit erledigen, den wir im Laboratorium nicht machen können. Wenn es schön ist, fahren wir mit den Rädern nach Sceaux; den Zug nehmen wir nur, wenn es in Strömen gießt."[18]

Zwei Jahre nach der Hochzeit schickt Pierre Curie seine hochschwangere Frau mit ihrem aus Polen angereisten Vater zur Erholung in die Bretagne und folgt selbst zwei Wochen später, um mit ihr Fahrradtouren zu unternehmen. Aber sie müssen vorzeitig nach Paris zurückkehren, wo Marie am 12. September 1897 ihre Tochter Irène zur Welt bringt.

Einige Tage später stirbt Pierres Mutter an Brustkrebs.

Die Entdeckung der Radioaktivität

Im März 1896 berichtete der Pariser Physikprofessor Antoine Henri Becquerel der Französischen Akademie der Wissenschaften, was er entdeckt hatte: Auch sorgfältig mit schwarzem Papier gegen Licht geschützte fotografische Platten schwärzen sich, wenn sie eine Weile in der Nähe von Uransalzen gelagert werden. Becquerel schloß von dieser Beobachtung auf eine unsichtbare Strahlung, die das Schwermetall Uran fortwährend abgibt.

Seine Mitteilungen sind zwar kaum beachtet worden, aber Marie Curie setzt hier einige Monate nach der Geburt ihrer Tochter mit ihrer Doktorarbeit an – nicht zuletzt, weil dieses Forschungsgebiet noch unerschlossen ist. Wie kann eine spontane Strahlung von einem festen Stoff ausgehen? „Es galt also, die Herkunft der übrigens sehr geringen Energie zu untersuchen, die von dem Uran in Form von Strahlung ständig ausgesandt wurde. ... Ich beschloß, mich der Bearbeitung dieses Themas zu widmen."[19] Sie kann nicht ahnen, daß sie damit auf eine wissenschaftliche Goldader stößt und ihrem Leben eine entscheidende Wendung gibt.

Pierre Curie bettelt darum, daß seiner Frau in der Physikschule ein Arbeitsraum zur Verfügung gestellt wird. In einer feuchten, ungeheizten Abstellkammer beginnt sie im Dezember 1897, die Strahlung des Urans systematisch zu messen.

Die Strahlungsintensität einer Probe bleibt gleich, auch wenn sie zum Beispiel die Temperatur oder die Feuchtigkeit ändert. Aus dieser Beobachtung schließt Marie Curie, daß die Strahlung unmittelbar von den Atomen ausgeht und sie prägt für diese Eigenschaft den Begriff „Radioaktivität". Das ist eine kühne Behauptung, mit der sie das klassische Weltbild der Physik in Frage stellt, denn das Atom gilt als unteilbarer und unveränderlicher Baustein der Materie; wenn es aber Atome gibt, die Energie abstrahlen, kann das nicht richtig sein! (Daß die Radioaktivität auf einer Element-Umwandlung durch den Zerfall instabler Atome beruht, erkennen Ernest Lord Rutherford von Nelson und Frederick Soddy wenig später.)

Es gibt gleich noch eine weitere Überraschung: Sie findet

heraus, daß Pechblende stärker strahlt als aufgrund der in dem Mineral enthaltenen Menge Uran erklärt werden kann. Birgt diese Substanz ein noch unbekanntes Element, das stärker als Uran strahlt?

Die aufgeworfenen Fragen und die vorgeschlagenen Antworten sind eine Sensation! Marie Curies Doktorvater Gabriel Lippmann beeilt sich, in einer Sitzung der Französischen Akademie der Wissenschaften über den Stand der Forschungen zu referieren.

Pierre Curie läßt seine eigene Arbeit liegen, um das gesuchte Element – das Marie in Erinnerung an ihre Heimat Polonium nennt – gemeinsam mit ihr nachzuweisen. Sie lösen hundert Gramm zerstoßene Pechblende in einer Säure auf und scheiden die inaktiven Bestandteile des Stoffgemisches ab. Auf diese Weise gewinnen sie eine von Stufe zu Stufe stärker strahlende Substanz, die offenbar Polonium enthält.

Nach einem ausgedehnten Fahrradurlaub arbeiten sie im November 1898 weiter. Verblüfft stellen sie fest, daß auch eine Fraktion der Pechblende, die kein Polonium enthält, unverhältnismäßig stark strahlt: Das Ausgangsmaterial enthält also mindestens zwei unbekannte Elemente! Am 26. Dezember 1898 kündigen sie die Entdeckung eines weiteren radioaktiven Elements in der Pechblende an. Radium nennen sie es.

Knochenarbeit

Marie Curie hat Radium und Polonium aufgrund ihrer Strahlungseigenschaften nachgewiesen. Nun will sie wenigstens eines der beiden radioaktiven Elemente chemisch isolieren. Die Proben, mit denen sie bis dahin arbeitete, sind dafür ungeeignet: Hundert Gramm Pechblende enthalten lediglich Spuren der gesuchten Elemente. Um eines davon in wägbaren Mengen isolieren zu können, benötigen die Forscher tonnenweise Pechblende – und entsprechend viel Platz.

In einem Hof der Physikschule wird ihnen eine verwahrloste Holzbaracke zur Verfügung gestellt, „eine Kreuzung zwischen Stall und Kartoffelkeller"[20] mit einem Asphaltboden und einem Glasdach, das den Schuppen im Sommer zum Treibhaus werden läßt. Im Winter reicht der Eisenofen gerade aus, die Temperatur über dem Gefrierpunkt zu halten, und wenn es regnet, tropft das Wasser auf Stellen, die Marie und Pierre markieren, um dort nicht versehentlich eine Materialprobe hinzustellen. Aber Marie Curie wird sich später erinnern: „In diesem dürftigen alten Schuppen verbrachten wir unsere besten und glücklichsten Jahre."[21]

Pechblende ist ein für Marie und Pierre Curie unerschwingliches Uranmineral, das am Südrand des Erzgebirges für die böhmische Glasindustrie abgebaut wird. Da sie aber am Uran gar nicht interessiert sind, können sie auch mit Rückständen aus der Urangewinnung arbeiten. Über die französische Akademie wenden sie sich hilfesuchend an die Wiener Akademie der Wissenschaften, und tatsächlich schickt man ihnen insgesamt sechzig Tonnen Pechblende-Abfall. Sie brauchen dafür nichts zu bezahlen, müssen aber für die Transportkosten aufkommen.

Während Pierre Curie die physikalischen Eigenschaften der Radioaktivität erforscht, schuftet Marie Curie jahrelang, um aus der Halde Substanzen zu gewinnen, die in immer stärkerer Konzentration Radium enthalten. Sie schmilzt das Mineral in riesigen Wannen, schleppt die schweren Behälter von einer Stelle zur anderen, um den Inhalt umzugießen, dann den Bodensatz noch weiter zu erhitzen und die Bestandteile der Pechblende Schritt für Schritt voneinander zu trennen.

Marie Curie sorgt zu Hause für die Tochter und den Mann, in der Laborbaracke rührt sie stundenlang blubbernde Schlammassen, sie verfaßt wissenschaftliche Berichte und übernimmt außerdem eine Teilzeit-Anstellung als Physiklehrerin an einem renommierten Mädchengymnasium in Sèvres. Wie schafft sie das? Indem sie mit außergewöhnlicher Härte – oder sagen wir: Besessenheit – auf alles andere verzichtet. Ihr rastloser Einsatz geht „zwangsläufig mit einer gewissen Monomanie und emotionellen Verarmung einher";[22] sie lebt „wie losgelöst von dieser Welt: selbstgenügsam und vollkommen zurückgezogen, im Elfenbeinturm ihrer wissenschaftlichen Interessen".[23]

Marie Curie selbst sieht das so: „Unser Leben bleibt sich immer gleich. Wir arbeiten viel, aber da wir gut schlafen, schadet es uns nicht. Die Abende verbringe ich mit der Kleinen. Am Morgen kleide ich sie an und gebe ihr zu essen, dann kann ich gewöhnlich gegen neun Uhr fortgehen. Wir waren ein ganzes Jahr weder im Theater noch in einem Konzert und haben nicht einen einzigen Besuch gemacht. Im übrigen fühlen wir uns wohl ...“[24]

„Im übrigen fühlen wir uns wohl." Schönfärberei ist das. Marie Curie verliert sieben Kilogramm Körpergewicht; leidet unter Überreiztheit und Schlaflosigkeit. Die Fingerspitzen entzünden sich und schmerzen. Ständige Müdigkeit und Muskelschmerzen machen auch Pierre Curie zu schaffen.

Niemand weiß zu diesem Zeitpunkt, daß die radioaktive Strahlung Körperzellen schädigt; aber auch als den Curies auffällt, daß die Haut in der Nähe radioaktiver Substanzen verbrennt, setzen sie ihre Arbeit bedenkenlos fort.

Wenn die Strahlung gesundes Körpergewebe zerstört, müßte man damit auch bösartige Geschwüre bekämpfen können. Deshalb untersucht Pierre mit zwei Medizinern therapeutische Anwendungsmöglichkeiten der Radioaktivität. Er klebt sich strahlendes Material zehn Stunden lang auf den Unterarm und beobachtet danach die entstandene Verbrennung, die erst nach sechs Wochen zu heilen beginnt.

Endlich ist es soweit: Am 28. März 1902 hält Marie Curie ein versiegeltes Glasröhrchen in der Hand. Gefüllt ist es mit einem Zehntel Gramm eines Pulvers, das sie in vierjähriger Arbeit aus sechzig Tonnen Pechblende gewonnen hat. Es enthält das gesuchte Element in einer so hohen Konzentration, daß sie das Atomgewicht bestimmen kann. „Wenn man die Summe der Arbeit überblickt, die es gekostet hat, ist es sicherlich das kostspieligste Element der Welt", schreibt Wladislaw Sklodowski seiner Tochter.[25] Aber es bedarf weiterer Anstrengungen, um anstelle des jetzt verfügbaren Radiumsalzes metallisches Radium zu isolieren.

Zunächst jedoch reist Marie Curie besorgt nach Warschau: Ihr Vater befindet sich nach einer Gallenblasenoperation in einem kritischen Zustand. Als sie eintrifft, ist er bereits tot.

Nobelpreis

Am 19. Juni 1903 nimmt das Forscherehepaar an einer Sitzung der Royal Society in London teil. Erstmals rang sich die älteste englische Wissenschaftsakademie dazu durch, eine Frau einzuladen: Sie darf wenigstens im Publikum sitzen, als Pierre Curie einen Vortrag über die gemeinsame Forschungsarbeit hält.

„Die englische Naturphilosophin Margaret Cavendish sprach für viele, als sie im 17. Jahrhundert schrieb, daß Frauenhirne einfach zu ‚kalt' und zu ‚schwach' seien, um die Strenge des Gedankens auszuhalten. ... Im späten 18. Jahrhundert nahm man an, daß die weibliche Schädelhöhle zu klein sei, um ein leistungsfähiges Gehirn zu bergen; im 19. Jahrhundert behauptete man, daß übermäßige Gedankentätigkeit die Eierstöcke der Frauen verkümmern ließe."[26] Und Max Planck meinte 1897: „Amazonen sind auch auf geistigem Gebiet naturwidrig."[27]

Sechs Tage nach ihrem Besuch bei der Royal Society steht Marie Curie vor einem Tisch, an dem drei Professoren im Frack sitzen. Bronislawa überredete sie, für diesen Anlaß ein schwarzes Kleid zu kaufen. Es handelt sich um die erste Promotion einer Frau in einem naturwissenschaftlichen Fach an der Sorbonne. Ruhig beantwortet die Fünfunddreißigjährige die ihr gestellten Fragen: Sie verteidigt erfolgreich ihre Dissertation „über radioaktive Stoffe" und erläutert den staunenden Prüfern ihre Forschungsergebnisse.

Im August wird Dr. Marie Curie von einem Mädchen entbunden, das jedoch nach wenigen Stunden stirbt – möglicherweise infolge der Strahlenbelastung der Mutter. „Ich habe meinem Organismus viel zugetraut, und nun bedauere ich es tief, denn ich habe es teuer bezahlt. Das Kind, ein kleines Mädchen, war in gutem Zustand und lebte. Und ich hatte es mir so sehr gewünscht!"[28]

Die Royal Society zeichnet das Ehepaar Curie mit der Davy-Medaille aus. Marie ist allerdings so geschwächt, daß Pierre im November allein zur Verleihungsfeier nach London reisen muß.

Noch im gleichen Monat erfährt das Forscherehepaar, daß der Physik-Nobelpreis an Antoine Henri Becquerel und sie beide verliehen werden soll, „als Anerkennung für die außerordentlichen Verdienste, die sie sich durch die Entdeckung der spontanen Radioaktivität und der Strahlungsphänomene erworben haben."[29]

Inzwischen fühlt sich auch Pierre Curie so krank, daß er ebensowenig wie seine Frau zur Preisverleihung nach Stockholm fahren kann. (Erst eineinhalb Jahre später holen sie die Reise nach: Am 6. Juni 1905 hält Pierre Curie vor der Schwedischen Akademie der Wissenschaften einen Vortrag über ihre gemeinsame Arbeit.)

Das Preisgeld versetzt sie in die Lage, einen Laborassistenten einzustellen und ihre Ausrüstung zu verbessern. Aber sie werden nun ständig von Journalisten belästigt. Die Presse entdeckt auflagensteigernde romantische Momente in Maries Leben: eine Polin in Paris, Jahre der Armut, die völkerübergreifende Liebe zweier Forscher, eine Baracke als Laboratorium, harte Arbeit, bahnbrechende Erfolge – und ein freudiges Ereignis: Am 6. Dezember 1904 bringt Marie Curie noch eine Tochter zur Welt: Eve.

Fast zur gleichen Zeit richtet die Sorbonne für Pierre Curie einen neuen Physik-Lehrstuhl ein. Dazu gehören ein Laboratorium und drei Assistentenstellen, von denen eine für Marie Curie vorgesehen ist: Endlich kann das Forscherehepaar unter angemessenen Bedingungen arbeiten. Überdies wird Pierre Curie am 3. Juli 1905 in die Französische Akademie der Wissenschaften aufgenommen. Marie Curie gratuliert ihrem Mann: Er hat es geschafft. Dem Sorbonne-Professor, Akademie-Mitglied und Nobelpreisträger stehen viele Türen offen.

Aber diese Lebensphase dauert nur einige Monate, dann endet sie mit einem Schicksalsschlag.

Tödlicher Unfall

Am 19. April 1906 regnet es den ganzen Tag. Pierre Curie, der nach wie vor von rheumatischen Beschwerden geplagt wird, zu Depressionen neigt und sich ständig erschöpft fühlt, geht nach einer Sitzung der Akademie der Wissenschaften zu seinem Verleger, kehrt aber wieder um, ohne etwas erreicht zu haben, weil das Büro wegen eines Druckerstreiks geschlossen ist. Mit aufgespanntem Schirm will er gerade hinter einer Droschke eine belebte Avenue überqueren. In der Eile übersieht er das Fuhrwerk auf der anderen Straßenseite, prallt gegen das linke der beiden Zugpferde, wird zu Boden geworfen. Der Kutscher reißt an den Zügeln; die Pferde bäumen sich auf, stehen. Zu spät: Pierre liegt mit zerquetschtem Schädel auf dem Pflaster.

Im Rahmen einer schlichten Zeremonie wird der Leichnam in Sceaux bestattet.

Marie Curie mietet im gleichen Ort ein einfaches Haus, in das sie mit ihrem Schwiegervater und den beiden Töchtern zieht.

Vier Wochen nach dem Tod ihres Mannes wird sie zur außerordentlichen Professorin an der Sorbonne ernannt.

Ihre Antrittsvorlesung hält sie am 5. November – zwei Tage vor ihrem 39. Geburtstag. Eine halbe Stunde vor dem Beginn öffnet man die Türen des Hörsaals; zehn Minuten später müssen sie wieder geschlossen werden, weil in dem Raum niemand mehr Platz findet. Pünktlich schreitet Professor Paul Appell zum Katheter und erklärt: „Madame Curie wird keine Ansprache halten und keine offizielle Einführung geben, sondern an der Stelle fortfahren, wo Professor Curie den Kurs abgebrochen hat."

1908 beruft die Sorbonne Marie Curie als ordentliche Professorin auf den Lehrstuhl ihres verstorbenen Mannes. Sie ist die zweite Frau in der europäischen Geschichte, die mit einem Ordinariat betraut worden ist.[30]

Mit widersprüchlichen Gefühlen nimmt sie die Glückwünsche entgegen.

Eve und Irène

Einer Freundin schreibt Marie Curie: „Mein Leben ist so zerstört, daß es sich nie mehr einrichten wird. So ist es, so wird es bleiben, und ich werde nicht versuchen, es zu ändern. Ich habe den Wunsch, meine Kinder so gut wie nur irgend möglich zu erziehen, doch sind auch sie nicht imstande, mich zum Leben zu erwecken. Sie sind beide lieb und gut und ziemlich hübsch. Ich tue, was ich kann, um ihnen Gesundheit und Widerstandskraft ins Leben mitzugeben. Wenn ich an die Jüngere denke, wird mir bewußt, daß es noch zwanzig Jahre dauern wird, ehe beide erwachsen sind. Ich muß bezweifeln, so lange durchzuhalten, denn ich führe ein höchst ermüdendes Leben, und Kummer ist nicht gerade des rechte Mittel, einen bei Kraft und Gesundheit zu erhalten."[31]

Marie Curie läßt ihre Töchter nicht taufen. Bei der freigeistigen Erziehung orientiert sie sich am Vorbild ihres Schwiegervaters. Auf Etikette legt sie keinen Wert, und gesellschaftliche Gepflogenheiten mißachtet sie. Es kommt ihr darauf an, daß Eve und Irène einmal selbst für ihren Lebensunterhalt sorgen können und nicht auf eine vorteilhafte Heirat angewiesen sind.

Zusammen mit einigen Kollegen organisiert Marie Curie eine Unterrichtsgemeinschaft: Abwechselnd geben sie ihren acht, neun Kindern Physik-, Chemie- und Mathematikstunden. Aber nach zwei Jahren scheitert das Experiment an der Arbeitsbelastung der Eltern, die ihre Sprößlinge nun doch auf öffentliche Schulen schicken.

Romanze

Nach wie vor konzentriert sich Marie Curie auf ihre Arbeit, scheut jegliche Ablenkung und vermeidet deshalb auch Bekanntschaften, die nichts mit ihrer Forschung zu tun haben.

Eine Ausnahme macht sie bei Paul Langevin.

Den um fünf Jahre jüngeren Physiker kennt sie seit Jahren, denn er war zunächst Schüler, später Mitarbeiter ihres Mannes, unterrichtete an derselben Schule wie sie und gehörte zu den Mitgliedern der gescheiterten Unterrichtsgemeinschaft für die eigenen Kinder.

Der hervorragende Wissenschaftler schlägt verlockende Angebote der Industrie aus, weil ihm seine eigene Forschung wichtiger als das Einkommen ist, aber der gutaussehende Mann lebt nicht nur für die Arbeit, sondern bewegt sich auch gewandt in der Gesellschaft; er besucht Konzerte und Theateraufführungen, verabredet sich gern mit anderen im Restaurant, genießt dann – ungeachtet seiner Magenbeschwerden – den Wein und das Essen und diskutiert über die politischen Ereignisse.

Paul Langevin ist für Marie Curie „die Inkarnation der Jugend ... Nicht nur seine äußere Erscheinung und sein jungenhaftes Wesen, auch sein wissenschaftliches Denken waren so ganz anders, als sie es von den Männern in ihrer Umgebung gewohnt war. Bisher hatte sie es meist mit erheblich älteren Männern zu tun gehabt. Intellektuelles Vorbild war einst ihr Vater gewesen, später dann ihr ein knappes Jahrzehnt älterer Mann. ... Nun sah sich Marie Curie plötzlich mehr als nur freundschaftlich verbunden mit einem Physiker der neuen Generation..."[32]

Obwohl jeder Schritt der Nobelpreisträgerin aufmerksam beobachtet wird, besucht Marie Curie den Freund häufig in seiner Wohnung. Wie unvorsichtig! Paul Langevin lebt von seiner Frau und den vier Kindern getrennt, aber solange er nicht geschieden ist, gilt ein Verhältnis als Ehebruch. Im November 1911 veröffentlichen Boulevardblätter kompromittierende Artikel über Marie Curie und Paul Langevin: „Das Feuer des Radiums hat im Herzen eines Wissenschaftlers eine Flamme entzündet; die Frau und die Kinder des Wissenschaftlers aber müssen nun bittere Tränen vergießen."[33] Einige der Briefe, die Marie Curie an Paul Langevin schrieb, werden gestohlen. Wochenlang befürchten die beiden, vor Gericht gezerrt zu werden. Das bleibt ihnen zwar erspart, aber die Belastung zerstört die Romanze.

Noch ein Nobelpreis

Am 8. November 1911 – vier Tage nach den ersten Zeitungs-
meldungen über ihre Beziehung zu Paul Langevin – erfährt
Marie Curie durch ein Telegramm, daß ihr die Schwedische
Akademie der Wissenschaften nach dem Physik- nun auch
noch den Chemie-Nobelpreis zugesprochen hat, „als Anerkennung des Verdienstes, das sie sich um die Entdeckung der Elemente Radium und Polonium, durch die Charakterisierung
des Radiums und dessen Isolierung in metallischem Zustand
und durch die Untersuchungen über die Natur und die chemi-
schen Verbindungen dieses Elements erworben hat".[34]

Ein Nobelpreis ist etwas Außerordentliches; zwei Nobel-
preise für eine Person: das ist eine Sensation, die sich ein halbes Jahrhundert lang nicht wiederholt![35]

Als Irène Curie ihre Mutter und ihre Tante Bronislawa im
Dezember nach Stockholm begleitet, kann sie nicht ahnen,
daß sie vierundzwanzig Jahre später erneut in die schwedische
Hauptstadt reisen wird, um ihren eigenen Nobelpreis entge-
genzunehmen.

Krieg

Am 31. Juli 1914 feiert Marie Curie einen weiteren Erfolg: An
diesem Tag wird das von der Sorbonne und dem Pasteur-Insti-
tut gegründete Radium-Institut in einer dreigeschoßigen Villa
hinter dem Panthéon bezugsfertig. Marie Curie und der Mediziner Claude Régaud übernehmen die Leitung.

Sie können mit der Arbeit aber noch nicht beginnen, denn
zwei Tage später besetzen deutsche Truppen Luxemburg, und
das Deutsche Reich erklärt Frankreich am 3. August den
Krieg.

Marie Curie nimmt den Zug nach Bordeaux, um ihre mit
zwanzig Kilogramm Blei ummantelten Radiumproben in
Sicherheit zu bringen. Frankreich macht mobil: Die Züge sind
überfüllt, und Fahrpläne gelten nur noch auf dem Papier. Die
Forscherin kommt so spät in Bordeaux an, daß ihr zunächst
nichts anderes übrigbleibt, als in einem Privatzimmer zu über-

nachten – mit dem Radium neben dem Bett. Erst am nächsten Morgen kann sie das ebenso kostbare wie gefährliche Material in einen Banktresor schließen und nach Paris zurückfahren.

Im Krieg leitet sie den Röntgendienst des Roten Kreuzes, richtet zwanzig fahrbare und zweihundert stationäre Röntgenstationen ein, befaßt sich mit Anatomie, lernt Autofahren und fährt von Lazarett zu Lazarett, um Ärzten und Krankenschwestern zu zeigen, wie Verwundete durchleuchtet, Knochenfrakturen mit Hilfe der Röntgenbilder beurteilt und Granatsplitter im Körper geortet werden.

Empfang beim US-Präsidenten

Als der Krieg zu Ende ist, können Marie Curie und Claude Régaud endlich das Radium-Institut eröffnen. An Mitarbeitern und finanziellen Mitteln fehlt es gleichermaßen, und auf den Staat können sie nach dem verlustreichen Krieg nicht zählen.

Andere verdienen inzwischen an der Gewinnung und Verwendung des Radiums, denn Marie und Pierre Curie waren stets dagegen, irgendwelche materiellen Vorteile aus ihrer Erfindung zu ziehen. „Von Anfang an haben wir die Methode der Radiumgewinnung mit allen Einzelheiten veröffentlicht. Wir haben kein Patent angemeldet und sicherten uns keine Vorteile bei den Produzenten. ... Die Menschheit braucht sicherlich praktisch denkende Menschen, die zwar für die Bedürfnisse der Allgemeinheit arbeiten, dabei aber vor allem an ihre eigenen Ziele denken. Sie braucht jedoch auch Schwärmer, deren Drang, gesteckte Ziele zu erreichen, derartig groß ist, daß sie ihre persönlichen Interessen völlig außer acht lassen, daß sie gar nicht in der Lage sind, an eigene materielle Vorteile zu denken. Man könnte auch sagen, daß diese Idealisten vielfach keinen Reichtum gewinnen, weil sie ihn nicht erstreben. Es scheint jedoch, daß eine fortschrittliche Gesellschaft die entsprechenden Mittel für eine erfolgreiche Tätigkeit dieser Schwärmer sicherstellen müßte, damit sie, befreit von materiellen Sorgen, sich voll und ganz dem Dienste der Wissenschaft widmen können."[36]

Von unerwarteter Seite erhält Marie Curie schließlich Hilfe: Im Mai 1920 dringt die angesehene Journalistin Marie Mattingley Meloney zu der pressescheuen Nobelpreisträgerin vor, und obwohl sich diese nur zögernd auf Beziehungen zu fremden Menschen einläßt, befreundet sie sich mit der um vierzehn Jahre jüngeren Amerikanerin, die – im Gegensatz zu ihr – Geselligkeit sucht, Luxus schätzt und ihre Ellbogen benutzt, um sich durchzusetzen.

Marie Mattingley Meloney beschließt, Marie Curie eine weitere Probe Radium zu verschaffen. In den USA, wo es inzwischen fünfzig Gramm Radium gibt, kostet das Gramm 100 000 Dollar. Um diese Summe aufzutreiben, wendet sich die Journalistin zunächst an einige der reichsten Damen der amerikanischen Gesellschaft, und als sie damit keinen Erfolg erzielt, gründet sie ein Komitee, um in mehreren Bundesstaaten zu sammeln.

Im Mai 1921 begleitet sie die Forscherin und deren Töchter auf einem Luxusdampfer von Southampton nach New York, wo Tausende am Kai warten und sie jubelnd empfangen, als sie im Blitzlichtgewitter der Reporter von Bord geht.

US-Präsident Warren Harding überreicht ihr im Weißen Haus ein Gramm Radium in einem Glasröhrchen – allerdings nur eine Attrappe, aus Sicherheitsgründen.

Noch am Abend zuvor ließ Marie Curie die notarielle Schenkungsurkunde abändern. Trotz des Wirbels bestand sie darauf, daß das Radium nicht ihr persönlich, sondern ihrem Institut übereignet wurde.

Marie Curie ist gesundheitlich angeschlagen und nicht in der Lage, all die vorgesehenen Reisen und Termine in den USA zu absolvieren. „Zu viel Gastfreundschaft" lautet eine Schlagzeile. Einige Male springen die Töchter für sie ein. Erschöpft von Ansprachen, Empfängen und Banketten, Kongressen, Universitätsveranstaltungen und Industriebesichtigungen tritt sie nach zwei Monaten die Heimreise an.

Spätfolgen der Strahlenbelastung

Irène Curie promoviert im März 1925 und heiratet im Jahr darauf Frédéric Joliot, einen Schüler Paul Langevins und Mitarbeiter ihrer Mutter. Sieben Jahre später entdeckt das Forscherehepaar die künstliche Radioaktivität. (1935 werden sie dafür mit dem Chemie-Nobelpreis ausgezeichnet.)

Marie Curie stolpert im Institut und bricht sich das rechte Handgelenk. Obwohl es sich um eine einfache Fraktur handelt, zieht sich die Heilung hin, und zugleich verschlimmern sich die Schmerzen in ihren Fingern.

An Ostern 1934 fährt sie mit ihrer Schwester nach Süden, um sich an der Riviera zu erholen. Aber wegen des schlechten Wetters und einer Erkältung Maries kehren sie und Bronislawa vorzeitig nach Paris zurück.

Ab Mai liegt Marie Curie im Bett. Weil die Ärzte Tuberkulose diagnostizieren, begleiten Eve und eine Krankenpflegerin sie in ein Schweizer Alpensanatorium. Dort sinkt die Zahl ihrer roten Blutkörperchen rapide, und es stellt sich heraus, daß sie nicht an Tuberkulose, sondern an perniziöser Anämie[37] leidet – möglicherweise eine Spätfolge der Strahlenbelastung.

Am 4. Juli 1934 stirbt Marie Curie im Alter von sechsundsechzig Jahren.

Albert Einstein meint in einem Nachruf: „Ich hatte das Glück, mit Frau Curie zwanzig Jahre lang durch eine schöne und ungetrübte Freundschaft verbunden zu sein, was mich lehrte, ihre menschliche Größe in immer steigendem Maße zu bewundern. Frau Curie war von einer Stärke und Lauterkeit des Willens, von einer Härte gegen sich selbst, von einer Objektivität und Unbestechlichkeit des Urteils, die selten in einem Menschen vereinigt sind. ... Hatte sie einen Weg für richtig erkannt, so verfolgte sie ihn ohne Kompromisse mit äußerster Zähigkeit."[38]

Coco Chanel

*Der märchenhafte Aufstieg
einer Näherin aus der Provinz
zur Pariser Modeschöpferin*

Aus Gabrielle wird Coco

Scharlachrote Hosen gehören in der malerischen Altstadt von Moulins zum gewohnten Bild: Hochaufgerichtet reiten die blasierten Offiziere des am Stadtrand stationierten Jägerregiments durch die belebten Straßen. Selbst an warmen Sommertagen öffnet keiner von ihnen die eng anliegende und bis unter das Kinn zugeknöpfte Uniformjacke mit den goldenen Epauletten.

Eine neue Uniform läßt man sich zwar nicht in der Provinz anfertigen, aber wenn eine abgerissene Tresse angenäht oder eine aufgeplatzte Naht geflickt werden muß, lohnt es sich nicht, dreihundert Kilometer weit nach Paris zu fahren; Ausbesserungsarbeiten überlassen die Herren Offiziere deshalb dem örtlichen Schneider.

Als einer von ihnen dort seine Uniform abholt, bemerkt er im hinteren Teil des Ladens zwei Näherinnen. Die neunzehnjährige Gabrielle und ihre drei Jahre ältere Tante Adrienne sind in einem Geschäft für Aussteuer und Babywaren angestellt, aber wenn es dort wenig zu tun gibt, helfen sie beim benachbarten Schneider aus.

Bald spricht es sich unter den Offizieren herum, daß zarte Hände die Reparaturen ausführen, und es dauert nicht lange, bis forsche Leutnants die armen aber hübschen Mädchen zum Tanz ausführen.

In der Gesellschaft der prahlerisch-spendablen Offiziere erblüht Gabrielle. Sie kündigt ihre Stelle und tritt in einem

Coco Chanel (1883–1971)
Foto: um 1930

Tingeltangel als „Poseuse" auf: Zusammen mit anderen Mädchen tanzt sie auf der Bühne um die „Stars" herum, trägt in den Pausen selbst Lieder vor und geht dann von Tisch zu Tisch, um von den vorwiegend männlichen Besuchern Geld einzusammeln. Sie näht sich ein Bühnenkostüm, das ihre knabenhafte Figur betont und schlitzt den langen Rock, um ihre schlanken Beine zu zeigen. „Qui qu'a vu Coco dans le Trocadéro?" – „Wer hat Coco im Trocadéro gesehen?" lautet der Titel eines Chansons über eine kleine Verkäuferin, die ihren armen Pudel Coco sucht. Gabrielle singt es immer wieder; deshalb nennen die Gäste sie „Coco".

In dem provinziellen Etablissement ist sie bald unzufrieden. Etienne Balsan, einer ihrer Bekannten, der inzwischen seinen Militärdienst bei dem Jägerregiment in Moulins beendete, verhilft ihr 1905 zu einer Anstellung als Sängerin in der fünfzig Kilometer entfernten Stadt Vichy. Aber dort wird sie ausgepfiffen.

Nach diesem Fehlschlag folgt Coco Etienne Balsans Einladung und richtet sich auf seinem Landsitz Royallieu in den Wäldern von Compiègne bei Paris neben seiner Kokotte als „Illegitime" ein. Emilienne d'Alençon ist dreiunddreißig Jahre alt und hat bessere Zeiten gesehen, aber sie gilt noch immer als „eine berühmte Gesellschaftsamazone, deren Reize in den abschätzigen, spöttischen Augen, den runden Wangen, der frechen Nase und dem kleinen kirschroten Mund" liegen; für Etienne Balsan ist sie „so etwas wie eine Touristenattraktion".[1] „Emilienne fühlte sich von Etiennes neuer Eroberung nicht bedroht, und Coco war klug genug zu wissen, daß sie Etiennes Mätresse nicht gewachsen war."[2]

Etienne Balsan führt Coco in die Gesellschaft sportlicher Junggesellen und unverheirateter Künstlerinnen ein, lehrt sie reiten und zeigt ihr, wie man mit Pferden umgeht. Sie liebt es, bis mittags im Bett zu liegen und den Rest des Tages mit ihrem Gastgeber und seinen lebenslustigen Freunden zu feiern.

„Etienne hatte aus seinem Haus alle tugendhaften Ehefrauen und gefürchteten Millionärswitwen verbannt, so daß man bei ihm vor dem ‚erbarmungslosen Lorgnettenblick', wie

146

Proust das nannte, sicher sein konnte."[3] In dieser Atmosphäre kann die kleine Näherin ihre Talente an den Mann bringen – und sie zögert nicht, ihre Chance zu nutzen.

Tochter eines Straßenhändlers

Henri Adrien Chanel wurde 1832 in Ponteils, einem Marktflecken in den Cevennen, als Sohn eines Gastwirts geboren. Im Alter von zweiundzwanzig Jahren verließ der Junggeselle seine Heimat und verdingte sich als Tagelöhner in einem fünfzig Kilometer von seinem Geburtsort entfernten Dorf. Noch im Jahr seiner Ankunft mußte er heiraten, weil er eine sechzehnjährige Bauerntochter verführt hatte. Nach der Geburt des Kindes hielt er es zu Hause nicht mehr aus und zog als fliegender Händler von Jahrmarkt zu Jahrmarkt.

1857 kam seine Frau in Nîmes zum zweiten Mal nieder, mit einem Sohn, der auf den Namen Albert getauft wurde.

Albert Chanel trat in die Fußstapfen seines Vaters: Er verdiente seinen Lebensunterhalt als Straßenhändler, und 1882 ließ er in der Nähe von Clermont-Ferrand ein neunzehnjähriges Dienstmädchen schwanger zurück. Jeanne Devolle stöberte ihn jedoch in einem Dorf im Tal der Ardèche auf und brachte dort eine Tochter zur Welt. Obwohl Albert Chanel nicht leugnete, der Vater zu sein, weigerte er sich, die Mutter des Kindes zu heiraten.

1883 kam das Paar mit dem Mädchen nach Saumur an der Loire, wo Jeanne Devolle am 19. August von einer weiteren Tochter entbunden wurde. Da Albert Chanel gerade wieder herumzog, gab Jeanne vor, er sei ihr Ehemann und habe die Heiratsurkunde bei sich. Tatsächlich wurde das Neugeborene mit dem Familiennamen des Vaters ins Taufregister eingetragen – aufgrund eines Schreibfehlers als „Gabrielle Chasnel".

Nachdem er Jeanne zum dritten Mal geschwängert hatte, gab Albert Chanel nach und heiratete sie. Weitere Schwangerschaften folgten bis 1891 im Abstand von jeweils zwei Jahren, und schließlich mußte Jeanne für drei Söhne und ebensoviele Töchter sorgen. Als ihr Mann in einem Dorf im Limousin eine

Stelle als Kellner fand, hoffte sie, er werde endlich das Wanderleben aufgeben und folgte ihm mit den beiden ältesten Töchtern, während sie die anderen vier Kinder in der Obhut eines Onkels zurückließ. Aber Jeanne war kein Glück vergönnt: Sie erkrankte bald darauf und starb 1895 im Alter von zweiunddreißig Jahren.

Bevor Albert Chanel weiterzog, setzte er die beiden elf bzw. zwölf Jahre alten Mädchen, die ihre Mutter begleitet hatten, „wie überflüssiges Gepäck" in einem Waisenhaus ab, „das nach Karbolseife und Armut roch".[4]

Arthur Capel

Als Coco Chanel Etienne Balsan 1908 zu einem Poloturnier nach Pau begleitet, lernt sie Arthur Capel kennen. Nach dem Turnier nimmt der Engländer die Fünfundzwanzigjährige im Schlafwagen mit nach Paris – und kommt von da an häufiger nach Royallieu.

Er bemerkt, wie geschickt sie Hüte aufputzt und ermutigt sie, sich als Modistin zu versuchen. Zu Etienne Balsan sagt er: „So häufig benützen Sie Ihre Wohnung in Paris doch gar nicht. Was halten Sie davon, Coco die Räume für ein Hutgeschäft zu überlassen?"

Eine Zeitlang arbeitet sie mit einer erfahrenen Hutmacherin zusammen. Und sie holt ihre jüngere Schwester Antoinette nach Paris, um sich von ihr helfen zu lassen.

„Coco konnte weder zeichnen noch Skizzen anfertigen, aber sie sah auf einen Blick, was richtig oder falsch war, wenn eine Kundin einen ihrer Hüte aufsetzte. Sie wußte auf Anhieb, was verändert, was noch umgearbeitet werden mußte. Ihr Talent steckte in ihren Händen und Augen."[5]

Durch den Erfolg ermutigt, will sie bereits im Jahr darauf ein größeres Geschäft eröffnen. Etienne Balsan, der ihre Begeisterung für eine Laune hält, verweigert ihr das erbetene Darlehen, doch Arthur Capel leiht ihr das Geld – und löst Etienne Balsan endgültig als Liebhaber ab.

Arthur Capel, den seine Freunde „Boy" nennen, besitzt

Bergwerke und läßt die Kohle mit seinen eigenen Frachtschiffen in verschiedene europäische Häfen transportieren. Er spielt begeistert Polo, liest viel, interessiert sich für Politik und Geschichte; zu seinen Bekannten gehören auch Künstler, und er führt Coco Chanel in die Welt des Theaters ein. (In ihrer Loge zupft sie ihn wiederholt am Ärmel, um ihn auf Damen im Publikum aufmerksam zu machen, die bei ihr Hüte kaufen.)

Am 28. Mai 1913 erlebt sie im Théâtre des Champs Elysées die Uraufführung des Balletts „Le sacre du printemps" mit der von Serge Diaghilew aus den besten russischen Tänzern und Tänzerinnen zusammengestellten Compagnie. Das Publikum ist auf die rhythmischen Urgewalten der Musik nicht vorbereitet, setzt Igor Strawinsky doch das gesamte Orchester als Perkussionsinstrument ein. Unerhört! Es kommt zu einem der größten Skandale in der Musikgeschichte: Die Leute springen auf, schreien durcheinander. „In einer Loge stand eine elegant gekleidete Dame plötzlich auf und schlug einem Mann, der in der angrenzenden Loge saß und zischte, ins Gesicht."[6] In dem Tumult hören die Tänzer zeitweise das Orchester nicht mehr. Der Komponist flüchtet durch einen Hinterausgang.

Als die Schauspielerin Gabrielle Dorziat einen von Coco Chanel kreierten Hut auf der Bühne trägt und ein Pariser Modejournal ein Foto veröffentlicht, spricht sich der Name der Modistin herum. Bald geben sich die Stars der Pariser Varietés und die Damen aus den Villengegenden in Coco Chanels Atelier die Klinke in die Hand.

Coco Chanel und Arthur Capel fahren im Sommer 1913 nach Deauville zu einem Poloturnier. Die Feriengäste in dem mondänen Seebad in der Normandie betrachten das Meer bloß als Kulisse, denn das Sonnenbaden ist noch unüblich, und ins Wasser gehen ohnehin nur die Fischerjungen. „Bis weit in die zwanziger Jahre hinein glaubte man, die Hitze sei lebensgefährlich und sich der Sonne ... auszusetzen, würde den sicheren Tod bedeuten."[7] „Statt zu schwimmen schlenderte man die Mole entlang, im Gehrock oder buntbedruckten Kleid, und betrachtete die Segelschiffe."[8] Doch Arthur Capel bringt seiner Geliebten das Schwimmen im Meer bei. Um den Skandal kümmern sich die beiden nicht.

Modeschöpferin

Noch im gleichen Jahr eröffnet Coco Chanel mit einem weiteren Kredit Arthur Capels in Deauville eine Boutique nicht nur für Hüte, sondern auch für Kostüme, Blusen, Handtaschen, Sportbekleidung und bequeme Schuhe. Sie stellt zwei Verkäuferinnen ein und überträgt ihrer Tante Adrienne die Leitung des Geschäfts.

Im Sommer 1914 entwirft sie den Körper locker umspielende Kleider – etwas völlig Neues in einer Zeit, in der es noch immer vorkommt, daß junge Damen mit Wespentaillen wegen der Korsettschnürung bewußtlos umsinken. „Hohe Absätze, Korsetts, Paniers, Reifröcke, Krinolinen waren ... weniger dazu bestimmt, die natürlichen Wölbungen des weiblichen Körpers zu betonen, als seine Ohnmacht zu fördern."[9] „Auf den ersten Blick wird man gewahr, daß eine Frau, einmal in eine solche Toilette verpanzert wie ein Ritter in seine Rüstung, nicht mehr frei, schwunghaft und grazil sich bewegen konnte, daß jede Bewegung, jede Geste und in weiterer Auswirkung ihr ganzes Gehabe in solchem Kostüm künstlich, unnatürlich, widernatürlich werden mußte."[10]

Doch bevor sich der ungewohnte Trend durchsetzen kann, bricht der Erste Weltkrieg aus.

Während des Krieges kommt sie an einen Restposten Jersey. Aus dem billigem Stoff würde niemand ein Kleid schneidern, aber Coco Chanel kreiert daraus eine neue Mode. Da das Material schwierig zu verarbeiten ist, verzichtet sie weitgehend auf Abnäher, achtet mehr auf klare Linien als auf Putz. So entsteht ein elegantes und zugleich bequemes Straßenkleid mit einem knöchelfreien Rock, zu dem statt eines Gürtels eine Schärpe locker über die Hüfte getragen wird. Die amerikanische Modezeitschrift „Harper's Bazaar" stellt noch im gleichen Jahr ein Chanel-Kleid im „Garçonne-Stil" vor: „Chanel's charming chemise dress". Und Jean Cocteau lobt Coco Chanels „sachlich-raffinierte Schneiderkunst"[11] als „Aufstand gegen den Firlefanz".[12]

Dreihundert Näherinnen beschäftigt sie mittlerweile. Das Geschäft geht so gut, daß sie Arthur Capel die Darlehen zurückzahlen und sich auf diese Weise von ihm unabhängig fühlen kann.

Ängstlich achtet Coco Chanel darauf, auch als Liebende ihre Eigenständigkeit nicht zu verlieren, niemand darf sich einbilden, sie „gehöre" ihm, und keinem Mann gibt sie sich vorbehaltlos hin – mußte sie doch als Kind mit ansehen, wie ihr Vater die Mutter vernachlässigte, diese darunter litt und trotzdem nicht von ihm loskam.

Der Preis, den sie dafür zahlt, ist die immer wiederkehrende Angst vor der Einsamkeit. Um sich davon abzulenken, arbeitet sie wie besessen. Impulsiv, unnachgiebig, und mit außergewöhnlicher Durchsetzungskraft führt sie ihr Geschäft; Ruhe und Ausgeglichenheit zählen nicht zu ihren Vorzügen. Jean Cocteau erwähnt ihre Wutanfälle und Launen – aber auch ihren Humor und ihre Großzügigkeit.

Bezeichnend ist der folgende Ausspruch Coco Chanels: „Man kann nicht gleichzeitig zwei Schicksale haben, das des Narren und Maßlosen und das des Weisen und Maßvollen. Man kann kein Nachtleben durchhalten und tagsüber noch etwas zuwege bringen. Man kann sich nicht Nahrungsmittel und alkoholische Getränke genehmigen, die den Körper zerstören und immer noch hoffen, daß man einen Körper hat, der mit einem Minimum an Selbstzerstörung funktioniert. Eine Kerze, die an beiden Enden brennt, mag zwar helleres Licht verbreiten, doch die Dunkelheit, die dann folgt, währt länger."[13]

Der russische Großfürst

Arthur Capel heiratet im Oktober 1918 eine Engländerin. Im Jahr darauf wird die erste Tochter geboren. Seine Frau ist erneut schwanger, als er am 22. Dezember 1919 an der Côte d'Azur mit seinem Auto ins Schleudern gerät und nur noch tot geborgen werden kann. (Selbst die „New York Times" meldet den Unfall unter der Schlagzeile „Britischer Diplomat tot. Arthur Capel, ein Freund Lloyd Georges, Opfer eines Autounfalls.")

Mitten in der Nacht wird Coco Chanel in Paris aus dem

Schlaf geklingelt. Unverzüglich läßt sie sich zum Unglücksort fahren. Der Chauffeur erzählt später: „Die Dame stieg aus, ging zurück zu dem Autowrack und betastete es wie eine Blinde mit beiden Händen. Danach setzte sie sich auf einen Kilometerstein, kehrte der Straße den Rücken zu und weinte."[14]

Im folgenden Jahr begleitet sie ihre zehn Jahre ältere Freundin Misia und deren frischgebackenen Ehemann, den Maler und Architekten José Sert, auf der Hochzeitsreise nach Italien – nicht zuletzt, um sich von dem Schmerz über den Verlust Arthur Capels abzulenken.

Als sie in Venedig in einer Bar sitzen, sieht Misia, „wie sich eine vertraute Gestalt ihren Weg durch die Menge bahnte, an jedem Tisch von einem Bekannten aufgehalten wurde und schließlich auf uns zukam. Wer hätte ihn nicht erkannt, riesig, wie er war, und mit jener kennzeichnenden Strähne weißen Haares, dem Monokel und den vorstehenden Schneidezähnen, die Cocteau veranlaßt hatten, ihn ‚Chinchilla' zu taufen ..."[15]: Serge Diaghilew, ein alter Freund Misia Serts, der an diesem Abend von Luchino Visconti begleitet wird. Der russische Ballettmeister, der „wie ein buntgefiederter Kolibri"[16] in Europa herumflattert, zählt bald auch zu Coco Chanels engstem Freundeskreis.

Auch Dimitri Pawlowitsch lernt sie in Venedig kennen. Bei dem Großfürsten handelt es sich um ein Mitglied der Zarenfamilie Romanow, einen Enkel Alexanders II. und Neffen Alexanders III. Weil er im Dezember 1916 maßgeblich an der Ermordung Rasputins[17] beteiligt gewesen war, mußte er nach Frankreich fliehen.

Dimitri Pawlowitsch und Coco Chanel werden rasch ein Paar: Der Russe zieht zu seiner zehn Jahre älteren Geliebten – sie ist jetzt siebenunddreißig – in die Villa „Bel Respiro" auf den Hügeln von Garches westlich von Paris.

Dort wohnt ab Herbst 1920 auch Igor Strawinsky mit seiner Frau Catherine und den vier Kindern. (Diaghilew überredete Coco Chanel, den in finanziellen Schwierigkeiten steckenden Komponisten bei sich aufzunehmen. Sie überweist ihm auch regelmäßig Geld und läßt Strawinsky glauben, es stamme aus einem Kunstförderungsfonds.)

Chanel No. 5

Henri Désiré Landru tötet elf Frauen, zerstückelt und verbrennt die Leichen. Gefaßt wird er, als er am 6. April 1919 in einem Porzellangeschäft einkauft, und eine Kundin den Liebhaber ihrer vermißten Schwester an dem Parfum „Mouchoir de Monsieur" erkennt.

Die Nachricht bringt Coco Chanel auf die Idee, ihr Angebot um ein exklusives Parfum zu erweitern.

Dimitri Pawlowitsch kennt den Parfumeur Ernest Beaux in La Bocca bei Cannes. Bei ihm bestellt Coco Chanel ein Parfum, das den ganzen Tag über duftet, dabei aber weder beim Einkaufsbummel am Vormittag noch beim Nachmittagstee oder abends im Theater unpassend wirkt. Tatsächlich schickt ihr Ernest Beaux zwei Sets von je fünf Probefläschchen, die er mit den Zahlen 1 bis 5 bzw. 20 bis 24 markiert hat. Coco Chanel entscheidet sich für die Nummer 5.

Der unverwechselbare Duft hält lange an, weil die Komposition nicht nur Essenzen tierischer und pflanzlicher Herkunft enthält, sondern auch synthetisch erzeugte. Das ist etwas völlig Neues.

Um die Kreation weltweit zu vermarkten, unterschreibt sie einen Vertrag mit Paul und Pierre Wertheimer. Die Besitzer der größten Parfum- und Kosmetikfirma Frankreichs gründen 1924 die Handelsgesellschaft „Parfums Chanel AG" und überlassen Coco Chanel zehn Prozent der Aktien.

Die goldfarbene Flüssigkeit wird nicht in einem der bis dahin üblichen reich verzierten Flakons angeboten, sondern in einem glatten Kristallkubus, der später im Museum of Modern Art in New York ausgestellt wird. Dazu paßt der schlichte Name „Chanel No. 5".

Der Herzog von Westminster

1921 verbrachten Coco Chanel und Dimitri Pawlowitsch die Sommerferien in einer gemieteten Villa an der Biskaya. Es war ihr letztes Zusammensein. Vielleicht wußten sie von Anfang an, daß ihre Beziehung nicht für dauernd sein konnte. Jedenfalls trennten sie sich, nachdem sie ein Jahr lang in ihrer Verliebtheit geschwelgt hatten.

Durch ihre Freundin Vera Bate lernt Coco Chanel in Monte Carlo einen vier Jahre älteren Mann kennen: Hugh Richard Arthur Grosvenor, den Herzog von Westminster, der als einer der reichsten Aristokraten Englands gilt und sich seine Wünsche unbekümmert wie ein Kind erfüllt. „Sein sagenhaftes Vermögen verlieh dem Herzog die kindliche Unschuld der Armen; er vergaß, daß er reich war, das zählte nicht mehr für ihn."[18]

Aufgrund ihrer unglücklichen Erfahrung mit Arthur Capel sträubt sich die Einundvierzigjährige gegen eine neue Liebesbeziehung. Aber gerade das reizt den Herzog: Die Chanel ist „hart, strahlend und teuer wie ein Diamant".[19] Und trotz seines grenzenlosen Reichtums kann er sie nicht kaufen! Er muß um sie werben, bis sie ihren Widerstand aufgibt.

Coco Chanels neuer Geliebter – zu dessen Freunden das Ehepaar Churchill gehört – nimmt sie in die elitären Kreise der Gesellschaft mit, und wie ein Chamäleon paßt sie sich ihrer Umgebung an. Winston Churchill schreibt über sie: „Ich war sehr von ihr angetan – eine äußerst fähige und angenehme Frau – wohl die stärkste Persönlichkeit, mit der Benny[20] je konfrontiert wurde."[21]

Als sich der Herzog von Westminister nach fünf Jahren Ehe von seiner zweiten Frau scheiden läßt, mit Coco Chanel auf der „Flying Cloud" im Mittelmeer kreuzt und Journalisten auf die Liebesaffäre aufmerksam werden, sorgt sich die erfolgreiche Modeschöpferin mehr denn je, daß ehrgeizige Reporter Einzelheiten über ihre Familie herausfinden könnten.

Schon als Jugendliche log Coco Chanel, ihr Vater sei als Weinhändler in den USA unterwegs, und zeitlebens versucht sie, ihre Herkunft durch widersprüchliche Legenden zu verschleiern: „,Weil mir mein Leben nicht gefiel, habe ich mir eines erfunden', sagte sie mir. ... In sehr jungen Jahren hatte sie bereits zu lügen begonnen, und diese Lügen waren mit ihr gealtert, bis sie zu ihrer Wahrheit geworden waren. Zu jedem Ereignis gab es mehrere Versionen, und jede ihrer Erzählungen stieß sich an der nächsten."[22]

Gesellschaftliche Anerkennung benötigt sie wie ein Vogel die Luft zum Fliegen. Aber sie ist nicht bereit, Wertschätzung durch angepaßtes Verhalten zu erkaufen, sondern verlangt, trotz ihres unkonventionellen Lebensstils respektiert zu werden.

Am 17. August 1929 besuchen Coco Chanel und Misia Sert den schwerkranken Serge Diaghilew in seinem Hotelzimmer am Lido von Venedig.

Da es so aussieht, als würde er sich erholen, segelt Coco Chanel am nächsten Tag mit dem Herzog von Westminster weiter nach Süden. In der Nacht gerät sie in Panik: „Ich habe so ein ungutes Gefühl. Wir müssen umkehren!" Als sie zu Serge Diaghilew eilt, begegnet sie Misia Sert auf der Straße und erfährt, daß der Freund gerade gestorben ist. Ihr bleibt nur noch, die Bestattung zu arrangieren.

Als Coco Chanel merkt, daß ihr Geliebter sie betrügt, erneuert sie ihr Verhältnis mit dem Dichter Pierre Reverdy, das sie wegen des Herzogs aufgab. Aber die Beziehung zerbricht nach wenigen Wochen endgültig.

Hollywood

Samuel Goldwyn bietet Coco Chanel eine Traumgage, um sie nach Hollywood zu locken, wo sie Kleider für seine Filmstars kreieren soll.

Im April 1931 reist sie erstmals nach Kalifornien. Greta Garbo läßt sich zusammen mit ihr fotografieren, und die Presse schreibt vom „Treffen zweier Königinnen". Aber die meisten Stars verweigern sich dem einheitlichen Look, der ihre Rundungen verbirgt, und auf die Kinobesucher wirken die Chanel-Kleider „zu schlicht, zu realistisch und zu elegant".[23] Im Gegenzug schimpft die Pariser Modeschöpferin über Hollywood als „Hochburg der Brüste und der Hinterbacken".[24]

Weil sie nicht bereit ist, ihren eigenen Stil zu verleugnen, wird der Vertrag mit Samuel Goldwyn im beiderseitigen Einvernehmen aufgehoben.

Operation „Modellhut"

An den im Mai 1936 in Paris ausgerufenen Streiks beteiligen sich auch die viertausend Mitarbeiter Coco Chanels. „Ein Sitzstreik auf meinen Kleidern ...", klagt sie mit ihrer Papageienstimme. „Das ist eine Idee aus den Vereinigten Staaten, ein Sitzstreik! Frauen auf ihrem Hintern, das ist obszön! Und kommen Sie mir nicht mit den Gehältern. Meine Gehälter sind völlig in Ordnung, bezahlter Urlaub noch dazu!"[25] Aber nach heftigen Auseinandersetzungen muß sie sich auf die Forderungen der Streikenden einlassen. Verständnis bringt sie dieser Entwicklung nicht entgegen.

Im Frühjahr 1939 stellt sie noch einmal eine neue Kollektion vor, aber als Frankreich am 3. September dem Deutschen Reich den Krieg erklärt,[26] entläßt sie die Näherinnen, beendet ihre Tätigkeit als Modeschöpferin und führt lediglich die Boutique weiter – wozu sie aufgrund der Vereinbarungen mit den Gebrüdern Wertheimer verpflichtet ist.

Sie argwöhnt, daß sie bei dem Vertragsabschluß über die Vermarktung ihrer Parfums übervorteilt worden sei, und ein von ihr beauftragter Anwalt versucht, die Abmachungen zu ändern – vergeblich. Eine neue Gelegenheit dafür sieht Coco Chanel, als die Deutschen große Teile Frankreichs besetzen[27] und von Juden geführte Unternehmen beschlagnahmen, doch Paul und Pierre Wertheimer haben ihre Anteile rechtzeitig einem französischen Flugzeugfabrikanten überschrieben und sich nach New York abgesetzt.

Niemand ist darüber wütender als Coco Chanels neuer Liebhaber, der dreizehn Jahre jüngere Hans Gunther Baron von Dincklage, ein Attaché der deutschen Botschaft in Paris, der vielleicht auch als Spion für die Nationalsozialisten arbeitet.

Als der Deutsche erfährt, daß seine Geliebte Winston Churchill kennt, bringt er sie auf eine Idee: „Du mußt versuchen, ihn wiederzusehen und für deutsch-englische Geheimgespräche über einen Separatfrieden zu gewinnen. Wenn du ihn wenigstens dazu überreden kannst, zuzuhören..."

Coco Chanel sieht die Chance, etwas für den Frieden zu tun;

vielleicht hält sie es auch für nützlich, bei dieser Gelegenheit weitere einflußreiche Deutsche kennenzulernen.

Baron von Dincklage weiht Rittmeister Theodor Momm ein. Der stellt die richtigen Kontakte her, und tatsächlich interessiert sich SS-Obersturmführer Walter Schellenberg, der Leiter des Auslandsnachrichtendienstes im Reichssicherheitshauptamt, für den Vorschlag.

Coco Chanel erinnert sich an ihre frühere Mitarbeiterin und Freundin Vera, die ebenfalls zu Winston Churchills Freundeskreis gehört hat: Im Oktober 1943 schreibt sie der inzwischen mit einem antifaschistischen Italiener in Rom verheirateten Engländerin: „Ich will mich wieder an die Arbeit machen, und ich möchte, daß Sie mir helfen. Tun Sie genau, was der Überbringer dieser Nachricht von Ihnen verlangt. Kommen Sie so schnell wie möglich! Vergessen Sie nicht, daß ich voller Freude und Ungeduld auf Sie warte."[28]

Vera ist mißtrauisch, zumal ein deutscher Offizier den Brief überbringt, denn ihr Mann hält sich verborgen, und die Nationalsozialisten könnten sie als Geisel mißbrauchen, um ihn aus seinem Versteck zu locken: Sie sträubt sich, Rom zu verlassen – aber sie wird kurzerhand verhaftet und zweieinhalb Wochen später von SS-Angehörigen nach Paris gebracht.[29]

Die beiden Damen reisen nach Madrid, um zunächst mit dem englischen Botschafter Kontakt aufzunehmen. Heimlich sucht Vera ihn als erste auf, verrät ihm den Plan, und er verspricht ihr zu helfen, damit sie bis zum Kriegsende in Spanien bleiben kann.

Am 16. Dezember 1943 wird bekanntgegeben, daß Winston Churchill – der seit der Konferenz von Teheran[30] in Marrakesch eine Lungenentzündung auskuriert – ernstlich erkrankt sei und bis auf weiteres keine Besucher empfangen könne.

Die Operation „Modellhut" ist gescheitert. Coco Chanel kehrt allein nach Paris zurück.

Dort marschiert Charles de Gaulle[31] am 26. August 1944 an der Spitze freifranzösischer Truppen durch den Arc de Triomphe und über die Champs Élysées. Die Bevölkerung jubelt. Aber nach der Befreiung beginnt eine Jagd auf alle, die ver-

dächtigt werden, mit den Nationalsozialisten zusammenge-
arbeitet zu haben. „Die *épuration*, die Säuberungen, eine
Mischung aus Volkszorn und privaten Abrechnungen, war in
vollem Schwange, und ein überführter Kollaborateur ... mußte
mit den schlimmsten Demütigungen rechnen. Verdächtige
wanderten auf Monate ohne Gerichtsverfahren ins Gefängnis,
Frauen, die sich mit Deutschen eingelassen hatten, wurde
öffentlich der Kopf geschoren, Besitz ohne viel Federlesens
beschlagnahmt, Karrieren endeten auf bloßes Hörensagen. ...
De Gaulle war bestürzt über den von der Kette gelassenen
Volkszorn, doch seine wacklige Koalitionsregierung ließ den
Rachezug seinen Lauf nehmen."[32]

Coco Chanel ist besorgt, denn sie könnte für einige ihrer
Aktionen während des Krieges zur Rechenschaft gezogen werden: Die antisemitischen Bestimmungen der Besatzungsmacht
wollte sie nutzen, um das Unternehmen der Gebrüder Wertheimer an sich zu reißen. Man sagt ihr nach, sie habe ihr
Modehaus geschlossen, um sich an den Arbeiterinnen für
einen Streik zu rächen; die Boutique, in der die nationalsozia-
listischen Offiziere für ihre Bräute und Geliebten einkauf-
ten, führte sie jedoch weiter. Obwohl Hakenkreuzfahnen vom
Hotel Ritz wehten, wohnte sie dort, war sogar die Geliebte
eines deutschen Diplomaten; und möglicherweise findet man
heraus, daß sie mit hochrangigen Nationalsozialisten konspi-
rierte.

Tatsächlich tauchen Mitte September zwei Männer mit
Armbinden im Ritz auf und führen sie ab. Nach ein paar Stunden wird Coco Chanel ins Hotel zurückgebracht. Was wurde
besprochen? Sie schweigt darüber.

Comeback

Nach dem Krieg lebt Coco Chanel meistens in der Schweiz, in
Genf, Zermatt, St. Moritz und Davos.

1953 ist die Siebzigjährige wieder in Paris, und im folgenden
Frühjahr führt die „ebenso aktive wie aggressive Altmeisterin
der französischen Haute Couture"[33] in ihrem vor vierzehn

Jahren geschlossenen, inzwischen von den Gebrüdern Wertheimer übernommenen Modehaus eine neue Kollektion vor. Obwohl die Presse mit beißendem Spott darüber berichtet, macht sie unbeirrt weiter.

„Chanel herrschte in ihrem Salon wie an einem königlichen Hof."[34] Coco Chanels langjährige Mitarbeiterin Lilou Marquand berichtet: „Ihre Tatkraft reichte für zehn, und ihr Lebenswille übertrumpfte den aller anderen ... Obwohl Mademoiselles Kräfte nachließen, arbeitete sie nicht weniger als früher. Ihre Zornesausbrüche übermannten sie vielleicht ein bißchen seltener, dagegen war ihre außergewöhnliche Kreativität ungebrochen ... Ich brauchte das Geschäft nur zu betreten, um zu wissen, ob Mademoiselle anwesend war. Etwas Unerklärliches lag dann in der Luft, etwas Unsichtbares war spürbar, ein Schimmern im Spiegelglas wahrzunehmen. Das Personal sprach leiser, die Kundinnen gaben sich anders. Chanel war der Schöpfer im Universum der Rue Cambon, und durch ihr Werk wähnte man sie allgegenwärtig."[35]

Noch einmal schafft sie es, ihren Stil durchzusetzen: Ausführlich berichtet „Life" 1955 über die schlichte Eleganz der wollenen Straßenkostüme. Jacqueline Kennedy und Fürstin Gracia Patricia, Marlene Dietrich und Elizabeth Taylor zeigen sich in Chanel-Kostümen; Luchino Visconti ersucht die Pariser Modeschöpferin, Romy Schneider für ihre Rolle in dem Episodenfilm „Boccaccio 70" einzukleiden – und Marilyn Monroe tritt zwar nicht in Chanel-Kostümen auf, behauptet jedoch in einem Interview, nachts lediglich „drei Tropfen Chanel No. 5" zu tragen.

Ende 1969 wird in New York das Musical „Coco" uraufgeführt, die bis dahin aufwendigste Broadway-Inszenierung.[36] (Coco Chanel glaubte zunächst, Audrey Hepburn spiele die Titelrolle – und schnaubte wütend, als sie erfuhr, daß sie sich getäuscht hatte: Tatsächlich wurde die zwanzig Jahre ältere Katherine Hepburn engagiert.)

Der internationale Erfolg hilft Coco Chanel nicht über die Einsamkeit hinweg: „Ich wollte unabhängig sein, nicht allein."[37] Aber sie war nicht in der Lage, sich einem anderen Menschen gegenüber vorbehaltlos anzuvertrauen. Wenn Arthur Capel ihr einen Heiratsantrag gemacht hätte, wäre sie vermutlich darauf eingegangen; nach seinem Tod fand sie zwar neue Liebhaber, jedoch nie mehr einen Mann für die Ehe.

Am 10. Januar 1971 – während der Vorbereitungen für die nächste Kollektion – ruht sich die siebenundachtzig Jahre alte Modeschöpferin in ihrem Schlafzimmer im Hotel Ritz aus. „Plötzlich schrie Coco: ‚Ich bekomme keine Luft! Céline, öffnen Sie das Fenster.' Céline eilte ins Schlafzimmer. Mademoiselle hielt die Spritze in der Hand, die sie immer griffbereit aufbewahrte.[38] Coco hatte nicht mehr die Kraft, das Röhrchen abzubrechen. Céline nahm die Spritze und schob Cocos Kleid hoch. ‚Sie bringen mich um', stammelte Coco. Ihr Gesicht war tränenüberströmt. Céline stach die Nadel in Cocos Oberschenkel und verlangte den Hotelarzt, doch weil es Sonntag abend war, war er nicht sofort verfügbar. Gabrielle war bis zum Schluß bei vollem Verstand. Ihre letzten Worte waren: ‚Sehen Sie, so ist das, wenn man stirbt.'"[39]

Frida Kahlo

Auseinandersetzung mit dem Schmerz: Die Tragödie einer großen mexikanischen Malerin

Der Unfall

Frida Kahlo und ihr Schulfreund Alejandro Gómez Arias stehen am 17. September 1925 an einer Haltestelle im Zentrum von Mexiko-Stadt, um nach dem Unterricht heimzufahren. Aus einem Bus stiegen sie wieder aus, weil die achtzehnjährige Gymnasiastin plötzlich ihren Schirm suchte. Ein verhängnisvoller Schritt! Nun warten sie auf den nächsten Bus.

„Der Bus nach Coyoacán war voll, aber Alejandro und Frida fanden noch Sitze im hinteren Teil des Wagens."[1] Sie sprechen über ihre Absicht, in San Francisco eine Wohnung zu suchen, und Frida bittet Alejandro um Rat: „Was meinst du? Wo soll ich mit dem Medizinstudium beginnen? Noch hier in Mexiko oder gleich in den USA?"

Auf einer Kreuzung kreischen die Räder einer elektrischen Straßenbahn; quietschend bremst der Bus; ein Knall, ein Schlag, Holz splittert, Metallstangen brechen; Frida spürt einen stechenden Schmerz im Leib; die Straßenbahn reißt den Bus herum, schiebt ihn noch ein Stück weiter. „Der Bus hatte eine eigentümliche Elastizität, bog sich mehr und mehr, ohne gleich auseinanderzubrechen. ... Als der Bus seine höchste Biegsamkeit erreicht hatte, zersplitterte er in tausend Stücke, und noch immer kam die Trambahn nicht zum Stehen, sondern begrub Leute und Trümmer unter sich."[2]

Alejandro, der unter die Straßenbahn geschleudert wurde, aber mit Prellungen, Quetschungen und Abschürfungen davonkommt, kriecht benommen zwischen den Trümmern

hervor, um Frida im Wrack des Busses zu suchen. Einige Fahrgäste sind tot. Er hört Menschen schreien, wimmern und stöh-
nen, aber von Frida keinen Laut. Sie liegt bewußtlos mit dem
Gesicht nach unten auf dem Bretterboden. Hilflos wirft er sich
neben ihr auf die Knie: Rock und Pullover sind zerrissen; ihr
entblößter Körper ist mit Goldstaub gepudert – eine aufgeplatzte Tüte mit Farbpulver liegt daneben. Blut sickert auf
den Boden. Als Alejandro versucht, Frida auf den Rücken zu
drehen, merkt er, daß in ihrer Hüfte eine abgebrochene
Metallstange steckt. Überzeugt davon, daß sie stirbt, breitet er
seinen Mantel über sie.

Später schreibt Frida Kahlo: „Ich ahnte nichts von der
Schwere meiner Verletzungen. Das erste, an das ich dachte,
war ein hübsches buntes hölzernes Spielzeug, das ich mir an
dem Tag gekauft hatte und das ich bei mir trug. Ich versuchte,
es zu suchen, und dachte gar nicht daran, daß der Unfall
größere Folgen gehabt haben könnte. Es ist nicht wahr, daß
man den Unfall merkt, es ist nicht wahr, daß man weint. In
mir waren keine Tränen."[3]

Eine Ärztin notiert: „Bruch des dritten und vierten Lenden-
wirbels, drei Beckenbrüche, ca. elf Brüche des rechten Beines,
Verrenkung der linken Schulter. Wunde im Unterleib, verur-
sacht durch eine Metallstange, die auf der linken Seite eintrat
und durch die Vagina herausstieß und dabei die linke Scham-
lippe verletzte. Akute Bauchfellentzündung. Blasenentzün-
dung."[4]

Monatelang liegt die Verletzte im Bett, zuerst in einer
Klinik, dann zu Hause, die meiste Zeit mit dem gesamten
Oberkörper starr in einem Gipskorsett – wie in einem
„orthopädischen Gefängnis"[5]. Können wir ermessen, wie sich
eine Achtzehnjährige dabei fühlt? „Alle sagen mir, ich solle
nicht so verzweifelt sein, aber sie wissen nicht, was es für
mich bedeutet, drei Monate lang im Bett zu liegen..., wo ich
doch mein Leben lang eine Herumtreiberin ... war."[6] (Zwei
Jahre nach dem Unfall klagt sie, es sei „ihr größter Wunsch
zu reisen, aber ihr bleibe nur die Melancholie der Leser von
Reiseberichten."[7])

In einem Brief an Alejandro Gómez Arias schreibt Frida

Frida Kahlo (1907–1954)
Foto: 1954

Kahlo: „Warum studierst Du so viel? Nach welchem Geheimnis suchst Du? Das Leben wird es Dich ohnehin bald lehren. Ich kenne es ja bereits ohne Lesen und Schreiben. Noch vor kurzem, es ist bloß ein paar Tage her, war ich noch ein Kind, das in einer Welt von Farben, von harten und berührbaren Dingen herumlief. Alles war geheimnisvoll, und irgendetwas war mir, wie mir schien, verborgen; wie im Spiel versuchte ich zu erraten, was es sein möchte. Aber wenn Du wüßtest, wie schrecklich es ist, plötzlich zu wissen – gleichsam als würde die Welt von einem Blitz erleuchtet. Jetzt lebe ich in einem schmerzvollen Planeten, durchsichtig wie Eis ... Ich weiß, daß nichts dahinter liegt; wenn da etwas wäre, würde ich es jetzt erkennen ..."[8]

Sie erinnert sich daran, daß ihr Vater in seiner Freizeit malt. „Mein Vater hatte jahrelang einen Malkasten mit Ölfarben in seinem Foto-Atelier ... Angeblich soll ich es von Kindesbeinen an auf diesen Farbkasten abgesehen haben, ohne recht zu wissen, warum. Als ich nun so lange das Bett hüten mußte, nahm ich die Gelegenheit wahr und bat meinen Vater, mit seinen Utensilien malen zu dürfen. Er ,lieh' mir den Malkasten wie ein Junge, dem seine Spielsachen für einen kleineren Bruder weggenommen werden."[9]

Die Mutter läßt eine Staffelei für das Bett anfertigen, damit Frida auf dem Rücken liegend malen kann. Jetzt kommt ihr der Zeichenunterricht zugute, den sie kurz vor dem Unfall von einem Werbegrafiker bekam.

Ihr erstes Porträt widmet sie Alejandro. Aber dessen Eltern wollen verhindern, daß sich aus der Schulfreundschaft eine feste Beziehung ihres Sohnes mit einer Verkrüppelten entwickelt, die noch dazu wegen ein oder zwei anderer Liebesaffären nicht den besten Ruf hat: Deshalb schicken sie ihn für ein dreiviertel Jahr zum Studium nach Europa. Obwohl er auch in dieser Zeit mit Frida Briefe wechselt, trennt er sich innerlich von ihr – und verliebt sich nach seiner Rückkehr in eine ihrer Freundinnen.

Eineinhalb Jahre nach dem Unfall versuchen es die Ärzte mit einem Spezialkorsett. „Am Freitag haben sie mir das Gipskorsett angepaßt, und seither erlebe ich ein unbeschreibliches

Martyrium; ich ersticke, ein grausamer Schmerz in den Lungen und im ganzen Rücken, das Bein kann ich nicht mal berühren und fast kann ich nicht mehr laufen, und schlafen noch weniger. ... Drei oder vier Monate lang werde ich dieses Martyrium ertragen müssen, und wenn es mir nicht hilft, möchte ich wirklich sterben ..."[10]

Frida Kahlo kann wieder ohne Krücken gehen, aber sie hinkt, und manchmal preßt sie vor Schmerzen den Mund zusammen. Sie befürchtet, daß eine Operation der Wirbelsäule unvermeidlich sein wird.

Gerade noch glaubte sie, frei über ihre Zukunft entscheiden zu können, aber jetzt weiß sie, daß sie ihren Lebensentwurf ändern muß: Ärztin kann sie nicht werden.

Eine Kindheit ohne Liebe

Wilhelm Kahlo, der Sohn eines jüdischen Goldschmieds in Baden-Baden, wanderte 1891 im Alter von neunzehn Jahren nach Mexiko aus und heiratete dort drei Jahre später. Als Maria Cardeña kurz nach der Geburt der zweiten Tochter starb, stand er mit den beiden Mädchen zunächst allein da. Es dauerte nicht lang, bis er wieder eine Frau fand; Matilde vergaß allerdings nie ihren früheren Verlobten, einen Deutschen, der sich vor ihren Augen umgebracht hatte.

Matildes Vater war Berufsfotograf, und auf der Hochzeitsreise durfte Wilhelm Kahlo eine seiner Kameras ausprobieren. Das gefiel ihm, und von da an verdiente er sein Geld ebenfalls mit Fotografieren, als „Spezialist für Landschaften, Gebäude, Interieurs, Fabriken"[11]. Davon konnte er sich 1904 in Coyoacán, im Süden der mexikanischen Hauptstadt, ein Haus bauen. Dort wuchs Frida Kahlo auf.

Am 6. Juli 1907 wurde sie geboren. Die Gefühlskälte, mit der eine indianische Amme sie stillte, wird sie später auf einem ihrer Gemälde zum Ausdruck bringen. Viel Liebe erfuhr sie nie: Ihre Mutter – die wohl „neben der Religion nur noch an Geld interessiert" war[12] – schob die zwei angeheirateten Töchter in ein streng katholisches Waisenhaus ab und hielt selbst ihre vier leiblichen Töchter auf Distanz. Frida beschreibt sie als „sehr sympathisch, aktiv, intelligent, aber auch als berechnend, grausam und fanatisch religiös."[13]

Die Einstellung der Mutter änderte sich nicht einmal während der neun Monate, in denen die sechsjährige Frida wegen einer spinalen Kinderlähmung im Bett liegen mußte. Daß ihr rechtes Bein verkrüppelt blieb, wirkt in diesem Zusammenhang wie eine Metapher für ihre psychische Verletzung.

„Ich war wohl sechs Jahre alt, als ich mir sehr lebhaft eine Freundschaft mit einem ungefähr gleichaltrigen Mädchen vorstellte. In meinem Zimmer, das auf die Allende-Straße ging, hauchte ich gegen die Fensterscheibe und zeichnete mit dem Finger eine Tür. In meiner Vorstellung lief ich nun aufgeregt und gespannt durch diese ‚Tür‘ hinaus, überquerte die große breite ‚Ebene‘, die ich vor mir liegen sah, bis ich bei der Molkerei Pinzón ankam. Dort schlüpfte ich durch das O von Pinzón und begab mich dann unverzüglich ins Innere der Erde, wo stets die Gespielin meiner Träume auf mich wartete. An ihre Gestalt und Farben kann ich mich nicht mehr erinnern; aber ich weiß, daß sie sehr lustig war und viel lachte, freilich völlig lautlos. Sehr beweglich war sie und konnte tanzen, wie wenn sie gänzlich schwerelos gewesen wäre. Ich imitierte sie in all ihren Bewegungen, und während wir gemeinsam tanzten, vertraute ich ihr alle meine geheimen Sorgen und Wünsche an. Welche das waren? Ich weiß es nicht mehr. Sie jedenfalls wußte alles über mich. Wenn ich nach meinem imaginären Ausflug zum Fenster zurückkehrte, kam ich wieder durch die ‚Tür‘ herein; dann wischte ich sie schnell mit den Fingern weg, um sie auf diese Weise verschwinden zu lassen."[14]

Der Elefant und die Taube

Im Januar 1907, kurz nach seinem zwanzigsten Geburtstag, reiste der mexikanische Maler Diego Rivera nach Europa, um sich in Spanien, Frankreich, Belgien und Italien umzusehen. Die meiste Zeit lebte er mit einer russischen Malerin zusammen, einige Zeit in einem Dreiecksverhältnis mit ihr und einer anderen Russin, die ein Kind von ihm empfing.

Allein kehrte er im Sommer 1921 nach Mexiko zurück, um „seine Malerei in den Dienst der politischen Erziehung seines Volkes zu stellen".[15]

Unterstützt von seinen Gehilfen bemalte er eine Fläche von eintausendsechshundert Quadratmetern in den Arkaden des Bildungsministeriums. Auf monumentalen Fresken stellte er folkloristisch-narrative Szenen aus dem Leben seines Volkes dar, die seine Sehnsucht nach dem von Kolumbus zerstörten Paradies zum Ausdruck brachten und marxistische Utopien veranschaulichten.

„Als außerordentlicher Künstler, militanter Politiker und exzentrischer Zeitgenosse spielte Diego Rivera eine Hauptrolle in einer herausragenden Epoche Mexikos ..."[16] Dabei sagte er über sich selbst: „Ich bin nicht bloß ‚Künstler', ich bin ein Wesen, das seine biologische Funktion erfüllt, wenn es Bilder malt, etwa so, wie ein Baum Blätter und Früchte tragen muß."[17]

Vor dem Unfall schaute Frida Kahlo Diego Rivera bei der Arbeit zu, als er in der Aula ihres Gymnasiums das Wandfresko „Die Schöpfung" malte. 1928 sucht sie den berühmten Künstler auf, zeigt ihm ihre Bilder und fragt ihn um Rat: „Bin ich begabt? Soll ich weitermachen?" Eine ermutigende Antwort erhofft sie, doch Diego Rivera „ist begeistert von der Frische und dem durch keine Ausbildung zurechtgestutzten Stil ihrer Bilder".[18]

In seiner Autobiographie erinnert er sich: „Da war nichts von den Tricks, mit denen ehrgeizige Anfänger oft fehlende Originalität übertünchen ... Für mich bestand gar keine Frage, daß dieses Mädchen bereits eine eigene und selbständige Künstlerpersönlichkeit vorstellte. Sie muß mir meine Begeisterung vom Gesicht abgelesen haben; denn bevor ich noch etwas sagen konnte, ermahnte sie mich nochmals in barsch abweisendem Ton: ‚Ich will keine Komplimente von dir hören, sondern die Kritik eines ernsthaften Menschen. Ich bin weder Sonntagsmaler noch Kunstliebhaber, ich bin bloß ein Mädchen, das sich seinen Lebensunterhalt verdienen muß.'"[19]

Diego Rivera besucht die junge Frau; sie treffen sich häufiger. Später erinnert sich Frida Kahlo: „Die Begegnung fand zu einer Zeit statt, als alle Leute mit Pistolen bewaffnet herumliefen ... So schoß auch Diego einmal auf das Grammophon bei einer von Tinas[20] Parties. Damals fing ich an, mich für ihn zu interessieren, obwohl er mir zugleich Angst machte."[21] Frida Kahlo verliebt sich in das „Feuer des flunkernden, sinnlichen, unkonventionellen, intuitiven, spöttischen und spaßenden, sehr neuweltlichen Rivera".[22]

Im August 1929 findet die Hochzeit statt: Die zierliche zweiundzwanzigjährige Braut steht während der Zeremonie im Rathaus neben einem doppelt so alten Mann mit barocker Leibesfülle und aufgedunsenem Gesicht, dem sie nur bis zur Schulter reicht. Fridas Eltern sprechen von einem „vollgefressenen Breughel" und vergleichen das Paar mit „einem Elefanten und einer Taube".[23]

„Was Fridas Schönheit an Vollkommenheit fehlte, trug nur dazu bei, ihre eigenwillige Anziehungskraft zu erhöhen. Die dunklen Augenbrauen zogen eine durchgehende, kräftige Linie über ihre Stirn, ihr Mund war sinnlich voll, und ein Anflug von Bartflaum lag als Schatten auf ihrer Oberlippe. Frida hatte dunkle, schrägstehende mandelförmige Augen. Leute, die die Künstlerin gut kannten, berichten, wie Fridas Intelligenz und Humor aus diesen Augen leuchteten und wie sie Stimmungen und Launen der Malerin verrieten. In ihrem Blick kam eine durchdringende Direktheit zum Ausdruck; ihr schien nichts zu entgehen, und Fridas Besucher fühlten sich von ihren Augen so unausweichlich scharf beobachtet wie von einem Ozelot. Fridas Lachen war tief und ansteckend; es brach aus ihr hervor, wenn sie sich freute, aber auch, wenn sie sich fatalistisch in die Absurdität ihrer Leiden schickte. Mit einer etwas rauhen Stimme sprudelte die Kahlo ihre Sätze hervor, intensiv, gefühlsbetont und lebhaft, und sie unterstrich sie mit raschen und zierlichen Gesten. Dazwischen lachte sie immer wieder aus vollem Halse, oder sie ließ einen gelegentlichen emotionalen Aufschrei hören."[24] Mit Vorliebe trägt sie mexikanische Bauernblusen und sie neigt dazu, „sich eher mit dem merkwürdigsten und schönsten, als mit dem kostbarsten Schmuck zu schmücken."[25] „Halsketten, Ringe, Kopfbedeckungen aus weißem Organdy, blumige Bauernblusen, granatapfelrote Umschlagtüchter, lange Röcke, das alles verhüllte den zerbrochenen Körper."[26]

Ein Jahr nach der Hochzeit begleitet Frida Kahlo ihren vielbeschäftigten Mann für sechs Monate nach San Francisco.

Vor der Abreise unterzog sie sich einer medizinisch notwendigen Abtreibung; 1932 erleidet sie eine Fehlgeburt, und zwei Jahre später muß eine weitere Schwangerschaft im dritten Monat abgebrochen werden. Über den Verlust der ungeborenen Kinder kommt sie nur schwer hinweg, und schließlich nimmt ihr ein Arzt jede Hoffnung, noch ein Kind auszutragen.

Als Frida Kahlo und Diego Rivera im Dezember 1933 von einem zweijährigen USA-Aufenthalt zurückkehren, beziehen sie ein Doppelhaus in San Angel, unweit von Frida Kahlos Geburtshaus am Rand von Mexiko-Stadt. Ein befreundeter Architekt gestaltete die beiden mit einer Metallbrücke verbundenen Kuben im Bauhaus-Stil: „getrennt verbunden".[27]

Dreimal innerhalb von drei Jahren wird Frida Kahlo an ihrem verkrüppelten rechten Bein operiert. Sie fühlt sich häufig erschöpft; immer wieder von Schmerzen und Depressionen gequält, beginnt sie zu trinken.

„Diego ist hemmungslos, exhibitionistisch, legendär durch die Geschichten, die man sich über ihn erzählt und die er selbst über sich erzählt."[28] Er liebt es, andere durch haarsträubende Äußerungen zu düpieren – etwa indem er das „Geheimnis" verbreitet, er sei der Vater des deutschen Generals Rommel –, oder er schockiert die Besucher, indem er ihnen von lesbischen Neigungen seiner Frau erzählt.

Über seine eigenen Seitensprünge berichtet die Regenbogenpresse. 1934 schläft er sogar mit seiner Schwägerin Cristina.

„Warum nenne ich ihn *meinen* Diego? Er war nie mein und wird es nie sein. Er gehört sich selbst."[29] Und Diego Rivera gesteht: „Je mehr ich sie liebte, um so mehr wollte ich sie verletzen."[30]

Frida Kahlo schreibt Leo Eloesser, dem Arzt, der sie in San Francisco behandelte und sich seither auch aus der Ferne um

sie kümmert: „Ich habe in den letzten Monaten so viel erlei-
den müssen, daß ich mich kaum so schnell erholen werde,
aber ich habe alles getan, um zu vergessen, was zwischen
Diego und mir vorgefallen ist, und um wieder wie früher leben
zu können. Ich glaube allerdings kaum, daß es mir ganz
gelingen wird, weil es Dinge gibt, die einfach stärker als eines
Menschen Wille sind; aber ich kann nicht endlos in dieser
äußersten Traurigkeit verharren, in der ich mich befunden
habe."[31]

Diego Rivera droht zwar, jeden Liebhaber seiner Frau zu
erschießen, aber Frida Kahlo beansprucht nun dasselbe Recht
auf sexuelle Freiheit wie er. Der aus Japan stammende amerikanische Bildhauer Isamu Noguchi ist mutig genug, sich auf
ein Verhältnis mit ihr einzulassen. Als Trotzkij und dessen
Frau im Januar 1937 durch den persönlichen Einsatz von Diego
Rivera in Mexiko Asyl finden und von 1937 bis 1939 in Coyoacán wohnen,[32] verdreht Frida Kahlo dem siebenundfünf-
zigjährigen russischen Revolutionär den Kopf, bis dessen
Anhänger für ein Ende der wochenlangen Affäre sorgen, weil
sie einen politischen Skandal befürchten.

Die Künstlerin

Im November 1938 stellt eine New Yorker Galerie erstmals
Bilder von Frida Kahlo aus. Die Hälfte davon wird verkauft,
und „Vogue" veröffentlicht drei Reproduktionen.

Der Elefant und die Taube: Im Gegensatz zu Diego Rivera
bevorzugt Frida Kahlo kleine Formate. Mit ihrer Malerei
knüpft sie an die Votivtafeln an, auf denen anonyme Künstler
im Auftrag von zumeist armen Leuten wie durch ein Wunder
überstandene gefährliche Situationen volkstümlich darstellen.

Durch Diego Rivera und Trotzkij lernt sie 1938 den surrea-
listischen Dichter André Breton kennen. Aber nicht erst seit
dieser Begegnung malt sie in einem eigenständigen surreali-
stischen Stil – auch wenn sie das Etikett „Surrealistin"
zurückweist: „Ich habe niemals Träume gemalt. Ich habe
meine Realität gemalt."[33]

In den Monaten, in denen sie wegen ihrer Verletzung liegen mußte, sah Frida Kahlo in einem Spiegel über ihrem Bett ständig sich selbst. Ist es da verwunderlich, daß die meisten ihrer Bilder Selbstporträts sind? „Ich male mich, weil ich sehr viel Zeit alleine verbringe und weil ich das Motiv bin, das ich am besten kenne."[34]

In ihren Selbstbildnissen manifestieren sich „ihre inneren Erfahrungen, Träume, Phantasien, Ängste und Hoffnungen";[35] es sind Metaphern konkreter Ereignisse, die ihre Qual zum Ausdruck bringen. Diego Rivera glaubt, daß sie über eine besondere Fähigkeit verfügt, „Wahrheit, Wirklichkeit, Grausamkeit und Leiden zu ertragen".[36] „Analytisch oder symbolisch, lyrisch oder burlesk"[37] wirken die Gemälde, auf denen sie sich „blutend, weinend, aufgebrochen"[38] darstellt. Nicht selten bildet sie ihren nackten Körper geöffnet ab; sie malt sich beispielsweise in einem Halbakt von vorn, wobei die Haut zwischen den Brüsten aufgerissen ist und in dem hohlen Innenraum eine einsturzgefährdete Marmorsäule sichtbar wird, die wie eine kaputte Wirbelsäule den Kopf stützt.[39]

Mit Hilfe der Kunst bewältigt Frida Kahlo das Dasein, denn auf diese Weise sucht und findet sie sich immer wieder aufs neue. Ihre Kraft schöpft sie aus dem Unterbewußten.

Sie selbst meint: „In bezug auf meine Malerei bin ich sehr unruhig. Vor allem, weil ich sie zu etwas Nützlichem umgestalten will, denn bisher habe ich damit lediglich einen aufrichtigen Ausdruck meiner selbst geschaffen ... Ich muß mit all meinen Kräften darum ringen, damit das wenige Positive, das meine Krankheit mir zu tun erlaubt, auch der Revolution[40] nützt. Das ist der einzig wirkliche Grund, zu leben."[41] „Ich möchte mich mit meinen Bildern meines Volkes würdig erweisen ... Ich möchte, daß mein Werk als ein Beitrag angesehen werden kann zu dem Kampf, den die Menschen um Frieden und Freiheit führen."[42]

1939 reist Frida Kahlo nach Paris zu einer von André Breton versprochenen Ausstellung. In einem Brief an einen Geliebten, den amerikanischen Porträtfotografen Nickolas Muray, beschwert sie sich: „...die Sache mit der Ausstellung ist ein saumäßiges Durcheinander. ... Bei meiner Ankunft waren die

Bilder immer noch im Zollbüro, weil dieser Mistkerl von Breton es nicht für nötig gehalten hat, sie abzuholen. ... So kam ich mir vor wie ein Narr und mußte eben warten, bis ich Marcel Duchamp traf (fabelhafter Maler!). Der ist wirklich der einzige hier, der auf dem Boden der Wirklichkeit steht – nicht wie all diese wahnwitzigen Spinner von Surrealisten. Er packte die Sache sofort richtig an, holte meine Bilder vom Zoll ab und suchte eine geeignete Galerie."[43] Unter dem Titel „Mexique" werden einige ihrer Bilder zusammen mit alten mexikanischen Gemälden, Skulpturen und Gegenständen der Volkskunst gezeigt – und der Louvre erwirbt eines ihrer Selbstporträts.

Von den Pariser Künstlern ist Frida Kahlo tief enttäuscht: „Du machst Dir keine Vorstellung, was das alles für verwahrloste Erscheinungen sind, einfach zum Kotzen! Sie gebärden sich alle so verdammt ‚intellektuell' und sind trotzdem so armselige Existenzen, daß ich sie wirklich nicht länger ertrage. ... Sie leben einfach als Schmarotzer auf Kosten einer Gruppe reicher Angeber, die das vermeintliche künstlerische Genie bewundern. Scheiße, nichts als Scheiße ist das. ... Es hat sich dennoch gelohnt, mal hierherzukommen, auch wenn es nur dazu dient, zu begreifen, warum Europa verfault und daß alle diese Taugenichtse der Grund für die Hitlers und Mussolinis sind. Ich wette mit Dir um mein Leben, daß ich, solange ich lebe, diesen Ort und seine Bewohner hassen werde."[44] Und sie wird noch deutlicher: „Diese Scheißdemokratien sind keinen Pfifferling mehr wert."[45]

„Getrennt verbunden"[46]

Nach Frida Kahlos Europareise beendet Nickolas Muray das Liebesverhältnis mit ihr: „Mir war sehr wohl bewußt, daß New York für Dich bloß vorübergehend eine Lücke ausfüllen konnte, und ich will hoffen, daß Du bei Deiner Rückkehr Deinen vertrauten Hafen unverändert vorgefunden hast. Von uns dreien wart stets Ihr das Paar, das habe ich immer gespürt. Es war an Deinen Tränen abzulesen, wenn Du seine Stimme am Telefon hörtest."[47]

Doch Frida Kahlo findet in Mexiko keinen vertrauten Hafen vor. Die Enttäuschung über die Zurückweisung durch Nickolas Muray verschärft ihren Unmut über das rücksichtslose Verhalten ihres Mannes. Am 6. November 1939 lassen sich Frida Kahlo und Diego Rivera nach zehnjähriger Ehe scheiden. Das hält sie nicht davon ab, weiterhin gemeinsam Gäste einzuladen und auszugehen. Diego Rivera erklärt einem Reporter: „... glaube ich, daß ich auf diese Weise dazu beitrage, Fridas zukünftiges Leben auf die bestmögliche Weise zu fördern. Sie ist jung und hübsch. Sie hat bereits in den anspruchsvollsten Kunstzentren der Welt Erfolge gehabt. Ihr stehen alle Möglichkeiten des Lebens offen, während ich aufs Alter zugehe und ihr nicht mehr viel zu bieten habe. Frida zählt für mich zu den fünf oder sechs bedeutendsten Malern der Gegenwart."[48]

Mit zwei Gemälden beteiligt sich Frida Kahlo im Januar 1940 an der Internationalen Surrealistenausstellung in Mexiko-Stadt. Sie, Diego Rivera und Alvarez Bravo sind die einzigen mexikanischen Künstler, deren Bilder zusammen mit Werken weltberühmter Maler wie Dalí, Max Ernst, Kandinsky, Klee, Magritte, Miró und Picasso gezeigt werden.

Zu diesem Zeitpunkt erholt sie sich gerade von einer Nierenentzündung, die sie sich in Paris zugezogen hat, und sie schafft das Leben jetzt auch wieder, ohne sich mit einer Flasche Brandy pro Tag zu betäuben.

Jemand schießt am 24. Mai 1940 mit einem Maschinengewehr auf Trotzkij, aber der Revolutionär bleibt unverletzt. Weil sich Diego Rivera vor einiger Zeit mit seinem früheren Idol überwarf, wird er verdächtigt, von dem Anschlag gewußt zu haben. Als die Polizei bereits sein Haus umstellt, schmuggelt ihn eine Bekannte im Auto durch die Absperrung; er versteckt sich einige Wochen lang und fliegt dann nach San Francisco.

Am 21. August 1940 erschlägt Ramón Mercader Trotzkij mit einem Eispickel. Diesmal wird Frida Kahlo zwei Tage lang verhört, weil es sich bei dem Mörder um einen ihrer Bekannten handelt. (Bereits während ihres Aufenthaltes in Paris bat er sie, ihm Zugang zu Trotzkij zu verschaffen, aber sie lehnte das ab.)

Vor Aufregung fühlt sich Frida Kahlo wieder so krank, daß sie keinen klaren Gedanken fassen kann.

Leo Eloesser fordert sie auf, nach San Francisco zu kommen: „Diego liebt Sie sehr, und ich weiß, daß auch Sie ihn lieben. Gewiß, es besteht kein Zweifel daran – und wem wäre das bewußter als Ihnen –, daß Diego außer Ihnen nur zwei Dinge liebt: 1. die Malerei und 2. Frauen im allgemeinen. Er war nie – und wird es auch nie sein – jemand, der in einer dauerhaften Zweierbeziehung lebt, was ja ohnehin töricht und wider die Natur ist. Denken Sie mal darüber nach, Frida, was sich auf dieser Basis machen ließe! Möglicherweise könnten Sie doch die Fakten hinnehmen, wie sie sind, und unter diesen Voraussetzungen trotzdem mit ihm zusammenleben ... Entscheiden Sie sich, liebe Frida, entweder für das eine oder das andere."[49]

Im September 1940 folgt Frida Kahlo der Einladung. Sie stellt jetzt Bedingungen. Diego Rivera erinnert sich später: „Sie wollte finanziell für sich selbst aufkommen und vom Erlös ihrer Arbeit leben; ich sollte die Hälfte des Haushaltsgeldes beisteuern, weiter nichts; Geschlechtsverkehr war ausgeschlossen. Sie erklärte diese Bedingung damit, daß es ihr unmöglich sei, die psychologische Barriere zu überwinden, die sich vor ihr aufbaue, wenn sie an alle meine anderen Frauen denken müsse. Ich war so glücklich, Frida wieder bei mir zu haben, daß ich mit allem einverstanden war."[50]

Am 8. Dezember 1940 – Diego Riveras 54. Geburtstag – findet in San Francisco die zweite Hochzeit statt.

Frida Kahlos Mutter starb 1932 bei einer Operation; ihr Vater erliegt im April 1941 einem Herzinfarkt. In das leere Elternhaus zieht sie nun mit Diego Rivera – der allerdings sein Studio in San Angel behält, nicht zuletzt, um sich dort mit wechselnden Geliebten treffen zu können. („Frauen waren wie Zugluft durch das Leben des Malers geweht."[51])

Die Lehrerin

Im Alter von sechsunddreißig Jahren übernimmt Frida Kahlo in einer staatlichen Kunstakademie im Zentrum von Mexiko-Stadt die Ausbildung der Anfänger. Aber die körperliche Belastung ist zu groß für die behinderte Frau. Damit sie den Unterricht in ihrem eigenen Haus fortsetzen kann, bezahlt die Schulleitung den Schülern die tägliche Fahrt nach Coyoacán.

Frida Kahlo zwingt ihre Schüler zu nichts, sondern sie beschränkt sich darauf, Anstöße und Anregungen zu geben, damit sie ihre eigenen Ideen entfalten, und wenn sie ihnen andere Gemälde zeigt, dann geschieht das nicht, um auf nachahmenswerte Vorbilder hinzuweisen. Sie engt ihre Rolle nicht auf die einer Kunsterzieherin ein, sondern diskutiert mit den jungen Menschen auch über ihre politischen Überzeugungen und ihre unkonventionelle Einstellung zum Leben: „Ihre Schüler erleben etwas ganz anderes als Unterricht im herkömmlichen Sinne. Zwar erfahren sie auch manches über Farbverhältnisse im Ganzen des Bildes, aber in Wirklichkeit ‚lernen' sie sehr viel mehr: Vertrauen in ihren unverwechselbar eigenen Weg als Maler und Liebe zur Alltagswirklichkeit, zu Sitten, Gebräuchen, Lebensformen, das heißt zur mexikanischen Kultur. Sie lernen verstehen, daß Malen zuallererst bedeutet, sich von der Wirklichkeit beeindrucken zu lassen. Nur wenn das möglich ist, hat es Sinn, das Malen als Handwerk richtig zu erlernen ... Die Studenten sollen spüren, daß es kein allgemeingültiges System, abgeleitet von einer Theorie, für die Malerei gibt, sondern daß ein Künstler seiner Freiheit selbst das Gesetz geben muß."[52]

Die vier Schüler, die ihr trotz des weiten Weges nach Coyoacán über längere Zeit treu bleiben, bemalen die Fassade einer Pulquería, einer dieser traditionsreichen Schenken, in der es nichts anderes als Pulque – das aus Agaven gewonnene Nationalgetränk der Mexikaner – zu trinken gibt. Aufgrund des Erfolgs werden sie beauftragt, auch die Wände im Festsaal eines Hotels neu zu bemalen. Im Februar 1945 eröffnet die Schule eine kleine Ausstellung mit Arbeiten der Frida-Kahlo-

Schüler („los Fridos"), die sich verpflichten, mit künstlerischen Mitteln gegen die Ausbeutung des Volkes und für die
sozialistische Revolution zu kämpfen.

„Sie hätte so viele Gründe gehabt, Schwäche zu zeigen ..."

Als sich die Schmerzen im Rücken und im rechten Bein verschlimmern, erhält Frida Kahlo 1944 nach einer Wirbelsäulen-
Operation ein neues Stahlkorsett.

Zwei Jahre später meißelt ein New Yorker Spezialist aus
ihrem Becken ein Stück Knochen heraus und verschraubt
damit die gebrochenen Lendenwirbel. Sechs weitere Wirbel-
säulen-Operationen und einige längere Krankenhausaufent-
halte folgen. Nach einem der chirurgischen Eingriffe infor-
miert ihre Schwester Leo Eloesser über Fridas Zustand: „Ihre
Verdauungsorgane waren gelähmt, und sie hatte ständig über
39° Fieber. Dazu kamen anhaltende Übelkeit, Erbrechen und
unaufhörliche Schmerzen im Rücken, sobald ihr das Korsett
angepaßt worden war und sie auf der operierten Stelle lag. ...
Außerdem merkte ich, daß von ihrem Rücken ein ganz übler
Geruch ausging. Ich sagte dies dem behandelnden Arzt bei der
Visite. Als sie das Korsett öffneten, hatte sich ein Abszeß oder
Tumor gebildet, die Wunde war tief entzündet, und sie muß-
ten wieder operieren."[53]

Ab 1951 – also von ihrem 44. Lebensjahr an – ist Frida Kahlo
auf einen Rollstuhl angewiesen und kommt nicht mehr ohne
Schmerzmittel aus.

Trotzdem setzt sie ihre Arbeit fort und beweist, „daß ihre
unendliche Vielfältigkeit weder durch Leiden verdorrt noch
durch Krankheit verkümmert"[54] ist. Wieder malen Schüler
Frida Kahlos eine Pulquería aus. Als am 13. April 1953 in
Mexiko-Stadt ihre erste Einzelausstellung eröffnet wird, läßt
sie sich in einem Krankenwagen hinbringen und auf einer
Bahre ins Gebäude tragen.

Einige Monate später wird ihr rechtes Bein bis zum Knie
amputiert. „... für mich war dies eine Jahrhundert-Folter, und

manchmal verlor ich fast den Verstand. Ich habe immer noch Lust, mich umzubringen. Aber Diego hält mich zurück, weil ich so eitel bin, zu glauben, daß ich ihm fehlen könnte. Er hat es mir gesagt und ich glaube es. Aber ich habe noch nie in meinem Leben so gelitten. Ich werde noch eine Weile warten ...."[55] Im April wird sie nach einem Selbstmordversuch im Krankenhaus behandelt.

Ihr politisches Engagement läßt sie auch jetzt nicht abflauen: Obwohl sie von einer Lungenentzündung noch kaum genesen ist, beteiligt sie sich am 2. Juli 1954 im Rollstuhl an einer Demonstration gegen den von der CIA unterstützten Sturz des sozialistischen Präsidenten von Guatemala.

Elf Tage später, sechs Tage nach ihrem 47. Geburtstag, stirbt Frida Kahlo.[56]

„Sie hätte so viele Gründe gehabt, Schwäche zu zeigen und zu resignieren. Aber sie schien gestärkt aus diesen Leiden zu kommen. Ihre Kräfte waren unerschöpflich. Ihre Willenskraft, ihre Intelligenz und ihre physische Kräfte schienen mit ihrem Leiden zu wachsen. Bis wenige Monate vor ihrem Tod war sie ununterbrochen tätig. Dabei von seltener Heiterkeit und positiver Einstellung – ein Beispiel von Arbeitsbesessenheit und Vitalität. ... Sie hätte wirklich Gründe zu klagen und zu weinen gehabt. Statt dessen zeigte sie eine tiefe Liebe zur Arbeit und zum Leben."[57]

Simone de Beauvoir

Mit den Männern von gleich zu gleich

„Schrecken des Alters"

„Da die Frau stärker ihren weiblichen Funktionen verhaftet bleibt, hängt ihre Geschichte viel mehr als die des Mannes von ihrem physiologischen Schicksal ab. Die Kurve ihres Schicksals hat daher auch mehr Knicke, verläuft diskontinuierlicher als die des Mannes. Jede Periode des weiblichen Lebens bleibt sich gleich monoton, doch die Übergänge von einem Stadium in ein anderes erfolgen mit gefährlicher Brutalität. Solche wie Pubertät, erste geschlechtliche Erfahrungen, Klimakterium geben sich durch viel entscheidendere Krisen zu erkennen als beim Mann. Während dieser kontinuierlich altert, wird der Frau die Weiblichkeit schlagartig genommen. Noch verhältnismäßig jung, verliert sie den erotischen Anreiz und die Fruchtbarkeit, aus denen sie in den Augen der Gesellschaft und in ihren eigenen Augen die Rechtfertigung ihrer Existenz und ihre Glücksmöglichkeiten ableitete: Ihrer ganzen Zukunft beraubt, hat sie etwa die Hälfte ihres Lebens als Erwachsene vor sich ...

Lange vor ihrer endgültigen Verstümmelung wird die Frau in ihren Vorstellungen vom Schrecken des Alters verfolgt. Der reife Mann ist mit wichtigeren Unternehmungen als denen der Liebe beschäftigt. Seine Liebesglut ist weniger lebhaft als in seiner Jugend. Und da von ihm keine passiven Eigenschaften eines Objekts verlangt werden, tut die Veränderung seiner Züge und seines Körpers seinen Anziehungsmöglichkeiten keinen Abbruch. Im Gegensatz dazu erreicht die Frau im allgemeinen mit 35 Jahren, nachdem sie endlich alle Hemmungen überwunden hat, ihre volle erotische Entfaltung. Dann

Simone de Beauvoir (1908–1986)
mit ihrem langjährigen Lebensgefährten Jean-Paul Sartre
Foto: um 1950

sind ihre Begierden am lebhaftesten, dann will sie sie am leidenschaftlichsten stillen. Viel mehr als der Mann hat sie auf die sexuellen Werte gesetzt, die sie besitzt. Um ihren Gatten zu fesseln, um sich in den meisten Berufen, die sie ausübt, einen Schutz zu sichern, muß sie notwendigerweise gefallen. Man läßt sie auf die Welt nur über den Mann als Mittler einwirken: Was wird aus ihr werden, wenn sie auf ihn nicht mehr einwirkt? ... Sie kämpft, aber Bemalung, Schälkur, Schönheitsoperationen ziehen immer nur das Sterben ihrer Jugend hinaus. Zum mindesten kann sie den Spiegel noch überlisten. Wenn aber der schicksalhafte, unwiderrufliche Prozeß sich abzeichnet, der in ihr das ganze in der Pubertät errichtete Gebäude zerstört, fühlt sie sich vom Verhängnis zu Tode getroffen."[1]

Diese Zeilen schreibt Simone de Beauvoir im Alter von vierzig Jahren.

Standesdünkel

Georges de Beauvoir macht sich nicht die Mühe zu promovieren, bevor er sich als Rechtsanwalt in Paris niederläßt. Ohnehin wäre er lieber Schauspieler geworden – aber das schickt sich nicht für den Sohn einer Familie, die ihren Stammbaum bis ins Mittelalter zurückverfolgen kann.

Als er achtundzwanzig Jahre alt ist, verheiratet ihn sein Vater mit der neunzehnjährigen Tochter des Bankiers Gustave Brasseur, der seinen Reichtum in der Wohnung, auf Jagdgesellschaften und bei Ferienaufenthalten in mondänen Badeorten bewußt zur Schau stellt: Am 31. Dezember 1906 wird Hochzeit gefeiert.

Obwohl Georges de Beauvoir infolge seiner Gleichgültigkeit wenig verdient, glaubt er, jeglichen Anschein von Sparsamkeit vermeiden zu müssen und mietet deshalb eine pompös eingerichtete Wohnung im Pariser Stadtteil Montparnasse. „Georges' Begriff von der eigenen Vornehmheit überstieg bei weitem seine Einkommensverhältnisse."[2] Das ändert sich auch nicht, als er zweieinhalb Jahre nach der Eheschließung jede Hoffnung auf eine Mitgift seiner Frau aufgeben muß, weil die Bank ihres Vaters zusammenbricht und dieser für fünfzehn Monate ins Gefängnis muß. (Er versuchte nämlich, das Unternehmen durch die Veruntreuung von Kundengeldern zu retten.)

Überzeugt davon, daß eine Frau nur das sei, was der Mann aus ihr mache, liest er Françoise ausgewählte Texte vor, während sie sich über eine Stickerei beugt. „Françoise fühlte sich immer ein wenig schuldig, wenn sie sich all diese ‚maskulinen‘ Ideen anhörte, daher versuchte sie gleichzeitig, diese Unschicklichkeit durch die Beschäftigung mit ‚femininer‘ Handarbeit auszugleichen.“[3] Sie unterwirft sich seinem Urteil, aber sein Agnostizismus steht in krassem Gegensatz zu ihrer im Klosterinternat geprägten Religiosität.

Die beiden Mädchen, die Françoise de Beauvoir am 9. Januar 1908 bzw. am 9. Juni 1910 zur Welt bringt, wachsen in dieser vom Standesdünkel vergifteten Welt des französischen Großbürgertums auf: Simone und Hélène dürfen beispielsweise erst dann mit fremden Kindern spielen, wenn eine der Mütter der anderen einen Besuch abgestattet hat – was nur in Betracht kommt, wenn sie sich als ebenbürtig akzeptieren. „Diese Gesellschaft erwartete von jedem dreijährigen Kind, daß es eine eigene Visitenkarte hatte. Auch Simone de Beauvoir besaß ihre: tiefschwarze Tintenlettern breit auf dickem weißem Büttenpapier. Noch bevor sie vier Jahre alt war, verstand sie es, nach dem Vorbild ihrer Mutter in ihr schwarzes Samthandtäschen zu greifen und die Karte so geschickt wie eine Erwachsene auf das ihr gereichte Silbertablett zu legen.“[4]

Die Erziehung hindert Simone jedoch nicht, ihren Willen durchzusetzen, indem sie aus vollem Hals brüllt bis sie rot anläuft und sich vor Erregung übergibt. Wenn sie mit anderen Kindern spielt, reißt sie stets die Rolle der Heldin an sich, und sobald Erwachsene zu Besuch kommen, fällt sie durch frühreife Äußerungen auf: Häufig steht sie im Mittelpunkt. Zwei der Geschichten, die sie im Alter von sieben Jahren verfaßt, muß Hélène abschreiben, denn die Mutter will sie Bekannten zu lesen geben. Diese loben artig die schöne Schrift – und beim nächsten Treffen zitieren sie begeistert aus dem Text.

In dem snobistischen Privatinstitut, in dem sie zur Schule geht, befreundet sich Simone mit „Zaza": Elisabeth Le Coin ist hochintelligent, keck und ungeniert, aber auch feinfühlig und verwundbar. „... wie ein schmales, elegantes Rennpferd, das immer drauf und dran war durchzugehen."⁵ Obwohl sie alles leicht und spielerisch angeht, während Simone ernst und verbissen büffelt, zählt sie zu den Besten in der Klasse, und in Musik oder Sport kann Simone es ohnehin nicht mit ihr aufnehmen. Während die anderen Schülerinnen die Überlegenheit Simones hinnehmen, verkehrt Zaza als einzige von gleich zu gleich mit ihr. Immer wieder staunt Simone, welche Frechheiten und Respektlosigkeiten sich Zaza gegenüber ihren Eltern ungestraft herausnimmt. „Dank Zaza habe ich die Freude zu lieben, das Vergnügen geistigen Austauschs und täglichen Einanderverstehens kennengelernt. Sie hat mich dazu gebracht, auf meine Rolle als braves Kind zu verzichten. Sie hat mich Unabhängigkeit und Respektlosigkeit gelehrt, aber doch nur obenhin."⁶

Absturz

Simone bewundert ihren Vater, den sie wegen seiner Belesenheit für den klügsten Menschen der Welt hält und der für sie – im Gegensatz zur Mutter – das intellektuelle Leben verkörpert: „Niemand aus ihrem Bekanntenkreis war so lustig, so interessant und so strahlend wie er. Kein anderer hatte so viele Bücher gelesen, wußte so viele Gedichte auswendig oder konnte so leidenschaftlich diskutieren wie er. Auf Gesellschaften und Familientreffen war immer er das Zentrum und die belebende Kraft des Gesprächs."⁷ Er verschafft ihrem außergewöhnlichen Denken ständig neue Anregungen und behauptet stolz: „Simone denkt wie ein Mann!"

Aber als sich ihr Körper weiblich formt, bricht seine Bewunderung zusammen, weil er mit intellektuellen Frauen nichts anfangen kann. Unverblümt sagt er der Zwölfjährigen: „Wie häßlich du bist!" Den Schock wird sie nie verwinden!

Nach dem Verlust ihrer familiären Vorrangstellung und in-

folge der nagenden Zweifel an ihrer Attraktivität vernach-
läßigt sie ihr Aussehen noch mehr und setzt statt dessen alles
daran, durch ihren Verstand aufzufallen. Sie lernt wie besessen, büffelt während des Essens Vokabeln und stellt detail-
lierte Zeitpläne auf, die sie krampfhaft einzuhalten versucht,
um keine Minute ungenutzt verstreichen zu lassen. Eine
Freundin wirft ihr später vor: „Sie sind eine Uhr in einem
Kühlschrank!"[8]

Nach dem Krieg, als das Geld vorn und hinten nicht mehr
reicht, muß Georges de Beauvoir mit seiner Familie in eine
kleine Wohnung im fünften Stock eines Mietshauses umziehen. Fließendes Wasser gibt es nur in der Küche; das Klosett
im Treppenhaus wird von mehreren Parteien benützt, und das
Zimmer, in dem Simone und Hélène schlafen, ist so winzig,
daß darin außer zwei Betten keine Möbel aufgestellt werden
können.

Kurz nach dem Umzug kündigt auch noch das Dienstmädchen, weil es heiratet.

Françoise, die jetzt selbst Strümpfe stopft, Essen kocht und
den Fußboden schrubbt, sitzt mit strähnigen Haaren bei Tisch.
Sie schämt sich, weil ihr Vater Schande über die Familie
brachte, ihre Mitgift verlorenging und ihr Mann beruflich
scheiterte.

Georges, der ebenfalls unter dem Niedergang leidet, hilft
sich darüber hinweg, indem er sonntags Pferderennen besucht
und immer häufiger die Nacht über fortbleibt – ganz im Ein-
klang mit den gesellschaftlichen Konventionen, die zwar im
Fall einer untreuen Ehefrau rücksichtslose Sanktionen verlangen, aber für das männliche Verhalten dehnbare Maßstäbe
zulassen. Simone de Beauvoir schreibt darüber später: „Als ich
zwischen fünfzehn und zwanzig Jahre alt war, habe ich ihn
mehr als einmal um acht Uhr morgens nach Hause kommen
sehen; er roch nach Alkohol und erzählte verlegen irgendwelche Bridge- oder Pokergeschichten. Mama empfing ihn, ohne
Szenen zu machen; vielleicht glaubte sie ihm, denn sie war
darin geübt, peinliche Wahrheiten zu übersehen. Mit seiner
Gleichgültigkeit aber fand sie sich nicht ab. Daß die bürgerliche Ehe eine widernatürliche Einrichtung ist, diese Überzeu-

gung konnte ich allein schon ihrem Falle entnehmen. Der Ehering an ihrem Finger hatte ihr das Recht gegeben, die Lust kennenzulernen; ihre Sinne waren anspruchsvoll geworden; mit fünfunddreißig, in den besten Jahren, durfte sie sie nicht mehr befriedigen. Noch immer lag sie an der Seite des Mannes, den sie liebte und der fast nie mehr mit ihr schlief: sie hoffte, wartete, verzehrte sich – vergebens."[9]

Ausbruch

Zaza lädt ihre Freundin ein, die Sommerferien 1928 mit ihr auf dem Landgut der Familie Le Coin zu verbringen. Dort wird Simone mit der Hochnäsigkeit der Bourgeoisie konfrontiert. Bei jeder Gelegenheit lassen Zazas Eltern und Schwestern ihren Gast spüren, daß sie die Familie de Beauvoir verachten. „Sie nannten sie ‚Zazas Sozialfall, ein völlig verarmtes Mädchen, dessen leichtsinniger Vater sein ganzes Vermögen verschleudert hatte'."[10] Sie darf nicht mit ihrer Freundin in deren Zimmer schlafen, sondern muß sich mit der Gouvernante Stépha Avdicovitch ein Zimmer teilen.

Simone de Beauvoir befreundet sich mit der vier Jahre älteren, aus der Ukraine stammenden Literaturstudentin, die vorübergehend als Erzieherin arbeitet, um Geld zu verdienen. Nach den Ferien, zurück in Paris, begleitet Simone die neue Freundin in Bars am linken Seine-Ufer. Dort lebt sie auf, weil sie sich in dem kosmopolitischen Durcheinander von Bohemiens, Künstlern, Intellektuellen und ausgewanderten Amerikanern nicht als „anders" empfindet.

Zaza versteht „nichts von dem Dämon ..., von dem sie besessen" ist.[11] Die beiden Freundinnen treffen sich seltener. Deshalb wird Simone de Beauvoir auch erst viel später erfahren, was Zaza durchmacht, bis sie 1929 im Alter von einundzwanzig Jahren an einer Gehirnhautentzündung stirbt.

Als Zaza sich in Maurice Merleau-Ponty[12] verliebt, beauftragt ihr Vater einen Privatdetektiv, dessen Familienverhältnisse zu durchleuchten. Auf diese Weise findet er heraus, daß der intelligente Philosophiestudent und dessen Schwester in einem ehebrecherischen Verhältnis gezeugt worden sind. Einen Bastard aber will Monsieur Le Coin nicht in seiner Familie dulden. Er droht deshalb Maurice Merleau-Ponty mit einem Skandal, und dieser verzichtet auf Zaza, um die bevorstehende Hochzeit seiner Schwester nicht zu gefährden. Zaza geht daran zugrunde.

Simone de Beauvoir weiß zunächst nichts von der Intrige, aber sie ahnt, daß ihre Freundin inhumanen Konventionen zum Opfer fiel. 1972 schreibt sie: „Meine Familie hat in mir von meinem sechzehnten Lebensjahr an das Verlangen geweckt, aus meiner Umwelt auszubrechen, jähzornig und rachsüchtig zu reagieren, aber speziell durch Zaza habe ich entdeckt, wie hassenswert das arrivierte Bürgertum war."[13]

Sie stellt nicht nur die Religion ihrer Mutter in Frage, sondern auch die Grundlagen ihrer Erziehung und will selbst den Maßstab für sich wählen – ohne zu ahnen, daß sie damit den Grundgedanken des Existentialismus vorwegnimmt.

Der Pakt

Bevor Simone de Beauvoir zu Zaza aufs Land fuhr, hatte sie ihr Philosophie-Grundstudium abgeschlossen. Trotz des exzessiven Nachtlebens bereitet sich die Einundzwanzigjährige auf die staatliche Ausleseprüfung (agrégation) für die Bewerber um eine Anstellung als Philosophielehrer vor. Wer dieses Examen besteht, zählt zur geistigen Elite Frankreichs.

Sie befreundet sich mit dem Kommilitonen René Maheu, der sie wegen ihres außergewöhnlichen Fleißes „Castor" (Biber) nennt. Wenn sie mit ihm und seinen Freunden Paul Nizan, Raymond Aron und Jean-Paul Sartre lernt, streicht Paul Nizans Frau Butterbrote und beobachtet nicht ohne Neid, daß Simone de Beauvoir gar nicht daran denkt, ihr dabei zu helfen, sondern statt dessen mit den Männern über philosophische Themen redet.

Dreizehn von sechsundsechzig Bewerbern bestehen 1929 die Philosophieprüfung.

René Maheu scheitert und verläßt Paris, ohne sich zu verabschieden. („Sag dem Biber, ich wünsche ihm viel Glück", schreibt er später Jean-Paul Sartre.[14]) Die besten Ergebnisse erzielen der vierundzwanzigjährige Jean-Paul Sartre und die drei Jahre jüngere Simone de Beauvoir – wobei die Professoren erst nach längerem Abwägen den ersten Platz an ihn und den zweiten an sie vergeben.

Nach dem Erfolg treffen sich die beiden nahezu jeden Tag. Aber den Sommer verbringt Simone de Beauvoir wie üblich mit ihrer Familie auf dem Land.

In der Provinz, wo jeder jeden kennt, achten ihre Eltern besonders streng auf die Einhaltung der Etikette. Um so bestürzter sind sie, als Jean-Paul Sartre auftaucht, in einem nahegelegenen Hotel übernachtet und tagsüber mit ihrer Tochter spazierengeht.

Simone glaubt, daß sie sich die Abscheu ihres Vaters vor dem Kommunismus zunutze machen kann und behauptet, sie arbeite mit Jean-Paul Sartre an einem kritischen Buch über den Marxismus – aber das Ablenkungsmanöver funktioniert nicht: Die Eltern stöbern das Paar auf, und Georges de Beauvoir erklärt dem Freund seiner Tochter, er schade dem Ruf der Familie, wenn er nicht unverzüglich abreise; die Leute fingen schon an zu tuscheln. Sartre weigert sich ebenso höflich wie bestimmt – und bleibt noch eine Woche lang.

Um der Kontrolle der Eltern zu entkommen und ihr eigenes Leben zu führen, zieht Simone de Beauvoir nach den Ferien zur Großmutter Brasseur, die seit dem Tod ihres Mannes Zimmer vermietet. „Als ich im September 1929 wieder nach Paris kam, berauschte mich vor allem meine Freiheit. Seit meiner Kindheit hatte ich von ihr geträumt, wenn ich mit meiner Schwester ‚große Mädchen' spielte. Ich habe schon gesagt, wie leidenschaftlich ich sie auch als Studentin ersehnte. Plötzlich besaß ich sie; bei jeder meiner Bewegungen staunte ich von neuem, wie leicht ich mich fühlte. Wenn ich morgens die Augen öffnete, strampelte und jauchzte ich vor Freude. Schon mit zwölf Jahren hatte ich darunter gelitten, zu Hause keinen Winkel für mich allein zu haben. Als ich in ‚Mon Journal' die Geschichte einer englischen Collegestudentin las, betrachtete ich sehnsüchtig den Farbdruck von ihrem Zimmer: ein

Schreibtisch, ein Sofa, Regale voller Bücher; zwischen fröhlich getönten Wänden arbeitete sie, las sie und trank Tee, ganz ungestört: wie ich sie beneidete! ... Als Heizung diente mir ein roter Petroleumofen, der sehr schlecht roch: mir schien, als verteidige dieser Geruch meine Einsamkeit, und ich mochte ihn gern. Wie herrlich, meine Tür schließen zu können und geschützt vor allen Blicken meine Tage zu verbringen."[15]

Den 14. Oktober, den Tag ihres Wiedersehens in Paris, feiern Simone de Beauvoir und Jean-Paul Sartre zeitlebens als ihren „Hochzeitstag". Sie treffen sich nun jeden Morgen zum Frühstück im Jardin Luxembourg und reden dann bis spät in die Nacht über sich, ihre Beziehung, ihr Leben, ihre Pläne, um sich über ihre Standpunkte klarzuwerden.

Als sie ihm ihre philosophischen Vorstellungen erläutert und Jean-Paul Sartre ihre Gedanken in einem dreistündigen Disput zerpflückt, beginnt Simone de Beauvoir sowohl an ihrem Weltbild als auch an ihrer Denkfähigkeit zu zweifeln – fragt sich aber nicht, mit welchen Manipulationen Sartre seine intellektuelle Überlegenheit demonstriert. Von da an behauptet sie immer wieder, sich als Philosophin nicht mit Sartre messen zu können. Sie begreift zwar philosophische Texte schneller als er, erklärt das aber damit, daß er im Gegensatz zu ihr schöpferisch denke und es ihm deshalb schwerer falle, sich in die Überlegungen anderer hineinzuversetzen.

Die beiden schließen einen Pakt: Sie lehnen die Monogamie ab, wollen nicht auf andere sexuelle Beziehungen verzichten. „Er formulierte die Theorie, daß es in seinem Leben eine ‚notwendige Liebe' geben werde, und das sei Simone. Daneben aber solle es viele ‚zufällige Liebschaften' geben, und das gelte sowohl für ihn wie für die geliebte Partnerin."[16] Aber sie nehmen sich vor, für die Dauer von zwei Jahren keinen Gebrauch von ihrer Freiheit zu machen und in dieser Zeit so eng wie möglich zusammenzuleben. Außerdem versprechen sie, einander weder zu belügen, noch voreinander etwas zu verbergen.

Berücksichtigt der Pakt Simones Bedürfnisse oder verleugnet sie sich, weil sie fürchtet, Sartre zu verlieren, wenn sie nicht auf seinen Vorschlag eingeht und ihm nicht seine Unab-

hängigkeit garantiert? Die Literaturwissenschaftlerin Toril
Moi meint letzteres,[17] und Josef Rattner schreibt: „Beauvoir
willigte in dieses Konzept nolens volens ein, denn sie erahnte
Sartres ‚Bindungsangst', und er war nur zu gewinnen und zu
halten, wenn man ihm mehr oder minder totale Unabhängigkeit gewährte."[18]

Gewiß ist, daß sie in dem Augenblick, in dem sie Jean-Paul
Sartres Anspruch auf sexuelle Freiheit akzeptiert, für sich
selbst die gleichen Rechte verlangt.

Das Beispiel ihrer Eltern vor Augen, lehnt sie die Ehe ab, um
Lügen und Täuschungen zu vermeiden. Da jedoch eine Le-
benspartnerschaft häufig nichts anderes als eine eheliche
Gemeinschaft darstellt, geht Simone de Beauvoir einen Schritt
weiter, um ihre Unabhängigkeit und Gleichberechtigung zu
bewahren: Sie weigert sich, Mutter zu werden oder auch
nur hausfrauliche Pflichten zu übernehmen, vermeidet „entschlossen jede Art von Häuslichkeit, denn sie hatte bei ihren
Eltern, Verwandten und Bekannten gesehen, wie sehr sie vor
allem die Frau, ob arm oder reich, gefangennahm."[19] Sie und
Jean-Paul Sartre wohnen deshalb stets getrennt, und gewöhnlich essen sie in einem einfachen Restaurant.

Trennung

Im November tritt Jean-Paul Sartre seinen Militärdienst an.

Alleingelassen erschrickt Simone de Beauvoir über ihr hefti-
ges sexuelles Verlangen, das sie so elementar wie Hunger oder
Durst empfindet und mit ihrer Willenskraft kaum zu bändigen
vermag. Sie begreift dieses Bedürfnis auch als Einschränkung
ihrer Freiheit. „Mein Körper hatte seine Launen, und ich war
unfähig, sie zu zügeln. Ihre Heftigkeit überrannte meine Verteidigung. … Ich hatte meine puritanische Erziehung gerade
weit genug abgeschüttelt, um meinen Körper ohne Hemmung
genießen zu können, aber nicht genug, um seine Aufdringlich-
keit hinzunehmen."[20]

Nachdem Sartre seine Dienstzeit beendet hat, weist ihm das
Kultusministerium die Stelle eines Philosophielehrers an

einem Gymnasium in Le Havre zu, und Simone de Beauvoir soll an einem Lyzeum in Marseille anfangen. Weil Ehepaare gewöhnlich an ein und demselben Ort eingesetzt werden, schlägt Sartre vor, pro forma zu heiraten. Aber obwohl sich Simone de Beauvoir vor der erneuten Trennung fürchtet, ist sie „nicht einen Augenblick in Versuchung, seinen Vorschlag anzunehmen",[21] und nach gemeinsam in Spanien verbrachten Ferien reisen sie im Herbst 1931 getrennt zu ihren Einsatzorten.

Um mit ihrer Einsamkeit fertig zu werden, wandert Simone de Beauvoir an ihren freien Tagen vom Morgengrauen bis zur Abenddämmerung in der Umgebung von Marseille und schafft dabei bis zu vierzig Kilometer am Tag. Sie schreckt auch nicht davor zurück, sich als Anhalterin an den Straßenrand zu stellen.

Selbst als ihre Schwester sie besucht, unterbricht sie das obsessive Wanderprogramm nicht, und Hélène bleibt nichts anderes übrig, als ihr so gut wie möglich zu folgen. Einmal kann sie nicht mehr weiter, aber statt sich um sie zu kümmern, rät Simone ihr lediglich, auf einer Bank sitzen zu bleiben und auf den Bus zu warten, während sie allein weitergeht.

Abends setzt sie sich mitunter in ein Bistro und arbeitet an einem Roman. Sie bezweifelt, daß sie über genügend Phantasie verfügt, macht aber weiter, weil Jean-Paul Sartre – der während des Studiums zu schreiben angefangen hat – sie dazu drängt.

Aufgrund eines Versetzungsgesuchs erhält Simone de Beauvoir nach einem Jahr eine Stelle als Philosophie- und Literaturlehrerin an einem Mädchengymnasium in Rouen – von wo aus sie in einer halben Stunde mit dem Zug nach Le Havre fahren kann.

Bald finden die Schülerinnen heraus, daß die neue Lehrerin die Wochenenden mit ihrem Liebhaber in Paris oder Le Havre verbringt. Naserümpfend erzählen sich die Kollegen, daß Simone de Beauvoir in einem lausigen Hotel im Bahnhofsviertel von Rouen wohnt, und sie stoßen sich gegenseitig an, wenn sie einen abgerissenen Knopf an ihrer Jacke oder ein Loch in ihren Strümpfen bemerken. „Ich habe nie verstanden, wie

Castor ihrer Umgebung so gleichgültig gegenüberstehen konnte. Sie war in der Lage, inmitten von Schmutz und Abfällen zu leben – das störte sie überhaupt nicht."[22]

Die „Familie"

Simone de Beauvoir befreundet sich in Rouen mit der aus Rußland stammenden Schülerin Olga Kosakiewicz. Im Frühsommer 1934 hilft sie ihr beim Lernen für das Abitur, und als das Mädchen im Jahr darauf zum zweiten Mal durch die Aufnahmeprüfung für das Medizinstudium fällt, bietet sie den Eltern an, die Achtzehnjährige privat auf ein Philosophiestudium vorzubereiten. Die verzweifelten Eltern sind einverstanden, aber ihre kapriziöse, lebenshungrige und nur für den Augenblick lebende Tochter ist nicht bereit, sich in irgendeiner Weise geistig anzustrengen; sie stellt ihre „launische Unangepaßtheit als höhere Form von Moral" hin und „huldigt der Reinheit des unmittelbaren Lebens – noch nicht zersetzt von den Giften des analytischen Denkens, den Säuren der Strategie und den Austrocknungen übermäßiger Hirnbildung."[23] Nach ein paar Wochen gibt Simone de Beauvoir auf.

Durch ihre neun Jahre ältere Freundin hat Olga auch Jean-Paul Sartre kennengelernt. Der schlägt seiner Lebensgefährtin nun vor, in einem „Trio" neue Erfahrungen zu sammeln. Simone de Beauvoir glaubt, über die Eifersucht erhaben zu sein, aber: „er hatte Anwandlungen von Unruhe, Wut und Freude, wie er sie mit mir nicht kannte. Mein Unbehagen ging über Eifersucht hinaus. Es gab Augenblicke, in denen ich mich fragte, ob mein Glück nicht allein auf einer ungeheuren Lüge beruhe."[24]

Tapfer bemüht sie sich, „Sartres lässige Verachtung normaler menschlicher Gefühle in sexuellen Beziehungen zu kopieren."[25]

Wenig später beweist Jean-Paul Sartre, daß die „notwendige Liebe" ungeachtet aller „zufälligen Liebschaften" für ihn unverzichtbar bleibt: Während Simone im Herbst 1936 an ein Gymnasium in Paris-Passy versetzt wird, bietet man ihm eine

Stelle in Lyon an, aber er schlägt sie aus, um in ihrer Nähe zu bleiben (und bekommt schließlich eine Anstellung in Laon).

Seine Eltern ärgern sich, als sie erfahren, daß er seine Karriere hintanstellt: Wenn es in ihrer Macht stünde, würden sie die unschickliche Liaison lieber heute als morgen beenden. Und die Beauvoirs denken ebenso: Georges de Beauvoir bezeichnet seine Tochter als „Hure eines Wurms".[26] Jedenfalls dürfen Jean-Paul Sartre und Simone de Beauvoir keines der Elternpaare gemeinsam besuchen.

Darauf legen sie ohnehin keinen Wert. Ihre „Familie" besteht aus einer Gruppe zumeist jüngerer Leute. Olga, deren um zwei Jahre jüngere Schwester Wanda und Sartres ehemaliger Schüler Jacques-Laurent Bost – der sich in Olga verliebt – sind von Anfang an dabei.

Später erinnert sich Simone de Beauvoir: „Wir zogen sie dem Gerede unserer Altersgenossen vor, die sich endlos über ihre Wohnungseinrichtung und die Intelligenz ihrer Babys ausließen und vor Selbstzufriedenheit trieften wegen der bürokratischen Sicherheit ihrer Existenz."[27]

„Nicht zufällig ist die Schar der Liebhaber(innen) viel jünger als die beiden Stifterfiguren im Zentrum des Bildes …; nicht zufällig sind sie psychologisch und finanziell im Banne ihrer ‚Adoptiv'eltern; nicht zufällig tauschen sich Castor und Sartre über Wonne und Weh mit ihren Blagen im Detail und in elterlichem Tonfall aus."[28] In der Familie heben Simone de Beauvoir und Jean-Paul Sartre ihre Intimität auf eine neue Stufe.

Während Jean-Paul Sartre auch Wanda erobert und ihr sogar einen Heiratsantrag macht, verbringt Simone de Beauvoir viel Zeit mit deren Schwester – der ersten Frau, von der sie sich auf den Mund küssen läßt.

Sie fühlt sich durch ihre konservative Erziehung „in die Heterosexualität gestoßen", aber sie rät den Frauen, „sich nicht länger ausschließlich auf das Begehren der Männer hin konditionieren zu lassen".[29] „Ideal wäre, ebensogut eine Frau lieben zu können wie einen Mann, einfach ein menschliches Wesen. Ohne Angst, ohne Zwänge, ohne Verpflichtungen."[30] Von manchen Frauen fühlt sie sich erotisch angezogen, aber sie wehrt sich dagegen, als Lesbierin bezeichnet zu werden, weil sie darunter eine Frau versteht, die ausschließlich am weiblichen Körper Gefallen findet[31] – und das trifft in der Tat nicht auf sie zu.

Als sie den Sommer 1938 mit Jacques-Laurent Bost in der Provence verbringt, während Olga, Wanda und Sartre in Paris zurückbleiben, überredet sie ihren Begleiter, mit ihr zu schlafen – und teilt es gleich darauf Jean-Paul Sartre in einem Brief mit: „Vor drei Tagen habe ich mit dem kleinen Bost geschlafen. Natürlich war ich es, die das vorgeschlagen hat."[32]

Fünfzehn Monate später berichtet Simone de Beauvoir ihrem Lebensgefährten über eine Nacht mit der achtzehnjährigen in Polen geborenen Jüdin Bianca Bienenfeld, einer ehemaligen Schülerin: „Wir haben eine leidenschaftliche Nacht miteinander verbracht ... Es hatte einen Hauch von Verderbtheit, den ich nicht genau benennen kann, aber ich glaube, daß es einfach das Fehlen von Zärtlichkeit war. Es war das Bewußtsein, sinnliche Lust ohne Zärtlichkeit zu empfinden – etwas, was mir grundsätzlich noch nie passiert ist."[33]

Trotz seiner zahlreichen Amouren scheint Jean-Paul Sartre kein leidenschaftlicher Liebhaber zu sein: „Er ist ein hitziger, quicklebendiger Mann – überall, außer im Bett."[34] Im Zusammenleben Simone de Beauvoirs und Jean-Paul Sartres spielt der Geschlechtsverkehr bald keine Rolle mehr, aber sie bleibt sein intellektuelles Alter ego, die unentbehrliche geistige Lebensgefährtin, die ihm durch verständnisvolle Fragen und Anregungen hilft, Ideen auszubauen, Widersprüche aufzudecken und Gedanken klar zu formulieren. Simone de Beauvoir schätzt an ihm, „daß er nie aufhörte zu denken, nie etwas als gegeben und sicher hinnahm."[35] Und trotz ihrer wiederholten Zweifel ist ihr klar, daß sie ohne Jean-Paul Sartre eine andere wäre.

Krieg

Am 31. August 1939 löst Adolf Hitler den Zweiten Weltkrieg aus, indem er der deutschen Wehrmacht befiehlt, am nächsten Morgen Polen anzugreifen. Frankreich ordnet die Mobilmachung an und erklärt dem Deutschen Reich den Krieg.

Jean-Paul Sartre, der sich wie Millionen anderer Franzosen pünktlich bei den Militärbehörden meldet, wird in die meteorologische Abteilung einer Artillerieeinheit im Elsaß abkommandiert, wo „den trainierten Individualisten das kollektive Leben in Behelfsunterkünften, die Rituale der Hierarchie ... kurz: das Soziale im militärischen Alarmzustand"[36] erwarten.

Vergeblich fragt Simone de Beauvoir im Oktober auf einem Polizeirevier nach einem Passierschein; sie muß schon eine mit dem Krebstod ringende Schwester im Elsaß erfinden, um in einer anderen Dienststelle eine Reiseerlaubnis zu bekommen. Da inzwischen das neue Schuljahr begonnen hat, benötigt sie außerdem eine Krankmeldung: Sie legt sich nachmittags ins Bett und läßt einen Arzt rufen. „Ich warte bis halb neun Uhr und lese. Ich habe fast den Eindruck, wirklich krank zu sein. Er kommt: ergrauendes, nach hinten gekämmtes Haar, Hornbrille, Berufsmiene. Er tastet mich ab, und – o Jammer! – er glaubt an einen simplen Muskelkater. ... Er holt trotzdem ein paar kleine Instrumente, um sicherzugehen, daß ich keine Blinddarmentzündung habe. Er sticht mich in den Finger, saugt mit einer Pipette Blut heraus und läßt es in eine grüne Flüssigkeit laufen. Er findet, daß ich 11 000 weiße Blutkörperchen habe; das sind zu viele, aber nicht genug für eine akute Appendizitis. Er horcht mich ab und erzählt mir gelehrte Dinge über die Folgen kalter Füße, dabei zieht er die Hosen hoch, um mir seine langen Unterhosen zu zeigen. Er spricht auch vom Kreislaufbogen der Neger und der Eskimos. ,Wenn der Neger aus seiner Hütte tritt und den Fuß aufs feuchte Gras setzt, spürt er sofort einen Eingeweide-Reflex', erklärt er mir. Endlich schreibt er mir ein Attest, das mir Krankenurlaub bis kommenden Montag verordnet. Munter stehe ich auf und packe meinen Koffer."[37]

Am 3. Juni 1940 explodieren die ersten Bomben in Paris. Simone de Beauvoir flieht aus der Stadt, aber als am 21. Juni Waffenstillstandsverhandlungen beginnen, kehrt sie sofort zurück, um Jean-Paul Sartre nicht zu verpassen. Sie wartet vergeblich: Ende Juli erfährt sie, daß ihn die Deutschen als Kriegsgefangenen festhalten.

Ein dreiviertel Jahr später trifft er unerwartet in Paris ein.

Simone de Beauvoir findet einen Zettel von ihm im Briefkasten, als sie vom Abendessen in ihr Hotel zurückkehrt. Sie rennt los, aber in dem Café, in dem er auf sie warten wollte, findet sie ihn nicht. Vom Kellner erfährt sie, daß er zwei Stunden gewartet habe und dann zu einem Spaziergang aufgebrochen sei.

In der schäbigen Pariser Absteige, in der die „Familie" nun unterkommt, zieht noch eine ehemalige – ebenfalls von Russen abstammende – Schülerin Simone de Beauvoirs ein: Nathalie („Natascha") Sorokine. Die Zwanzigjährige bringt zwar ihren Freund mit, verführt aber auch Simone de Beauvoir.

Zwei Jahre später, im März 1943, taucht plötzlich Nataschas Mutter auf. Sie ist verzweifelt. Wie kann sie erreichen, daß ihre Tochter ins Elternhaus zurückkehrt? Sie verlangt von Simone de Beauvoir dafür zu sorgen, aber diese beharrt darauf, daß Natascha sich selbst entscheiden müsse. Daraufhin wendet sich deren Mutter an die Leitung der Schule, an der Simone de Beauvoir unterrichtet, weist auf Indizien für lesbische Neigungen der Lehrerin hin und erreicht damit, daß Simone de Beauvoir ihre Berufstätigkeit beenden muß.

Dolores

Im Januar 1945 fliegt Jean-Paul Sartre als Zeitungskorrespondent mit anderen französischen Journalisten nach New York: Das US-Außenministerium hat sie eingeladen, sich zwei Monate lang in den Vereinigten Staaten von Amerika umzusehen.

Während die Kollegen in verschiedene Bundesstaaten reisen und dann wie vorgesehen nach Europa zurückkehren, um ihre Berichte zu schreiben, bleibt Sartre vier Monate lang in New York, wo er Dolores Vanetti Ehrenreich begegnet ist, einer zierlichen, temperamentvollen Französin, die sich zu Beginn des Krieges nach Amerika abgesetzt und einen reichen Arzt geheiratet hatte.

Im Dezember fliegt Sartre noch einmal für ein Vierteljahr nach New York, und Simone de Beauvoir teilt er mit, er beabsichtige, von nun an in jedem Jahr einige Monate mit Dolores zu verbringen. (Nach fünf Jahren wird auch diese leidenschaftliche Liebesaffäre zu Ende sein.)

Existentialismus

In Simone de Beauvoirs 1945 veröffentlichtem Roman „Das Blut der anderen" bemüht ein Mann sich verzweifelt, nicht die Schicksale von Mitmenschen zu tangieren, aber er begreift am Ende, daß dies unmöglich ist und er bereit sein muß, auch das Leben Unbeteiligter zu gefährden, um für die Résistance Anschläge durchführen zu können. „In Kriegs- und Revolutionszeiten besteht der wahre Mut darin, sich nicht zu stellen und die anderen sterben zu sehen ..."[38]

Hier handelt es sich um ein grundlegendes Dilemma, zumal Simone de Beauvoir Freiheit, Selbstbestimmung und Gleichberechtigung als Fundamente aller Werte betrachtet und davon ausgeht, daß der einzelne sich erst durch seine Handlungen definiert. „Die Existenz geht der Essenz voraus." So formuliert Sartre die Grundthese des Existentialismus und meint damit, daß es anfangs nur die bloße Tatsache des Daseins gebe, eine Phase, in der das menschliche Individuum weder gut noch böse, sondern neutral wie die unbelebte Realität sei. Der einzelne sei „in eine endliche, an ihren beiden Enden vom Nichts begrenzte Existenz geworfen".[39] „Zunächst ist der Mensch einmal da, allein, ohne Entwurf, wesenlos. Aus seinem nackten Dasein muß er selbst erst sein Sosein machen, aus seiner bloßen Existenz eine Essenz."[40]

Da das Leben keinen Sinn habe, sei jeder auf sich selbst angewiesen, ohne sich an vorgegebenen Werten orientieren zu können; es komme darauf an, sich zu entscheiden, ohne sich hinter Traditionen und Religionen, Doktrinen und Ideologien zu verstecken – auch wenn die Verdammung zur Freiheit Angst hervorrufe.

„Wenn die Moral des Eigennutzes, wenn die naturalistische Tristesse sich so großer Gunst erfreut, dann deshalb, weil die darin zum Ausdruck kommende Verzweiflung den Charakter von Wohligkeit und Behaglichkeit besitzt; sie setzt einen Determinismus voraus, der dem Menschen die Last der Freiheit abnimmt. ... Wenn der Mensch sein Wesen nicht verändern kann, wenn er über sein Schicksal keine Macht besitzt, bleibt ihm nur, sich mit Nachsicht so zu akzeptieren, wie er ist: das erspart ihm die Anstrengung des Kampfes. Der Existentialismus, der dem Menschen sein Schicksal wieder in die eigenen Hände legt, stört seine Ruhe ... Wenn der Existentialismus beunruhigt, liegt das also nicht daran, daß er am Menschen verzweifelt, sondern daß er von ihm eine permanente Anstrengung verlangt."[41]

Die von Jean-Paul Sartre, Simone de Beauvoir und Albert Camus vertretene Philosophie trifft den Nerv der Nachkriegszeit und wird von vielen Menschen aufgegriffen. „Innerhalb weniger Monate hatte der Existentialismus Paris überflutet."[42] Allerdings engen die meisten den Existentialismus auf das Postulat der individuellen Freiheit ein und verwechseln die Theorie mit einer Lebensart, deren Anhänger sich durch unkonventionelles Verhalten und eine betont nachlässige Kleidung zu erkennen geben.

Nachdem sie sich anfangs dagegen wehrten, finden sich Jean-Paul Sartre und Simone de Beauvoir schließlich damit ab, daß sie als die Idole der Bewegung angesehen werden und Scharen von Neugierigen an den Straßencafés in Saint-Germain-des-Près vorbeistreichen, um sie zu begaffen.

Simone de Beauvoir verkörpert den Existentialismus. „Mein wichtigstes Werk ist mein Leben", sagt sie.[43] Und genau hier, im Zusammenklang von Werk und Leben, liegt der Schlüssel ihres Erfolgs.

Nelson Algren

Im Januar 1947 trifft Simone de Beauvoir in New York ein, um von dort aus eine Vortragsreise durch die Vereinigten Staaten von Amerika anzutreten.

Man empfiehlt ihr, sich mit Nelson Algren in Verbindung zu setzen. Der amerikanische Schriftsteller, der ein Jahr jünger als Simone ist, wuchs im Einwanderer- und Arbeiterviertel Chicagos auf und verwendet diese Erfahrungen als Hintergrund naturalistischer Romane und Kurzgeschichten, mit denen er die Pervertierung des amerikanischen Traums anprangert und sich für die Ausgestoßenen einsetzt.

Eineinhalb Tage lang hält sich Simone de Beauvoir wegen eines Referats in Chicago auf. Die Gastgeber fahren mit ihr am Abend durch die hell erleuchtete Innenstadt und laden sie in ein teures Restaurant ein. Nelson Algren führt sie durch die Elendsviertel im Westen der Stadt und zieht mit ihr durch zwielichtige Bars. Im Alter von neununddreißig Jahren erlebt sie ihren ersten Orgasmus[44] und schwärmt von der wahren Liebe, in der Seele und Körper eins sind.

Als sie zwei Monate später ihre Rundreise beendet, fliegt sie nochmals nach Chicago, um Nelson Algren nach New York zu holen und bis zu ihrer Rückkehr nach Europa mit ihm zusammenzusein. Den Ring, den er ihr am 10. Mai schenkt, trägt sie bis zu ihrem Tod; sie bezeichnet Nelson Algren lange Zeit als ihren „Mann" und betrachtet den 10. Mai – wie den 14. Oktober – als „Hochzeitstag".

In einem ihrer zahlreichen Briefe versucht sie, Nelson Algren zu erklären, daß sie trotz ihrer stürmischen Liebe zu ihm nicht an seiner Seite leben könne, weil sie sich mit Jean-Paul Sartre verbunden fühle. Aber der Amerikaner versteht das nicht.

Im September besucht sie ihn zwei Wochen lang, und ein dreiviertel Jahr später fliegt sie erneut nach Chicago, um mit ihm durch die USA und Mexiko zu reisen. Als jedoch Jean-Paul Sartre klagt, er könne seine Arbeit ohne sie nicht termingerecht bewältigen, kehrt sie vorzeitig zurück und stößt damit ihren Liebhaber vor den Kopf.

Im Dezember 1948 schreibt Nelson Algren, er wolle nach Paris kommen, aber Simone de Beauvoir bittet ihn, noch einige Monate zu warten, damit sie zuvor die Arbeit an dem umfangreichen Essay „Das andere Geschlecht" abschließen könne.

„Das andere Geschlecht"

Vor drei Jahren dachte sie darüber nach, ihre Memoiren zu schreiben, aber Jean-Paul Sartre lenkte ihre Aufmerksamkeit auf die Frage, was es bedeutet, eine Frau zu sein, und 1949 erscheinen die beiden Bände ihres Buches „Das andere Geschlecht".

Sie untersucht das Bild der Frau in der Biologie, in der Psychoanalyse und im historischen Materialismus, beschreibt die tatsächlichen Lebensbedingungen der Frau im Verlauf der Geschichte, setzt sich mit Mythen über das Wesen der Frau auseinander und beschäftigt sich mit aktuellen Frauenrollen, mit den Besonderheiten verschiedener Lebensphasen und der weiblichen Sexualität. „Ich habe die Möglichkeiten untersucht, die diese Welt den Frauen bietet, und die Möglichkeiten, die sie ihnen vorenthält, ihre Begrenzungen, ihr Glück und Unglück, ihre Ausflüchte, ihre Leistungen."[45]

Die zentrale Aussage lautet: „Man kommt nicht als Frau zur Welt, man wird es."[46] Damit behauptet die Autorin, daß Kultur und Sozialisation mehr als die Natur das Wesen der Frau bestimmen. Das kulturelle Leitbild werde jedoch vom Mann geprägt, der sich stets als Subjekt verhalte und die Frau als Objekt, als „das andere Geschlecht" betrachte. Es sei kein Zufall, daß das französische Wort „homme" sowohl den Mann im besonderen als auch den Menschen schlechthin bezeichnet.

Simone de Beauvoir distanziert sich von der Ehe, attackiert die repressiven Gesetze gegen Abtreibung und Empfängnisverhütung, verwirft die Mystifizierung der Mutterschaft, die nur dazu diene, die Frau über ihre Abhängigkeit zu täuschen, denn man könne der Frau zwar nicht sagen, es sei ihre heilige Pflicht, Töpfe zu spülen, aber man könne ihr sehr wohl einreden, daß es ihre vordringliche Aufgabe sei, Kinder aufzuziehen – und der Rest ergebe sich von selbst.

Simone de Beauvoir träumt von einer Welt, in der Männer und Frauen gleichberechtigt miteinander leben, „wo der weibliche und der männliche Mensch nicht mehr definiert wird durch sein biologisches Geschlecht, sondern in erster Linie Mensch ist und versuchen kann, sich ... zu realisieren, ohne daß man ihm sagt: ‚Du bist ein Mann, du darfst das nicht tun. Und du bist eine Frau, du darfst nur das machen.'"[47] Als Hauptaufgabe der Frauenbewegung betrachtet sie es, diese Vision zu verwirklichen – und den Feminismus damit überflüssig zu machen.

Das Buch löst eine ebenso heftige wie kontroverse Diskussion aus, wobei die Anerkennung in einem Sturm der Entrüstung und in einer Flut wütender Briefe unterzugehen droht. François Mauriac, zum Beispiel, schreibt einem Mitarbeiter Simone de Beauvoirs: „Nun weiß ich alles über die Vagina Ihrer Chefin."[48]

Das unglückliche Ende einer Liebe

Simone de Beauvoir graut es vor dem Altern, und die Furcht vor dem Sterben peinigt sie. Vielleicht verdrängt sie auf diese Weise auch die Angst vor Trennung und Einsamkeit, Leere und Liebesverlust.

Als der siebenundzwanzig Jahre alte Claude Lanzmann die Vierundvierzigjährige anruft und ins Kino einlädt, bricht sie in Tränen aus, denn sie hielt sich bereits für zu alt, um noch von einem Mann begehrt zu werden. Seine Spontaneität erfüllt sie mit neuem Schwung; er zieht schließlich in ihrem Appartement ein – und ist damit der einzige Mann, mit dem sie sich jemals eine Wohnung teilt.

Überglücklich berichtet sie Nelson Algren von der Entwicklung, und als sie erfährt, daß er seine geschiedene Frau erneut heiraten will, hofft sie auf einen Neubeginn ihrer Freundschaft in Form einer rein geistigen Beziehung.

Als sie sich drei Jahre später in einer großzügigen Atelierswohnung gegenüber dem Friedhof von Montparnasse einrichtet, kommt Claude Lanzmann nicht mit. Doch er und Simone de Beauvoir bleiben für immer befreundet.

Auch in der neuen Wohnung besucht Jean-Paul Sartre sie jeden Nachmittag, um Gedanken mit ihr auszutauschen und zu arbeiten. Und wenn er danach nicht mit einer anderen Frau verabredet ist, verbringt er den Abend bei seiner Lebensgefährtin, um mit ihr Schallplatten zu hören und eine Flasche Scotch zu trinken.

Jahr für Jahr werden die beiden weltberühmten Schriftsteller zu ausgedehnten Reisen aufgefordert, weil sich Organisationen oder Regierungen davon positive Schlagzeilen versprechen. Auch privat reisen sie häufig in andere Länder, um die politisch-sozialen Verhältnisse besser zu verstehen. Über ihre Beobachtungen unterrichten sie die Öffentlichkeit und tragen so zu Veränderungen bei. Das Reisen ist „für sie ein Akt der Fraternisierung mit der Welt".[49] Sie verlangen „für die Menschen Gesundheit, Bildung, Wohlbefinden, Muße, auf daß ihre Freiheiten nicht im Kampf gegen Krankheit, Unwissenheit, Not aufgezehrt werden."[50]

Im Februar 1960 fliegen Jean-Paul Sartre und Simone de Beauvoir nach Kuba, wo Fidel Castro sie persönlich mit einem Motorboot zu seinem Heimatort Ciénaga de Zapata bringt.

Als sie einige Wochen später nach Paris zurückkehren, wartet Nelson Algren – der bereits wieder geschieden ist – in Simone de Beauvoirs Wohnung. Ein halbes Jahr will er in Europa bleiben. Aber nachdem Simone im Hochsommer einige Wochen mit ihm in der Türkei und in Griechenland verbrachte, läßt sie ihn in ihrer Wohnung zurück, um Jean-Paul Sartre nach Brasilien zu begleiten.

Auf die Briefe, die sie während der Reise an Nelson Algren schreibt, erhält sie keine Antwort, und in Paris findet sie ihn nicht mehr vor.

Zwar nehmen sie ihren Briefwechsel[51] später wieder auf, aber Nelson Algren verzeiht Simone de Beauvoir nie, daß sie ihre gemeinsame Liebesgeschichte in „Die Mandarins von Paris"[52] preisgibt, und als sie in ihrer Autobiographie „Der Lauf der Dinge"[53] erneut darüber schreibt, bricht er endgültig mit ihr.

Arlette und Sylvie

Im Sommer 1956 rief die achtzehn Jahre alte, ebenso hübsche wie intelligente Studentin Arlette Elkaim Jean-Paul Sartre an, um ihn über seine Bücher zu befragen.

Bald gehörte sie zur „Familie".

Vier Jahre nachdem Arlette in Jean-Paul Sartres Leben getreten war, wurde Simone de Beauvoir ebenfalls von einer achtzehnjähren Studentin – Sylvie le Bon – um ein Gespräch über ihr Werk gebeten, und auch in diesem Fall entwickelte sich allmählich eine enge Beziehung.

Als Sylvies Mutter heimlich in deren Tagebuch blätterte und dadurch von der Liaison erfuhr, sah sich Simone de Beauvoir mit einer ähnlichen Situation konfrontiert wie neunzehn Jahre zuvor mit Natascha. Sylvie mußte zu ihren wohlhabenden, konservativen Eltern nach Rennes zurückkkehren – aber als sie im Jahr darauf volljährig wurde, zog sie erneut nach Paris.

Obwohl sich Sylvie und Jean-Paul Sartre mögen und Arlette und Simone de Beauvoir zunächst ebenfalls gut miteinander auskommen, ist ein „Quartett" unmöglich, weil sich die beiden jungen Frauen nicht vertragen: Außer ihrer hohen Intelligenz und ihrer Begeisterung für Philosophie und Literatur gibt es wenig Gemeinsames zwischen der stillen und nachdenklichen, finanziell völlig von Sartre abhängigen Arlette und der redefreudigen, als Philosophielehrerin selbst für ihren Lebensunterhalt sorgenden Sylvie.

Sartre hält sich immer häufiger in Arlettes Wohnung auf, aber Simone de Beauvoir, die längst an seine amourösen Abenteuer gewöhnt ist, fühlt sich nicht alarmiert. Um so heftiger trifft sie der Schlag, als sie 1965 von Jacques-Laurent Bost erfährt, daß Sartre die Adoption Arlettes beantragt hat. Zur Rede gestellt, begründet er den Schritt damit, daß er zum einen die aus Algerien stammende Jüdin zur französischen Staatsbürgerin machen wolle und zum anderen eine junge und sowohl geistig als auch charakterlich geeignete Person gesucht habe, die einmal seinen literarischen Nachlaß ordnen könne.

Das bringt Simone de Beauvoir auf die Idee, Sylvie auf die Bearbeitung ihres Nachlasses vorzubereiten. (Mit der Adoption wartet sie, bis Jean-Paul Sartre gestorben ist.)

Frauenbewegung

1970 formiert sich die Frauenbewegung in Frankreich. Simone de Beauvoir – sie ist jetzt zweiundsechzig – arbeitet in Frauenorganisationen mit, beteiligt sich an Demonstrationszügen für das Recht auf Schwangerschaftsabbruch, bezichtigt sich gemeinsam mit 342 weiteren Frauen, illegal abgetrieben zu haben und gründet die „Liga für Frauenrechte".

Das Engagement für den Feminismus betrachtet Simone de Beauvoir als konsequente Fortentwicklung ihres Einsatzes für die Freiheit des menschlichen Individuums. Sie tritt für die Gleichberechtigung der Geschlechter ein und mißt dem Anderssein der Frau keinen Wert bei, weigert sich auch, neue Normen für spezifische weibliche Verhaltensweisen aufzustellen, weil sie als Existentialistin von jeder einzelnen Frau verlangt, daß diese sich durch ihr Handeln selbst definiert.

„Der Männerhaß geht bei manchen Frauen so weit, daß sie alle von den Männern anerkannten Werte verwerfen und alles ablehnen, was sie, die Frauen, als ‚männliche Modelle' bezeichnen. Ich kann dem nicht zustimmen, da ich nicht glaube, daß es spezifisch feminine Eigenschaften, Werte oder Lebensweisen gibt. Daran zu glauben, hieße, die Existenz einer weiblichen Natur anzuerkennen, mit anderen Worten: einem Mythos anzuhängen, der von den Männern eigens erfunden wurde, um die Unterdrückung der Frau aufrechtzuerhalten. Es geht für die Frauen nicht darum, sich als Frauen zu bestätigen, sondern als ‚ganze', ‚vollständige' menschliche Wesen anerkannt zu werden."[54]

Vom Feminismus läßt sich Simone de Beauvoir ebensowenig wie von anderen Bewegungen vereinnahmen; sie widersetzt sich jeder Festlegung.

„Einerseits beschrieb man Simone de Beauvoir als Verrückte, als Exzentrikerin mit ausschweifenden Sitten, die alle

Laster praktiziert und ein Leben wie im Karneval führt; anderenteils erkannte man an, daß sie ihr Leben am Arbeitstisch verbrachte, einen scharfen Verstand hatte und sich mit ihren flachen Schuhen und ihrem festgezogenen Haarknoten wie eine Pfadfinderführerin benahm. So oder so war sie nicht normal. Sie widerstand jeglicher Einordnung: sie war links, aber bei den Kommunisten nicht gut angesehen, sie lebte im Hotel, war aber keine Bohemienne, sie war berühmt, aber lehnte es ab, in der feinen Welt zu verkehren. Dank ihrer Bücher war sie reich, führte aber kein Leben, wie man es gewöhnlich mit dem Erfolg verknüpft."[55]

„Die Zeremonie des Abschieds"

Jean-Paul Sartre ißt reichlich, liebt Süßigkeiten, raucht, trinkt Unmengen Scotch und Rotwein, schluckt abwechselnd Barbiturate und Amphetamine. Da ist es nicht erstaunlich, daß er 1971 im Alter von sechsundsechzig Jahren zwei Gehirnschläge erleidet.

Auf dem rechten Auge ist er seit seiner frühen Kindheit nahezu blind, und nun verschlechtert sich die ohnehin eingeschränkte Sehkraft seines linken Auges so, daß er nur noch groß gedruckte Texte mit dem Vergrößerungsglas lesen kann und seine eigene Handschrift nicht mehr zu entziffern vermag.

Simone de Beauvoir findet ihn am Morgen des 19. März 1980 auf der Bettkante sitzend, nach Luft ringend. In der Klinik diagnostizieren die Ärzte ein Lungenödem, Leberzirrhose und Durchblutungsstörungen des Gehirns.

Am 15. April erhält Simone de Beauvoir einen Telefonanruf von Arlette: Jean-Paul Sartre ist tot.

Sylvie fährt sie ins Krankenhaus. Dort versammeln sich auch die Freunde des Schriftstellerpaares, um die Nacht im Sterbezimmer zu verbringen. Am anderen Morgen schlägt Simone de Beauvoir – durch Alkohol und Beruhigungstabletten fast besinnungslos – das über den Toten gebreitete Laken zurück und will sich zu ihm ins Bett legen. Das Pflegepersonal hält sie davon ab.

Bei der Beerdigung muß sich Simone de Beauvoir sogar am Grab auf einen Stuhl setzen, und an der Einäscherung vier Tage später vermag sie überhaupt nicht teilzunehmen.[56]

Als Claude Lanzmann und Sylvie nach der Feuerbestattung zu ihr kommen, sitzt sie mit hohem Fieber auf dem Fußboden und deliriert. Im Krankenhaus behandelt man sie einen Monat lang gegen Lungenentzündung, Leberzirrhose, Kreislaufbeschwerden und neurologische Ausfälle.

Wie auch in anderen Krisen – beim Tod ihrer Mutter[57] und in ihrer Angst vor dem Alter[58] – versucht sie, Jean-Paul Sartres Sterben durch Schreiben zu verarbeiten: Sie verfaßt einen Bericht über das letzte Jahrzehnt seines Lebens, der 1981 unter dem Titel „Die Zeremonie des Abschieds" veröffentlicht wird. Viele seiner Freunde lesen das Buch mit Abscheu und werfen der Autorin vor, ungeschönt über seine Inkontinenz und andere Funktionsstörungen nach den beiden Schlaganfällen berichtet zu haben. Simone de Beauvoir wundert sich darüber: „Sie können mit einer beliebigen Kombination von Menschen in jedem Schlafzimmer dieses Landes machen, was Sie wollen, aber wehe Sie erwähnen, daß jemand in die Hosen geschissen hat, weil er alt und krank war – ah, wie Sie da die Prüderie der Leute verletzen!"[59]

Simone de Beauvoir pflegt zwar keine Aufputsch- und Beruhigungsmittel zu nehmen, wie es Jean-Paul Sartre tat, trinkt aber bereits vor dem Mittagessen Wodka und nachmittags zwei, drei Gläser Scotch.

Seit ihrem Zusammenbruch beim Tod Sartres fällt ihr das Gehen so schwer, daß sie kaum die paar Schritte zum Kühlschrank schafft, um die Whiskyflasche herauszunehmen. Damit bringt sie ihre Gäste in Verlegenheit: Sollen sie ihr helfen oder lieber so tun, als bemerkten sie nichts? („... stand sie langsam vom Sofa auf und schlurfte gebückt in die Küche, um zwei Gläser zu holen, dann zum Kühlschrank hinüber, wo sie eine riesige Flasche Scotch aufbewahrte. Mir ist zum Weinen zumute, wenn ich so an sie zurückdenke..."[60])

Am 20. März 1986 klagt sie über Magenkrämpfe und wird deshalb in eine Klinik eingeliefert, wo man sie einige Tage später operiert und bis Anfang April auf der Intensivstation versorgt. Die Diagnose lautet ähnlich wie bei Jean-Paul Sartre: Lungenödem und Lungenentzündung als Folgen einer Leberzirrhose.

Simone de Beauvoir stirbt am 14. April 1986 im Alter von achtundsiebzig Jahren – fast auf den Tag genau sechs Jahre nach Jean-Paul Sartre.

Ihr wichtigstes Werk war ihr Leben.

Ulrike Meinhof

Moral und Terror

Das Fahndungsplakat

„Mordversuch in Berlin.

10 000 DM Belohnung.

Am Donnerstag, dem 14. Mai 1970, gegen 11.00 Uhr, wurde anläßlich der Ausführung des Strafgefangenen Andreas Baader in Berlin-Dahlem, Miquelstr. 83, und seiner dabei durch mehrere bewaffnete Täter erfolgten Befreiung der Institutsangestellte Georg Linke durch mehrere Pistolenschüsse lebensgefährlich verletzt. Auch zwei Justizvollzugsbeamte erlitten Verletzungen.

Der Beteiligung an der Tat dringend verdächtigt ist die am 7. Oktober 1934 in Oldenburg geborene Journalistin Ulrike Meinhof, geschiedene Röhl.

Personenbeschreibung: 35 Jahre alt, 165 cm groß, schlank, längliches Gesicht, langes mittelbraunes Haar, braune Augen.

Die Gesuchte hat am Tattage ihren Wohnsitz in Berlin-Schöneberg, Kufsteiner Str. 12, verlassen und ist seitdem flüchtig. Wer kann Hinweise auf ihren jetzigen Aufenthalt geben?

Für Hinweise, die zur Aufklärung des Verbrechens und zur Ergreifung der an der Tat beteiligten Personen führen, hat der Polizeipräsident in Berlin eine Belohnung von 10 000.– DM ausgesetzt...

Berlin im Mai 1970

Der Generalstaatsanwalt bei dem Landgericht Berlin"

Ulrike Meinhof (1934–1976)
Foto: undatiert

Verwaist

Der Kunsthistoriker Werner Meinhof erlag 1940 einem Krebs-
leiden – vier Jahre nachdem er sich mit seiner Familie in Jena
niedergelassen hatte, um dort die Direktion des Stadtmu-
seums zu übernehmen.

Trotz des Krieges holte die Witwe nun das Studium der
Kunstgeschichte nach, auf das sie wegen der Heirat verzichtet
hatte. Ingeborg Meinhof wurde zwar von der Stadtverwaltung
unterstützt; um aber für sich und ihre beiden Töchter Wienke
und Ulrike etwas mehr Geld zu haben, entschloß sie sich, die
Kommilitonin Renate Riemeck als Untermieterin aufzunehmen. Aus der Mitbewohnerin wurde eine enge Freundin. Ingeborg Meinhof und Renate Riemeck blieben auch nach dem
Studium und der Promotion zusammen, wurden Lehrerinnen
und traten gleich nach dem Krieg in die SPD ein.

Als Wienke achtzehn Jahre alt war und Ulrike vierzehn,
mußte sich ihre Mutter einer Brustkrebsoperation unterziehen.
Sie überstand den chirurgischen Eingriff, aber kurz darauf starb
sie an einer Infektion. Renate Riemeck blieb bei den Waisen,
kümmerte sich um sie und übernahm die Vormundschaft.

Ulrike, die sich sonst wie eine wilde Hummel als Anführe-
rin hervortat, die Schwachen beschützte und sich mit den
Starken herumbalgte, nahm „den Tod der Mutter gelassen auf,
jedenfalls äußerlich. Ihre Ruhe und geradezu verbissene
Schweigsamkeit hätten auffallen müssen, besonders eine Art
Wildheit oder Trotz in ihrem Gesichtsausdruck, der nicht zu
deuten war. Man hätte ihn als Trotz oder Wut gegenüber dem
Schicksal oder der Krankheit deuten können, aber auch als
Trotzhandlung gegenüber der an sie gestellten Forderung, nach
dem Tod der Mutter Trauer und Verzweiflung zu zeigen."[1]

Wienke geht 1950 ihren eigenen Weg und läßt sich zur Kin-
derkrankenschwester (und später zur Sonderschulpädagogin)
ausbilden. Mit Ulrike zieht Renate Riemeck 1952 nach Weil-
burg an der Lahn, wo sie eine Professur am Pädagogischen
Institut übernimmt.

Die offene, intelligente, kontakt- und diskutierfreudige
Gymnasiastin Ulrike ist sowohl bei den Lehrern als auch

unter den Mitschülerinnen beliebt. Sie betet vor dem Essen, nimmt Violinunterricht, tanzt aber auch leidenschaftlich Boogie-Woogie und raucht Pfeife oder selbstgedrehte Zigaretten. Lachen hört man sie selten. Auf ihr Aussehen und ihre Kleidung achtet sie wenig. Für das Geld, das sie durch Nachhilfestunden verdient, kauft sie am liebsten Bücher. „Die Begeisterung für Bücher, für Literatur und Geschichte hat Ulrike Meinhof von ihrer Mutter und von Renate Riemeck erworben. Sie liest viel, oft bis tief in die Nacht hinein ... Hermann Hesse wird Ulrikes Lieblingsautor ... Sie befaßt sich in den letzten Schuljahren mit der Geschichte der alten Kirche, vor allem mit dem Urchristentum, wobei es sie besonders interessiert, wie ein praktischer, ein gelebter Glaube auszusehen habe."[2]

Einladungen von Mitschülern zu Spaziergängen und Tanzveranstaltungen nimmt sie an; wenn einer jedoch zudringlich wird, „kann sie ihn mit der Frage, ob die Abgeordneten des zukünftigen Europa-Parlaments nun direkt gewählt oder delegiert werden sollten, aus der Fassung" bringen.[3]

Sie läßt sich in die Schülermitverwaltung wählen und engagiert sich in der Schülerzeitung für die Europa-Bewegung, weil sie überzeugt ist, daß der Nationalismus überwunden werden muß, um die Gefahr eines dritten Weltkriegs zu bannen.

Kampf dem Atomtod

Unmittelbar nach dem Abitur im März 1955 zieht Ulrike Meinhof nach Marburg, um dort Pädagogik und Psychologie zu studieren.

Sie verlobt sich mit einem Physik-Doktoranden, der Atomwaffen ablehnt, aber die friedliche Nutzung der Kernenergie befürwortet, obwohl er sich bewußt ist, daß dieser Bereich nicht klar von der militärischen Entwicklung getrennt werden kann. Auf Halbheiten wie diese läßt sich Ulrike Meinhof nicht ein; für sie gilt es, eindeutig Stellung zu beziehen und vor den praktischen Konsequenzen der eigenen Überzeugung nicht zurückzuschrecken.

An Konflikten wie diesem und Ulrikes politischem Engagement zerbricht die Beziehung.

„Ulrike Meinhof liebt das Diskutieren – und sei es nur aus Spaß oder um den Advocatus Diaboli zu spielen."[4] In politischen Diskussionen glänzt sie nicht als intellektuelle Theoretikerin, sondern drückt sich eher bieder aus; doch wenn sie mit ihrer Altstimme das Wort ergreift, hören alle zu, weil sich Ulrikes Betroffenheit überträgt: „Sie war in ihrem Widerspruch ganz echt, persönliche Verlorenheit und ein auf Allgemeines abzielender Grimm, das Sorgenkind, die Furie."[5] Auch die radikalste Position trägt sie schnörkellos vor; sie gilt als ehrlich, geradlinig und standhaft.

Als Bundeskanzler Konrad Adenauer beteuert, bei den Atomwaffen handele es sich lediglich um „eine Weiterentwicklung der Artillerie"[6], wenden sich achtzehn namhafte deutsche Naturwissenschaftler am 12. April 1957 an die Öffentlichkeit, um gegen die Verharmlosung der Kernwaffen zu protestieren. Eineinhalb Wochen später warnt Albert Schweitzer im norwegischen Rundfunk vor Atomwaffen. In den USA fordern Linus Pauling und zweitausend andere Wissenschaftler die Einstellung der Kernwaffenversuche.

Der NATO-Rat ignoriert die Bedenken und beschließt am 19. Dezember 1957, in Europa Raketen mit atomaren Sprengköpfen aufzustellen. Daraufhin treten vierundvierzig deutsche Hochschullehrer – unter ihnen Renate Riemeck – für die Schaffung einer atomwaffenfreien Zone in Mitteleuropa ein. SPD-Politiker, Gewerkschafter und andere Gegner der atomaren Aufrüstung formieren sich im Ausschuß „Kampf dem Atomtod". Und auf dem Trafalgar Square in London findet am Karfreitag 1958 eine Massenkundgebung gegen Atomwaffen statt, aus der die internationale „Ostermarsch-Bewegung" hervorgeht.

Ulrike Meinhof tritt im Mai 1958 in Münster – wo sie seit dem Vorjahr studiert – dem Sozialistischen Deutschen Studentenbund (SDS) bei und organisiert als Sprecherin des „Studentischen Arbeitskreises für ein kernwaffenfreies Deutschland" Aufrufe und Veranstaltungen.

„konkret"-Kolumnistin

Wie ihre Pflegemutter Renate Riemeck geht Ulrike Meinhof von der Realität zweier deutscher Staaten aus und setzt sich dafür ein, die quer durch Deutschland verlaufende Kluft zwischen den weltpolitischen Machtblöcken zu überbrücken.

Im Frühjahr 1959 gelingt es ihr auf zwei Studentenkongressen, erfahrenen Sozialdemokraten das Ruder zu entreißen: Gegen deren Widerstand verabschieden die überrumpelten Delegierten Resolutionen für eine Verständigung der Bundesregierung mit dem DDR-Regime.

Diese Erfolge feiert sie mit Redakteuren des linksradikalen Politmagazins „konkret".

Den „konkret"-Chef Klaus Rainer Röhl lernte sie bereits im Jahr zuvor bei einer Pressekonferenz von Atomwaffengegnern kennen, aber „es war Abneigung auf den ersten Blick. Auf beiden Seiten."[7] Sie kann mit dem zynischen Bonvivant („Genießt den Kapitalismus, der Sozialismus wird hart."[8]) nichts anfangen, während „K2R" ihre Humorlosigkeit und Kompromißlosigkeit unerträglich findet.

Trotzdem zieht Ulrike Meinhof nach Hamburg, um in der „konkret"-Redaktion mitzuarbeiten: Im Oktober 1959 schreibt sie ihre erste Kolumne; hundert weitere folgen im Verlauf von zehn Jahren, und die Mischung aus Kommentar, Leitartikel und politisch-literarischem Essay wird zum Markenzeichen der erfolgreichen Journalistin, der Klaus Rainer Röhl nach wenigen Monaten die Chefredaktion anvertraut.

Ernst und ungeduldig tritt sie für ihre Überzeugungen ein: Sie versucht Konrad Adenauers Kommunistenhetze lächerlich zu machen, mißbilligt die kritiklose Anbindung der Bundesrepublik Deutschland an die USA und verlangt den Verzicht auf Atomwaffen. Immer wieder fragt sie, warum die Deutschen das Hitler-Regime hinnahmen; umgetrieben wird sie von der Sorge, daß ihre eigene Generation ebenfalls versagt und nicht laut genug protestiert gegen Kernwaffen, den Vietnamkrieg und die Notstandsgesetzgebung[9]: „Wie wir unsere Eltern nach Hitler fragen, werden wir eines Tages nach Herrn Strauß gefragt werden."[10]

Ehefrau und Mutter

Die Abneigung zwischen Ulrike Meinhof und dem sechs Jahre älteren Klaus Rainer Röhl löst sich allmählich auf: Gerade das Konträre in ihren Charakteren zieht sie gegenseitig an.

„Das Anti-Puritanische, das Genußhafte, was Röhl ja auch amüsant vorzustellen wußte, das übte eine unerhörte Anziehungskraft auf Ulrike aus. Dieses ‚evangelische Blockflöten-Mädchen' erlebt – mit ihrer ganzen Strenge so nach Hamburg gekommen – in Gestalt von Klaus Rainer Röhl die ihr bislang sozusagen aus Purismus weit weg liegende Welt des Lebens."[11] Und Klaus Rainer Röhl entdeckt, daß er sich auf Ulrike Meinhof verlassen kann: „Ein guter Kumpel, diese Frau. ... Sie strahlt Ruhe aus. Keine Angst. Wir kommen schon hin, klar. Ein Kumpel. Ein wirklich guter Kumpel. Zum Pferdestehlen."[12]

1960 verloben sie sich, und am 27. Dezember 1961 heiraten sie.

Im Jahr darauf klagt die siebenundzwanzigjährige Frau über bohrende Kopfschmerzen. Zunächst hält sie ihre Schwangerschaft für die Ursache, aber als sie die Schmerzen kaum noch erträgt, läßt sie sich von einem Spezialisten untersuchen. Die Diagnose ist niederschmetternd: Verdacht auf Gehirntumor! Um das ungeborene Leben zu schützen, schieben die Ärzte die erforderliche Operation auf und raten ihr von der Einnahme schmerzlindernder Mittel ab.

Ulrike Meinhof durchleidet qualvolle Wochen, bis sie im achten Monat der Schwangerschaft durch einen Kaiserschnitt von Zwillingen entbunden wird.

Als Regine und Bettina aus dem Brutkasten genommen und von Renate Riemeck betreut werden können, öffnen die Chirurgen Ulrike Meinhofs Schädeldecke und stellen fest, daß es sich nicht um eine Krebsgeschwulst, sondern um ein Hämatom handelt. Sie schneiden es nicht heraus, sondern klemmen es mit einem Silberdraht ab. (Später wird die Polizei Ulrike Meinhof anhand dieses Merkmals identifizieren.)

Nach dem Eingriff leidet die Patientin zunächst unter Sehstörungen und besonders heftigen Kopfschmerzen. Ihre

„starke, runde, intakte Persönlichkeit zerbrach nicht, aber sie bekam einen Riß, eine offene Wunde, die nie wieder ganz heilte. Sie lernte in diesen Monaten etwas, was es in ihrem Leben nie gegeben hatte und was ihrer Persönlichkeit fremd war: Angst. Die rasende, panische Angst, irgendwann, durch irgendein Ereignis könnten diese Schmerzen, die nach langsamer Absetzung der Medikamente allmählich nachließen, wiederkommen, es könnten ihre Hilflosigkeit, ihre Hilfrufe noch einmal ungehört durch den Raum gellen."[13]

Da Ulrike Meinhof in den letzten Wochen ihrer Schwangerschaft nicht mehr dazu in der Lage war, hat Klaus Rainer Röhl die Leitung der „konkret"-Redaktion wieder selbst übernommen. Auch als es ihr wieder besser geht, beschränkt sie sich auf das Schreiben ihrer Kolumnen und widmet die restliche Zeit ihrer Familie. „Obwohl ihr die Rolle der Ehefrau und Mutter anfänglich sehr schwer fällt, wie sie Freunden gegenüber zugibt, bemüht sie sich mit der ihr eigenen Konsequenz, auch diese Aufgabe zu erlernen. Wann immer Kollegen und Freunde ... zu Besuch sind, sie erleben ‚eine überzeugte Ehefrau und Mutter'."[14]

Leid und Elend

Der Hessische Rundfunk überredet Ulrike Meinhof 1964, sozialkritische Hörfunk-Features zusammenzustellen.

In ihrem ersten Beitrag berichtet sie über den Prozeß gegen Karl Wolff, einen ehemaligen SS-General, und kritisiert besonders die Kameraderie der Entlastungszeugen mit dem Angeklagten. „Es sind ‚Unbelehrbare, Unbeeindruckte, Unverbesserliche' ... allesamt Biedermänner, erfolgreich und angesehen, mit Nachkriegs-Karrieren in Industrie und Verwaltung. Schreibtischtäter."[15]

Für weitere Features schaut sie sich in Erziehungsheimen, Fabrikhallen und Obdachlosensiedlungen um, sie befaßt sich mit der Situation von Fürsorgezöglingen, Sonderschülern, Hilfs- und Fließbandarbeiterinnen.

Immer geht es ihr darum, Ungerechtigkeiten anzuprangern,

um die Welt ein bißchen humaner zu machen. „Wir glauben, daß der Mensch in jeder Situation, unter jedem System, in jedem Staat die Aufgabe hat, Mensch zu sein und seinen Mitmenschen zur Verwirklichung des Menschseins zu helfen."[16] Anfangs hofft sie, die Öffentlichkeit aufrütteln zu können, denn ihre Features werden zur besten Sendezeit ausgestrahlt und erreichen viele Zuhörer, aber im Lauf der Jahre wird sie realistischer und fordert statt dessen die Betroffenen auf, sich selbst gegen die Ungerechtigkeiten zur Wehr zu setzen.

„Ulrike Meinhof gerät bei ihren Recherchen in eine Welt des sozialen Elends und persönlichen Leids, der Unterdrückung und Benachteiligung, der Angst und Hoffnungslosigkeit."[17]

Sie berichtet darüber auch auf den schicken Parties, zu denen sie als prominente Journalistin häufig eingeladen wird. Die Gäste hören ihr aufmerksam zu und geben sich verständnisvoll, aber sie erleben ihre Schilderungen „wie exotische Reiseberichte aus einer fernen Welt".[18] Ihre politischen Überzeugungen findet man gescheit – aber sobald die Zuhörer glauben, ausreichend soziale Betroffenheit gezeigt zu haben, füllen sie ihre Teller am Büffet.

Napalm und Pudding

Als SPD, CDU und CSU im November 1966 eine große Koalition bilden, steht den 447 Abgeordneten der Regierungsparteien im Bundestag ein Häuflein von 49 FDP-Mitgliedern gegenüber: Die parlamentarische Opposition verkommt zur Farce.

In dieser Situation bilden Neomarxisten[19], Studenten, die eine längst überfällige Hochschulreform verlangen („Unter den Talaren Muff von 1000 Jahren"[20]) und Gegner der Notstandsgesetzgebung die Außerparlamentarische Opposition (APO). Sie betrachten den Staat „als ein Geflecht von Mechanismen, deren letzter – immer ideologisch getarnter – Zweck die Ausbeutung der nicht zum ‚Establishment' Gehörenden sei."[21] Die Kritik an den bestehenden politischen und gesellschaftlichen Verhältnissen entzündet sich auch an Ereignissen und Entwicklungen im Ausland, besonders am Vietnamkrieg. Heftig diskutiert wird über die Form des Widerstands gegen den Staat: Einig sind sich die APO-Mitglieder, daß die Öffentlichkeit durch Demonstrationen wachgerüttelt werden muß. Eine Berliner Popmusik-Gruppe singt: „Macht kaputt, was Euch kaputt macht." Gegen Personen gerichtete Gewalttaten lehnen die meisten ab; zahlreicher sind die Befürworter der „Gewalt gegen Sachen".

Hans-Dietrich Genscher, der im Oktober 1969 als Innenminister der neuen sozialliberalen Regierung vereidigt wird, erinnert sich später: „Daß die Achtundsechziger-Generation damals gegen ihre Eltern aufbegehrte, lag einmal an deren unbefriedigenden Antworten auf die Frage, wie sie sich im Dritten Reich verhalten hatten. Das konnte ich verstehen. Hinzu kam der wachsende Materialismus der bundesrepublikanischen Gesellschaft, gegen den sich viele Jüngere wehrten. Auch hierfür hatte ich Verständnis. Schon lange hatte ich damit gerechnet, daß die in unserer Gesellschaft vorhandene Selbstzufriedenheit, oft sogar Selbstgerechtigkeit eines Tages dramatische Reaktionen auslösen würde. ... Bei allem Verständnis habe ich jedoch von Anbeginn darauf bestanden, daß es keinen Unterschied zwischen Gewalt gegen Sachen und gegen Personen gebe. Das eine sei nur die Vorstufe des anderen, war meine Meinung, und Gewalt sei in jeder Form in einer demokratischen Gesellschaft inakzeptabel."[22]

Die von Fritz Teufel und Rainer Langhans gegründete „Kommune 1" in Berlin-Charlottenburg sorgt nicht nur durch ihr unkonventionelles Sexualleben für Schlagzeilen: Am 5. April 1967, einen Tag vor dem Besuch des US-Vizepräsidenten Hubert H. Humphrey in der geteilten Stadt, verhaftet die Polizei die Mitglieder der Wohngemeinschaft. Von einem im letzten Augenblick vereitelten Bombenattentat berichten einige Zeitungen: „Maos Botschaft in Ost-Berlin liefert die Bomben gegen Vizepräsident Humphrey", „Attentat auf Humphrey von Kripo vereitelt. FU-Studenten fertigen Bomben mit Sprengstoff aus Peking".[23] Tatsächlich enthalten die sichergestellten Plastikbeutel, mit denen der Staatsgast aus Protest gegen den Vietnamkrieg beworfen werden sollte, keinen Sprengstoff, sondern Mehl, Farbpulver und Pudding.

Ulrike Meinhof schreibt darüber in einer „konkret"-Kolumne: „Nicht Napalmbomben auf Frauen, Kinder und Greise abzuwerfen, ist demnach kriminell, sondern dagegen zu protestieren. ... Es gilt als unfein, mit Pudding und Quark auf Politiker zu zielen, nicht aber, Politiker zu empfangen, die Dörfer ausradieren lassen und Städte bombardieren."[24]

„Bild hat mitgeschossen"

Während das iranische Herrscherpaar – Schah Mohammed Resa Pahlawi und Farah Diba – am 2. Juni 1967 im Rahmen seines Staatsbesuches eine Aufführung der „Zauberflöte" in der Deutschen Oper in Berlin genießt, treffen vor dem Gebäude vierzehn Krankenwagen ein, dann rücken fünftausend Polizisten gegen achthundert Demonstranten vor: „Nehmen wir die Demonstranten als Leberwurst, dann müssen wir in die Mitte hineinstechen, damit sie an den Enden auseinanderplatzt."[25] Fliehende werden von Polizeitrupps gejagt. Der sechsundzwanzigjährige Student Benno Ohnesorg reißt sich los, wird eingeholt, verprügelt. Als er zu Boden sackt, schießt ein Beamter aus einem halben Meter Entfernung, trifft den Demonstranten in den Hinterkopf.

Dessen Tod treibt auch besonnene APO-Mitglieder ins Lager der Radikalen.

Die Tendenz verstärkt sich, nachdem am 11. April 1968 „der charismatische Studentenführer Rudi Dutschke, der seinerseits immer um die Grenze zwischen provokativer Aktion und offener Gewaltanwendung wußte und auch innerhalb der APO konsequent gegen Gewalt und Inhumanität aufgetreten war"[26], schwer verwundet wurde: Ein vierundzwanzigjähriger Gelegenheitsarbeiter fuhr eigens mit dem Zug von München nach Berlin, fragte sich zu Rudi Dutschkes Wohnung durch und wartete, bis dieser aus der Haustür trat und sich aufs Fahrrad schwang. „Bachmann lief auf Dutschke zu, der auf dem Weg zur Apotheke war, um Medizin für seinen drei Monate alten Sohn zu besorgen. Bachmann stellte sich vor ihn und fragte: ‚Sind Sie Rudi Dutschke?' ‚Ja.' ‚Du dreckiges Kommunistenschwein', sagte Bachmann. Dann zog er seine Pistole. Dutschke ging ein paar Schritte auf ihn zu. Der erste Schuß traf Rudi Dutschke in die rechte Wange. ... Bachmann schoß noch zweimal, traf Dutschke am Kopf und in der Schulter."[27]

APO-Sprecher machen dafür auch die hetzerische Berichterstattung der Springer-Presse verantwortlich: „Bild hat mitgeschossen!"

Brennende Kaufhäuser

Über eine Katastrophe, die sich am 22. Mai 1967 in Brüssel ereignete, schreiben Fritz Teufel und Rainer Langhans: „Ein brennendes Kaufhaus mit brennenden Menschen vermittelt zum erstenmal in einer europäischen Großstadt jenes knisternde Vietnam-Gefühl, das wir in Berlin bislang noch missen mußten ... Dreihundert saturierte Bürger beenden ihr aufregendes Leben, und Brüssel wird Hanoi ... Wann brennen die Berliner Kaufhäuser?"[28]

Andreas Baader, Gudrun Ensslin, Thorwald Proll und Horst Söhnlein nehmen die provokative Frage wörtlich und legen am 2. April 1968 tatsächlich Feuer: Um Mitternacht lösen umgebaute Wecker in zwei Frankfurter Kaufhäusern die Zünder von vier Brandsätzen aus.

Im „Club Voltaire", einem Treffpunkt der Frankfurter Linken, spricht Andreas Baader über kaum etwas anderes als über den Anschlag, sagt, da sei endlich nicht nur geredet, sondern auch gehandelt worden und deutet prahlerisch an, mehr darüber zu wissen. Nach drei Tagen werden die Brandstifter verhaftet und im Oktober zu drei Jahren Haft verurteilt.

Ulrike Meinhof fliegt nach Frankfurt, um die Täter im Gefängnis aufzusuchen. Dann schreibt sie darüber folgendes: „Gegen Brandstiftung im allgemeinen spricht, daß dabei Menschen gefährdet sein könnten, die nicht gefährdet werden sollen. Gegen Warenhausbrandstiftung im besonderen spricht, daß dieser Angriff auf die kapitalistische Konsumwelt ... eben diese Konsumwelt nicht aus den Angeln hebt, sie nicht einmal verletzt ... Das progressive Moment einer Warenhausbrandstiftung liegt nicht in der Vernichtung der Waren, es liegt in der Kriminalität der Tat, im Gesetzesbruch ... Das Gesetz, das da gebrochen wird durch Brandstiftung, schützt nicht die Menschen, sondern das Eigentum. Das Gesetz bestimmt, daß fremdes Eigentum nicht zerstört, nicht gefährdet, nicht beschädigt, nicht angezündet werden darf. Die da Schindluder treiben mit dem Eigentum, werden durch das Gesetz geschützt ... Es bleibt aber auch, was Fritz Teufel auf der Delegiertenkonferenz des SDS gesagt hat: ‚Es ist immer noch besser ein Warenhaus anzuzünden, als ein Warenhaus zu betreiben.' Fritz Teufel kann manchmal wirklich sehr gut formulieren."[29]

Scheidung

Immer schwerer fällt es Ulrike Meinhof, über die Liebesaffären ihres Mannes hinwegzusehen, der „seine Frau mit Schwung und Lärm betrog, der aber andererseits vor Stolz auf diese vielbestaunte, vielbegehrte Frau nur so zu platzen schien."[30] Lange Zeit versucht sie, ihren beiden Kindern eine Scheidung zu ersparen: „Ich möchte, daß die Kinder erleben, was ein Vater ist."[31] Auf einen Neuanfang hofft sie, als sie sich für eine zum Verkauf stehende Jugendstil-Villa in Hamburg-Blankenese begeistert. Im Frühjahr 1967 beginnt sie, das Haus einzurichten, und im Herbst laden die Röhls Gäste zur Einweihung ein – aber im Winter trennen sie sich, und Ulrike Meinhof zieht mit den Kindern nach Berlin.

In einer der Kolumnen, die sie weiterhin für „konkret" schreibt, setzt sie sich selbstkritisch mit ihrer journalistischen Arbeit auseinander: „Da wird auf Termine gearbeitet ... Ein guter Journalist ist auf Zack, schafft das, schafft alles, schreibt, auch wenn er nichts hat, schreibt, auch wenn er noch nicht fertig nachgedacht hat, schreibt, auch ohne die notwendigen Bücher vorher gelesen zu haben. Ein guter Journalist macht seinen Gegenstand zum Objekt, macht mit dem Objekt, was er will, die Leute, die entsetzt sind über das, was sie nachher über sich selbst lesen, haben eben keine Ahnung vom Journalismus, verdammt, es mußte alles so schnell gehen." Und weiter: „Indem sich der Verleger die Originalität, den Nonkonformismus und Eigensinn des Kolumnisten etwas kosten läßt, läßt er sich den schönen Schein etwas kosten, nicht nur um des Profits willen seine Zeitung zu machen ... Man muß Kolumnist sein, um Kolumnistenfreiheit als Kehrseite redaktioneller Unfreiheit beschreiben zu dürfen."[32]

Mit Sex and Crime steigert Klaus Rainer Röhl die Auflage seines Magazins, aber Ulrike Meinhof und einige andere Redakteure wollen „konkret" von dem unpolitischen Beiwerk reinigen. Die Kolumnistin kündigt im April 1969 ihre Mitarbeit bei „konkret" auf, und einige Wochen später versucht sie, mit einer Besetzung der Redaktionsräume in Hamburg eine Änderung zu erzwingen. Aber die Aktion scheitert.

„Ulrike Meinhof ist fest entschlossen, den Anspruch der Neuen Linken, daß eine grundlegende Veränderung der Gesellschaft mit der Umwälzung der privaten Verhältnisse einhergehen müsse, persönlich einzulösen – kompromißlos und mit allen Konsequenzen, wie immer, wenn sie glaubt, etwas als richtig erkannt zu haben. Doch sie stößt dabei schnell auf die eigenen Grenzen ... Eingespannt in politische Aufgaben, in Atem gehalten von einem Beruf, der Nerven kostet und Ruhe verlangt, fällt es ihr äußerst schwer, den eigenen Ansprüchen gerecht zu werden."[33] Es bedrückt sie, daß die Zwillinge bei einer Mutter aufwachsen, die von morgens bis tief in die Nacht mit anderen über Politik und Soziales diskutiert, schreibt und kaum Zeit für sie aufbringt. „Das ist das Problem aller politisch arbeitenden Frauen, mein eigenes inklusive, daß sie auf der einen Seite gesellschaftlich notwendige Arbeit machen, daß sie den Kopf voll wichtiger Sachen haben, daß sie eventuell auch wirklich reden und schreiben und agitieren können, aber auf der anderen Seite mit ihren Kindern genauso hilflos dasitzen wie alle anderen Frauen auch."[34] „Von den Bedürfnissen der Kinder her gesehen, ist die Familie bzw. der stabile Ort mit stabilen menschlichen Beziehungen notwendig und unerläßlich. Das ist natürlich viel einfacher, wenn man ein Mann ist und wenn man also eine Frau hat, die sich um die

Kinder kümmert ... Wenn man eine Frau ist und also keine Frau hat, die das alles für einen übernimmt, muß man das alles selber machen, und das ist unheimlich schwer."[35]

Ulrike Meinhof beginnt zu bezweifeln, ob sie mit ihren journalistischen Beiträgen die sozialen Verhältnisse ändern kann. Auch wenn sie Fürsorgezöglinge aufnimmt und sich um Arbeitsplätze für sie kümmert, bleibt sie eine privilegierte Außenstehende. Ist es richtig, die sozialen Mißstände anzuprangern und dabei Geld zu verdienen und Karriere zu machen? Zu Renate Riemeck sagt sie: „Es hat alles keinen Zweck mehr."[36]

Andreas Baader und Gudrun Ensslin

Die Kaufhaus-Brandstifter werden am 13. Juni 1969 bis zur Entscheidung über ihren Revisionsantrag aus der Haft entlassen.

Ulrike Meinhof trifft Gudrun Ensslin und Andreas Baader wieder, als sie in Frankfurt am Main über ein Fürsorgeprojekt recherchiert.

Andreas Baader ist sechsundzwanzig, drei Jahre jünger als Gudrun Ensslin und neun Jahre jünger als Ulrike Meinhof. Da sein Vater nicht aus dem Krieg zurückkehrte, wuchs er als Einzelkind in einem Haushalt mit drei Frauen auf: Mutter, Tante und Großmutter. Das Gymnasium mußte er ohne Abschluß verlassen. Ständig focht er Machtkämpfe aus und forderte andere zu Mutproben auf. „Andreas Baader prügelte sich in der Schule so oft, daß sich der Schulleiter schriftlich bei der Mutter beschwerte: ‚Einen zweiten Baader könnte meine Schule nicht tragen.'"[37] Wie man Frauen dazu bringt, das zu tun, was man von ihnen will, das wußte er bald so gut wie ein Zuhälter. Andreas Baader lebte wie ein Anarchist, aber politische Debatten interessieren ihn erst, seit er Gudrun Ensslin kennt.

Gudrun Ensslin wuchs mit drei älteren und drei jüngeren Geschwistern in einem zweihundert Jahre alten Pfarrhaus auf. Nach dem pädagogischen Hochschul-Examen studierte sie Anglistik und Germanistik. Im Wahlkampf 1965 engagierte sie sich für die SPD, aber nach der Bildung der großen Koalition stieß sie zur APO. 1967 brachte sie ihren Sohn Felix Robert zur Welt, und kurz darauf lernte sie Andreas Baader kennen.

Fünf Monate nach der Haftentlassung verwirft der Bundesgerichtshof die Revision: Andreas Baader und Gudrun Ensslin setzen sich zunächst ins Ausland ab, dann kehren sie zurück und schlüpfen als „Hans" und „Grete" bei Ulrike Meinhof in Berlin unter, bis Horst Mahler – Baaders Verteidiger – ihnen nach zwei Wochen eine Wohnung besorgt.

Andreas Baader versucht Waffen zu beschaffen, aber ein Spitzel des Verfassungsschutzes lockt ihn dabei am 3. April 1970 in eine als Verkehrskontrolle getarnte Falle der Polizei.

Der Sprung in den Untergrund

Gudrun Ensslin will ihn aus dem Gefängnis in Berlin befreien und drängt Ulrike Meinhof, mitzumachen: Sie wirft ihr vor, Schreiben genüge nicht – und die Journalistin, die ohnehin am Sinn ihrer Arbeit zweifelt, glaubt ihr. Gemeinsam arbeiten sie einen Plan aus: Der Verleger Klaus Wagenbach behauptet in einem Brief an die Haftanstalt, daß Andreas Baader an einem Buch Ulrike Meinhofs über „randständige" Jugendliche mitarbeitet, und diese ersucht die Gefängnisleitung, dem Häftling zu gestatten, mit ihr zusammen im Deutschen Zentralinstitut für soziale Fragen wissenschaftliches Material durchzusehen.

Tatsächlich begleiten zwei Beamte den Strafgefangenen am 14. Mai 1970 zu der Villa, in der das Institut untergebracht ist.

Als sie eintreffen, sitzt Ulrike Meinhof bereits im Lesesaal. Sie fragt die Beamten, ob sie verheiratet sind, Kinder haben – und scheint über die bejahende Antwort irritiert zu sein.

Kurze Zeit später klingeln zwei junge Frauen, die ebenfalls in den Lesesaal möchten, aber von dem zweiundsechzig Jahre alten Institutsangestellten Georg Linke zurückgehalten werden und daraufhin in der Eingangshalle Platz nehmen – angeblich um dort zu arbeiten.

Nachdem Georg Linke in sein Büro zurückgekehrt ist, öffnen die beiden Frauen die Außentüre; Gudrun Ensslin stürmt mit einem Begleiter herein – beide vermummt. Plötzlich steht Georg Linke vor ihnen. Der Maskierte schießt: Die Kugel durchschlägt den Oberarm des Institutsmitarbeiters und bleibt in seiner Leber stecken. Während der Getroffene zusammensackt, stürmen der Schütze und die drei Frauen in den Lesesaal, feuern Gaspistolen ab. Die Beamten stellen sich in den Weg, schießen, können aber nicht verhindern, daß Andreas Baader und seine Befreier durch das geöffnete Parterrefenster entkommen.

Ulrike Meinhof sollte im Institut zurückbleiben und sich vor den Kriminalbeamten überrascht zeigen. Es wäre kaum möglich gewesen, ihr eine Komplizenschaft nachzuweisen – und die Fünfunddreißigjährige hätte ihren publizistischen Kampf weiterführen können. Doch sie flieht mit den anderen und vergißt dabei ihre Handtasche. Eine Kurzschlußreaktion. „Mit ihrem Satz aus dem Fenster an diesem 14. Mai sprang Ulrike Meinhof nicht nur 1,50 Meter tief auf den Rasen, sondern zugleich auch von ihrem sicheren Tribünenplatz als Journalistin in die Arena. Es ist die Geburtsstunde der RAF."[38] Die Rote Armee Fraktion entsteht nicht aufgrund eines durchdachten Plans, sondern als Zufallsergebnis eines mißglückten Verbrechens, und die polizeiliche Fahndung engt den Handlungsspielraum der Gruppe drastisch ein.

Drei Wochen später treffen sich Andreas Baader, Gudrun Ensslin und Ulrike Meinhof in einer Berliner Wohnung mit der französischen Journalistin Michèle Ray, um sie über ihre Absichten zu unterrichten. Ein von Ulrike Meinhof besprochenes Tonband übergibt Michèle Ray dem „Spiegel", der Auszüge veröffentlicht: „Wenn wir mit einer Gefangenenbefreiung anfangen, dann auch deswegen, um wirklich klarzumachen, daß wir es ernst meinen."[39] Während die Linken immer nur redeten, würden Andreas Baader und seine Befreier jetzt handeln, und dabei werde es nicht bei Sandkastenübungen bleiben. In diesem Kampf dürfe man in einem Polizisten nicht den Menschen sehen, sondern nur den Feind, dessen Aufgabe es sei, das verbrecherische System zu schützen: „… und wir sagen, natürlich, die Bullen sind Schweine, wir sagen, der Typ in der Uniform ist ein Schwein, das ist kein Mensch, und so haben wir uns mit ihm auseinanderzusetzen. Das heißt, wir haben nicht mit ihm zu reden, und es ist falsch, überhaupt mit diesen Leuten zu reden, und natürlich kann geschossen werden."[40]

Andreas Baader und die an seiner Befreiung Beteiligten tauchen ab. Die APO und die Linke distanzieren sich von ihnen: Sie sind isoliert. Was sollen sie tun? Welche Möglichkeiten bleiben ihnen?

Guerillaausbildung

Aufgrund der guten Zusammenarbeit der ehemaligen „konkret"-Journalistin mit den Kommunisten wäre Ulrike Meinhof in der DDR willkommen – aber das gilt nicht für Andreas Baader und die anderen. Einen Alleingang lehnt sie ab und fliegt deshalb mit zwanzig Gesinnungsgenossen nach Jordanien, um sich zwei Monate lang in einem Lager der Al Fatah[41] für den Guerillakampf ausbilden zu lassen: Auf diese Weise bereitet sich die Bande auf ein Leben im Untergrund vor.

„Die Lebensbedingungen im Camp sind karg, das Essen entspricht dem in den Flüchtlingslagern. Die Ausbildung findet wegen der großen Hitze in den frühen Morgenstunden statt, so daß der Tag für die Gruppe bereits um 4 Uhr in der Frühe beginnt. Die Anforderungen der Ausbildung ähneln denen einer soldatischen Grundausbildung. Neben Waffenkunde und Übungen im Gelände gehören Selbstverteidigungsmethoden wie Judo und Karate zum Programm, aber auch die Herstellung von Sprengstoff."[42]

Ulrike Meinhof fällt der Umgang mit Waffen schwer: Einmal folgt sie den Anweisungen eines Ausbilders und zieht eine Handgranate ab, wartet dann auf weitere Instruktionen – bis sie begreift, daß sie den scharfgemachten Sprengkörper schleunigst fortwerfen muß.

Sie weiß zunächst nicht, wer längerfristig für ihre Töchter sorgen soll. Unmittelbar nach der Befreiungsaktion waren sie von Bekannten in Bremen aufgenommen worden. Als ein Gericht Klaus Rainer Röhl das Sorgerecht zusprach, ließ sie

Bettina und Regine in ein sizilianisches Barackenlager bringen, wo sich Hippies um sie kümmerten. Aber in Jordanien verlangt Andreas Baader von ihr, sich von den Kindern zu trennen, „es sei ein Relikt aus Ulrikes bürgerlicher Vergangenheit, noch immer an den Kindern zu hängen."[43] „Sie müsse sich entscheiden: Illegalität und Kampf seien nur möglich, wenn man alle Brücken hinter sich abbreche. Schließlich stimmt Ulrike Meinhof einem Beschluß der Gruppe zu, die Zwillinge in ein jordanisches Waisenlager der PLO[44] zu geben. Der Wille, gegenüber der Gruppe Entschlossenheit zu demonstrieren, die Befürchtung, aufgrund der Kinder erpreßbar zu sein, und nicht zuletzt Gudrun Ensslins Beispiel, die sich ebenfalls von ihrem Kind getrennt hat, mögen diese Zustimmung bewirkt haben. Wie verschiedene Beteiligte später berichteten, hat Ulrike Meinhof dennoch unter ihrer Entscheidung sehr gelitten."[45]

Im letzten Augenblick erfährt der Journalist Stefan Aust, wo sich die Kinder aufhalten, und es gelingt ihm, sie für ihren Vater aus Sizilien zu „entführen".

Logistik im Untergrund

Für einen Guerillakampf gibt es 1970 in der Bundesrepublik Deutschland weder Ressourcen noch Stützpunkte.

Um das erforderliche Geld zu beschaffen, überfallen Mitglieder der in Jordanien trainierten Bande am 29. September innerhalb von zehn Minuten drei Banken in Berlin. Mit den erbeuteten 200 000 Mark bauen sie eine illegale Infrastruktur auf, besorgen Autos, mieten in mehreren Großstädten konspirative Wohnungen, richten Depots ein und knüpfen ein Kommunikationsnetz. Das hält sie eineinhalb Jahre lang in Atem.

Bei dem „Dreierschlag" am 29. September ließ sich Ulrike Meinhof von einem Bankangestellten mit 8000 Mark abspeisen und übersah in der Aufregung weitere 100 000 Mark. Im November verschickt sie ein Paket mit Dienstsiegeln und Ausweisvordrucken, die sie mit anderen aus einem Rathaus stahl, aber sie irrt sich beim Schreiben der Adresse – und die

Aktion muß eine Woche später in einer anderen Stadt wiederholt werden.

Das Leben in der Illegalität zerrt an ihren Nerven: Wie die anderen auch, muß Ulrike Meinhof fortwährend damit rechnen, daß sie trotz Perücke und Sonnenbrille erkannt oder von der Polizei aufgespürt wird. Mißtrauisch achtet sie im Fahrstuhl, beim Einkaufen und während des Essens im Restaurant darauf, ob sich ein Augenpaar weitet, wenn der Blick auf sie fällt.

Wie berechtigt die ständige Sorge vor der Entdeckung ist, erweist sich, als Horst Mahler und vier weibliche Mitglieder der Bande[46] am 8. Oktober in Berlin verhaftet werden.

Verschärft wird dieser Streß durch den Gruppenzwang – um nicht zu sagen: Psychoterror –, den Andreas Baader und Gudrun Ensslin aufrechterhalten. Andreas Baader, „der aus Langeweile, Zynismus und Verzweiflung über die Welt zum Pistolero"[47], zum „Räuberhauptmann" geworden ist, handelt „im Rahmen seines irrwitzigen Denksystems nur konsequent. Die Gruppe mußte etwas nach außen deutlich Wahrnehmbares tun, wenn nicht die ganze Flucht- und Vorbereitungszeit als reiner Selbstlauf, als Bankräuberkarriere ohne politischen Hintergrund dastehen sollte."[48]

„Konzept Stadtguerilla"

Den Begriff „Baader-Meinhof-Bande" prägt die „Bild-Zeitung". Andreas Baader und Ulrike Meinhof ergänzen sich: Während er in seinem Tatendrang kaum auf Programme achtet, fungiert sie als Ideologin und PR-Managerin.

Sie verfaßt im Frühjahr 1971 das „Konzept Stadtguerilla", um Horst Mahlers unauthorisiertem Traktat über die Gruppenziele ein mit den Führungsmitgliedern abgestimmtes Manifest gegenüberzustellen.

Auf dem Titelblatt tauchen das Kalaschnikow-Signet[49] und die Bezeichnung „Rote Armee Fraktion" auf. Nachträglich rechtfertigt die Autorin, was mehr oder weniger zufällig geschehen ist: Unversehens ist eine Gruppe sozial und politisch engagierter Menschen zu einer Untergrundorganisation mutiert, die sich als Weiterentwicklung der APO versteht: Die RAF will den Rechtsstaat durch Terroranschläge provozieren und aufgrund der Gegenmaßnahmen als Unterdrückungssystem entlarven.

Ein Jahr später folgt Ulrike Meinhofs sechzig Seiten langer Traktat „Rote Armee Fraktion: Stadtguerilla und Klassenkampf". Sie läßt sich von ihrem Wunschdenken mitreißen und behauptet, die RAF kämpfe als Teil einer globalen Revolutionsarmee gegen Imperialismus und Kapitalismus.

Horst Mahler schreibt 1998: „Ihre Kombattanten waren in der Tradition der französischen Revolution sozusagen amoralische Moralisten, die die Herrschaft der Tugend auf den Terror gründen wollten (das ist die gefährlichste Sorte der Moralisten). ... Der Irrtum der Kombattanten der RAF besteht darin, daß sie glauben, Tugendhaftigkeit mit Sprengstoff herbeizwingen zu können. ... Die RAF hielt die Repräsentanten des Kapitals und des bürgerlichen Staates für die Stützpfeiler eines menschen- und lebensfeindlichen Systems, die herausgerissen werden sollten."[50]

Helmut Schmidt: „Sie waren größenwahnsinnig; größenwahnsinnig – ursprünglich aus idealistischen, aber ideologisch völlig verrückten Vorstellungen kommend, sich selbst zu Verbrechern wandelnd –, größenwahnsinnige Verbrecher."[51]

Heinrich Böll in einem vom „Spiegel" im Januar 1972 veröffentlichten Essay: „Will Ulrike Meinhof Gnade oder freies Geleit? ... Selbst wenn sie keines von beiden will, einer muß es ihr anbieten. ... Ulrike Meinhof will möglicherweise keine Gnade, wahrscheinlich erwartet sie von dieser Gesellschaft kein Recht. Trotzdem sollte man ihr freies Geleit anbieten, einen öffentlichen Prozeß, und man sollte auch Herrn Springer öffentlich den Prozeß machen, wegen Volksverhetzung."[52]

Im gleichen Aufsatz meint Heinrich Böll, es handele sich bei den RAF-Mitgliedern um verzweifelte Theoretiker, Verfolgte und Denunzierte, „die sich in die Enge begeben haben, in die Enge getrieben worden sind und deren Theorien weitaus gewalttätiger klingen, als ihre Praxis ist..."[53]

Im Mai 1972 schlägt die RAF zu. Genau zwei Jahre nach der

Befreiung Andreas Baaders versetzt die RAF zwei Wochen lang die Menschen in Angst und Schrecken: Bomben explodieren in Frankfurt am Main, Augsburg, München, Karlsruhe, Hamburg und Heidelberg. Vier Menschen sterben, zahlreiche werden verletzt.

Erstmals werden nicht nur Sachen zerstört, um gegen die politischen Verhältnisse zu demonstrieren, sondern absichtlich Menschen getötet.

Verhaftungen

1971 begann eine Sonderkommission („SoKo B/M") nach den RAF-Mitgliedern zu suchen, und Bundesinnenminister Hans-Dietrich Genscher holte Horst Herold, den siebenundvierzig Jahre alten Polizeichef von Nürnberg, als neuen Präsidenten des Bundeskriminalamts nach Wiesbaden. „Herold war ein hochintelligenter, psychologisch arbeitender Kriminalist und nahezu besessen vom Gedanken der Modernisierung, der Nutzung elektronischer Datenverarbeitung."[54] Er baut einen High-Tech-Fahndungsapparat auf, verdreifacht die Zahl der Beamten und verfünffacht das Budget innerhalb von zehn Jahren.

Polizisten mit kugelsicheren Westen verhaften am 1. Juni 1972 – acht Tage nach dem Anschlag in Heidelberg – Andreas Baader, Holger Meins und Jan-Carl Raspe in Frankfurt am Main vor laufenden Fernsehkameras: Um 5.50 Uhr steigen die Gesuchten aus einem Porsche. Jan-Carl Raspe wird als erster überwältigt. Die beiden anderen Terroristen verschanzen sich in einer Garage. Obwohl sie nicht wissen, daß die Polizei in der Nacht den eimerweise dort deponierten Sprengstoff gegen Knochenmehl vertauscht hat, rauchen sie und schießen auf die Beamten, die Tränengasgranaten in die Garage werfen. Ein Scharfschütze trifft Andreas Baader in den Oberschenkel. Er stürzt und schreit. Holger Meins kommt mit erhobenen Händen aus dem Unterschlupf, muß sich bis auf die Unterhose ausziehen und abführen lassen. Danach wird Andreas Baader an Händen und Füßen aus der Garage gezerrt.

Gudrun Ensslin fällt am 7. Juni in einer Hamburger Boutique auf und wird festgenommen.

Ein Terroristenpaar findet am 15. Juni in der Wohnung eines der APO nahestehenden Lehrers in Hannover-Langenhagen Unterschlupf: Die beiden betreten das Haus, nicht ahnend, daß der verunsicherte Lehrer zur Polizei gegangen ist und sie deshalb observiert werden. Als der Terrorist etwas später eine nahegelegene Telefonzelle benützt, schnappt die Falle zu. Nachdem er abgeführt worden ist, läuten vier Polizisten in der zweiten Etage an der Wohnungstür des Lehrers. Die schwarz gekleidete Frau mit struppigen kurzen Haaren, die wohl ihren Begleiter zurück erwartet, öffnet, wird gepackt. „Ihr Schweine!" kreischt sie erschöpft.

Die Polizisten wissen zunächst nicht, wen sie festgenommen haben. Als sie es ahnen, lassen sie die Frau in eine Klinik bringen. Eine gegen ihren Willen erzwungene Röntgenaufnahme beweist: Es handelt sich um die vor zehn Jahren am Kopf operierte Ulrike Meinhof.

Isolation

Ulrike Meinhof wird in Köln-Ossendorf inhaftiert. Nur die engen Verwandten dürfen sie besuchen – alle zwei Wochen einmal eine halbe Stunde.

Ihre Zelle befindet sich in einem Trakt, in dem nur sie allein untergebracht ist. Noch nicht einmal Geräusche anderer Häftlinge sind zu hören. Sie beschreibt, was sie in der Isolierung erlebt: „Das Gefühl, es explodiert einem der Kopf (das Gefühl, die Schädeldecke müßte eigentlich zerreißen, abplatzen) – das Gefühl, es würde einem das Rückenmark ins Gehirn gepreßt – das Gefühl, das Gehirn schrumpelt einem allmählich zusammen, wie Backobst z. B. – das Gefühl, man stünde ununterbrochen, unmerklich, unter Strom, man würde ferngesteuert – das Gefühl, die Assoziationen würden einem weggehackt – das Gefühl, man pißte sich die Seele aus dem Leib, als wenn man das Wasser nicht halten kann ... – das Gefühl, man verstummt – man kann die Bedeutung von Worten nicht mehr identifizieren, nur noch raten – der Gebrauch von Zischlauten – s, ß, tz, sch – ist absolut unerträglich – Wärter, Besuch, Hof erscheint einem wie aus Zelluloid – Kopfschmerzen – flashs – Satzbau, Grammatik, Syntax – nicht mehr zu kontrollieren. Beim Schreiben: zwei Zeilen – man kann am Ende der zweiten Zeile den Anfang der ersten nicht behalten – das Gefühl innerlich auszubrennen ... – rasende Aggressivität, für die es kein Ventil gibt. ... – Das Gefühl, Zeit und Raum sind ineinander verschachtelt – das Gefühl, sich in einem Verzerrspiegelraum zu befinden – torkeln – ... das Gefühl, als sei einem die Haut abgezogen worden."[55]

Nach vergeblichen Haftbeschwerden treten die RAF-Häftlinge Anfang 1973 in einen vierwöchigen Hungerstreik. Daraufhin wird Ulrike Meinhof zwar in einen Gefängnistrakt verlegt, in dem auch andere einsitzen, aber sie bleibt weiterhin in strenger Einzelhaft.

Zwei der Verteidiger gründen Komitees gegen die „Isolationsfolter" und sorgen für Aufmerksamkeit in den Medien. Sie handeln nicht aus Mitleid, sondern es kommt ihnen darauf an, der Öffentlichkeit die Brutalität des Staates vorzuführen und das politische System bloßzustellen.

Ihre beiden Töchter sah Ulrike Meinhof Anfang Oktober 1972 nach zweieinhalb Jahren erstmals wieder. Sie schreibt ihnen aufmunternde Briefe, erkundigt sich über ihren Fortschritt in der Schule, fragt, was ihre Pflegemutter Emma Biermann – die Mutter des Protestsängers Wolf Biermann – mit ihnen unternimmt und gibt ihnen Tips für eine bevorstehende Geburtstagsfeier.

„Also ich mach' mir jetzt ziemlich viele Gedanken über Euch. Oma soll mal schreiben, wie's läuft. Sagt ihr das. Und besucht mich! Und schreibt – los! Oder malt mir was, ja? Ich finde, ich brauch' mal wieder ein neues Bild. Die ich hab', kenn' ich jetzt auswendig. Meine Idee, daß Ihr mal sagen sollt, wie ich denn nun bei Euch heiße, war, glaube ich, eine Schnapsidee. Ich bin eben Eure Mami, fertig."[56]

Im Advent 1973 malen und basteln die elf Jahre alten Zwillinge für ihre Mutter. Kurz vor Weihnachten kommt das Paket zurück – ohne ein Wort. Regine und Bettina erfahren, was die

Medien über Ulrike Meinhof berichten, aber von ihr selbst hören sie nichts mehr.

Erst nach fast zwanzig Monaten endet die Isolierung: Am 5. Februar 1974 werden Ulrike Meinhof und Gudrun Ensslin in zwei benachbarten Zellen untergebracht, und sie dürfen jeden Tag mehrere Stunden gemeinsam verbringen.

Die beiden Frauen werden im April in einen speziell eingerichteten Hochsicherheitstrakt der Justizvollzugsanstalt Stuttgart-Stammheim verlegt. Ein halbes Jahr später kommen Andreas Baader und Jan-Carl Raspe dazu.

Holger Meins – der zusammen mit Hans Baader, Gudrun Ensslin, Ulrike Meinhof und Jan-Carl Raspe unter Mordanklage steht – ist durch den seit 13. September dauernden dritten Hungerstreik der RAF-Häftlinge bereits so geschwächt, daß er nicht von Wittlich nordöstlich von Trier nach Stuttgart transportiert werden kann – „während Andreas Baader bei einer ärztlichen Zwangsuntersuchung Hähnchenfleisch aus dem Magen gepumpt wird."[57] Obwohl man Holger Meins zwangsweise ernährt, magert er auf 39 kg ab und stirbt am 9. November 1974.

Am folgenden Abend klingelt ein Blumenbote bei Günter von Drenkmann, dem Präsidenten des Berliner Kammergerichts. Als er öffnet, treffen ihn drei tödliche Schüsse: Die Rache der RAF für Holger Meins' Tod.

Aufgrund einer Bitte Ulrike Meinhofs besucht Jean-Paul Sartre am 4. Dezember Andreas Baader in Stuttgart-Stammheim und prangert auf einer anschließenden Pressekonferenz die „Folterhaft" an.[58]

Das Ende

Der Mordprozeß gegen Andreas Baader, Gudrun Ensslin, Ulrike Meinhof und Jan-Carl Raspe beginnt am 21. Mai 1975 in einer eigens dafür auf einem Kartoffelacker gebauten fensterlosen Mehrzweckhalle.

„Im Sitzungssaal, 610 Quadratmeter groß und hoch wie eine Turnhalle, konnten 200 Zuhörer untergebracht werden ... Reiter der Polizei patrouillierten um das mit Stacheldraht abgesicherte Gebäude. Der Luftraum über dem Gefängnis und der Mehrzweckhalle war gesperrt. Innenhof und Dach des Prozeßgebäudes waren mit einem Netz aus Stahl überspannt, so daß auch Sprengkörper aus der Luft keinen Schaden anrichten konnten ... Anwälte, Zuschauer und Journalisten wurden vor Betreten des Sitzungssaals einer Leibesvisitation unterzogen. Hosentaschen mußten geleert werden, ihr Inhalt wurde in Klarsichthüllen verpackt und eingeschlossen. Selbst angebrochene Zigarettenpackungen mußten abgegeben werden ... Kugelschreiber wurden konfisziert; Journalisten erhielten als Ersatz behördeneigene Bleistifte."[59]

Die jetzt vierzig Jahre alte Ulrike Meinhof ist abgemagert, und es fällt ihr schwer, sich zu konzentrieren.

Dem Gericht und der Bundesanwaltschaft wirft sie Fanatismus vor: „In Südafrika werden politische Gefangene maximal drei Monate in den Trakt gesperrt. Wenn sie dann immer noch nicht ausgesagt haben, weiß man, daß sie eher unter Folter sterben als auszusagen und erschießt sie. Ich will damit nicht sagen, daß man in Südafrika mit politischen Gefangenen humaner umgeht, ich will sagen, daß, wo der Zweck der Folter – erst einmal Aussageerpressung, Informationsbeschaffung – gelaufen ist, nur noch der Tod, die Vernichtung und die vollständige Zerstörung der Gefangenen sein kann: Haftzweck ist der Tod der Gefangenen!"[60]

Auch während der Haft halten Gudrun Ensslin und Andreas Baader den psychologischen Druck auf die anderen RAF-Mitglieder aufrecht, und in der Enge des Gefängnisses verschärfen sich die Spannungen, häufen sich die Auseinandersetzungen. „Von einem freundschaftlichen, solidarischen Verhältnis der Gefangenen untereinander kann keine Rede sein. Besonders das Verhältnis Gudrun Ensslins zu Ulrike Meinhof war gekennzeichnet durch Mißtrauen, Rivalität und Haß."[61] Ulrike Meinhof leidet unter Demütigungen: Jede Zeile, die sie im Namen der RAF schreibt, wird von Gudrun Ensslin geprüft, korrigiert und erst dann an Andreas Baader weitergereicht, der die Formulierungen der ehemaligen Starkolumnistin nicht selten mit dem Vermerk „Scheiße" zurückweist.

231

Nach fast vier Jahren Haft ist Ulrike Meinhof am Ende. Als der diensthabende Beamte am 9. Mai 1976 frühmorgens die Zellentür aufschließt, hängt Ulrike Meinhofs Leiche in einer Schlinge am Fenstergitter. Einen Abschiedsbrief hinterläßt die Einundvierzigjährige nicht.

Eine im Herbst 1976 vom internationalen Komitee zur Verteidigung politischer Gefangener in Westeuropa einberufene Untersuchungskommission stellt am 15. Dezember 1978 fest: „Die Behauptung der staatlichen Behörden, Ulrike Meinhof habe sich durch Erhängen selbst getötet, ist nicht bewiesen, und die Ergebnisse der Untersuchungen der Kommission legen den Schluß nahe, daß sich Ulrike Meinhof nicht selber erhängen konnte. Die Ergebnisse der Untersuchungen legen vielmehr den Schluß nahe, daß Ulrike Meinhof tot war, als man sie aufhängte, und daß es beunruhigende Indizien gibt, die auf das Eingreifen eines Dritten im Zusammenhang mit diesem Tod hinweisen."[62]

„Ulrike Marie Meinhof
Beerdigung Samstag, 15. Mai 1976, 10.00 Uhr, Dreifaltigkeitskirche Berlin-Tempelhof, Eisenacher Str. Nr. 61.
Statt Kranzspenden bitten wir um Spenden auf den Rechtshilfefonds für die Verteidigung politischer Gefangener, Postscheckkonto Stuttgart 6838702 – Sonderkonto Rechtshilfe –
Wienke Zitzlaff, geb. Meinhof"[63]

Der Verteidiger Otto Schily sagt am 11. Mai 1976 vor Gericht: „In der Öffentlichkeit ist der Name Ulrike Meinhof, jenseits aller Diffamierung, mit einem hohen moralischen Anspruch, man kann auch sagen, mit einer hohen moralischen Rigorosität verbunden."[64]

„Man hat ihr nachgesagt, ein verantwortungsbewußter Mensch von hoher ethischer Integrität zu sein, und sie zugleich verdammt als militante Top-Terroristin mit fanatischem Haßpotential. ... Wild gewordenes Flintenweib oder Leitfigur im Engagement für eine bessere Welt? Eine Person im Widerspruch, die sich jedem eindeutigen Urteil entzieht."[65]

„Diejenigen unter uns, denen vielleicht die Entschiedenheit und Strenge Ulrike Meinhofs zu fremd ist, erinnern wir an die beiden Zeilen von Bert Brecht: ‚Ach, wir / Die wir den Boden bereiten wollten für Freundlichkeit / Konnten selber nicht freundlich sein.‘"[66]

Der Theologe Helmut Gollwitzer bezeichnet Ulrike Meinhof am Grab als einen „Menschen mit einem schweren Leben, der sich das Leben dadurch schwergemacht hat, daß er das Elend anderer Menschen sich so nahegehen ließ."[67]

Und Gustav Heinemann mahnt: „Mit allem, was sie getan hat, so unverständlich es war, hat sie uns gemeint."[68]

Anmerkungen

Johanna von Orléans, S. 9–37

1 Karl von Orléans wurde erst 1440 – als Johanna von Orléans bereits tot war – gegen ein immenses Lösegeld freigelassen.
2 Will und Ariel Durant, Kulturgeschichte der Menschheit. Band 9: Das Zeitalter der Reformation. Köln 1985, S. 95. – Angeblich borgte Karl VII. sogar von einem seiner Köche Geld.
3 zitiert nach: Herbert Nette, Jeanne d'Arc. Reinbek 1995[6], S. 16
4 Gemeint ist Isabella von Bayern, die Gemahlin des geisteskranken Königs Karl VI. und Mutter des Dauphins. Sie stimmte einem Vertrag zu, den Philipp der Gute von Burgund und Heinrich V. von England im Mai 1420 schlossen: Der englische König wurde mit der Regentschaft Frankreichs beauftragt und statt Karls VII. als Thronanwärter anerkannt.
5 zitiert nach: Herbert Nette, a.a.O., S. 16
6 Jacques Cordier, Johanna von Orléans. Wiesbaden 1966, S. 90 f. – Elfriede Husstedt (Die Stimmen der Jeanne d'Arc enträtselt. Kirchliche Manipulation und tödliche Intrige. Aachen 1998) ist überzeugt davon, daß Johanna nicht halluzinierte, sondern auf die schauspielerischen und bauchrednerischen Fähigkeiten ihrer Brüder und ihres Beichtvaters hereinfiel. Die Inszenierungen hätten dazu gedient, Johanna wie eine Marionette zu führen, und zwar im Auftrag einer Gruppe von Männern, die den König und das Heer zum Kampf gegen die Feinde aufstacheln wollten.
Daß Johanna von Orléans als politisches Werkzeug mißbraucht worden sei, wurde bereits im 16. Jahrhundert behauptet. (Gerd Krumeich, Jeanne d'Arc in der Geschichte. Historiographie – Politik – Kultur. Sigmaringen 1989, S. 232) Elfriede Husstedt glaubt es nun beweisen zu können. Ihr Argument: Halluzinationen beschränken sich auf das Wissen und die Erfahrungen des Halluzinierenden. Wenn also die Stimmen von etwas sprachen, das Johanna nicht wissen konnte – wie es z. B. bei den Prophezeiungen ihrer Verletzung vor Orléans und ihrer Verhaftung der Fall war –, sei bewiesen, daß andere Menschen diese Mitteilungen inszenierten.
7 Vita Sackville-West, Jeanne d'Arc. Die Jungfrau von Orléans. Frankfurt am Main / Berlin 1992, S. 167
8 ebd.
9 Leo Linder, „Ah, mein kleiner Herzog, du hast Angst?" Jeanne d'Arc. München / Düsseldorf 1998, S. 50
10 Diesen Wortlaut überlieferte Raoul de Gaucourt, ein Vertrauter des Königs; zitiert nach: Régine Pernoud und Marie-Véronique Clin, Johanna von Orléans. Der Mensch und die Legende. Bergisch Gladbach 1991, S. 45 f.
11 zitiert nach: Régine Pernoud und Marie-Véronique Clin, a.a.O., S. 46
12 Leo Linder, a.a.O., S. 47
13 Ruth Schirmer-Imhoff (Hg.), Der Prozeß Jeanne d'Arc. Akten und Protokolle 1431 – 1456. München 1978[3], S. 35 f.
14 Leo Linder, a.a.O., S. 70
15 ebd., S. 43
16 Hedwig Röckelein, Jeanne d'Arc als Konstruktion der Geschichte. In: Hedwig Röckelein, Charlotte Schoell-Glass, Maria E. Müller (Hg.), Jeanne d'Arc oder Wie Geschichte eine Figur konstruiert. Freiburg / Basel / Wien 1996, S. 15
17 zitiert nach: Herbert Nette, a.a.O., S. 31
18 „Bastard" wurde Johann Graf von Dunois genannt, weil es sich bei ihm um einen unehelichen Sohn des ermordeten Herzogs Ludwig von Orléans handelte.

19 zitiert nach: Régine Pernoud und Marie-Véronique Clin, a.a.O., S. 76
20 zitiert nach: Régine Pernoud und Marie-Véronique Clin, a.a.O., S. 87
21 Leo Linder, a.a.O., S. 66
22 Vita Sackville-West, a.a.O., S. 475
23 zitiert nach: Régine Pernoud und Marie-Véronique Clin, a.a.O., S. 90
24 Barbara Tuchman, Der ferne Spiegel. Das dramatische 14. Jahrhundert. München 1982, S. 519
25 Vita Sackville-West, a.a.O., S. 204
26 Sabine Tanz, Jeanne d'Arc. Spätmittelalterliche Mentalität im Spiegel eines Weltbildes. Weimar 1991, S. 225
27 Gerd Krumeich, a.a.O., S. 16
28 „Die Versuche, zwischen der ,authentischen Jeanne' und den Phantasien und Legenden, die sich um ihr Leben ranken, zu trennen, sind ebenso zahlreich wie erfolglos." (Hedwig Röckelein, a.a.O., S. 9)
29 zitiert nach: Régine Pernoud und Marie-Véronique Clin, a.a.O., S. 102
30 Von 988 bis 1825 wurden hier die französischen Könige gekrönt.
31 Papst Gregor XI. beendete 1376 die jahrzehntelange „Babylonische Gefangenschaft" der Kirche in Avignon und residierte wieder in Rom. Als er zwei Jahre später starb, wählten die Kardinäle unter dem Druck des aufgebrachten Volkes keinen Franzosen als Nachfolger, sondern den Erzbischof von Bari. Kurz darauf erklärten die französischen Kardinäle, die Wahl sei erpreßt worden und ernannten einen Franzosen zum Papst, der 1379 nach Avignon zog. Damit begann das Große Schisma der abendländischen Kirche: 38 Jahre lang gab es jeweils einen Papst in Rom und einen in Avignon, die sich und ihre Anhänger gegenseitig exkommunizierten.
    Um die Spaltung zu beenden, wählte ein Konzil 1409 anstelle der beiden rivalisierenden Päpste ein neues Oberhaupt der Kirche. Weil das aber keiner der beiden Abgesetzten akzeptierte, gab es fortan drei Päpste. Erst mit der Wahl Martins V. auf dem Konstanzer Konzil im November 1417 konnte das Schisma überwunden werden – auch wenn es noch einige Zeit dauerte, bis alle Christen Martin V. als rechtmäßigen Papst anerkannten.
32 beide Zitate: Ruth Schirmer-Imhoff, a.a.O., S. 34 f.
33 Der nachfolgende fiktive Dialog ist einem Spielfilm entnommen: Johanna, die Jungfrau. 2. Teil: Der Verrat (Regie: Jacques Rivette, 1993)
34 Perceval de Cagny um 1436, zitiert nach: Régine Pernoud und Marie-Véronique Clin, a.a.O., S. 140
35 zitiert nach: Ruth Schirmer-Imhoff, a.a.O., S. 161 f.
36 Einige Autoren (z. B. Elfriede Husstedt, a.a.O., S. 222) behaupten, der Stadthauptmann Guillaume de Flavy habe Johanna verraten und das Tor nur geschlossen, um sie dem Feind auszuliefern. (Vgl.: Leo Linder, a.a.O., S. 178 f.)
37 zitiert nach: Régine Pernoud und Marie-Véronique Clin, a.a.O., S. 161
38 Schreiben an Pierre Cauchon vom 21. November 1430, zitiert nach: Régine Pernoud und Marie-Véronique Clin, a.a.O., S. 180 f.
39 Herbert Nette, a.a.O., S. 78. –
    Das von einem ungebildeten Bauernmädchen nicht erwartete Verhalten nährte auch Spekulationen über Johannas Herkunft. Einige Autoren vermuten, sie sei mit den Bourbonen bzw. den Herzögen von Orléans verwandt gewesen: z. B.: Pierre Caze, La vérité sur Jeanne d'Arc ou éclaircissements sur son origine. Paris / London 1819; Jean Jacoby, Le secret de Jeanne d'Arc, Pucelle d'Orléans. Paris 1932; Jean Bancal, Jeanne d'Arc, princesse royale. Paris 1971
40 Edward Lucie-Smith, Johanna von Orleans. Eine Biographie. Düsseldorf 1977, S. 279
41 zitiert nach: Georges und Andrée Duby, Die Prozesse der Jeanne d'Arc. Berlin 1985, S. 31

42 zitiert nach: Régine Pernoud und Marie-Véronique Clin, a.a.O., S. 208
43 „Unam Sanctam" (eine heilige [Kirche]) lautet der Titel der Bulle, mit der Papst Bonifatius VIII. 1302 den Vorrang der geistlichen vor der weltlichen Macht betonte, um den französischen König Philipp den Schönen in seine Schranken zu weisen. (1303 ließ der König den Papst in Rom überfallen und gefangennehmen. Bonifatius wurde zwar nach zwei Tagen befreit, aber vier Wochen später starb er.)
44 Ruth Schirmer-Imhoff, a.a.O., S. 71
45 Will und Ariel Durant, a.a.O., Köln 1985, S. 99
46 Zeugenaussage des Arztes Jean Tiphaine am 2. April 1456 in Paris, zitiert nach: Ruth Schirmer-Imhoff, a.a.O., S. 187
47 zitiert nach: Ruth Schirmer-Imhoff, a.a.O., S. 79
48 zitiert nach: Herbert Nette, a.a.O., S. 101
49 zitiert nach: Elfriede Husstedt, a.a.O., S. 88
50 Herbert Nette, a.a.O., S. 101
51 Der Dominikaner Martin Ladvenu sagte 1450 aus: „Ich hörte von Johanna, ein hoher englischer Herr sei heimlich des Nachts zu ihr ins Gefängnis gekommen und habe versucht, ihr Gewalt anzutun." (zitiert nach: Régine Pernoud und Marie-Véronique Clin, a.a.O., S. 241)
52 zitiert nach: Régine Pernoud und Marie-Véronique Clin, a.a.O., S. 241f.
53 Faksimile in: Leo Linder, a.a.O., S. 207
54 Aussage Jean Toutmouillés vom 5. März 1450, zitiert nach: Régine Pernoud und Marie-Véronique Clin, a.a.O., S. 243. –
Ein reiner Leib, der nie geschändet wurde? Scheiterten die Vergewaltigungsversuche im Kerker daran, daß ihre Vagina nur rudimentär vorhanden war, weil es sich um einen Fall von Pseudohermaphroditismus handelte? (Anders als der echte Zwitter, der sowohl über Hoden als auch über Eierstöcke verfügt, weist der Pseudohermaphrodit die Keimdrüsen eines Geschlechts und die sekundären Geschlechtsmerkmale des anderen auf.) Bei den Untersuchungen der Jungfräulichkeit könnte der Fundus einer ansatzweise vorhandenen Vagina mit dem Hymen verwechselt worden sein – und eine Penetration wäre dann gar nicht möglich gewesen. (Robert B. Greenblatt, Johanna von Orléans. Syndrome of Feminizing Testes. In: British Journal of Sexual Medicine, August 1981; Walter Rost, Die männliche Jungfrau. Das Geheimnis der Johanna von Orléans. Reinbek 1983)
55 Régine Pernoud und Marie-Véronique Clin, a.a.O., S. 247
56 Leo Linder, a.a.O., S. 226
57 Der Hundertjährige Krieg endete 1453 – zunächst ohne förmlichen Friedensvertrag.

Maria Ward, S. 38–58

1 Vater, ich habe gesündigt.
2 Es lauert die Schlange im Gras.
3 Er sei verflucht.
4 durch Gottes Gnade
5 genug davon!
6 Notizen Maria Wards über das Gespräch mit Pater George Keynes SJ blieben erhalten. Siehe: Henriette Peters, Mary Ward. Ihre Persönlichkeit und ihr Institut. Innsbruck / Wien 1991, S. 135ff.
7 Will und Ariel Durant, Kulturgeschichte der Menschheit. Band 10: Gegenreformation und Elisabethanisches Zeitalter. Köln 1985, S. 453
8 Henriette Peters, a.a.O., S. 137f.
9 zitiert nach: Henriette Peters, a.a.O., S. 165f.; Walter Nigg, Mary Ward. Eine Frau gibt nicht auf. München 1985², S. 40
10 Helmut Kaiser, Maria Sibylla Merian. Eine Biographie. Düsseldorf 1997, S. 38

11 „Es wurde also in der vorfreudianischen Zeit die Vereinbarung als Axiom durchgesetzt, daß ein weibliches Wesen kein körperliches Verlangen habe, solange es nicht vom Manne geweckt werde ... Da aber die Luft ... voll gefährlicher erotischer Infektionsstoffe war, mußte ein Mädchen aus gutem Hause von der Geburt bis zu dem Tage, da es mit seinem Gatten den Traualtar verließ, in einer völlig sterilisierten Atmosphäre leben." (Stefan Zweig, Die Welt von Gestern. Erinnerungen eines Europäers. In: Walter Jens und Marcel Reich-Ranicki (Hg.), Bibliothek des 20. Jahrhunderts, Stuttgart / München o. J., S. 100. Vgl.: Thea Leitner, Fürstin, Dame, Armes Weib. Ungewöhnliche Frauen im Wien der Jahrhundertwende. München / Zürich 1996³, S. 302)

12 Henriette Peters, a.a.O., S. 200

13 Schule der seligen Maria

14 Immolata Wetter, Mary Ward. Aschaffenburg 1985, S. 41

15 zitiert nach: Mathilde Köhler, Maria Ward. Ein Frauenschicksal des 17. Jahrhunderts. München 1984, S. 123 f.

16 Das Tridentinum tagte von 1545 bis 1547 in Trient, von 1547 bis 1548 in Bologna, von 1551 bis 1552 und von 1562 bis 1563 wieder in Trient. Es reformierte die römisch-katholische Kirche grundlegend und gab Antworten auf Fragen zur Kirchenlehre, die durch die Reformation aufgeworfen worden waren.

17 Diese Worte sprach der Jesuit Georg Stengel. Er war ein paar Monate älter als Maria Ward. – Zitiert nach: Rudolf Reiser, Einst Kampfzentrale des Katholizismus. Süddeutsche Zeitung, 3. Januar 1997

18 Mathilde Köhler, a.a.O., S. 265

19 Theresia von Avila (1515 – 1582), zitiert nach: Mathilde Köhler, a.a.O., S. 129

20 Fischer Weltgeschichte. Band 24: Richard van Dülmen, Entstehung des frühneuzeitlichen Europa. 1550 –1648. Frankfurt am Main 1982, S. 291

21 Immolata Wetter, Mary Ward, a.a.O., S. 35 f.

22 ebd., S. 45

23 Der Kardinalvikar verwaltet als Stellvertreter des Papstes das Bistum Rom.

24 Immolata Wetter, Mary Ward, a.a.O., S. 45 f.

25 Maria Ward, zitiert nach: Mathilde Köhler, a.a.O., S. 152

26 Der bayerische Herzog Maximilian I. zog als Vorkämpfer der von ihm 1609 gegründeten katholischen Liga in den Dreißigjährigen Krieg und trug die finanzielle Hauptlast des Kriegs. Mit einem festlichen Akt erhob Kaiser Ferdinand II. seinen Vetter Maximilian I. 1623 zum Kurfürsten.

27 Ferdinand von Habsburg wurde 1617/18 König von Böhmen und Ungarn, 1619 Kaiser. Am Aufstand des böhmischen Adels gegen Ferdinand entzündete sich 1618 der Dreißigjährige Krieg (siehe Seite 239 f., Anm. 6). Melchior Klesl gehörte zu Ferdinands Gegnern, die dessen Inthronisierung in dem nicht von den Türken besetzten Rumpfstaat Ungarn verhindern wollten. Deshalb wurde er verbannt.

28 Carola Stern, Der Text meines Herzens. Das Leben der Rahel Varnhagen. Reinbek 1994, S. 61

29 Dem in Wien akkreditierten Nuntius Carlo Carafa trat im Mai 1627 der außerordentliche Nuntius Giovanni Battista Pallotto zur Seite.

30 Carlo Carafa am 7. Juni 1627 an Francesco Barberini in Rom, zitiert nach: Henriette Peters, a.a.O., S. 705

31 Mathilde Köhler, a.a.O., S. 207

32 Immolata Wetter, Maria Ward. Mißverständnisse und Klärung. Vortrag anläßlich der Verleihung der Ehrendoktorwürde durch die Katholisch-Theologische Fakultät der Universität Augsburg am 19. Februar 1993. In: Augsburger Universitätsreden. Band 22, Augsburg 1993, S. 16

33 ebd., S. 18

34 ebd., S. 18 f.
35 zitiert nach: Mathilde Köhler, a.a.O., S. 264
36 Henriette Peters, a.a.O., S. 861
37 ebd., S. 862
38 Maria Ward am 13. Februar 1631 in einem Kassiber an Elizabeth Cotton; zitiert nach: Immolata Wetter, Mary Ward, a.a.O., S. 66; Henriette Peters, a.a.O., S. 865.
39 zitiert nach: Ida Friederike Görres, Das große Spiel der Maria Ward. Das Leben einer wagemutigen Frau. Freiburg im Breisgau 1960, S. 150 f.
40 zitiert nach: Henriette Peters, a.a.O., S. 880; Immolata Wetter, Mary Ward, a.a.O., S. 68
41 zitiert nach: Immolata Wetter, Mary Ward, a.a.O., S. 70
42 So lautet der lateinische Name Maria Wards.
43 zitiert nach: Immolata Wetter, Mary Ward, a.a.O., S. 71
44 Immolata Wetter, Maria Ward. Mißverständnisse und Klärung. a.a.O., S. 13
45 Diese 2500 Englischen Fräulein unterstehen seit 1953 dem Generalat in Rom. Dazu kommen 1500 Mitglieder des irischen und 400 des kanadischen Generalats – die Loreto-Schwestern –, die Maria Ward ebenfalls als die Gründerin ihrer Kongregationen ansehen.

Maria Sibylla Merian, S. 59–74

1 Sein bedeutendstes Werk ist die „Topographia" (30 Bände, 1621–1687), eine Sammlung von mehr als 2000 europäischen Stadtplänen und -ansichten, die sein gleichnamiger Sohn weiterführte. Die Texte verfaßte Martin Zeiller (1589–1661).
2 zitiert nach: Helmut Kaiser, Maria Sibylla Merian. Eine Biographie. Düsseldorf 1997, S. 15
3 Will und Ariel Durant, Kulturgeschichte der Menschheit. Band 11: Europa im Dreißigjährigen Krieg. Köln 1985, S. 282 f.
4 Die ersten Tulpen wurden in der zweiten Hälfte des 16. Jahrhunderts aus der Türkei nach Mitteleuropa gebracht. Während des Dreißigjährigen Kriegs brach eine regelrechte Manie des Tulpenhandels aus. „Man erzählt die sonderbarsten Geschichten von Transaktionen im privaten Tulpenhandel. Eine einzige Zwiebel wurde mit einem Zweispänner abgegolten, eine andere gar mit zwölf Morgen Land." (Tyler Whittle, Pflanzenjäger. München 1971, S. 12)
5 Charlotte Kerner, Seidenraupe, Dschungelblüte. Die Lebensgeschichte der Maria Sibylla Merian. Weinheim / Basel 1988, S. 28
6 Der – durch die Zugeständnisse der Habsburger Rudolf und Matthias – erstarkte böhmische Adel wehrte sich gegen die Ernennung des Erzherzogs Ferdinand zum böhmischen König. Am 23. Mai 1618 warfen Abgesandte eines Prager Protestantentages zwei kaiserliche Statthalter aus dem Fenster ihrer Kanzlei auf dem Hradschin und gaben damit das Zeichen für einen Aufstand des protestantischen Adels gegen die katholischen Landesherren. Die Rebellen konstituierten einen Landtag – eine der ersten revolutionären Nationalversammlungen der Geschichte –, wählten eine Regierung aus dreißig Direktoren und stellten eine Armee auf. Am 31. Juli 1619 gaben sich die Böhmen eine ständische Verfassung, am 22. August 1619 setzten sie Ferdinand als König von Böhmen ab, ein paar Tage später wählten sie an seiner Stelle den calvinistischen pfälzischen Kurfürsten Friedrich V. und beriefen sich dabei auf das von Matthias zugesagte Recht der freien Königswahl. Am 28. August 1619 wurde Ferdinand zum Nachfolger des verstorbenen Kaisers Matthias gewählt, aber die Böhmen weigerten sich, dem neuen Kaiser zu huldigen. Damit wurde der böhmische Streit zur Reichsangelegenheit und entzündete einen europaweiten Krieg,

in dem Frankreich seine Hegemonialstellung durchsetzen konnte. 1648 schrieb der Westfälische Frieden die volle Landeshoheit der Reichsstände fest und verhalf ihnen damit gegenüber der kaiserlichen Zentralgewalt endgültig zum Sieg: Nach dem Dreißigjährigen Krieg bestand das Reich nur noch aus einem lockeren Verband von etwa dreihundert souveränen Territorien.

7 Will und Ariel Durant, a.a.O., S. 369f.
8 Utta Keppler, Die Falterfrau. Heilbronn 1963, S. 95
9 Helmut Kaiser, a.a.O., S. 87
10 Londa Schiebinger, Schöne Geister. Frauen in den Anfängen der modernen Wissenschaft. Stuttgart 1993[2], S. 122
11 Maria Sybilla Merian, Der Raupen wunderbare Verwandlung und sonderbare Blumennahrung. Nürnberg 1679
12 Rudolf Suter im Geleitwort zu: Margarete Pfister-Burkhalter, Maria Sibylla Merian. Leben und Werk 1647–1717. Basel 1980, S. 7
13 Charlotte Kerner, a.a.O., S. 42f.
14 Das Albumblatt mit einer aquarellierten Rose wird in der Staatsbibliothek in Bamberg aufbewahrt. Die Widmung galt vermutlich dem Geistlichen Christoph Arnold. – Maria Sibylla Merian. Künstlerin und Naturforscherin zwischen Frankfurt und Surinam. Ausstellung im Historischen Museum Frankfurt am Main, 18. Dezember 1997 bis 1. März 1998
15 Ruf der Schmetterlinge. Die Falterfrau. Film von Dietrich von Ruffer (ZDF 1991)
16 zitiert nach: Helmut Kaiser, a.a.O., S. 29 / 107
17 ebd., S. 123
18 Holland erhielt Surinam 1667 im Frieden von Breda von England als Ersatz für den Verzicht auf Neu-Amsterdam, das spätere New York. Verwaltet wurde die holländische Kolonie von einer Sozietät der Westindischen Kompanie, der Stadt Amsterdam und der Familie des Gouverneurs Cornelis van Sommelsdijk.
19 Helmut Kaiser, a.a.O., S. 149. – Bei dieser Schilderung bezieht sich Helmut Kaiser auf die 1544 bis 1650 in 44 Auflagen veröffentlichte „Kosmographie" von Sebastian Münzer.
20 Werner Quednau (Maria Sibylla Merian. Gütersloh 1961) ging noch davon aus, daß Johanna Helena ihre Mutter nach Surinam begleitete. Das war die gängige Meinung, bis J. Stuhldreher-Nienhuis (Verborgen Paradijzen. Het leven en de werken van Maria Sibylla Merian. 1647–1717. Arnheim 1952) den Irrtum aufdeckte.
21 Alexander von Humboldt und der französische Botaniker Aimé Bonpland bereisten von 1799 bis 1804 Lateinamerika.
22 Brief von Nicolaus de Graaff aus dem Jahr 1649; zitiert nach: Natalie Zemon Davis, Drei Frauenleben. Glikl. Marie de l'Incarnation. Marie Sibylla Merian. Berlin 1996, S. 201
23 zitiert nach Helmut Kaiser, a.a.O., S. 151. –
Der französische Physiker und Zoologe René-Antoine Ferchault de Réaumur (1683–1757) schlug eine der drei allgemein beachteten Thermometerskalen vor. (Die beiden anderen stammen von Anders Celsius und Gabriel Daniel Fahrenheit.)
24 Charlotte Kerner, a.a.O., S. 77
25 Maria Sibylla Merian, zitiert nach: Natalie Zemon Davis, a.a.O., S. 210
26 ebd., S. 211
27 zitiert nach: Elisabeth Rücker, Maria Sibylla Merian. 1647–1717. Ihr Wirken in Deutschland und Holland. In: „Nachbarn", Heft 24, Bonn 1980, S. 22f.
28 „Surinam war wegen der Greueltaten, die die Plantagenbesitzer an den Schwarzen verübten, verrufen: Widerspenstige Sklaven wurden in Tonnen

ertränkt, auf kleinen Feuern eingeäschert, von Pferden zerrissen, lebend in Kisten eingenagelt oder mit Fleischerhaken im Brustkorb aufgehängt." (Siggi Weidemann, Sagenhafte Profite aus dem Menschenhandel. Süddeutsche Zeitung, 16. Juli 1998)

29 Charlotte Kerner, a.a.O., S. 89
30 Die wissenschaftlichen Benennungen sowie die lateinische Übersetzung stammen von Caspar Commelin (1668–1731).
31 Elisabeth Rücker, Maria Sibylla Merian, 1647–1717. Katalog zur Ausstellung im Germanischen Nationalmuseum Nürnberg, 12. April–4. Juni 1967, S. 14

Madame de Pompadour, S. 75–98

1 „Königliche Romanzen. Liebe, die Geschichte machte." Heft 33: Ludwig XV. und Madame Pompadour. Hamburg 1992, S. 13
2 ebd., S. 15
3 Claus Süßenberger, Abenteurer, Glücksritter und Maitressen. Virtuosen der Lebenskunst an europäischen Höfen. Frankfurt am Main 1996, S. 43
4 l'étoile = Stern
5 Edmond und Jules de Goncourt, Madame Pompadour. Ein Lebensbild. (Neuübertragung von Ulrike Nikel) Düsseldorf / Zürich 1998, S. 49
6 ebd., S. 13
7 Der neue Namen war zwar adelig, aber er bedeutete auch nichts Großartiges: étioler = verkümmern lassen.
8 Dufort de Cheverny, zitiert nach: Nancy Mitford, Madame de Pompadour. Geliebte des Königs. München 1991[4], S. 26
9 Forstmeister LeRoy, zitiert nach: Edmond und Jules de Goncourt, a.a.O., S. 212
10 Forstmeister LeRoy, zitiert nach: Nancy Mitford, a.a.O., S. 27
11 „Mitte des 17. Jahrhunderts erreicht die Salonkultur in Frankreich eine erste Blüte. In den Häusern gebildeter Frauen ... treffen sich regelmäßig Gruppen illustrer Gäste in der Absicht, sich durch Konversation und Gesprächsspiele kultiviert zu unterhalten. ... Die Treffen in den Salons beginnen meist am späten Nachmittag und enden oft erst nach Mitternacht. Immer ist die Dame des Hauses Dreh- und Angelpunkt der geselligen Zusammenkünfte. Sie sorgt dafür, daß die Konversation nicht abbricht, daß alle Anwesenden an den Gesprächen beteiligt werden und daß die Atmosphäre der kultivierten Geselligkeit gewahrt bleibt." (Annette Kuhn (Hg.), Die Chronik der Frauen. Dortmund 1992, S. 266)
12 Der Staat bin ich. – Der berühmte Ausspruch, der angeblich von Königin Elisabeth I. stammt, wird v. a. König Ludwig XIV. in den Mund gelegt.
13 Caroline Hanken, Vom König geküßt. Das Leben der großen Mätressen. Darmstadt 1996, S. 115
14 Nancy Mitford, a.a.O., S. 12
15 Pierre Ambroise François Choderlos de Laclos veranschaulicht so ein raffiniert-maliziöses Netzwerk von Intrigen in seinem 1782 veröffentlichten Briefroman „Gefährliche Liebschaften".
16 Will und Ariel Durant, Kulturgeschichte der Menschheit. Band 12: Europa im Zeitalter der Könige. Köln 1985, S. 44
17 Will und Ariel Durant, Kulturgeschichte der Menschheit. Band 14: Das Zeitalter Voltaires. Köln 1985, S. 39
18 Edmond und Jules de Goncourt, a.a.O., S. 33
19 August der Starke, der in Sachsen als Kurfürst und in Polen als König regierte, mußte nach seiner vernichtenden Niederlage gegen die Schweden 1706 zugunsten von Stanislaus Leszczynski auf die polnische Krone verzichten. Als jedoch die schwedische Großmachtstellung unter dem Druck

Rußlands zusammenbrach, rückte August der Starke erneut in Polen ein, und Stanislaus Leszczynski floh. Nach dem Tod Augusts des Starken im Februar 1733 kam Stanislaus Leszczynski erneut an die Macht, aber er scheiterte im Polnischen Erbfolgekrieg und verzichtete 1735 endgültig auf die Krone. Ludwig XV. entschädigte seinen Schwiegervater mit dem Herzogtum Lothringen.

20 Als Ludwig XV. 1744 in Metz so schwer erkrankte, daß man um sein Leben fürchtete, spendete ihm der Bischof von Soissons die Sterbesakramente erst, als die Herzogin von Châteauroux abgereist war. (Friedrich der Große mokierte sich darüber: Geschichte meiner Zeit, München o. J., S. 255/293.) Ähnliches geschah dreißig Jahre später: Ludwig XV. mußte die Gräfin Dubarry ins Kloster verbannen, um drei Tage vor seinem Tod die Letzte Ölung zu erhalten.

21 Caroline Hanken, a.a.O., S. 46ff.

22 Madame de Pompadour in einem Brief, zitiert nach: Claus Süßenberger, a.a.O., S. 178

23 zitiert nach: Claus Süßenberger, a.a.O., S. 181

24 ebd., S. 152

25 Madame de Pompadour in einem Brief, zitiert nach: Claus Süßenberger, a.a.O., S. 161

26 zitiert nach: Tibor Simanyi, Madame de Pompadour. Eine Biographie. Düsseldorf 1979, S. 108

27 Albert Soboul, Die Große Französische Revolution. Frankfurt am Main 1973³, S. 45

28 Encyclopédie ou Dictionnaire raisonné des sciences, des arts et des métiers; 28 Bände erschienen von 1751 bis 1772, und bis 1781 folgten sieben Ergänzungs- und Registerbände.

29 Nancy Mitford, a.a.O., S. 132 (fiktives Zitat)

30 Edmond und Jules de Goncourt, a.a.O., S. 93f. (fiktives Zitat)

31 Caroline Hanken, a.a.O., S. 141

32 Jacques Ange Gabriel, der auch die Place de la Concorde gestaltete, entwarf das Gebäude neben dem Hôtel des Invalides.

33 Edmond und Jules de Goncourt, a.a.O., S. 164

34 zitiert nach: Caroline Hanken, a.a.O., S. 139f.

35 Claus Süßenberger, a.a.O., S. 177; vgl.: Will und Ariel Durant, a.a.O. (Band 14), S. 39

36 Madame de Pompadour in einem Brief, zitiert nach: Claus Süßenberger, a.a.O., S. 177

37 Edmond und Jules de Goncourt, a.a.O., S. 199

38 ebd., S. 115

39 ebd., S. 163 (fiktives Zitat)

40 ebd., S. 165

41 Caroline Hanken, a.a.O., S. 208

42 Edmond und Jules de Goncourt, a.a.O., S. 68

43 Auf der Reise begleitete ihn zeitweise Jacques-Germain Soufflot, der Hauptmeister des französischen Klassizismus.

44 zitiert nach: Claus Süßenberger, a.a.O., S. 154

45 Franz Herre, Maria Theresia. Die große Habsburgerin. Köln 1994, S. 221

46 Edmond und Jules de Goncourt, a.a.O., S. 110

47 In den Schlesischen Kriegen (1740–1742, 1744/45) riß Friedrich der Große Schlesien an sich und verteidigte diesen Besitz. Österreich wollte sich jedoch mit dem Verlust nicht abfinden. Um einem möglichen Angriff zuvorzukommen und um sich eine günstige Ausgangsposition für die erwarteten Auseinandersetzungen zu schaffen, marschierte der preußische König am 29. August 1756 in Sachsen ein. Am 15. Oktober kapitulierte die sächsische Armee. Aber im Jahr darauf sah sich Preußen überall Feinden

gegenüber: im Süden Österreich, im Osten Rußland, im Norden Schweden und im Westen Frankreich. Trotz einiger existenzbedrohender Rückschläge gelang es Friedrich, sich im Siebenjährigen Krieg zu behaupten, und der Friedensvertrag vom 15. Februar 1763 bestätigte seine Herrschaft in Schlesien.

Mit dem Krieg in Europa verknüpft waren die Kriege um Indien und Kanada, in deren Verlauf die Briten die Franzosen aus Indien, Kanada und dem Osten Louisianas sowie die Spanier aus Florida und dem Westen Louisianas verdrängten.

48 zitiert nach: Edmond und Jules de Goncourt, a.a.O., S. 112
49 Brief vom 9. Juni 1756, zitiert nach: Tibor Simanyi, a.a.O., S. 224
50 Nancy Mitford, a.a.O., S. 189
51 ebd., S. 193
52 Madame de Pompadour, zitiert nach: Otto R. Gervais, Die Frauen um Friedrich den Großen. Versuch einer Deutung des Liebeslebens Friedrichs II. Salzburg 1996, S. 440
53 Edmond und Jules de Goncourt, a.a.O., S. 125
54 Otto R. Gervais, a.a.O., S. 240
55 Hermann Schreiber, Die ungekrönte Geliebte. Liebe und Leben der großen Mätressen. München 1992, S. 151
56 zitiert nach: Olivier Bernier, Ludwig XV. Eine Biographie. Zürich / Köln 1986, S. 453
57 zitiert nach: Otto R. Gervais, a.a.O., S. 444

Rahel Varnhagen, S. 99–120

1 Rahel Varnhagen, zitiert nach: Hannah Arendt, Rahel Varnhagen. München / Zürich, 1997[9], S. 146 f.
2 Gordon A. Craig, Über die Deutschen. München 1982, S. 147
3 „Sind Christ und Jude eher Christ und Jude, / Als Mensch? Ah! Wenn ich einen mehr in Euch / Gefunden hätte, dem es genügt, ein Mensch / Zu heißen!" (Gotthold Ephraim Lessing, Nathan der Weise, 2. Aufzug, 5. Auftritt)
4 Stefan Zweig, Die Welt von Gestern. Erinnerungen eines Europäers. In: Walter Jens und Marcel Reich-Ranicki (Hg.), Bibliothek des 20. Jahrhunderts, Stuttgart / München o. J., S. 28 f.
5 Friedrich Daniel Ernst Schleiermacher in einem Brief an seine Schwester; zitiert nach: Konrad Feilchenfeldt, Die Berliner Salons in der Romantik. In: Barbara Hahn und Ursula Isselstein (Hg.), Rahel Levin Varnhagen. Die Wiederentdeckung einer Schriftstellerin. In: Zeitschrift für Literaturwissenschaft und Linguistik, Beiheft 14, Göttingen 1987, S. 156
6 siehe Seite 242 f., Anm. 47
7 Marie-Claire Hoock-Demarle, Die Frauen der Goethezeit. München 1990, S. 156
8 Carola Stern, Der Text meines Herzens. Das Leben der Rahel Varnhagen. Reinbek 1994, S. 35
9 Ursula Isselstein, Emanzipation wovon und wofür? Das Beispiel der Familie Levin aus Berlin. In: Norbert Altenhofer und Renate Heuer (Hg.), Jüdinnen zwischen Tradition und Emanzipation. Jahrbuch des Archivs Bibliographia Judaica. Bad Soden 1990, S. 86
10 Marie-Claire Hoock-Demarle, a.a.O., S. 157
11 zitiert nach: Hannah Arendt, a.a.O., S. 103
12 Heide Thomann Tewarson, Rahel Varnhagen. Reinbek 1992[3], S. 21
13 In seinem Haus trafen sich 1804 Rahel Varnhagen und Madame de Staël. Während die berühmte Französin von ihrer noch unbekannten deutschen Gesprächspartnerin beeindruckt war, schrieb diese über Madame de Staël:

„...sie hat nichts gehört, nichts gesehen, nichts verstanden." (Christopher Herold, Madame de Staël. Dichterin und Geliebte, München 1982, S. 268)

14 Die acht Jahre ältere Freundin Rahel Varnhagens war von 1783 bis 1799 mit dem Bankier Simon Veit verheiratet, aber seit 1797 die Geliebte Friedrich Schlegels, dem sie nach seiner Scheidung 1804 angetraut wurde.

15 Gerhard Danzer, Rahel Varnhagen oder der Ausgang des Menschen aus seiner selbstverschuldeten Unmündigkeit. In: Gerhard Danzer (Hg.), Frauen in der patriarchalischen Kultur. Literaturpsychologische Essays über Germaine de Staël, Rahel Varnhagen, Karen Horney und Simone de Beauvoir. Würzburg 1997, S. 48. – Vgl.: Marie-Claire Hoock-Demarle, a.a.O., S. 157

16 Gabriele Hoffmann, Frauen machen Geschichte. Von Kaiserin Theophanu bis Rosa Luxemburg. Bergisch Gladbach 1991, S. 257

17 Tibor Simanyi, Madame de Pompadour. Eine Biographie. Düsseldorf 1979, S. 283

18 Wilhelm von Humboldt in einem Brief an Charlotte Diede vom November 1834, zitiert nach: Ursula Isselstein, a.a.O., S. 106

19 Dieter Bähtz (Hg.), Rahel Varnhagen. Briefe und Aufzeichnungen. Frankfurt am Main 1986, S. 366

20 zitiert nach: Dieter Bähtz, a.a.O., S. 407 f.

21 So äußerte sich Goethe gegenüber einem Kommilitonen David Veits. Zitiert nach: Gerhard Danzer, a.a.O., S. 19.

22 Rahel Varnhagen, 1832, zitiert nach Carola Stern, Große Frau und große Geister. Rahel Varnhagen. In: Marianne Lienau und Wolf Dieter Ruppel (Hg.), ZeitZeichen – Frauen. Köln / Frankfurt am Main 1978, S. 30

23 Hannah Arendt, a.a.O., S. 41; vgl.: Gerhard Danzer, a.a.O., S. 20

24 zitiert nach: Heidi Thomann Tewarson, a.a.O., S. 63 f., und Hannah Arendt, a.a.O., S. 54

25 Rahel Varnhagen, zitiert nach: Hannah Arendt, a.a.O., S. 150 f.

26 Gerhard Danzer, a.a.O., S. 25. – Das klingt wie „Bokelmann" und bedeutet: der schöne Kelmann.

27 Hannah Arendt, a.a.O., S. 86

28 ebd., S. 103 f.

29 Marie-Claire Hoock-Demarle, a.a.O., S. 190. – Purgatorium: Fegefeuer

30 1805 wurde zwar die französische Flotte von Admiral Nelson vor Trafalgar vernichtet, aber aus der Dreikaiserschlacht bei Austerlitz ging Napoleon siegreich hervor. Das Heilige Römische Reich Deutscher Nation erlosch am 6. August 1806. Drei Tage später ließ der preußische König mobilmachen, und nach zwei Monaten erklärte er Frankreich den Krieg. Eilends stieß Napoleon nach Thüringen vor und schlug die beiden preußisch-sächsischen Armeen am 14. Oktober bei Auerstedt und Jena.

31 Aufruf des Stadtkommandanten Friedrich Wilhelm Graf von Schulenburg vom 17. Oktober 1806: „Der König hat eine Bataille verloren. Jetzt ist Ruhe die erste Bürgerpflicht. Ich fordere die Einwohner Berlins dazu auf. Der König und seine Brüder leben!" (Faksimile in: Michael Freund, Deutsche Geschichte. Von den Anfängen bis zur Gegenwart. München 1981, S. 319)

32 Golo Mann, Deutsche Geschichte des 19. und 20. Jahrhunderts, Stuttgart / Hamburg 1958, S. 89

33 Heinrich Heine schrieb dazu in Paris: „Man befahl uns den Patriotismus und wir wurden Patrioten; denn wir tun alles was uns unsere Fürsten befehlen. Man muß sich aber unter diesem Patriotismus nicht dasselbe Gefühl denken, das hier in Frankreich diesen Namen führt. Der Patriotismus des Franzosen besteht darin, daß sein Herz erwärmt wird, durch diese Wärme sich ausdehnt, sich erweitert, daß es nicht mehr bloß die nächsten Angehörigen, sondern ganz Frankreich, das ganze Land der Zivilisation, mit seiner Liebe umfaßt; der Patriotismus des Deutschen hingegen besteht

243

darin, daß sein Herz enger wird, daß es sich zusammenzieht wie Leder in der Kälte, daß er das Fremdländische haßt, daß er nicht mehr Weltbürger, nicht mehr Europäer, sondern nur ein enger Deutscher sein will." (Über Deutschland. In: Die Bibliothek der deutschen Klassiker. Band 38. München / Wien 1982, S. 379)

34 zitiert nach: Daniel Jonah Goldhagen, Hitlers willige Vollstrecker. Ganz gewöhnliche Deutsche und der Holocaust. Berlin 1996., S. 87; vgl.: Gordon A. Craig, a.a.O., S. 150. (Das Zitat soll aus einem Brief Ludwig Börnes stammen. Craig gibt kein Datum an. Bei Goldhagens Zeitangabe – 1859 – muß es sich um einen Druckfehler handeln, weil der Publizist 1837 starb.)

35 Gordon A. Craig, a.a.O., S. 150. –
Rahel „war eine Jüdin, die ihre Herkunft verfluchte und doch nie, in keinem Augenblick, von ihr loskam." (Walter Jens, Rahel Varnhagens Briefe. In: Walter Jens und Hans Thiersch (Hg.), Deutsche Lebensläufe in Autobiographien und Briefen, Frankfurt am Main 1991, S. 85)

36 Tagebuch-Eintragung vom 5. Juli 1809; zitiert nach: Hannah Arendt, a.a.O., S. 257

37 Brief an Karl Gustav von Brinckmann in Paris, Anfang 1808; zitiert nach: Heide Thomann Tewarson, a.a.O., S. 74; Hannah Arendt, a.a.O., S. 133/157

38 Brief vom 12. März 1810; zitiert nach: Roman Gleissner, Das liebliche Sagen des Wissens. Rahel Levin über die weibliche Seite des Sprechens. In: Norbert Altenhofer und Renate Heuer (Hg.), a.a.O., S. 118

39 Carola Stern, Der Text meines Herzens, a.a.O., S. 106

40 Heidi Thomann Tewarson, a.a.O., S. 93

41 zitiert nach: Hannah Arendt, a.a.O., S. 158

42 ebd., S. 159

43 Napoleon hielt im Mai 1812 einen glanzvollen Fürstentag in Dresden ab und marschierte dann mit 400 000 Mann gegen die Russen, die jedoch einer Entscheidungsschlacht auswichen und Moskau räumten. Nachschubschwierigkeiten und der einbrechende Winter zwangen die Franzosen, sich zurückzuziehen – während Partisanen ihnen zusetzten und Kälte, Hunger und Krankheiten die „Grande Armée" vollends auflösten.

44 Heinrich Eduard Jacob, Felix Mendelssohn und seine Zeit. Frankfurt am Main 1981, S. 35

45 siehe Seite 99 f.

46 Rahel Varnhagen in einem Brief vom 12. März 1810 an Pauline Wiesel, zitiert nach: Hannah Arendt, a.a.O., S. 185 / 262

47 Dieter Bähtz, a.a.O., S. 414

48 1826 stellte sich heraus, daß Varnhagen seinen Adelstitel zu Unrecht trug. Um einen Skandal zu verhindern, wurde ihm in aller Stille nachträglich der Adelsbrief ausgehändigt.

49 Auf dem Wiener Kongreß (1. November 1814 bis 9. Juni 1815) wurde das von Napoleon befreite Europa neu aufgeteilt. Napoleon kehrte zwar während der Verhandlungen aus der Verbannung auf Elba zurück, aber nach der verlorenen Schlacht bei Waterloo internierten ihn die Alliierten auf der britischen Südatlantik-Insel St. Helena.

50 Der Kongreß tanzt viel, aber er geht nicht [voran]. Das heißt: Die Gesandten amüsieren sich, statt zu arbeiten.

51 zitiert nach: Ursula Isselstein, a.a.O., S. 108

52 Carola Stern, Der Text meines Herzens, a.a.O., S. 229

53 Henriette Mendelssohn in einem Brief an Ludwig Robert, zitiert nach: Heidi Thomann Tewarson, a.a.O., S. 111

54 ebd.

55 Manfred Firnkes, „Restauration" und „Vormärz". Reaktionäre Fürstenmacht und liberale Bürgeropposition. 1815–1848. In: Heinrich Pleticha

(Hg.), Deutsche Geschichte. Band 9: Von der Restauration bis zur Reichs-
gründung. 1815–1871. Gütersloh 1987, S. 44
56 Golo Mann, a.a.O., S. 126f.
57 Carola Stern, Der Text meines Herzens, a.a.O., S. 241. (Dore ist eine Haus-
angestellte.)
58 Heinrich Eduard Jacob, a.a.O., S. 16
59 Carola Stern, „Ich möchte mir Flügel wünschen" Das Leben der Dorothea
Schlegel, Reinbek 1990, S. 258
60 Rahel Varnhagen litt zeitlebens unter rheumatischen Beschwerden.
61 Franz Grillparzer, Sämtliche Werke, herausgegeben von August Sauer.
Band 19. Stuttgart 1930/31, S. 127; vgl.: Humbert Fink, Franz Grillparzer.
Innsbruck / Frankfurt am Main 1990, S. 63
62 Gabriele Hoffmann, a.a.O., S. 266
63 Heidi Thomann Tewarson, a.a.O., S. 41
64 Roman Gleissner, a.a.O., S. 122
65 Brief vom 22. Januar 1819, zitiert nach: Hannah Arendt, a.a.O., S. 287f.
66 Carola Stern, Große Frau und große Geister, a.a.O., S. 30f.

Marie Curie, S 121–143

 1 Robert Reid, Marie Curie. Biographie. Düsseldorf / Köln 1980, S. 32
 2 Eve Curie, Madame Curie. Berlin 1938, S. 113
 3 Marie Curie am 18. März 1894 in einem Brief an ihren Bruder Josef; zitiert
nach: Eve Curie, a.a.O., S. 122
 4 Robert Reid, a.a.O., S. 9
 5 Ulla Fölsing, Marie Curie. Wegbereiterin einer neuen Naturwissenschaft.
München / Zürich 1990, S. 10
 6 siehe Seite 245, Anm. 49
 7 Cordula Tollmien, „Das kostspieligste Element der Welt". In: Charlotte
Kerner (Hg.), Madame Curie und ihre Schwestern. Frauen, die den Nobelpreis bekamen. Weinheim und Basel 1997, S.14
 8 Robert Reid, a.a.O., S. 25
 9 Marie Curie am 10. Dezember 1885 in einem Brief an ihre Cousine Hen-
rika Michalowska, zitiert nach: Eve Curie, a.a.O., S. 67
10 zitiert nach Peter Ksoll & Fritz Vögtle, Marie Curie. Reinbek 1993[3], S. 25f.
11 Brief vom 18. März 1888, zitiert nach Peter Ksoll und Fritz Vögtle, a.a.O.,
S. 28
12 Brief vom 12. März 1890, zitiert nach Peter Ksoll und Fritz Vögtle, a.a.O.,
S. 31f.
13 Marie Sklodowska-Curie, Selbstbiographie. Leipzig 1962, S. 23
14 Wenn bestimmte Kristalle durch Druck oder Zug verformt werden, polari-
sieren sie sich elektrisch, und in ihrer Umgebung baut sich ein elektrisches Feld auf. Umgekehrt führt ein elektrisches Feld dazu, daß sich die
Kristalle verformen.
15 Pierre Curie in einem Brief vom 17. September 1894, zitiert nach: Robert
Reid, a.a.O., S. 53
16 Maries Kosename
17 zitiert nach: Peter Ksoll und Fritz Vögtle, a.a.O., S. 51
18 Marie Curie am 23. November 1895 in einem Brief an ihren Bruder Josef,
zitiert nach: Peter Ksoll und Fritz Vögtle, a.a.O., S. 52
19 Marie Curie, zitiert nach: Peter Ksoll und Fritz Vögtle, a.a.O., S. 56
20 So der deutsche Chemiker Wilhelm Oswald, der sie dort besuchte. Zitiert
nach: Karl Rolf Seufert, Magie des blauen Lichts. Marie Curie entdeckt das
Radium. Bindlach 1989, S. 205.
21 Marie Sklodowska-Curie, a.a.O., S. 34
22 Ulla Fölsing, a.a.O., S. 9

23 ebd., S. 58
24 Marie Curie, 1899, zitiert nach: Peter Ksoll und Fritz Vögtle, a.a.O., S. 66
25 Brief vom Mai 1902, zitiert nach: Cordula Tollmien, a.a.O., S. 32 f.
26 Londa Schiebinger, Schöne Geister. Frauen in den Anfängen der modernen Wissenschaft. Stuttgart 19932, S. 13 f.
27 zitiert nach: Cordula Tollmien, a.a.O., S. 8
28 zitiert nach: Peter Ksoll und Fritz Vögtle, a.a.O., S. 73 f.
29 zitiert nach: Ulla Fölsing, a.a.O., S. 37. – Beinahe wäre Marie Curie von der Preisverleihung ausgeschlossen worden, denn man hatte sie zwar 1902, nicht aber 1903 als Kandidatin für den Nobelpreis nominiert.
30 Die Russin Sofja Kowalewskaja lehrte 1884 bis 1891 als ordentliche Professorin an der Stockholmer Universität Mathematik.
31 Brief an Kazia Przyborowska, 1907, zitiert nach: Peter Ksoll und Fritz Vögtle, a.a.O., S. 86
32 Ulla Fölsing, a.a.O., S. 73
33 „Le Journal", 4. November 1911, zitiert nach: Robert Reid, a.a.O., S. 169
34 zitiert nach: Ulla Fölsing, a.a.O., S. 39
35 Es gibt bis heute insgesamt nur drei Personen mit zwei Nobelpreisen: Der amerikanische Chemiker Linus Pauling erhielt 1954 den Chemie- und acht Jahre später den Friedensnobelpreis. Der amerikanische Physiker John Bardeen bekam 1956 und 1972 einen Nobelpreis für Physik, den ersten gemeinsam mit William Shockley und Walter Houser Brattain für Arbeiten über Halbleiter und den zweiten zusammen mit Leon N. Cooper und John Robert Schrieffer für die Theorie der Supraleitung.
36 Diese Worte setzt Marie Curie an den Schluß ihrer Selbstbiographie. (Marie Sklodowska-Curie, a.a.O., S. 68 f). – Übrigens verzichtete auch Wilhelm Conrad Röntgen auf eine Patentanmeldung für die von ihm entdeckten Strahlen.
37 bösartige Blutarmut
38 Albert Einstein 1935, zitiert nach: Peter Ksoll und Fritz Vögtle, a.a.O., S. 136 f. bzw. S. 145

Coco Chanel, S. 144–160

1 Axel Madsen, Chanel. Die Geschichte einer einzigartigen Frau. Bergisch-Gladbach 1995², S. 46
2 ebd., S. 52
3 Edmonde Charles-Roux, Coco Chanel. Ein Leben. Frankfurt am Main 1991, S. 118
4 Patricia Soliman, Coco. Der Roman. München 1992, S. 11
5 Axel Madsen, a.a.O., S. 81 f.
6 Barbara W. Tuchman, Der stolze Turm. Ein Portrait der Welt vor dem Ersten Weltkrieg 1890–1914. München / Zürich 1969, S. 407
7 Patrick O'Brian, Pablo Picasso. Eine Biographie. Hamburg 1979, S. 309
8 Axel Madsen, a.a.O., S. 84
9 Simone de Beauvoir, Das andere Geschlecht. Reinbek 1970, S. 170
10 Stefan Zweig, Die Welt von Gestern. Erinnerungen eines Europäers. In: Walter Jens und Marcel Reich-Ranicki (Hg.), Bibliothek des 20. Jahrhunderts, Stuttgart / München o. J., S. 94
11 „Der Spiegel", Heft 4 vom 18. Januar 1971, S. 126
12 Jean Cocteau, Vollendete Vergangenheit. Band 1: Tagebücher 1951–1952. München / Zürich 1989, S. 59
13 Coco Chanel 1931; zitiert nach: Djuna Barnes, Solange es Frauen gibt, wie sollte da etwas vor die Hunde gehen? Berlin 1991, S. 88
14 Axel Madsen, a.a.O., S. 127

15 Patricia Soliman, a.a.O., S. 194
16 Barbara W. Tuchman, a.a.O., S. 399
17 Der sibirische Bauernsohn Grigorij Jefimowitsch Rasputin hatte sich als
    wundertätiger Mönch das Vertrauen der Frau des Zaren Nikolaus II. er-
    schlichen und auf diesem Weg großen Einfluß auf die Regierung erlangt.
    Deshalb planten Mitglieder der Zarenfamilie ein Attentat auf ihn. Dimitri
    Pawlowitsch und ein weiterer Verwandter des Zaren luden ihn Ende De-
    zember 1916 ein und setzten ihm vergiftetes Teegebäck vor. Das Gift er-
    wies sich allerdings als unwirksam; Rasputin versuchte zu fliehen, wurde
    aber erschossen.
18 Marcel Haedrich, Coco Chanel. Eine Nahaufnahme. Frankfurt am Main /
    Berlin 1989, S. 86
19 Arthur Gold und Robert Fizdale, Misia. Muse, Mäzenin, Modell. Das
    ungewöhnliche Leben der Misia Sert. Bern / München 1981, S. 244
20 der Herzog von Westminster
21 Winston Churchill 1927 in einem Brief an seine Frau, zitiert nach: Axel
    Madsen, a.a.O., S. 210
22 Lilou Marquand, Coco Chanel hat mir erzählt ... Berlin 1991, S. 47
23 Rudolf Kinzel, Die Modemacher. Die Geschichte der Haute Couture.
    Wien / Darmstadt 1990, S. 194
24 Coco Chanel, zitiert nach: Marcel Haedrich, a.a.O., S. 164
25 zitiert nach: Axel Madsen, a.a.O., S. 260 f.
26 Mit dem deutschen Überfall auf Polen begann am 1. September 1939 der
    Zweite Weltkrieg. Der englische und der französische Botschafter in Ber-
    lin forderten die Deutschen ultimativ auf, die Kämpfe einzustellen; nach
    Ablauf der Fristen am 3. September befanden sich auch England und Frank-
    reich im Krieg gegen das Deutsche Reich.
27 Deutsche Truppen griffen am 10. Mai 1940 Belgien und die Niederlande
    an, um von dort nach Nordfrankreich vorzustoßen. Am 14. Juni besetzten
    sie Paris.
28 Coco Chanel in einem Brief vom 17. Oktober 1943 an Vera Lombardi (ge-
    borene Sarah Gertrude Arkwright, geschiedene Vera Bate); zitiert nach:
    Axel Madsen, a.a.O., S. 304
29 Nach der Landung der Alliierten auf Sizilien wurde Mussolini am 25. Juli
    1943 gestürzt. Ein SS-Kommando befreite ihn, und er rief im Oktober am
    Gardasee eine faschistische Republik aus, aber tatsächlich beherrschten
    zunächst die deutschen Streitkräfte Italien (bis auf die von den Alliierten
    kontrollierten Gebiete im Süden).
30 Vom 28. November bis 1. Dezember 1943 berieten Stalin, Churchill und
    Roosevelt in Teheran über die geplante Invasion, und vom 2. bis 6. De-
    zember konferierten Churchill und Roosevelt in Kairo.
31 Während Staatspräsident Pétain von Vichy aus die unbesetzten Gebiete
    Frankreichs regierte und sich dabei mit den Deutschen zu arrangieren ver-
    suchte, rief General de Gaulle von London aus zur Fortsetzung des Krieges
    gegen Deutschland auf, erklärte sich zum einzigen legitimen Vertreter
    Frankreichs und bildete im Mai 1944 eine Provisorische Regierung.
32 Axel Madsen, a.a.O., S. 314
33 „Der Spiegel", Heft 4 vom 18. Januar 1971, S. 126
34 Axel Madsen, a.a.O., S. 363
35 Lilou Marquand, a.a.O., S. 78 / 111 / 24
36 Drehbuch: Alan Jay Lerner; Partitur: André Previn; Regie: Frederick Bris-
    son (vgl.: „Der Spiegel", Heft 52 vom 22. Dezember 1969, S. 135)
37 Coco Chanel; zitiert nach: Marcel Haedrich, a.a.O., S. 147
38 Bei Angina-pectoris-Anfällen spritzte sie Nitroglycerin.
39 Axel Madsen, a.a.O., S. 393 f. –
    Die Trauerfeier fand in der Pariser Kirche Madeleine statt. Bestattet wurde

der Leichnam in Lausanne. Die Erben der Gebrüder Wertheimer beauftragten 1983 Karl Lagerfeld, das Haus Chanel weiterzuführen.

Frida Kahlo, S.161–177

1 Hayden Herrera, Frida Kahlo. Ein leidenschaftliches Leben. Frankfurt am Main 1998, S. 46
2 Alejandro Gómez Arias, zitiert nach: Heyden Herrera, a.a.O., S. 47
3 zitiert nach: Linde Salber, Frida Kahlo. Reinbek 1997, S. 30
4 Krankengeschichte, aufgenommen 1946 von Dr. Henriette Begun; zitiert nach: Raquel Tibol, Frida Kahlo. Frankfurt am Main 1980, S. 139
5 Carlos Monsiváis, Frida und ihre Freunde. In: Erika Billeter (Hg.), Das Blaue Haus. Die Welt der Frida Kahlo. Schirn Kunsthalle Frankfurt am Main, Ausstellung vom 11. März bis 23. Mai 1993, Ausstellungskatalog, S. 190
6 Frida Kahlo, zitiert nach: Linde Salber, a.a.O., S. 31
7 Frida Kahlo in einem Brief an Alejandro Gómez Arias vom August 1927, zitiert nach: Linde Salber, a.a.O., S. 56
8 Brief vom 29. September 1926, zitiert nach: Erika Billeter (Hg.), Das Blaue Haus, a.a.O., S. 245
9 Frida Kahlo zu Antonio Rodriguez, zitiert nach: Erika Billeter (Hg.), Einsame Begegnungen. Lola Alvarez fotografiert Frida Kahlo. Bern 1992, S. 53
10 Frida Kahlo am 31. April 1927 in einem Brief an Alejandro Gómez Arias; zitiert nach: Erika Billeter (Hg.), Das Blaue Haus, a.a.O., S. 245f.
11 Linde Salber, a.a.O., S. 15
12 ebd., S. 39
13 zitiert nach: Andrea Kettenmann, Frida Kahlo. Leid und Leidenschaft. Köln 1992, S. 9
14 Frida Kahlo, zitiert nach: Hayden Herrera, a.a.O., S. 25
15 Linde Salber, a.a.O., S. 45. –
   Der seit 1877 herrschende mexikanische Diktator Porfirio Diaz war durch den Aufstand von 1911 hinweggefegt worden. (Er starb vier Jahre später in Paris.) Nach jahrelangem revolutionären Chaos gab sich Mexiko 1917 eine sozialistische Verfassung und nahm bereits 1924 diplomatische Beziehungen zur Sowjetunion auf.
16 Andrea Kettenmann, Diego Rivera. Ein revolutionärer Geist in der Kunst der Moderne. Köln 1997, S. 7
17 Diego Rivera, zitiert nach: Heyden Herrera, a.a.O., S. 68
18 Linde Salber, a.a.O., S. 47
19 zitiert nach: Heyden Herrera, a.a.O., S. 75, und Linde Salber, a.a.O., S. 42
20 Gemeint ist hier die Fotografin Tina Modotti. –
   Es wird auch berichtet, Tina Modotti habe Frida Kahlo und Diego Rivera miteinander bekannt gemacht: „Es scheint so viele Varianten zu geben wie Erzähler, und auch Frida erzählte die Begebenheit zu verschiedenen Zeiten ihres Lebens jeweils anders." (Heyden Herrera, a.a.O., S. 74)
21 zitiert nach: Heyden Herrera, a.a.O., S. 74
22 Carlos Fuentes, Frida Kahlo. In: Vera Eckstein (Hg.), Kultfrauen. Fünfzehn Begegnungen. Mannheim 1996, S. 199
23 Frida Kahlo, zitiert nach: Hayden Herrera, a.a.O., S. 84. –
   Mit „Der Elefant und die Taube. Diego Rivera und Frida Kahlo de Rivera" überschreibt Wieland Schmied seinen Beitrag in Olaf Münzberg und Michael Nungesser (Hg.), Diego Rivera. 1886–1957. Retrospektive. Berlin 1987.
24 Hayden Herrera, a.a.O., S. 8
25 Diego Rivera Anfang Mai 1953 in einem Gespräch mit Raquel Tibol, zitiert nach: Raquel Tibol, a.a.O., S. 87

26 Carlos Fuentes, a.a.O., S. 203
27 Linde Salber, a.a.O., S. 75
28 Carlos Monsiváis, a.a.O., S. 187
29 Frida Kahlo, Gemaltes Tagebuch. München 1995, S. 61/235
30 zitiert nach: Carlos Fuentes, a.a.O., S. 198
31 Brief vom 24. Oktober 1934, zitiert nach: Hayden Herrera, a.a.O., S. 155
32 Lew Dawidowitsch Trotzkij unterlag Stalin in dem nach Lenins Tod 1924 ausgebrochenen Machtkampf, verlor seine Ämter, wurde 1927 aus der Kommunistischen Partei der Sowjetunion verstoßen, 1928 nach Kasachstan verbannt und 1929 ausgewiesen. Am 9. Januar 1937 kam er mit Natalia Sedova nach Mexiko und wohnte bis April 1939 im Geburtshaus Frida Kahlos.
33 zitiert nach: Rauda Jamis, Frida Kahlo. Malerin wider das Leiden. München 1991, S. 205
34 Frida Kahlo, zitiert nach: Andrea Kettenmann, Frida Kahlo, a.a.O., S. 18/27
35 Keto von Waberer in: Frida Kahlo, Meisterwerke. München 1992, S. 10
36 Diego Rivera, zitiert nach: Linde Salber, a.a.O., S. 68 f. – Vgl.: Erika Billeter, Frida Kahlo. Welt der Wahrheit – Welt der Utopie. In: Erika Billeter (Hg.), Das Blaue Haus, a.a.O., S. 11
37 Raquel Tibol, a.a.O., S. 54
38 Hayden Herrera, a.a.O., S. 10
39 Frida Kahlo, Die zerbrochene Säule, 1944
40 siehe Seite 249, Anm. 15
41 Frida Kahlo, zitiert nach: Linde Salber, a.a.O., S. 49
42 Frida Kahlo, zitiert nach: Erika Billeter, Einsame Begegnungen, a.a.O., S. 32
43 zitiert nach: Linde Salber, a.a.O., S. 90
44 Frida Kahlo im Februar 1939 in einem Brief an Nickolas Muray, zitiert nach: Andrea Kettenmann, Frida Kahlo, a.a.O., S. 51
45 Frida Kahlo in einem Brief vom 17. März 1939 an Ella und Bertram Wolfe, zitiert nach: Linde Salber, a.a.O., S. 91
46 siehe Seite 169
47 Nickolas Muray in einem Brief vom Mai 1939, zitiert nach: Hayden Herrera, a.a.O., S. 239
48 zitiert nach: Hayden Herrera, a.a.O., S. 244
49 zitiert nach: Hayden Herrera, a.a.O., S. 268
50 zitiert nach: Hayden Herrera, a.a.O., S. 272
51 Elena Poniatowska, Das Blaue Haus von Frida Kahlo. In: Erika Billeter (Hg.), Das Blaue Haus, a.a.O., S. 24
52 Linde Salber, a.a.O., S. 115 f.
53 zitiert nach: Hayden Herrera, a.a.O., S. 341 f.
54 Carlos Fuentes, a.a.O., S. 184
55 Tagebucheintragung vom Februar 1954, zitiert nach: Erika Billeter (Hg.), Das Blaue Haus, a.a.O., S. 262
56 „Damals wurde als offizieller Todesgrund eine Lungenembolie mitgeteilt, aber angesichts der Umstände kann ein Selbstmord nicht ausgeschlossen werden." (Gislind Nabakowski, Frida Kahlo. In: Ulrike Becker und Imke Krüger (Redaktion), Frei und Frau. Sieben eigenwillige Lebensbilder. Bensheim / Düsseldorf 1993, S. 162)
57 Lola Alvarez Bravo, zitiert nach: Erika Billeter, Einsame Begegnungen, a.a.O., S. 11 f.

Siehe auch: Helga Prignitz-Poda, Salomón Grimberg und Andrea Kettenmann (Hg.), Frida Kahlo. Das Gesamtwerk. Frankfurt am Main 1988

1 Simone de Beauvoir, Das andere Geschlecht. Reinbek 1970², S. 550 f. –
Siehe dazu auch das folgende Zitat aus dem Roman „Die Unsterblichkeit"
von Milan Kundera: „Eine Frau verbringt sehr viel mehr Zeit mit Diskussionen über ihre physischen Beschwerden; es ist ihr nicht vergönnt, ihren
Körper sorglos zu vergessen. Es beginnt mit dem Schock der ersten Blu-
tung; der Körper ist plötzlich da, und die Frau sieht sich in die Rolle eines
Maschinisten, der eine kleine Fabrik in Gang halten muß: täglich den Bü-
stenhalter zuhaken, jeden Monat Tampons benutzen, Tabletten
schlucken, bereit sein zur Produktion. Deshalb beneidete Agnes alte Männer; ihr schien, daß sie anders alterten: der Körper ihres Vaters hatte sich
langsam in seinen eigenen Schatten verwandelt, hatte sich entmateriali-
siert, war nur noch als reine, unvollkommen verkörperte Seele auf der
Erde geblieben. Demgegenüber wird der Körper der Frau immer mehr Körper, je unbrauchbarer, belastender und schwerer er wird; er gleicht einer
alten, abbruchreifen Manufaktur, bei der das Ich der Frau bis zum Schluß
als Wächter ausharren muß." (Frankfurt am Main 1994, S. 123 f.)
2 Deidre Bair, Simone de Beauvoir. Eine Biographie. München 1990, S. 46
3 ebd., S. 35
4 ebd., S. 19
5 Simone de Beauvoirs Schwester Hélène, zitiert nach: Deidre Bair, a.a.O.,
S. 158
6 Simone de Beauvoir, Alles in Allem. Reinbek 1974, S. 17
7 Axel Madsen, Jean-Paul Sartre und Simone de Beauvoir. Die Geschichte
einer ungewöhnlichen Liebe. Reinbek 1982, S. 15
8 Nathalie Sorokine, zitiert nach: Simone de Beauvoir, In den besten Jahren.
Reinbek 1961, S. 408 (Axel Madsen schreibt das Zitat irrtümlich Jean-Paul
Sartre zu: a.a.O., S. 45)
9 Simone de Beauvoir, Ein sanfter Tod. Reinbek 1984, S. 39 f.
10 Deidre Bair, a.a.O., S. 137
11 Claude Francis und Fernande Gontier, Simone de Beauvoir. Die Biographie. Weinheim / Berlin 1986, S. 98
12 französischer Philosoph, 1908–1961
13 Simone de Beauvoir, Alles in Allem, a.a.O., S. 17
14 zitiert nach: Deidre Bair, a.a.O., S. 173
15 Simone de Beauvoir, In den besten Jahren, a.a.O., S. 13
16 Josef Rattner, Simone de Beauvoir. In: Gerhard Danzer (Hg), Frauen in der
patriarchalischen Kultur. Literaturpsychologische Essays über Germaine
de Staël, Rahel Varnhagen, Karen Horney und Simone de Beauvoir. Würzburg 1997, S. 175
17 Toril Moi, Simone de Beauvoir. Die Psychographie einer Intellektuellen.
Frankfurt am Main 1997, S. 343 ff.
18 Josef Rattner, a.a.O., S. 175
19 Christiane Zehl Romero, Simone de Beauvoir. Reinbek 1978, S. 31. –
Vgl.: „Denn wenn das, was man eine freie Verbindung nennt, unter den
gleichen Bedingungen abläuft wie eine Ehe – wenn man also eine gemeinsamen Haushalt hat, wo regelmäßig gegessen wird –, wird die Frau
trotz allem die Frauenrolle spielen. Da gibt's zu einer Ehe kaum einen
Unterschied." (Simone de Beauvoir 1973 in einem Interview mit Alice
Schwarzer. In: Alice Schwarzer, Simone de Beauvoir heute. Gespräche aus
zehn Jahren. Reinbek 1983, S. 47)
20 Simone de Beauvoir, In den besten Jahren, a.a.O., S. 57 f.
21 Simone de Beauvoir, zitiert nach: Axel Madsen, a.a.O., S. 44
22 Sylvie le Bon über Simone de Beauvoir in einem Interview am 20. Oktober
1986; zitiert nach: Deidre Bair, a.a.O., S. 805

23 Walter van Rossum, Simone de Beauvoir und Jean-Paul Sartre. Die Kunst der Nähe. Berlin 1998, S. 122
24 Simone de Beauvoir, In den besten Jahren, a.a.O., S. 223. – Wie verwirrt und verzweifelt Simone de Beauvoir durch die Dreiecksbeziehung war, ahnt man beim Lesen ihres Romans „Sie kam und blieb". (Der Roman entstand in den Jahren 1938 bis 1941.) Pierre Labrousse und Françoise Miquel bilden ein unkonventionelles Paar, das sich vor allem durch die gemeinsame Arbeit am Theater verbunden fühlt. Dieses „allzu harmonische Verhältnis" (Toril Moi, a.a.O., S. 153) zerbricht, als Françoise begreift, daß Xavière – ein junges Mädchen, das bei ihnen ein- und ausgeht – kein reizendes Kind mehr ist, sondern ihre Rivalin. Aus der Verstrickung ihrer Gefühle befreit sich Françoise durch die Ermordung Xavières.
25 Toril Moi, a.a.O., S. 199
26 Walter van Rossum, a.a.O., S. 67; vgl.: Claude Francis und Fernande Gontier, a.a.O., S. 229
27 zitiert nach: Deidre Bair, a.a.O., S. 322
28 Walter van Rossum, a.a.O., S. 45
29 Simone de Beauvoir 1976 in einem Interview mit Alice Schwarzer; zitiert nach: Alice Schwarzer, a.a.O., S. 118
30 ebd., S. 78 f.
31 Simone de Beauvoir, Das andere Geschlecht, a.a.O., S. 383
32 Simone de Beauvoir am 27. Juli 1938 in einem Brief an Jean-Paul Sartre, zitiert nach Toril Moi, a.a.O., S. 199. – Simone de Beauvoir verarbeitete die Verführungsszene auch in ihrem Roman „Sie kam und blieb".
33 Brief vom 10. November 1939, zitiert nach: nach Toril Moi, a.a.O., S. 357
34 Simone de Beauvoir, zitiert nach: „Der Spiegel", Heft 27 vom 30. Juni 1997, S. 195
35 Axel Madsen, a.a.O., S. 10
36 Walter van Rossum, a.a.O., S. 13
37 Simone de Beauvoir, In den besten Jahren, a.a.O., S. 353
38 Morvan Lebesque, Camus. Reinbek 1963[4], S. 93
39 Richard Tarnas, Idee und Leidenschaft. Die Wege des westlichen Denkens. Frankfurt am Main 1997, S. 490
40 Willy Hochkeppel, Vom Existentialismus zur Analytischen Philosophie. In: Hilmar Hoffmann und Heinrich Klotz (Hg.), Die Kultur unseres Jahrhunderts. Band 4: 1945–1960. Düsseldorf / Wien / New York 1991, S. 48
41 Simone de Beauvoir, Auge um Auge. Artikel zu Politik, Moral und Literatur, 1945–1955, herausgegeben von Eva Groepler, Reinbek 1987, S. 53, 55
42 Morvan Lebesque, a.a.O., S. 69
43 zitiert nach: Alice Schwarzer, a.a.O., S. 47
44 Deidre Bair, a.a.O., S. 410
45 Simone de Beauvoir, Der Lauf der Dinge. Reinbek 1966, S. 183
46 Simone de Beauvoir, Das andere Geschlecht, a.a.O., S. 265
47 Alice Schwarzer in einem Film von Karl Heinz Götze und Ralph Quinke mit dem Titel „Simone de Beauvoir" (NDR / Arte 1997)
48 zitiert nach: Claude Francis und Fernande Gontier, a.a.O., S. 336
49 Josef Rattner, a.a.O., S. 198
50 Simone de Beauvoir, zitiert nach: Christiane Zehl Romero, a.a.O., S. 69
51 1997 veröffentlichte der Verlag Gallimard Simone de Beauvoirs Briefe an Nelson Algren: Simone de Beauvoir, Lettres à Nelson Algren. Un amour transatlantique 1947–1964.
52 Schlüsselroman über den moralischen Verfall der linksintellektuellen Führungsgruppe von Saint-Germain-des-Près aus dem Jahr 1954. Jean-Paul Sartre ist unschwer in der Romanfigur des Schriftstellers und Literaturprofessors Robert Dubreuilh wiederzuerkennen; die mit Dubreuilh verhei-

ratete Psychologin Anne entspricht Simone de Beauvoir, und als Vorbild für den amerikanischen Autor Lewis Brogan wählte die Autorin Nelson Algren – dem der Roman gewidmet ist.

53 Simone de Beauvoirs Autobiographie umfaßt vier Bände: Memoiren einer Tochter aus gutem Hause (1958), In den besten Jahren (1960), Der Lauf der Dinge (1963), Alles in allem (1972)
54 Simone de Beauvoir, Alles in allem, a.a.O., S. 465; vgl.: Barbara Sommerhoff, Frauenbewegung. Reinbek 1995, S. 33
55 Claude Francis und Fernande Gontier, a.a.O., S. 294
56 In Frankreich ist es nicht unüblich, eine Leiche zuerst zu beerdigen, sie dann zu exhumieren und einzuäschern.
57 Simone de Beauvoir, Ein sanfter Tod. Reinbek 1968
58 Simone de Beauvoir, Das Alter. Reinbek 1977
59 zitiert nach: Josef Rattner, a.a.O., S. 210
60 Margaret A. Simons, Simone de Beauvoir. In: Vera Eckstein (Hg.), Kultfrauen. Fünfzehn Begegnungen. Mannheim 1996, S. 43

Ulrike Meinhof, S. 206–233

1 Klaus Rainer Röhl, Die Genossin. Wien / München / Zürich 1975, S. 25 f.
2 Mario Krebs, Ulrike Meinhof. Ein Leben im Widerspruch. Reinbek 1995, S. 24 f.
3 Klaus Rainer Röhl, Die Genossin, a.a.O., S. 29
4 Mario Krebs, a.a.O., S. 24
5 Christa Rotzoll, Frauen und Zeiten. Porträts. Stuttgart 1987, S. 114 / München 1991, S. 91
6 Terence Prittie, Konrad Adenauer. Vier Epochen deutscher Geschichte. Frankfurt am Main 1976, S. 326
7 Klaus Rainer Röhl, Fünf Finger sind keine Faust. Köln 1974, S. 130
8 zitiert nach: „Der Spiegel", Heft 20/21, 17. Mai 1976, S. 14
9 Wenn ein demokratischer Staat ohne Vorwarnung militärisch angegriffen oder von einer Naturkatastrophe heimgesucht wird, bleibt keine Zeit, die notwendigen Entscheidungen kontrovers zu diskutieren. „In dieser Lage muß dem Gemeinwohl Vorrang eingeräumt und damit notfalls die individuelle Freiheit beschränkt werden." (Ernst Benda, Die Notstandsverfassung, München 1966, S. 11) Um der Exekutive im Fall eines Notstands die Möglichkeit zum raschen Handeln zu geben und zugleich einem Machtmißbrauch vorzubeugen, sprach sich der damalige Bundesinnenminister Gerhard Schröder am 9. Oktober 1955 dafür aus, entsprechende Ausnahmeregelungen in das Grundgesetz einzufügen. Die Gegner einer Notstandsgesetzgebung befürchteten, „daß im Grundgesetz verankerte Rechte ... eingeschränkt werden können und der demokratische Inhalt des Grundgesetzes ... verfälscht wird." (so die Gewerkschafter Fritz Thomas 1965, zitiert nach: Eric Waldman, Notstand und Demokratie, Boppard am Rhein 1968, S. 174) Vom 11. bis 13. Mai 1968 zogen 30 000 Gegner der Notstandsgesetze nach Bonn, aber sie konnten ebensowenig wie 53 SPD-Abgeordnete und das Häuflein der oppositionellen FDP-Abgeordneten verhindern, daß der Bundestag am 30. Mai 1968 die Grundgesetzänderungen mit der erforderlichen Zweidrittel-Mehrheit verabschiedete.
10 Ulrike Meinhof, Hitler in Euch. In: „konkret" 5/1966. –
In der Nacht vom 26./27. Oktober 1962 durchsuchten Beamte des Bundeskriminalamtes Büroräume des Hamburger Nachrichtenmagazins „Der Spiegel", das Franz Josef Strauß häufig kritisierte. Verhaftet wurden der Herausgeber Rudolf Augstein, die Chefredakteure Claus Jacobi und Johannes K. Engel, und – von der spanischen Polizei in Malaga – der stellvertretende Chefredakteur Conrad Ahlers. Bei den Ermittlungen ging es

um den angeblichen Verrat militärischer Staatsgeheimnisse in einem Artikel über ein NATO-Manöver mit dem Titel „Bedingt abwehrbereit". Die Vorwürfe ließen sich nicht aufrechterhalten; Innenminister Hermann Höcherl gab am 8. November zu, das Vorgehen sei „etwas außerhalb der Legalität" gewesen. Obwohl Verteidigungsminister Franz Josef Strauß beteuerte: „Ich habe mit der Sache nichts, im wahrsten Sinne des Wortes nichts zu tun!", stellte sich schließlich heraus, daß er den deutschen Militärattaché in Madrid angerufen hatte, um auf die Verhaftung Conrad Ahlers zu drängen. Am 19. November traten die fünf FDP-Minister zurück, um eine Neubildung der Bundesregierung zu erzwingen, und dem neuen Kabinett gehörte Franz Josef Strauß nicht mehr an. (Vgl.: Terence Prittie, a.a.O., S. 422 ff.; Bernt Engelmann, Das neue Schwarzbuch. Franz Josef Strauß. Köln 1980, S. 130 ff.)

11 Reinhard Opitz, zitiert nach: Mario Krebs, a.a.O., S. 64
12 Klaus Rainer Röhl, Die Genossin, a.a.O., S. 67
13 ebd., S. 167 f.
14 Mario Krebs, a.a.O., S. 98 (das Zitat im Zitat stammt von Jürgen Holtkamp)
15 ebd., S. 119
16 Ulrike Meinhof, zitiert nach: Mario Krebs, a.a.O., S. 44
17 ebd., S. 122
18 ebd., S. 125
19 Als Neomarxisten oder Neue Linke werden Philosophen bezeichnet, die sich nach dem Zweiten Weltkrieg zwar auf der Grundlage des Marxismus, aber in kritischer Distanz zu den kommunistischen Systemen und Parteiprogrammen mit gesellschaftlichen, wirtschaftlichen und politischen Fragen auseinandersetzten. In Deutschland waren dies Wolfgang Abendroth, Ernst Bloch, Theodor W. Adorno, Jürgen Habermas, Max Horkheimer, Herbert Marcuse u. a. (Vgl: Wolfgang Kraushaar (Hg.), Frankfurter Schule und Studentenbewegung. Von der Flaschenpost zum Molotowcocktail. 1946–1995. Hamburg 1998; Wolfgang Kraushaar, 1968. Das Jahr, das alles verändert hat. München 1998; Oskar Negt, Achtundsechzig. Politische Intellektuelle und die Macht. Hamburg 1998)
20 Ein Transparent mit dieser Aufschrift entfalteten Studenten bei der Feier anläßlich des Rektorenwechsels am 9. November 1967 in der Hamburger Universität.
21 Carlo Schmid, Erinnerungen. München 1981, S. 807
22 Hans-Dietrich Genscher, Erinnerungen. Berlin 1995, S. 173
23 „Der Abend", „Berliner Morgenpost"– zitiert nach: Mario Krebs, a.a.O., S. 130
24 Ulrike Meinhof, Napalm und Pudding. In: „konkret" 5/1967
25 So zitiert Stefan Aust den Berliner Polizeipräsidenten: Der Baader-Meinhof-Komplex. München 1989, S. 51
26 Peter Lauritzen, „Unruhige Jugend". Politisches Engagement von der APO bis zur „Friedensbewegung". In: Heinrich Pleticha (Hg.), Deutsche Geschichte. Band 12: Geteiltes Deutschland. Nach 1945. Gütersloh 1987, S. 360
27 Stefan Aust, a.a.O., S. 63 f.
28 zitiert nach: Hermann Glaser, Die Kulturgeschichte der Bundesrepublik Deutschland. Band 3: Zwischen Protest und Anpassung. 1968–1989. Frankfurt am Main 1990, S. 299; Stefan Aust, a.a.O., S. 42 f. – Fritz Teufel und Rainer Langhans wurden wegen „Aufforderung zur Brandstiftung" angeklagt, aber am 22. März 1968 freigesprochen.
29 Ulrike Meinhof, Warenhausbrandstiftung. In: „konkret" 14/1968
30 Christa Rotzoll, a.a.O., S. 114 / S. 91
31 Ulrike Meinhof zu Renate Riemeck, zitiert nach: Mario Krebs, a.a.O., S. 139

32 Ulrike Meinhof, Kolumnismus. In: „konkret" 21/1968
33 Mario Krebs, a.a.O., S. 182f.
34 Ulrike Meinhof 1969 in einem Fernseh-Interview, zitiert nach: Mario Krebs, a.a.O., S. 180
35 ebd.
36 Renate Riemeck in einem Interview mit Alice Schwarzer, zitiert nach: Alice Schwarzer, Warum gerade sie? Weibliche Rebellen. Begegnungen mit berühmten Frauen. Frankfurt am Main 1992², S. 266
37 Stefan Aust, a.a.O., S. 18
38 Butz Peters, RAF. Terrorismus in Deutschland. Stuttgart 1991, S. 81
39 „Der Spiegel", Heft 25 vom 15. Juni 1970, S. 71ff.
40 ebd.
41 1958 im Untergrund gegründete Palästinenser-Organisation, heute die stärkste Gruppierung innerhalb der Organisation zur Befreiung Palästinas (PLO).
42 Mario Krebs, a.a.O., S. 218
43 Klaus Rainer Röhl, Linke Lebenslügen. Eine überfällige Abrechnung. Frankfurt am Main / Berlin 1994, S. 83
44 Palestine Liberation Organization: Organisation zur Befreiung Palästinas
45 Mario Krebs, a.a.O., S. 219
46 Ingrid Schubert, Monika Berberich, Brigitte Asdonk und Irene Goergens
47 Hans Leyendecker, Der Dandy und der Polizist. Dorothea Hauser über Horst Herold und Andreas Baader. Süddeutsche Zeitung, 27. Oktober 1997
48 Klaus Rainer Röhl, Linke Lebenslügen. a.a.O., S. 92
49 Zumeist wird angenommen, daß es sich bei dem Signet um eine Kalaschnikow Ak-47 handelt. Tatsächlich aber sei eine Heckler & Koch MP 5 mit Schulterstütze abgebildet, meint Dirk Growe in einem Leserbrief an die Süddeutsche Zeitung (2. August 1997).
50 Horst Mahler, Sonst kommt die Moral. Für das Verstehen der RAF fehlen die Begriffe. Süddeutsche Zeitung, 27. April 1998
51 Helmut Schmidt in dem Film „Todesspiel" (Regie: Heinrich Breloer, 1997)
52 zitiert nach: Gabriele Dietz, Maruta Schmidt, Anne Honkomb, Elvira Schmiel (Redaktion), Klamm, Heimlich & Freunde. Die siebziger Jahre. Berlin 1987, S. 120
53 ebd., S. 119
54 Hans-Dietrich Genscher, a.a.O., S. 139
55 Ulrike Meinhof, hier zitiert nach: Peter Brückner, Ulrike Marie Meinhof und die deutschen Verhältnisse. Berlin 1995, S. 152f. – „Der Spiegel" (Heft 20-21/1976 vom 17. Mai 1976, S. 16) datiert diesen Brief auf den 231. Tag ihrer Haft in Köln-Ossendorf.
56 Brief vom Oktober 1973, zitiert nach: Klaus Rainer Röhl, Linke Lebenslügen. a.a.O., S. 107f.
57 ebd., S. 109
58 Axel Madsen, Jean-Paul Sartre und Simone de Beauvoir. Die Geschichte einer ungewöhnlichen Liebe. Reinbek 1982, S. 289
59 Stefan Aust, a.a.O., S. 323f.
60 zitiert nach dem authentischen Film „Stammheim" (Regie: Reinhard Hauff, Drehbuch: Stefan Aust, 1986)
61 Klaus Rainer Röhl, Linke Lebenslügen, a.a.O., S. 114
62 Der Tod Ulrike Meinhofs. Bericht der Internationalen Untersuchungskommission. Tübingen 1979, Reprint: Münster 1996, S. 5f; vgl. Stefan Aust, a.a.O., S. 376ff; Mario Krebs, a.a.O., S. 264ff.
63 Todesanzeige, zitiert nach: Im Fadenkreuz. Deutschland und die RAF. Die Familien. Ein Film von Sabine Zurmühl (SFB / ORB 1997). (Im Original steht „Rechtshilfefond".)
64 zitiert nach: Stefan Aust, a.a.O., S. 381

65 Leona Siebenschön, ... und natürlich kann geschossen werden. In: Bärbel Becker (Hg.), Wild women. Furien, Flittchen, Flintenweiber. Berlin 1992, S. 136
66 Klaus Wagenbach in seiner Grabrede für Ulrike Meinhof am 15. Mai 1976; zitiert nach: Peter Brückner, a.a.O., S. 197ff.
67 zitiert nach: Stefan Aust, a.a.O., S. 384
68 zitiert nach: Mario Krebs, a.a.O., Umschlag

Bildnachweis

LETTERA A UN BAMBINO MAI NATO

Oriana Fallaci

Lettera
a un bambino
mai nato

Rizzoli

ISBN 88-17-85371-2

Trentasettesima edizione riveduta e corretta dall'autore: settembre 1993
Trentottesima edizione: novembre 1993
Trentanovesima edizione: gennaio 1994
Quarantesima edizione: maggio 1995
Quarantunesima edizione: febbraio 1996
Quarantaduesima edizione: maggio 1996
Quarantatreesima edizione: marzo 1997
Quarantaquattresima edizione: giugno 1997

A chi non teme il dubbio
a chi si chiede i perché
senza stancarsi e a costo
di soffrire di morire
A chi si pone il dilemma
di dare la vita o negarla
questo libro è dedicato
da una donna
per tutte le donne

Stanotte ho saputo che c'eri: una goccia di vita scappata dal nulla. Me ne stavo con gli occhi spalancati nel buio e d'un tratto, in quel buio, s'è acceso un lampo di certezza: sì, c'eri. Esistevi. È stato come sentirsi colpire in petto da una fucilata. Mi si è fermato il cuore. E quando ha ripreso a battere con tonfi sordi, cannonate di sbalordimento, mi sono accorta di precipitare in un pozzo dove tutto era incerto e terrorizzante. Ora eccomi qui, chiusa a chiave dentro una paura che mi bagna il volto, i capelli, i pensieri. E in essa mi perdo. Cerca di capire: non è paura degli altri. Io non mi curo degli altri. Non è paura di Dio. Io non credo in Dio. Non è paura del dolore. Io non temo il dolore. È paura di te, del caso che ti ha strappato al nulla, per agganciarti al mio ventre. Non sono mai stata pronta ad accoglierti, anche se ti ho molto aspettato. Mi son sempre posta l'atroce domanda: e se nascere non ti piacesse? E se un giorno tu me lo rimproverassi gridando "Chi ti ha chiesto di mettermi al mondo, perché mi ci hai messo, perché?". La vita è una tale fatica, bambino. È una guerra che si ripete ogni giorno, e i suoi momenti di gioia sono parentesi brevi che si pagano un prezzo crudele. Come faccio a sapere che non sarebbe giusto buttarti via, come faccio a intuire che non vuoi essere restituito al silenzio? Non puoi mica parlarmi. La tua goccia di vita è soltanto un nodo di cellule appena iniziate. Forse non è nemmeno vita ma possibilità di vita. Eppure darei tanto perché tu potessi aiutarmi con un cenno, un indizio. La mia mamma sostiene che glielo detti, che per questo mi mise al mondo.

La mia mamma, vedi, non mi voleva. Ero incominciata per sbaglio, in un attimo di altrui distrazione. E perché non nascessi ogni sera scioglieva nell'acqua una medicina. Poi la beveva, piangendo. La bevve fino alla sera in cui mi mossi, dentro il suo ventre, e le tirai un calcio per dirle di non buttarmi via. Lei stava portando il bicchiere alle labbra. Subito lo allontanò e ne rovesciò il contenuto per terra. Qualche mese dopo mi rotolavo vittoriosa nel sole, e se ciò sia stato bene o male non so. Quando sono felice penso che sia stato bene, quando sono infelice penso che sia stato male. Però, anche quando sono infelice, penso che mi dispiacerebbe non essere nata perché nulla è peggiore del nulla. Io, te lo ripeto, non temo il dolore. Esso nasce con noi, cresce con noi, ad esso ci si abitua come al fatto d'avere due braccia e due gambe. Io, in fondo, non temo neanche di morire: perché se uno muore vuol dire che è nato, che è uscito dal niente. Io temo il niente, il non esserci, il dover dire di non esserci stato, sia pure per caso, sia pure per sbaglio, sia pure per l'altrui distrazione. Molte donne si chiedono: mettere al mondo un figlio, perché? Perché abbia fame, perché abbia freddo, perché venga tradito ed offeso, perché muoia ammazzato alla guerra o da una malattia? E negano la speranza che la sua fame sia saziata, che il suo freddo sia scaldato, che la fedeltà e il rispetto gli siano amici, che viva a lungo per tentar di cancellare le malattie e la guerra. Forse hanno ragione loro. Ma il niente è da preferirsi al soffrire? Io perfino nelle pause in cui piango sui miei fallimenti, le mie delusioni, i miei strazi, concludo che soffrire sia da preferirsi al niente. E se allargo questo alla vita, al dilemma nascere o non nascere, finisco con l'esclamare che nascere è meglio di non nascere. Tuttavia è lecito imporre tale ragionamento anche a te? Non è come metterti al mondo per me stessa e basta? Non mi interessa metterti al mondo per me stessa e basta. Tanto più che non ho affatto bisogno di te.

— 2 —

Non mi hai tirato calci, non mi hai inviato risposte. E come avresti potuto? Ci sei da così poco: se ne chiedessi conferma al medico, sorriderebbe di scherno. Ma ho deciso per te: nascerai. L'ho deciso dopo averti visto in fotografia. Non era proprio la tua fotografia, evidente: era quella di un qualsiasi embrione di tre settimane, pubblicata su un giornale insieme a un reportage sul formarsi della vita. E, mentre la guardavo, la paura m'è passata: con la stessa rapidità con cui m'era venuta. Sembravi un fiore misterioso, un'orchidea trasparente. In cima si scorgeva una specie di testa con le due protuberanze che diverranno il cervello. Più in basso, una specie di cavità che diverrà la bocca. A tre settimane sei quasi invisibile, spiega la didascalia. Due millimetri e mezzo. Eppure cresce in te un accenno di occhi, qualcosa che assomiglia a una spina dorsale, a un sistema nervoso, a uno stomaco, a un fegato, a intestini, a polmoni. Il tuo cuore è già fatto, ed è grande: in proporzione, nove volte più grande del mio. Pompa sangue e batte regolarmente dal diciottesimo giorno: potrei buttarti via? Che m'importa se sei incominciato per caso o per sbaglio, anche il mondo in cui ci troviamo non incominciò per caso e forse per sbaglio? Alcuni sostengono che in principio non c'era nulla fuorché una gran calma, un gran silenzio immobile, poi si verificò una scintilla, uno strappo, e ciò che non era fu. Allo strappo seguirono presto altri strappi: sempre più imprevisti, sempre più insensati, più ignari delle conseguenze. E tra le conseguenze sbocciò una cellula, anche lei per caso, forse per sbaglio, che subito si moltiplicò a milioni, a miliardi, finché nacquero gli alberi e i pesci e gli uomini. Tu credi che qualcuno si ponesse un dilemma prima dello scoppio o prima della cellula? Credi che si domandasse se gli sarebbe piaciuto o no? Credi che si preoccupasse della sua fame, del suo freddo, della sua infelicità? Io lo escludo. Anche se il qualcuno fosse esistito, ad esempio un Dio paragonabile all'inizio dell'inizio, al di là del tempo e al di là dello spazio, io temo che non si sarebbe curato del bene e del male. Tutto avvenne perché poteva avvenire, quindi doveva avvenire, secondo una prepotenza che era l'unica prepotenza legittima. E lo stesso discorso vale per te. Mi prendo la responsabilità della scelta.

Me la prendo senza egoismo, bambino: metterti al mondo, lo giuro, non mi diverte. Non mi vedo camminare per strada col ventre gonfio, non mi vedo allattarti e lavarti e insegnarti a parlare. Sono una donna che lavora: ho tanti altri impegni, curiosità. Te l'ho già detto che non ho bisogno di te. Però ti porterò avanti lo stesso, che ti piaccia o no. Te la imporrò lo stesso quella prepotenza che fu imposta anche a me, e ai miei genitori, ai miei nonni, ai nonni dei miei nonni: su fino al primo essere umano partorito da un essere umano, che gli piacesse o no. Probabilmente, se a costui o a costei fosse stato concesso di scegliere, si sarebbe impaurito e avrebbe risposto non voglio nascere, no. Ma nessuno gli chiese un parere, e così nacque e visse e morì dopo aver partorito un altro essere umano cui non aveva chiesto di scegliere, e costui fece lo stesso, per milioni di anni fino a noi, e ognivolta fu una prepotenza senza la quale non esisteremmo. Coraggio, bambino. Pensi che il seme di un albero non abbia bisogno di coraggio quando buca la terra e germoglia? Basta un colpo di vento a staccarlo, la zampina di un topo a schiacciarlo. Eppure lui germoglia e tiene duro e cresce gettando altri semi. E diventa un bosco. Se un giorno griderai "Perché mi hai messo al mondo, perché?" io ti risponderò: "Ho fatto ciò che fanno e hanno fatto gli alberi, per milioni e milioni di anni prima di me, e credevo di fare bene".

L'importante è non cambiare idea ricordando che gli esseri umani non sono alberi, che la sofferenza di un essere umano è mille volte più grande della sofferenza di un albero perché è cosciente, che a nessuno di noi giova diventare un bosco, che non tutti i semi degli alberi generano alberi: nella stragrande maggioranza vanno perduti... Un simile voltafaccia è possibile, bambino: la nostra logica è piena di contraddizioni. Appena affermi qualcosa, ne vedi il contrario. E magari ti accorgi che il contrario è valido quanto ciò che affermavi. Il mio ragionamento di oggi potrebb'essere rovesciato così, con uno schiocco di dita. Infatti ecco: mi sento già confusa, disorientata. Forse perché non posso confidarmi con nessuno al di fuori di te. Sono una donna che ha scelto di vivere sola. Tuo padre non sta con me. E non me ne dolgo sebbene, ognitanto, il mio sguardo cerchi la porta da cui egli uscì, col suo passo deciso, senza che io lo fermassi, quasi non avessimo più nulla da dirci.

— 3 —

Ti ho portato dal medico. Più che la conferma, volevo qualche consiglio. Per risposta ha scosso la testa dicendo che sono impaziente, che non può ancora pronunciarsi, ripassi tra quindici giorni, pronta a scoprire che eri un prodotto della mia fantasia. Tornerò solo per dimostrargli che è un ignorante. Tutta la sua scienza non vale il mio intuito, e come fa un uomo a capire una donna che sostiene anzitempo di aspettare un bambino? Un uomo non resta incinto e, a proposito, dimmi: è un vantaggio o una limitazione? Fino a ieri mi sembrava un vantaggio, anzi un privilegio. Oggi mi sembra una limitazione, anzi una povertà. V'è un che di glorioso nel chiudere dentro il proprio corpo un'altra vita, nel sapersi due anziché uno. A momenti ti invade addirittura un senso di trionfo e, nella serenità che accompagna il trionfo, niente ti preoccupa: né il dolore fisico che dovrai affrontare, né il lavoro che dovrai sacrificare, né la libertà che dovrai perdere. Sarai un uomo o una donna?

Vorrei che tu fossi una donna. Vorrei che tu provassi un giorno ciò che provo io: non sono affatto d'accordo con la mia mamma la quale pensa che nascere donna sia una disgrazia. La mia mamma, quando è molto infelice, sospira: «Ah, se fossi nata uomo!». Lo so: il nostro è un mondo fabbricato dagli uomini per gli uomini, la loro dittatura è così antica che si estende perfino al linguaggio. Si dice uomo per dire uomo e donna, si dice bambino per dire bambino e bambina, si dice figlio per dire figlio e figlia, si dice omicidio per indicar l'assassinio di un uomo e di una donna. Nelle leggende che i maschi hanno inventato per spiegare la vita, la prima creatura non è una donna: è un uomo chiamato Adamo. Eva arriva dopo, per divertirlo e combinare guai. Nei dipinti che adornano le loro chiese, Dio è un vecchio con la barba bianca mai una vecchia coi capelli bianchi. E tutti i loro eroi sono maschi: da quel Prometeo che scoprì il fuoco a quell'Icaro che tentò di volare, su fino a quel Gesù che dichiarano figlio del Padre e dello Spirito Santo: quasi che la donna da cui fu partorito fosse un'incubatrice o una balia. Eppure, o proprio per questo, essere donna è così affascinante. È un'avventura che richiede un tale coraggio, una sfida che non annoia mai. Avrai tante cose da intraprendere se nascerai donna. Per incominciare, avrai da batterti per sostenere che se Dio esistesse potrebbe anche essere una vecchia coi capelli bianchi o una bella ragazza. Poi avrai da batterti per spiegare che il peccato non nacque il giorno in cui Eva colse la mela: quel giorno nacque una splendida virtù chiamata disubbidienza. Infine avrai da batterti per dimostrare che dentro il tuo corpo liscio e rotondo c'è un'intelligenza che chiede d'essere ascoltata. Essere mamma non è un mestiere. Non è neanche un dovere. È solo un diritto fra tanti diritti. Faticherai tanto a ripeterlo. E spesso, quasi sempre, perderai. Ma non dovrai scoraggiarti. Battersi è molto più bello che vincere, viaggiare è molto più divertente che arrivare: quando sei arrivato o hai vinto, avverti un gran vuoto. Sì, spero che tu sia una donna: non badare se ti chiamo bambino. E spero che tu non dica mai ciò che dice mia madre. Io non l'ho mai detto.

— 4 —

Ma se nascerai uomo io sarò contenta lo stesso. E forse di più perché ti saranno risparmiate tante umiliazioni, tante servitù, tanti abusi. Se nascerai uomo, ad esempio, non dovrai temere d'essere violentato nel buio di una strada. Non dovrai servirti di un bel viso per essere accettato al primo sguardo, di un bel corpo per nascondere la tua intelligenza. Non subirai giudizi malvagi quando dormirai con chi ti piace, non ti sentirai dire che il peccato nacque il giorno in cui cogliesti una mela. Faticherai molto meno. Potrai batterti più comodamente per sostenere che, se Dio esistesse, potrebb'essere anche una vecchia coi capelli bianchi o una bella ragazza. Potrai disubbidire senza venir deriso, amare senza svegliarti una notte con la sensazione di precipitare in un pozzo, difenderti senza finire insultato. Naturalmente ti toccheranno altre schiavitù, altre ingiustizie: neanche per un uomo la vita è facile, sai. Poiché avrai muscoli più saldi, ti chiederanno di portare fardelli più pesi, ti imporranno arbitrarie responsabilità. Poiché avrai la barba, rideranno se tu piangi e perfino se hai bisogno di tenerezza. Poiché avrai una coda davanti, ti ordineranno di uccidere o essere ucciso alla guerra ed esigeranno la tua complicità per tramandare la tirannia che instaurarono nelle caverne. Eppure, o proprio per questo, essere un uomo sarà un'avventura altrettanto meravigliosa: un'impresa che non ti deluderà mai. Almeno lo spero perché, se nascerai uomo, spero che tu diventi un uomo come io l'ho sempre sognato: dolce coi deboli, feroce coi prepotenti, generoso con chi ti vuol bene, spietato con chi ti comanda. Infine, nemico di chiunque racconti che i Gesù sono figli del Padre e dello Spirito Santo: non della donna che li partorì.

Bambino, io sto cercando di spiegarti che essere un uomo non significa avere una coda davanti: significa essere una persona. E anzitutto, a me, interessa che tu sia una persona. È una parola stupenda, la parola persona, perché non pone limiti a un uomo o a una donna, non traccia frontiere tra chi ha la coda e chi non ce l'ha. Del resto il filo che divide chi ha la coda da chi non ce l'ha, è un filo talmente sottile: in pratica si riduce alla facoltà di poter crescere o no una creatura nel ventre. Il cuore e il cervello non hanno sesso. E neanche il comportamento. Se sarai una persona di cuore e di cervello, ricordalo, io non starò certo tra quelli che ti ingiungeranno di comportarti in un modo o nell'altro in quanto maschio o femmina. Ti chiederò solo di sfruttare bene il miracolo d'essere nato, di non cedere mai alla viltà. È una bestia che sta sempre in agguato, la viltà. Ci morde tutti, ogni giorno, e son pochi coloro che non si lasciano sbranare da lei. In nome della prudenza, in nome della convenienza, a volte della saggezza. Vili fino a quando un rischio li minaccia, gli umani diventan spavaldi dopo che il rischio è passato. Non dovrai evitare il rischio, mai: anche se la paura ti frena. Venire al mondo è già un rischio. Quello di pentirsi, poi, d'esserci venuti.

Forse è troppo presto per parlarti così. Forse dovrei tacerti per ora le brutture e le malinconie, forse dovrei raccontarti un mondo di innocenze e gaiezze. Ma sarebbe come attirarti in un inganno, bambino. Sarebbe come indurti a credere che la vita è un tappeto morbido sul quale si può camminare scalzi e non una strada di sassi. Sassi contro cui si inciampa, si cade, ci si ferisce. Sassi contro cui bisogna proteggerci con scarpe di ferro. Ma neanche questo basta perché, mentre proteggi i piedi, c'è sempre qualcuno che raccoglie una pietra per tirartela in testa e... E per oggi ho finito, figlio mio, figlia mia. La lezione ti è giunta? Chissà che direbbero alcuni se mi ascoltassero. Mi accuserebbero d'essere pazza o semplicemente crudele? Ho guardato la tua ultima fotografia e, a cinque settimane, sei lungo meno di un centimetro. Stai cambiando molto. Più che un fiore misterioso ora sembri una graziosissima larva, anzi un pesciolino cui spuntano svelte le pinne. Quattro pinne che diverranno gambe e braccia. Gli occhi sono già due minuscoli granelli neri, con un cerchio

intorno, e in fondo al corpo hai una codina! La didascalia
dice che in questo periodo è quasi impossibile distinguerti
dall'embrione di un qualsiasi mammifero: se tu fossi un
gatto, appariresti più o meno ciò che sei ora. Infatti il
volto non c'è. Non c'è nemmeno il cervello. Io ti parlo,
bambino, e tu non lo sai. Nel buio che t'avvolge ignori addirittura d'esistere: potrei buttarti via e non sapresti mai
che t'ho buttato via. Non sapresti mai se ti ho fatto un
torto o un regalo.

— 5 —

Ieri ho avuto un cedimento di malumore. Devi scu-
sare il discorso sul fatto che potrei buttarti via e tu non
sapresti nemmeno se ti ho fatto un torto o un regalo. È un
discorso e basta. La mia scelta non è affatto mutata anche
se, intorno a me, ciò solleva sorpresa. Stanotte ho parlato
con tuo padre. Gli ho detto che c'eri. Gliel'ho detto al telefono perché si trova lontano e, a giudicare da quello che
ho udito, non gli ho dato una buona notizia. Ho udito,
anzitutto, un profondo silenzio: neanche fosse caduta la
comunicazione. E poi ho udito una voce che balbettava,
roca: «Quanto ci vorrà?». Gli ho risposto con allegria:
«Nove mesi, suppongo. Anzi meno di otto, ormai». E
allora la voce ha smesso d'essere roca per diventare fredda:
«Parlo di denaro». «Che denaro?» ho replicato. «Il denaro
per disfarsene, no?» Sì, ha detto proprio «disfarsene».
Neanche tu fossi un fagotto. E quando, più serenamente
possibile, gli ho spiegato che avevo tutt'altra intenzione, s'è
perduto in un lungo ragionamento dove le preghiere si al-
ternavano ai consigli, i consigli alle minacce, le minacce alle
lusinghe. «Pensa alla tua carriera, considera le responsabilità, un giorno potresti pentirtene, cosa diranno gli altri.»

Io sorridevo, quasi divertita. Però mi sono divertita assai meno quando, incoraggiato dal fatto che ascoltassi zitta, ha concluso che la spesa potevamo sostenerla a metà: dopotutto eravamo «colpevoli entrambi». Mi ha colto la nausea. Mi sono vergognata per lui. E ho abbassato il ricevitore pensando che un tempo lo amavo. Lo amavo? Un giorno io e te dovremo discutere un poco su questa faccenda chiamata amore. Perché, onestamente, non ho ancora capito di cosa si tratti. Il mio sospetto è che si tratti di un imbroglio gigantesco, inventato per tener buona la gente e distrarla. Di amore parlano i preti, i cartelloni pubblicitari, i letterati, i politici, coloro che fanno all'amore, e parlando di amore, presentandolo come toccasana di ogni tragedia, feriscono e tradiscono e ammazzano l'anima e il corpo. Io la odio questa parola che è ovunque e in tutte le lingue. Amo-camminare, amo-bere, amo-fumare, amo-la-libertà, amo-il-mio-amante, amo-mio-figlio. Io cerco di non usarla mai, di non chiedermi nemmeno se ciò che turba la mia mente e il mio cuore è la cosa che chiamano amore. Infatti non so se ti amo. Non penso a te in termini di amore. Penso a te in termini di vita. E tuo padre, guarda: più ci penso, più credo di non averlo mai amato. L'ho ammirato, l'ho desiderato, ma amato no. Così coloro che vennero prima di lui, fantasmi deludenti di una ricerca sempre fallita. Fallita? A qualcosa servì, dopotutto: a capire che nulla minaccia la tua libertà quanto il misterioso trasporto che una creatura prova verso un'altra creatura, ad esempio un uomo verso una donna, o una donna verso un uomo. Non vi sono né cinghie né catene né sbarre che costringano a una schiavitù più cieca, a un oblio altrettanto cieco dei tuoi diritti, della tua dignità, della tua libertà. Guai se ti regali a qualcuno in nome di quel trasporto. Come un cane che annaspa nell'acqua cerchi invano di raggiungere una riva che non esiste, la riva che ha nome Amare ed Essere Amato, e finisci neutralizzato deriso deluso. Nel caso migliore finisci col chiederti cosa ti spinse a buttarti nell'acqua: lo scontento di te stesso, la speranza di trovare in un altro ciò che non vedevi in te stesso? La paura della solitudine, della noia, del silenzio? Il bisogno di possedere ed essere posseduto? Secondo alcuni è questo l'amore. Ma io temo che sia molto meno: una fame che, una volta saziata, ti lascia una specie di indigestione. E tuttavia, tuttavia, deve pur esserci qualcosa in grado di rivelarmi il significato di quella maledetta parola, bambino. Deve pur esserci qualcosa in grado di farmi scoprire cos'è, e che c'è. Ne ho tanto bisogno, tanta fame. Ed è in questo bisogno che penso: forse è vero ciò che ha sempre sostenuto mia madre. L'amore è ciò che una donna sente per suo figlio quando lo prende tra le braccia e lo sente solo, inerme, indifeso. Almeno fino a quando è inerme, indifeso, lui non ti insulta, non ti delude. E se toccasse a te farmi scoprire il significato di quelle cinque lettere assurde? Proprio a te che mi rubi a me stessa e mi succhi il sangue e mi respiri il respiro?

Un indizio esiste. Gli innamorati lontani si consolano con le fotografie. Ed io ho sempre in mano le tue fotografie. È diventata ormai un'ossessione. Appena rientro in casa agguanto quel giornale, calcolo i giorni, la tua età, e ti cerco. Oggi hai compiuto sei settimane. Eccoti a sei settimane, ripreso di spalle. Come sei diventato bellino! Non più pesce, non più larva, non più cosa informe, sembri già una creatura: con quel testone calvo e rosa. La spina dorsale è ben definita, una striscia bianca e sicura nel mezzo, le tue braccia non sono più protuberanze confuse né pinne ma ali. Ti sono spuntate le ali!

Viene voglia di accarezzarle, accarezzarti. Come si sta lì nell'uovo ? Secondo le fotografie, sei sospeso in un diafano uovo che ricorda le uova di cristallo dentro cui si mette una rosa. Al posto della rosa, tu. Dall'uovo parte un cordone che si conclude in una palla bianca, lontana, con venature di rosso e macchie di azzurro. Vista così sembra la Terra, osservata da migliaia e migliaia di miglia. Sì, è proprio come se dalla Terra partisse un filo interminabile, lungo quanto l'idea della vita, e da quelle distanze remote giungesse a te. In modo così logico, così sensato. Ma come fanno a dire che l'essere umano è un incidente della natura ?

Il medico aveva detto di tornare da lui dopo sei settimane. Domani ci vado. E aghi di inquietudine mi bucano l'anima alternando vampate di gioia.

— 6 —

Con un tono che oscillava tra il solenne e l'allegro, ha alzato un foglietto ed ha detto: «Congratulazioni, signora». Automaticamente ho corretto: «Signorina». È stato come tirargli uno schiaffo. Solennità ed allegria sono scomparse, e fissandomi con voluta indifferenza, ha risposto: «Ah!». Poi ha preso la penna, ha cancellato signora e ha scritto signorina. Così, in una stanza gelidamente bianca, attraverso la voce di un uomo gelidamente vestito di bianco, la Scienza mi ha dato l'annuncio ufficiale che c'eri. Non mi ha impressionato per niente, visto che lo sapevo già e molto prima di lei. Però mi ha sorpreso che si sottolineasse il mio stato civile e si portasse quella correzione sul foglio. Aveva l'aria di un'avvisaglia, di una complicazione a venire. Perfino il modo in cui subito dopo la Scienza mi ha detto di spogliarmi e stendermi sul lettuccio non era cordiale. Sia il medico che l'infermiera si comportavano come se gli fossi antipatica. Non mi guardavano in faccia. In compenso si scambiavano occhiate per dirsi chissacché. Quando sono stata sul lettuccio, l'infermiera s'è adirata perché non avevo divaricato le gambe e non le avevo appoggiate sulle due stampelle di metallo. Lo ha fatto lei, con fastidio, e dicendo: «Qui, qui!». Io mi sentivo ridicola e vagamente oscena. Le sono stata grata quando mi ha coperto il ventre con un asciugamano. Ma allora è successo il peggio perché il medico ha infilato un guanto di gomma e ha pigiato, frugato, pigiato di nuovo, quasi volesse schiacciarti perché non ero sposata. Infine lo ha tirato fuori e ha sentenziato: «Tutto bene, tutto regolare». Mi ha anche dato alcuni consigli: che non fumi troppo, non compia sforzi eccessivi, non mi lavi con acqua troppo calda, non mi proponga soluzioni criminali. «Criminali?» ho chiesto, stupita. E lui: «La legge lo proibisce. Ricordi!». Per rafforzar la minaccia mi ha perfino prescritto alcune pillole di luteina e mi ha ingiunto di tornare da lui ogni quindici giorni. Me l'ha ingiunto senza un sorriso, prima di informarmi che il pagamento si regolava alla cassa. Quanto all'infermiera, non mi ha salutato nemmeno. E, mentre chiudeva la porta, m'è parso che scotesse la testa con disapprovazione.

Temo che dovrai abituarti a simili cose. Nel mondo in cui ti accingi ad entrare, e malgrado i discorsi sui tempi che mutano, una donna che aspetta un figlio senza esser sposata è vista il più delle volte come una irresponsabile. Nel migliore dei casi, come una stravagante, una provocatrice. O un'eroina. Mai come una mamma uguale alle altre. Il farmacista da cui ho comprato le pillole di luteina mi conosce e sa bene che non sono sposata. Quando gli ho dato la prescrizione, ha alzato le sopracciglia e mi ha fissato con sgomento. Dopo il farmacista sono andata dal sarto, per ordinargli un cappotto. Si avvicina l'inverno, voglio che tu stia al caldo. Con la bocca piena di spilli per appuntarmi addosso il modello di tela, il sarto ha incominciato a prender le misure. E quando gli ho spiegato che doveva prenderle molto abbondanti perché ero incinta, d'inverno sarei stata grossa, è violentemente arrossito. Ha spalancato la bocca e ho temuto che inghiottisse gli spilli. Non li ha inghiottiti, graziaddio, ma gli son caduti per terra. Gli è caduto anche il metro, e ho provato come un dispiacere ad imporgli tanto imbarazzo. Lo stesso col commendatore. Che ci piaccia o no, il commendatore è colui che compra il mio lavoro e ci dà i soldi per vivere: sarebbe stato disonesto non informarlo che tra qualche mese non potrò più lavorare. Così sono entrata nel suo ufficio e l'ho informato. È rimasto senza fiato. Poi s'è ripreso e ha balbettato che rispettava la mia decisione, anzi mi ammirava moltissimo per averla presa, mi considerava assai coraggiosa, però sarebbe stato opportuno non raccontarlo a tutti. « Una cosa è parlarne tra noi, gente di mondo, e una cosa è parlarne con chi non può capire. Tanto più che lei potrebbe cambiare idea, no ? » Ha insistito parecchio su questa faccenda del cambiare idea. Almeno fino al terzo mese avrei avuto tutto il tempo di ripensarci, diceva, e ripensarci avrebbe dimostrato saggezza : la mia carriera era così bene avviata, perché interromperla per un sentimentalismo ? Ci pensassi bene, non si trattava neanche di interromperla per pochi mesi o un anno. Si trattava di mutare l'intero corso della mia vita : non avrei più potuto disporre di me stessa. E non dimentichiamo che la ditta mi aveva lanciato puntando proprio sulla disponibilità che offrivo. Lui teneva in serbo tanti bei progetti per me. Davvero, se ci ripensavo, non avevo che da dirlo. E mi avrebbe aiutato.

Tuo padre ha telefonato una seconda volta. Gli tremava la voce. Voleva sapere se ho avuto conferma. Gli ho risposto di sì. Mi ha chiesto una seconda volta quando avrei "sistemato la cosa". Ho posato una seconda volta il ricevitore senza ascoltarlo. Quel che non capisco è perché, quando una donna annuncia d'essere legalmente incinta, tutti si mettono a farle feste e toglierle di mano i pacchetti e supplicarla di non strapazzarsi, restare tranquilla. Che bella cosa, felicitazioni, si accomodi qui, si riposi. Con me rimangono fermi, zitti, o fanno discorsi sull'abortire. La diresti una congiura, un complotto per dividerci. E vi sono momenti in cui mi sento inquieta, in cui mi chiedo chi vincerà: noi o loro? Forse è per via di quella telefonata. Ha rinverdito amarezze che credevo dimenticate, offese che credevo superate. Quelle inflittemi dai fantasmi grazie a cui compresi che l'amore è un imbroglio. Le ferite son chiuse, le cicatrici appena visibili, ma una telefonata così basta a farle dolorare di nuovo. Come vecchie ossa rotte quando cambia il tempo.

— 7 —

Il tuo universo è l'uovo dentro il quale galleggi, rannicchiato e quasi privo di peso, da sei settimane e mezzo. Lo chiamano sacco amniotico e il liquido che lo riempie è una soluzione salina che serve a non farti combattere con la forza di gravità, a proteggerti dai colpi provocati dai miei movimenti, ed anche a nutrirti. Fino a quattro giorni fa, anzi, era la tua sola fonte di nutrimento. Con un processo complicatissimo e quasi incomprensibile, tu ne inghiottivi una parte, ne assorbivi un'altra, ne espellevi un'altra ancora, e ne producevi di nuovo. Da quattro giorni, invece, la tua fonte di nutrimento son io: attraverso il cordone ombelicale. Sono successe tante cose in questi giorni: io mi esalto e t'ammiro a pensarci. La placenta che avvolge il tuo uovo come una pelliccia calda s'è rafforzata, il numero delle tue cellule sanguigne è aumentato, e tutto procede a una velocità pazza: l'impalcatura delle tue vene è ormai visibile. Sono perfettamente visibili anche le due arterie, e la vena del cordone ombelicale che ti porta il mio ossigeno e le sostanze chimiche di cui tu hai bisogno. Inoltre ti sei sviluppato il fegato, ti sei abbozzato tutti gli organi interni: perfino il tuo sesso e i tuoi organi riproduttivi hanno incominciato a sbocciare! Lo sai già, tu, se sarai un uomo o una donna. Ma quel che mi esalta di più, bambino mio, è che ti sei fatto anche le manine. Ti si vedono ormai le dita. Ed hai una piccola bocca, ormai: con le labbra! Hai un principio di lingua. Hai le cavità per venti dentini. Hai gli occhi. Così minuscolo, neanche un centimetro e mezzo, così lieve, neanche tre grammi, hai gli occhi! A me sembra addirittura impossibile che tutte queste cose siano successe nello spazio di poche settimane. Mi sembra irreale. Eppure l'inizio del mondo, quando si formò quella cellula e tutto ciò che nasce e respira e muore per rinascere ancora, dev'essere avvenuto come avviene in te: in un brulicare, un gonfiarsi, un moltiplicarsi di vita sempre più complicata, sempre più difficile, sempre più veloce e ordinata e perfetta. Quanto lavori, bambino! Chi ha detto che dormi tranquillo, cullato dalle tue acque? Non dormi mai, tu, non riposi mai. Chi ha detto che te ne stai in pace, in un'armonia di suoni che giungono alla tua membrana dolcemente ovattati? Sono certa che è un continuo sciaguattare da te, un continuo pompare, soffiare, frusciare, un esplodere di rumori brutali. Chi ha detto che sei materia inerte, quasi un vegetale estirpabile con un cucchiaio? Se voglio liberarmi di te, sostengono, è questo il momento. Anzi il momento incomincia ora. In altre parole, avrei dovuto aspettare che tu diventassi un essere umano con gli occhi e le dita e la bocca per ammazzarti. Prima no. Prima eri troppo piccolo per essere individuato e strappato. Sono pazzi.

— 8 —

La mia amica afferma che la pazza son io. Lei, che è sposata, ha abortito quattro volte in tre anni. Aveva già due figli, averne un terzo sarebbe stato inammissibile: dice. Anche i polli non mettono al mondo tutti i figli che potrebbero avere. Se da ogni uovo gallato nascesse un pulcino, questo pianeta sarebbe un pollaio. Lo sai che tante galline si bevon le uova? Lo sai che le covano solo una volta o due all'anno? E i conigli: lo sai che certe coniglie mangiano i neonati più deboli per poter allattare gli altri? Eliminarli all'inizio non sarebbe meglio che metterli al mondo per mangiarli o farli mangiare? Secondo me sarebbe ancora meglio non concepirli affatto. Ma, appena azzardo quel ragionamento, lei si arrabbia. Risponde che la prendeva la pillola, certo. Le faceva male, eppure la prendeva. Poi una sera se ne dimenticò, e di qui il primo aborto. Con la sonda, mi dice. Non ho capito bene cosa sia questa sonda. Suppongo un ago che uccide. In compenso ho capito che la usano molte e sapendo che procura sofferenze infinite, a volte la prigione.

Ti chiedi perché da qualche giorno non faccio che parlarti di questo? Non lo so. Forse perché gli altri me ne parlano in modo ossessivo. Forse perché a un certo punto ci ho pensato anch'io senza dirmelo. Forse perché non voglio confidare a nessun altro un dubbio che mi avvelena l'anima. La sola idea di ucciderti, oggi, mi uccide e tuttavia mi capita di considerarla. Mi confonde quel discorso sui polli. Mi confonde l'ira della mia amica quando le mostro la tua fotografia e indico i tuoi occhi, le tue mani. Lei risponde che per vederli davvero, i tuoi occhi, per vederle davvero, le tue mani, non basterebbe il microscopio. Grida che vivo di fantasia, che pretendo di razionalizzare i miei sentimenti, i miei sogni. Ha perfino esclamato: «Allora i girini che togli dalla vasca del tuo giardino perché non diventino ranocchi e non ti disturbino la notte gracidando?». Lo so, continuo senza pietà ad informarti sulle infamie del mondo in cui ti prepari ad entrare, sugli orrori quotidiani che noi commettiamo, e ti espongo concetti troppo complicati. Ma a poco a poco va maturandosi in me la certezza che tu li capisca perché sai già tutto. Incominciò il giorno in cui mi seviziavo il cervello per tentar di spiegarti che la terra è rotonda come il tuo uovo, che il mare è composto d'acqua come quella in cui galleggi, e non riuscivo ad esprimere ciò che volevo. D'un tratto mi paralizzò l'intuizione che il mio sforzo fosse inutile, che tu sapessi già tutto e molto più di me, e il sospetto d'avere intuito il giusto non mi abbandona più. Se nel tuo uovo c'è un universo, perché non dovrebbe esserci anche il pensiero? Non dicono, alcuni, che il subconscio sia il ricordo dell'esistenza vissuta prima di venire alla luce? Lo è? Allora dimmi, tu che sai tutto: quando incomincia la vita? Dimmi, ti supplico: è davvero incominciata la tua? Da quanto? Dal momento in cui la stilla di luce che chiamano spermio bucò e scisse la cellula? Dal momento in cui ti sbocciò un cuore e prese a pompar sangue? Dal momento in cui ti fiorì un cervello, un midollo spinale, e ti avviasti ad assumere una forma umana? Oppure quel momento deve ancora venire e sei solo un motore in fabbricazione? Cosa darei, bambino, per rompere il tuo mutismo, penetrare nella prigione che ti avvolge e che avvolgo, cosa darei per vederti, ascoltare la tua risposta! Certo siamo una ben strana coppia, io e te. Tutto in te dipende da me e tutto in me dipende da te: se tu ti ammali io mi ammalo, se io muoio tu muori. Però io non posso comunicare con te e tu non puoi comunicare con me. In quella che è forse la tua sapienza infinita, non conosci nemmeno la faccia che ho, l'età che ho, la lingua che parlo. Ignori da dove vengo, dove mi trovo, cosa faccio nella vita. Se tu volessi immaginarmi, non avresti neanche un elemento per indovinare se sono bianca o nera, giovane o vecchia, alta o bassa. Ed io mi chiedo ancora se sei o no una persona. Mai due estranei legati allo stesso destino furono più estranei di noi. Mai due sconosciuti uniti nello stesso corpo furono più sconosciuti, più lontani di noi.

— 9 —

Ho dormito male e avevo dolori giù in fondo al ventre: eri tu? Mi giravo angosciata nel letto, e il sonno era un'ossessione di incubi assurdi. In uno c'era tuo padre, e piangeva. Non lo avevo mai visto piangere, non credevo che ne fosse capace. Le sue lacrime cadevano in tonfi di piombo nella vasca del mio giardino e la vasca era piena di nastri interminabili e gelatinosi. Dentro i nastri c'erano piccole uova nere che si allungavano in una specie di coda: i girini. Io non badavo a tuo padre, mi preoccupavo soltanto di ammazzare i girini perché non diventassero ranocchi e non mi tenessero sveglia gracidando la notte. Il sistema era semplice: bastava sollevare i nastri con un bastone e posarli sull'erba del prato dove il sole li avrebbe soffocati, seccati. Ma i nastri sgusciavano via, scivolosi, in svelte volute che ricadevano nell'acqua e affondavano dentro il limo: non riuscivo a posarli sul prato. Poi tuo padre non ha pianto più e s'è messo ad aiutarmi: riuscendoci senza difficoltà. Con un ramo d'albero tirava su dall'acqua quei nastri che a lui non scivolavano via, li ammucchiava sull'erba. Metodico, calmo. E io ne soffrivo. Perché era come vedere decine, centinaia di bambini che soffocavano e seccavano al sole. Sconvolta, gli ho tolto il ramo dalle mani e ho gridato: « Lasciali stare! Tu sei nato, no? ». Nell'altro incubo c'era un canguro. Era un canguro femmina, dal suo utero è uscita una cosa tenera e viva: una specie di delicatissimo verme. S'è guardato intorno sbalordito, quasi a tentar di capire dove fosse, ed ha preso ad arrampicarsi su per il corpo peloso. Procedeva lentamente, faticosamente, inciampando, sdrucciolando, sbagliando, ma alla fine ha raggiunto la sacca e con un ultimo sforzo tremendo ci si è buttato dentro a capofitto.

Io mi rendevo conto che non eri te, che era l'embrione del canguro il quale nasce così perché esce presto dalla prigione dell'uovo e completa la sua formazione all'aperto. Però gli parlavo come se si fosse trattato di te. Lo ringraziavo per esser venuto a mostrarmi di non essere una cosa ma una persona. Gli dicevo che ora non eravamo più due estranei, due sconosciuti, e ridevo felice. Ridevo... Ma è arrivata la nonna. Era molto vecchia, e molto triste. Sulle sue spalle curve sembrava che stagnasse tutto il peso del mondo. Tra le mani sciupate teneva un bambolottino con gli occhi chiusi e la testa sproporzionata. Diceva: « Sono tanto stanca. Sto pagando per gli aborti. Io ho avuto otto figli e otto aborti. Se fossi stata ricca avrei avuto sedici figli e nemmeno un aborto. Non è vero che ci si fa l'abitudine, ogni volta è la prima volta. Ma questo il prete non lo capiva». Il bambolottino era grande come un crocifisso, di quelli che si portano in tasca. Levandolo come un crocifisso, la nonna è entrata in una chiesa dove s'è inginocchiata a un confessionale e ha incominciato a bisbigliare qualcosa alla grata. Dall'interno del confessionale s'è alzata una voce cattiva, la voce del prete: «Lei ha ucciso una creatura! Ha ucciso una creatura!». La nonna tremava per il terrore che gli altri ascoltassero. Si raccomandava: «Non gridi, reverendo, la prego! Lei mi fa arrestare! La prego!». La voce del prete però non si abbassava, e allora la nonna è scappata. Per strada correva, inseguita dai poliziotti, ed era straziante vedere una vecchia che correva così. Io mi sentivo svenire per lei e pensavo: le scoppierà il cuore, morirà. I poliziotti l'hanno raggiunta sulla porta di casa. Le hanno rubato il bambolottino e le hanno legato le braccia. Lei ha detto, fiera: «Sono pentita ma lo rifarò. Non lo faccio mai volentieri ma non posso mantenere tanti figli. Non posso». Mi hanno svegliato quei dolori giù in fondo al ventre.

Non devo veder più la mia amica. Sono i suoi discorsi che mi provocano gli incubi. Ieri sera mi ha invitato a cena: suo marito non c'era, le è sembrata una buona occasione per parlarmi di te, ed è stato un tormento. Sembra infatti che un fisico, il dottor H. B. Munson, sia d'accordo con lei. Perfino il feto, dichiara costui, è materia pressoché inerte, quasi un vegetale estirpabile con un cucchiaio. Al massimo lo si può considerare un «sistema coerente di capacità irrealizzate». Secondo alcuni biologi, invece, l'essere umano incomincia col concepimento perché l'uovo fertilizzato contiene DNA: l'acido desossiribonucleico che è la base delle proteine che formano un individuo. Tesi cui il dottor Munson replica che anche lo spermatozoo, anche l'uovo non fertilizzato contiene DNA: vorremmo considerare l'uovo e lo spermatozoo come esseri umani? Poi c'è un gruppo di medici pei quali un essere umano diventa un essere umano dopo ventotto settimane, cioè al momento in cui può sopravvivere fuori dell'utero anche se la gestazione non è completata. E c'è un gruppo di antropologi per cui un essere umano non è nemmeno un neonato ma qualcuno che è stato plasmato da influenze culturali e sociali. È esploso quasi un litigio. La mia amica giudicava con favore l'opinione degli antropologi ed io ero portata ad accettare quella dei biologi. Irritata, m'ha accusato di stare dalla parte dei preti: «Sei cattolica, cattolica, cattolica!». Non sono cattolica e lei lo sa. Inoltre rifiuto ai preti ogni diritto di interferire in questa faccenda, e lei lo sa. Ma non posso, assolutamente non posso accettare gli arbitrari principii del dottor Munson. Non posso, assolutamente non posso capire chi si infila la sonda come se prendesse una purga con cui eliminare un cibo indigesto. Ammenoché...

Ammenoché cosa? Sto tradendo la mia decisione? Mi sembrava d'essere ormai così sicura, d'aver superato così gloriosamente tutte le incertezze, tutti i dubbi. Perché ora tornano, camuffati da mille pretesti? È per via di questo malessere che mi fa girare la testa, per via di questi dolori che mi accoltellano il ventre? Devo essere forte, bambino. Devo tener fede a me stessa ed a te. Devo portarti in fondo perché da grande tu sia qualcuno che non assomiglia né al prete che urlava nel sogno, né alla mia amica e al suo dottor Munson, né ai poliziotti che legavan le braccia alla nonna. Il primo ti considera proprietà di Dio, la seconda ti considera proprietà della madre, i terzi ti considerano proprietà dello Stato. Non appartieni né a Dio né allo Stato né a me. Appartieni a te stesso e basta. Dopotutto sei tu che hai preso l'iniziativa ed io sbagliavo a credere d'importi una scelta. Tenendoti, non faccio che piegarmi al comando che mi impartisti quando s'accese la tua goccia di vita. Non ho scelto nulla, ho obbedito. Fra me e te, la possibile vittima non sei te, bambino: sono io. Non è questo che vuoi dirmi quando ti avventi come un vampiro contro il mio corpo? Non è questo che vuoi confermare quando mi regali la nausea? Sto male. Da una settimana lavoro con fatica. Mi si è gonfiata una gamba. Sarebbe terribile se dovessi rinunciare a quel viaggio ormai stabilito. E il commendatore sembra averlo compreso. In tono quasi minaccioso oggi mi ha chiesto "se potrò" ed ha aggiunto che se lo augura. Si tratta di un progetto importante, costruito su misura per me. Ci tiene, e ci tengo anch'io. Se non potessi andare... Certo che vi andrò. Il dottore non disse che la gravidanza non è una malattia, è uno stato normale, che devo continuare a fare ciò che ho sempre fatto? Tu non mi tradirai.

— 10 —

È successo qualcosa che non prevedevo: il dottore mi ha messo a letto. E qui mi trovo, immobile. Devo stare ferma e distesa. Non è facile, capisci, visto che vivo sola: se qualcuno suona il campanello, devo alzarmi per aprire la porta. E poi devo mangiare, devo lavarmi: per fare un caffè o andare nel bagno, sono costretta a lasciare il letto. Sì o no? Al cibo, per ora, ci pensa la mia amica. Le ho dato le chiavi e due volte al giorno viene a portarmelo, poveretta. Ho esclamato: «Non hai voluto un terzo figlio ed ecco che ti trovi ad adottarne una adulta». Ha risposto che una adulta è meglio di una neonata: non si deve allattare. Ci credi se ti dico che la mia amica è buona? Lo è. E non solo perché viene qui: ma perché non parla più di quel Munson, dei suoi antropologi. All'improvviso, sembra preoccupatissima dal timore che ti perda. Non ti allarmare: il pericolo non esiste. Il medico ha ripetuto gli esami e concluso che procedi bene, l'immobilità è una precauzione dovuta ai dolori che egli attribuisce a cause ben diverse. Hai compiuto due mesi, e i due mesi segnano un passaggio molto delicato: quello durante il quale l'embrione diventa feto. Stai formando le tue prime cellule ossee, che rimpiazzano le cartilagini. Stai allungando le gambe, proprio come un albero che spinge avanti i suoi rami, e anche ai tuoi piedini fioriscono ormai le dita. Dovremo stare cauti fino al terzo mese, poi potremo riprendere le nostre abitudini: questa storia di restare ferma e distesa non durerà che quindici giorni. Infatti al commendatore ho inventato che ho una forte bronchite. Ci ha creduto e mi ha assicurato che il viaggio può attendere: tanti particolari vanno ancora organizzati. Menomale: se sapesse la verità, potrebbe sostituirmi. Al limite, licenziarmi. E sarebbe un bel guaio per me e per te: chi ci camperebbe? Tra l'altro, tuo padre non s'è più fatto vivo. A quanto pare, non vuol essere coinvolto. Ti dispiace? A me no: il poco che provavo per lui s'è estinto in due telefonate. Anzi nel fatto stesso che m'abbia parlato al telefono anziché fissandomi negli occhi. Al ritorno poteva presentarsi, ti pare? Sa bene che non gli chiederei di sposarmi, che non gliel'ho mai chiesto, che non voglio sposarmi, che non lo vorrei mai: cosa lo trattiene dunque? Si sente forse colpevole d'avermi amato in un letto? Un giorno la nonna andò a confessarsi davvero e il prete le dette il seguente consiglio: «Non vada a letto con suo marito, non vada!». In fondo, per certa gente, la vera colpa di un uomo e di una donna consiste nell'amarsi in un letto. Per non avere bambini, dicono, basterebbe diventare casti. D'accordo:

visto che è un po' difficile stabilire chi debba essere casto e chi no, diventiamo tutti casti e trasformiamoci in un pianeta di vecchi. Milioni e milioni di vecchi incapaci di generare, mentre la razza umana si estingue, come nei racconti di fantascienza ambientati su Marte, sullo sfondo di meravigliose città che si sgretolano: abitate solo da fantasmi. I fantasmi di tutti coloro che avrebbero potuto essere e non sono stati. I fantasmi dei bambini mai nati. Oppure diventiamo tutti omosessuali, tanto il risultato sarebbe lo stesso: un pianeta di persone incapaci di generare, sullo sfondo di meravigliose città che si sgretolano, abitate solo dai fantasmi dei bambini mai nati...

E se invece li utilizzassimo, i vecchi? Ho letto da qualche parte che è possibile effettuare il trapianto degli embrioni. Una conquista della biologia tecnologica. Si toglie l'uovo fertilizzato dal ventre della madre e lo si trasferisce nel ventre di un'altra donna disposta a ospitarlo. Lo si fa crescere lì. Ecco, se un'altra donna ti ospitasse, ad esempio una vecchia per cui rimanere immobile non costituisse uno strazio, nasceresti ugualmente e non starei qui a tormentarmi. Fare bambini, in fondo, è un'impresa da vecchi. Sono così pazienti, i vecchi. Ti offenderebbe essere trapiantato in un ventre che non è il mio? Un buon vecchio ventre che non ti rimprovera mai? E perché dovresti? Non ti negherei mica alla vita. Ti darei solo un altro alloggio. Perdonami. Sto vaneggiando. Il guaio è che questa immobilità mi innervosisce, mi incattivisce.

— 11 —

Oggi ho avuto una buona sorpresa. È suonato il campanello, ed era il postino con un pacchetto spedito via aerea. Lo mandava mia madre insieme a una lettera firmata da lei e mio padre. Li avevo informati su te, giorni fa. M'era sembrato un dovere. E ogni giorno aspettavo la loro risposta, con angoscia, rabbrividendo al pensiero delle cose dure o addolorate che forse m'avrebbero scritto. Sono due persone all'antica, sai. Invece questa lettera dice che, pur sentendosi disorientati e colpiti, si rallegrano e ti danno il benvenuto. «Ormai noi siamo due alberi secchi, non abbiamo più nulla da insegnarti. Ormai sei tu che hai qualcosa da insegnare a noi. E, se hai deciso così, vuol dire che è giusto così.» Dopo la lettera ho aperto il pacchetto. Conteneva una scatolina di plastica, e dentro c'erano due scarpine. Piccole piccole, lievi lievi... Le tue prime scarpe. Mi stanno sulla palma della mano, non la coprono nemmeno tutta. E mi si chiude la gola a toccarle. Mi si scioglie il cuore. Ti piacerà la mia mamma. Ti piacerà perché pensa che senza i bambini il mondo finirebbe. Ti piacerà perché è grossa e morbida, con una pancia grossa e morbida per sederci sopra, due braccia grosse e morbide per proteggerti, e una risata che è un concerto di campanelli. Non ho mai capito come faccia a ridere in quel modo: ma penso che sia perché ha pianto molto. Solo chi ha pianto molto può apprezzare la vita nelle sue bellezze, e ridere bene. Piangere è facile, ridere è difficile. Imparerai subito questa verità. Il tuo incontro col mondo sarà un pianto disperato, nei primi tempi riuscirai a piangere e basta. Tutto ti farà piangere: la luce, la fame, il sonno... Passeranno settimane, mesi, prima che la tua bocca si schiuda a un sorriso, prima che la tua gola gorgogli una risata. Ma non dovrai scoraggiarti. E quando il sorriso verrà, quando la risata verrà, dovrai regalarla a me: per dimostrarmi che ho fatto bene a non servirmi della biologia tecnologica, a non trasferirti al ventre di una madre più buona e più paziente di me.

— 12 —

Ho ritagliato la fotografia che ti ritrae a due mesi esatti: un primo piano del tuo volto ingrandito di quaranta volte. L'ho attaccata sul muro, e qui dal letto la guardo: ossessionata dai tuoi occhi. Sono così grandi rispetto al resto del corpo, così spalancati. Che vedono? L'acqua e basta? Le pareti della prigione e basta? Oppure ciò che vedo anch'io? Un sospetto delizioso mi turba: il sospetto che vedano attraverso di me. Mi dispiace che presto tu li chiuda. Sull'orlo delle palpebre si sta formando una sostanza collosa che fra qualche giorno appiccicherà i due bordi per proteggere le pupille durante la loro formazione finale. Non le solleverai più fino al settimo mese, le tue palpebre. Per venti settimane vivrai nel buio completo. Peccato! O forse no? Senza cose da guardare, mi ascolterai meglio. Ho ancora tanto da dirti e queste giornate immobili me ne forniscono il tempo, visto che la mia unica attività consiste nel leggere o guardare la televisione. Per esempio, ho da prepararti ad alcune verità molto scomode. La speranza che tu sappia già tutto, e molto più di me, non mi convince. Ma spiegarti certe cose è difficile perché il tuo pensiero, se esiste, agisce su fatti troppo diversi da quelli che troverai. Tu sei solo, magnificamente solo là dentro. La tua sola esperienza è te stesso. Noi siamo molti, invece: milioni, miliardi. Ogni nostra esperienza dipende dagli altri, ogni nostra gioia, ogni nostro dolore, e...

Ecco, incomincio da qui. Incomincio annunciandoti che non sarai più solo quaggiù e che, se vorrai liberarti

34

degli altri, della loro compagnia forzata, non ci riuscirai. Quaggiù una persona non può provvedere a se stessa da sola, come fai tu. Se prova, impazzisce. Nel migliore dei casi, fallisce. A volte qualcuno ci prova. E scappa nel bosco o sul mare giurando che non ha bisogno degli altri, che gli altri non lo ritroveranno mai più. Lo ritrovano, invece. Magari è lui che torna. E così rientra sconfitto a far parte del formicaio, dell'ingranaggio: per cercarvi inutilmente, disperatamente, la sua libertà. Udrai molto parlare di libertà. Qui da noi è una parola sfruttata quasi quanto la parola amore che, te l'ho detto, è la più sfruttata di tutte. Incontrerai uomini che si fanno fare a pezzi per la libertà, subendo torture, magari accettando la morte. Ed io spero che sarai uno di essi. Però, nello stesso momento in cui ti farai straziare per la libertà, scoprirai che essa non esiste, che al massimo esisteva in quanto la cercavi: come un sogno, un'idea nata dal ricordo della tua vita prima di nascere, quando eri libero perché eri solo. Io continuo a ripetere che sei prigioniero lì dentro, continuo a pensare che hai poco spazio e che d'ora innanzi starai perfino al buio: ma in quel buio, in quel poco spazio, tu sei libero come non lo sarai mai più in questo mondo immenso e spietato. Non devi chiedere permesso a nessuno, aiuto a nessuno, lì dentro. Perché non hai accanto nessuno ed ignori cosa sia la schiavitù. Qui fuori, invece, avrai mille padroni. E il primo padrone sarò io che senza volerlo, magari senza saperlo, ti imporrò cose che sono giuste per me non per te. Quelle belle scarpine, ad esempio. Sono belle per me ma per te? Griderai ed urlerai quando te le infilerò. Ma io te le infilerò lo stesso, magari sostenendo che hai freddo, e un po' alla volta ti ci abituerai. Ti piegherai, domato, fino a soffrire se ti mancheranno. E questo sarà l'inizio di una lunga catena di schiavitù dove il primo anello verrà sempre rappresentato da me, visto che tu non potrai fare a meno di me. Io che ti nutrirò, io che ti coprirò, io che ti laverò, io che ti porterò in braccio. Poi incomincerai a camminare da te, a mangiare da te, a scegliere da te dove andare e quando lavarti. Ma allora sorgeranno altre schiavitù. I miei consigli. I miei insegnamenti. Le mie raccomandazioni. La tua stessa paura di darmi dolore facendo cose diverse da quelle che ti avrò insegnato. Passerà molto tempo, ai tuoi occhi, prima ch'io ti lasci partire come gli uccelli che i genitori buttano fuori dal nido, il giorno in cui sanno volare. Infine quel tempo verrà, e io ti lascerò partire, ti lascerò attraversare la strada da solo, col verde e col rosso. Ti ci spingerò. Ma questo non aumenterà la tua libertà perché mi resterai incatenato con la schiavitù degli affetti, la schiavitù del rimpianto. Alcuni la chiamano schiavitù della famiglia. Io non credo alla famiglia. La famiglia è una menzogna costruita da chi organizzò questo mondo per controllare meglio la gente, sfruttarne meglio l'obbedienza alle regole. Ci si ribella più facilmente quando si è soli, ci si rassegna più facilmente quando si vive con altri. La famiglia non è che il portavoce di un sistema che non può lasciarti disubbidire, e la sua santità non esiste. Esistono solo gruppi di uomini e donne e bambini costretti a portare lo stesso nome ed abitare sotto lo stesso tetto: detestandosi, odiandosi, spesso. Però il rimpianto esiste, e i legami esistono, radicati in noi come alberi che non cedono neanche all'uragano, inevitabili come la fame e la sete. Non te ne puoi mai liberare, anche se ci provi con tutta la tua volontà, la tua logica. Magari credi di averli dimenticati e un giorno riaffiorano, irrimediabilmente, spietati, per metterti la corda al collo più di qualsiasi boia. E strozzarti.

Insieme a quelle schiavitù, conoscerai quelle imposte dagli altri e cioè dai mille e mille abitanti del formicaio. Le loro abitudini, le loro leggi. Non immagini quanto siano soffocanti le loro abitudini da imitare, le loro leggi da rispettare. Non fare questo, non fare quello, fai questo e fai quello... E se ciò è tollerabile quando vivi tra brava gente che ha un'idea della libertà, diventa infernale quando vivi tra prepotenti che ti negano perfino il lusso di sognarla, la libertà: realizzarla nella tua fantasia. Le leggi dei prepotenti offrono solo un vantaggio: ad esse puoi reagire lottando, morendo. Le leggi della brava gente, invece, non t'offrono scampo perché ti si convince che è nobile accettarle. In qualsiasi sistema tu viva, non puoi ribellarti alla legge che a vincere è sempre il più forte, il più prepotente, il meno generoso. Tantomeno puoi ribellarti alla legge che per mangiare ci vuole il denaro, per dormire ci vuole il denaro, per camminare dentro un paio di scarpe ci vuole il denaro, per riscaldarsi d'inverno ci vuole il denaro, che per avere il denaro bisogna lavorare. Ti racconteranno un mucchio di storie sulla necessità del lavoro, la gioia del lavoro, la dignità del lavoro. Non ci credere, mai. Si tratta di un'altra menzogna inventata per la convenienza di chi organizzò questo mondo. Il lavoro è un ricatto che rimane tale anche quando ti piace. Lavori sempre per qualcuno, mai per te stesso. Lavori sempre con fatica, mai con gioia. E mai nel momento in cui ne avresti voglia. Anche se non dipendi da nessuno e coltivi il tuo pezzo di terra, devi zappare quando vogliono il sole e la pioggia e le stagioni. Anche se non ubbidisci a nessuno e il tuo lavoro è arte cioè creazione, liberazione, devi piegarti alle altrui esigenze o soprusi. Forse in un passato molto lontano, tanto lontano che se ne è smarrito il ricordo, non era così. E lavorare era una festa, un'allegria. Ma esistevano poche persone a quel tempo, e potevano starsene sole. Tu vieni al mondo dopo millenovecentosettantacinque anni la nascita di un uomo che chiamano Cristo il quale venne al mondo centinaia di migliaia di anni dopo un altro uomo di cui si ignora il nome, e di questi tempi le cose vanno come t'ho detto. Una recente statistica afferma che siamo già quattro miliardi. In quel mucchio entrerai. E quanto rimpiangerai il tuo sguazzare solitario nell'acqua, bambino!

— 13 —

Ti ho scritto tre fiabe. O meglio, non le ho scritte perché stando distesa a letto non posso: le ho pensate. Te ne racconto una. C'era una volta una bambina innamorata di una magnolia. La magnolia stava in mezzo a un giardino e la bambina passava giornate intere a guardarla. La guardava dall'alto perché abitava all'ultimo piano di una casa affacciata su quel giardino, e la guardava da una finestra che era la sola finestra aperta in quel punto. La bambina era molto piccina, per vedere la magnolia doveva arrampicarsi sopra una sedia dove la mamma la sorprendeva gridando «Oddio casca, casca!». La magnolia era grande, con grandi rami e grandi foglie e grandi fiori che si aprivano come fazzoletti puliti e che nessuno coglieva perché stavano troppo in alto. Infatti avevano tutto il tempo di invecchiare e ingiallire e cadere con un piccolo tonfo per terra. La bambina sognava lo stesso che qualcuno riuscisse a cogliere un fiore finché era bianco, e in questa attesa stava alla finestra: le braccia appoggiate sopra il davanzale e il mento appoggiato sopra le braccia. Di fronte e dintorno non c'erano case, solo un muro che si alzava ripido al lato del giardino e finiva in una terrazza coi panni tesi ad asciugare. Si capiva quand'erano asciutti per gli schiaffi che davano al vento e allora arrivava una donna che li raccoglieva dentro una cesta e li portava via. Ma un giorno la donna arrivò e invece di raccogliere i panni si mise anche lei a guardare la magnolia: quasi studiasse il modo di cogliere un fiore. Restò lì molto, a pensarci, mentre i panni sbattevano al vento. Poi fu raggiunta da un uomo che l'abbracciò. Lo abbracciò anche lei, e presto caddero insieme per terra dove insieme sussultarono a lungo, infine giacquero addormentati. La bambina era sorpresa, non capiva perché i due se ne stessero a dormire sulla terrazza anziché occuparsi della magnolia, tentare di cogliervi un fiore, e aspettava paziente che si svegliassero quando apparve un altro uomo: molto arrabbiato. Non disse nulla ma era chiaro che fosse molto arrabbiato perché si gettò immediatamente sui due. Prima sull'uomo che però fece un balzo e scappò, dopo sulla donna che incominciò a correre tra i panni. Correva anche lui, per agguantarla, e alla fine l'agguantò. La sollevò come se non pesasse e la scaraventò giù: sulla magnolia. La donna impiegò tanto tempo per giungere alla magnolia. Ma poi vi giunse, e si posò sui rami con un tonfo più sordo dei fiori che cadevano gialli per terra. Un ramo si ruppe. E nello stesso momento in cui il ramo si ruppe, la donna si aggrappò ad un fiore. E lo colse. E rimase lì ferma col suo fiore in mano. Allora la bambina chiamò la sua mamma. Le disse: «Mamma, hanno buttato una donna sulla magnolia ed ha colto un fiore». La mamma venne, gridò che la donna era morta, e da quel giorno la bambina crebbe convinta che per cogliere un fiore una donna dovesse morire.

Quella bambina ero io, e Dio voglia che tu non apprenda nel modo in cui l'appresi io che a vincere è sempre il più forte, il più prepotente, il meno generoso. Dio voglia che tu non lo comprenda presto come lo compresi io, oltretutto convincendomi che una donna è la prima a pagare per tale realtà. Ma io sbaglio a sperarlo. Devo augurarti di perderla presto quella verginità che si chiama infanzia, illusione. Devo prepararti fin d'ora a difenderti, ad essere più svelto, più forte, e buttare lui giù dal terrazzo. Specialmente se sei una donna. Anche questa è una legge: o me o te. O mi salvo io o ti salvi te. E guai a dimenticarla: qui da noi ciascuno fa del male a qualcuno, bambino. Se non lo fa, soccombe. E non ascoltare chi dice che soccombe il più buono. Soccombe il più debole, che non è necessariamente il più buono. Io non ho mai preteso che le donne fossero più buone degli uomini, che per bontà meritassero di non morire. Essere buoni o cattivi non conta: la vita quaggiù non dipende da quello. Dipende da un rapporto di forze basato sulla violenza. La sopravvivenza è violenza. Calzerai scarpe di cuoio perché qualcuno ha ammazzato una vacca e l'ha scuoiata per farne cuoio. Ti scalderai con una pelliccia perché qualcuno ha ammazzato una bestia, cento bestie, per strappargli via la pelliccia. Mangerai il fegatino di pollo perché qualcuno ha ammazzato un pollo che non faceva del male a nessuno. E nemmeno questo è vero perché anche lui faceva del male a qualcuno: divorava i vermetti che se ne andavano in pace brucando insalata. C'è sempre uno che per sopravvivere mangia un altro o scuoia un altro: dagli uomini ai pesci. Anche i pesci si mangiano fra loro: i più grossi inghiottiscono i più piccini. E così gli uccelli, così gli insetti, chiunque. Che io sappia, solo gli alberi e le piante non divoran nessuno: si nutrono d'acqua, di sole, e basta. Però a volte si rubano il sole e l'acqua, anche loro, soffocandosi,

sterminandosi. Ed è proprio il caso che tu venga a conoscere simili orrori, tu che vivi e ti nutri e ti scaldi senza
ammazzare nessuno?

— 14 —

Anche questa è una fiaba. C'era una volta una bambina cui piaceva la cioccolata. Però più le piaceva, meno
ne mangiava. E sai perché? Perché un tempo ne aveva
mangiata quanta volesse. Il tempo in cui abitava in una
casa piena di cielo che entrava dalle finestre. Ma un
giorno s'era svegliata in una casa senza cielo. Dalle finestre, poste quasi al soffitto e protette da una grata, si vedevano soltanto piedi che andavano su e giù. Si vedevano anche cani, e lì per lì era un piacere perché i cani si vedevano
interi: fino alla testa. Però subito dopo alzavan la zampa e
facevano pipì sulla grata, mentre la mamma della bambina piangeva: «Questo no, questo no!». La sua mamma
piangeva sempre, del resto, anche quando si rivolgeva al
pancione che le tirava il grembiule, e parlava a qualcuno
chiuso lì dentro dicendogli: «Non avresti potuto scegliere
momento peggiore!». Al che il babbo incominciava a tos-
sire, nel letto, una tosse che lo lasciava come morto. Il
babbo stava a letto anche di giorno, col viso giallo e gli occhi lucidi. Tristi. Secondo i calcoli della bambina, la fine
della cioccolata aveva coinciso con la malattia del babbo e
il trasloco in quella casa senza cielo e senza gioia. Insomma con la mancanza di soldi.

Per trovare i soldi, la mamma della bambina andava
a pulire la casa di una bella signora cui dava del tu e
che le dava del tu. Era costei una zia ricca, che cambia-
va sempre vestito. Si diceva perfino che avesse una borsa

per ogni vestito e un paio di scarpe per ogni borsa. La sua casa era sul fiume e dalle finestre vi entrava tutto il cielo della città. Ma la bella signora non era contenta lo stesso. Si lamentava sempre: perché un cappello non le stava bene, o perché il suo gatto starnutiva, o perché la sua cameriera era andata da un mese in campagna e non accennava a tornare. La mamma della bambina, dunque, sostituiva la cameriera screanzata: tutti i giorni dalle nove alle una. Lasciava il marito soltanto per questo, e portava la bambina con sé sostenendo che prendere aria le faceva meglio che restare accanto a un uomo coi polmoni bucati. Ce la portava a piedi, in un lungo viaggio attraverso strade che non finivano mai. Camminando si chiedeva quali infelicità avrebbe ascoltato stavolta dalla bella signora e, prima di suonare il campanello, mormorava a se stessa: «Coraggio!». Al suono del campanello rispondeva una voce strascicata, poi un passo ancor più strascicato, e la porta si apriva su una vestaglia lunga fino ai piedi: ora bianca, ora rosa, ora azzurra. Entravano calpestando tappeti, la mamma della bambina posava la bambina su uno sgabello: quasi fosse un pacco. Le raccomandava di stare ferma, zitta, di non disturbare, e poi spariva in cucina a lavare i piatti. La bella signora invece si adagiava su un divano, a leggere il giornale e a fumare col bocchino. Chiaramente non aveva altro da fare. E la bambina non capiva il motivo per cui essa non si lavasse i piatti da sé, invece di farli lavare alla mamma che aveva il pancione.

Quel mattino la bella signora si lamentava per una faccenda di soldi. «Capisci» ripeteva «solo quella cifra vuol darmi.» E quando la mamma della bambina rispose «con quella cifra mi sentirei una principessa», si arrabbiò.

Disse: «A me bastano appena per il taxi. Non vorrai mica paragonarti con me!». La mamma della bambina arrossì e con la scusa di spolverare il tappeto si inginocchiò per terra abbassando il viso. La bambina sentì come un pizzicare alla gola. E stava per sciogliere le lacrime che le bruciavano gli occhi quando la sua attenzione fu rapita da alcuni oggetti d'oro che luccicavano al sole: una bomboniera di vetro, colma di gianduiotti. Però non gianduiotti normali: gianduiotti grandi due volte, tre volte, quelli che s'era abituata a mangiare nei giorni remoti della casa col cielo. Infatti, di colpo, il pizzicare alla gola scomparve e al suo posto si formò un liquido che aveva il sapore della cioccolata. La mamma se ne accorse. La fulminò con lo sguardo per avvertirla: se chiedi qualcosa, te ne pentirai! La bambina capì e si mise a fissare il soffitto con dignità. Stava fissando il soffitto quando la bella signora si alzò e con aria annoiata andò sul balcone dove rimase ad accarezzarsi un polso. Il balcone si affacciava su un secondo balcone, più grande. E sul secondo balcone c'erano due bambini ricchi. La bambina lo sapeva perché li aveva visti, una volta, e aveva capito che erano ricchi perché erano belli. La stessa bellezza della signora. Sempre accarezzandosi il polso, questa li scorse. Sorrise, estasiata, si affacciò per chiamarli: «Bonjour, mes petits pigeons! Ça va, aujourd'hui?». E poi: «Attendez, attendez! Il y a quelque chose pour vous!». Rientrò in casa, prese la bomboniera di vetro, la scoperchiò, la portò sul balcone reggendola con delicatezza, cominciò a gettar gianduiotti di sotto. Li gettava e diceva: «Gianduiotti pour mes petits pigeons, gianduiotti per i miei piccioncini!». Ne gettò più di metà, tra uno scoppiettar di risate, infine posò di nuovo la bomboniera sul tavolo e tirò fuori un altro gianduiotto. Lo spogliò lentamente della sua carta d'oro, lo sollevò un attimo pensando chissacché, e se lo mangiò. Mentre la bambina guardava.

È da quel giorno che non posso mangiar cioccolata. Se la mangio, vomito. Ma spero che la cioccolata ti piaccia, bambino, perché voglio comprartene tanta. Voglio coprirti di cioccolata: affinché tu la mangi per me, fino alla nausea, fino all'oblio di quell'ingiustizia che mi porto ancora addosso con il rancore. Conoscerai l'ingiustizia quanto la violenza: devo prepararti anche a questo. E non intendo l'ingiustizia di uccidere un pollo per mangiarlo, una vacca per scuoiarla, una donna per punirla: intendo l'ingiustizia che divide chi ha e chi non ha. L'ingiustizia che lascia questo veleno in bocca, mentre la madre incinta spolvera il tappeto altrui. Come si risolva un tale problema non so. Tutti coloro che ci hanno provato sono riusciti soltanto a sostituire chi spolvera il tappeto. In qualunque sistema tu nasca, qualunque ideologia, c'è sempre un tale che spolvera il tappeto di un altro, e c'è sempre una bambina umiliata da un desiderio di gianduiotti. Non troverai mai un sistema, mai un'ideologia, che possa mutare il cuore degli uomini e cancellarne la malvagità. Quando ti diranno da-noi-è-diverso, rispondigli: bugiardi. Poi sfidali a dimostrarti che da loro non esistono cibi pei ricchi e cibi pei poveri, case pei ricchi e case pei poveri, stagioni pei ricchi e stagioni pei poveri. L'inverno è una stagione da ricchi. Se sei ricco, il freddo diventa un gioco perché ti compri la pelliccia e il riscaldamento e vai a sciare. Se sei povero, invece, il freddo diventa una maledizione e impari a odiare perfino la bellezza di un paesaggio bianco sotto la neve. L'uguaglianza, bambino, esiste solo dove stai tu:

come la libertà. Nell'uovo e basta siamo tutti uguali. Ma è proprio il caso che tu venga a conoscere tali ingiustizie, tu che lì vivi senza servire nessuno ?

— 15 —

Questa non lo so se è una fiaba, ma te la racconto lo stesso. C'era una volta una ragazzina che credeva nel domani. Infatti le insegnavano tutti a credere nel domani : assicurandole che il domani è sempre meglio. Glielo assicurava il prete quando tuonava le sue promesse in chiesa e annunciava il Regno dei Cieli. Glielo assicurava la scuola quando le dimostrava che l'umanità va avanti e che un tempo gli uomini vivevano nelle caverne poi in case senza termosifone poi in case col termosifone. Glielo assicurava suo padre quando le portava ad esempio la storia e sosteneva che i tiranni finiscono sempre sconfitti. Al prete, la ragazzina aveva tolto fiducia assai presto. Il suo domani era la morte, e alla ragazzina non importava nulla di abitare dopo la morte in un lussuoso albergo chiamato Regno dei Cieli. Alla scuola aveva tolto fiducia un po' dopo, e cioè durante un inverno in cui le sue mani e i suoi piedi s'eran coperti di geloni, di piaghe. Sì, era una gran cosa che gli uomini fossero passati dalle caverne al termosifone : ma lei non aveva il termosifone. Di suo padre aveva continuato a fidarsi, invece, a occhi chiusi. Suo padre era un uomo molto coraggioso e testardo. Da vent'anni combatteva certi prepotenti vestiti di nero e ognivolta che questi gli rompevan la testa diceva, coraggioso e testardo : « Domani verrà ». C'era la guerra in quegli anni. I prepotenti vestiti di nero avevano tutta l'aria di vincerla. Ma lui scoteva la testa e diceva, coraggioso e testardo : « Domani verrà ».

La ragazzina gli credeva perché aveva visto una notte di luglio. Quella notte i prepotenti vestiti di nero eran stati cacciati e sembrava che la loro guerra fosse finita per dare il via al domani. Ma venne settembre ed essi tornarono, con nuovi prepotenti che parlavan tedesco: la guerra raddoppiò. La ragazzina si sentì tradita e interrogò suo padre. Suo padre rispose che il domani non poteva tardare perché non eran più soli ad attenderlo, stavano arrivando gli amici, un esercito intero di amici detti alleati, e il giorno dopo la città della ragazzina venne bombardata dagli amici detti alleati. Una bomba cadde proprio dinanzi a casa sua. La ragazzina ne rimase disorientata. Se erano amici, perché facevano questo? Ma suo padre rispose che purtroppo dovevano farlo, che ciò non diminuiva per niente la loro amicizia, e per convincerla meglio portò in casa due di coloro che gli gettavan le bombe. Già prigionieri dei prepotenti, i due eran fuggiti da un campo di concentramento. Bisognava nasconderli, spiegò, aiutarli. La ragazzina ubbidì. Li nascose, li aiutò, li salvò. E poi, carica di speranza, si mise ad aspettare l'esercito che avrebbe portato il domani. Che attesa lunga mentre le bombe continuavano a cadere e i prepotenti vestiti di nero a picchiare, arrestare, torturare, ammazzare... Un giorno, anche il padre della ragazzina fu arrestato, torturato, quasi ammazzato. Però neanche quel giorno lei rinunciò alla speranza. E, quando andò a trovarlo in prigione, credette di nuovo a ciò che di nuovo egli disse: «Domani verrà».

E il domani giunse, alla fine. Era un'alba d'agosto e durante la notte la città era stata squassata da orrende esplosioni. Erano saltati i ponti, le strade, erano morti nuovi innocenti. Poi era sorta quest'alba, splendida come campane di Pasqua, ed aveva portato gli amici. Avanzavano belli, sorridenti, festosi, angeli in uniforme, e la gente gli correva incontro buttandogli fiori, gridandogli grazie. Il padre della ragazzina, ormai libero, veniva salutato da tutti con gran deferenza e i suoi occhi brillavano la luce di chi ha conosciuto la fede. Ma si avvicinò qualcuno e gli disse di correre al comando alleato: succedeva una cosa gravissima. Il padre della ragazzina corse. E la cosa gravissima era un uomo che singhiozzava su un prato, col volto immerso nell'erba. Indossava un abito blu, chiaramente scelto per ricever gli amici, all'occhiello della giacca gli fioriva una gran rosa rossa, di carta, e dinanzi a lui stava un angelo in uniforme: con le gambe divaricate e il mitragliatore puntato. Il padre della ragazzina chiese di parlare col colonnello. Il colonnello lo ricevette agitando un frustino: «Lei è un rappresentante del popolo?». Il padre della ragazzina rispose di sì. «In tal caso la informo che il suo popolo ci ha dato il benvenuto rubando! Quell'uomo ha rubato!» Il padre della ragazzina chiese che cosa avesse rubato. «Un saccapane pieno di cibo e di documenti» sibilò il frustino. Il padre della ragazzina chiese quali documenti. «Il libretto di congedo del sergente proprietario del saccapane» sibilò il frustino. Il padre della ragazzina chiese se il libretto era stato ritrovato. «Sì, ma stracciato!» sibilò il frustino. Il padre della ragazzina osservò che forse lo si poteva incollare. Ed il cibo? Era stato ritrovato anche quello? «Il cibo è stato mangiato! L'intera razione di un'intera giornata!» gridò il frustino impazzito. Il padre della ragazzina rispose che ciò era molto spiacevole: per rimediare, avrebbe preso il ladro in consegna e chiesto di rimborsare il sergente coi danni di guerra. Allora il frustino disegnò una gran voluta nell'aria e tuonò che nell'esercito inglese i ladri venivan fucilati. Quanto al rappresentante del popolo, fuori! Fuori, il ladro continuava a piangere col volto immerso nell'erba, mamma-mamma-mamma, l'angelo in uniforme continuava a stare dinanzi a lui con le gambe divaricate e il mitragliatore puntato. Le gambe erano tozze, pelose, il mitragliatore era puntato contro la nuca. Passando la ragazzina udì uno schiocco metallico, lo schiocco della sicura quando viene tolta.

Dopo l'esercito inglese, venne l'esercito americano. Tutti dicevano che gli americani sarebbero stati più cordiali, più buoni, e la ragazzina ci credette perché molti di loro ridevano grasse risate colme di umanità. Presto però s'accorse che, con le loro grasse risate, anch'essi si comportavano da padroni: il domani era una paura nuova. La fame, invece, era sempre la stessa. E per placarla alcune donne si prostituivano, altre lavavano i panni dei nuovi padroni. Ogni terrazza, ogni cortile era un ciondolar di uniformi e calzini e magliette; un vantarsi di chi ne lavava di più. Sei paia di calzini, un pane a cassetta. Tre maglie, una scatoletta di carne e fagioli. Una uniforme, due scatolette di carne... Il padre della ragazzina non permetteva che sua moglie e sua figlia toccassero quei panni sporchi. Diceva che bene o male il domani era incominciato, che bisognava difenderlo con dignità, e per dimostrarlo invitava a mangiare gli "amici". Gli dava la sua razione di cibo fresco. Una sera gli dette perfino il suo orologio d'oro, pronunciando un bel discorso dove ricordava i due prigionieri aiutati per il domani che restava una causa comune. Gli amici presero l'orologio d'oro e, per risposta, offrirono panni da lavare. La ragazzina si offese. Ma la fame è una bestia piena di tentazioni. Pochi giorni dopo, di nascosto a suo padre, ci ripensò e accettò di lavare i panni... Giunsero due sacchi. Uno di roba sporca e uno di cibo. Quello del cibo fu subito aperto e vuotato di tre scatolette di fagioli col sugo, due pani a cassetta, un vasetto di noccioline, un barattolo intero di gelato alla fragola. Quello della roba sporca fu aperto più tardi. E quando la ragazzina lo rovesciò nel lavatoio, arrossì di rabbia. Erano tutte mutande sporche.

Fu lavando le mutande sporche degli altri che me ne resi conto: il nostro domani non era giunto, e forse non sarebbe mai giunto. Avrebbero sempre continuato a imbrogliarci con le promesse: in un rosario di delusioni alleggerite da falsi sollievi, miserandi regali, pietose comodità per tenerci quieti. Giungerà mai per te il mio domani? Ne dubito. Sono secoli, sono millenni che la gente mette al mondo figli fidando nel domani, sperando che domani essi stiano meglio di loro. E quel meglio si risolve al massimo nella conquista di un misero termosifone. D'accordo, un termosifone è gran cosa quando si ha freddo: ma non ti dà certo la felicità e non difende affatto la tua dignità. Col termosifone continui a subire prepotenze, dispiaceri, ricatti, e il domani resta una bugia. Io ti dicevo all'inizio che nulla è peggiore del nulla, che il dolore non deve incuter spavento, nemmeno morire perché se uno muore vuol dire che è nato, ti dicevo che nascere merita sempre, visto che l'alternativa è il vuoto e il silenzio. Ma era giusto, bambino? È giusto che tu nasca per morire sotto una bomba o il fucile di un sergente peloso cui hai rubato per fame una razione di rancio? Più cresci, più io mi impaurisco. È quasi totalmente scomparso l'entusiasmo in cui mi esaltavo all'inizio, la gloriosa certezza d'aver colto il vero del vero. E nel dubbio mi consumo sempre di più. Questo dubbio che subdolo gonfia e si abbassa come la marea, ora coprendo in ondate la spiaggia della tua esistenza, ora ritirandosi per lasciarvi detriti. Non voglio scoraggiarti, credimi, indurti a non nascere:

voglio solo dividere con te la mia responsabilità, e chiarire a te stesso la tua. Hai ancora tempo per pensarci, bambino, anzi ripensarci. Per quel che mi riguarda e sia pure attraverso le alte maree, le basse maree, sono pronta. Ma tu? Ti ho già chiesto se sei disposto a veder scaraventare una donna su una magnolia, a veder piovere la cioccolata su chi non ne ha bisogno. Ora ti chiedo se sei disposto a correre il rischio di lavare le mutande degli altri e scoprire che il domani è un ieri. Tu che te ne stai dove ogni ieri è domani, e ogni domani è una conquista. Tu che non conosci ancora la peggiore delle verità: il mondo cambia e resta come prima.

— 16 —

Dieci settimane. Stai crescendo con rapidità impressionante. Quindici giorni fa misuravi meno di tre centimetri e pesavi appena quattro grammi. Ora misuri sei centimetri e pesi otto grammi. Ci sei tutto. Dell'antico pesciolino è rimasto solo il fatto che inali ed esali acqua attraverso i polmoni. Il tuo scheletro di umano è formato, con le ossa che rimpiazzano le cartilagini. Le tue costole stanno incollandosi l'una con l'altra alle estremità quasi che il tuo corpo si abbottonasse davanti come un cappotto. E il tuo uovo, pur lievitando, diventa sempre più angusto. Presto lo troverai scomodo. Ti agiterai, ti stirerai, le tue braccia e le tue gambe faranno i primi movimenti. Un colpo di gomito qui, un colpo di ginocchio là. È questo che aspetto. Il primo colpo sarà un segno, un assenso. Io feci così, ricordi, per dire a mia madre di non bere più la medicina. E allora lei buttò via la medicina. Certo è un'attesa inversamente proporzionale al tuo crescere: tanto più lenta quanto più quello è veloce: mi ricorda l'esercito amico che non giungeva mai. La colpa è dell'immobilità. Due settimane immobili, a letto, son troppe. Come fanno le donne che ci stanno anche sette, otto mesi? Sono donne o larve? L'unico punto su cui mi trovo d'accordo è che fa bene. Scomparsi gli spasmi, le coltellate giù in fondo al ventre. Svanita la nausea, e la gamba non è più gonfia. Però è subentrata una specie di spossatezza, un'ansia che assomiglia all'angoscia. Da che cosa viene? Forse dall'ozio, dalla noia. Non conoscevo l'ozio, non mi aveva mai sfiorato la noia. Non vedo l'ora che passino gli ultimi due giorni, mi preparo ad affrontarli come se fossero due anni. Stamani ho litigato con te. Ti sei offeso? Mi ha colto una specie di isteria. Ti ho detto che anch'io avevo i miei diritti, che nessuno era autorizzato a dimenticarlo e quindi nemmeno te. Ti ho gridato che mi avevi esasperato, che non ne potevo più. Mi ascolti? Da quando so che hai chiuso gli occhi mi sembra che tu non presti attenzione a ciò che ti racconto, che tu ti culli in una specie di incoscienza. Svegliati, su. Non vuoi? Allora vieni qui, accanto a me. Appoggia la testina su questo guanciale, così. Dormiamo insieme, abbracciati. Io e te, io e te... Nel nostro letto non entrerà mai nessun altro.

— 17 —

È venuto. Non credevo che l'avrebbe mai fatto. Era sera, la chiave ha girato dentro la toppa e ho pensato che fosse la mia amica. Di regola è lei che sale a trovarmi prima di cena. Infatti le ho gridato ciao, certa di vederla entrare ansimante col suo pacchettino: scusa-ho-frettati-porto-un-poco-di-carne-fredda-e-un-po'-di-frutta-torno-domattina. Invece era lui. Dev'essersi insinuato in punta di piedi: mi sono girata, ed eccolo lì, col volto serrato e un mazzo di fiori in mano. La prima cosa che ho provato è stata una morsa nel ventre. Non la solita coltellata: una morsa. Quasi che tu ti fossi spaventato a vederlo e mi avessi afferrato coi pugni per ripararti dietro le mie viscere, nasconderti. Poi mi è mancato il respiro e un'onda di ghiaccio mi ha intirizzito. L'hai sentita anche tu? Ti ha fatto male? Se ne stava lì in silenzio, col suo volto serrato e i suoi fiori. Ho odiato il suo viso e i suoi fiori. Perché piombare a quel modo, come un ladro? Non lo sa che alle donne incinte bisogna evitare ogni trauma? Gli ho chiesto: «Che cosa vuoi?». Ha posato i fiori sul letto, in silenzio. Li ho subito tolti dicendo che i fiori sul letto portano disgrazia, i fiori sul letto si mettono ai morti. E li ho posati sul tavolino. Erano fiori gialli, comprati all'ultimo momento, scommetto: senza scelta e senza convinzione. Lui è rimasto zitto e fermo: un'ombra alta e scura contro il bianco della parete. Però non guardava me. Guardava la tua fotografia sul muro: quella che ti ritrae a due mesi, ingrandito quaranta volte. Avresti detto che non riuscisse a staccare gli occhi dai tuoi occhi e più ti guardava più gli si affondava la testa dentro le spalle. Infine si è coperto il volto con le mani ed è scoppiato in un pianto. Leggermente all'inizio, senza far rumore. Più forte dopo. S'è anche seduto sul letto per piangere meglio, e a ciascun singhiozzo il letto si scuoteva. Infatti gli ho detto: «Stai scuotendo il letto. Le vibrazioni lo disturbano». E lui ha staccato le mani dal volto, si è asciugato col fazzoletto, ed è andato a sedersi su una sedia. Quella sotto la tua fotografia. Era strano vedervi accanto. Tu con le tue pupille ferme, misteriose, lui con le sue pupille tremule, senza segreti. Poi ha schiuso le labbra ed ha detto: «È anche mio».

L'ira mi ha travolto. Sono balzata a sedere sul letto e gli

ho gridato che non eri né mio né suo : eri tuo. Gli ho gridato che detestavo questa retorica da melodramma, questa melensaggine da canzonette, e dovevo stare tranquilla, l'aveva ordinato il dottore : cos'era venuto a fare ? A ucciderti senza aborto perché risparmiassi denaro ? Ho anche sbattuto il mazzo di fiori sul tavolino : tre, quattro volte, finché le corolle si sono staccate volando in aria come coriandoli. Quando son ricaduta sopra i guanciali ero così sudata che il pigiama mi aderiva alla pelle, e il dolore al ventre era così forte che non lo sopportavo. Lui non s'è mosso, invece. Ha chinato la testa e ha sussurrato : «Quanto sei dura, quanto puoi esser cattiva». Poi s'è abbandonato a una specie di interminabile arringa centrata sul fatto che sbagliavo, che eri mio e suo, che ci aveva tanto riflettuto, tanto sofferto, che da due mesi si dilaniava per te, che infine aveva capito quanto la mia scelta fosse nobile e giusta, che un figlio non si dovrebbe mai buttare perché un-figlio-è-un-figlio-non-una-cosa. Ed altre banalità. Infatti l'ho interrotto per esclamare : «Tanto non ce l'hai mica tu dentro il corpo, non devi mica portarlo tu dentro il corpo per nove mesi». E lui ha spalancato la bocca, sorpreso : «Credevo che tu lo volessi, che tu lo facessi volentieri».

Allora è successa una cosa che non capisco : mi son messa a piangere io. Non avevo mai pianto, lo sai, e non volevo piangere : perché mi umiliava, perché mi imbruttiva. Ma più respingevo le lacrime più esse sgorgavano : quasi si fosse rotto qualcosa. Ho provato anche ad accendere una sigaretta. Le lacrime hanno bagnato la sigaretta. E così tuo padre ha lasciato la sedia, è venuto verso di me, mi ha accarezzato la testa. Timidamente. Poi ha mormorato «ti faccio un caffè» ed è andato in cucina a fare il caffè. Quando è tornato, avevo ripreso il controllo di me stessa. Lui no. Reggeva la tazzina come se fosse un gioiello, esagerava in premura. Ho bevuto il caffè. Mi son messa ad aspettare che se ne andasse. Non se n'è andato. Mi ha chiesto che cosa volevo mangiare. E così ho ricordato che la mia amica non era venuta, ho capito che lo aveva mandato lei. E l'ira si è trasferita su lei, su tutti coloro che credono di aiutarti con le leggi del formicaio, il loro arbitrario concetto del giusto e dell'ingiusto. Maria, Gesù, Giuseppe. Perché Giuseppe? Sta così bene Maria col suo bambino e basta. L'unica cosa accettabile, nella leggenda, è proprio quel rapporto a due: la meravigliosa bugia di un uovo che si riempie per partenogenesi. Che ci fa all'improvviso Giuseppe? A chi serve? Tira l'asino che non vuol camminare? Taglia il cordone ombelicale e si accerta che la placenta sia uscita intera? Oppure salva la reputazione di una screanzata che rimase incinta senza marito? Ammenoché non la segua come un domestico per farsi perdonare la colpa d'averle chiesto di abortire.

Lo guardavo raccogliere le corolle dei fiori, chino sul pavimento, e non sentivo nemmeno un po' di amicizia. S'era infranto un equilibrio, al suo ingresso. S'era rotta una simmetria, turbata una complicità: quella che esisteva fra me e te. Era giunto un estraneo, capisci. E s'era messo fra noi ed era come se ci avesse imposto un mobile di cui non si ha bisogno. Anzi ingombra la stanza togliendo luce, rubando aria, facendo inciampare. Forse, se fosse stato con noi fin dall'inizio, ora la sua presenza ci sarebbe sembrata normale e perfin necessaria: non avremmo potuto concepire altro modo di prepararci al tuo arrivo. Ma vederlo piombare così, all'improvviso, con l'indiscrezione e l'inopportunità dell'intruso che si siede al tuo tavolo sebbene tu non l'abbia né invitato né incoraggiato, era quasi offensivo. Avrei voluto dirgli: "Vattene via, per favore. Non abbiamo bisogno né di te, né di Giuseppe, né del Signore

Iddio. Non ci serve un padre, non ci serve un marito, tu sei di troppo". Ma non potevo. Forse mi frenava la timidezza di chi non sa cacciare chi si siede al tuo tavolo senza domandare permesso. Forse mi frenava una pietà che a poco a poco diventava comprensione, rimpianto. Al di là delle sue debolezze, delle sue viltà, chissà quanto s'era tormentato, anche lui. Chissà quanto gli era costato tacere, imporsi di venire con un brutto mazzo di fiori. Non si nasce per partenogenesi, la stilla di luce che aveva bucato l'uovo era sua, metà del nucleo che aveva dato l'avvio al tuo corpo era suo. E il fatto ch'io me ne dimenticassi era il prezzo che pagavamo per l'unica legge che nessuno ammette: un uomo e una donna si incontrano, si piacciono, si desiderano, forse si amano, e dopo un certo tempo non si amano più, non si desiderano più, non si piacciono più, magari vorrebbero non essersi mai incontrati. Ho trovato ciò che cercavo, bambino: tra un uomo e una donna ciò che chiamano amore è una stagione. E se al suo sbocciare questa stagione è una festa di verde, al suo appassire è solo un mucchio di foglie marce.

Gli ho lasciato preparare la cena. Gli ho lasciato aprire quella assurda bottiglia di champagne. (Dove l'aveva nascosta, entrando?) Gli ho lasciato fare un bagno. (Fischiettava, nel bagno, come se tutto fosse sistemato.) E gli ho permesso di dormire qui, nel nostro letto. Ma appena se ne è andato, stamani, ho provato una specie di vergogna. E ora mi sembra d'aver mancato a un impegno, d'averti tradito. Speriamo che non torni mai più.

— 18 —

Camminare per strada dopo tanti giorni in un letto! Sentire il vento sul viso, il sole sugli occhi, vedere altra gente che va, assistere alla vita! Se lo studio del medico non fosse stato lontano, ci sarei andata a piedi: cantando. Ho fermato quel taxi a malincuore. L'autista era un bruto. Fumava un sigaro grasso che mi nauseava, guidava bombardandomi di frenate brusche ed inutili. Dopo qualche metro ho sentito uno spasmo e l'allegria è annegata nel solito nervosismo. Nello studio del medico c'era una fila di donne con la pancia gonfia. Quando la segretaria mi ha pregato di attendere, mi sono irritata. Non mi piaceva allinearmi con le donne dalla pancia gonfia: non avevo nulla in comune con loro. Nemmeno la pancia. La mia è scarsa, si vede e no. Finalmente sono entrata, mi sono spogliata, mi sono distesa sul lettuccio. Il medico ti ha tormentato col dito, pigiando, frugando, poi si è tolto il guanto di gomma e con voce di gelo mi ha chiesto: «Ma lei vuole davvero questo figlio?». Non credevo ai miei orecchi. «Naturalmente. Perché?» gli ho risposto. «Perché molte donne dicono di volerlo e poi, nel subconscio, non lo vogliono affatto. Senza realizzarlo magari, fanno di tutto perché non nasca.» Mi sono indignata. Non ero lì per subire processi alla mia buonafede e nemmeno per discutere di psicanalisi, ho detto, ero lì per sapere come stavi tu. Ha cambiato tono, si è spiegato con garbo. V'erano cose che non capiva in questa gravidanza. Riteneva che l'uovo fosse inserito bene, in sede normale. Riteneva che la crescita del feto avvenisse bene, in modo regolare. E tuttavia qualcosa non funzionava. Ad esempio l'utero era troppo sensibile, si contraeva con eccessiva facilità: ciò alimentava il sospetto che il sangue non affluisse perfettamente alla placenta. Ero stata immobile come mi aveva ordinato? Ho risposto sì. Avevo evitato di bere alcool, avevo fumato meno come s'era raccomandato? Ho risposto sì. Non avevo mai compiuto sforzi, strapazzi? Ho risposto no. Avevo avuto rap-

porti sessuali ? Di nuovo ho risposto no ed era vero, lo sai:
non gli ho permesso di avvicinarsi, l'altra notte, sebbene
lui ripetesse che era una crudeltà. Allora è apparso per-
plesso: «Ha preoccupazioni?». Gli ho risposto sì. «Ha
avuto qualche trauma psicologico, che so, un dispiacere?»
Gli ho risposto sì. Mi ha fissato senza chiedere che tipo di
trauma, che tipo di dispiacere, poi mi ha esposto la sua
tesi. A volte le preoccupazioni, le ansie, gli shock sono più
pericolosi delle fatiche fisiche perché causano spasmi, contrazioni uterine, e minacciano seriamente la vita dell'embrione o del feto. Non dimenticassi che l'utero è in rela-
zione con l'ipofisi, che ogni stimolo si trasmette subito agli
organi genitali. Una sorpresa violenta, un dolore, una collera, possono provocare il distacco parziale dell'uovo. Lo
può addirittura un nervosismo costante, un perpetuo stato
d'angoscia. Al limite, e lungi da lui l'intenzione di sconfi-
nare nella fantascienza o nella fantapsicologia, si poteva
parlare di un pensiero che uccide. Al livello inconscio,
s'intende, e per questo dovevo assolutamente impormi
d'esser tranquilla. Dovevo rigorosamente evitare ogni
emozione, ogni pensiero nero. Serenità, placidità erano le
parole d'ordine. Dottore, ho risposto, è lo stesso che chiedermi di cambiare il colore degli occhi: come faccio ad essere placida se la mia natura non lo è? Mi ha squadrato di
nuovo con freddezza: «Questo è affar suo. Si arrangi. In-
grassi». Poi mi ha prescritto antispastici e altre medicine.
Se per caso appare una goccia di sangue, corra da lui.

Sono impaurita. Ed anche adirata con te. Cosa credi
che sia: un contenitore, un barattolo dove si mette un
oggetto da custodire? Sono una donna, perdio, sono una
persona. Non posso svitarmi il cervello e proibirgli di
pensare. Non posso annullare i miei sentimenti o proibirgli di manifestarsi. Non posso ignorare una rabbia, una
gioia, un dolore. Ho le mie reazioni, io, i miei stupori, i

miei scoramenti. Anche se potessi, non vorrei disfarmene per ridurmi allo stato di un vegetale o di una macchina fisiologica che serve a procreare e basta! Quanto sei esigente, bambino. Prima pretendi di controllare il mio corpo e privarlo del suo più elementare diritto: muoversi. Poi pretendi addirittura di controllare la mia mente e il mio cuore: atrofizzandoli, neutralizzandoli, derubandoli della loro capacità di sentire, pensare, vivere! Accusi perfino il mio inconscio. Questo è eccessivo, è inaccettabile. Se vogliamo restare insieme, bambino, dobbiamo scendere a patti. Eccoli. Ti faccio una concessione: ingrasso, ti regalo il mio corpo. Ma la mia mente no. Le mie reazioni no. Me le tengo. E con quelle pretendo una mancia: i miei piaceri spiccioli. Infatti ora bevo uno whisky, e fumo un pacchetto di sigarette, una dopo l'altra, e riprendo a lavorare, ad esistere come persona e non come barattolo, e piango, piango, piango: senza chiederti se ti fa male. Perché sono stufa di te!

— 19 —

Perdonami. Dovevo essere ubriaca, impazzita. Guarda quante cicche, e guarda questo fazzoletto. È ancora bagnato. Che crisi di furore imbecille, che scena disgustosa. Egoista. Come stai, bambino? Meglio di me, spero. Io sono esausta. Sono così stanca che vorrei resistere altri sei mesi, il tempo di portarti alla luce, e poi morire. Tu prenderesti il mio posto nel mondo e io mi riposerei. Non sarebbe neanche troppo presto: mi sembra d'avere ormai visto tutto ciò che v'era da vedere, d'avere ormai capito tutto ciò che v'era da capire. E comunque, una volta uscito dal mio corpo, non avrai più bisogno di me. Qualsiasi donna capace di amarti sarà un'ottima madre per te: la voce del sangue non esiste, è un'invenzione. La mamma non è colei che ti porta nel ventre, è colei che ti cresce. O colui che ti cresce. Potrei regalarti a tuo padre. Tuo padre è tornato poco fa e mi ha portato una rosa blu. Ha detto che il blu è il colore del maschio. Ora pensa anche al colore. Ovviamente desidera che tu sia maschio: nascere maschio per lui è un merito maggiore, un segno di superiorità. Poveretto. Non è colpa sua, hanno raccontato anche a lui che Dio è un vecchio con la barba bianca, che Maria era un'incubatrice, che senza Giuseppe non avrebbe trovato nemmeno una stalla, che ad accendere il fuoco fu un uomo chiamato Prometeo. Io non lo disprezzo per questo. Tuttavia dico che non ho, non abbiamo bisogno di lui. Né della sua rosa blu. Gli ho ordinato di andarsene, di lasciarci in pace. Ha barcollato come sotto una legnata, s'è avviato verso la porta, se n'è andato senza rispondere. Tra poco ce ne andiamo anche noi: a lavorare. Il commendatore mi ha ricordato la sua comprensione però ha aggiunto che bisogna rispettare gli impegni: una donna incinta può lasciare l'impiego solo al sesto mese. Mi ha ricordato anche il viaggio: minacciando con perfido garbo di trasferire l'incarico a un uomo perché a-un-uomo-non-accadono-certi-incidenti. Ho frenato a stento la tentazione di aggredirlo, e mi son messa a tergiversare. I prossimi dieci giorni saranno duri, devo guadagnare il tempo perduto. Ma ti dirò: l'idea di riprendere le mie attività mi scuote da questo torpore, da questa rassegnazione che mi fa sognare la morte. Menomale che è già incominciato l'inverno: sotto il cappotto, il ventre gonfio non si noterà. E, d'ora innanzi, crescerà parecchio. Stamani ad esempio è più gonfio. Il vestito mi tira. A quattordici settimane, sai quanto sei lungo? Almeno dieci centimetri. Perfino la placenta, ormai troppo piccola per avviluppare il sacco amniotico, sta tirandosi da parte. E tu stai invadendomi senza pietà.

— 20 —

Non sono una persona che si spaventa alla vista del sangue. Ed essere donne è una scuola di sangue: tutti i mesi offriamo a noi stesse il suo spettacolo odioso. Ma quando ho visto quella minuscola macchia sopra il cuscino, i miei occhi si sono annebbiati e le mie gambe si sono piegate. M'ha invaso il panico, poi la disperazione, e mi son maledetta. Mi sono accusata di ogni colpa verso di te che non potevi proteggerti, non potevi ribellarti, così piccino e indifeso e alla mercé di ogni mio capriccio, ogni mia irresponsabilità. Non era nemmeno rossa, la macchia. Era rosa, d'un pallido rosa. E tuttavia era più che sufficiente a trasmettermi il messaggio, ad annunciarmi che stavi forse finendo. Ho agguantato il cuscino e son corsa. Il medico è stato inaspettatamente gentile. Mi ha ricevuto sebbene fosse sera, mi ha detto di calmarmi: non stavi morendo, non t'eri staccato, avevi sofferto e basta, si trattava di una minaccia e basta, il riposo assoluto avrebbe sistemato ogni cosa. Purché fosse assoluto. Purché non scendessi dal letto nemmeno per andare nel bagno. E per questo era meglio che mi ricoverassi in ospedale.

Siamo all'ospedale. Una camera triste di questo mondo triste. Ci siamo da una settimana che ho trascorso quasi sempre dormendo, obnubilata dai sedativi. Ora li hanno sospesi ma è peggio: non so come impiegare il tempo che gocciola vuoto. Ho chiesto i giornali e non me li hanno portati. Ho chiesto una televisione e me l'hanno negata. Ho chiesto un telefono e non funziona. La mia amica non viene, tuo padre nemmeno, il silenzio mi abbrutisce e

60

mi schiaccia. Prigioniera d'una belva vestita di bianco che ognitanto arriva con un'iniezione di luteina, non riesco nemmeno a trasmetterti un po' di tenerezza. Ma riflessioni a lungo sopite, invano soffocate, salgono alla superficie della mia coscienza e gridano cose che non sapevo di sapere. Queste. Perché dovrei sopportare una tale agonia? In nome di che cosa? Di un reato commesso abbracciando un uomo? Di una cellula scissa in due cellule e poi in quattro e poi in otto, all'infinito, senza che io lo volessi, senza che io lo ordinassi? Oppure in nome della vita? E va bene, la vita. Ma cos'è questa vita per cui tu, che esisti non ancora fatto, conti più di me che esisto già fatta? Cos'è questo rispetto per te che toglie rispetto a me? Cos'è questo tuo diritto ad esistere che non tiene conto del mio diritto ad esistere? Non c'è umanità in te... Umanità! Ma sei un essere umano, tu? Bastano davvero una bollicina d'uovo e uno spermio di cinque micron a fare un essere umano? Essere umano son io che penso e parlo e rido e piango e agisco in un mondo che agisce per costruire cose ed idee. Tu non sei che un bambolottino di carne che non pensa, non parla, non ride, non piange, e agisce soltanto per costruire se stesso. Ciò che vedo in te non sei te: sono io! Ti ho attribuito una coscienza, ho dialogato con te, ma la tua coscienza era la mia coscienza e il nostro dialogo era un monologo: il mio! Basta con questa commedia, con questo delirio. Non si è umani per diritto naturale, prima di nascere. Umani lo si diventa dopo, quando si è nati, perché si sta con gli altri, perché ci aiutano gli altri, perché una madre o una donna o un uomo o non importa chi ci insegna a mangiare, a camminare, a parlare, a pensare, a comportarsi da umani. L'unica cosa che ci unisce, mio caro, è un cordone ombelicale. E non siamo una coppia. Siamo un persecutore e un perseguitato. Tu al posto del persecutore e io al posto del perseguitato... Ti insinuasti in me come un ladro, e mi rapinasti il ventre, il sangue, il respiro. Ora vorresti rapinarmi l'esistenza intera. Non te lo permetterò. E giacché sono arrivata a dirti queste verità sacrosante, sai cosa concludo? Non vedo perché dovrei avere un bambino. Non mi sono mai trovata a mio agio, io, coi bambini. Non sono mai riuscita a trattare con loro. Quando mi avvicino con un sorriso, strillano come se li picchiassi. Il mestiere di mamma non mi si addice. Io ho altri doveri verso la vita. Ho un lavoro che mi piace e intendo farlo. Ho un futuro che mi aspetta e non intendo abbandonarlo. Chi assolve una donna povera che non vuole altri figli, chi assolve una ragazza violentata che non vuole quel figlio, deve assolvere anche me. Essere povere, essere violentate, non costituisce la sola giustificazione. Lascio questo ospedale e parto per il mio viaggio. Poi sarà quel che sarà. Se riuscirai a nascere, nascerai. Se non ci riuscirai, morirai. Io non ti ammazzo, sia chiaro: semplicemente, mi rifiuto di aiutarti ad esercitar fino in fondo la tua tirannia e...

Questo non era il nostro patto, me ne rendo conto. Ma un patto è un accordo dove ciascuno dà per ricevere, e quando lo firmammo ignoravo che avresti preteso tutto per darmi nulla. Del resto tu non lo firmasti per niente, lo firmai soltanto io. Ciò ne incrina la validità. Non lo firmasti e da te non mi giunse mai un assenso: il tuo unico messaggio è stato una goccia rosa di sangue. Ch'io sia maledetta davvero, e per sempre, che la mia vita diventi un rimpianto perpetuo, al di là della morte, se stavolta cambio la mia decisione.

— 21 —

Mi ha definito assassina. Chiuso dentro il suo camice bianco, non più medico ma giudice, ha tuonato che vengo meno ai doveri più fondamentali di madre e di donna e di cittadina. Ha gridato che lasciar l'ospedale sarebbe già un misfatto, scendere dal letto già un crimine, ma intraprendere un viaggio è omicidio premeditato e la legge dovrebbe punirmi come punisce un qualsiasi assassino. Poi s'è fatto supplice, ha tentato di convincermi con la tua fotografia. Che ti osservassi bene se avevo un minimo di cuore: eri ormai un bambino in tutto e per tutto. La tua bocca non era più l'idea di una bocca ma una bocca. Il tuo naso non era più l'idea di un naso: ma un naso. Il tuo viso non era più l'abbozzo di un viso: ma un viso. E lo stesso il tuo corpo, le tue mani, i tuoi piedi dove le unghie erano evidenti. Era evidente anche un principio di capelli sulla testolina ben formata. Che mi rendessi conto, al tempo stesso, della tua fragilità. Che studiassi la tua pelle: così delicata, così diafana che attraverso di essa traspariva ogni vena, ogni capillare, ogni nervo. Non eri neanche più minuscolo: misuravi almeno sedici centimetri e pesavi due etti. Se avessi voluto abortirti non avrei potuto: sarebbe stato tardi. Eppure mi accingevo a fare qualcosa che era peggio di un aborto. L'ho ascoltato senza battere ciglio. Ho firmato un foglio con cui egli declinava ogni responsabilità per la tua vita e la mia, ed io me le assumevo al suo posto. L'ho guardato uscire dalla camera in preda a un furore che lo rendeva paonazzo. E, quasi in quel momento, tu ti sei mosso. Hai fatto ciò che avevo aspettato, agognato, per mesi. Ti sei allungato, forse hai sbadigliato, e mi hai tirato un piccolo colpo. Un piccolo calcio. Il tuo primo calcio... Come quello che tirai a mia madre per dirle di non buttarmi via. Le mie gambe son diventate di marmo. E per qualche secondo son rimasta con il fiato mozzo, le tempie che mi pulsavano. Ho sentito anche un bruciore alla gola, una lacrima che mi accecava. Poi la lacrima è ruzzolata giù, è caduta sul lenzuolo facendo: paf! Ma sono scesa ugualmente dal letto. Ho preparato ugualmente la valigia. Domani si parte, ho detto. In aereo.

— 22 —

Ma era proprio il caso di pigliarsela tanto? Stiamo benissimo nel paese in cui siamo venuti. Siamo stati benissimo durante l'intero viaggio e all'arrivo e dopo. Mai uno spasmo, un dolore, una nausea. Non è successo nulla di ciò che il medico aveva annunciato: ho la conferma della dottoressa che mi ha visitato ieri. Simpatica. Dopo averti garbatamente palpato ha concluso che non vede ragioni per allarmarsi, il suo collega eccedeva in pessimismo e prudenza, una goccia di sangue cos'è? Vi sono donne che perdono sangue per l'intera durata della gravidanza e poi mettono al mondo figli sanissimi. Secondo lei stare a letto è contro natura. Ed anche eccedere nelle precauzioni. Una sua cliente, ad esempio, ballerina di professione, aveva continuato a esibirsi nel pas à deux fino a dopo il quinto mese. Di me la meravigliava soltanto lo scarso gonfiore del ventre. Però anche la ballerina aveva un ventre pressoché piatto. Che continuassi pure coi medicamenti prescritti dal collega, se desideravo, ma soprattutto lasciassi la natura provvedere da sé. Unico consiglio, non guidare troppo l'automobile. Le ho spiegato che in automobile dobbiamo fare un viaggio di almeno dieci giorni. Mi ha chiesto se fosse proprio necessario. Le ho risposto di sì, e allora è rimasta zitta per qualche minuto. Ma poi ha concluso pazienza, le strade di questo paese sono comode e lisce, le macchine di questo paese sono ben molleggiate: l'importante è non strapazzarsi e concedersi ogni due o tre ore un riposo. Mi ascolti? Sto dicendo che ho fatto pace con te, che ora siamo amici! Sto dicendo che mi dispiace averti maltrattato, sfidato. E ancora di più mi dispiace se resti offeso e non mi tiri colpetti. Non me ne hai tirati più, dopo l'ospedale. A volte, pensandoci, aggrotto la fronte.

Dura poco però. Subito dopo ritrovo la tranquillità: intuisci quanto sono cambiata? Dacché ho ripreso la vita di sempre, mi sembra d'essere un'altra: un gabbiano che vola. Davvero ci fu un momento in cui desideravo la morte? Pazza. È così bella la vita, la luce. Sono così belli gli alberi e la terra e il mare. C'è molto mare qui: te ne arriva il profumo, il fragore? È bello anche lavorare se dentro di te guizza una gioia. Sbagliavo a sostenere che in ogni caso il lavoro stanca e umilia. Devi scusarmi: la collera, l'ansia, mi facevano veder tutto buio. E a proposito del buio: è sorta di nuovo in me l'impazienza di tirartene fuori. Con quella, il timore di averti scoraggiato attraverso le chiacchiere sulla libertà che non esiste e sulla solitudine che è l'unica condizione possibile. Dimentica certe sciocchezze: stare gomito a gomito serve. La vita è una comunità per darci la mano, consolarci, aiutarci. Anche le piante fioriscono meglio una accanto all'altra, e gli uccelli migrano a gruppi, i pesci nuotano a branchi. Che faremmo soli? Ci sentiremmo come astronauti sulla Luna, soffocati dalla paura e dalla fretta di tornare indietro. Sbrigati, trascorri alla svelta i mesi che ti rimangono, non aver paura di vedere il sole. Lì per lì ti abbaglierà, ti spaventerà, ma presto diverrà un'allegria di cui non potrai fare a meno. Io mi pento d'averti fornito sempre gli esempi più brutti, di non averti mai raccontato lo splendore di un'alba, la dolcezza di un bacio, il profumo di un cibo. Io mi pento di non averti fatto ridere mai. Se tu mi giudicassi dalle fiabe che narravo, saresti autorizzato a concludere che sono una specie di Elettra sempre vestita di nero. D'ora innanzi devi immaginarmi come un Peter Pan sempre vestito di giallo di verde di rosso e sempre intento a stendere nastri di fiori sui tetti, sui campanili, sulle nuvole che non diventano pioggia. Saremo felici insieme perché, in fondo, sono un bambino anch'io. Lo sai che mi diverto a giocare? Stanotte rientrando in albergo ho scambiato tutte le scarpe messe fuori delle camere ed anche le richieste delle colazioni. Al mattino è scoppiato il subbuglio. Una signora aveva trovato un paio di mocassini da uomo e reclamava i suoi sandali col tacco, un uomo aveva trovato due scarpette da tennis e reclamava i suoi stivali, un tale protestava perché non aveva chiesto un pranzo di Natale ma un tè col limone. L'orecchio appoggiato alla porta, ascoltavo e ridevo in modo così divertito che mi sembrava d'esser tornata alla mia fanciullezza. Quand'ero felice perché ogni gesto era un gioco.

— 23 —

Ti ho comprato una culla. Dopo averla comprata m'è venuto in mente che, secondo alcuni, possedere una culla prima che il bambino nasca porta disgrazia come i fiori sul letto. Ma le superstizioni non mi toccano più. È una culla indiana, di quelle che si portano a zaino dietro le spalle. È gialla e verde e rossa come Peter Pan. Ti caricherò sulle spalle, ti porterò ovunque così, e la gente sorriderà dicendo: guarda quei due fanciulli matti. Ti ho comprato anche un guardaroba: magliette, tutine, e un bel carillon che suona un valzer festoso. Quando l'ho detto alla mia amica, per telefono, ha commentato che manco di qualsiasi equilibrio. Però aveva una voce contenta, lavata

dell'inquietudine che la serrava il giorno in cui partimmo:
e-se-lo-perdi-in-aereo? Lei che mi consigliava di elimi-
narti all'inizio! È davvero una brava donna. Infatti non
sono mai riuscita a rimproverarla per avermi mandato tuo
padre. E quanto a lui, sai che dico? Un uomo che accetta
di farsi cacciare come lo cacciai io non è un uomo da but-
tar via. Mi ha scritto una lettera, dopo. Mi ha commosso.
Sono un vigliacco, mi ha scritto, perché sono un uomo;
però devo essere assolto perché sono un uomo. Un atavico
istinto, suppongo, lo induce ormai a desiderarti. Vedremo
cosa fare di lui: a volte un mobile di cui non si ha bisogno
finisce col dimostrarsi utile. Ed è certo che non ho più voglia di essergli nemica. In questo armistizio col formicaio
c'entrano tutti: lui, i medici, il commendatore. Se tu avessi
visto il commendatore mentre gli annunciavo la nostra
partenza. Ripeteva: «Ecco una buona notizia. Brava, non
se ne pentirà!».

No, non me ne pentirò. È solo rispettando se stessi che
si può esigere il rispetto degli altri, è solo credendo in se
stessi che si può essere creduti dagli altri. Buonanotte,
bambino. Domani incomincia il viaggio in automobile.
Vorrei scriverti una poesia per narrare il mio sollievo, la
mia fiducia ritrovata, e questa voglia di tendere nastri di
fiori sui tetti, sui campanili, sulle nuvole, questa sensazione di volare come un gabbiano dentro l'azzurro, lontano dalle sporcizie, dalle malinconie, su un mare che dal-
l'alto sembra sempre pulito. In fondo il coraggio è ottimismo. Io non ero ottimista perché non ero coraggiosa.

— 24 —

Le strade di questo paese sono comode e lisce, le au-
tomobili di questo paese sono ben molleggiate: dottores-

sa, lei mente. Ed io non sono un gabbiano. Cosa faccio, bambino? Vado avanti, torno indietro? Se torno indietro è peggio: devo rifare lo stesso tratto impossibile. Se vado avanti, invece, ho speranza che migliori. Avendo il coraggio della retorica, potrei dire che sto guidando lungo una strada uguale alla mia vita: tutta buche e sassi, difficoltà. Una volta conobbi uno scrittore che diceva: ciascuno ha la vita che si merita. Come dire che un povero merita d'essere povero, che un cieco merita d'essere cieco. Era un uomo stupido, sebbene fosse uno scrittore intelligente. Anche il filo che divide l'intelligenza dalla stupidaggine è un filo talmente sottile, te ne accorgerai. Infatti, quando si rompe, le due cose si fondono insieme come l'amore e l'odio, la vita e la morte, che tu sia uomo o donna. Sono tornata a chiedermi se sei un uomo o una donna ed ormai vorrei che tu fossi un uomo. Così non avresti la scuola mensile di sangue, un giorno non ti giudicheresti colpevole di guidare lungo una strada sconvolta dalle buche e dai sassi. Non ti sentiresti male come in questo momento mi sento io e potresti librarti su nell'azzurro molto più seriamente di quanto faccia io: i miei sforzi per volare non vanno mai oltre il balzo di un tacchino. Le donne che bruciano il reggiseno hanno ragione. Hanno ragione? Nessuna di loro ha scoperto un sistema perché il mondo non finisca se non fai bambini. E i bambini nascono dalle donne. Conosco un racconto di fantascienza che si svolge su un pianeta dove per procreare bisogna essere in sette. Ma è molto difficile trovarsi in sette ed è ancor più difficile mettersi d'accordo in sette perché la gravidanza, non solo il concepimento, coinvolge tutti e sette. Perciò la razza si estingue e il pianeta si vuota. Conosco un altro racconto dove al protagonista basta una soluzione alcalina, per riprodursi, o un bicchiere d'acqua col sale. Ci salta dentro e paf! Diventano due. Si tratta di una normale scissione cellulare e, nell'attimo in cui il protagonista si scinde, cessa d'esser se stesso: compie una specie di suicidio del suo io. Però non muore e non soffre nove mesi d'inferno. D'inferno? Per alcune, sono nove mesi di gloria. La soluzione migliore resta quella che ti dissi in principio. Si toglie l'embrione dal ventre della madre, lo si mette nel ventre di un'altra disposta ad ospitarlo, una più paziente di me, più generosa di me... Credo d'avere la febbre. Gli spasmi sono ricominciati. Devo ignorarli. Ma come? Pensando a tutt'altre cose, suppongo. Potrei raccontarti una fiaba. È tanto che non ti racconto una fiaba... Eccola.

— 25 —

C'era una volta una donna che sognava un pezzetto di luna. Anzi, nemmeno un pezzetto: un po' di polvere le sarebbe bastata. Non era un sogno irrealizzabile, tantomeno bizzarro. Lei conosceva gli uomini che andavano sulla luna, andarci era una gran moda a quel tempo. Gli uomini partivano da un punto della Terra non lontano da qui, con piccole navi di ferro, agganciate sulla cima di un altissimo razzo, e ogni volta che il razzo schizzava nel cielo, tuonando, seminando fiori di fuoco come una cometa, la donna era molto felice. Gridava: «Go, go, go! Vai, vai, vai!». Poi seguiva trepidante e gelosa il viaggio degli uomini che volavano tre giorni e tre notti, nel buio.

Gli uomini che andavano sulla luna erano uomini sciocchi. Avevano sciocchi volti di pietra e non sapevano ridere, non sapevano piangere. La luna per loro era un'impresa scientifica e basta, una conquista della tecnologia. Durante il viaggio non dicevano mai qualcosa di bello, solo numeri e formule e informazioni noiose, se al-ternavano lampi di umanità era per chieder notizie su una squadra di football. Una volta sbarcati sulla luna sapevano dire ancor meno. Al massimo pronunciavano due o tre frasi fatte. Poi piantavano una bandiera di latta, con movimenti da automa si abbandonavano a un cerimoniale di gesti scontati, e ripartivano dopo aver sporcato la luna coi loro escrementi che così restavano a testimoniare il passaggio dell'Uomo. Gli escrementi eran chiusi dentro scatolette, le scatolette venivano lasciate lì con la bandiera, e se lo sapevi non riuscivi a guardare la luna senza pensare: «Lassù ci sono anche i loro escrementi». Infine tornavano pieni di sassi, di polvere. Sassi di luna, polvere di luna. La polvere che la donna sognava. E rivedendoli lei elemosinava (io elemosinavo): «Mi dai un poco di luna? Ne hai tanta!». Ma loro rispondevano sempre: non-si-può-è-proibito. Tutta la luna finiva nei laboratori, sulle scrivanie dei personaggi per cui andarci era un'impresa scientifica e basta, una conquista della tecnologia. Erano uomini sciocchi, perché erano uomini privi di anima. Eppure ce n'era uno che a me sembrava migliore. Infatti sapeva ridere e piangere. Era un omino brutto, coi denti radi e una gran paura addosso. Per nasconderla rideva buffe risate e portava buffi cappelli. Io gli ero amica per questo e perché sapeva di non meritare la luna. Incontrandomi brontolava: «Cosa dirò lassù? Io non sono un poeta, non so dire cose belle e profonde». Pochi giorni prima di andar sulla luna venne da me, per salutarmi e chiedermi cosa dire sulla luna. Gli risposi che doveva dire qualcosa di vero, qualcosa di onesto, ad esempio che era un omino colmo di paura perché era un omino. Ciò gli piacque e giurò: «Se torno ti porto un poco di luna. Polvere di luna». Partì e tornò. Ma tornò cambiato. Se gli telefonavo per ricordargli la promessa, rispondeva evasivo.

Poi, una sera, mi invitò a cena nella sua casa e io mi precipitai credendo che volesse darmi finalmente la luna. A tavola ero inquieta, la cena non finiva mai. Quando finì, lui disse: «Ora ti faccio vedere la luna». Non disse ora-ti-do-la-luna. Disse ora-ti-faccio-vedere-la-luna. Ma io non notai la differenza. Portava ancora quei buffi cappelli, rideva ancora quelle buffe risate, non sospettavo che in cielo avesse perduto anche il goccio d'anima che gli attribuivo.

Mi accompagnò nel suo studio, ammiccando. Aprì un armadio chiuso a chiave, giocando. Dentro l'armadio c'erano alcuni oggetti: una specie di vanga, una specie di zappa, un tubo... Tutti coperti da una polvere strana, color grigio argento. La polvere di luna. Il mio cuore prese a battere forte. Col cuore che batteva forte allungai una mano, agguantai delicatamente la vanga. Era una vanga leggera, quasi priva di peso, e la polvere era una specie di cipria, un velo d'argento che sulla pelle restava come una seconda pelle d'argento, e non saprei dirti che cosa provai a vedere la luna sulla mia pelle. Forse la sensazione di espandermi nel tempo e nello spazio, o di raggiungere l'irraggiungibile, l'idea stessa dell'infinito. Cose che penso ora, però. In quel momento non potevo pensare. Anche ora che cerco, frugando nel ricordo della coscienza, riesco a dirti soltanto che me ne stavo lì sbalordita, tenendo in mano la vanga, e non mi accorgevo nemmeno che lui diventava impaziente: quasi temesse di vedersi rubare un tesoro di cui non era disposto a conceder nemmeno il ricordo. Quando me ne accorsi, gliela restituii e sussurrai: «Grazie. Ora dammi la polvere di luna». Divenne subito duro: «Che polvere di luna?». «Quella che mi hai promesso...» «L'hai appena avuta. Te l'ho lasciata toccare». Credevo che scherzasse. Impiegai minuti più lunghi di anni per rendermi conto che non scherzava, che la sua promessa s'era esaurita nell'atto di lasciarmi toccare la vanga. Proprio quel che si fa coi poveri quando gli si consente di ammirare un gioiello in vetrina o di guardar da lontano una festa cui non devono partecipare. Nella sorpresa, il dolore, non riuscivo neanche a rinfacciargli l'imbroglio, rimproverargli tanta meschinità. Mi ripetevo soltanto: se riuscissi a convincerlo che ciò è troppo malvagio. E in questa pazza speranza cominciai a supplicarlo, spiegargli che non gli chiedevo un pezzetto di luna, gli chiedevo soltanto la polvere di luna che mi aveva promesso, pochina, ne aveva tanta dentro l'armadio, ogni oggetto ne era coperto, bastava che mi permettesse di raccoglierne un po' sopra un foglio; su qualcosa che non fosse la mia pelle, per guardarla di nuovo negli anni a venire, era sempre stato un desiderio per me, lo sapeva, non un capriccio. Ma, più mi umiliavo, più lui diventava duro. Mi fissava con gelidi occhi e taceva. Infine, tacendo, richiuse l'armadio ed uscì dalla stanza. Dal salotto sua moglie chiedeva se volevamo un caffè.

Non risposi. Me ne rimasi ferma a guardar la mia mano coperta di luna. Avevo la luna in mano e non sapevo dove appoggiarla, come conservarla: al minimo contatto sarebbe sparita. Il mio cervello cercava invano una soluzione, uno stratagemma che offrisse la via di salvare il salvabile, ma trovava solo una nebbia, e dentro la nebbia una frase: «Sarebbe come toglier la cipria. Ovunque la spalmi è perduta». Ed era questo il tormento più grande, la sevizia che Tantalo non aveva mai conosciuto. Tantalo si vedeva sfuggire il frutto nell'attimo in cui stava per afferrarlo, non se lo vedeva svanire dopo averlo afferrato. Poi detti un'ultima occhiata alla mia mano d'argento, spalancata in un gesto di supplica assurda, inghiottii un desiderio di lacrime, sorrisi con amarezza. Da lontananze infinite la luna era giunta a me, s'era posata sulla mia pelle, ed io mi accingevo a buttarla via. Per sempre. Anche volendo non avrei potuto restare così, con le dita tese, senza toccare altre cose. Prima o poi le avrei posate in un posto, capisci, e tutto sarebbe svanito come svanisce il fumo : per la beffa crudele di un imbecille crudele. Strinsi la mano con rabbia. La spalancai di nuovo. Ora sulla palma si vedeva appena un arabesco di righe sporche, contorte, e guardarle mi dava un ribrezzo. Per arrivare a questo ribrezzo avevo tanto sognato, aspettato ?

Quando me ne andai, la luna era bianca e illuminava la notte di bianco. La fissavi con occhi appannati e pensavi : appena esiste una cosa bianca, pulita, c'è sempre qualcuno che la insozza con i suoi escrementi. Poi ti chiedevi : perché ? Ma perché ? In albergo aprii il rubinetto dell'acqua, ci posai sotto la mano. Ne colò un liquido nero che presto scomparve in un vortice nero e sai che ti dico, bambino ? Tu sei come la mia luna, la mia polvere di luna. Gli spasmi sono raddoppiati, non posso più guidare. Se trovassi un motel, se potessi fermarmi, riposarmi. Col cervello più lucido, forse, scoprirei una soluzione per salvare il salvabile : non buttare via la mia luna. Non voglio perder di nuovo la luna, vederla sparire in fondo a un lavabo. Ma è inutile. Con la stessa certezza che mi paralizzava la notte in cui seppi che esistevi, ora so che stai cessando di esistere.

— 26 —

Ho interrotto il viaggio. Sono tornata in città e ho telefonato alla dottoressa che non ci credeva. Ripeteva sia calma, quindici giorni fa tutto andava bene : certo è la sua fantasia. Le ho risposto che il sangue non è fantasia, che per una settimana sono stata ferma in un motel con il solo risultato di vedere uno stillicidio di sangue. Mi ha ordinato di raggiungerla immediatamente. Sulla porta sorrideva, col consueto ottimismo. Mi sono spogliata alla svelta, prima che me lo dicesse. Mi sono distesa sul lettuccio e lei m'ha appoggiato una mano sul cuore. Ha esclamato: «Come batte! Fa rumore quanto un tamburo». Non ho risposto né alla sua dolcezza né al suo sorriso. L'altrui comprensione non mi serviva più e v'era in me la sicurezza di partecipare a una cerimonia superflua, segretamente attesa, in fondo, e forse voluta. Ero pronta, rassegnata, convinta che non avrei reagito perché tutto quello che c'era da dire l'avevo già detto, tutto quello che c'era da patire l'avevo già patito. Ma quando la cerimonia è iniziata ho compreso che non sarei mai stata pronta, mai. Perfino ascoltare le sue domande mi faceva male, perfino rispondervi. «Lo ha sentito muovere, recentemente?» «No.» «Si è sentita più pesante, più goffa?» «No.» «E quando s'è messa in testa l'idea che...» «Sulla strada accidentata, prima di arrivare al motel.» «Piuttosto insufficiente per cavarne giudizi. E tocca a me esprimer giudizi, sì o no?» Poi mi ha scoperto il ventre, ha notato che in realtà sembrava più piatto di prima. Mi ha palpato i seni, ha osservato che in realtà sembravano meno turgidi di prima. Si è infilata il guanto di gomma, ti ha cercato. E la sua fronte s'è corrugata, i suoi occhi si sono rabbuiati mentre diceva: «L'utero ha perso tono. Si presenta avvizzito. È lecito sospettare che il bambino non cresca bene, che non cresca più. Dovremmo fare un esame biologico, aspettare ancora qualche giorno.» Poi si è sfilata il guanto, lo ha buttato via. Si è appoggiata con entrambe le mani al lettuccio. Mi ha fissato con mestizia: «Tanto vale che glielo dica subito. Ha ragione lei. Non cresce più. Almeno da due settimane e forse da tre. Si faccia coraggio, è finita. È morto».

Non ho risposto nulla. Non ho fatto un gesto. Non ho battuto un ciglio. Sono rimasta lì con un corpo che era pietra e silenzio. Anche il cervello era pietra e silenzio. Non vi si annidava un pensiero, una parola. L'unica sensazione era un peso insopportabile sopra lo stomaco, un piombo invisibile che mi schiacciava come se il cielo mi fosse precipitato addosso: senza far rumore. Nell'immobilità assoluta, nella mancanza di suoni assoluta, il suo invito è esploso col fragore di uno sparo: «Coraggio, si alzi. Si vesta». Mi sono alzata e le gambe eran pietra dentro la pietra, bisognava che compissi uno sforzo disumano per indurle a obbedire. Mi sono vestita e ho udito la mia voce che chiedeva cosa avrei dovuto fare, un'altra voce che rispondeva: «Niente. Lui starà lì ancora per un poco. Poi se ne andrà spontaneamente». Ho annuito. Allora l'altra voce ha ammucchiato frasi su frasi, un incessante ronzio che mi pregava di non avvilirmi, molti bambini se ne vanno perché non sono perfetti, non sono formati bene, chi vuole mettere al mondo un bambino che non è perfetto, non formato bene, non dovevo condannarmi, non dovevo rimproverarmi per colpe incommesse, la gravidanza è tale quando si svolge con naturalezza, lei era contraria al sistema di coloro che costringono una donna a letto per mesi e impediscono alla natura di fare il suo corso. Ho pagato. L'ho salutata con un cenno della testa. Sono uscita tra due filari di pance gonfie, le pance gonfie si offrivano provocatorie al mio ventre piatto che chiudeva un morto, e finalmente il mio cervello ha pensato qualcosa. Ha pensato: "È andata come doveva andare. Dunque ci vuole coerenza". E la parola coerenza mi ha accompagnato fino all'albergo,

martellante, ossessiva: coerenza, coerenza, coerenza. Ma
quando sono entrata nella mia stanza e ho visto la culla,
ho visto il carillon, le magliette del tuo guardaroba, ho
vomitato un gemito lungo. E son caduta sul letto, mentre
un altro gemito si aggiungeva a quel gemito, poi un altro,
e un altro ancora, finché dal profondo del corpo dove
ormai giaci come un pezzettino di carne che non conta
più nulla è salito un gran pianto, e ha schiantato la pietra rompendola in mille pezzetti, sbriciolandola in polvere. E ho urlato. E sono svenuta.

— 27 —

Forse è successo durante il sonno cui mi sono abban-
donata dopo aver ripreso i sensi. O forse durante il
delirio. Comunque è successo: me ne ricordo con luci-
dità. C'era una sala candida, con sette scanni e una gabbia. Io ero dentro la gabbia e loro sugli scanni, remoti e
irraggiungibili. Sullo scanno centrale stava il medico che
mi curava prima del viaggio. Alla sua destra stava la
dottoressa, alla sua sinistra il commendatore. Accanto al
commendatore stava la mia amica e accanto alla mia
amica stava tuo padre. Accanto alla dottoressa stavano
i miei genitori. Nessun altro. E nessun oggetto intorno o
alle pareti o per terra. Ma ho capito subito che si stava
celebrando un processo dove ero io l'accusata, e che i sette
costituivano la giuria. Non ho provato panico, né smarri-
mento. Con infinita rassegnazione mi son messa a stu-
diarli, uno a uno. Tuo padre singhiozzava piano, copren-
dosi il viso come il giorno in cui s'era seduto sul letto. I
miei genitori tenevano il capo chino, quasi fossero oppressi
da una mortale stanchezza o da un mortale dolore. La mia
amica sembrava triste. Gli altri tre, impenetrabili. S'è al-

zato il medico e ha incominciato a leggere un foglio: «Presente l'imputata, questa giuria si riunisce per giudicarla del reato di omicidio premeditato per aver voluto e provocato la morte di suo figlio mediante incuria, egoismo, mancanza del più elementare rispetto verso il suo diritto alla vita». Poi ha posato il foglio, ha spiegato in che modo si sarebbe svolto il processo. Ciascuno avrebbe parlato come testimone e come giudice, quindi avrebbe dato ad alta voce il suo voto: colpevole o non colpevole. La maggioranza dei voti avrebbe determinato il verdetto e dopo quello, in caso di condanna, si sarebbe scelta la pena. Ecco, incominciava. Toccava a lui prendere la parola. La prima frase s'è levata come un vento di ghiaccio.

«Un figlio non è un dente cariato. Non lo si può estirpare come un dente e buttarlo nella pattumiera, tra il cotone sporco e le garze. Un figlio è una persona, e la vita di una persona è un continuum dall'attimo in cui viene concepita al momento in cui muore. Alcuni di voi contesteranno il concetto stesso del continuum. Ripeteranno che nell'attimo in cui si è concepiti, non esistiamo come persona. Esistiamo solo come cellula che si moltiplica e che non rappresenta la vita. O non più di quanto la rappresenti un albero che non è delitto tagliare, un moscerino che non è delitto schiacciare. Da scienziato rispondo subito che un albero non diventa un uomo, e nemmeno un moscerino. Tutti gli elementi che compongono un uomo, dal suo corpo alla sua personalità, tutti i quozienti che costituiscono un individuo, dal suo sangue alla sua mente, sono concentrati in quella cellula. Essi rappresentano molto di più che un progetto o una promessa: se potessimo esaminarli con un microscopio capace di vedere al di là del visibile, ci butteremmo in ginocchio e crederemmo tutti in Dio. Già in tale fase, dunque, e per quanto ciò possa apparire paradossale, io mi sento autorizzato a usare la parola assassinio. Ed aggiungo: se l'umanità dipendesse dal volume, l'assassinio dalla quantità, dovremmo dedurne che uccidere un uomo di cento chili è più grave che ucciderne uno di cinquanta. La collega che mi sta a fianco non sorrida. Sulle sue tesi io risparmio giudizi ma sul suo modo di esercitare la professione medica non risparmio commenti: in quella gabbia dovrebbero starci due donne, non una.» Poi ha guardato la dottoressa con sprezzante severità. Lei ha sostenuto lo sguardo tranquilla, fumando, e ciò mi ha consolato come un tepore. Ma subito dopo il vento di ghiaccio ha ripreso.

«Tuttavia non siamo qui per giudicare la morte di una cellula. Siamo qui per giudicare la morte di un bambino che aveva raggiunto almeno i tre mesi della sua esistenza prenatale. Chi, che cosa, ne provocò la morte? Circostanze a noi ignote ma naturali, qualcuno che è sfuggito alla cattura, o la donna che vedete in gabbia? Io vi posso fornire le prove che mi permettono di affermare: a provocarne la morte fu la donna che vedete in gabbia. Non a caso io la sospettai fin dal primo incontro. L'esperienza mi fa riconoscere un'infanticida anche dietro una maschera, ed era una maschera che lei portava sul volto dicendo di volere il bambino. Era una menzogna offerta a se stessa prima che agli altri. Mi colpì, ad esempio, la sua durezza ferrigna. Il giorno in cui mi congratulai con lei perché l'esame era stato positivo, rispose secca che lo sapeva già. Mi colpì anche l'ostilità con cui reagì all'ordine di mettersi a letto non appena fu colta da spasmi dovuti a contrazioni uterine. Non poteva permettersi simili lussi, replicò, e quindici giorni era il limite massimo cui si sarebbe piegata. Dovetti insistere, adirarmi, mortificarmi in raccomandazioni. E ciò mi convinse che non le piaceva accettare i doveri di madre, che la sua non era una maternità responsabile. Del resto mi telefonava in continuazione affermando che stava bene, che non c'era ragione di tenerla a letto, o protestando che aveva un lavoro e doveva alzarsi. Il mattino in cui la rividi era il ritratto dell'infelicità. E, proprio nel corso di quella visita, si maturarono i miei sospetti che costei meditasse un delitto. Anatomicamente e fisiologicamente non si spiegava infatti perché la gravidanza fosse così dolorosa: gli spasmi potevano avere soltanto un'origine psicologica, cioè volontaria. La interrogai. Ammise, laconica, di sentirsi angosciata per molte preoccupazioni. Alluse anche a un dispiacere che non cercai di chiarire giacché mi parve ovvio che fosse il dispiacere d'essere incinta. Infine le domandai se volesse davvero il bambino e le spiegai che a volte il pensiero uccide: era necessario che mutasse il suo nervosismo in placidità. Ma con un lampo d'ira rispose che sarebbe stato come chiederle di mutare il colore degli occhi. Pochi giorni dopo si presentò di nuovo. Aveva ripreso la vita normale e le cose erano peggiorate. La ricoverai in clinica. Qui, per una settimana, la immobilizzai e ottenni il controllo della sua psiche attraverso la farmacologia.

«E siamo al delitto, signori. Ma prima di illustrarvelo, dico: supponiamo che uno di voi sia gravemente ammalato e abbia bisogno di una medicina. La medicina è a portata di mano, la salvezza consiste nel semplice gesto di qualcuno che ve la porge. Come chiamate colui che invece di darvi la medicina la butta via o la sostituisce con un veleno? Pazzo, dispettoso, colpevole di omissione di soccorso? Eh, no: troppo poco. Io lo chiamo assassino. Signori giurati, non v'è dubbio che il bambino fosse ammalato e che la medicina a portata di mano fosse l'immobilità. Ma questa donna non solo gliela negò: gli somministrò il veleno di un viaggio che avrebbe danneggiato una gravidanza più facile. Ore e ore in aereo, in automobile, per strade sconnesse, luoghi accidentati, da sola. Io la scongiurai. Le dimostrai che a quel punto suo figlio non era più un moltiplicarsi di cellule ma un vero bambino. Le annunciai che lo avrebbe ucciso. Mi oppose la sua durezza ferrigna, firmò un foglio col quale si assumeva ogni responsabilità, partì, lo uccise. D'accordo: se fossimo dinanzi a un tribunale di leggi scritte, mi sarebbe arduo sostenerne la colpevolezza. Non vi furono sonde né farmaci né interventi chirurgici: secondo le leggi scritte, questa donna dovrebbe andarsene assolta perché il fatto non esiste. Ma noi siamo una giuria della vita, signori, e in nome della vita io vi dico che il suo comportamento fu peggio delle sonde e dei farmaci e degli interventi chirurgici. Perché fu ipocrita, vile, e senza rischi legali.

«Darei molto per riconoscerle le circostanze attenuanti, assolverla in parte. Ma non vedo dove, non vedo come. Era povera forse, affogava in ristrettezze economiche tali da non poter mantenere suo figlio? Assolutamente no. Lo riconosce lei stessa. Doveva difendere il suo onore in quanto apparteneva a una società che l'avrebbe perseguitata se avesse messo al mondo un illegittimo? Neppure. Appartiene a un establishment culturale che anziché respingerla avrebbe fatto di lei un'eroina, e comunque non crede alle regole della società. Rifiuta Dio, la patria, la famiglia, il matrimonio, gli stessi principii del vivere insieme. Il suo delitto non ha attenuanti, signori. Perché lo commise in nome di una illegittima libertà: la libertà personale, egoista, che non tiene conto degli altri e dei loro diritti. Ho pronunciato la parola diritti. L'ho fatto per prevenirvi sulla parola eutanasia. L'ho fatto anche perché non mi rispondiate che lasciando morire quel figlio essa esercitò un suo diritto: risparmiare alla comunità il fardello di un individuo malato e cioè sbagliato. Non spetta a noi stabilire a priori chi sarà sbagliato e chi no, se sarà sbagliato oppure no. Omero era cieco e Leopardi era gobbo. Se gli spartani li avessero gettati dalla rupe Tarpea, se le loro madri si fossero stancate di portarli in seno, oggi l'umanità sarebbe più povera: escludo che un campione olimpionico valga più di un poeta cieco o storpio. Quanto al sacrificio di custodire nel ventre il feto di un campione olimpionico o di un poeta cieco o storpio, io vi ricordo che la specie umana si propaga così: piaccia o non piaccia. E concludo: colpevole!»

* * *

Mi sono rattrappita a quell'urlo. Ho chiuso gli occhi e così non ho visto la dottoressa che si alzava per parlare. Quando li ho riaperti lei aveva già incominciato e diceva: «Il mio collega si è dimenticato di sottolineare che per ogni Omero nasce un Hitler, che ogni concepimento è una sfida carica di splendide e orrende possibilità. Io non so se questo bambino sarebbe stato un Omero o un Hitler: quando è morto, era soltanto una sconosciuta possibilità. Però so chi è questa donna: una realtà da non distruggere. E fra una possibilità sconosciuta e una realtà da non distruggere, io scelgo quest'ultima. Il mio collega sembra ossessionato dal culto della vita. Però quel culto egli lo riserva a chi potrebb'essere, non lo estende a chi è già. Il culto della vita è una bella chiacchiera e basta. Anche la battuta un-figlio-non-è-un-dente-cariato è una bella battuta e basta. Scommetto che il mio collega è stato alla guerra. E ha sparato e ha ucciso dimenticando che nemmeno a vent'anni un figlio è un dente cariato. Non conosco infanticidio peggiore della guerra. La guerra è un infanticidio in massa, rinviato di vent'anni. Eppure lui l'accetta, in nome di chissà quali altri culti, e non applica ad essa la tesi del suo continuum. Anche come scienziata non posso prendere sul serio il suo continuum: se lo facessi, dovrei portare il lutto ognivolta che un uovo muore non fecondato, ognivolta che i duecento milioni di spermii non arrivano a bucarne la membrana. Peggio: dovrei portare il lutto anche quando viene fecondato: pensando ai centonovantanove milioni e novecentonovantanovemilanovecentonovantanove spermii i quali muoiono sconfitti dall'unico spermio che ha bucato la membrana. Anch'essi sono creature di Dio. Anch'essi sono vivi e contengono gli elementi che compongono un individuo. Il mio collega non li ha mai osservati al microscopio? Non li ha mai visti correre scodinzolando come un branco di girini, non li ha mai visti faticare e lottare contro la zona pellucida, battendoci il capo disperatamente, sapendo che fallire è morire? Si tratta di uno spettacolo straziante: ignorandolo, il mio collega non è generoso verso il suo sesso. Non vorrei indulgere a facili ironie ma, visto che egli crede tanto alla vita, come può lasciar morire miliardi e miliardi di spermii senza farci nulla? Omissione di soccorso o crimine? Crimine, ovvio: dentro quella gabbia dovrebbe starci anche lui. Se non ci va, e subito, significa che ci ha mentito, che il suo perbenismo è turbato da chi dice che il problema non consiste nel far nascere un gran numero di individui ma nel rendere meno disgraziata possibile l'esistenza di coloro che sono già nati.

«Sempre a proposito del mio collega, evito di prender sul serio la sua insinuazione di correità. Al massimo potrei essere accusata di errato giudizio, e neanche una giuria della vita può condannare l'errato giudizio. Del resto non fu tale: fu semplicemente un giudizio, del quale non mi pento. La gravidanza non è una punizione inflitta dalla natura per farti pagare il brivido di un momento. È un miracolo che deve svolgersi con la stessa spontaneità che benedice gli alberi, i pesci. Se non procede in modo normale, non puoi chiedere a una donna di stare mesi e mesi distesa in un letto come una paralitica. In altre parole, non puoi esigere da lei la rinuncia della sua attività, della sua personalità, della sua libertà. Lo esigi forse da un uomo che con quel brivido gode altrettanto e forse di più? Evidentemente il mio collega non riconosce alle donne il diritto che riconosce agli uomini: disporre del proprio corpo. Evidentemente egli considera l'uomo un'ape cui è permesso svolazzare di fiore in fiore, la donna un sistema genitale che serve solo alla procreazione. Capita a molti nel nostro mestiere: le pazienti preferite dai ginecologi sono fattrici placide, grasse, senza problemi di libertà. E comunque non siamo qui per giudicare i medici. Siamo qui per giudicare una donna accusata di omicidio premeditato e compiuto col pensiero anziché coi ferri. Rifiuto l'accusa, in base ad elementi precisi. Il giorno in cui diagnosticai che tutto andava bene, vidi un gran sollievo in lei. Il giorno in cui ammisi che il feto era morto, vidi un gran dolore in lei.

«Ho detto feto e non bambino: la scienza mi permette questa distinzione. Sappiamo tutti che un feto diventa un bambino solo al momento della viabilità, e che tale momento sopraggiunge al nono mese. In casi eccezionali, al settimo mese. Ma ammettiamo pure che non fosse più un feto, che fosse già un bambino: il crimine non esisterebbe ugualmente. Caro collega, costei non voleva la morte del suo bambino: voleva la propria vita. E purtroppo in certi casi la nostra vita è la morte di un altro, la vita di un altro è la nostra morte. A chi ci spara, si spara. Le leggi scritte chiamano ciò legittima difesa. Se mai questa donna desiderò inconsciamente la morte del figlio, lo fece per legittima difesa. Quindi non è colpevole».

* * *

Poi s'è alzato tuo padre che non piangeva più. Ma appena ha mosso le labbra per dire qualcosa, il suo mento ha incominciato a tremare e le lacrime sono sgorgate di nuovo. Si è portato di nuovo le mani agli occhi ed è ricaduto a sedere. «Rinuncia alla parola dunque?» ha detto il medico con irritazione. Tuo padre ha abbassato il capo impercettibilmente, come a rispondere sì. «Non può rinunciare al voto però» ha insistito l'altro. Tuo padre ha raddoppiato i singhiozzi. «Il voto, la prego!» Tuo padre s'è soffiato il naso, tacendo. «Colpevole o no?» Tuo padre ha tirato un sospiro lungo e ha mormorato: «Colpevole». E a quel punto è successa una cosa tremenda: la mia amica s'è voltata e gli ha sputato addosso. E mentre lui si detergeva, pallido, la mia amica ha gridato: «Vigliacco. Ipocrita vigliacco. Tu che le telefonavi soltanto perché lo buttasse via. Tu che per due mesi sei rimasto nascosto come un disertore. Tu che sei andato da lei solo perché ti ho pregato. Fate sempre così, vero? Vi spaventate e ci lasciate sole e al massimo tornate da noi in nome della paternità. Tanto che vi costa la paternità? Un ventre sfasciato da un ingrossamento ridicolo? La pena del parto, la tortura dell'allattamento? Il frutto della paternità vi viene scodellato dinanzi come una minestra già cotta, posato sul letto come una camicia stirata. Non avete che dargli un cognome se siete sposati, neanche quello se siete fuggiti. Ogni responsabilità è della donna, ogni sofferenza, ogni insulto. Puttana, le dite se ha fatto l'amore con voi. La parola puttano non esiste nel dizionario: usarla è un errore di glottologia. Sono millenni che ci imponete i vostri vocaboli, i vostri precetti, i vostri abusi. Sono millenni che usate il nostro corpo senza rimetterci nulla. Sono millenni che ci imponete il silenzio e ci relegate al compito di mamme. In qualsiasi donna cercate una mamma. A qualsiasi donna chiedete di farvi da mamma: perfino se è vostra figlia. Dite che non abbiamo i vostri muscoli e poi sfruttate la nostra fatica anche per farvi lucidare le scarpe. Dite che non abbiamo il vostro cervello e poi sfruttate la nostra intelligenza anche per farvi amministrare il salario. Eterni bambini, fino alla vecchiaia restate bambini da imboccare, pulire, servire, consigliare, consolare, proteggere nelle vostre debolezze e nelle vostre pigrizie. Io vi disprezzo. E disprezzo me stessa per non saper fare a meno di voi, per non gridarvi più spesso: siamo stanche d'esservi mamme. Siamo stanche di questa parola che avete santificata per il vostro interesse, il vostro egoismo. Dovrei sputare anche su lei, signor dottore. Lei che in una donna vede soltanto un utero e due ovaie, mai un cervello. Lei che dinanzi a una donna incinta pensa: "Prima si è divertita e poi viene da me". Non si è mai divertito, lei, signor dottore? Non lo ha mai dimenticato il culto della vita? Lo difende così bene al livello cellulare che la si direbbe invidioso di ciò che la sua collega chiama miracolo della maternità. Ma no, lo escludo. Quel miracolo sarebbe un sacrificio per lei. In quanto uomo, non saprebbe affrontarlo. Signor dottore, qui non si fa il processo a una donna: si fa il processo a tutte le donne. Ho quindi il diritto di rovesciarlo su lei e dirle: la maternità non è un dovere morale. Non è nemmeno un fatto biologico. È una scelta cosciente. Questa donna aveva fatto una scelta cosciente, non voleva uccider nessuno. Era lei che voleva ucciderla, signor dottore, negandole perfino l'uso del proprio intelletto. Perciò dentro la gabbia dovrebbe starci lei, e non per mancato soccorso a miliardi di stupidi spermii bensì per tentato donnicidio. Dopodiché mi pare addirittura superfluo dichiarare che l'accusata non è colpevole».

* * *

Poi s'è alzato il commendatore, con un'espressione di falso imbarazzo. Non sapeva come pronunciarsi, ha iniziato, perché in questa giuria si sentiva un estraneo. Gli altri erano legati all'imputata da un vincolo professionale o affettivo che includeva il bambino: lui, invece, era il suo datore di lavoro. In quanto tale, poteva solo rallegrarsi all'idea che le cose fossero andate com'erano andate: pur cedendo alla magnanimità, egli aveva sempre considerato quella gravidanza un ostacolo. Peggio: una catastrofe che gli sarebbe costata un mucchio di denaro. Bastasse pensare allo stipendio da pagarle, secondo una legge assurda e riprovevole, anche nei mesi di inerzia. Oh, sì: il bambino era stato saggio, più saggio della madre. Oltretutto, morendo, aveva difeso il nome della ditta. Che avrebbe pensato il pubblico a veder la sua dipendente, non sposata per giunta, con un neonato in braccio? Non si peritava di confessarlo: se la donna avesse accettato, lui l'avrebbe aiutata a disfarsi dell'inopportuno. Però lui non era solo un industriale: era un uomo. E i giurati che lo avevano preceduto, i due giurati maschi s'intende, avevan provocato nella sua coscienza un ripensamento. Il dottore, attraverso la logica e la moralità; il padre del bambino, attraverso il cordoglio. Riflettendo, non poteva non associarsi ai ragionamenti del primo e al pianto del secondo. Un figlio appartiene in uguale misura al padre e alla madre: se il delitto era stato commesso, si trattava di un doppio delitto perché, oltre ad eliminare la vita di un infante, aveva stroncato la vita di un adulto. Quanto a decidere se il delitto fosse stato commesso o no: ma esistevano dubbi in proposito? Era necessaria una prova più schiacciante della testimonianza offerta dal medico? Il medico era stato indulgente a parlare di vago egoismo. Lui, il commendatore, poteva svelarne il motivo e il movente: l'imputata temeva che il famoso viaggio venisse affidato a un collega rivale. Per questo era balzata dal letto ed era partita, senza alcun riguardo per la vita che portava in seno. Senza nessuna misericordia. Che la sua alleata sputasse pure, insultasse pure. L'imputata era colpevole.

* * *

Così ho cercato con gli occhi mio padre e mia madre. E li ho implorati, in silenzio, perché erano la mia ultima possibilità di salvezza. Mi hanno risposto con uno sguardo avvilito. Apparivano talmente esausti, molto più vecchi di quando il processo era incominciato. La testa gli ciondolava in avanti come se non potessero sostenerne il peso, il corpo gli tremava come se avessero freddo, e tutto in loro cedeva stroncato da un mesto abbandono che li isolava dagli altri: chiudendoli dentro un'unica disperazione. Chiusi in quell'unica disperazione, e sempre con lo sguardo avvilito, hanno chiesto il permesso di restare seduti. Il permesso gli è stato concesso e li ho visti confabulare: per stabilire, suppongo, chi dovesse incominciare il discorso. Lo ha incominciato lui. Ha detto: « Io ho avuto due dolori. Il primo, a sapere che quel bambino c'era. Il secondo, a sapere che non c'era più. Spero che qui mi venga risparmiato un terzo dolore: veder condannare mia figlia. In che modo si siano svolte le cose io non lo so. E voi nemmeno. Nessuno può saperlo. Perché nessuno può entrare nell'anima altrui. Però questa è mia figlia: e per un padre i figli non sono colpevoli. Mai». Subito dopo ha parlato mia madre. Ha detto: «È la mia bambina. Sarà sempre la mia bambina. E la mia bambina non può fare cose cattive. Quando mi scrisse che aspettava un figlio, io le risposi: "Se hai deciso così, vuol dire che è giusto così". Se mi avesse scritto che non lo voleva, io avrei risposto la medesima cosa. Non tocca a noi giudicare. Né a voi. Non avete né il diritto di accusarla né quello di difenderla. Perché non siete né dentro la sua mente né dentro il suo cuore. Nessuna delle vostre testimonianze ha valore. V'è solo un testimone, qui, che potrebbe spiegarci come sono andate le cose. Questo testimone è il bambino che non può...». E a questo punto gli altri l'hanno interrotta, in coro: «Il bambino, il bambino!». Ed io mi sono aggrappata alla gabbia, ho gridato: «Il bambino no! Il bambino no!». Ed è stato mentre gridavo così che...

— 28 —

Sì, è stato mentre gridavo così che ho udito la tua voce: «Mamma!». E mi son sentita svuotare perché era la prima volta che qualcuno mi chiamava mamma, e perché era la prima volta che udivo la tua voce, e perché non era la voce di un bambino. Era la voce di un adulto, di un uomo. E ho pensato: "Era un uomo!". Poi ho pensato: "Era un uomo, mi condannerà". Infine ho pensato: "Lo voglio vedere!". E le mie pupille hanno frugato ovunque, dentro la gabbia, fuori della gabbia, tra gli scanni, al di là degli scanni, per terra, sui muri. Ma non ti hanno trovato. Non c'eri. C'era solo una quiete di tomba. E in questa quiete di tomba la tua voce s'è levata, di nuovo.

«Mamma! Lasciami parlare, mamma. Non avere paura. Non bisogna aver paura della verità. Del resto la verità è già stata detta. Ciascuno di loro ha detto una verità, e tu lo sai: me lo hai insegnato tu che la verità è fatta di molte verità differenti. Sono nel giusto coloro che ti hanno accusato e coloro che ti hanno difeso, coloro che ti hanno assolto e coloro che ti hanno condannato... Però quei giudizi non contano. Tuo padre e tua madre hanno ragione a dire che non si può entrare nell'anima altrui, che l'unico testimone son io. Soltanto io, mamma, posso affermare che mi hai ucciso senza uccidermi. Soltanto io posso spiegare come l'hai fatto e perché. Io non avevo chiesto di nascere, mamma. Nessuno lo chiede. Laggiù nel nulla non v'è volontà. Non v'è scelta. V'è il nulla. Quando avviene lo strappo e ci accorgiamo di incominciare, non ci chiediamo nemmeno chi l'ha voluto e se ciò sia bene o male. Semplicemente, accettiamo e poi aspettiamo di scoprire se ci piaccia aver accettato. Scoprii fin troppo presto che mi piaceva. Sia pure attraverso i tuoi timori, le tue esitazioni, eri stata così brava a convincermi che nascere è bello e scappare dal nulla una gioia. Una volta nato non dovrai scoraggiarti, dicevi: neanche a soffrire, neanche a morire. Se uno muore vuol dire che è nato, che è uscito dal niente, e niente è peggiore del niente: il brutto è dover dire di non esserci stato. La tua fede mi seduceva, la tua prepotenza. Sembrava davvero la prepotenza dei tempi remoti in cui la vita era esplosa nel modo che mi narravi. Io ti credevo, mamma. Insieme all'acqua che mi immergeva io bevevo ogni tuo pensiero. E ogni tuo pensiero aveva il sapore di una rivelazione. Poteva avvenire altrimenti? Il mio corpo era solo un progetto che si sviluppava in te, grazie a te; la mia mente era solo una promessa che si realizzava in te, grazie a te. Apprendevo esclusivamente ciò che mi davi, ignoravo ciò che non mi davi: le mie sorsate di luce e di coscienza eri tu. Se sfida tutto e tutti per condurmi alla vita, pensavo, la vita è davvero un dono sublime.

«Ma poi crebbero le tue incertezze, i tuoi dubbi, e prendesti ad alternare lusinghe e minacce, tenerezza e rancore, coraggio e paura. Per lavarti della paura un giorno attribuisti a me la decisione di esistere. Affermasti d'avere obbedito a un mio ordine, non alla tua scelta. Mi accusasti d'essere il tuo padrone: tu la mia vittima, non io la tua. E passasti a rimproverarmi, biasimarmi perché ti facevo soffrire. Giungesti addirittura a sfidarmi spiegando cos'era la vita da voi: una trappola priva di libertà, di felicità, di amore. Un pozzo di schiavitù e di violenze cui non mi sarei potuto sottrarre. Non ti stancavi mai di dimostrarmi che non c'è salvezza nel formicaio, che non si sfugge alle sue leggi cupe. Le magnolie servono per scaraventarci le donne, la cioccolata la mangiano quelli che non ne hanno bisogno, il domani è un uomo fucilato per un pezzo di pane e poi un sacco di mutande sporche. Si concludevano sempre con una domanda triste, le tue fiabe tristi: ma è proprio il caso che tu esca dal tuo nido di pace per venire quaggiù? Non mi raccontasti mai che un fiore di magnolia si può cogliere senza morire, che un gianduiotto si può mangiare senza umiliarsi, che il domani può essere meglio di ieri. E quando te ne accorgesti era troppo tardi: mi stavo già suicidando. Non piangere, mamma: io mi rendo conto che facevi questo anche per amore, per prepararmi a non cedere il giorno in cui l'orrore di esistere mi avrebbe investito. Non è vero che non credi all'amore, mamma. Ci credi tanto da straziarti perché ne vedi così poco, e perché quello che vedi non è mai perfetto. Tu sei fatta d'amore. Ma è sufficiente credere all'amore se non si crede alla vita? Non appena compresi che tu non credevi alla vita, che facevi uno sforzo ad abitarci e portare me ad abitarci, io mi permisi la prima e l'ultima scelta: rifiutar di nascere, negarti per la seconda volta la luna... Ormai potevo, mamma. Il mio pensiero non era più il tuo pensiero: ne possedevo uno mio. Piccolo forse, abbozzato, ma in grado di trarre questa conclusione: se la vita è un tormento, approdarci perché? Non mi avevi mai detto perché si nasce. Ed eri stata abbastanza onesta da non imbrogliarmi con le leggende che avete inventato per consolarvi: il Dio onnipotente che crea a sua immagine e somiglianza, la ricerca del bene, la corsa al paradiso... La tua sola spiegazione era stata che eri nata anche tu, e prima di te la tua mamma, prima della tua mamma, la mamma della tua mamma: all'indietro verso uno ieri di cui si perdevan le tracce. Si nasceva insomma perché altri eran nati e perché altri nascessero: in un prolificare affine a se stesso. Se non accadesse così, mi dicesti una sera, la specie umana si estinguerebbe. Anzi non esisterebbe. Ma perché dovrebbe esistere, perché deve esistere, mamma? Lo scopo qual è? Te lo dico io: un'attesa della morte, del niente. Nel mio universo che tu chiamavi uovo, lo scopo esisteva: era nascere. Ma nel tuo mondo lo scopo è soltanto morire: la vita è una condanna a morte. Io non vedo perché avrei dovuto uscire dal nulla per tornare al nulla».

* * *

Allora ho compreso quanto fosse profondo e irrimediabile il male che ti avevo inflitto e che avevo inflitto a me stessa, alle cose in cui mi costringo a credere: nascere per essere felici, liberi, buoni, per battersi in nome della felicità, della libertà, della bontà, nascere per tentare, sapere, scoprire, inventare. Nascere per non morire. E in preda al panico mi sono augurata che tutto ciò fosse un sogno, un incubo da cui sarei uscita per ritrovarti vivo, bambino dentro di me, e ricominciare daccapo, senza spaventarmi, senza mostrarmi impaziente, senza rinunciare alla fede che ha nome speranza, e ho scosso la gabbia: dicendo a me stessa che non esisteva. La gabbia ha resistito. Era davvero una gabbia ed era davvero un tribunale e s'era svolto davvero un processo dove tu mi avevi giudicato colpevole perché io mi giudicavo colpevole, mi avevi condannato perché io mi condannavo. Restava soltanto da decider la pena e questa era ovvia: rifiutare la vita e tornare al nulla con te. Ti ho teso le braccia. Ti ho supplicato di portarmi via con te, perdonarmi... E tu mi sei venuto accanto, mi hai detto: «Ma io ti perdono, mamma. Non tornare al nulla con me. Nascerò un'altra volta».

Splendide parole, bambino, ma parole e basta. Tutti gli spermii e tutti gli ovuli della terra uniti in tutte le possibili combinazioni non potrebbero mai creare di nuovo te, ciò che eri e che avresti potuto essere. Tu non rinascerai mai più. Non tornerai mai più. Ed io continuo a parlarti per pura disperazione.

— 29 —

Sono giorni che te ne stai chiuso lì dentro, senza vivere e senza andar via. La dottoressa ne è stupita e impaurita. Posso morire, dice, se non ti tolgo. Lo capisco benissimo e aggiungo: non ho alcuna intenzione di punirmi fino a quel punto, servirmi di te per applicare l'autocondanna di quell'assurdo processo. La durezza del rimpianto mi basta. Allo stesso tempo, però, non ho alcuna fretta di toglierti e sarebbe difficile individuarne il motivo. Forse l'abitudine a stare insieme, addormentarci insieme, svegliarci insieme, sapermi sola senza essere sola? Forse il sospetto illogico che si tratti di un errore e convenga attendere ancora? O forse perché tornare ad essere ciò che ero prima di te non mi interessa più? Avevo tanto agognato di diventar nuovamente padrona della mia sorte. Ora che lo sono, non mi interessa più. Ecco un'ennesima realtà che hai perso l'occasione di scoprire nascendo, bambino: uno si consuma per ottenere una ricchezza o un amore o una libertà, si affatica per conquistare un suo diritto, e, quando lo conquista, non ne gioisce. O lo sciupa o lo ignora, magari pensando che gli piacerebbe tornare indietro, ricominciare daccapo con le battaglie e i tormenti. Aver raggiunto il traguardo lo fa sentire perduto... Se almeno riuscissi a convincermi che tu sei stato una fermata e basta, che la morte non cancella la vita, che la vita non aveva bisogno di te, che questo dolore è servito a qualcosa e a qualcuno. Ma a chi serve un bambino che muore e una mamma che rinuncia ad essere mamma? Ai moralisti, ai giuristi, ai teologi, ai riformatori? In tal caso c'è da domandarsi chi sfrutterà questa storia e quale sarà il verdetto del loro tribunale. Merito solidarietà o vituperio? Ho reso un servigio ai moralisti o ai giuristi, ai teologi o ai riformatori? Ho peccato istigandoti al suicidio e uccidendoti, oppure ho peccato attribuendoti un'anima che non possedevi? Senti come discutono, come gridano: ha offeso Dio, no, ha offeso le donne; ha dileggiato un problema, no, vi ha contribuito; ha capito che la vita è sacra, no, ha capito che la vita è una beffa. Quasi che il dilemma esistere o non esistere si potesse risolvere con una sentenza o un'altra, una legge o un'altra, e non toccasse ad ogni creatura risolverlo da sé e per sé. Quasi che intuire una verità non aprisse interrogativi su una verità opposta, ed entrambe non fossero valide. Qual è il fine dei loro processi, dei loro litigi? Stabilire ciò che è lecito e ciò che non lo è? Decidere dove sta la giustizia? Avevi ragione, bambino: stava in tutti. Anche la coscienza è fatta di molte coscienze: io sono quel medico e quella dottoressa, la mia amica e il commendatore, mia madre e mio padre, tuo padre e te. Io sono ciò che ciascuno di voi mi ha detto. E vallate di tristezza si stendono dinanzi a me, invano fiorite d'orgoglio.

— 30 —

Tuo padre mi ha scritto di nuovo. Stavolta è una lettera che mi induce a riflettere. Dice: «Ti conosco abbastanza per evitare di consolarti affermando che hai fatto bene a sacrificare il bambino a te stessa anziché te stessa a lui. Sai meglio di me (sei stata tu a gridarlo cacciandomi) che una donna non è una gallina, che non tutte le galline covano le uova, che molte le abbandonano, che altre se le bevono. Né noi le condanniamo per questo, o non più di quanto si condanni la natura che uccide con le malattie e i terremoti. Ti conosco abbastanza anche per evitare di ricordarti che la crudeltà della natura contiene una logica e una saggezza: se ogni possibilità di esistenza diventasse esistenza, morremmo per mancanza di spazio. Sai meglio di me che nessuno è indispensabile, che il mondo se la sarebbe cavata ugualmente se Omero e Icaro e Leonardo da Vinci e Gesù Cristo non fossero nati: il figlio che hai voluto perdere non lascia vuoti, la sua scomparsa non reca danno né alla società né al futuro. Ferisce soltanto te, e oltremisura, perché il tuo pensiero ha ingigantito un dramma il quale, forse, non è nemmeno un dramma. (Povera cara: hai scoperto che pensare significa soffrire, che essere intelligenti significa essere infelici. Peccato che ti sia sfuggito un terzo punto fondamentale: il dolore è il sale della vita e senza di esso non saremmo umani.) Non ti scrivo dunque per compiangerti. Ti scrivo per congratularmi, per riconoscere che hai vinto. Ma non perché ti sei scrollata di dosso la schiavitù di una gravidanza e di una maternità: perché sei riuscita a non cedere al bisogno degli altri, incluso il bisogno di Dio. Proprio il contrario di ciò che è successo a me. Eh, sì. L'invidia verso coloro che credono in Dio mi ha talmente assalito in questi ultimi mesi da diventar tentazione. E ho ceduto alla tentazione. Lo riconosco ammettendo la mia stanchezza. Dio è un punto esclamativo con cui si incollano tutti i cocci rotti: se uno ci crede vuol dire che è stanco, che non ce la fa più a cavarsela da sé. Tu non sei stanca perché sei l'apoteosi del dubbio. Dio è per te un punto interrogativo, anzi il primo punto interrogativo di infiniti punti interrogativi. E solo chi si strazia nelle domande per trovare risposte, va avanti; solo chi non cede alla comodità di credere in Dio per aggrapparsi a una zattera e riposarsi, può incominciare di nuovo: per contraddirsi di nuovo, smentirsi di nuovo, regalarsi di nuovo al dolore. La nostra amica mi informa che il bambino è ancora dentro di te e rifiuti di liberartene, quasi tu volessi servirti di lui per punire la tua incoerenza e proibirti di vivere. Suppongo che me ne informi perché ti preghi di non insistere in questa follia. Anziché pregarti, ti annuncio che non vi insisterai a lungo. Ami troppo la vita per non avvertirne il richiamo. Quando esso verrà, tu gli obbedirai come quel cane di Jack London che segue i lupi ululando e diventa lupo con loro».

Infatti domani torniamo a casa, bambino. E sebbene la parola domani mi sembri un'offesa per te, una minaccia per me, non posso fare a meno di guardarmi intorno ed accorgermi che domani è un giorno colmo di opportunità.

— 31 —

Mi hanno salutato con grande entusiasmo, come se fossi stata ammalata a un piede o a un orecchio ed ora mi accingessi a trascorrere una convalescenza. Si sono congratulati per il lavoro che son riuscita a condurre a termine malgrado-le-difficoltà. Mi hanno portato a mangiare. E non una parola su te. Quando ho tentato io, hanno assunto un'aria tra evasiva e imbarazzata: quasi alludessi a un argomento sgradevole o volessero dirmi non-ci-pensiamo-più-quel-che-è-stato-è-stato. Più tardi la mia amica m'ha preso da parte e, col tono di ricordarmi un appuntamento importante, ha detto d'essersi consultata col medico il quale sostiene che non è il caso di contare su una tua partenza spontanea: se non ti faccio togliere, muoio di setticemia. Sì, bisogna che mi decida: sarebbe paradossale se, per ristabilir l'equilibrio, tu uccidessi me. Ho ancora tante cose da fare. Tu non le hai incominciate, ma io sì. Ho da sviluppare la mia carriera, ad esempio, e dimostrare che non sono meno brava di un uomo. Ho da battermi contro le comodità dei punti esclamativi, ho da indurre la gente a porsi più perché. Ho da spegnere la pietà per me stessa, e convincer me stessa che il dolore non è il sale della vita. Il sale della vita è la felicità, e la felicità esiste: consiste nel darle la caccia. Infine devo ancora chiarire il mistero che chiamano amore. Ma non quello che si divora in un letto, toccandoci: quello che mi accingevo a conoscer con te... Mi manchi, bambino. Mi manchi quanto mi mancherebbe un braccio, un occhio, la voce: e tuttavia mi manchi meno di ieri, meno di stamani. È strano. Si direbbe che di ora in ora il tormento si affievolisca per chiudersi in una parentesi. I lupi hanno già incominciato a chiamarmi, e non importa se sono lontani: quando si avvicineranno, lo sento, li seguirò. Davvero ho sofferto così profondamente ed a lungo? Me lo chiedo con incredulità. Una volta lessi in un libro che la durezza di una pena sopportata si avverte soltanto quando ce ne siamo liberati e, stupefatti, si esclama: come ho fatto a tollerare un simile inferno? Dev'essere davvero così, e la vita è straordinaria: rimargina le ferite a una velocità folle. Se non restassero le cicatrici, non ci ricorderemmo nemmeno che di lì sgorgò il sangue. Del resto anche le cicatrici svaniscono. Impallidiscono e infine svaniscono. Succederà anche a me.

Succederà? Deve succedere! Perché lo pretendo, lo esigo. Infatti ora stacco il tuo ritratto dal muro, la smetto di farmi impressionare dai tuoi occhi spalancati. E nascondo le altre fotografie. Anzi le strappo. E faccio a pezzi questa culla che mi son portata dietro come una bara. La scaravento nell'inceneritore. E regalo il tuo guardaroba. Anzi lo straccio. E prendo l'appuntamento col medico, gli dico che sono d'accordo, che bisogna strapparti via. E magari chiamo tuo padre, o non importa chi, e stasera vado con lui. Perché io sono viva... così viva che non accetto processi, non accetto verdetti, neanche il tuo perdono... E perché i lupi non sono lontani. Sono già qui, ed io posso partorirti cento volte senza implorare soccorso né da Dio né da nessuno... Dio, che male! Mi sento male, ad un tratto. Cos'è? Di nuovo le coltellate. Si allungano fino al cervello come allora, per bucarlo come allora... Sto sudando. Mi sale la febbre. È arrivato il nostro momento, bambino... Il momento di separarci... E non vorrei... Non voglio... Non voglio che ti strappino come un dente cariato, per gettarti nella pattumiera tra il cotone sporco e le garze... Ma non ho scelta. Se non ti strappano via, mi ammazzi. E tu sbagliavi, tu sbagli, a pensare che io non creda alla vita... Ci credo, ci credo! E mi piace. Anche con le sue ingiustizie, le sue tristezze le sue infamie... E intendo viverla ad ogni costo. Io corro, bambino. E ti dico addio con fermezza.

— 32 —

Sopra di me c'è un soffitto bianco e accanto a me, dentro un bicchiere, ci sei tu. Non volevano che ti vedessi ma li ho convinti affermando che era mio diritto e ti hanno posato lì: con una smorfia di disapprovazione. Ti guardo, finalmente. E mi sento beffata perché non hai proprio nulla in comune con il bambino della fotografia. Non sei un bambino: sei un uovo. Un uovo grigio che galleggia in un alcool rosa e dentro il quale non si scorge nulla. Finisti assai prima che se ne accorgessero: non arrivasti mai ad avere le unghie e la pelle e le infinite ricchezze che io ti regalavo. Creatura della mia fantasia, riuscisti appena a realizzare il desiderio di due mani e due piedi, qualcosa che assomigliava ad un corpo, l'abbozzo di un volto con un nasino e due microscopici occhi. In fondo amai un pesciolino. E per amore di un pesciolino mi inventai un calvario in seguito al quale rischio di finire anch'io. È inaccettabile. Ma perché non ti ho fatto togliere prima? Perché ho perso tanto tempo prezioso lasciando che tu mi avvelenassi? Sto male, sembrano tutti allarmati. Mi hanno infilato aghi nel braccio destro e nel polso sinistro, dagli aghi partono tubi sottili che salgono come serpenti fino ai boccioni. L'infermiera si aggira con passi d'ovatta. Ognitanto entra il dottore con un altro dottore e si scambiano frasi che non capisco ma che suonano come minacce. Darei molto perché arrivassero la mia amica o tuo padre, meglio ancora i miei genitori: m'era parso di udirne le voci. Invece non viene nessuno fuorché quei due col camice bianco: uno è lo stesso che mi condannò? Un momento fa s'è arrabbiato. Ha detto: «Raddoppiate la dose!». La dose di che? Della pena? L'ho già scontata, devo ricominciare? Poi ha detto: «Svelti, non capite che se ne va?». Chi se ne va? Non tu... Tu sei già morto... Morto senza sapere cosa significa essere vivo: senza sapere cosa sono i colori, i sapori, gli odori, i suoni, i sentimenti, il pensiero. Mi dispiace: per te e per me. Mi umilia. Perché a cosa serve volare come un gabbiano dentro l'azzurro se non si generano altri gabbiani che ne genereranno altri ancora ed ancora per volare dentro l'azzurro? A cosa serve giocare come bambini se non si generano altri bambini che ne genereranno altri ancora ed ancora per giocare e divertirsi? Dovevi resistere. Dovevi combattere, vincere. Hai ceduto troppo presto, ti sei rassegnato troppo alla svelta: non eri fatto per la vita. Chi si spaventa per un paio di fiabe, per due o tre avvertimenti? Eri simile a tuo padre: lui trova comodo riposarsi in Dio, tu trovasti comodo riposarti non nascendo. Chi di noi due ha tradito? Non io. Sono molto stanca, non sento più le gambe, a intervalli mi si annebbiano gli occhi e il silenzio m'avvolge come un ronzio di vespe. Eppure non cedo, io, guarda. Tengo duro, io, guarda. Siamo talmente differenti. Non devo addormentarmi. Devo stare sveglia e pensare. Se penso, forse, resisto. Da quando stai in quel bicchiere? Da ore, da giorni, da anni? Magari sono giorni e a me sembrano anni: non posso lasciarti ancora in un bicchiere. Bisogna che ti sistemi in un posto più dignitoso: ma dove? Forse ai piedi della magnolia. Il fatto è che la magnolia è lontana: si trova nel tempo in cui anch'io ero piccina. Il presente non ha magnolie. Nemmeno la mia casa. Dovrei portarti a casa. Al mattino, però. Ora è notte: il soffitto bianco sta diventando nero. E fa freddo. Meglio che infili il cappotto per scendere giù. Via, andiamo: ti porto. Vorrei tenerti fra le braccia, bambino. Ma sei così minuscolo: non posso tenerti fra le braccia. Posso appoggiarti sulla palma di una mano ed è tutto. Purché un colpo di vento non ti rubi. Ecco una cosa che non capisco: può rubarti un colpo di vento e tuttavia pesi tanto, barcollo. Dammi la mano, ti prego: così. Bravo. Ora sei tu che mi conduci, mi guidi. Ma allora non sei un uovo, non sei un pesciolino: sei un bambino! Mi arrivi già al ginocchio. No, al cuore. No, alla spalla. No, al di sopra della spalla. Non sei un bambino, sei un uomo! Un uomo con dita forti e gentili. Ne ho bisogno ormai: sono vecchia. Non riesco nemmeno a scendere i gradini se non mi sorreggi. Ricordi quando andavamo su e giù per questa scala, attenti a non cadere, stretti l'uno all'altra in un abbraccio di complicità? Ricordi quando ti insegnavo ad andarci da solo, camminavi da poco, e contavamo i gradini ridendo? Ricordi come imparavi aggrappandoti ad ogni sporgenza, ansimando, mentre io ti seguivo con le mani tese? E il giorno in cui ci litigammo perché non ascoltavi le mie raccomandazioni? Dopo mi dispiacque. Volevo chiederti scusa ma non mi riusciva. Ti cercavo di sotto le ciglia e anche tu mi cercavi di sotto le ciglia finché ti fiorì sulle labbra un sorriso e compresi che avevi compreso. Poi cosa accadde? Il mio pensiero si appanna... le mie palpebre sembrano piombo... È il sonno o la fine? Non devo cedere al sonno, alla fine. Aiutami a restare sveglia, rispondimi: fu difficile usare le ali? Ti spararono in molti? Gli sparasti a tua volta? Ti oppressero nel formicaio? Cedesti alle delusioni e alle rabbie oppure rimanesti dritto come un albero forte? Scopristi se c'è la felicità, la libertà, la bontà, l'amore? Spero che i miei consigli ti siano serviti. Spero che tu non abbia mai urlato l'atroce bestemmia "perché sono nato?". Spero che tu abbia concluso che ne valeva la pena: a costo di soffrire, a costo di morire. Sono così orgogliosa d'averti tirato fuori dal nulla a costo di soffrire, a costo di morire. Fa davvero freddo e il soffitto bianco ora è proprio nero. Ma siamo arrivati, ecco la magnolia. Cogli un fiore. Io non ci sono mai riuscita, tu ci riuscirai. Alzati sulla punta dei piedi, allunga un braccio. Così. Dove sei? Eri qui, mi sorreggevi, eri grande, eri un uomo. E ora non ci sei più. C'è solo un bicchiere di alcool dentro il quale galleggia qualcosa che non volle diventare un uomo, una donna, che non aiutai a diventare un uomo, una donna. Perché avrei dovuto, mi chiedi, perché avresti dovuto? Ma perché la vita esiste, bambino! Mi passa il freddo a dire che la vita esiste, mi passa il sonno, mi sento io la vita. Guarda, s'accende una luce... Si odono voci... Qualcuno corre, grida, si dispera... Ma altrove nascono mille, centomila bambini, e mamme di futuri bambini: la vita non ha bisogno né di te né di me. Tu sei morto. Ora muoio anch'io. Ma non conta. Perché la vita non muore.

Finito di stampare nel mese di maggio 1997
presso Legatoria del Sud
Via Cancelliera 40, Ariccia RM

Printed in Italy